## Praise for Heir of Darion

"Swordfights and leading a sea raider crew are one thing, but now Wilde brings our Everyman Hero with a Past closer to the perils of the royal court. That means mystery heritages, faction fighting, and a kingdom that could tear itself apart unless Nagaro can protect an innocent man -- and resist getting too close to the Princess who just might remember who he used to be. For intricate worlds, an irresistible hero and the varied friends he attracts, and more twists than you can shake a cutlass at, Nagaro never disappoints."

Ken Hughes, author of the *Spellkeeper Flight* books

**Also by Carol Louise Wilde**

## Books of the Nagaro Chronicle

Gift of Chance (1)

Covenant of the Sword (2)

Return to Lankura (3)

Thief of Slaves (4)

Heir of Darion (5)

## Future Titles in this Series

Brothers of the Blood (6)

Legacy of Loros (7)

The *Nagaro* Chronicle 5

# Heir of Darion

## Carol Louise Wilde

Rivulus Books Trade Paperback Edition



Text, maps, and internal artwork by Carol Louise Wilde



Published in the United States of America by Rivulus Books, Arcadia, CA. The Rivulus Books name and Rivulus Books logo are trademarks of Rivulus Books.

ISBN: 978-1-944492-13-7

Cover art copyright by Cherie Foxley

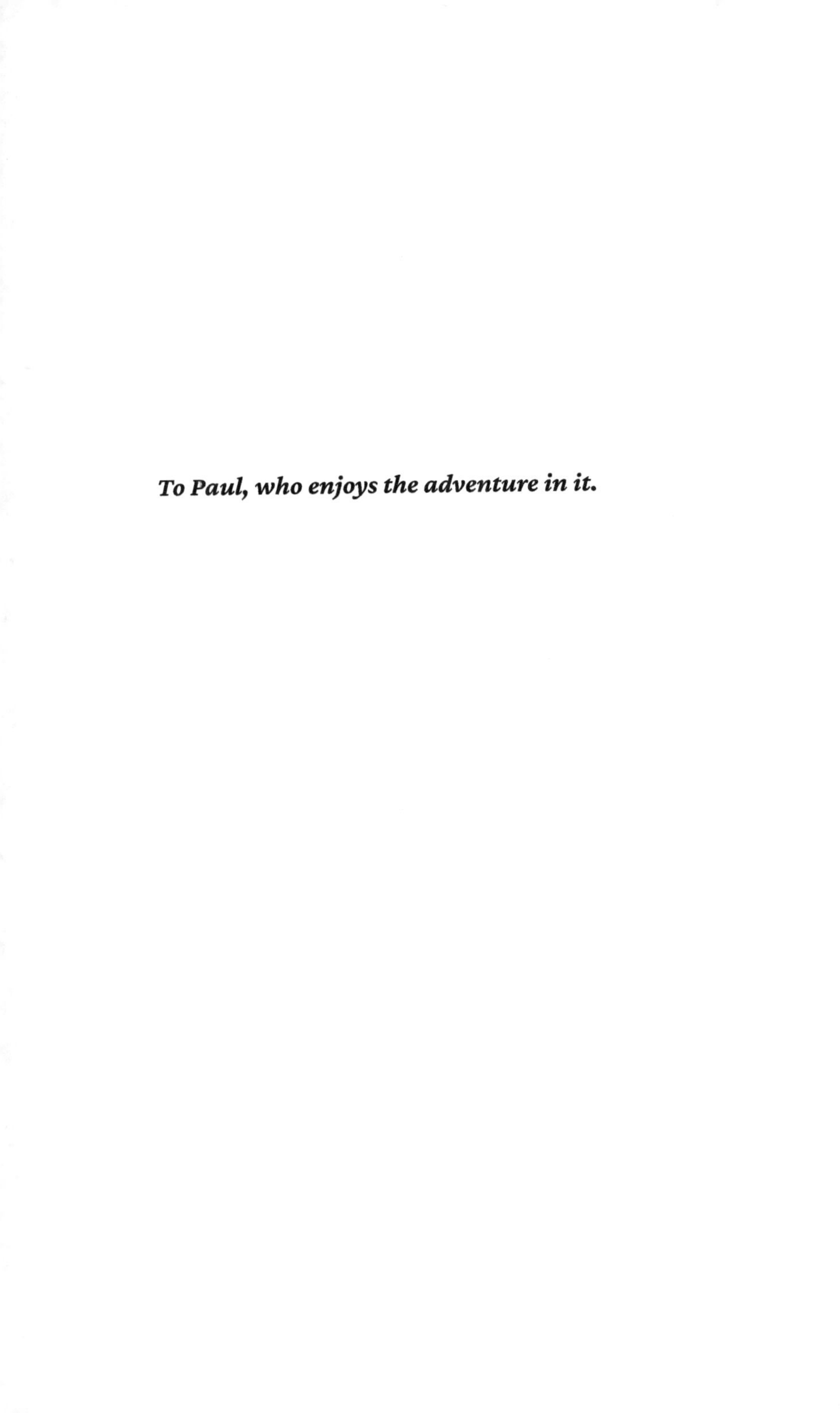

*To Paul, who enjoys the adventure in it.*

# MAPS

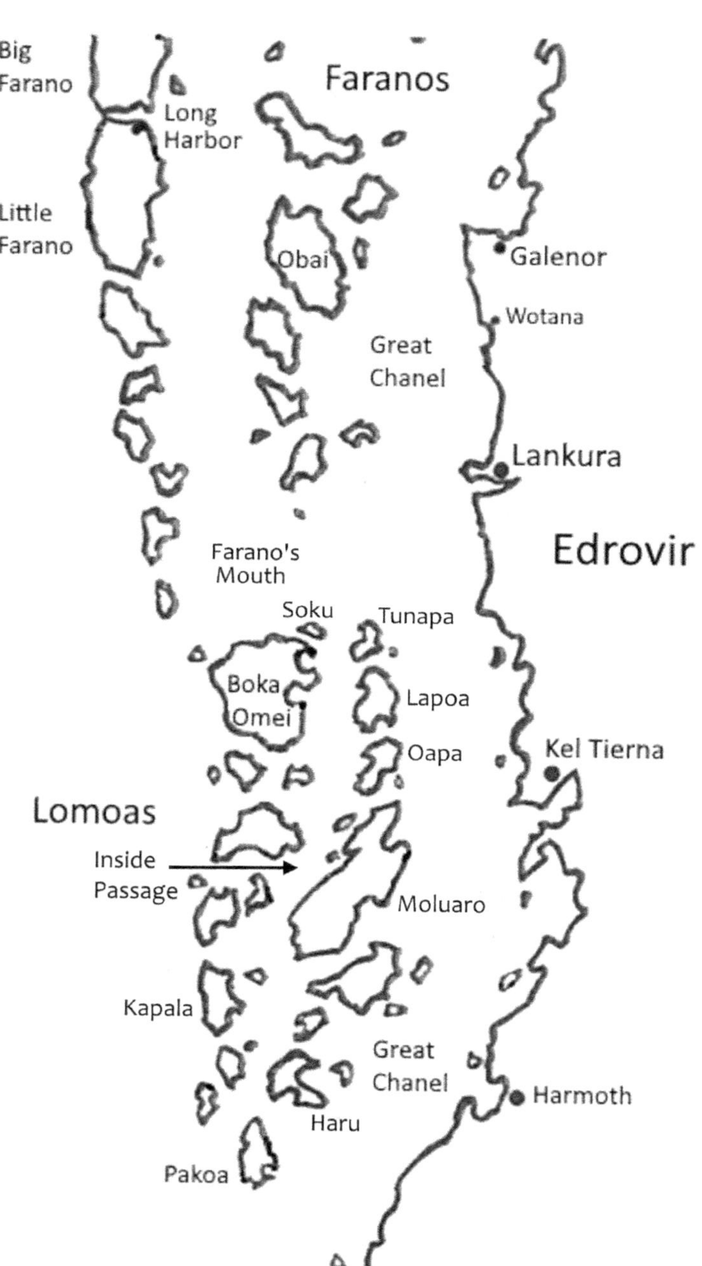

Big Farano
Long Harbor
Little Farano
Faranos
Obai
Galenor
Wotana
Great Chanel
Lankura
Edrovir
Farano's Mouth
Soku
Tunapa
Boka
Lapoa
Omei
Oapa
Kel Tierna
Lomoas
Inside Passage
Moluaro
Kapala
Great Chanel
Harmoth
Haru
Pakoa

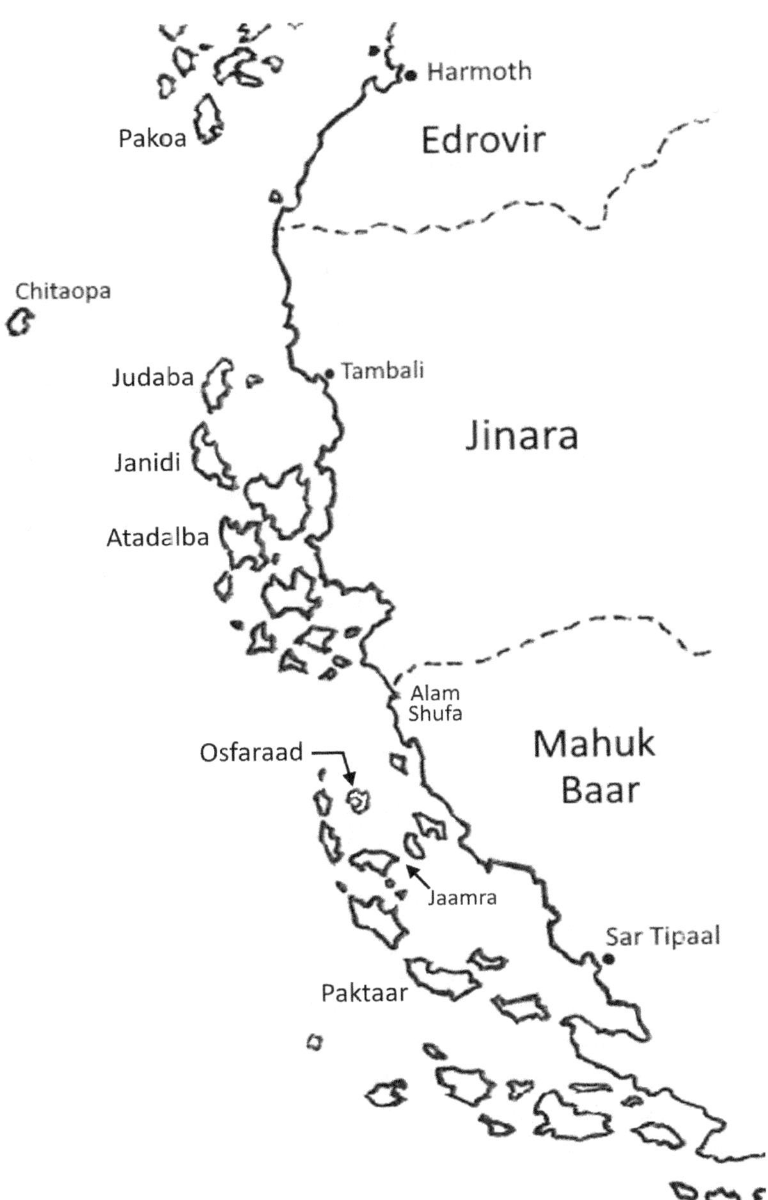

Harmoth
Edrovir
Pakoa
Chitaopa
Judaba
Tambali
Janidi
Jinara
Atadalba
Alam
Shufa
Osfaraad
Mahuk
Baar
Jaamra
Sar Tipaal
Paktaar

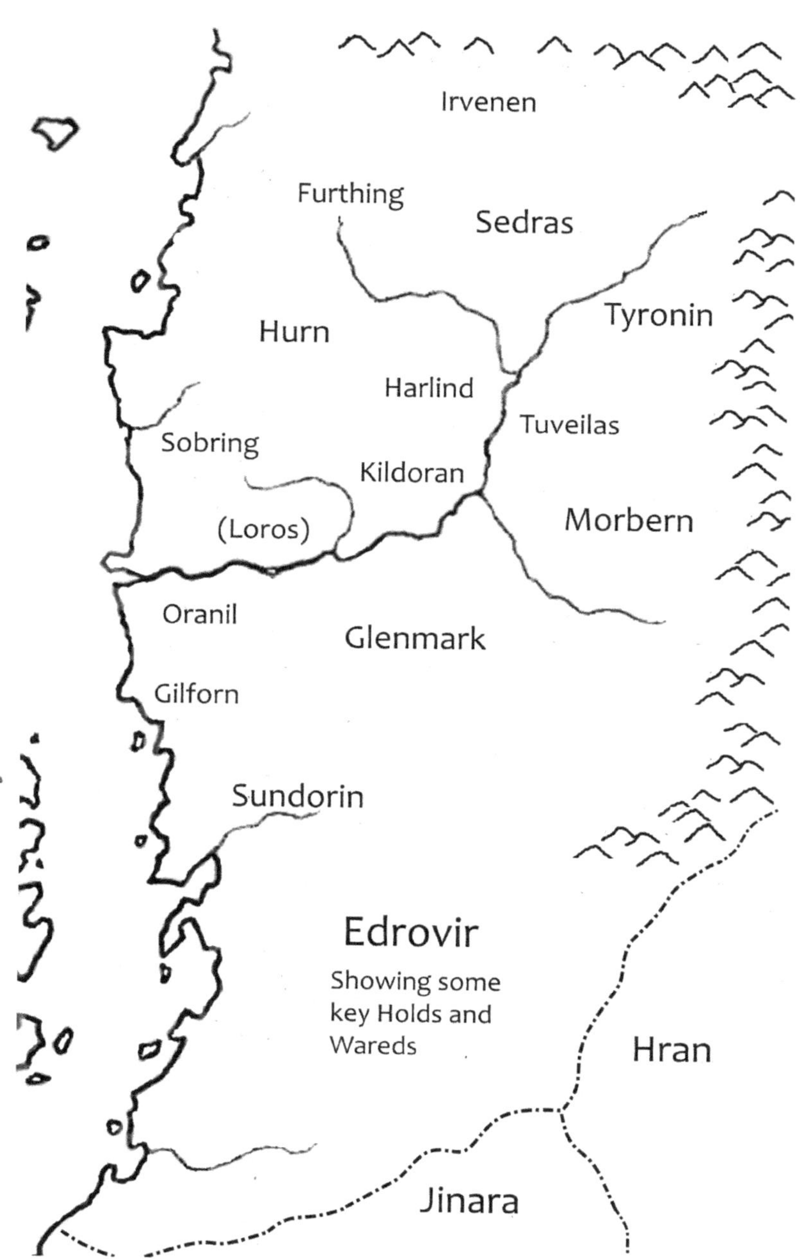

Irvenen
Furthing
Sedras
Tyronin
Hurn
Harlind
Tuveilas
Sobring
Kildoran
Morbern
(Loros)
Oranil
Glenmark
Gilforn
Sundorin
Edrovir
Showing some
key Holds and
Wareds
Hran
Jinara

↑ (Irvenen) ↑
Furthing
Sedras
Hurn
Glenarl
Galenor
Harlind
Huring
Wotana
Fendred
Sobring
Virden
Devenrul
Kildoran
Kel
(Loros)
Lankura
Glenmark
Oranil
River
Road
Border
Town
Hall
Gilforn
Sundorin

CONTENTS

## Chapter 1

# In Exile

The southern end of the Inside Passage between the isles of Haro and Kapala was being whipped into whitecaps by the eratic Madrel wind. The sun, a little past its zenith, shown clear and bright, and scattered puffs of cloud chased their shadows over the blue-green sea. Foaming surf tossed itself over rocks along Haro's shore where it ended in a jutting headland. Two ships followed the shoreline, one behind the other, as close to the rocks as they dared. The first ship was making desperately for the headland, seeking to round it and enter the Great Channel where she might find a clear path past Pakoa Island to the south. She wore all her canvas despite the blustering wind, and her oars rose and dipped in a rapid rhythm. From her masthead flew a banner of red and black. The second ship was gaining on the first, also under the power of both oars and sail, under a banner that bore a white hawk upon a field of blue.

As the first ship approached the tip of the headland and began to adjust the set of her sails, Nagaro, on the captain's platform of the second ship, shouted an order to his second mate.

"Take up the painted canvas, Pavo! Let them see who we are!"

Pavo gave the order, the main deck crew of the *Sword of Freedom* leaped to obey, and the dark gray sheets of canvas that had swathed the vessel's sides were lifted, pulled inboard, and made fast along the rails on either side. A row of alternating black and white diamonds was thus revealed, running along each side of the ship above the oar ports. On the captain's platform, Nagaro smiled grimly to himself. When their quarry made her turn to port around the headland, everyone on her deck would have a clear view of the pursuing ship's distinctive markings. The Mautep crewmen were unlikely to keep silent, and the slaves would hear the news, even if they could get no glimpse for themselves through the oar ports.

As the Mahuk galley turned, shouts were heard across the water, broken by the wind. Soon after that, the galley's oars began to falter.

Nagaro called another order to Pavo, who sent a man to the *Sword's* forecastle with a speaking trumpet in his hand to issue a cry aimed at the other vessel: "*Ship oars for Kiraam Shaku-Tal! Ship oars for Captain Nagaro!*"

Moments later Pavo ordered an adjustment of the *Sword's* sails. Nagaro watched as the headland came abreast, then gave the order to put the tiller over, and the *Sword of Freedom* executed her own turn to port, continuing to bear down on her prey.

The Mahuk craft was floundering now, though the path of escape lay clear before her. The Mautep oar deck crew were having to deal with slaves who answered to neither command nor lash, and oars were being drawn in irregularly along both sides of the galley as the *Sword* came on, closing fast. Pavo had his crew aloft, taking in sail so the wind wouldn't hinder them in close quarters. The crew of the Mahuk craft belatedly attempted to do the same. They'd probably been loath to slacken sail with the ship already losing way for lack of her oars, and the craft had begun to heel dangerously in the wind. There was confusion on her deck amid cries in Hashti of, "*Row, shaku! Row!*"

As if in answer, a new cry to ship oars came from the pursuing craft, this time directed at her own oar deck crew, and the *Sword's* oars were drawn in as she swept alongside her quarry and the grapples began to fly. The Mautep crewmen remaining on the deck cried out in alarm and drew their swords or frantically took up the long fending pikes to thrust against the *Sword's* rail, even as the *Sword's* oar deck crew came pouring up through doors and hatches.

Nagaro was at the center of the fray, down among the main deck crew working to dislodge the pikes. He waited only for Taru and the others from below to swarm about him before giving a shout and leaping onto the rail, sword in hand. Pavo leaped up beside him on his left, Taru on his right, and half a dozen others of his best-trained swordsmen flanked the three officers on either side. The last pike fell, and the men manning the *Sword's* grapples hauled on the ropes, narrowing the gap between the two ships, while the Mautep sea warriors hacked desperately at the grappling ropes.

Nagaro stood on the Sword's rail, balancing to the regular heave of the ship and gaging the distance, until he saw his moment. Then, with another shout, he leaped across the remaining gap onto the opposite rail. His comrades came with him, moving as one, and the Mautep crew abruptly found themselves in a fight as the entire Droviri line came leaping down onto the deck of the Mahuk craft. More Droviri sea warriors poured after the first rank as the two ships' sides came together with a grinding thud.

Nagaro drove forward, making for where the Mautep captain stood, only taking care not to outdistance the rest of the line. His sword rang against the blades of his foes, and they retreated before him. He felled one man who lunged at him under another man's sword, cut the other so that his sword fell from his grasp, and beat aside the blade of a third with a stroke so forceful that the man leaped back with a cry, clutching his wrist.

Nagaro halted only when he had the captain of the Mahuk war galley crouching directly before him. The man was a seasoned veteran, square-faced and broad-shouldered. Nagaro regarded him with a feral smile.

The captain sprang at him with an oath and a well-aimed sword thrust, but Nagaro's answering stroke was lightning-quick, turning the blade aside. The captain staggered back, recovered, and tried again— and again— only to find himself thwarted each time by a blade that was always, somehow, exactly where it needed to be, as if the mind that controlled it anticipated his every thought.

"*Keshaal!*" The captain of the Mahuk vessel backed away as if he were retreating from some horror.

Nagaro advanced to follow him, and now he wasn't smiling. "*Kia kaar hanuk-tak!*" he grated, speaking loud enough to be clearly heard across the deck. It meant, "Put down your sword," and when the Mautep didn't immediately comply, Nagaro moved so quickly that the poor captain uttered a cry of sheer astonishment as his sword was twisted from hand and fell with a clatter to the deck. Beside Nagaro, Pavo took one stride and set his boot on the fallen blade before any man among the Mautep could even think of picking it up. "Kia kaar hanuk-tak," the Hashtep said, and his teeth flashed in a sudden grin.

Nagaro spread his arms, gesturing along the line. He raised his voice, speaking in Hashti. "All now put down your sword! Surrender and keep your life!"

The weaponless captain swallowed. He gave a sign and spoke a word. All along the line, swords clattered to the deck. The Droviri crew moved swiftly to gather them up.

The Mautep captain had his eyes on Nagaro. "What will you take, thief?" he asked with a show of bravado.

Nagaro sheathed his sword. "All your slave are now free," he answering the man's Hashti in kind, "and we will take what is needed to help them live again as free man."

The captain spread his hands. "My slave all belong to Emperor. Why must you take them? This is hard to bear after Emperor have given you your life and your sword and your ship."

Nagaro regarded the Mautep captain coldly. "Your Emperor did right to pardon me," he said levelly. "Because it is wrong to make man slave. But we will see if you have any man of Edrovir on your oar deck," he added. "Already my man have gone down. Now they come up."

Indeed the first denizens of the oar deck were just emerging from the forecastle, escorted by a half dozen rescuers. Forty men, filthy and ragged, stepped out onto the main deck and stood blinking and staring about them. It was immediately apparent that roughly half of them were men of Edrovir, mostly Turowan and some Kelorin.

The Mautep captain licked his lips. "Lord Kiraam," he said in a more ingratiating tone, "perhaps it is right that you take Droviri man, but Hashtep man belong to Emperor."

Nagaro looked the captain up and down with some disdain. "In these water they all are free. In Edrovir no man is permitted to keep slave. Droviri you cannot keep, and Hashtep will choose if they will go back to Emperor, or stay in Edrovir. And I will give you your life, and sword, and ship, if you will swear on your honor not to sail again into these water with slave on your oar deck."

The captain raised both hands in protest. "You will leave me no one to row my ship, Lord! We would be out of your water very soon if you did not follow us so fast and make attack." He pointed to the south where the boundary of Edroviran waters lay but a few leagues away.

Nagaro's brow darkened. "This is no valid complaint!" he snapped. "You are in our water now, with oar deck full of slave, and you have man enough to row and to sail." He indicated the Mautep crew with a gesture. "Now, do you swear as I have asked?"

The Mautep captain read the steel in Nagaro's eyes. "Yes, Lord. I will swear," he said quickly.

Nagaro waited long enough to hear the man's oath, then turned on his heel and began to walk away. A voice stopped him and he turned back.

"Why do you still sail under Droviri flag, Lord Kiraam? We hear you are outcast. Your own king sends man to hunt you!"

It wasn't the Mautep captain who had spoken, but a younger man whose uniform marked him as the ship's first mate. Nagaro met the man's gaze. "I keep my oath," he said flatly. "My oath is not to king, but to land and people of Edrovir."

***

Stripped of her slaves and valuables, the Mahuk craft was allowed to limp away, sailing southward under sails alone. Nagaro spared only enough time to use the longboats to put the newly-freed Edroviran slaves ashore on the eastern coast of Pakoa where he knew they would find immediate shelter and assistance. Then he directed the *Sword* to follow the Mahuk craft, at a distance, to the southern boundary of Edroviran waters. This action ensured that the Mahuk galley made no effort to turn northward again to possibly meet some compatriot and cause further mischief along Edrovir's coast. It also placed the *Sword* in a position to make her own run southward to Alam Shufa to set ashore the freed Hashtep slaves who wished to return to their homeland. While Nagaro would later personally deliver a handful to his contact on Pakoa, the majority would choose Alam Shufa—an option Nagaro preferred not to mention to their former masters.

While these men's lives would be difficult in the Mahuk Baar where they would have to take on new identities and conceal the fact that they had ever been slaves, assimilation into Edrovir's very limited Hashtep population wasn't easy either. The prospect was daunting to many, and so it was that most newly freed Hashtep chose Alam Shufa, a place where an uninhabited stretch of coast just inside the boundary of Mahuk territory offered a safe landing. Getting there meant traversing the full length of the coast of Jinara that lay between Edrovir and the Baar, on a journey the *Sword* had made many times before when Nagaro and her crew had been simply pirates.

Now that Nagaro, Pavo, and Taru were viewed as renegade officers, hunted by the Royal Fleet of Edrovir, the maneuver was a little more difficult than it had been in happier days. Nagaro would take his time making the southward run and take care to enter Mahuk waters in the dark of night, after the moons had set, and to keep the *Sword* in those waters no longer than was as absolutely necessary. This was safest for the freed slaves and would also preserve the appearance of respect for Mautep sovereignty if they should be seen and reported to the Emperor of the Mahuk Baar. Nagaro's actions were intended to enforce the rules he had once advised King Elgurn to impose on Mautep sea warriors who entered Edroviran waters, while offering no further offense to Emperor Baalkir.

The transit of Jinari waters was also complicated, owing to the intermittent border war between Edrovir and Jinara, combined with the rather delicate status of the *Sword* and her crew. In his pirate days, Nagaro had largely ignored the border dispute, going freely among the Jinari islands and doing business with his Jinari acquaintance, Utabala, whenever it suited him. The *Sword*'s markings and colors had become well-known to the folk of those islands, and her peaceful intentions well established. Nagaro's only real concession in those days had been to avoid anchoring openly in Tambali Harbor if he knew the war was on.

All was different now. Though Nagaro still considered himself a Fleet officer, Edrovir's king and council and most of her lords disputed it. He sailed under Edrovir's flag to make no doubt of his allegiance, but covered the distinctive black-and-white diamonds along the *Sword*'s sides with canvas as a matter of survival. The latter tactic had been Taru's idea, and the disguise was aimed less at the Mautep than at Lord Kuran's Fleet warriors. The difficulty was that it confused the Jinari fishermen and merchant captains, and the Edroviran flag atop the *Sword*'s mainmast potentially marked her as an enemy when the war-winds were blowing. Jinara had no warships, but Nagaro didn't like to frighten folk unnecessarily or have his intentions misconstrued. He might have solved the problem by steering well out to sea, clear of the Jinari coast and islands, but passing warships—either Mahuk or Edroviran—sometimes made it necessary to hide.

So it was that on this occasion Nagaro spent the remainder of the night, after landing at Alam Shufa, anchored in the lee of one of Jinara's smaller, less populated southern isles, before cautiously heading northward at first light along the western shores of the outer Jinari islands with the *Sword*'s lookout on high alert.

It was just past the noon hour, and they were nearing the northern end of the Jinari archipelago, when the lookout spotted a small boat emerging from the strait between the islands of Janili and Judaba with all sails spread and on a course to directly intercept the *Sword*. Nagaro raised his spyglass and quickly noted that the boat bore a black and a white telltale tied to one of her mast stays. It was a sign that the boat carried one of Utabala's couriers bearing news intended for Nagaro. Accordingly, he gave orders to slacken sail and meet the small craft. He soon recognized the single man on board and hailed him as the boat drew along side.

"Well met, Matapili! What news do you have? How is the war right now?

Matapili was tall and lean, and like all of his people, dark of skin, hair, and eyes. He grinned up at Nagaro, showing strong white teeth, and answered in rapid, strongly accented Common Speech. "Right now de war is not so much, Cap-i-tan. May de sun always shine upon you. My master have ting he want to show you. You follow me. Come see!"

"Right now?" Nagaro was surprised. "In broad daylight?"

Matapili bobbed his head. "De war is not so much, as I say. Take down de blue flag on de top, and leave up de can-vas on de side, and come. It will be good. You will see!"

Nagaro frowned. "Why such a hurry?"

The man in the boat shrugged. "It is not hurry. Only you are hard to find, and maybe next time dere will be more war, Cap-i-tan."

Nagaro knew he *was* hard to find, so he decided to trust Matapili's judgement. He ordered the flag lowered and they followed the Jinari's little boat back through the strait between the two islands and across the expanse of open water on the other side, trying to ignore the stares of men in the fishing boats they passed. They anchored the *Sword* well out in Tambali Harbor, away from the docks and any merchant ships. From there, Nagaro let Matapili ferry him to shore. He decided to go alone this time, reasoning that one man was less conspicuous than two.

"Are ye sure it's safe?" Taru demanded as Nagaro went over the rail.

Nagaro laughed. "No," he said. "But I think it is. I know of no one here that wishes me harm."

On shore, Matapili led Nagaro between the long warehouses to the building that housed Utabala's office, and Nagaro was soon shown into the presence of the merchant's agent.

Utabala greeted him warmly, as always, in Common Speech that was equally rapid, though smoother and somewhat less accented than Matapili's. "Captain Nagaro! May de Un-named One keep you ever in His hand. It is good to see you, my friend. Please sit down and be comfortable."

Nagaro sat down on the padded leather seat of an elegantly carved wooden chair across a small table from Utabala's desk, which was half hidden beneath stacks of ledgers. "Well met, Utabala. It's good to see you also. I must say you look well."

Utabala beamed. In fact, he was looking positively sleek. The contours of his hawk-featured face had the smoothness of a comfortably well-fed man. The distinguished gray at his temples was only slightly more pronounced than the last time Nagaro had seen him. His shirt was crisp linen, his vest a dark green satin embroidered in black and gold.

"I haven't much time," Nagaro continued. "There are still some newly-freed Hashtep I must assist. And I confess it makes me a little nervous to be anchored here even if the war is 'not so much' as Matapili says."

Utabala returned an understanding nod. "Always I believe dat you do de work of de Un-named One, Captain, when you set slaves free," he said. "But I have someting that is maybe important to show you." He opened one of the drawers of his desk and withdrew a sheet of folded paper. He rose and unfolded it carefully as he came around the desk and laid it on the table in front of Nagaro. He then sat down in the table's other chair to watch his guest's reaction.

Nagaro studied the paper. There were three little pictures on it, each a kind of crudely rendered silhouette drawn in black ink. The first appeared to be three bull's heads facing the viewer and arranged in a triangle, two above and one below. The second showed what looked like a sheaf of grain with two sticks that might have been either staffs or spears crossed above it. The third represented a figure mounted on a prancing horse, facing to the left.

Nagaro examined the little pictures. "What are they?" he inquired, puzzled. "Are they merchants' marks of trade?"

Utabala shook his head. "Dey are not de marks of any of de merchants of Jinara. I checked dem all against de Book of Lists. I had hoped dat you could perhaps tell me what dey were," he added with evident disappointment. "You have not seen dem before?"

Nagaro frowned. "No," he said. "Where did they come from?"

"I will tell you dat." The Jinari leaned forward and his black eyes glittered. "It concerns de secret shipments dat my men have been investigating—all de poisons and oder tings. You recall dat my man discovered—a year ago—a little warehouse outside de town of Patamtala on de island of Judaba, where all of de tings are being sent and where de Droviri men wit yellow hair come to get dem in deir little boats?"

Nagaro felt a chill. "Yes, I remember."

"Do you remember dat dere were papers dat de yellow-haired men brought wit dem? Papers sealed wit wax?"

Nagaro nodded.

Utabala moistened his lips. "De last man I sent to Patamtala was able to look at some of de papers." He leaned out to tap the paper on the table. "Dese are de marks in de wax."

Nagaro frowned darkly. "They could still be merchant's marks," he said. "But they would belong to Edroviran merchants—Leithian merchants."

Utabala leaned back again in his chair. "I do not know what it means to you dat dey are—as you say—Leithians," he said carefully. "But I must tell you dat de members of de High Council of Jinara—may de Unnamed One give dem long life—have heard rumors of de secret trade, and dey have es-started to ask questions of de merchants because dey want to es-stop de trade." Utabala paused, looking uncomfortable. "So far I have only been asked about what my master is doing *now*, and I have answered what I was asked. It is fortunate dat my master es-stopped doing de secret trade some years ago. I have not told anyone dat dere are tings going to Droviri men. I have not shown anyone dese marks." Again Utabala indicated the paper. He was watching Nagaro carefully. "I also have not told dem dat *you* are interested in dis trade, Captain." And here Utabala stopped speaking. His black eyes held a question.

Nagaro thought he understood, and he fully appreciated Utabala's caution. "I also would like to stop the secret trade," he said. "I don't like to see dangerous things going into my country. I have a suspicion of who may be involved in this, but it's only a suspicion, and there may be others involved who are innocent in the sense that they don't know the true nature of the things they are procuring. Also, it's likely that *politics* are involved."

Utabala nodded in comprehension. "I do not much under-es-stand your politics," he said delicately. "But I do know dat you, yourself, have at dis time, some... *difficulty*... wit de king of your country. Dis is a great shame. Is your king perhaps likely soon to find de wisdom to see dat he has made a mistake?"

Nagaro grimaced. "It doesn't depend on the king so much as on a young Leithian named Peldred Gilforn. A young man who must find the courage to tell the truth."

Utabala bent his head then and touched the heel of his hand to his forehead in the familiar ritual gesture of his people. "Den I pray dat de One Whose Name We Do Not Es-speak will touch de heart of dis young man wit courage," he intoned. He paused then, apparently considering. Finally he said, "If it happens dat de High Council—blessings of de Un-named be upon dem—should wish to es-speak to someone in Edrovir about dis matter, how would you advise dem to proceed?"

Nagaro thought for a moment, frowning. "They should send out a boat to contact the Lord of the Fleet," he said at length. "Lord Kuran's first concern is the good of Edrovir, he keeps clear of politics, and he has the ear of the king. Also he is a man who will talk first rather than attack."

"De last is good to know." Utabala smiled tightly. "But I had heard dat Lord Kuran was hunting for *you*."

"He's hunting without finding. It's very important right now that he keep doing that."

"Ah." Utabala nodded sagely. "I under-es-stand, and I give you my tanks for de advice."

"You are most welcome." Nagaro picked up the paper and began to re-fold it. He was thinking about the fact that Dreigen served the king of Edrovir, and also the fact that merchants could be caught up in something they didn't fully understand. "For now, I will take this," he said. "Perhaps I can make some inquiries."

***

The night was clear and bright with stars. A gentle breeze from the sea caressed the little houses of Pakoa's Hashtep quarter. Candles showed in some of the windows, casting splashes of yellow light across the narrow street. In the shadow beside a garden wall, Nagaro paused, clutching his dark cloak about him and motioning to the men who crept after him to wait.

"Stay here," he said to them, in Hashti. "I will soon return."

Heads nodded. The leader murmured an acknowledgment. Nagaro turned away from them, rounded the corner of the wall, and approached the door of the house to which the garden belonged. He knocked softly and waited. Presently he heard footsteps within, there was the sound of a bolt being slid, and the door opened a crack.

"Who is there?" It was a man's voice.

"Well met, Chatef. I bring you friends in need. Five of them."

"So many? Sheptuum is good. Bring them around to the garden gate."

***

Half an hour later Nagaro knocked at a different door.

"Who's there?" A woman's voice responded.

"Let me in, Yuli. The night is chill."

"Tor Nagaro!" A diminutive Turowa, with her graying hair tightly braided down her back, opened the back door just wide enough to let him pass. "Get ye in here quick, afore someone sees ye."

Gratefully, he slipped through into the warmth of the kitchen. "I thought you might have already gone to your room upstairs, Yuli, but I saw the light in the window." The room smelled of fresh-baked bread and there were three large loaves set out to cool on the table.

She sighed and wiped her brow. "I'm just waiting for the last loaf t' bake—that I made for tomorrow. What brings ye to Pakoa Town this time? The Spirits know I've missed ye all winter."

"The Hashtep folk of Pakoa are good people," he said. "As many as I bring, they find places for."

"Oh, aye." She nodded understanding. "Some o' them will go to the new settlement on Kapala. Sit ye down, Zirda, while I get ye some hot sothiril. I've some cold meat for ye too, and we can sample the bread. I expect ye'll be wanting news."

He hung his cloak on a peg, then sat down and waited while Yuli stirred the fire. There was still sothiril in the pot and it was soon hot again. In the meantime she brought him a plate with the promised meat before taking the last loaf from the oven and setting it on the table beside the others. She cut two slices from a cool loaf before pouring them each a cup of sothiril and joining him at the table. "There's quite a few things to tell," she said as she sat down and picked up her cup. "For one, ye just missed Tulara's wedding t' my Habu. It was two weeks ago."

He picked up his own cup. "I'm sure they'll be very happy."

Yuli eyed him for a moment before nodding. She knew how little chance he had of achieving such happiness himself. "Ye're a good man, Tor Nagaro," she said at length. "But there's more important things t' tell than that. We had four Fleet ships here two days after the wedding, and your Lord Kuran was here in this very kitchen. I knew him, this time, from when he was here more 'n a year ago, asking after ye. He was sittin' on that very stool, pretending he was just one o' the crew—just like the last time. He asked for news o' ye. So I told him the truth—that I hadn't seen ye since afore the turning o' the year, and I didn't know where ye'd wintered." Yuli sniffed. "I *also* told him I was onto his little play-act this time, and I wouldn't tell him anything t' hurt ye even if I knew!"

Nagaro washed a bite of meat down with sothiril. "That was bold, Yuli. What did he have to say to it?"

She smiled over her bread. "He looked me straight in the eye, and said, 'What would ye like to know, Tira Yuli?' Just like that!"

"Meaning he knows that anything he tells you will get back to me. So what did you ask?"

"I asked how things stood in Lankura. He said that ye and Taru have been charged with 'aiding the escape of a convicted traitor.' That was his words exactly."

Nagaro frowned over his bread and meat. "That's better than being charged with treason ourselves, Yuli, although we would still have to face a tribunal and a prison sentence. And they'd find us guilty, of course, unless Pavo can be cleared of treason."

Yuli digested this. "He also said the Fleet's orders was not t' waste time or ships in searchin' for ye. Just to take ye if they chanced to see ye."

"Which they won't. We're one ship in all the islands."

"Aye," Yuli said. But she looked worried. "Except he also said that any lord what finds ye on his land is to take ye if he can. Ye're not safe anywhere on the mainland."

Nagaro shrugged. "I already knew that. Anything else?"

Yuli shifted in her chair. "They found that shipment o' gold ye left hidden for 'em on the far side o' Kapala. He said the letter ye left with it, explaining things, raised some hackles in Lankura. It seems some folk didn't like t' have ye keepin' one tenth share of it."

Nagaro put down his bread. "I didn't keep it. It went to Moraga and Timegar and their men. We couldn't have re-taken the shipment without them, and it was Kuran himself that told me our men could keep one tenth for expenses and for charity in the islands. I explained that in the letter!"

Yuli shrugged. "He said as much. But I guess there's some as would like t' say ye've gone back to pirating."

There was a pause during which Nagaro picked up his cup and studied the contents. "Is there any *other* news? From Lankura?" She knew of his feelings for Nevien. And there *had* to be news about the outcome of the princess's courtship.

"Well, there's the coming o' the heir of Darion." Yuli's eyes shown. "That's such a wonderful thing! I do so hope he'll put things back as they were in the old days."

Nagaro shifted his seat impatiently. *Surely she could guess what he wanted to know.* "What's the man doing?" he asked. He didn't really care, though he knew he ought to.

"They're sayin' there was another battle—bigger than the one last fall—though the tidings aren't very clear about who won."

"I don't think these battles are a good thing, Yuli. Who's the man fighting anyway?"

Yuli blinked in surprise. "Why the Leithians o' course! It was always the Leithians that were against him—against his father, King Tevren, I should say."

Nagaro scowled. "It was never *all* of the Leithians that were," he pointed out. "Darion, in his time, was opposed to anyone who interfered with the people living together peacefully under one rule—which was not just Leithians by any means."

"Well, perhaps not," Yuli conceded hastily. "It's all a bit complicated. But I'm sure those folk in Lankura will sort it out."

Nagaro wasn't so sure, knowing what he did about the men who governed Edrovir. He would have to ask elsewhere for the details of these events. *But right now...* "Isn't there *any other news?*" he asked her rather pointedly.

And there was so much pity in the look she gave him then that it made him wince.

"Finish your bread and meat, and I'll tell ye about the princess," she said.

Nagaro gave her a resentful look, but he picked up his bread again and wolfed it down, following it with the remainder of his meat and a few hasty gulps of sothiril. "There," he said. "Are you satisfied?"

"It's not for *my* sake," she said. "Ye won't be helping anyone if ye don't eat."

"I'm eating well enough, Yuli! Now will you just tell me which one of her suitors she married?"

Yuli was watching him worriedly. "She hasn't married anyone, Tor Nagaro."

His heart leaped absurdly at the words, only to crash back to earth in the next instant. What did it matter that she was unwedded, since *he* could never have her? And then the other implications of the news struck him. "Why not?" he asked. "What's happened, Yuli?"

She reached across the table to put a hand on his arm. "It's the queen," she said. "She's been very ill. They're saying that the princess has hardly left her side all winter, and King Elgurn has said there's to be no more courting—and no wedding—until... well... I guess until Queen Semorel is dead and buried and properly grieved for."

"*All winter?*" Nagaro shook off her hand and was on his feet. "Vothra'a Eyes! Poor Nevien!"

"Tor Nagaro, I'm sorry—"

He began to pace the kitchen. "I should have been there," he muttered. "I should be there *now!*"

Yuli watched in growing alarm. "What could ye possibly have done?" she cried. "What could ye do now?"

He turned on her, forgetting all pretense. "*Comfort* her, Yuli! Her mother is dying!"

For an instant Yuli gaped, stunned by the intensity of his emotion. "But how could ye *do* that?" she managed at last. "They wouldn't let ye near her, surely! Not at the queen's bedside."

He sagged. "No... of course not... She used to send me invitations to feasts at the palace, where we could talk, or to picnics at her country house where we could go riding together. But she wouldn't be sparing time for those things now." He came back to the table and sat down, brooding. "Who is there now to give her comfort?" he wondered aloud.

Yuli stared at him. She had naturally imagined that he'd fallen in love with the princess from a distance, and these glimpses of how things had really been were revelations to her. She shifted uncertainly. "She has her father—"

"Elgurn?" His head came up. "The king loves her, Yuli, but he's cold comfort, I'm afraid."

"Well then, there's her *ladies*, surely!"

He grimaced, picturing the princess's ladies one by one in his mind. He started to open his mouth, only to check himself when he saw the growing dismay on Yuli's face. Belatedly he remembered that Nevien had long been Yuli's distant adopted darling. The thought of her being left with no one to turn to was obviously upsetting the innkeeper's wife.

"Yes, of course. She has her ladies." He tried to sound relieved, and was gratified to see Yuli relax visibly.

He didn't stay long after that. He thanked her for the food and the news, and took his cloak and his leave, slipping out into the night.

Yuli stayed for a time, tiding up her kitchen. As she banked the fire, she shook her head and murmured, "Oh Spirits, ye're too cruel! I know I've asked ye often enough t' send the princess a good man. And now ye've finally gone and done it, but ye've sent her one she can't have." She paused as a thought occurred to her. *If the heir of Darion got to be king, would it set Nevien free, because she wouldn't be a princess anymore?* But then she sighed. It wouldn't work that way, of course. The man would just want to marry her like everybody else.

***

Nagaro threaded his way through the back streets and alleys of Pakoa Town, a shadow among shadows. It took some care, by starlight, to climb the ridge again that he and the newly freed Hashtep and traversed earlier that evening. From the top of the ridge, he looked down into the narrow valley where his six-year-old daughter, Narei, lived with her Aunt Animara and Uncle Sudano and their family. Nagaro could just make out the small stone house on the far side of the valley, beside the secret cove where the *Sword of Freedom* lay at anchor, another silent shadow under the stars.

He went down the zig-zag path as quickly as he could and through the grove of cedar trees at the bottom of the ravine. There was just a single small light flickering in one of the windows of the house as he crept past it to the beach where the longboat was drawn up. He would have liked to stop at the house, to visit with Animara and Sudano and their three children, to talk to his daughter and hold her in his arms. He missed them all, and most especially Narei, after wintering on far-off Chitaopa. In his pirate days, winter had always been the season when he saw the most of his adopted family. Now it was safer for them not to even know he had come this way. Narei would likely be abed already in any case, and it looked as if Animara and Sudano would be soon as well.

Yet Nagaro paused beside the longboat on the pebble beach and stood, gazing at the wavering glow in the window. "Vothra keep you, Ani," he murmured, "and all those under your roof. And sleep well, my little Narei."

Then he pushed off the boat, climbed into it, and began to ply the oars. A few minutes later he was on the deck of the *Sword* with the longboat safely stowed, giving orders to his crew. The anchor was quickly weighed, the ship's oars were extended, and the long, lean war galley slid out of the little cove as quietly as she had come. The sound of her passing was lost in the soughing of the wind and the gentle rush and slap of waves against the rocks.

Later that night, as the ship rocked easily at anchor in a different secret cove, Nagaro sat intently studying the pieces on the game board. He and his friends were in the great cabin of the *Sword of Freedom*, playing *kasadrin*, or King's Men, by lantern light. It had been a long day and they were taking their ease together before retiring for the night. He moved one of his horsemen. "There," he said. "I've trapped you, Taru. Do you yield?"

Taru stared at the board. "Hakura Kili!" he exclaimed. "I don't know what demon possesses ye, Nagaro!"

Nagaro looked up in surprise. "What do you mean?"

"That's the fifth time ye've beaten me this week, and it's only Third Day! It used t' be I could best ye two times out o' three, but ye've been catching me up—ever since last winter."

"I'm just paying more attention. It's only a game, and I only gave it half a mind before."

Pavo, who had been watching the game, said, "I think maybe you do not play well tonight, Taru. You are thinking maybe still about how Tulara have marry Habu."

Taru shot Pavo a scowling look. "She can marry whoever she likes!" He turned back to Nagaro. "I tell ye I think ye've changed since we left Lankura, Nagaro. It's not just King's Men. Ye were like a demon for sword practice all winter on Chitaopa—and rowing practice too. Ye drove the men so hard! And ye're taking more chances with the *Sword*. Ye never used t' go against ships one to one if ye could help it. And I swear ye were positively short-tempered with that last Mautep captain—not that he didn't deserve it, the way he was whining about having no slaves to row his ship!"

Nagaro frowned and shifted uncomfortably in his chair. He hadn't yet told either of his friends about how his heart had betrayed him. He knew he would have to eventually, and he felt a bit guilty, but keeping his secret close was easier, not to mention safer. He'd been trying to focus fully on whatever task was at hand—throwing himself into his work—as the best way to avoid thinking about Nevien.

"I had to train all those new recruits very quickly," he pointed out defensively. "And our safety now depends more on keeping clear of the Fleet than on avoiding Mahuk ships. I think we'd fare better in Emperor Baalkir's hands than in an Edroviran tribunal."

"I think you are right, Nagaro," Pavo put in. Then he turned his narrow dark eyes on Taru. "If you do not care about Tulara and Habu, why do you look like you have taste something bad ever since Nagaro have told us about it?"

Taru drew himself up. "I've just been thinking what a poor, silly fool Tulara is, if ye must know," he said stiffly. "And not because she threw me over for that wretched Habu! She could have had Nagaro, that's what I'm thinking. Nagaro's ten times the man Habu 'll ever be!"

For once Pavo's surprise showed in his face as he looked from one of his friends to the other. "She could have *Nagaro?*"

Nagaro covered his eyes with his hand. "I asked if I could court her once, after she'd said no to Taru. But it seems her heart had already gone to Habu, and she said no. And it doesn't matter to me." He uncovered his eyes. "Nor do I think she's any kind of a fool for marrying a man she loves, and who loves her."

"Huh!" Taru snorted. "Well, *I* feel sorry for her."

Pavo regarded him narrowly. "I think this is why you want to sail to Wotana," he said. "Tulara having marry Habu have make you remember very pretty girl in Wotana named Jitali."

"I hadn't ever forgot about Jitali!" Taru retorted. "I mean to court her, too. And it's time we went back to Wotana anyway, to see Gama." He stood up. "What d' ye say, Nagaro?"

Nagaro frowned. The suggestion raised conflicting emotions. "Wotana is rather close to Lankura," he pointed out cautiously. "We'd have to cross Farano's Mouth, and pass Lankura, to get there."

"So?" Taru gestured dismissively. "*I'm* not afraid. The fishermen 'll tell us where the Fleet ships are, and we can always outrun them. I say we can do it!"

"What about you, Pavo," Nagaro asked, turning to the Hashtep. "Being convicted of treason, you have the most to lose if we're caught."

Pavo shrugged his great shoulders. "I think we can do it," he said calmly. "And I also am not afraid."

Nagaro heaved an internal sigh. He might do worse than let his friends decide since he didn't entirely trust his own judgement under the circumstances. "All right," he said, as casually as he could. "We'll sail north in the morning."

"Good!" Taru spoke with obvious satisfaction. "I've had enough o' this game," he added, gesturing at the board. "I'm for my bunk. Good night t' ye both." So saying, he stood up and exited through the cabin door.

"Will you play, Pavo?" Nagaro inquired as the door closed behind Taru.

The Hashtep shook his head. "Already you have beaten me tonight, Nagaro. Maybe I go to my bunk also."

"All right." Nagaro found the bag and began to put the pieces away. "I have some bookkeeping to do anyway."

Pavo got up. "You do book-keeping now? Maybe Taru is right about demon inside you, Nagaro. You work too much."

Nagaro paused with the last playing piece in his hand. "Do you think I've been acting differently, Pavo?"

Pavo regarded him with his unreadable Hashtep eyes. "I think you do not like to be exile," he said. "When you save me, you do right thing because I am not traitor, but it is not according to law. I think you do not like that."

Nagaro gave him a wan smile. "You're right," he said. There was more to it than that, but it wasn't false and it was a good thing for Pavo to believe. He put the last playing piece into the bag and drew the string tight. "Pavo," he said on a sudden impulse as his friend was turning to go, "How do *you* manage to act the same as ever? You're under sentence of death and scarcely dare set foot on Edroviran soil. You can't even go to see Tenepti and your little son."

Pavo had turned back. "I trust in Sheptuum," he said calmly.

"Well, of course." *And Pavo believed that Sheptuum was somehow protecting Nagaro too.* It didn't help at all. It was like saying he should trust in Lokundas—the personification of fate. Kelorin folk always said that only a fool put his trust Lokundas.

Pavo was still watching him. The big Hashtep must have guessed some of his thoughts, for he said, "Long time ago, very wise man have say this: Thing that is in past, you maybe know, but you cannot change it. Thing that is in future you can maybe change, but you do not yet know what it is. Thing that is happen right now is only thing you can both know *and* change."

"Is that it, Pavo? You only think about *right now*—this moment in time?"

Pavo nodded his shaggy head. "Yes. Past is gone, and who knows what future will be? Does this help, Nagaro?"

"Maybe. Thank you."

The Hashtep gave Nagaro a brief, knowing smile. "Maybe Taru will not be in so bad temper now that we will go to Wotana."

Nagaro grinned back. "Let's hope so. Good night, Pavo."

He got out his ledger after Pavo had gone and tried to do some bookkeeping, but he found he couldn't concentrate. When he tried to think about *now*, rather than the past or future, he kept picturing Nevien at her mother's sickbed. Finally he gave it up. He put the book away, turned down the lantern, and flung himself on his bunk. "You're not there," he told himself, "and you couldn't do anything if you were." At last he tried imagining how Narei might have spent her day, and that worked well enough that he finally fell asleep.

# Chapter 2

# The Lingering Vigil

Nevien awakened out of an unpleasant dream, into an even more unpleasant reality. Frowning, she made an effort to retreat back into the dream. *Something about trying to climb a slope, but she kept slipping.... The bits of root and tufts of grass she tried to grasp had kept coming loose in her hands and...*

It was no good. The dream was gone. She blinked in the pale dawn light that suffused her chamber and sat up with a little groan, to find that she'd been sleeping in her shift. Vaguely she remembered Lady Merriel helping her struggle out of her gown and tucking her into bed. She couldn't actually recall how she'd gotten from her mother's room to her own. She had a half recollection of being carried—which couldn't have been by Merriel, of course. It must have been her father.

She rose and washed, exchanged her rumpled shift for a fresh one, and dressed—picking a gown at random from one of her wardrobes. Belatedly, she remembered that she was going to the Temple of Solbrid that morning and she picked up a black veil and the heavy gray hooded cloak she always wore to the Temple Compound. She carried both things with her when she went down the hall to her mother's chamber.

She entered the sickroom quietly without knocking. The heavy curtains were drawn across the windows, and a lamp burned low on the dressing table. The room was dim and close. One of her mother's ladies was there, a dark-haired Kelorin woman who rose gratefully and relinquished the seat by the bedside, murmuring some empty words of intended comfort before going to seek her own bed. Nevien dropped her cloak and veil on the dressing table beside the lamp and took the seat the other woman had just vacated. Queen Semorel stirred a little, moaning wordlessly. Her dark hair, streaked with gray, spread over the pillow. Her face looked as if it had been carved from wax. Her eyes were closed, and a folded, dampened cloth lay across her brow.

Mechanically Nevien removed the cloth and laid it aside in an empty wash bowl. She dipped a fresh one in the basin of water that rested on the floor beside the bed. Squeezing out the cloth a little, she folded it twice lengthwise and laid it gently across her mother's brow. It was a ritual she could have performed in her sleep.

Two hours later, Merriel came. The small, flaxen-haired Leithian woman brought her some breakfast on a tray.

"How is she, child?"

"Sleeping, Merriel. But she's been growing more restless this last half hour, as if the pain is getting worse. She needs more opa. Will Master Ambras come soon?

"Yes. Soon. Try to eat something now, dear." Merriel sat down at the dressing table.

Nevien ate a few bites, but couldn't force herself any further. As she was finishing, her father came in. The king stood silently for a long moment beside the sickbed, looking down at his wife, his arms rigid at his sides, his fingers curling tensely. Then he turned to Nevien.

"Are you ready, Daughter, to go to the temple?"

"Yes, Father."

She rose, quickly donning her veil and hanging her cloak about her shoulders. With a rustle of skirts, Merriel sat down at the bedside to take her place.

***

One of the royal coaches carried Nevien and her father to the Temple Compound. They rode in silence, having long since run out of words to comfort one another. At the compound, the king alighted first and offered his hand to help his daughter down the little steps to the ground. Again wordlessly, they then went their separate ways, he to the Temple of Hrathgard, she to the Temple of Solbrid.

Nevien pulled her hood closer about her veiled face as she stepped through the temple portico. The shapes of other people moved in the cool dimness of the central hall, some passing inwards ahead of her, others passing outwards. Many were ordinary folk dressed in ordinary garments. Others were attired as she was, hooded and cloaked from head to foot, seeking anonymity. No one ever completely found it, of course. There was stature, breadth of shoulders, the shape of hands. And of course the shoes. Boots or buskins or dainty embroidered slippers always showed.

Nevien usually wore her oldest, most worn pair of shoes when coming to the Temple Compound. She'd never liked the thought that other folk might look at her feet and think, *princess*, or even simply, *lady*. On this particular day, she was wearing whatever she'd put on her feet that morning, hardly heeding, before going to her mother's side. She glanced down ruefully. *The black ones, finely fashioned of soft, supple, leather with gold stitching... "lady" at least...* Her lips twisted bitterly. Of course, anyone who had noticed the royal carriage in which she and her father had arrived wouldn't be fooled by shoes. She couldn't possibly be any less a person than the wife of some lord who happened to be staying in one of the palace's many guest chambers.

Nevien frowned as she moved along the hallway towards her destination. She didn't ordinarily come to the Temple Compound with her father. She preferred coming with Merriel. Her father was *conspicuous*—and not as accepting as Merriel. He tended to ask questions if anything surprised him. *But of course Merriel was taking Nevien's place at her mother's side. Helping to keep what must surely be the final vigil...* Tears welled unexpectedly. For days she'd been too numb and weary to weep. Hastily she brushed them away. She drew a sigh and focused her mind on what she was doing.

The central hall of the Temple of Solbrid had numerous doors along its length on either side, leading to alter chambers dedicated to various causes that lay within the province of Queen Solbrid, the Mother Goddess of the Leithians. Nevien was making for the entrance to the chamber of the Altar of Life and Death, and she found herself more of less following a shabbily-dressed elderly woman who was going the same way. The woman was moving too quickly to be gracefully overtaken before reaching the doorway, and Nevien understood that she must graciously wait her turn. She wouldn't have minded... *except that she didn't like to be too long away from her mother's side...*

Her steps faltered as her tears sprang for a second time. With an effort, she pulled her thoughts away from the brink of the pit that opened before her at the thought of losing her mother. Desperate for some other thought, she fixed her attention on the old woman who would reach the doorway of the chamber of Life and Death before her. The woman must have some trouble and pain of her own. *Perhaps she, too, had left a sickroom to come here. Perhaps she had left it unattended.* Certainly she was in a hurry, hobbling along at a surprising rate, her offering clutched in her hand. Nevien caught a glimpse of the offering bag as the old woman turned at the altar chamber door. It was nothing more than a rag drawn up around a handful of coins, but it bulged surprisingly large. It had to contain twenty rins at least. How could this ragged old woman afford to part with so much?

Nevien slipped through the doorway, entering the chamber's vestibule close behind the woman. She was frowning now, momentarily drawn out of herself by her interest in this other sufferer. She stopped in the vestibule, however, knowing she shouldn't intrude on the woman's supplication. The inner doorway on the other side of the little space was covered by a heavy curtain hanging from a high rod at the top of the opening. The old woman seemed not to have noticed Nevien, for she didn't look back, but hurriedly tugged the curtain aside and passed through into the altar chamber.

In her hurry, the woman failed to get the curtain properly closed. A two-inch gap remained between its edge and the stone of the doorframe. Nevien crossed the vestibule and grasped the curtain edge, intending to close it. She stopped however, instead, for she could quite clearly see the old woman's retreating back and the interior of the chamber through the gap. *It would really do no harm to watch. She could easily withdraw before the woman turned around, and it was better than being left alone with her own thoughts.*

The chamber of the Altar of Life and Death was shadowy, lit only by two lamps set on a pair of slender four-foot pillars, one on each side of the altar, and to a lesser extent by a flickering fire in a great bronze brazier on the raised bed of the huge ceremonial hearth located behind the altar stone. The pillar on the left was of pale translucent alabaster, while the one on the right was of jet-black marble. They represented life and death, respectively. The altar between the pillars was a massive slab of white stone standing three feet high, three feet deep, and six feet wide. Behind it, to the left of the brazier, stood a priestess robed and masked in purest white and bearing a long staff.

The kneeling-stone before the altar lay some twenty feet from the curtained doorway, and the old woman soon reached it and sank down onto her knees. Nevien saw her empty the little bag she carried onto the top of the altar with shaking hands. A quantity of coins spilled out. The dark patina of copper rins, nearly two dozen of them, stood out in contrast to the white stone.

The old woman bowed her bare head, clutching her raised hands together in supplication. She spoke, and Nevien heard the sound but not the words because the room swallowed them. The woman spoke at some length, swaying a little from side to side. When she stopped, the priestess waited a moment before extending a hand over the brazier. The flames flared up briefly before sinking again to their previous level. The old woman got painfully to her feet, bowing, and bowing again, to the altar, the brazier, the priestess. At last she turned around and began hobbling back across the polished stone floor. Nevien let go of the curtain and stepped back. Just before she lost her view of the chamber, she saw quite clearly a figure, robed and hooded in gray, rise up from behind the altar and deftly scoop up the scattered rins, then quickly duck down again.

*So that is how it's done,* Nevien thought. The credulous believed that the goddess herself took the coins. Nevien had always imagined that the priestess must remove them before the next supplicant came in. She frowned fleetingly. *It didn't really matter.* She moved to the back of the vestibule as the old woman twitched aside the curtain and passed through the doorway. Nevien caught a glimpse of the woman's pale face, wrinkled and ruinous and lined with sorrow, and her heart was moved suddenly to overwhelming sympathy.

"Wait, good mother," she said as she thrust her hand into her own offering bag and drew out a silver trokin. She held out the coin. "Here is something for your need."

The old woman stared in apparent shock for a moment. The single coin was worth four times what she had just left on the altar. Then she reached out and took it. "Blessed be the name of our Mother Solbrid," she murmured, and shuffled out through the outer doorway into the central hall with the prize clutched in her bony fist.

Nevien stood alone, her head bowed. The silver in the bag she held seemed to weigh like lead. It didn't matter, it was said, how large or small the offering might be. It was supposed to be in proportion to what one possessed, and to be a sacrifice in proportion to the magnitude of one's need. She had probably brought a hundred times what the old woman had brought, and yet in proportion to what they each possessed she suspected the woman had made the greater sacrifice, and she felt humbled. The trokin coin meant little to Nevien. To the old woman it was a bounteous windfall.

The woman's words had made it clear that she believed the coin had been sent by the Goddess. Perhaps she believed Nevien had been sent by Mother Solbrid in answer to her prayer. *And maybe, just maybe, some part of the old woman's sorrow was something to which money might make some difference.*

Nevien sighed, feeling unexpectedly a little easing of the emptiness inside her. Then she thought of something. The image of the single coin brought it to her mind, and her face clouded. *She'd almost forgotten.* Hastily she withdrew a second coin from her offering bag and guiltily slipped it into the sash of her gown, under her concealing cloak. Then she lifted her head. Moving to thrust the curtain aside, she began her own journey to the Altar of Life and Death.

She knelt on the cushioned kneeling-stone and poured her offering of silver coins onto the altar's top. She clasped her hands, bowed her head, and after a moment found her voice. "Good and merciful Queen Solbrid, mother of us all, hear my prayer. If you are going to take my mother, I beg you, please, to do it soon. Her suffering is great, and has been very long." Nevien paused and swallowed, her throat so tight it hurt to speak.

Still, she drew a breath and continued. "I know she has been all her life an unbeliever..." She faltered. "Yet she's been a good woman, a good wife, a good mother to me... And she's done much good in the world through her charity. I don't know where her spirit will dwell, but please, Mother Solbrid, be merciful and end her pain."

Nevien stopped. She huddled where she knelt, pressing her hands to her eyes, squeezing back the tears. It had been a hard choice to make, to stop asking for life—to ask for death instead. It felt like a defeat, though it was only an admission of the inevitable. Presently she heard, rather than saw, the flames in the brazier flare up, rushing and crackling, marking the end of her time... her dismissal.

She rose unsteadily, blindly, resisting the impulse to steady herself by placing a hand on the altar stone, which was forbidden. Turning, she stumbled out of the chamber and through the vestibule. No stranger stepped out of the shadows to hand her a miracle.

Once in the central hall, she found her balance again, or some of it. These days she always felt perilously near the brink, when she felt anything at all. She was glad of the veil that hid her face from the eyes of strangers as she moved, almost unseeing, threading her way among the many supplicants. Her feet eventually brought her out through the wide entranceway into the temple's high portico.

She stopped at the top of the long flight of stairs that led down to the broad courtyard of the Temple Compound. That wide space was by this time thronged with folk. Here and there were waiting wagons, carriages, or tethered horses. Her eyes found the royal carriage, standing where she and her father had left it. The driver sat in the open door, enjoying a bit of late breakfast. This observation told her that her father was most likely still in the Temple of Hrathgard where he'd gone to pray for guidance—Hrathgard being the ruler of the gods, and therefore also the god of rulers. It meant she had time to do... the other thing.

She turned to the side of the portico where a small door opened in the wall, a narrow rectangle of deeper shadow within the shadow of the out-thrust temple roof. She approached the doorway cautiously, halting once while a man emerged and hurried away. Above the door were inscribed the words *Altar of the Lost.*

Nevien slipped through the doorway. The space inside was little more than a large alcove, windowless and dim. She waited a moment for her eyes to adjust to the lack of light. Here there was no kneeling-stone, no priestess. The altar stone was set against the right-hand wall of the alcove, which was the temple wall. It was waist-high, four feet wide by two feet deep, gray and rough, with a hole the size of a large coin in the middle of the top of it. A single candle burned in a little glass box set in a narrow niche in the wall at about eye level. Nevien advanced to stand before the altar. Withdrawing the last silver coin from her sash, she stood with it clutched in her hand and spoke a whispered prayer whose words flowed easily, made familiar by frequent repetition.

"This is for Leyel, wherever he may wander, be he living or dead. Wherever his spirit may dwell, keep him safe... and bring him peace."

With a sigh, she dropped the coin into the hole. It rang hollowly inside the stone. The ritual of the single coin was the time-worn tradition of the Altar of the Lost, its origin lost in the passing of years. The coin might be of any denomination, but Nevien had settled nearly eight years before on a silver trokin. She had come every month throughout those eight years, never once forgetting the duty she'd set for herself.

She turned away from the altar stone—and nearly collided with her father in the doorway. She knew him as much by the color and fabric of his cloak as by the bearded features under the shadow of his hood. "I hardly think your pirate captain is as lost as *that*, Daughter," he said sternly. "He seems to have no trouble evading capture."

"It wasn't for him." Nevien was startled and defensive. "It was for Leyel—" And she stopped, wishing she had played to her father's inaccurate guess instead, for she saw his features darken.

"*Still?*" he asked sharply. "Just because we didn't find a body? He is certainly dead. We searched outside the wall—as much as it made sense to search. If he was the one they saw go over the wall, he could have wandered anywhere, or fallen in the stream and been carried to the sea! But most likely he died of a fit and the Mahuk raiders threw his body overboard."

Nevien looked at the ground and bit her lip. It was an old argument between them and she hadn't meant to open it again, especially not now when they would soon have nothing left but one another. "If he's dead, Father," she said meekly, "his spirit may still wander."

"But *you* shouldn't have to do this—" The king bit off his words.

"Yes, I do, Father," she said quietly. "Because I feel the need. I didn't care for him... *properly*." It was all she dared say of what had troubled her for so long. She half expected her father to argue, but he made no direct reply. He was looking at the ground, and she couldn't make out his face under his hood.

"I have a duty here," he said gruffly. "And then I'll go into Solbrid's Temple, as well. Go to the carriage and wait, if you're finished." With that, he ushered her past him with a gesture, and stepped into the alcove.

Nevien moved on a little, away from the doorway, but something held her. She turned back to watch her father through the door, where he stood before altar. She saw him reach under his cloak, draw something out, then stand with hand outstretched. She heard him murmur words she couldn't understand, and heard distinctly the ring of his coin as it fell.

She would have left then, but she saw his hand reach again for something under his cloak. Again he stood with outstretched hand, again he spoke, and a coin dropped. This time, however, Nevien caught her breath in surprise before turning quickly to hurry down the steps and put as much distance as she could between them before her father emerged. The first coin had winked silver, but the second coin, when it caught the light of the candle as it fell, had flashed with the color of pure gold.

She was still puzzling over this when she reached the carriage, climbed inside, and took a seat. She knew her father went regularly to the Temple of the Lost to offer prayers for Kale. That would explain one coin, but who had the golden coin been for? If it had been even a half dokan, it seemed out of proportion to anything in her father's life of which she was aware. It wouldn't be for her mother. That was what he would go into the main temple for. The Altar of the Lost was for those who were *lost*—in body, or mind, or spirit. It really wouldn't have been appropriate for her to have left a coin there for Nagaro, except perhaps because he was Vothrin, an unbeliever. But she'd never thought of him as *lost* for that reason, any more than she did her mother. They were both too strong and steady in their convictions.

Nagaro was strong and steady in many ways, in fact. As Nevien leaned wearily against the cushioned seat and closed her eyes, she remembered the comfort of his arm around her shoulders the last time they had sat together in the little room on the third floor of the palace after Kale had nearly strangled her. She'd felt so safe, so protected... so cared for. *If only he were here now to hold her so again.*

She opened her eyes only briefly when her father climbed into the carriage and sat down across from her. He didn't look at her, but stared moodily out of the carriage window. His face in the light from the window looked drawn, his mouth set in a hard line. She knew better than to disturb him. He had other concerns in addition to her mother's condition. So she shut her eyes again and didn't open them until the carriage had nearly reached the stable yard.

She found her father looking at her then, gravely. "You should get more rest, Nevien," he said.

"I rest when I can, Father." *I'll rest when it's over. Perhaps it won't be long.* She looked away guiltily, avoiding his eyes.

The carriage halted with a jingle of harness and her father swung the door open, descended, then held up a hand to assist her. Soon she stood beside him. "Father," she said on impulse, looking up almost fearfully, "I... I prayed this time for Solbrid to take her—to take her quickly." She felt as if she were confessing a betrayal, but he only nodded.

"So did I, Nevien. I prayed so the last time as well."

She looked down again then, hiding her frown, momentarily distressed that their prayers might have been working at cross-purposes. But she let the thought go. Queen Solbrid would do what she would do, in her own time. There had been nothing in Nevien's life to lead her to expect that her prayers would be answered promptly—if indeed they were answered at all. Still she prayed when the need was great and the matter beyond her control—because there was nothing else she could do.

They were intercepted, as they walked towards the palace's side door, by Lord Kuran. The Fleet Lord had apparently just arrived in the stable yard, by horse, and he approached Elgurn, saying something about making his report before putting to sea again. The king made some reply as they all passed through the side door and into the small entry hall at the base of what they called the back stairs. But Nevien's thoughts were elsewhere and she wasn't listening until her father spoke her name.

"Will you escort Nevien back to her mother's chamber, Kuran? Before joining me? I have something urgent to attend to, and my daughter is worn out with lack of food and sleep."

"Of course, My Lord. I'm glad to be of service."

Nevien frowned. "I'm all right, Father," she protested, although she took Kuran's arm gratefully as they approached the foot of the stairs.

Her father continued along the hall with a murmured word, leaving them to climb the stairs to the third floor without him.

Halfway up the first flight, Nevien felt herself dragging and began to lean on Kuran's arm. "I'm sorry," she murmured. "I guess I am more tired than I thought."

The Lord of the Fleet gave her a look of concern. "You really should rest more, My Lady. All Lankura is worried about you."

"Mmm." She stopped when they reached the second floor landing to catch her breath, feeling a little hazy. They stood there under the shy, serious gaze of Leyel Virden's portrait, hanging on the wall. She barely glanced at it. She was thinking of a different man, another arm to lean on. Because she'd been thinking of him in the carriage as well, she asked, "Is there any news of Captain Nagaro?"

Lord Kuran laughed a little. "I wondered how long it would take you to ask. As it happens, I've just returned from a patrol of the southern isles, where I stopped at Pakoa and made inquiries. Nothing had been heard of him there since before the turning of the winter."

Nevien looked at him in some alarm. "You don't think he's been taken by the Emperor, do you?"

Kuran shook his head. "It's more likely that he wintered in some out-of-the-way place. But I wouldn't fear for him in the Emperor's hands, My Lady. I fancy those two might just sit down across a table and have a pleasant little chat."

The last words were spoken lightly, and Nevien feared that Kuran was being overly sanguine for her benefit. "But he's been freeing more slaves, hasn't he?" she persisted. "The Emperor nearly killed him for that!"

The Lord of the Fleet regarded her seriously. "As far as I can tell, he's freed slaves only in Edroviran waters. And the Emperor apparently let him go without any stipulations. Honor begets honor, so Vothra says. And honor respects honor besides."

At this point they were interrupted by the sound of a door opening above them and a hurried, booted tread descending the stairs. In a moment, Lord Odus appeared at the top of the flight, coming rapidly down. "Ah, Kuran!" he exclaimed, pausing in his descent as he reached them."Do you know where Elgurn has gotten to?"

Kuran cleared his throat. "The king is somewhere downstairs. He said he had something to attend to."

Odus frowned in annoyance. "Well, since I've just seen that he isn't *upstairs*, of course he must be down," he observed testily. "Lord Madred is downstairs, demanding an audience concerning this latest supposed heir of the House of Loros. Since Rastyl is there as well, the two of them have very nearly come to blows!"

Nevien frowned a little. She knew there'd been increasing troubles involving a man who it was claimed was the son of King Tevren, and therefore the grandson of Darion the Great of the long-disbanded House of Loros, but her father was convinced the man was a fraud. Compared to her mother's plight, it all seemed rather distant to her. Kuran, however, cocked and eyebrow and said, "How so?"

Odus waved an exasperated hand. "Madred kept insisting on telling Rastyl to 'curb his dog,' and Rastyl was adamant that the man is no 'dog' of his—or some such nonsense. How he expects anyone to believe that when the man comes out of *his* Wared, is beyond my comprehension!" Odus paused, apparently to catch his breath after this tirade, and abruptly frowned hard at Kuran. "Have you caught that pirate yet?" he demanded.

Kuran returned him a bland smile. "Not yet, My Lord. The man likely wintered outside of Edroviran waters, and he may not yet have re-entered them." He coughed significantly. "And it's hardly just to call him a pirate. As far as anyone can tell, he's been subsisting entirely on charity."

Odus grimaced. "Oh, *yes*," he snapped. "He knows how to play the crowd, doesn't he? He's *quite* the hero." The Leithian threw up his hands in furious frustration. "I don't understand it! The man surrenders and is nearly beaten to death for it, and he's a hero! He frees a convicted Mahuk traitor, and he's a hero! Obviously the common folk have no intelligence whatsoever."

He swept past them then, fuming, turning back just long enough to say,"But *you* should know better, Kuran. One would almost think you didn't want to find him. See that you attend to your duty, *My Lord!*" He went on down the stairs, grumbling. "The Council should obviously have taken my suggestion! But Elgurn is always much too squeamish."

Kuran shook his head and gave Nevien a wink. "Are you ready for the next flight?"

She nodded. "I think I can manage it." They started up the stairs once more, and she focused her energy on the climb. When they reached third floor landing, she said a little breathlessly, "Is it true, Kuran, that Captain Nagaro is still a hero to the people?"

He snorted. "Half of those I've spoken to are prepared to accept Pavo's innocence on his say-so alone. Most of the rest think Pavo is probably guilty, but they believe Nagaro is honestly deceived and they admire his loyalty and sacrifice on his friend's behalf."

"Good. I'm glad the people haven't abandoned him."

They passed through the door into the third floor hallway.

"He still must fear the worst if he's taken on Edrovirn soil, My Lady. The lords of all the coastal Holds and Wareds and their soldiers are supposed to be watching for him."

Nevien frowned as they walked, then fastened upon the last few words. "*Supposed to be,* Kuran?"

He smiled a little grimly. "Some are hotter for it than others, I'm sure. And anyone suspected of *knowingly* letting him escape would be in rather serious trouble. It means the islands are safest for him, where the power of authority is weakest."

"Might there be an end of it soon, Kuran? What about the young Leithian? What was his name?"

"Peldred? There's been no word from him."

"Can't you send to Geldoran and ask to have him brought back to Lankura?"

Kuran's feet paused. They had reached the door of the queen's bedchamber. "Not without a formal charge, Nevien. And there isn't much hope of getting one."

"Oh." She heaved a small sigh and knocked lightly on the door. After a moment Merriel opened it a crack. "How is Mother?" Nevien asked. "Is she in a fit state to receive a visitor?"

Merriel's brow puckered. "She's had more opa—Master Ambras is here—and she's wandering."

Nevien sighed. "I'm sorry, Kuran," she said. "You'd best not come in."

"It's just as well," he replied gravely. "I still have my report to make."

Lady Merriel seemed to become aware of Kuran's presence for the first time. "Oh! Good morning, Kuran," she said, rather too eagerly. "I've missed seeing you—since we... since we've had no outings, I mean" She faltered, blushing pink, and dropped her eyes."

Kuran looked faintly puzzled. "I've missed seeing you as well, Merriel," he said with apparent sincerity. "I've been in the palace a number of times, bringing my reports, but there was no excuse to come to the third floor until today."

He bowed and Lady Merriel turned even pinker, which he seemed not to notice, merely bowing to them both and making for the main stair.

Nevien moved past Lady Merriel into the room, and Merriel hastily closed the door and leaned against it, looking flustered. "Sweet Lissafel!" she murmured weakly. "What *must* he think of me?"

"He doesn't think anything, Merriel, because he hasn't any idea how you feel," Nevien said wearily as she shed her cloak and veil. "I still think you should just tell him."

"I couldn't possibly! A well-bred Leithian woman *never* approaches a man. It's *terribly* forward."

"But Kuran isn't Leithian," Nevien pointed out. "He won't think it's forward at all—"

"Nevien...? My child... is that you?" The queen's quavering voice interrupted them.

Nevien instantly dropped her things on the dressing table and hurried to the bedside. Master Ambras the healer, seated on a chair on the opposite side of the bed, acknowledged her with a somber nod.

"Yes, Mother. I'm here."

Queen Semorel was propped up on a pair of pillows. Her hair still streamed loose. Her eyes were open and very bright, but the gaze she now directed at her daughter was vague and dreamy. "Oh yes... there you are, Nevien..." she murmured. "But where is he?"

"He? Where is who, Mother?"

"Your gallant young man, of course, dear. Captain Nagaro... I thought I heard him..."

Nevien sat down. "You must have heard Kuran, Mother. I'm afraid Captain Nagaro isn't here. He's, ah, away sailing, in the south."

"*Away? Sailing?* But that won't do, dear... He must be here... for the wedding..."

Nevien bit her lip. "Mother, I told you," she said gently. "We've postponed the wedding." Her voice died. She couldn't explain to her mother why the courtship—and any thought of a wedding—had been postponed, any more than she dared to truthfully explain Nagaro's absence.

"You've postponed it?" The queen's wandering gaze fastened on her daughter. "Well you would have to... wouldn't you? You can't very well marry him... if he isn't *here*..."

Nevien stared in shock. "Oh, *Mother*," she murmured. "I can't... I mean *he* can't—" She broke off. On the other side of the bed, Ambras was desperately shaking his head and mouthing, *"humor her!"* Nevien drew a breath, swallowed hard, and said, "Yes, Mother, we've postponed the wedding until Captain Nagaro returns."

A spasm suddenly crossed the queen's face, and her hands fluttered briefly at her breast. Her eyes closed and she seemed scarcely to breathe.

*"Mother!"* Nevien grasped one thin, pale hand and chafed it, her heart in her throat. She was seized with terror at the thought that Solbrid had already taken the queen's spirit—although she'd prayed for that very thing not an hour before.

It wasn't so, however. The queen's eyes opened again, and dreamily sought her daughter's face. "Dearest Nevien," she murmured, smiling beatifically. "It's given me such joy to see him court you. My heart is glad… so very glad… I know you'll be happy. He'll take care of you… as your father always took care of me. But tell me, dear," The queen frowned vaguely. "Where is he? He must be here for the wedding…"

Nevien struggled to hide her anguish as she explained for the second time that Nagaro was sailing in the south, then listened to more ramblings about the imagined wedding. She glanced across at Master Ambras, and saw him wincing as well. Yet the healer always advised that she not try to dissuade her mother from her happy fantasies. In fact, Nevien had found it all but impossible to do so. Under the influence of opa, the queen seemed often to hear only what she wished to hear.

Nevien could easily see how her mother had come to this particular notion. Fearing for her daughter's future, and wandering in opa dreams, she'd sought amongst the men she'd seen consorting with her daughter and picked the one who was most appealing, forgetting—*or perhaps not caring*—that he was of unknown parentage. It would embarrass Nagaro terribly, of course, Nevien knew. The poor man had only sought to be her friend. Perhaps it was for the best that he couldn't set foot in Lankura right now. *But oh, Sweet Lissafel, how she missed him.*

# Chapter 3

# Pursuits

Nagaro grasped the tree limb above him and reached high with the pruning hook. The blade found the base of a small dead branch, he sawed at it, and it came down with a crack and a swish, falling past him and landing on the ground below among the others. He squinted against the light that came through the apple tree's canopy of pale new leaves and lingering blossoms, looking for more dead wood—black and bare among the leafy twigs. Satisfied at length that there was no more to be found, he tossed the pruning hook down on top of the pile of dead branches and descended from the tree. On the ground, he gathered an armload of cut branches, picked up the pruning hook, and set off down the short slope beside Gama's small stone house to the little slanting woodshed. It leaned against the corner of the house not far from where an intermittent hedge separated Gama's garden from the road.

The road beyond the hedge was a bare dirt track that lay warming under the pale spring sun. The morning mist had burned away here on the outskirts of the town of Wotana, though its veil still hung over the bay. The road was empty of folk at that hour since it was past time for going out to work and not yet time for a mid-day meal.

Nagaro hung up the hook and took his time arranging his load of future kindling in the dim recesses of the woodshed. When he came out again he paused in the doorway, shielding his eyes against the brightness of the morning. Standing there, squinting, he saw that someone was coming along the road.

It was a young Turowan woman, hurrying with her head down, her dark hair hiding her face. As she drew near, he could tell that she was crying. She raised her head just as she drew abreast of the hedge, turning back to look over her shoulder. She hadn't seen him yet, but he'd caught enough of a glimpse of her face to recognize her as the elder of the two daughters of the man who owned the house on the other side of the road and a little way along it in the direction of the edge of the town.

She had a blunt, broad face, with a chin too square and a nose too flat for beauty, but with eyes wide and dark that were usually kind and often merry. He was so shocked by seeing those eyes full of tears, that he stepped quickly out of the shed's doorway and towards a break in the hedge to intercept her. Over the years he'd exchanged a little speech with her from time to time, and she often came of her own choosing to help Gama with odd tasks about the house and garden.

"Hamani!" he cried. "Whatever is the matter?"

She started violently as she turned towards him. "N-nothing, Tor Nagaro," she stammered, wiping hastily at her eyes. "I washed my face at the pump, and... and I had no way o' drying it."

"Have you some errand in the town then?" he asked, pretending to accept her explanation.

Apparently she couldn't think of one quickly enough, for she said, "No... I... I hadn't."

"Then, perhaps you could help me gather up these branches," he said easily. "It would make the work go more quickly, and I need to be finished soon because we mean to sail within the hour."

For a moment, she looked torn, glancing back at her father's house as if thinking of returning to it, but almost immediately turning away again. Nagaro guessed that she didn't want to go back but had no excuse to go forward. Finally she gave him a weak smile and said, "All right, I'd be glad t' help." Having made her decision, she quickly stepped through the break in the hedge.

They worked side by side with few words for a time, gathering branches and twigs under the apple tree. They were quite alone together there in Gama's garden, yet in full view from the road so there should be no question of impropriety. "Let me take the bundles into the shed," he told her when she started to follow him there. "I wouldn't want anyone to say I had my way with you in Gama's woodshed."

"Oh, Tor Nagaro!" she exclaimed in embarrassed astonishment. "Who would ever imagine ye 'd think o' doing that with an ugly old thing like me?"

He stopped in the act of reaching for her bundle. "Hamani!" he admonished her. "You are neither old nor ugly!"

"Ye're very kind." She said with a little sniff. "But I know I'm not beautiful like my sister."

"Well," he said, piling her bundle of sticks on top of his own. "Maybe not, but you have a beauty of your own. You're kind and generous and good-hearted, and it shines in your face and in your eyes when you smile. Your name means 'spirit,' doesn't it?"

"Ye-es, it does."

"Well, it's a good name for you, Hamani, because you have such a beautiful spirit."

"*Oh!*" She was staring at him, searching his eyes and finding only earnestness. "Tor Nagaro, I think that's the nicest thing anyone has ever said t' me!" The light that had kindled in her eyes faded an instant later, however. "But even if it's true, it doesn't matter if nobody else notices."

He ducked into the woodshed. "Someone else is bound to," he said over his shoulder. "You just wait."

He piled up the branches on top of those he'd brought earlier and emerged to find that Hamani was picking up more twigs under the apple tree. He hurried to rejoin her.

"Why are ye trimming Gama's tree, anyway, Tor Nagaro?" she asked when she saw him. "It should be Taru's task."

"Perhaps. But we're both visiting Gama, and I had nothing better to do while Taru went about his... ah... his own affairs."

She straightened and turned around, and he saw to his dismay that she was crying again. "He's courting my sister!" she exclaimed bitterly. "Why don't ye just say it?"

"Well, I think he did go to see if your father will allow it," Nagaro conceded, startled as much by her vehemence as by her tears. "We're both under warrants of arrest right now, after all, and that might make a difference."

"Well, Father let him in—that's all I know!" she interrupted in a choking voice. "And he made me put out the plate of honey cakes that *I* just baked! Jitali hardly knows how t' cook a thing, so Father has me put things out, and lets folk think *she* made them. He says he'll set folk straight after she's married and then maybe someone 'll take me for my cooking. He says it's the only way he's ever likely t' see me wed!"

Having finished her tirade, Hamani flung down the sticks she had gathered, and threw herself down on the grass.

Nagaro hastily sat down beside her. "That's a rather dreadful thing for him to do. And an even worse thing for him to say—and I doubt it's true."

"What does it matter if it's true," she demanded, lifting her head a little, "if Taru marries Jitali?" She huddled with her arms around her knees. "Jitali's not ready t' be wed! She's just a girl! All she knows how to do is sing, and braid her hair, and make flower chains to wear in it!"

Nagaro frowned. "Are you afraid Taru won't make her happy?"

"*No!*" She wiped at her eyes with one sleeve, without meeting his gaze. "I'm afraid *she* won't make *him* happy! She could have any man she wants in a year or two, so why must she have Taru now?" The bitterness in Hamani's voice was unmistakable as she plunged on. "She doesn't care about him—not the way *I* do! We used t' play games together—Taru and me—years ago, when we were children. Jitali's so much younger, she scarcely even *knows* him! She just thinks it would be grand to be his wife because he's handsome and dashing, and because he sails on your ship." Her voice failed.

Nagaro sat stunned for several seconds. Finally he said, "I didn't know you felt that way about Taru." In fact, he had found out quite by chance that Hamani had cared for Taru when he'd first come to Wotana. But that was seven years ago!

She hunched her shoulders. "Well I *do!* Ever since when we were children. But I can't exactly *tell* anyone, can I?" She still wasn't looking at him. Then she added, "Ye must think I'm a terrible sister."

He sighed. "Not really. It's not as if you want to hurt Jitali. It's not as if they're in love—"

Hamani turned on him at that. "He doesn't love her *either?*" she blurted.

Nagaro grimaced. "I don't think so." He hesitated, then said, "There was a young woman in Pakoa Town, named Tulara, that he had his eye on for a long time. But he never said anything, or did anything—for years—and eventually she found someone else and married him a few weeks ago. Taru hasn't said it in so many words, but I think it hurt him—hurt his pride as much as anything—and he means to be married too, just to show he can do it. And if he can marry a girl who's younger and prettier than Tulara, so much the better."

"Oh dear!" Hamani's eyes were wide with dismay. "We have t' stop him, Tor Nagaro! We can't let him make a mistake like that!"

Nagaro ran a hand through his hair. "I agree it could be a mistake," he said. "But as for *stopping* him, I can't see how. I've been hoping he'll figure it out for himself."

"Can't ye *talk* to him?"

Nagaro heaved a sigh. "Taru and I have never thought the same way about women," he said carefully. "He thinks I'm a perfect idiot on the subject." He frowned. "Maybe I am," he added in low voice. "I set out to be a friend to a lady, and ended by losing my heart."

"Ye have a *lady?*"

He cast her a rueful glance. "I don't *have* her. In fact, I can't ever have her. But my heart's run away from me, and I can't seem to get it back."

"Oh, Tor Nagaro! I had no idea!"

"That's because I haven't told anyone—except Animara, who's like a sister to me. And of course Tira Yuli at the Bay Tree Inn guessed it." He saw her astonished look and added, "You told me your secret, so I know I can trust you with mine."

"But it must be horrible for ye!" Hamani's brown eyes brimmed with sympathy.

He shrugged. "It is as it is," he said quickly, not wanting her to pity him. He gave her a wry smile. "The point is, Taru warned me about trying to be friends with the lady, and I didn't listen. I haven't told him he was right, though he'll find out sooner or later. But in any case, he's not likely to listen to me about Jitali just as a matter of principle. If I try to give him advice, I'm afraid he'll do the opposite. In fact, I told him months ago, when I first learned he'd taken an interest in your sister, that I thought you were the better choice."

Her eyes widened. "Oh, Tor Nagaro! Ye surely didn't!"

"I did. And you see how much difference it's made."

"Oh. Aye." Hamani looked at the ground, picking at the new blades of grass with slim, brown fingers.

"I think it might make a difference if he found out that Jitali can't cook," he ventured, "and that you can."

"Ye do?" She looked up again, her eyes hopeful.

"Oh yes. Cooking is very important to Taru. Or eating is, I should say."

She actually laughed. "He hasn't changed then. When we were children he always had a way of coming 'round whenever Mama was baking." She gathered her feet under her and stood up, starting to re-gather the branches she had dropped. "We should finish this, if ye want t' sail soon."

He got to his feet and gathered a new armful of sticks. They walked to the woodshed together. After he'd stowed the sticks inside, he reemerged to find her standing there, looking nervous. "I... I want to thank ye, Tor Nagaro," she said. "Ye've been awfully kind."

"No more so than you deserve, Hamani. Come on. One more armful each." He started back up the slope.

She came after him. "Ye're much easier t' talk to than I thought ye'd be."

His mouth twisted bitterly. "Oh yes. *Talking* is something I'm very good at. Talking is what got me into trouble." He stooped, frowning, to pick up some of the remaining branches.

"And listening." She gave him a shy smile. "Ye're good at that too."

"Well, I suppose..." He added sticks to his bundle, without looking at her.

She began to gather the smaller twigs. Presently she stopped and straightened. "I don't think ye're any kind o' idiot, Tor Nagaro," she said. "I think ye talk good sense."

He straightened as well, since he had all the larger branches in his arms. He smiled fleetingly. "That means something coming from you, Hamani. Thank you."

She bit her lip. "I was always afraid t' tell ye this," she said. "But I think I spoiled things between ye and Aramei, years ago, when I told her what your name meant. I've always felt bad about that."

"That was you?" He wasn't actually surprised, since Aramei had told him. "It doesn't matter, and you needn't apologize. Aramei thought I might have a girl somewhere that I didn't remember, and she was right to be worried. I had no right to take an interest in her when I had so little memory of my past..." His voice trailed. He was remembering the gray-eyed blacksmith's daughter and imagining how differently his life might have gone. "I don't actually think we were well suited to one another," he added after a moment. "I heard she married a tanner's son, and that she's happy. That's what's important." He became aware of Hamani's gentle gaze.

"Ye're a very good man, Tor Nagaro, to care about Aramei being happy when your heart's gone to another."

He shifted his bundle. "I'd like it if everyone were happy," he said. "Or at least not too *unhappy*." He studied her wide brown eyes in her plain, broad face. "If the worst comes, Hamani, and Taru marries Jitali, maybe I'll court you myself."

"*Tor Nagaro!*" she exclaimed. "Ye must be jesting! Ye couldn't possibly want t' marry me!"

"Only if you're willing," he said hastily. "I'd be no more than second best, but we could at least be kind to each other."

"*Second best?*" She gaped at him. "Now I *know* ye're jesting!"

He held her eyes. "I could do far worse than marry you, Hamani. I hope it won't come to that for you, though. You still have hope—"

There came the sound of voices from back along the road in the direction of Hamani's house. She stiffened. "Oh my little heart!" she cried, pressing her hand to her breast. "That's Taru's voice, and he'll be coming back this way! I don't want him to see me. He'll know I've been crying." She gave Nagaro a look like a frightened deer.

He reached out and took her little bundle of twigs to pile on top of his. "There's a thin spot in the hedge at the top of the garden." He gestured with the bundle of sticks. "You can get out that way onto the path behind the house."

Hamani gave him one quick, grateful glance and fled, calling, "Thank you, Tor Nagaro!" over her shoulder.

Nagaro hastily turned and made for the woodshed. When he came out he was just in time to see Taru coming along the road, carrying a small bundle in one hand and frowning introspectively. The frown instantly disappeared when Nagaro stepped through a gap in the hedge and hailed him.

Taru raised his free hand in greeting. "Ah! Hoy there, Nagaro."

Nagaro advanced to meet his friend. "Well," he ventured as casually as he could. "What did Jitali's father say?"

A flicker of the same frown crossed Taru's face, but was quickly wiped it away again. "That I'm free t' court her," he said easily. "I just can't be thinking about a wedding until the arrest warrant is past and done with. How long do ye think it'll be 'til the truth comes out?"

Nagaro fell in beside Taru as they continued towards Gama's house. "I've heard the same news here as in every other port we've visited this spring," he said. "Peldred wintered with the garrison at Long Harbor in the Faranos. He's likely heard that we took Pavo away from Lankura under our protection, so we've spared him the guilt of having another man die for his silence. And we're not in Lankura to trouble him if he goes back there. The question is whether he'll decide to let matters stand as they are. If he does that—"

"We'd be left skulking about like sneak-thieves 'til the fish fly to market!"

Nagaro laughed. "More or less."

Taru scowled. "It's no laughing matter! Jitali's father wouldn't swear not t' let anyone else court her—and there's at least three that's interested."

They had come to Gama's front gate. Taru shifted the cloth-wrapped bundle he was carrying from one hand to the other and reached for the gate latch.

"What's that you have?" Nagaro asked, indicating the cloth bundle.

Taru brightened. "I almost forgot. I brought one for ye and one for Gama." He unknotted the cloth. "See if this isn't the best honey cake ye ever tasted!"

Nagaro took the offered cake and bit into it. "Mmmm!" He nodded appreciatively. "That *is* good!" He took another bite, and another.

Taru grinned. "It's good that she's beautiful too," he said with obvious pride. "But when a woman cooks like *that*— Well, I could marry her no matter what she looked like!"

Nagaro nearly inhaled a bit of honey cake and struggled to keep from choking. When he could speak, he said as casually as he could, "Are you sure Jitali made them?"

"Well, o' course!" Taru looked affronted. "I mean, her father as good as said it."

Nagaro licked his fingers. "If I were you, I'd ask."

"What d' ye mean?"

Nagaro shrugged. "Oh, I don't know," he said. "It's just that if there's two women living under one roof, and you want to marry the one that's the better cook, it seems to me you ought to ask who made the honey cakes, that's all."

"Well she doesn't have t' be the *better* cook," Taru protested. "As long as she's good enough!" He brandished what remained of his bundle.

Nagaro shrugged again. "Well, if you think Jitali's good enough for you," he said easily, "I guess you wouldn't mind if I were to court Hamani for myself." He stepped through the gate that Taru was holding open and the young Turo came quickly after him.

"Ye can't mean that, Nagaro! *You* courtin' Hamani? Ye're only saying that t' tweak me!"

Nagaro started up the little path to the house. "I spoke to her about it this very morning and she didn't say no. So I may ask her father—if you marry Jitali. You've known Hamani longer than I have, so I'd give you the first chance with her."

"But Hamani's as plain as a fencepost!" Taru was incredulous.

Nagaro halted with his hand on the handle of Gama's front door. "I don't see her so," he said seriously. "Sometimes you have to look close to see the beauty of a thing." He opened the door, calling out a greeting to Gama as he entered.

Taru's grandmother emerged from her tiny kitchen beaming at them. She was small and bent, white-haired and bright-eyed. "Are ye back from your courtin', Taru?" she piped. She paused to sniff. "Somethin' surely smells wonderful! What have ye brought for your poor old Gama?"

Taru gave Nagaro one more quick frowning look, then unwrapped the remaining cake and presented it to the old woman with a flourish. "Sweets for my sweet Gama."

Gama's smile broadened by an inch, revealing several missing teeth. "Now bless ye, lad," she cried, delighted. "It's just as I thought. Ye've brought me one o' Hamani's perfect honey cakes. No one makes honey cakes like Hamani!"

Taru emitted a small strangled sound, but seemed otherwise to be speechless. Nagaro didn't trust himself to look at his friend's face, but he smiled at Gama who smiled back blissfully at him over her treasure.

They stayed only a short while after that. Gama was instantly solicitous when Nagaro said they had to sail. "O' course ye must go at once," she admonished. "I've dearly loved seeing ye both, but it makes my poor heart flutter, thinking what 'd happen if the Fleet ships found ye here."

Nagaro bent to give her a farewell embrace. "There aren't any Fleet ships within a dozen leagues of Wotana," he told her. "The fishermen told us so."

Taru nodded agreement and embraced her in his turn. "That's right, Gama, so don't fret. We'll go the same way we came, by the old mill path and down the road t' the sand spit. Hardly anyone saw us come in and hardly anyone 'll see us go."

Gama stood in the doorway as they started down the path. "The Spirits keep ye both!" she called after them. "Maybe they'll get some sense in Lankura an' crown Darion's heir—he'd set things t' rights, and pardon all three o' ye!"

***

*There is no past... there is no future... only now...*

Nagaro stood on the captain's platform with his hands on the stern castle rail, feeling the sun and the wind, and the sense of freedom that came with the ship's motion—trying to keep his mind fixed in the moment.

The *Sword of Freedom* leaped over the bright water. The sun was high. Its rays struck flecks of fire from the wave-crests. The air was crisp and clean and smelled of salt, and the mists of morning were long gone. Farano's Mouth lay open before them. They were sailing across it on a south by south-westerly course.

*Don't turn your head... don't look to the east...*

The last island of the Inner Faranos lay behind them and to starboard. Before them rose the rocky outline of Tunapa, closest of the Lomoas, just a little off their port bow. The low, pale silhouette of the little isle of Soku lay ahead and to starboard, with Boka Omei beyond. Intermittent white spray showed where several of the Mouth's "teeth" lay, but the *Sword*'s course steered well clear of the partially-submerged rocks.

The ship's sails were filled with a brisk spring breeze so there was no need for the oars, allowing the ship's three officers to stand together on the stern castle, gazing forward. Taru gripped the rail on Nagaro's right, and Pavo stood on his left, surveying the scene with dark, narrow eyes, the expression on his face as unreadable as always.

Abruptly Taru spoke. "Do ye think the heir o' Darion would pardon us if he was king, Nagaro? Like Gama said?"

Nagaro stirred and frowned, his mood broken. He didn't think much of the idea, but he hadn't wanted to disillusion Taru's grandmother. Now he said, "Even assuming he's the legitimate heir, I don't think it likely he'd be crowned without a war, Taru, and we shouldn't wish for war. And he'd still have to follow the law, so I don't think we should expect a pardon either."

"Why not?" Taru asked. "After all, Peldred's a Leithian, I mean, and Darion's heir is Kelorin."

Nagaro's frown deepened. "*That*," he said, "is *not* a good reason."

Taru angrily slapped the rail. "Then we should turn this ship about and sail north to Long Harbor t' find Peldred an' squeeze the truth out of him! We could find the *Tiger* and the *North Wind*—get Moraga and Timegar to join us. Ye know they would!"

Nagaro had been expecting something like this ever since hearing what Jitali's father had said. "We should give Peldred a chance before we consider anything like that," he said earnestly. "He has a choice between continuing to endure his guilt, or openly facing shame and the anger of the elders of his House. It can't be easy for him."

Taru snorted. "Am I supposed to weep?"

Pavo turned his level gaze on Taru. "Peldred must choose to do right thing, for his honor, Taru. There is no honor for him if we do what you say."

"*Bodjer honor!*" Taru scowled. "I don't trust Peldred to have any! What if he never chooses t' tell the truth? What's t' become of us then?"

Pavo regarded him steadily, but then lowered his head. "I am sorry, Taru, that you have so much trouble. Maybe you should not have saved me."

Taru opened his mouth and shut it again. "Oh, no ye don't," he muttered. "Ye won't catch me that way, Pavo. We *had* t' save ye. I'd do it again in a minute. But there's got t' be *something* we can do besides just wait!" He paused, frowning, but suddenly brightened. "We could find Geldoran and explain to *him* about Peldred. I'll wager Geldoran would make the little stinker talk if he only understood."

Nagaro sighed. "Before we try that, Taru, we'd have to be prepared to surrender ourselves. Geldoran would surely want to take us all back to Lankura to have the thing sorted out properly."

"If the *Tiger* and the *North Wind* were with us, we could fight our way out!"

"I've told you, Taru. I won't fight Fleet men."

Taru scowled again. "Well, if ye're going t' tie your hands like that—*our* hands, I should say—" He broke off. "Oh, hang it all! I'm going below."

With that he turned and stalked off, making for the ladder to the main deck.

Pavo watched him go. Once the young Turo was well out of earshot, the Hashtep turned to Nagaro. "If Peldred do not tell truth when he was in Lankura, Nagaro, why do you think he will tell it now?"

Nagaro grimaced. "For one thing, he doesn't have those other men of his House looking over his shoulder and telling him what to do. He left them behind in Lankura."

"I cannot go onto shore," Pavo said seriously. "So I cannot hear how man talk. Are there more man who are angry about what you have done, or more man that are pleased?"

Nagaro passed a hand over his eyes. "It depends on where you go ashore," he said. "In the southern isles, where we're headed, almost everyone favors us, because they know you, Pavo. On the mainland it's a different tale. I'm afraid there are a good many there who think I'm wrong about you. Not all of them are *angry* at me, but they expect I'll see my mistake in time and fetch you back to be hanged. Then of course I'll be forgiven for having believed in my 'guilty' friend, and all will be right with the world."

Pavo's dark eyes clouded. "I am sorry, Nagaro. I did not want to make all this trouble."

"I know you didn't. But I also know you would have done the same for me or for Taru. You mustn't take Taru's words too much to heart. I told him when we set about the task that our exile might be permanent. He was willing to accept the possibility then. He's just out of sorts right now because he can't move quickly to marry Jitali. Myself, I think it may be for the best. He shouldn't be so hasty."

"It does not make you very sad to think that maybe you can never go back to Lankura?"

Nagaro met the young Hashtep's earnest gaze. "No, Pavo. It doesn't make me very sad." He hoped he sounded sincere.

Pavo seemed satisfied. He nodded his head and said, "Thank you, Nagaro. I will go now to be ready for change of sail."

Nagaro heaved another sigh as he watched Pavo depart. The truth was, he had very mixed feelings about the possibility of returning to Lankura. Part of him longed to see Nevien again. But a more rational part foresaw the morass he'd be walking into. *How could he ever be her friend again? And how could he cease to be her friend without seeming to abandon her? He couldn't possibly explain the need to stop seeing her without telling her how he felt.*

And he couldn't possibly tell her that. It would be one more thing to cause her distress, which she certainly didn't need. Ani had said she'd be wed again before the year's end, but it hadn't happened because Queen Semorel was dying—by slow, painful inches—and Nevien was spending every possible moment at her mother's side. Nagaro felt his throat tighten. *If only he could be there.*

Before he could stop himself, he had turned to look eastward across the breadth of the Great Channel to the mouth of the River Edro, to Lankura. He saw it, just as he had known he would: the little notch in the mainland coast—the river's mouth—and just to the left of that notch, a little white speck he knew was the royal palace of Edrovir on its promontory.

*And of course he couldn't be there... shouldn't be there. Perhaps not ever again...*

With a wrench he pulled his gaze back to the sweeping panorama before him, the glittering sunlight on the waves under a perfect blue sky. He made an effort to put himself back into the moment. *There is no past... there is no future...* But the words now had an ominous and fatal ring.

***

"Do you see it?" Nagaro asked.

Taru lowered the spyglass, frowning. "Aye. She's a galley all right. But I can't tell the color of her banner."

The two men stood atop the Stone Head, the high ridge that jutted from Boka Omei's eastern shore out into the sea channel known as the Inside Passage. They were looking southward, surveying the Passage, the entire northern portion of which lay open to their view from that high vantage point. The warship under discussion was well down the channel, almost as far as they could see.

"I can't be sure of it," Nagaro admitted. "But I'm fairly certain it isn't a white hawk on blue. There's no lighter spot in the middle of it."

Taru grunted. "She looks like she's heading south. We could leave her to Timegar and Moraga."

Nagaro retrieved the spyglass from his friend. "If she turns towards the Great Channel, between the islands, Timegar and Moraga might miss her," he said. "We should go after her."

"I don't know..." Taru chewed a fingernail. "It'd be a long run t' catch her. She could get away from us."

Nagaro lowered the glass and looked hard at his friend. "What's gotten into you, Taru? You're usually spoiling for a good chase."

Taru shrugged. "I'm thinking that if we stay up here at the north end o' the Lomoas, we could move quick if we got any news—about Peldred owning up."

Nagaro frowned. "Any news will surely reach us wherever we are. A few days or even a few weeks won't make much difference. And sitting here thinking about it will only make the wait seem longer. Come on now. Let's get back to the ship as quick as we can."

Taru grimaced, knowing the debate was over. He hastily followed Nagaro down the path that led in long switchbacks to Omei Bay, below. The *Sword of Freedom* was anchored there, looking like a toy ship on a slab of polished jade. The town of Omei half-encircled the bay, the houses looking like toy houses, the moving townsfolk like children's playthings.

The Mahuk warship led them on a merry chase down the Inside Passage, dodging among the islands. They were hampered by fog in the northern Lomoas and by erratic winds once they got south of the fog. Still, they gained on the Mahuk craft, and the galley wasn't much more than half a mile ahead by the time they neared the southernmost end of the Passage, two days after they had first sighted her.

As the *Sword* was approaching the northern end of the island of Kapala, the *Tiger* and the *North Wind* suddenly emerged from behind an islet almost due west of their course. The Mautep captain very predictably altered course at first sight of the two pirate ships, making with all speed for the north Haru passage into the Great Channel.

To Nagaro's surprise, neither the *Tiger* nor the *North Wind* altered their courses to give chase.

"I do not understand!" Pavo shouted up from the main deck through cupped hands to keep his words from being blown away. "Why they do not chase ship of Tuluptak? Do they not see?"

"They must have seen her!" Nagaro shouted back from the captain's platform. "But they've seen us too, and they're steering for us!"

He put his spyglass to his eye and trained it on the nearer ship, the *North Wind*, which was slightly in the lead. A moment later he lowered the glass, and called down to Pavo. "Something must have happened! Timegar is signaling he wants to talk."

"What shall we do, Capt'n?" Taru's voice came through the speaking tube from the oar deck below. Apparently he'd heard at least Nagaro's half of the conversation.

Nagaro glanced again, frowning, at the rapidly receding stern of the Mahuk warship they had been chasing. It was hard to let the quarry go, carrying a shipload of slaves, but Timegar must have seen the ship, so whatever the former Fleet officer wanted to talk about must be important. *Besides,* he reminded himself, *they still might catch their prey by sailing around the south end of Haru.*

He bent over the speaking tube. "Steady ahead, Taru!" he said. "I want to see what Timegar has to say."

The three ships converged, the *Sword* drawing alongside the *North Wind* as both craft slowed and drew in their oars. A pair of fending pikes were put to gentle use to bring the ships' sides into contact, and a pair of ropes quickly made them fast. The *Tiger* came to a halt not quite so close to the *North Wind's* other side.

Nagaro was already on the main deck as the *Sword of Freedom* was being secured to her compatriot. He stepped quickly to the rail even as

Timegar approached it from the other side. "Have you some ill news, Timegar?" Nagaro asked, seeing the bearded Kelorin's grim look.

"I have," the pirate captain answered shortly. "Nagaro, they've taken Narei!"

The world seemed to give a sudden lurch. "Taken *Narei*, Timegar? *Who has?*"

"We don't know for sure, but Ani said the men were yellow-haired Leithians. They anchored just outside the cove and rowed a boat in, it seems, and took Narei as she was playing on the rocks—afore Ani could call Sudano or the lads."

*"Keshaal!"* Nagaro felt a blinding rage well up inside him, and his hand went to his sword hilt. *If this was Elgurn's doing and she came to any harm...* He fought for control, and found it, barely. "Where did they go, Timegar? Do you know? I have to go after them! *By the Eyes, if they hurt her—"*

Timegar vaulted over the railing onto the *Sword's* deck and took Nagaro by the shoulders. "Steady, lad," he said urgently. "They're not likely to harm her. It's *you* they want!"

Nagaro shook himself loose. "What do you mean?" he demanded. "How do you know?"

"Ani said one o' them shouted at her as they made off, saying, '*Tell him to come to Lankura if he wants her back*'."

Nagaro hadn't noticed Taru's arrival on deck, but his friend was suddenly beside him. "Nagaro, ye mustn't go!" he cried. "They're just tryin' to lure ye back so they can take ye."

"Well it's going to work then!" Nagaro shot back. "I have no choice! They may not hurt her, but they can hide her away somewhere—make sure I never see her again! I can't let them keep her!"

"Of course ye can't," Timegar hurriedly put in. "But we may be able to overtake them afore they reach the city. Will ye listen t' me for a minute?"

Nagaro put a hand to his forehead and drew a long breath, striving for better control. He and Timegar—as well as Taru and Pavo—were by now standing at the center of a circle of men, all members of his crew and all listening. "All right... yes," he said. "How much lead do they have and which way did they go?

"They took her late yesterday, and it's now—" Timegar squinted at the sun— "about an hour 'til noon. And Moraga and I have been trying to find out which way they went. From what Ani said, it seemed they went 'round Pakoa to the seaward side, but we saw no sign o' them out there. So we started asking the fishermen, and it seems there was a ship o' the right description that cut back through this way yester-eve."

"What was description?" Pavo spoke for the first time, his dark eyes hard as slivers of obsidian.

Timegar glanced warily at the massive Hashtep. "It's a merchant ship—no oars, or ram, or oar ports—and she's flying the flag of Edrovir. Ani said there was something that flashed like gold at the top of her mainmast. And the ship the fishermen saw had something like a ring painted gold atop her main-sprit, and one o' them that could read said the name on her was the *Golden Crown*."

Nagaro nodded, thinking, his gaze intense. "We've seen no such ship coming up the Inside Passage as we were going down it, so they must have gone into the Great Channel. And if it's a merchant ship, we can outpace her over a short haul using our oars, though she'd outrun us over a longer distance with a favorable wind. The wind's been very uneven these past two days. We may have a chance."

Timegar coughed. "That's true, Nagaro. We *may* have a chance. But when I say 'we,' I mean Moraga an' me. Ye shouldn't risk yourself. Just leave it to us. We'll bring her back if it can be done."

Nagaro stiffened. "And if it *can't* be done?"

"We can try to bargain for her in Lankura—"

Nagaro shook his head. "You know that won't work! Not if they want *me*. It will save time, in that case, if I'm near at hand to surrender myself. And if we do catch the ship in time, there's no harm to my being there. But the *Sword* and her crew needn't come. I can ship with you on the *North Wind*."

Pavo stirred. "If you go, Nagaro, then I must go. Because you have swear you will watch me very close."

Nagaro frowned. "No, Pavo," he said. "You stay with Taru. He also swore to watch you."

"But ye know what they'll say, don't ye?" Taru burst in. "If ye come to Lankura without Pavo, they'll say they can't trust Nagaro the pirate—that ye didn't stand by your oath t' watch your friend! They won't care what *I* do. I'm nothing t' those great folk. Besides, I don't like bein' left out o' the danger—or out o' the fight, if there is one!"

Pavo gave a decisive nod of his great head. "You see we must all go, Nagaro. Whole ship must go. All man will want to do it."

"Aye! That we will!" There was an immediate chorus from the encircling crewmen.

Nagaro had a sinking feeling in his stomach. "What if I have to surrender myself, Pavo? What if they insist on taking you too? That may be exactly what they have in mind."

Pavo shrugged impassively. "Then maybe is time to make end of exile. It is not right you lose your daughter for helping me."

Timegar had been listening tensely, his gaze shifting from one to another of the three friends as they spoke. "All right then," he said, holding up a hand for their attention. "If you're all determined to stick your necks into this noose, so be it. I know better than to argue with the stubborn lot o' ye. We'll sail with all three ships, though I hope there'll be no need for anyone to do any surrendering."

Nagaro was silent for a long moment, looking first at Pavo's stoic face, then turning to study Taru and to sweep the faces of Timegar and the gathered crewmen with his eyes. He swallowed. "Thank you, my friends," he said, with feeling. Then he squared his shoulders and raised his voice to carry across the *Sword*'s main deck and to the men on the deck of the *North Wind* as well. "There's no time to lose! Set course for the Great Channel through the north Haru passage!"

# Chapter 4

# Hunting The Golden Crown

"**D**o you think that is ship we look for?" Pavo pointed at what were obviously large, square sails, some leagues to the north.

Nagaro had been studying those sails through his spyglass ever since they'd come into view. "Possibly," he said, lowering the glass. "At least she's a merchant craft and her captain is taking her north, straight as the arrow flies, with sails full-spread. We're gaining on her now only because we're rowing."

The sun was mid-way between the zenith and the western horizon. The *Sword* and her two companion craft were sailing north up the coast of the large island of Moluaro. They'd been making the best speed they could, alternately by oars and by sails alone, resting the oarsmen as often as they dared and changing men out in rotation to serve as deck crew. The waters of the Great Channel were dotted with the small triangular sails of fishing boats, but there were only four larger craft presently in sight in the channel to the north of them, and the other three were unlikely to be their quarry. The nearest was southbound. A second was plainly making for the harbor of Kel Tierna, ahead and to starboard. And the third was crossing the channel from the mainland to the islands. The ship Nagaro was watching was the only northbound craft, standing well out from the mainland coast in the deep blue waters of mid-channel.

"Do you think captain will turn and hide between island when he see us?" Pavo asked.

Nagaro's slim black brows came together. "Perhaps. But there's no good place to hide until he gets north of Moluaro. Though if he changes course as we approach, it would certainly suggest a guilty conscience." His gray eyes narrowed speculatively. They had to avoid aggressively pursuing the wrong ship, and the one they were watching was, to all appearances, a harmless merchant vessel going about her business under the Edroviran flag. The *North Wind* and the *Tiger* were flying the pirate banner of his own devising, the white sword on a sable field. The identity of the *Sword of Freedom* could be easily guessed in such company even though she was flying the blue and white hawk banner of Edrovir. Nagaro knew he could lose the trust of the common people if it appeared that he and his pirate comrades were attacking Edroviran merchant craft.

He put his mouth to the speaking tube. "We may have her in sight, Taru. Be ready for my order to increase speed. I mean to see if we can make the rabbit jump."

The response came from below. "Aye, Zirda!"

Nagaro reached for the speaking trumpet that hung from a hook on the railing. Raising it, he shouted across the water to the other two ships that were running parallel, to starboard. "Make ready to match speed! And watch that sail dead ahead!" He waited only for shouts of acknowledgment from the other two captains before bending again to the speaking tube.

"Now, Taru! All speed!"

He heard the drumbeat quicken in response to Taru's command and felt the *Sword* surge rhythmically ahead. The *North Wind* and the *Tiger* increased speed a few seconds later. He raised the spyglass and watched grimly, counting the oar strokes. Five... six... seven... He thought he saw a subtle shifting of the distant sails, and then the supposed merchant ship abruptly changed course, angling to port as if preparing to take advantage of the first gap between islands—the north Moluaro passage. Lowering the glass, Nagaro made a quick survey of the channel and confirmed that none of the other large craft had made any visible response.

Pavo and the other men on deck had seen the change as well and excited cries were echoed by many voices.

"What's happened?" Taru's voice came from the speaking tube.

"She jumped—if it wasn't just by chance. How long can the men hold this pace?"

"Not long, Nagaro. They've rowed too much today already."

*Bodjer it!* Nagaro tensely chewed his lip. "Well, keep it up as long as you think wise," he said after a moment into the tube. "Then ship oars and let them rest." There was no help for it. Their quarry would begin to pull ahead again once the oars stopped, but they would get as close to her as they could before that happened. He leaned on the railing, his eyes locked on those sails that were becoming steadily larger even as the ship they were driving continued to veer towards the western side of the channel. *If Narei was on that ship, how were they treating her? Was she frightened, or did she think it was all just a game?*

"Will you not change course also?" Pavo inquired. "Sail more close to island?"

Nagaro shook his head. "Not yet. Perhaps her captain will think he was wrong to fear us—that we don't know it's his ship we should be chasing, or that we're only here by chance."

Pavo nodded sagely.

Nagaro's hands tightened on the rail. "I'd feel better knowing if that's really the *Golden Crown*, Pavo. If you get a chance to hail any fishermen, find out if they noticed something gold on her masthead when she passed." Worriedly he checked the position of the sun. "In this season, there'll almost certainly be mist off the open sea tonight. We probably have less than two hours before we'll have to find somewhere to lie up. So will they, of course, but we may lose track of them when the fog comes in."

By the time the oars were shipped, the merchant vessel's lead had narrowed to less than a league. She'd been running all that time close in along Moluaro's long eastern coastline, while the three pursuing craft had remained in the deeper water near the middle of the Great Channel. For the next half hour Nagaro watched grimly as their prey's lead slowly increased again until the merchant vessel began to turn, rounding the northern end of Moluaro and entering the passage separating it from the much smaller island of Oapa. He shook his head, frowning darkly. The ship's captain apparently hadn't been lulled, and he intended to try to lose his pursuers among the islands as Pavo had guessed.

As soon as their quary disappeared from view around Moluaro's shoulder, Nagaro ordered his own course change to make directly for the mouth of the north Moluaro passage. Shortly thereafter, Pavo hailed a Turowan fisherman who told them that the ship they were following did indeed have a carved golden crown atop her masthead. The man couldn't read, and so could make nothing of the letters painted on her bow and stern.

The afternoon was far advanced by the time the three pursuers reached the passage the *Golden Crown* had taken. The *Sword of Freedom* was in the lead, and Nagaro was thus the first of the three captains to get a clear view down the length of the north Moluaro passage. The channel was empty of anything but fishing boats. Its waters, reflecting the sun's slanting rays, looked like molten silver, while the shadows on the islands' hills on either side were already deepening to blue and violet. Beyond the end of the channel lay the Inside Passage and Nagaro could see the fog bank there already, coming in off the open ocean like a great, gray wave breaking over the seaward isles.

"*Bishka!*" He groaned. "She's already sailed out the other end! And the fog bank is coming in early!"

Pavo had come up to the stern castle deck to stand beside Nagaro. He glanced worriedly at his friend. "Passage here is short," he observed. "I did not think ship would be still there to see. Probably she have turn north to go around Oapa."

Nagaro's gray gaze was intense under his frowning brows. "Yes," he agreed. "They wouldn't cross the Inside Passage into the fog, and going south would mean back-tracking all the way around Moluaro— *unless* their captain is clever enough to think of hiding in a cove at this end of Moluaro until we've gone north around Oapa. Then he could cut back out to the Great Channel the way he came in. He might even get all the way across to the mainland side before the fog overtakes him."

Pavo looked startled. "Yes, that is so—"

Nagaro was already reaching for the speaking trumpet. He seized it and turned to shout over the stern rail. "Moraga! Turn about! Watch for her coming out north or south of Oapa! We'll flush her if we can!"

"Aye, Capt'n!" Moraga's shout came back. The *Tiger* had been just about to complete her turn into the passage, but now continued in a tighter arc that carried her back the way she'd come.

The *Sword* and the *North Wind* continued westward, but the wind was unfavorable, being off the sea, and Nagaro called on the weary men to row once more. He went down to join them himself, but returned to the deck when word came from Pavo that the *Sword* was nearing the Inside Passage. The *North Wind* was close behind her as she swung clear of the western tip of Oapa and turned north. By that time, the wall of mist had advanced half-way across the width of the Inside Passage and the sun was on the verge of sinking behind the crests of the fog-shrouded islands on the farther side.

Nagaro stood at his post at the stern castle rail as the *Sword* finished her turn. The spyglass was clutched in his hand as he tensely waited for a clear view up the Inside Passage to the north. The view, when it finally came, lasted only a few seconds before the sun's glowing disk slipped behind a western island and plunged the scene into a deep gray gloom.

In those few seconds, Nagaro was able to see the entire western shore of Oapa to beyond its northern end where the island of Lapoa was a dimmer silhouette. The local fishermen had all sought the shelter of their harbors and coves, and there was only one ship visible in the waning daylight. Kunao, aloft in the crow's seat, pointed it out with a cry. Nagaro had just time to note the vessel's position and to catch a brief, pale gleam of gold from her masthead through his glass before the light died from the world.

"*Keshaal!*" He lowered the glass and smote the railing with his fist.

Pavo looked up at him from the main deck below,s where he had been directing the re-trimming of the sails during the turn. "You have see her, Nagaro?"

Nagaro scowled. "She's gone *past* the north Oapa passage, Pavo! Her captain must mean to shelter for the night somewhere on the western coast of Lapoa so he can go on up the Inside Passage tomorrow as soon as the mist clears. But *we'll* have to turn in between Oapa and Lapoa, and lie up in Lapoa Harbor tonight. There is no closer shelter!"

He shook his head. "And we'll have to be quick to get there, too, before the fog closes in!"

***

Lapoa Harbor was a small bay on the northern shore of the passage separating the isles of Oapa and Lapoa. The *Sword* and the *North Wind* reached it safely, which was fortunate since the night that fell was dark and damp, with fog so thick that the watchmen on the *Sword's* deck couldn't see one end of the ship from the other.

Their situation now posed a dilemma. Coming to Lapoa Harbor had brought the two ships nearly back to the Great Channel, making it unclear which direction they should go in the morning—east to the Great Channel, where their quarry must ultimately be headed, or west to the Inside Passage, where they had last seen her. Without knowing exactly where the *Golden Crown* had put in for the night, they couldn't know which was the shorter path to their prey. The mass of the island of Lapoa, lying in between, would make it impossible to spot the merchant ship before having to make their choice.

Nagaro called a council with Taru, Pavo, and Timegar in the *Sword's* great cabin, where he laid out the problem as he saw it.

Timegar promptly suggested a third possibility. "Why must we choose one or the other?" he asked. "If ye lot take the *Sword* back to the Inside Passage, and I make for the Great Channel with the *North Wind*, one of us is sure to catch her."

Nagaro suspected that Timegar was motivated in part by a desire to keep him and his two friends from risking capture, though he didn't say so. Instead, he argued against further dividing their forces.

Taru agreed, adding, "We should go east t' the Great Channel, to meet the *Tiger*. If we go west, Moraga could miss us completely."

Pavo shook his head. "I think we should go west, where merchant ship have gone," he said. "Maybe captain of *Golden Crown* will not take north Lapoa channel. Maybe he will keep to Inside Passage and go past Tunapa, all of way to Farano's Mouth."

"But that would give him a longer course t' reach Lankura!" Taru pointed out.

"Aye," Timegar agreed. "But not by much, and it would increase the chances we could miss him. Which argues again for my plan to send one ship each way."

Nagaro could easily imagine failure with all three choices, and he was getting no consensus from his councillors. So he broke off the fruitless discussion and suggested that they all go to bed and hope for greater clarity in the morning. After the others had gone, he went out onto the foggy deck to try to think, only to find himself pacing.

His feet carried him back and forth as his mind ran endlessly over the possibilities. At last, he sought his bed, telling himself that the morning could bring some news to help him choose his course. He lay long awake, however, imagining Narei, held in some cabin aboard that fleeing merchant ship. Was she sleeping now? Or lying awake as he was on this second night of her captivity? She was a bold child, not much given to fear, but if she tried to defy her captors, what would they do?

In the end he fell asleep from sheer exhaustion.

He was awakened by Taru coming in with his breakfast on a tray. The great cabin was awash in diffuse gray light from the stern windows.

"Taru!" he exclaimed in dismay as he sat up. "I gave orders to be roused an hour before dawn!"

Taru gave an easy shrug. "Ye haven't missed anything, Nagaro. I decided t' let ye sleep, seeing as how ye were late going to bed and the mist is still thick as my mother's porridge."

"Still?" Nagaro rose and went to unlatch the window, throwing it open for a clearer view. He found that although the sun had plainly risen, he could make out no more than the outlines of several nearby fishing boats, rocking on the gray water. The shore of the bay where the sea met the shingle was barely discernable some fifty feet beyond, and the slope of the nearest hillside was a featureless presence, a slightly darker gray than the low ceiling of mist into which it disappeared.

"You're right," he said. "We can't safely sail in *that*." He closed the window and sat down at the table to help himself to hot porridge, cold smoked meat, and sothiril from the tray. "But we should send a man up to the top of the ridge to see if he can get above it. The fog might be breaking up over the Great Channel."

Taru sat down across from him. "Timegar already sent a man up there, and he hasn't come down yet. So ye might as well eat your breakfast. Have ye decided what t' do?"

Nagaro gave his friend a rueful glance over his cup of sothiril. "I hadn't when I went to bed last night, but now, as the fog rolls back, it'll likely clear the passage to eastward first, meaning we should go east. We could get a head start on the *Golden Crown* that way and make up some of the time we lost last night coming to this harbor." He smiled a little grimly to himself at the thought that the lingering fog was actually giving him clarity of purpose.

Taru looked smug. "That's what I said last night."

Nagaro grunted. "You said it *before* you knew that the mist would linger so late. And if it were to clear to westward first, it would make more sense to go west."

Taru's grin barely faltered. "But ye won't be dividing us at least," he said cheerfully. "So Timegar'll have to swallow it."

Nagaro shook a spoon at him. "Timegar and Moraga would have tried to do the whole task themselves. And it would have been wiser for us to have let them."

"If ye think we're being such fools," Taru retorted, "why are ye here?"

Nagaro frowned and bent over his porridge. "Narei will expect her papa to come for her," he said. "She's too young to understand why I might not. I wonder what they're telling her..." His voice trailed.

Taru shifted uncomfortably. "Nagaro, we'll catch that ship. We'll get her back."

Nagaro raised his eyes to meet his friend's encouraging glance. "I hope so, Taru. But the *Golden Crown*'s a fast ship, and the closer we get to Lankura, the greater the risk that we'll meet ships of the Fleet. And if we fail, I'll have to surrender myself."

"No! Nagaro ye can't—"

"I'd *have* to surrender, Taru. But I'd rather you and Pavo remained free."

Taru shook his head. "Pavo won't hear of it. He'll go anywhere ye go, if he can. I'd have to knock him down to stop him." Taru made a fist with his right hand and studied it ruefully. "I've threatened to do it before, but t' tell ye truth, I'm not sure I could."

Nagaro heaved a sigh. "Well," he said, "we'll have to see what fate Lokundas sends us."

At that moment, there came a shout from somewhere outside. Nagaro dropped his spoon and sprang to his feet. "What's that?"

"It must be news!" Taru was on his feet as well.

A moment later, both men burst out of the stern castle and onto the main deck. The crewmen there were already gathered at the port rail, but they parted to let the two officers through.

Nagaro immediately saw that Timegar's lookout was apparently returning, rowing himself across the water to the two ships waiting side by side only a dozen feet apart. The wind was so still and the morning so quiet that a man could be heard speaking from one ship to the other almost without raising his voice.

Timegar stood at the *North Wind's* rail, tension in his stance as the lookout came up the rope ladder. The one-time Fleet warrior didn't let the man catch his breath before demanding, "Well, man, what did ye see?"

The man answered in short sentences, between gasps of air. "The hilltop's out o' the mist Capt'n. The Great Channel's nearly clear too. An' there's ships moving in it!"

Nagaro felt immediately uneasy. He called across the water. "What kind of ships?"

The lookout turned towards him. "Warships, Zirda. Four Fleet ships t' the north of us—Kuran's flagship among 'em—coming south. An' down towards the south end o' Moluaro, there's two Mahuk warships coming north! The banners might be Tuluptak's."

*"Vothra!"* Nagaro clutched at the rail, uneasiness displaced by a sharp pang of guilt. Since learning of Narei's abduction, he had given no thought to the ship they'd chased south all the way to Haru. What if it had found a compatriot and come back, bent on mischief? *He'd forgotten the oath he had sworn.*

Taru gripped his shoulder. "Kuran will run 'em off, Nagaro. He's headed their way with four ships t' their two."

Nagaro shook off the hand. "I know," he said. "But I should have caught that warship we were chasing and saved the slaves aboard her."

Timegar must have heard Nagaro's words because he answered them from the deck of the *North Wind.* "Ye can't be everywhere, Nagaro, and never thinking o' yourself. It's Kuran's task. Let him do it!" The veteran sea warrior turned back to his lookout. "Did ye see any sign o' the *Tiger?*"

Nagaro stood silent, still feeling the sting of having let his own need overshadow his duty. *It was the first time he had truly faced such a test, and he had failed it.* Distracted, he listened with only half an ear as the lookout continued his report.

The man had seen the top-sprit of a mast that could be the *Tiger's* poking through the fog bank right up against Lapoa's shore, at the position of a well-known cove. To the north of their position, the mist still covered most of the width of the Great Channel, so Kuran's ships were sailing south along the far side of it where the air was clear. There was less mist to southward, with the full width of the channel open at the southern end of Moluaro. This had likely allowed the two Mahuk galleys to get through the south Moluaro passage earlier, and they were now coming boldly up the middle of the Great Channel at good speed.

This last observation was strange enough to shake Nagaro out of his abstraction, and it caused considerable discussion among the others who had heard it. Mautep captains rarely sailed openly in the Great Channel—between the islands and the mainland. What were these two doing there? Did they mean to attack Kel Tierna with only two ships?

Or were they hoping to catch some fishermen they could take for slaves? They must not yet have seen Kuran's small fleet when the lookout had spied them. Indeed, probably neither group of ships had sighted the other without having a high vantage point like the ridge top.

Everyone admitted that they couldn't guess what the two Mahuk craft were about, but they also agreed that the presence of Kuran's ships limited their own course of action. With the fog still thick to westward, they couldn't escape into the Inside Passage and were forced to wait where they were until Kuran's fleet had sailed past, at least far enough to allow them to safely enter the Great Channel.

While all of this did nothing to ease Nagaro's guilt, it did at least force him to concede that there was no serious argument against continuing his pursuit of the *Golden Crown*—as long as he didn't linger over it. Accordingly, he gave his approval to the plan to go north by the Great Channel as soon as the way was clear, knowing that Kuran and his ships would likely pass by without noticing the *Sword* and her companions, sparing the Lord of the Fleet any need to choose between chasing them or chasing the Mautep.

With the decision made, Timegar sent his lookout back to the hilltop to watch how things unfolded, bidding him come down as soon the fog showed signs of clearing in their vicinity.

There passed an hour of tense waiting. Having chosen his course, Nagaro was eager to be about it. He paced the deck, trying to judge whether the light through the mist was growing any brighter. He told himself over and over that the fog must be thick all up and down the Inside Passage, at least from Moluaro to Farano's Mouth, and his quarry must be just as immobilized as he was.

Finally there came a stirring of the damp air, harbinger of a wind off the mainland. The fog began to shift and separate, revealing ragged gaps through which the morning sun made its presence felt. Soon after that, there came another shout as the lookout returned again.

"Kuran an' his lot should be past us by now," the man told them breathlessly. "They were just coming level with the passage here, when I started t' come down."

Nagaro shifted impatiently. "What about the Mahuk ships? Have they turned about?"

"Aye, Zirda. Kuran must ha' seen 'em. He changed his course t' make straight for 'em. They kept comin' on for a while after that—don't really know why—but they've turned now, and they're on the run!"

"What of the *Tiger?*"

"She was still lyin' low in the last bit o' fog when I left my place on the ridge. Moraga's likely waitin' for the Fleet ships to clear this part o' the Channel, I'm thinking."

The mist was lifting above the water of the bay now, streaming by on a stiffening breeze, and Nagaro gave the order to sail. Out over the south Lapoa passage, the first patches of blue sky were showing. The anchors were quickly hoisted, and the two ships moved cautiously out of the little harbor under the power of their oars, watchful of the last drifting rags of mist.

The fishermen who were readying their boats for the day's work waved farewell as the warships departed, and their voices rose in cheers of encouragement. "The Spirits bless ye, Captain Nagaro!" "Fair sailing, and good luck t' ye!"

Hearing them, Nagaro raised his hand in a parting salute.

As the *Sword* and the *North Wind* rounded Lapoa's southeast headland into the Great Channel, they came suddenly into full sun and a fair wind. They immediately saw the *Tiger*, now out of her cove and heading north a quarter mile ahead, close to Lapoa's shore. The four Fleet ships under Kuran were a mile to the south and southward bound, out in mid channel and plying their oars.

The *Tiger* was soon seen to shorten sail, slowing to let her companions catch up. Kuran's ships continued pursuing their prey, taking no notice of the renegade Fleet ship and the two pirate craft.

With a sigh of relief, Nagaro turned his full attention to overtaking the *Tiger*. He called to both Taru and Pavo for more speed, and he soon heard the drumbeat from the oar deck quicken and saw the unreefing of the sails. The *North Wind* promptly followed the *Sword*'s example.

As they closed with the loitering *Tiger*, Moraga hailed them to say that he'd seen no sign of the *Golden Crown*, and to ask for their news.

Nagoro raised the speaking trumpet to shout back. "She went up the west side of Lapoa! She'll likely come out the north Lapoa passage. Let's try to be there first!"

"Aye, Capt'n! We'll catch her yet!"

The wind was brisk off the mainland, sweeping across the unobstructed width of the Great Channel. With its aid, they made good use of their sails while plying their oars at a moderate pace with frequent rests. Lapoa's eastern shore slid by, close off their port rail. The island's slopes were now completely free of mist. Every rock, tree, and bush stood out in clear relief, and the upland pastures gleamed a brilliant green, dotted with the tiny figures of goats and goatherds. The sun was mounting the sky and all around them, the sea sparkled in its light.

Nagaro was in no mood to enjoy the scenery. He knew that the warming of the day, and movement of the air, must be clearing the mist from the island's western shore as well. The Inside Passage would be opening, and the *Golden Crown* had likely already left her night's harbor and headed north. If she was already ahead of them, she would come out of the north Lapoa passage before they could reach it. He raised his spyglass and sought the spot where the shore of Lapoa came to an end in the distance. Beyond it, the fog had cleared enough that he could make out Tunapa's gray-green silhouette. He told himself that they might have a small advantage as things stood. The *Golden Crown* had no oars, and with the wind out of the east, she'd be sailing in Lapoa's lee with less wind to drive her.

Though his attention was focused mainly to the north, Nagaro had told Kunoa to keep watch in all directions, and he scanned the sea to the east and south as well. The sails of the four Fleet vessels gradually dwindled to stern, and there were as yet no merchant ships abroad. The smaller sails of fishing boats were soon out in full force, however, all around them and along the mainland shore across the channel.

Presently, one of the fishing boats swung in beside the *Sword*, almost under the port rail. Her master, a stout old Turo, steadied the tiller with one hand as he cupped the other to his mouth. "What are ye after in these waters, Capt'n Nagaro?" he cried.

Nagaro called back, "We seek a merchant ship with a gold crown at the top of her mainmast. Have you seen her?"

"Aye, she plies these waters, but the last I saw of her, she was headed south four days ago. What d' ye want with her, Zirda?"

"There's Leithian men aboard her that have taken my daughter and are carrying her to Lankura!"

At this, the fisherman let go the tiller and threw up his hands in dismay. "*Hamanei mata noa!*" he exclaimed. "Those filthy swine! The Spirit's speed ye, Capt'n, an' fetch her home again!" The last of the man's words were almost carried away by wind as the fishing boat dropped away to stern. Nagaro raised a hand in farewell.

Soon after that, the wind dropped, and then it came around from east to almost due west, blowing strongly off the open ocean. Any advantage the east wind had given them had just been turned against them, and Nagaro scowled. "Take us a little way out into the channel," he told the helmsman, "to see if we can get out of the lee of the island. And be ready to turn again at my word."

***

They were still a mile from the northernmost tip of Lapoa when they caught sight of the *Golden Crown*. Kunoa saw her first and gave a wild shout. Nagaro quickly focused his glass on the ship emerging from the north Lapoa passage on a northeasterly heading. She was sporting all her canvas, running swift and light, and he caught unmistakably the flash of gold from her mainsprit.

"*Bishka!*" He ground his teeth as he watched the merchant ship alter her course to a heading north by northeast.

"What's happening up there?" Taru's voice came to him from the speaking tube.

"She just came out of the passage, Taru. She's beaten us! We're more than a mile short, and she's running straight for Lankura."

"Only a mile? We can catch her, Nagaro! It must be almost forty miles t' Lankura from here."

"Yes, but she has a favorable wind, and she's running light—high in the water. And she's heading into the heart of Fleet territory! There could be other ships lying in wait for us. We can't let them tempt us in too close—"

"Then we'll have to catch her fast, Nagaro. But we know Kuran's busy away t' the south, chasing those Mautep. So at least *he* isn't lying in wait for us. There can't be many Fleet ships left in Lankura's harbor."

"Maybe..." Nagaro shifted uneasily, his dark brows knitting into a sharp line above his storm-gray eyes. He couldn't help thinking of all the possibilities, but he had to try. "Helmsman, take us a half point to starboard," he called. "Pavo, set her sails to that new course, and put as much canvas on her as you can!"

"Aye, Capt'n!"

"Aye, Zirda!"

The ship's bow swung to a new heading, describing a line that would intersect the course of the *Golden Crown* some distance in advance of her current position.

"How much speed can you give me, Taru? Speed that you can hold for half an hour?"

"A little more than we're making now."

"All right. Do it."

The throb of the drum increased its rhythm even as Pavo's deck crew scrambled aloft. The *Sword of Freedom* gave a little lunge forward. Aboard the *North Wind* and the *Tiger*, Timegar and Moraga gave orders of their own, and the two pirate ships turned to match the *Sword's* course and speed, slightly behind and flanking her.

The three galleys plowed the bright waters under a brighter sky, their oars adding speed to what their sails could give them. They gained steadily on the *Golden Crown*, and by the end of a half hour they had cut the distance between them nearly in half. During the next half hour, however, while the rowers rested, the merchant ship inched ahead again, being lighter and propelled by sails carried on three masts instead of two.

Nagaro adjusted the course of his small fleet again in an attempt to follow a line that would bring them between the merchant ship and the mainland coast before she could come too close to the mouth of the River Edro. He was foiled, however, when his quarry altered course to port, forcing him to swing the *Sword* to port as well. Every move the *Sword* made, the *Tiger* and the *North Wind* followed with only seconds delay.

Nagaro paced the deck of the stern castle, watching in frustration as the *Golden Crown* edged away from him. At the same time, he searched the surrounding sea for signs of danger. He saw none, but he could only watch helplessly as half of the distance they had gained by rowing was lost again when they rested.

When the rest period ended, he went down to take a turn at an oar himself, after reiterating his admonishment to Kunoa to watch the sea on all sides. The labor did him good, being too strenuous to let his mind wander along disturbing paths. He came up again at the beginning of the next rest period, slick with sweat, his back, arms, and legs all aching from the exertion.

The *Golden Crown* was now running only a quarter mile ahead of the pursuit. Through the spyglass he could see yellow-haired men on the deck of her stern castle. There was no sign of Narei, but they'd likely have her in some cabin below decks. *What had they told her? Did she even know he was so close?* He glanced about. There was still no sign of any Fleet ship, but Lankura was less than fifteen miles distant now. The mouth of the Edro lay dead ahead of them, the white shape of the royal palace visible to its left.

And with their oars shipped, the sleek merchant craft was drawing away from them once again. Nagaro's frown deepened as he imagined how much distance she would gain before he could ask the men to row again. He put his mouth to the speaking tube. "We should try to catch her on the next oar-leg, Taru. This rest may be a little shorter, and I may have to ask for more from the men when they row again."

"Aye, Zirda. We'll be ready!"

Nagaro took up the speaking trumpet and informed Timegar and Moraga of his intentions.

Some time later, Pavo mounted to the deck of the stern castle to stand beside his captain.

"What do you wait for, Nagaro?"

Nagaro's gray eyes were narrowed as he watched his prey. There was no need now for the spyglass. For the task at hand, he was better without it. "I'm letting the rowers rest 'til the last minute I can," he answered grimly. "We'll try to overtake her with one more hard row. Are the sails giving us their best speed?"

Pavo nodded. "I can not do more with them."

"Good." Nagaro's full attention was on the widening gap between the stern of the *Golden Crown* and the *Sword's* iron-clad prow. He moved his shoulders and flexed his arms, assessing his own readiness for renewed exertion, remembering that the rest of the crew had all rowed more than once that morning. The sweat had long since dried on his skin, fanned by the cool sea air. He was ready, but for the men, just a little more rest... The other ship's lead was nearly a third of a mile already. He couldn't let her get so much as half a mile ahead.

He counted a dozen heartbeats... two dozen... three dozen... until he felt he should wait no longer.

"Taru, ready the oars!"

"Aye Zirda!"

Another dozen heartbeats as the oars were thrust from their ports all along the *Sword's* sides.

"*Now*, Taru!"

The drum beat twice and on the third beat, the oars dipped and bit the water and the *Sword of Freedom* leaped ahead, followed seconds later by the *Tiger* and the *North Wind*.

Nagaro raised the spyglass and had the satisfaction of seeing the Leithians aboard the *Golden Crown* gesticulating and hurrying about the deck. There was nothing more they could do, however. Their vessel's sails were already trimmed for the best speed. The wind was steady. They had no oars.

The three pursuing craft came relentlessly on, narrowing the gap that had been widening.

The *Golden Crown* was racing ahead, healing to the wind, her hull cleaving the waves on a long diagonal across the Great Channel, bearing north-northeast, straight for the river's mouth. The *Sword* and her two companion ships were gaining steadily, oars flashing in the sun. Nagaro's hands were clenched, gripping the stern castle rail, his gray gaze locked on the quarry.

Pavo stood beside him, his black eyes also fixed on the fleeing ship, his face impassive. "I think we are go to catch her, Nagaro," he observed after a time. "Already we have made up distance we have lost when we stop rowing."

"Yes. Very nearly." Nagaro didn't take his eyes from his prey, now four hundred yards ahead.

A minute later Pavo shifted his gaze to the *Sword's* bellying main sail. "Wind is dropping," he observed.

"Good. That will act in our favor." Nagaro had felt the change as well. The *Sword* was losing a little way, and he could feel more strongly the rhythmic surge of each oar stroke. The *Golden Crown*, propelled by wind alone, was slowing even more. The merchant craft was now three hundred yards distant.

Pavo called for the deck crew to shorten the lines. The men moved quickly to do his bidding. Nagaro watched them. He was feeling every oar stroke now, imagining the increasing weariness of the oarsmen. Less wind meant harder work for them. Silently he prayed for them not to falter. *Two hundred yards now and still closing.* The *North Wind* and the *Tiger* were still matching the *Sword's* pace, but Nagaro was scarcely aware of them, one to starboard, the other to port. He caught himself unconsciously tensing and untensing his shoulders and arms with each rise and fall of the oars, in sympathy with the straining men below.

*One hundred yards...*

His attention was drawn to a sudden commotion on the merchant ship's stern castle deck, and he had the spyglass to his eye in an instant.

"*Narei!*" There was a small child among the yellow-haired men—dressed more like a boy than a girl. That was his daughter's preference, and Ani indulged it. Her long black hair was unmistakable, blowing loose in the wind.

"You see her, Nagaro?" Pavo was still at his side, but Nagaro had the glass, his eye glued to it.

"They've brought her on deck—or she got out of her cabin. She's fighting with one of them— Oh! Vothra!" He'd caught the flash of a steel blade.

"*Nagaro!* What have happened?"

"I think she got hold of his sword somehow. They've gotten it away from her again, but she had it in her hand for a moment! There's a... a woman with her now. In a skirt—dark-haired... She's holding Narei—"

"*Smoke!*" It was Kunoa's frantic cry from the crow's seat. "Dead ahead! Smoke over Lankura!"

*Smoke over Lankura?*

Nagaro's heart jumped into his throat. He lowered the spyglass, and was shocked to see how close they'd come to the mainland coast while his attention was elsewhere. The shore was only seven or eight miles ahead, the palace on its little peninsula plainly visible without the glass, and there was a long black streamer of smoke rising from somewhere just beyond it. He put the spyglass to his eye again and scanned the river mouth. The tops of several masts were sticking up above the river bank, and the flags flying from them were *not* the blue and white of Edrovir. Some of them, at least, were red and black.

"*Mautep!*" he exclaimed. "Attacking Lankura! By the Eyes of Vothra!"

"*Again?*" Taru's outraged voice came through the speaking tube. "Didn't they bloody our noses enough a year ago at Paktaar?"

"Emperor Baalkir must not think so. Some of those ships are flying the colors of the house of jir-Akaan. Rest the oars, Taru. This changes everything."

Taru gave the order and the ship slowed. Then he asked, "How did they *get* there?"

"They must have come in by Farano's Mouth from the Seaward Passage, early this morning, and slipped across before we came close enough to see them." Nagaro's voice died. *And Kuran was too far away to the south to see the smoke—chasing Mautep. Mautep that he should have been chasing instead...*

Pavo spoke beside him. "Leithian captain have see smoke too. He is changing his course."

It was true. The *Golden Crown* was turning sharply to starboard, taking a southeasterly tack. Nagaro could no longer see Narei or the woman who had stood with her. He caught himself wondering whether Narei had seen the smoke, whether she had any idea what it meant.

"Shall I put the tiller over, an' follow 'er, Capt'n?" the steersman inquired from behind them.

Nagaro shook his head. His duty was crystal clear. *Narei would have to understand.* "No. I'm a Fleet officer. I have an oath to keep." He bent to the speaking tube again. "Taru, I must go to Edrovir's defense."

"I'm with ye then!" Taru's response came with only an instant's hesitation.

Pavo, beside him, said, "I also will come."

Nagaro met his friend's narrow dark eyes. "I'll have to surrender myself when it's over, Pavo. I have to get Narei back."

"Then I also will surrender."

"They'll lock you up, Pavo! They may kill you. I won't be able to rescue you again."

Pavo's glance didn't waver. "I also have swear oath, Nagaro," he said calmly. "If they kill me for keep my oath, it is great shame on them, but for me only honor. You have made me part of your story. It is too late to try to make me go out of it."

Nagaro saw the set of his friend's jaw. "All right," he said. "So be it." He raised his voice, speaking loudly enough to be heard through the speaking tube and by the deck crew as well.

"I ask you, men, to take this ship to Lankura! Taru, Pavo, and I will fight for Edrovir because we have so sworn. Are you also willing to fight in this cause?"

Cries of affirmation came to him immediately, rising from all those present. "Aye, Capt'n, we're with ye!"

Timegar and Moraga had called a halt to their oarsmen. The *Sword* and her pirate companions were still under power of their sails and on a course towards Lankura, while the *Golden Crown* was drawing away from them, bearing to the southeast, making for the mainland coast somewhere south of the river's mouth.

Timegar shouted across the water. "She's getting away, Nagaro! Shall we follow her?"

Nagaro grabbed for the speaking trumpet. "The *Sword* is bound for Lankura for the defense of Edrovir! Will you join us in the fight?"

There was a pause while Timegar presumably put the matter to his men, then, "Aye, Captain. We're with ye, ship and man!"

Moraga must have caught the words being shouted back and forth, for he now called to the other captains with his own speaking trumpet. "Do we go 'round t' the north side o' the palace, Capt'n? Same as last time?"

But Nagaro shook his head as he made his answer, for he'd already formed a plan. "*No!* We're going straight up the river. We'll take their ships while they're looting the city. This time they won't escape!"

Chapter 5

# In Defense Of Lankura

The queen stirred restlessly and murmured something unintelligible. Her pale fingers tightened spasmodically on the bedclothes.

Nevien, drifting in her weariness, jerked back to full alertness and hastily reached out to take her mother's hand. "It's all right, Mother. I'm still here."

*It wasn't all right, of course. It was never going to be all right again.* And now the city was under attack.

The queen's eyes fluttered open. "Elgurn..." she murmured, her voice weak, but distinct and agitated. "Elgurn... where are you?"

The king had been standing in the open doorway that connected his bedchamber and that of his wife. He often stood there—for minutes at a time—his face frozen in rigid lines of pain. To Nevien it seemed that he was torn between a desire to be near his wife and an unwillingness to witness to her suffering. Now, however, he came immediately and swiftly, crossing the floor in long strides. He dropped to his knees beside the bed, reaching for the hand that Nevien hastily relinquished.

"Yes, Semorel," he said. "I'm here."

The dying woman turned him a too-bright gaze. "You mustn't let them dig up the pear tree..."

"The... *pear tree?*" he sounded puzzled, hurt. "What pear tree do you mean?"

"The little one by the kitchen garden..." A frown marred the queen's brow. "You must know the one, dear. It's just begun to bear fruit... and we may be glad of it one day. And it's a sin to destroy a tree if you don't have to. Surely they can run the wall around it..."

A spasm crossed the king's face. "But, Semorel... that tree... Don't you remember?"

Nevien put a restraining hand on her father's arm. She knew that the pear tree of which her mother spoke had stood in its place for more than twenty years, growing to great height and breadth. It had produced pears by the bushel the previous autumn. "No one will harm that tree as long as there's life in it, Mother," she said quickly.

The queen's eyes turned to her daughter and the frown returned. It seemed she was having trouble focusing her gaze. "Nevien?" she inquired vaguely. "What are you doing here...?"

"Mother, I'm here to listen—and to do anything I can for you."

"Ah...? Oh, yes. Of course." Semorel smiled weakly. "You're a good daughter, Nevien..." Her eyes closed again and she emitted a gentle sigh, seeming to drift once more into sleep.

Elgurn had sat rigid, watching his wife. After a moment, when she didn't speak again, he rose, letting go of her hand, and bent over her as if to be certain she still breathed. Apparently satisfied, he straightened and cast Nevien an agonized look. He backed away from the bedside, beckoning her to follow. Nevien got up from her chair and moved after him to stand a dozen paces from the queen's bed.

"Why did she ask me about the pear tree, Nevien?" He spoke low and urgently, his face drawn, his blue eyes full of pain. "She called for me, and when I came, she asked only about the tree!"

"It's the opa, Father, that's all. She wanders, sometimes in the past and sometimes in the present."

"Yes, yes—but I spared that tree twenty *years* ago for her sake. I wouldn't touch a twig of it for all the gold in the islands! She should know that! We never built the wall around the kitchen garden because of that tree. Why must she remember that I once talked of uprooting the wretched thing?"

Nevien shook her head. "Father, it doesn't mean anything. You mustn't take it so. If Master Ambras were awake, he'd tell you—"

"Master Ambras!" Elgurn's eyes sought the recumbent form of the healer, stretched on a narrow pallet near the foot of the queen's great carved bed. "I think he gives her too much opa. When next he wakes, I'll have a word with him."

Before Nevien could say what was in her mind—that Ambras only gave her mother as much opa as was needed to keep her out of pain—they were interrupted by the sound of booted feet and voices coming from the adjoining room, the king's bedchamber. A dark-haired youth in the uniform of the palace guard appeared in the doorway that separated the two royal bedrooms. The young man halted nervously. "M-My Lord King—" he stammered.

"Yes, what is it now?" Elgurn was suddenly crisp and commanding. "Guardsman Delvin, I believe?"

Nevien had also recognized the young guardsman as the one who was often posted at the main entrance of the palace. She watched him bob a quick bow.

"Aye, My Lord. Commander Worling sent me to make the report ye asked for. About th-the battle, Zirda."

"Yes. *And...?*"

"Well, ah, there's not much we *know*. It's all still inside the city wall—"

"So they haven't breached the gate?"

Delvin shook his head. "Not yet, My Lord. The City Guard must be holding it, but we can't see much from the second floor balcony."

"Why not? That should give you a view over the wall and out to the river, as well."

Delvin licked his lips. "It's the smoke from the burned shipyard, Zirda. The wind's dropped, and it's all just drifting."

"You've seen nothing then?" Elgurn demanded.

Delvin shifted his feet. "There's been some movements. Of ships..."

"Well, out with it! Speak up, lad!"

"W-we thought we saw three ships going *up* the river nearly an hour ago, Zirda, but there was too much smoke t' see their banners. And just now we saw six—or seven—ships, going *down* the river. Some o' them at least had red banners."

The king's frown had deepened as he listened, and now he began to pace the floor. "*Down* the river? But the fighting continues, you say," he muttered. "Where are they sending their ships? *What can they be plotting?*" He halted abruptly and turned on Delvin. "What does Worling think?"

Delvin jumped, dismayed by the sharpness of the king's tone. "Th-the commander's not sure what t' think, My Lord. I—I heard him saying he thinks they might be sending their ships 'round t' the north side—that they could mean t' break through the city gate and go over the north wall, an' make off that way."

"Mmm... yes... Or they could mean to storm the palace before they make off by the north cove with any captives they take. Which means we should—" The King broke off, glancing at Nevien as if he'd just noticed she was still standing there. "Go back to your mother, Nevien," he told her curtly. Turning again, he strode to the door where Delvin was standing, causing the youth to skip out of his way. Elgurn swept past the young guardsman with a peremptory gesture and a terse, "Follow me, lad."

Nevien stood still for a moment after the two men disappeared into her father's bedroom. A glance at her mother showed that the queen was moving a little, restlessly, but her eyes were still closed. Nevien debated for a few seconds, then moved closer to the door, which her father had failed to close completely behind him. His voice came clearly to her ears through the gap.

"—six men, at least, or as many as Commander Worling can spare us."

"Aye, My Lord!"

Nevien could practically hear the snap of Delvin's salute, and his words were followed by the sound of departing footsteps.

"And you, Brandle, you and Gilian gather up the women and take them to the queen's sitting room. If we have to defend them, I want them all in one place."

"Aye Zirda!" That was Brandle's response, and his heavy, booted tread could be heard also retreating from the adjoining room.

Knowing that her father would very likely return to his chosen place in the doorway, Nevien immediately crossed back to the chair at her mother's bedside. She knew from long experience that whenever her father clearly didn't wish to alarm her, her best course was to appear not to be alarmed.

She did her best to appear not to notice when, some time later, she heard the sound of more booted feet in the corridor outside, and then of men's voices in her father's chamber.

Elgurn left his place in the doorway long enough to carry on a muttered conversation with the new arrivals. Shortly thereafter, Brandle entered the queen's chamber through its other door, from the hallway. Closing the door behind him, the tall Leithian quietly moved Semorel's dressing table to stand in front of the door and sat down on it with studied nonchalance.

Nevien kept her eyes on her mother, who was sleeping fitfully, and desperately busied herself by cooling the Queen's forehead with a damp cloth, hoping that no one would notice how her hands shook. The disturbing knowledge of the ongoing battle was looming ever larger in her mind. *What if the enemy warriors forced their way onto the third floor... to this room? What could any of them possibly do then to spare the suffering of the dying woman?*

The king reappeared at the bedroom doorway. He stood there for a time, then advanced into his wife's chamber and began pacing the floor.

After perhaps a half an hour, which seemed much longer, Delvin came with another report. This time Elgurn went into his chamber to receive it, and Nevien caught the sound of their voices but not the words. When her father returned, she made sure to be diligently applying the dampened cloth.

"What's the news, My Lord?" Brandle spoke low, but not low enough.

"*Shh!* They've breached the gate." Elgurn's responding whisper would have been inaudible if the room hadn't been so silent. "There's fighting in the courtyard."

All was tensely quiet for a time after that. The queen seemed to rest more easily and Nevien must have dozed in her chair. She awoke groggily to the sound of more voices.

"Hush, my dear! Try to lie quiet."

"—*where is he—?*"

Nevien opened her eyes to find her father kneeling at the bedside, attempting to quiet his wife by speaking to her softly and stroking her brow.

"I'm here, Semorel."

"—*please! You have to find him... I need him—*

"Semorel, I'm here. It's all right."

The queen's eyes were open, but she stared wildly this way and that, murmuring. Her eyelids fluttered and she groaned aloud.

As if in answer to his patient's pain, Master Ambras suddenly woke and started up from his pallet. "Here, My Lady Queen! I'm coming." The healer stumbled blearily to his bag where it rested on a small table on the farther side of the bed. He returned with the vial of opa in his hand and froze when he caught the king's expression.

Elgurn's piercing blue gaze was fixed on the healer's face. "I don't want you to give her any more of that, Ambras. She's had enough!"

The queen shuddered and groaned again. "*Oh! Oh! Please... where is he—?*"

"But see, My Lord!" Ambras protested. "She suffers!"

The king's frown deepened. "We might as well have lost her already when she's under it. She doesn't know who she's talking to half the time, or what she's saying!"

Master Ambras opened his mouth to reply, but he was interrupted by the sound of running feet in the corridor outside. The steps seemed to stop outside the king's bedchamber, followed by raised voices. Someone could be heard calling for the king, and there was a confusion of voices from the adjoining room.

More rapid strides followed, coming on along the corridor, and a fist thudded heavily on the outer door of the queen's bedchamber. A man's voice reached their ears, and this time they could clearly make out the words.

"*Open! Open, I beg you!* If anyone there can bear a sword, we need your help!"

"*Nagaro!*" Nevien started to her feet. "It's Captain Nagaro," she said urgently as the eyes of the two men turned to her. "I know his voice."

Elgurn was instantly on his feet. With an oath, he strode to the door. Motioning Brandle away with a fierce wave of his hand, he shoved the dressing table violently aside and wrenched open the door, "*By the Gods!*" he bellowed. "Can't you leave a dying woman in peace?"

Nagaro stood revealed in the open doorway. He wasn't dressed as a pirate, nor in a Fleet uniform, but simply clad in black boots and pants and a plain white shirt. The shirt was spattered with blood, though it didn't appear to be his. He held a naked sword in his hand and the blade ran crimson. He met the king's gaze with a glance that was every bit its equal in intensity and command.

"They're on the second floor, My Lord," he said in a voice that cut like steel. "We've cut off their retreat by taking their ships, and they're fighting like demons bent on blood or death. If we can't hold them below, you'll be fighting them at this very door!"

Before the king could respond, a new commotion erupted from somewhere farther along the corridor to the left.

Nagaro stiffened as he turned to look. *"Keshaal!"* he cried. "They've come up the back stair!" Then he plunged away at a dead run in the direction of the sounds, shouting, "Pavo! Taru! To me!"

Two other men, one large, one small, dashed after him and within seconds there came the sound of steel on steel.

Elgurn stepped forward to take one quick look after the departing figures. Then he backed into the room, yanked the door closed, and pulled the dressing table back in front of it. Turning to Brandle, who stood as if rooted to the spot, the king leveled a finger and spoke in a voice taut enough to snap. "You! Guard this chamber with your life!"

"Aye, Zirda!" Brandle came to life, saluting crisply.

Elgurn gave him a curt nod of acknowledgment. Then he unsheathed his sword and exited through the other door without another word or a backward glance.

Master Ambras stood frozen, staring after the king and looking severely shaken.

Brandle sat down again on the dressing table barricade, laying his drawn sword across his knees and looking anything but nonchalant.

Nevien remained standing numbly beside her mother's sickbed. *Nagaro was here... and he hadn't even looked at her.* She frowned. *Of course he wouldn't—not in the middle of a battle.* It sounded as if the fighting was already in the hallway!

*"He's come at last!"*

Nevien shook herself, realizing that it was her mother who had spoken. She turned to stare at the frail figure on the bed. The queen was sitting up, leaning forward, her gaze fixed upon the chamber's outer door. Her breathing was ragged, her face very pale, her eyes bright.

"Who, Mother?" Nevien wondered aloud. *Not Brandle, surely.*

Semorel closed her eyes as a spasm of pain crossed her face. *"Oh!"* She sank back onto the pillows. After several seconds she spoke again, brokenly.

*"—Captain Nagaro... He's here!"*

The queen gasped, and winced again before continuing, speaking more steadily this time.

"When he's finished fighting, he will call Vothra to me. And Vothra will set my spirit free!"

***

Elgurn paused in his bedchamber only long enough to issue two quick commands to the half dozen men who waited there. "You, Sergeant! Hold this door. The rest of you, come with me."

Outside in the corridor, Nagaro and his two companions could be seen arrayed across the hallway near the door issuing from the back stairs. They were trying to prevent a group of Mautep sea warriors from advancing up the hallway. Though outnumbered two to one, they were managing to hold their own, though barely.

Elgurn hadn't seen the man called Captain Nagaro, or his men, fight before. What he saw now was impressive. Nagaro held the middle position of the three, but his blade ranged widely and he moved with such speed that he was covering more than his share of the width of the hall. Still, he would have been overwhelmed without the superb support of his companions. The man on his left was fighting with a focused intensity, which, together with his sheer size, was holding the attackers in front of him at bay. He swiftly covered the gap whenever Nagaro moved to the right. The smaller man, on Nagaro's right hand, reminded Elgurn of nothing so much as an armed and angry grasshopper. The apparent erraticness of his movements was deceptive, however, and what he lacked in size he made up for in energy.

The enemy were all still on their feet, fighting desperately, trying to focus their assault on Nagaro. They were giving ground only slowly as the king and his five guardsmen approached. The sight of reinforcements for their foes apparently daunted the Mautep, however, for they faltered at last, and the defenders took immediate advantage, pressing forward. Nagaro was in and out like lightning and one of the Mautep went down just as Elgurn and his men joined the fray.

The work went quickly after that. Captain Nagaro's men made room for the fresh fighters, who tripled their numbers, and the defenders took the offensive. Three more Mautep quickly went down, one slain by the king, one by Nagaro, and the third by Nagaro's massive left-hand man. The remaining two Mautep made a scrambling retreat through the door and onto the stairs, crying *"Kiraam! Kiraam!"*

Nagaro lunged after them but stopped on the landing. He peered down into the stairwell, breathing heavily. Presently he backed up, shaking his head and wiping his brow with the back of his hand. "They're on the second floor landing," he gasped. "It's held in force against us."

Elgurn considered him narrowly. "It was well done all the same, Captain. Your service to Edrovir is duly noted, as is that of these other two men—whom I presume are Pavo Maat and Taru Nareyo."

Nagaro's teeth flashed in his best pirate smile. "You are correct, My Lord."

"Where are the rest of your men?"

"Those who were with me on this sally—about a dozen—are on the second floor, helping defend the main stair with Worling's men."

"A dozen? You brought so few?"

Nagaro was already getting his breath back. "I came with three galleys full," he replied. "Some had to be left with the captured Mahuk ships, because the former slaves who are manning them needed direction to sail down the river and into the channel. The rest are somewhere out there—" Nagaro gestured toward the front of the palace, "—under Captain Timegar's command. We all joined the force that followed the Mautep when they broke through the city gate, but I left most of them in the courtyard and led a small foray to break through to the palace. We succeeded, but were cut off in the press. Worling opened the front door to us—"

"And the enemy came in after you?"

Nagaro shook his head. "We got the door closed and barred again. This lot got into the Great Hall by a side door. Commander Worling ordered a retreat to the base of the main stairs—then to the second floor—trying to stay ahead of them and keep them from reaching *this* floor. So the second floor is now the battleground. Things were at an impasse when the three of us came upstairs seeking aid."

The king had listened grimly. Now he nodded. "Then we should be down there." He squared his shoulders. "But we shouldn't leave this door unguarded."

"It's too narrow for two men to pass through it abreast," Nagaro pointed out. "Two or three men could hold it almost indefinitely."

The king nodded, frowning. "I'd set you and your men to it, but I think I'd rather have your talents elsewhere." He quickly chose three men from his own small company, telling them, "This is your task. Don't let them pass!" Turning then, he started back along the corridor with long strides.

Nagaro fell in beside him. Taru and Pavo came behind Nagaro and the two remaining guardsmen followed the king. "Are there no more under your command who could join us?" Nagaro asked as they passed the royal bedchambers.

Elgurn shook his head. "There are two guardsmen in the queen's sitting room with most of the women—and two more guarding her bedchamber. My daughter is in there, and Ambras the healer—but he's no fighter. Dreigen no doubt is in his own chambers, but I won't trouble *him!* Any man foolish enough to disturb Dreigen's sanctum does so at his own peril."

They had reached the top of the main stair and Elgurn paused, listening. A confusion of voices reached their ears. "How many Mautep are down there?" he asked.

"Within these walls, between fifty and sixty I'd guess. There must have been about two hundred to begin with, that came ashore."

"Hnnh." The king looked sober. "And how many of ours?"

"Mine and Worling's together? Perhaps thirty."

Elgurn chewed his lip. "What chance of reenforcements?"

"As things stood when I last saw, the Mautep are more likely to get reenforcements than we are. The bulk of their force stood between our men and the palace."

The king winced. "I don't care for the odds," he said, hefting his sword in his hand. "But we must do what we can." So saying he started down the stairs. "Thirty six against sixty," he muttered.

"Aye, but one of ours is Nagaro!" Taru paused, as the king shot him a questioning glance. "They're afraid of Nagaro, Zirda," he explained hastily. "And they should be! Just put him in the middle, with Pavo an' me, and stand back!"

"Taru!" Nagaro frowned.

The king returned his attention to the stairs. "I intend to put him close to the middle," he said quietly. "But I'm not going to stand back. I'll be right beside him, with these two." He jerked a thumb at the two guardsmen, who looked grim and well-seasoned.

The main stair descended in an enclosed stairwell, spiraling down through a full turn to the second floor landing. They were halfway down when sounds erupted from below—shouts, and the clash of arms.

"*Quickly!*" Nagaro hissed, springing ahead. Beckoning to his two officers, he took the remaining stairs at a run, Taru and Pavo a step behind him.

Elgurn, accustomed to giving the commands, was caught off guard, but only for a second. With a muttered exclamation of "*Kroneg's Blood!*" he sprang after the three comrades, beckoning his guardsmen to follow.

The stairwell opened at the second floor landing by means of a wide archway facing east. The arch turned out to be held by several members of the palace guard, crouching with swords drawn. Nagaro paused half a dozen steps behind them to get a view over the men's heads of the intersection of hallways that lay beyond.

When he'd left this scene, the defenders had been in possession of the crossing and of the north, west, and south halls. The Mautep force had been confined to the long east hallway that now lay straight before him, running all the way to the infamous back stair at the end of it. Based on what he could see from his present vantage point, things had gone badly in his absence. The wood-paneled hall was choked with men wielding bloodied swords. The polished floor was strewn with corpses. The Edroviran line that had held the Mautep at bay was being pushed back, stretching and buckling under a heavy onslaught from a mass of enemy warriors, several ranks deep. Commander Worling was in the thick of things, trying to rally his troops to stand their ground.

Elgurn, arriving beside Taru, immediately took stock of the scene and swore.

Nagaro shouted over the noise of battle. "Delvin! What happened?"

One of the guardsmen at the foot of the stairs twisted about. "They pulled back—like they meant t' retreat—but as soon as some o' the men went after 'em, they turned and rushed us full on!"

Elgurn spoke commandingly. "Stand aside, guardsmen! Make way for your king, and for Captain Nagaro!"

The men holding the stairwell entrance turned at the sound of the king's voice, then hastily parted, moving to right and left. Elgurn turned to Nagaro with a cocked eyebrow. He made a gesture of invitation with his sword. "Captain."

Nagaro's reply was a quick nod. He raised his blade. *"Forward for Edrovir!"*

*"For Edrovir!"* The chorus of voices rang all around him.

Taru and Pavo leaped to their positions at his sides as Nagaro sprang forward, charging across the floor towards the seething melee. He was aware of the king and his flank-men coming up on Taru's right as new shouts arose, crying, *"Nagaro!"* and others, fewer in number, crying, *"Edrovir!"* or *"Elgurn!"*

Nagaro had no time to think about who was shouting what, or why. The line of the defenders was right in front of him, the enemy immediately beyond. A gap opened in the line to let him pass, and he was through it with Taru and Pavo at his sides. He began to ply his blade with a mixture of fury and finesse. The high, wild song of battle was running through his veins like fire. It was powerful, exhilarating, and he let it carry him forward, careful only not to let it become his master.

The Edroviran line was rallying. Nagaro was aware of men closing ranks and advancing on either side of him. Worling was among them, on his left. The king was on his right, fighting hard. The enemy sea warriors were falling back, some literally falling, cut down by his blade or those of his companions. Still there came the rallying chant of *"Nagaro! Nagaro!"*

Other cries—alarmed cries—rose over the din, coming from the throats of the Mautep warriors: *"Kiraam! Kiraam! Sheptuum hanuk-par!"*

But there was one at least among the Mautep who was not dismayed—a broad-shouldered, square-faced man, gray about the temples and sporting a small pointed beard, his uniform bearing the insignia of a high-ranking officer. He fought near the center of the Mautep line, a little to Nagaro's right, and his shouts rang with command and with cold rage, rather than fear.

Nagaro understood enough of the man's words to know that he was calling on his men to fight and die with honor. Some were heeding the call, and where some came, others followed. They rallied to their commander, and their commander began to maneuver his way sideways through the press, trying to confront his nemesis, the accursed Kiraam Shaku-Tal.

Nagaro saw this clearly, and he knew, just as clearly, that if the man meant to challenge him it was best to take that challenge and waste no time about it. So he moved also, edging sideways until he and the Mautep commander were face to face. As soon as the bearded Mautep was within range, the man lunged with his sword, straight at Nagaro's chest.

Nagaro caught the blade on his, turning it aside with a high, thin skreel of metal on metal. The Mautep swore, but he recovered swiftly and mounted a fresh assault. Nagaro parried again, and again—stroke after stroke. He hadn't expected this to be an easy fight, and it wasn't. He'd been watching the man fight, and he knew the Mautep commander was fast, highly skilled, and desperate. He was grateful that Taru and Pavo were keeping the blades of other enemy warriors busy so he could focus his full attention on this determined adversary. Still, the man might possibly be the key. He was plainly in command and his men were cut off from retreat, in hostile territory. *If he could be convinced that dying wasn't the only path of honor...*

Nagaro frowned in concentration, watching the man's eyes, which were furious and red-rimmed in a face contorted with rage. Disarming his opponent wasn't likely to work here. The man was too impassioned and there were fallen men all around him. It would be too easy for the commander to take up another sword.

*If he could just slow the man...* A particularly adroit thrust by his opponent nearly found it's mark. Nagaro twisted out of the way in the nick of time, but in doing so he saw an opportunity, and his own blade pierced the fabric of the other man's tunic, slicing through it and cutting into the flesh beneath. As he sprang back, he saw the enemy commander grimace in pain.

The Mautep faltered then, falling back, his chest heaving. Sweat ran in tracks down his face—which had gone suddenly pale—trickling into the little pointed beard. He looked nearly spent. All along the line, other Mautep faltered as well.

Nagaro was not so nearly winded. He held his sword at the ready. "If you make surrender," he said in Hashti, "all your man will keep their life."

"*Never!*" The man spat the word and sprang at Nagaro again, but he was feeling both his wound and his weariness. Twice he struck and parried, and the third time his blade rang against Nagaro's it was sent arcing over the heads of the Mautep warriors to clatter against the wall of the corridor. The disarmed man came to halt, swaying where he stood, as if unable to comprehend what had happened.

"Now will you make surrender?"

The man backed up a pace, crouching at bay. "I do not trust Droviri honor!" His eyes flicked sideways even as he spoke, and he ducked to the side, scooping up the weapon of a fallen compatriot. "Die, slave-dog!" he cried as he made a lightning-fast lunge from his crouching position, his blade aimed straight at Nagaro's belly.

Nagaro's answering move caught the other man's blade with the hilt of his sword and deflected it. In the next split second he brought his own weapon into position—level with his opponent's chest, just left of center. All he had to do then was hold steady while the other man impaled himself with the force of his own lunge. The Mautep commander fell, toppling to the side as Nagaro pulled his sword free and came on his guard again, ready for the next assailant.

There was regret in his eyes, rather than triumph, as he surveyed the faces of the opposing Mautep. He saw that some were dismayed, hesitating, but others wore expressions of angry determination. Those latter came on with the look of men resolved to avenge their leader or follow him into death. Nagaro swallowed grimly, wishing the Mautep commander had given him some other choice. This was likely to be a bloody day indeed, and he was by no means sure how it would end.

It was at that moment that a voice was raised at the other end of the long east corridor, crying loudly in Hashti. Nagaro looked through the thinning ranks of his assailants and saw a second force of red-tunicked Mautep charging towards him up the hallway. Part of the enemy force must have been held back at the other end of the corridor, and these had just been joined by reenforcements. Now they were all coming to the aid of their comrades, and it was the turn of the Edroviran forces to cry out in dismay and draw back. Commander Worling was visibly faltering, with a wound to his sword-arm taken in the last exchange.

"*Stand!*" Nagaro cried. "We must hold them!"

"*Stand for Edrovir!*" came Elgurn's command.

Shaken though they were, the Edroviran defenders rallied yet again, forming a solid line with Nagaro's un-uniformed men prominent among them, their swords ready for the approaching onslaught. Blades began to ring as the charging enemy broke against that line. Nagaro waded forward, Taru and Pavo at his flanks, all three plying their swords with devastating effect. No less determined, King Elgurn was also making an impression on the foe.

But the reenforcing Mautep warriors had brought a new commander to the fight, and this man now raised his voice above the clamor.

"*Nagaro Kiraam! What you do here?*"

Nagaro, beset though he was, still managed a glance at the speaker, for the timber of the voice, as well as the words, caught his attention. The man was young, not tall, and rather slight. He sported a narrow mustache, impeccably trimmed. Nagaro felt a jolt of recognition as he locked eyes with the young Mautep. He took only an instant to consider. Then he lowered his sword and flung up his hand.

"*Hold!*" he cried, and repeated the command in Hashti. He spoke in a voice so clear and commanding that Edroviran and Mautep alike froze in mid-stroke. Even Elgurn came to a halt, his blade poised to strike a man who stood gaping in astonishment.

"Well met, Roheed jir-Akaan." Nagaro addressed the young Mautep officer in the Common Speech. "If you surrender now, you will save the lives of all your men."

Roheed stepped over a fallen man and moved into the front rank, and he also lowered his sword. He raised his own hand to indicate that he accepted the opportunity for parlay. All along the line, raised swords came down as men stepped back from their opponents.

"There is honor in surrender to you, Nagaro Kiraam Shaku-Tal, because you have honor," Roheed observed cautiously. "But word have come to Mahuk Baar that you are out-cast. That king of Edrovir do not give you honor because you have save—*that man.*" Here he pointed at Pavo. "How I can trust honor of Edrovir?"

Nagaro frowned. "You heard aright," he admitted. "I do not command here. You must make your surrender to the king, and see what promise of honor he will make. The King of Edrovir stands there." He indicated Elgurn, who still stood with his sword in hand, listening and observing all that passed, his ice-blue eyes narrowed shrewdly. "And when this fight is done," Nagaro added, "I must make my surrender to him also."

Roheed immediately transferred his gaze to Elgurn. "This is king?" he murmured as if to himself, looking Elgurn up and down.

As it chanced, Elgurn was not wearing the narrow golden circlet that served as the crown of Edrovir. Still, he wore a finely tailored tirka of black velvet trimmed with scarlet satin, with matching britches and elegantly tooled black boots. He now drew himself up to his full height and assumed a very stern demeanor. Though he had aged much in recent years, and the strain of his wife's long illness was wearing on him, he now managed to appear both regal and commanding. "Yes," he said, speaking formally, "I am Elgurn Harlind, King of Edrovir. And you, if I understand correctly, are Roheed jir-Akaan, nephew of the Emperor of the Mahuk Baar."

Roheed didn't flinch as he met Elgurn's gaze. He made a small, stiff bow. "Yes, I am Roheed jir-Akaan," he said with matching formality. "And I have word for you, Lord King. Man that stand there is not traitor to you." He indicated Pavo, who was standing impassively at Nagaro's side. "He do not tell your plan. Man who tell your plan is very young man with yellow hair. This I have see with my eye, and hear with my ear, and I swear it on my honor and in name of Sheptuum." He lifted his chin a little. "What will you do now, Lord King?"

Elgurn stood for several seconds considering the young Mautep officer. "The word of so noble and high-born a witness is worth much," he said at length, speaking with evident care. "And Pavo Maat has done good service to Edrovir this day. If you surrender all your men, I swear to you that you will all be honored prisoners. I believe I know the young yellow-haired man of whom you speak. He shall be brought to Lankura and questioned at a new tribunal that will decide the fate of Pavo Maat, and of Captain Nagaro and Taru Nareyo. And I promise that you will be allowed to speak at this tribunal. All of this I swear on my honor and by the Gods of Seralind. What do you say to that, Roheed jir-Akaan?"

Roheed had listened, frowning, and he now turned to Pavo and spoke some rapid words in Hashti with a questioning inflection.

Pavo seemed to come unfrozen as if with an effort. He made a little half-bow to Roheed and answered at somewhat greater length, also in Hashti. Then he turned to Elgurn, bowing again. "Lord King," he said quickly, "I have just make sure that he understand you."

Elgurn had raised an eyebrow slightly, but he turned his attention back to Roheed. "What do you say?" he asked again. "Will you surrender all your men?"

Rather than answering the king, however, the young Mautep officer turned yet again and spoke to Nagaro. "Nagaro Kiraam," he said, and there was something like reverence in his voice. "You have say you also will make surrender. Do you trust honor of your king?"

Nagaro had been standing silently, observing the progress of the parlay. He flinched inwardly at this open expression of Roheed's lack of trust in Elgurn. The king shifted his stance and frowned, but held his peace. It took Nagaro the space of several heartbeats to make his answer, for there flashed through his mind all that he knew of the man who wore the crown of Edrovir, and he found himself hesitating as he weighed the bad against the good. He also remembered the sight of Narei on the deck of the *Golden Crown*. He'd had no opportunity so far to question Elgurn about his daughter's abduction—but this was not the time. He cleared his throat. "Yes," he said. "I trust the honor of Elgurn Harlind."

Roheed gave a short decisive nod. "If Nagaro Kiraam trust, then I trust," he said firmly. Facing Elgurn squarely, he drew himself to his full height and said loudly and clearly. "Lord King, I make surrender of all my man. All that are inside, and all that are outside." So saying he advanced and laid his sword on the floor at Elgurn's feet. A ripple and a murmur swept through the ranks of the Mautep.

Elgurn's brows shot up. "You command *all* the Mautep force that is attacking us?" he inquired bluntly.

Roheed straightened and regarded him impassively. "That man was command all force," he replied, pointing to the body of the officer Nagaro had dispatched. "Now he is dead, so I command."

The king nodded gravely. "Then I accept your surrender. Let your men who can hear us lay down their swords, and we will go at once to a balcony overlooking the courtyard and make the surrender known to all."

Roheed made a small bow. Turning and raising both hands, he spoke in Hashti in a ringing voice, addressing his men. The ripple of movement and murmured words that followed his speech was punctuated by the clatter of weapons being laid down on the polished oak floor of the corridor. Elgurn caught Commander Worling's eye and indicated by gestures that the swords should be collected and the prisoners taken in hand. The Leithian officer nodded, moving promptly to the task, issuing orders to those under his command.

As the collection of weapons proceeded, Nagaro approached the king. Taru and Pavo moved with him, and the remaining members of the crew of the *Sword of Freedom* separated themselves from the uniformed Palace Guard and moved protectively to encircle their three officers. Nagaro put a hand to the buckle of his sword belt in preparation to surrender the weapon. "I will trust the promise you gave to Roheed, My Lord," he observed. "Since I'm not likely to get a better one myself."

Pavo moved promptly, and Taru a little more slowly, to surrender their weapons. The king allowed this but stayed Nagaro's movement with a gesture. "The swords of Pavo Maat and Taru Nareyo I accept," he said gravely. "But I would have you keep your sword yet awhile, Captain, since I want you to join us on the balcony. This surrender will go more smoothly, I fancy, if you are seen to stand at my side."

Nagaro storm-gray eyes held the king's ice-blue ones. "I'll do as you wish, My Lord," he said evenly. "But I would think you might find it awkward to have such help from me and then have to turn around and say that I, also, am a prisoner."

Elgurn shrugged. "I will face whatever consequence there may be of my actions. I'm curious, though, Captain," he added, cocking an eyebrow.

"Did you come here to surrender yourself, and find the fight in progress? Or did you come to the fight, and now find yourself forced to surrender?"

Nagaro's teeth flashed white in the midst of his beard. "If I chose to leave even now, My Lord, I'm not certain you could stop me," he said rather coolly, indicating with a gesture the company of men who stood around him. "But the truth is, I came seeking to retrieve my daughter."

"Your *daughter?*" The king's tone and expression both suggested genuine puzzlement.

"She was abducted from her home by yellow-haired Leithians and carried off aboard a merchant ship called the *Golden Crown*, to your very doorstep as it were, My Lord," Nagaro informed him. "Our pursuit of that ship was interrupted by the discovery of the attack on the city. 'If he wants her back he must come to Lankura.' That's what those Leithians said to my daughter's guardian. Well, I've come to Lankura, My Lord, to surrender as I am sure was the intention. And I fully expect to have my daughter freed and restored to me."

A frown had been gathering on Elgurn's brow as he listened. "Do you imagine that I had something to do with this?" he demanded as soon as Nagaro ceased speaking.

Nagaro stood his ground. "I'm waiting to hear you swear that you did not, My Lord."

"*By the Gods!*" The king exploded, his eyes flashing. "What do you take me for? I'd see myself in Hel before I'd use a man's child against him!"

This time Nagaro took a step backward before the obvious sincerity of the king's wrath. "I beg your pardon, My Lord," he said earnestly. "It seems I've misjudged you. But it had occurred to me that not many folk in Lankura would have known where to find my daughter's dwelling. Kuran Kel I suspect would have known. And what Kuran knows, he makes known to you."

Elgurn's anger receded visibly, and he looked uncomfortable. "I confess that such a plan was spoken of in the Council," he admitted. "And Kuran did give us the benefit of his knowledge—reluctantly, I might add. I forbade the use of it, however. I assure you that I'll look into the matter. It had none of my approval."

Nagaro nodded his acceptance. "I'm grateful for your assistance, My Lord."

The king's attention was already elsewhere. "Come," he said briskly. "The surrender of this lot appears to be complete. It's time we made our appearance on the balcony."

It was true. Looking about, Nagaro saw that the Mautep warriors were grouped together and guarded by Worling's men. Taru and Pavo stood a little apart from them, also nominally under guard. Nagaro gave his two friends an encouraging glance and a fleeting smile. To the rest of his men who stood watchfully nearby, he said, "Wait only to hear that the fighting is truly over. Then go find Timegar and follow his command. The *Sword of Freedom*, I expect, will be returned to the Fleet, however this turns out."

He turned then to follow Elgurn and Roheed as a four-man honor guard closed around them.

Chapter 6

# Midnight Ministration

Nagaro numbly regarded his reflection in the gilt-framed mirror that hung above the porcelain wash basin. The room that was to serve as his cell this time was very similar to the one he'd shared with Tredhold during his previous incarceration—and considerably more elegant than anything he would have chosen for himself. This time he would not be sharing it with anyone, of course. At least this time Pavo, and also Taru, were similarly housed in separate chambers somewhere farther along the corridor. Nagaro smiled fleetingly at the thought of his two friends using porcelain wash basins and sleeping on feather mattresses. Roheed and several other Mautep officers were also being held in some of the palace guest chambers, which probably suited *them* perfectly well. This arrangement had been settled on for all of the officers involved once it had been realized that the rank and file of the captured Mautep sea warriors would fill both the palace dungeon and the holding cells in the Fleet Compound to capacity.

Nagaro heaved a heartfelt sigh. It had been a bloody day indeed. Before the fighting had ended, nearly half of the invading Mautep had found honorable death. The surrender of those who remained alive outside the palace walls had proceeded remarkably smoothly once Roheed had appeared on the second floor balcony above the palace's front portico, flanked by Elgurn and Nagaro.

Exactly how much his own presence had contributed to the ease of that surrender Nagaro was uncertain, although Roheed's oration—delivered in ringing Hashti—had contained the name Kiraam Shaku-tal at several points. Nagaro hadn't been able to follow the details, but he knew that his endorsement of the king's honor had been conveyed to the assembled Mautep warriors. He grimaced at the thought, hoping Roheed wouldn't regret having put his faith in that endorsement.

As for Pavo's ultimate fate, there was considerable reason to hope. Roheed's appearance, and his offer to give testimony, were unlooked for and encouraging—if only other men besides the king were prepared to trust the words of the nephew of the Emperor of the Mahuk Baar.

Nagaro heaved another sigh as he poured some water from the delicate china pitcher into the matching basin. He splashed his face and wiped it dry with the towel provided. Unbuttoning his blood-stained shirt, he shrugged it off, rinsed it as best he could in the wash basin, wrung it out, and draped it over the back of a chair to dry. Then he sponged himself off with the moistened towel and flung himself down on the bed. Now that the excitement was over, he found he was exhausted, despite the fact that the light from the room's two high windows suggested it was only mid-afternoon. He'd already eaten some food that had been brought for him—bread, meat, and cheese, with a large ceramic cup of sothiril—and had left the dishes and tray on the small table beside the door. Since he probably wouldn't be disturbed again until someone came with his dinner, he resolved to try to sleep.

This turned out not to be easy. First he thought of Narei, wondering where she was and how she was faring. Had she been frightened when she realized that her papa wasn't going to rescue her? He knew he'd done the right thing, but it nagged at him to think that his daughter might feel abandoned.

From Narei, his thoughts turned to Nevien. He'd been aware of the princess's presence in the queen's bedchamber, but had deliberately avoided letting his gaze stray in that direction, not daring to let himself be distracted in such dire circumstances. Now, of course, he regretted his own good sense. He wanted very much to know how Nevien was bearing up under the strain of her mother's long illness and her own impending bereavement.

Eventually his weariness must have won out, for he was roused out of a deep slumber by an insistent rapping on the chamber door. He opened his eyes to find that the room had grown quite dark. Hours must have passed, and night had fallen. Shaking himself groggily, he rose and stumbled to the door, finding it by means of the light shining through the crack under its bottom edge. He wondered as he put his hand on the door handle why the guard didn't simply open the door if it was just his dinner being brought to him.

But it wasn't his dinner that waited in the corridor. It was the king. Elgurn looked pale and drawn, and an almost equally weary-looking Brandle stood behind him. The door guard—it was he who had been knocking—stepped hastily aside when Nagaro finally opened the door, returning to his stiff attitude of attention.

Nagaro could only stare at his two visitors in astonishment. "My Lord?" he managed at last, addressing the king.

Elgurn wasted no time on preliminaries. "I have a favor to ask of you, Captain," he said tersely. "The queen wishes to see you."

"The queen?" Nagaro was baffled. "Why would she wish to see *me?*"

The king looked uncomfortable. "That I will explain, if you come." He glanced significantly at the door guard who was studiously appearing not to listen. "*Will* you come, Captain?"

Nagaro ran a hand through his hair. "For Queen Semorel? Of course, My Lord. Let me get my shirt."

At this, the king put out a hand to stay him. "I took the liberty of bringing you a clean one, Captain. I don't wish to distress the women with the sight of blood stains." So saying, Elgurn hastily retrieved a small bundle of white cloth from Brandle and thrust it into Nagaro's hands.

Nagaro took it with a nod because it made sense. He stepped a little back into the room to put the garment on and found in handling it that it was silk, though it was otherwise plain and unadorned. Fleetingly he wondered whose shirt it was, but he didn't trouble to ask. The fit was acceptable. As he stepped forward again, he noticed for the first time that the tray on the table beside the door no longer bore the remains of his earlier meal. He instead saw fresh bread, sothiril, and a plate of stew that looked quite cold. Apparently he'd slept through the arrival of his dinner. "What time is it?" he inquired, frowning, as he stepped through the doorway into the hall outside.

"About an hour before midnight." It was Brandle who answered. The king had already moved a few steps away in the direction he intended to go and was hovering impatiently. Brandle had been eyeing him appraisingly through the door and now gave a broad wink as Nagaro moved past him to follow the king. "The three brands are quite decorative," the big Leithian observed out of the side of his mouth. "The matched set is rather elegant. A pity about your back, though. They've made rather a mess of it."

Nagaro felt the blood in his face. He considered Brandle a friend of sorts, or at least an ally, but the crossed man's unabashed frankness embarrassed him. "My back was well-scarred long before Osfaraad," he said, as easily as he could manage. "Slaves take a lot of the lash. And I could do quite well without the matching brands."

The door guard made a hesitant move to follow them, saying, "My Lord?"

The king gestured the man back to his post. "There's no need, Guardsman," he said quickly. "I've brought a guard, as you see, and I would vouch for Captain Nagaro's good behavior in any case."

After that, Elgurn set out at a brisk pace, leading the way along the hallway with Nagaro just behind him and Brandle bringing up the rear. They proceeded through several turnings, until they reached the main stair and so ascended to the third floor. Once there, however, Elgurn's steps slowed as if he felt some new reluctance. He led them, not to the queen's chamber door, but to the door of his own bedchamber. Opening it, he ushered Nagaro through and indicated with a nod that Brandle should join them.

The room contained, in addition to its other furnishings, a small table with a pair of chairs set against one wall. The king dropped wearily onto one of the chairs and indicated the other with a wave.

"Please sit down, Captain."

Nagaro complied. Brandle took a position beside the door without being bidden, assuming a resting guardsman's posture with feet slightly apart and hands behind his back.

Elgurn heaved a sigh and passed a weary hand over his eyes before meeting Nagaro's questioning gaze. "My wife is dying, Captain," he said with an air of fatalism. "Slowly and painfully."

Nagaro shifted. "There's nothing more the healer can do then? The princess mentioned something once about a rather harsh but effective medicine."

Elgurn shook his head. "Another dose of that, I'm told, would kill her outright—and rather horribly. And so she lingers, suffering. And Ambras gives her opa so she will suffer less, and then she *wanders...*"

"And in her wandering she's asked for me? Is that it?"

Elgurn nodded. "She... ah... seems to desire your assistance."

"Assistance? With what, My Lord?"

Elgurn bowed his head and massaged his temples. "Do you recall the... ah... service you once rendered to Prince Elyan?" He raised his eyes.

"Oh." Comprehension dawned and Nagaro felt his stomach drop. "She wants to die, with Vothra's help. She wants me to call Vothra for her."

Elgurn sighed and nodded again. "At least that's how my daughter interprets her words. As I've said, she wanders."

Nagaro frowned. "She could call Vothra herself. Anyone can."

But the king shook his head. "I doubt her mind is coherent enough for that."

Nagaro's frown deepened. "In that case, Vothra may have difficulty reaching her. The Spirit couldn't reach me once, when I had been given a sleeping drought."

Elgurn grimaced as if reliving painful choices. "She hasn't had opa in nearly two hours. But of course that means she'll be in pain. Will you at least *try*, Captain?"

Nagaro had placed his hands on the table. Now he studied them. "I can try to call the Spirit," he said seriously. "And Vothra may come, but it's the queen who must have the strength to let go of her life. Vothra can only guide her spirit in its passage into the void—"

*"Into the void..."*

Nagaro looked up to find that Elgurn was looking blindly past him, abstracted. There was deep pain in the older man's eyes as he murmured, *"Is this to be the end of all my efforts after all?"*

Again Nagaro frowned. "I thought you wanted—"

The king's gaze came sharply back to focus on him. "*She* wants it! And I want her suffering to end. But it's against Solbrid's law to seek one's own death. All these years I've let no evil touch her—kept her free of any taint or stain— all so her spirit might enter Seralind... and now *this!*"

Nagaro sucked a breath. *This was Leithian teaching.* "My Lord," he said levelly, "Semorel is Vothrin, and so she doesn't believe in Seralind. What I believe, and what she believes, is that if we are successful, her spirit will pass into the void for a time and then be born into a new life. This is what Vothra tells us. Is it so terrible?"

"Perhaps not—*if you believe it.*"

Nagaro pushed back his chair and rose. "Are you sure you wish me to try this, My Lord? Or should I return to my room? Remember, it may not even succeed."

Elgurn gave him a look of agonized outrage. "*Yes, yes, go on!*" He gestured in the direction of the closed door that separated his chamber from that of the queen. "Go! And be quick about it."

Nagaro drew a steadying breath. As he started across the room, he became aware that Brandle had left his place by the door and was following him. He grimaced at the realization that he was still under guard. The door handle yielded to his touch. He pulled the door open a little, hesitantly.

Immediately the sounds of the queen's suffering smote his ears, and, looking into the room beyond, he beheld a shocking scene. The chamber was dimly lit, the atmosphere close. The air that breathed into his face was pungent with medicinal herbs. Semorel was gasping and moaning aloud as she twisted and writhed upon the bed. Nevien was on the nearer side of the bed with her back to him, bending over her mother and attempting to raise her head and to steady her. Master Ambras, the healer, was on the far side, holding a small cup.

"My Lady Queen, if you would drink this— Nevien, hold her!"

"*—Oh! Ohh! Ahh! Mmmm—*"

"Mother, please! Try to hold your head up!"

"*—I... nn-no! Mmmm... Ohh! Ohhh!—*"

Nagaro took a panicked step backward, pulling the door closed. "*Vothra's Eyes!*" he murmured. "How can they bear it?"

He nearly collided with Brandle in his haste to shut out both the sight and the sound. They brought back a terrible memory, long buried, of a different lady—the Lady Maramine, *his Lady Guardian*—writhing on a different bed, screaming in the agony of heskial withdrawal, while he had been made to watch, enslaved by the same drug. *Unable to move of his own accord... unable to help her... unable even to weep...*

Elgurn must have risen from his own seat, for he suddenly blocked Nagaro's retreat, "Captain," he cried urgently, "*You must help her!*"

Nagaro turned on the king, remembering all too well the part this man had played on that other day. "*I* must help her?" he demanded. "Help her to die? Why not *you*, My Lord? It should be an easy thing to kill a woman who is so ill and frail. Then she won't have sought her own death—and that should please you!"

Elgurn recoiled, his face ashen. "*Oh Gods!*" he murmured, clutching at his head. "You may not believe me, but I did that once! I could never do it again! What it cost me, you couldn't possibly imagine!"

Staring at the king's stricken face, reading an agony of horror in those pale blue eyes, Nagaro felt something relent inside him. He was suddenly ashamed of his bitter outburst. "I'm sorry, My Lord," he said, "but I'm not sure I can do this—"

"Try! *Please!*" Elgurn grasped his shoulder.

Nagaro shook off the hand, and gave his head a shake to clear it. He tried to imagine going back into that room... standing beside that bed... attempting to empty his mind so that he could call Vothra. He felt his chest tighten. *Was he going to fail the queen because of his own weakness?*

"Maybe if I call Vothra *here* in this room..." he said, speaking his thought aloud. "If I let the Spirit enter into me *before* I go in there—" He stopped, remembering something. "Ambras was trying to give her something in a cup," he said urgently. "If it's opa—"

"We have to stop him!" Elgurn made a movement towards the door, but then he quailed and groaned aloud.

"I'll do it." Brandle had been standing there through the whole exchange and it was he who had spoken. In the next instant, the big Leithian put his hand on the door handle, opening the door and closing it quickly behind him as he passed through.

The king made no move to stop the lieutenant, or to follow him. He stood with his head down, looking more defeated than Nagaro had ever seen him.

Nagaro shook himself out of his own inaction and went back to the table. "Turn down the lamp," he said over is shoulder to Elgurn, who was still standing frozen and mute. "And please be quiet for a few minutes."

He sat down, placing his elbows on the table and resting his forehead in his hands. He closed his eyes and tried to calm himself, to steady the beating of his heart, to clear his mind. He was aware of the sound of the king's footsteps, and of the light dimming as he perceived it through his closed eyelids. He drew a series of long breaths, letting each one out slowly, trying to empty his mind of all but his quest for the Spirit's aid.

"Vothra," he murmured. "I have need of you. Spirit, will you come to me?"

He waited, but there was nothing. No voice in his head. No sense of presence. He shifted his position in the chair. He hadn't spoken with the Benevolent Spirit since the incident at Osfaraad, nearly a year ago. There was nothing particularly strange about this, since he hadn't tried to call the Spirit in all that time. Still, he felt a fleeting fear that he had somehow lost his connection. He tried again.

"Vothra, Lord of My Choosing, it is not for myself that I call, but for another. It is for Queen Semorel."

*There is no need for your fear, Spirit called Nagaro. I am here.*

The words inside his head came so suddenly that Nagaro started in his chair. He felt an intense flood of relief. "Thank you, Spirit," he said, still speaking aloud. "For a moment, I thought I might have lost you."

*I have been keeping a greater distance.* The voice was apologetic. *Hoping to avoid temptation.*

"Temptation? I don't understand."

*The temptation to interfere again in the events of the world to save your life, as I did at Osfaraad. But there is no time for this. I can see all that is in your mind. Are you ready for me to in-dwell in you as I did before?*

Nagaro straightened in the chair, lowering his hands and raising his head, still keeping his eyes closed. "Yes, I am ready."

In the next instant he caught his breath in a strangled gasp. A bud had burst into brilliant bloom inside of him, followed by an intense wave of something—*energy?*—that flowed outward from the center of his being to the very tips of his extremities. He felt as if he had been filled with blinding light and immense power. "*Oh!*" he exclaimed, opening his eyes in shock. "Spirit, you've become so much stronger!"

*Yes. I have grown. Now stand up, and let us be about this!*

Nagaro pushed his chair back, and got to his feet a little cautiously. It wasn't that his body didn't obey him, but he had the sense that if he weren't very careful, something—either inside or outside of him—might break.

Elgurn had indeed turned down the oil lamp and the room was sunk in shadow. The king stood eyeing him uncertainly. As Nagaro started to move towards the door that led to the queen's chamber, the older man moved to intercept him and asked, "Are you all right, Captain?"

"Yes. Please stand aside, My Lord."

The king started, as if at something in the sound of Nagaro's voice, and looked harder at him, then mutely stepped out of the way.

Nagaro went to the door and put his hand on the handle, but he hesitated fractionally before turning it. "Vothra, give me strength," he murmured. It was a hopeful prayer, not a request.

A low, gentle laugh rippled through him, followed by words. *I will do what I can. Now open the door.*

Nagaro did as he was bidden, this time passing through into the room beyond. He closed the door behind him and leaned his back against it. The scene was much the same as it had been before, except that Master Ambras had put down his cup and was holding the queen's left hand while Nevien held her mother's right. Brandle stood nearby, looking helpless.

The queen was, if anything, more agitated.

"—*Ohh! Ohh! ...mmmhh... Aaai!*—"

Nagaro's memories rose as before, but they were pushed away as words came into his mind to take their place.

*There is a task to be done here.*

"Yes..." He started to speak aloud, then thought, silently, instead, *Can you take away her pain as you did for me at Osfaraad? Can you do it for long enough?*

The answer came immediately. *I believe so. As I said, I have grown.*

*I don't wish to see inside this time... her pain or her sickness.*

*There is no need. Her husband has already given his permission for what we mean to do.*

Nagaro had taken two steps into the room, and Ambras, who was facing him, must have seen him. The healer said something, and Nevien turned to look. Then she spoke quickly to Brandle, who approached the bed and took the queen's hand that Nevien had been holding. She then rose from her stool and left the bedside, allowing Brandle to take her place. Turning to Nagaro, she indicated with a raised hand that he should stay where he was as she approached him.

Nagaro's eyes were only for the princess in that moment. His heart leaped ecstatically as she came towards him, then lodged in his throat when he saw how thin and pinched her face had become. There were dark smudges under her eyes from lack of sleep, and her honey-colored hair hung lank, obvious evidence of self-neglect. Acutely aware of her suffering, he was seized by a powerful desire to enfold her in his arms, to offer her any comfort that he could.

*Oh my. This is new.*

Vothra's thought broke upon Nagaro's mind. He had momentarily forgotten the Spirit's presence, and he responded with a mental protest. *I thought you said you could see what was in my mind.*

*I had not looked into all the corners. Ah, the love of the world... how well I remember it! But, Spirit called Nagaro, you must set this aside as best you can.*

Nevien had stepped up quite close to him by this time and his pulse quickened in defiance of Vothra's admonition. She bent close to speak to him, her voice urgent and low, and he forced himself to focus on her words.

"I'm so very glad you're here, Nagaro, but I have to warn you. My mother hasn't been in full possession of her faculties for days. Master Ambras has given her so much opa and… well… we've had to humor her. I'm not sure how much she'll remember, or what she thinks is real…" Her words trailed.

He nodded. "I think I understand. I've had some experience with opa."

She shot him a grateful glance. "We hadn't told her you had been banished. And there are other things—" again she broke off, biting her lip, then hastily resumed. "It's just… well… promise me you won't contradict her about anything that pleases her—no matter how much it surprises you. There mustn't be anything to make her feel she has to stay."

Again he nodded. "I promise."

Nevien appeared relieved, but still on edge. "Will you… will you call Vothra now?"

"Vothra is already here." He touched his forehead.

"Oh!" She looked harder at him. "I thought you seemed somehow *different.*"

Her scrutiny made him uncomfortable. "We should begin," he said. "I can't promise this will work. It's really up to her."

"Yes, I know. Come."

She led the way back to the queen's bedside and he followed with trepidation. Semorel was writhing on the bed and crying out so piteously that he could scarcely bring himself to look or listen.

*Do not be afraid, Spirit called Nagaro. You know what to do?*

*I think so.*

Semorel's eyes abruptly turned towards him. "*Ohh… Ohhh…*" she moaned. "Mm-mercy—" Then her eyes clenched shut as a spasm crossed her face, and she closed her mouth hard as if making an effort not to give further voice to her agony.

Nagaro cleared his throat. "We will make a circle of hands," he said quickly, before he could lose his nerve. "Any who wish to be part of this. You will feel Vothra's spirit—hear Vothra's voice. And you mustn't break the circle—no matter what happens. Ambras, I expect you'll join us?"

The healer nodded.

"Nevien?"

He saw her draw a sudden breath, but she nodded as well. "Yes. I will join."

He turned to Brandle and saw the Leithian's consternation. "If you don't wish to join, it would be good to have someone stand outside the circle," he offered quickly. "In case anything is needed."

"R-right," Brandle stammered. "I can do that."

"Good." Nagaro motioned Brandle out of the way and sat down on the stool beside the bed, reaching to take Queen Semorel's right hand in his left.

The woman's eyes snapped open at his touch. She took his hand with a gasp and a moan, then closed her eyes again. He was at first encouraged at the strength of the dying woman's grip, until he realized that she must be using it to help herself fight the pain. He turned to Nevien, who had seated herself on the bed, and reached for her left hand with his right.

*The last time they had touched, they'd been sitting in the blue-and-green sitting room. He'd put his arm around her shoulders to comfort her after Kale had nearly strangled her— Don't think about that!*

"Close the circle," he said urgently.

Ambras already held the queen's left hand in his right. He looked anxious but resolute. Nevien was very pale, but she gave Nagaro's hand a quick squeeze and leaned across the bed to take Master Ambras's free hand with her right, making the circle complete.

Nagaro released a breath he hadn't realized he'd been holding. "Remember," he said to both Nevien and Ambras, "You mustn't break the circle until I say it's all right." He waited just long enough for their answering nods, then, "Vothra," he said aloud, though he knew it was unnecessary, "We're ready to begin."

*I will move into the one called Nevien first, then through her into Ambras. Tell them.*

Quickly Nagaro conveyed this to the other members of the circle. A moment later he saw Nevien's eyes suddenly go wide as he felt a slight ebbing the spirit energy that filled him.

"Oh!" Nevien exclaimed. "It's like being filled with light!" Then, as if she were answering some internal voice, she added, "No, it's all right. I just didn't expect it to feel like this."

A moment later, Nagaro felt a further diminishing of Vothra's presence inside him as Master Ambras suddenly gave a little gasp and sat up straighter. "Yes it is..." he murmured softly, as if speaking to himself.

*And now I will enter into Semorel.*

Nagaro heard the words and knew, even without reading the confirmation in the other's faces, that Vothra was addressing all three of them together.

*I will move through both of her hands at once, because that way is more certain. Hold fast!*

Nagaro felt a further ebbing of the energy that filled him. Watching the queen, he saw her suddenly flinch. Her hand jerked in his, but he held it tight.

*Spirit that calls itself Semorel, I mean you no harm. I will try now to come between you and the pain you feel so that you will be free to speak and to choose.*

These words, though addressed to Semorel, were clearly heard by the entire circle. The queen's eyelids fluttered. She gasped and then emitted a long sigh. Her face that had been contorted by pain relaxed, and her entire body, so thin and frail beneath the bedclothes, seemed to go limp.

Nevien stirred. *"Mother?"* she said in some alarm.

*Speak to us, Semorel!*

As if with an effort, the queen opened eyes that were markedly sunken. The skin of her face looked as if it were stretched thin over her cheekbones but her gaze was clear and steady. "Oh Blessed Spirit, thank you for this respite," she murmured. "This is *wonderful!*"

*I cannot hold it so for very long, Spirit called Semorel. What is your wish?*

The queen sighed. "It is time for me to go, Gentle Spirit, to whatever new life awaits me. Will you aid my spirit's passing?"

*I will help as I am able, though it is you who must let go. If you have words to speak to any of those present, speak them now, and quickly.*

Semorel's eyes swept the room. "Where is my husband?"

Nagaro cleared his throat. "He is in the adjoining chamber, My Lady Queen. We could send Brandle for him."

But the queen shook her head. "There is no need. He has allowed this, and that is enough. He need not witness it. And we have already said all that we need to say to one another, he and I." Her gaze grew momentarily abstracted. "It was the last time we walked together on the balcony, at the turning of the year. It was a cold day with a wind from the sea. He will remember. There is nothing I would add to what I told him then."

Once more she sighed and her gaze shifted to the healer. "Ambras, I thank you for all your care, all that you have done for me."

Master Ambras spoke no word of answer, but bowed his head in acknowledgment.

"Nevien..." The queen's eyes sought her daughter's face. "Best of daughters that could be, I wish you peace, and love, and joy. It will be some time before you can feel it, I know. But you will. Be strong, child, and let your heart ever guide you to what is right."

Nevien was blinking back welling tears. "I love you, Mother," she murmured, and seemed unable to say more. In answer, the queen gave her a tender, beatific smile.

The smile remained as she turned to Nagaro. "And here at last," she said, "is my gallant young man—returned from the pursuit of the enemies of Edrovir."

Embarrassed, Nagaro could only nod and murmur, "My Lady Queen." He knew he had been one of her favorites since the day he'd found the missing princess hiding atop her bed canopy.

The queen gave a small contented sigh. "I'm so glad that Nevien has found you, Nagaro. And I know you'll make a very fine king—"

"*King!*" The word slipped out before Nagaro could stop it. In his shocked astonishment he very nearly let go of the queen's hand, catching himself just in time.

"Hadn't they told you?" Still the queen favored him with her gentle smile. "Whatever man weds Nevien, they will almost certainly make him king. Elgurn has been waiting only for the right man so that he can relinquish the crown, and with it the burden."

"Oh, *that*—" Nagaro began, but stopped speaking as the full import of the queen's words sank in. *Whatever man weds Nevien...* He glanced desperately at the princess, but she gave him a quick shake of her head. This must be one of the things she didn't want him to contradict—that Queen Semorel thought *he* was going to marry Nevien. *Well of course that would please her more than any of the likely matches.*

"I'm sorry I shall have to miss the wedding." The queen continued. "But I know it will be beautiful. And you'll both be very happy. Promise me you'll take good care of her."

Nagaro swallowed hard. "I'll do my best," he managed. "Always."

The queen managed to laugh, although the effort made her cough. When she recovered her breath, she said, "As if your best could possibly disappoint!" Then she turned to her daughter. "And he will have an honored place in my procession?"

Tears stood in Nevien's eyes, but she nodded. "Of course, Mother."

*Lady Semorel, my strength wears thin.* Vothra's words broke into the minds of all who were part of the circle.

Once more the queen sighed. "I'm sorry, good Spirit," she said. "It's been so long since I've been without pain—since I could speak so. But I am ready. What must I do?" She appeared to listen to a voice that no one else could hear. After a moment she asked, "Is that all?" After listening again, she spoke one final time to the circle.

"I must go now. Farewell, and may the Spirit bring you peace." With that, she closed her eyes and seemed to compose herself. Her breast rose and fell in a slow, steady rhythm.

Nagaro felt the gentle grip of her hand in his. He closed his eyes, trying not to hold his own breath. The easing of the pressure of the queen's fingers was so gradual that he nearly missed it. Much more obvious was the departure of Vothra's in-dwelling spirit. The superabundance of energy drained away, leaving him so empty that for a moment he thought he couldn't bear it. Then he breathed a ragged sigh and opened his eyes to look upon Semorel's still form. Her face had the appearance of being carved from translucent alabaster. The expression it wore was one of utter peace. Her body lay motionless beneath the bedclothes. He swallowed and managed to find his voice.

"It is over," he said. "Her spirit has gone with Vothra. The circle may now be broken."

Very gently he laid the queen's hand on her breast, letting go of the princess's hand at the same time. He was aware of Master Ambras, across the circle, releasing the hands he held as well. The healer then bent over the queen, feeling for a pulse and murmuring confirmation of what did not need to be confirmed.

Now that it was over, Nagaro felt suddenly grief-stricken, bereft and hollow, as if his heart encompassed the void. *It was finally finished. Queen Semorel—that good and kind and gracious lady, beloved of all Edrovir—was dead. And he had in some measure been the instrument of her passing. He had brought death into this room, and Nevien had lost her mother.*

*Nevien!* The thought of her pulled his mind back from the brink on which it teetered. He turned to look at the princess, still seated on her mother's bed. Her hands were raised before her as if grasping at empty air. Her eyes were fixed upon her mother's face. She scarcely seemed to breathe.

"Nevien?" he ventured, his throat painfully tight. And then, a little louder, "Nevien?"

Slowly she turned towards him. Then suddenly she was on her feet, stretching out her arms to him. "Hold me," she said. "Just hold me—"

He rose at her bidding and mutely folded her into his arms.

She clung to him, resting her head against his shoulder, and in that moment he was too overcome by his own emotion to think of doing anything more than holding her encircled and sheltered in his embrace. He bowed his own head until his cheek rested gently on the crown of her head, heedless of the fact that his tears were dampening her disheveled hair.

For a long moment, time stood still.

A soft, apologetic cough brought him back to an awareness of his surroundings.

Brandle had approached and was apparently the author of the cough. "I'm sorry, Captain," the big Leithian said, "but I'm afraid I must escort you back to your room."

Numbly, Nagaro nodded. "All right." Reluctantly he relaxed his embrace and opened his arms, stepping away from the princess. "I have to go," he told her. "Will you be all right?"

She met his eyes. "Yes," she said, and she seemed steadier, though there were tears on her cheeks. "I think I will be now. Thank you."

He turned, then, and let Brandle lead the way across the room and through the door into the king's chamber. He didn't dare look back.

Elgurn turned to face them as they entered. He had plainly been pacing the floor and his agitation was obvious despite the dim light. "Well?" he demanded. "Did it work?"

"Yes. Her spirit has departed."

Elgurn stepped closer. "Did she...? Was it her own doing?"

Nagaro nodded. "Yes. Her spirit must be strong. In the end it was very quick."

"*Kroneg's Blood!*" The king swore, his face contorting in anguish. "Neither one of us will now see Seralind!"

Nagaro was taken aback. "Do you mean, *she*, because she chose the moment of her passing? And *you*, because you allowed it?"

"It's worse than that!" Elgurn spun away to resume his distracted pacing. "She's gone to another life—or to some shadow place—I don't know where! But wherever it is, it's outside of Solbrid's keeping. And what have I done, with all my efforts to preserve her innocence, but earn myself a place in Hel? *Oh, the things I've done!*"

For a moment Nagaro stood frozen in astonishment. He was moved by Elgurn's remorse, but his own emotions were too frayed to let him be patient with the man's confession. *Did the king include among his misdeeds his handling of the young Leyel Virden?*

His mind recoiled from the thought, and he roused himself. Moving to intercept Elgurn, he caught him by the arm, bringing the older man to a halt, confronting him. His words, when they came, were less gentle than they might have been.

"I don't believe there's any such place as Hel, My Lord—unless you make it for yourself in your own mind! When we die, our spirits go into the void, and from there to a new life—in which we have no memory of the old one."

Elgurn's right hand had come up as if he meant to strike the man who dared speak to him so, but he checked himself and jerked free of Nagaro's grasp instead, staring into his face, breathing hard. "If that is so," he said raggedly, "I've still lost her!"

"That's right," Nagaro told him flatly. "You'll never meet her again, unless it's as two spirits passing in the void. In which case you will know each other, but distantly. You'll remember all the bad—*and* all the good—of this life, intertwined with the memories of all the other lives you've ever lived. None of it will seem so *very* bad, or so *very* good, as it did in living it. Everything will be brought into proportion."

Elgurn was frowning, calmer now and less apologetic. "I can't say I see great comfort in that," he said darkly.

Nagaro turned away. "It wasn't devised for your comfort, My Lord. It's only what is true, as Vothra tells us. Make what use of it you will." He started for the chamber's outer door. "If I were you, I'd try to choose deeds, henceforth, that will leave better memories."

Brandle had been standing as still as a statue throughout this interchange with a look of shock on his face. Now he seemed to come back to life and hastened to follow his charge. He reached the door just in time to open it and usher Nagaro through.

The king came after them. "That would seem to be good advice, whether there's a Hel or not, Captain," he said, apparently having missed the bitterness in Nagaro's voice. "And I thank you for what you did here this night. For my wife's sake, I'm grateful."

Nagaro came up short, his anger softening. He turned back, remembering something. "Semorel told us that you'd already said everything to each other that mattered," he said earnestly. "She spoke of a cold day at the turning of the year, when you walked together on the balcony and the wind was from the sea. She said you would remember."

"Yes... I remember..." Elgurn sagged in the doorway, gripping the doorframe for support. "Sweet Solbrid's tears, I will always remember! Thank you, Captain."

Nagaro felt some relief, glad that the queen hadn't been recalling some opa dream. "If you would choose a deed to show your gratitude, My Lord," he said quietly, "find my daughter." Then he turned again and strode toward the stairs, moving at such a pace that Brandle was hard pressed to keep up with him.

Elgurn's voice came after them. "You may be sure I will, Captain!" There was a pause. "And you may as well keep the shirt. I've no great need of it."

Nagaro and Brandle reached the prison-corridor without either having spoken. At the door of his chamber, Nagaro turned to the Leithian and said, "Good night, Lieutenant."

Brandle shot him a glance. "Aye. Good night, Captain." Then he lowered his voice as he opened the door. "You're a bolder man than I, Nagaro. I'd never have dared to speak to the king like that, much less lay a hand on him."

Nagaro put a weary hand to his head. "I'm just tired, Brandle."

"Is it hard, then? Letting a spirit possess you like that?"

Nagaro shook his head as he stepped into the room. "It's more like sharing than possession. Vothra calls it 'in-dwelling.' And it isn't hard. What's hard is watching pain... death... grief..."

Brandle shook his own head. "I'd have said it was an easy death in the end. Dying gloriously in battle is all very well, but if I could choose, I'd rather go that way—in my own bed, quickly and quietly."

Nagaro gave the other man a bitter smile. "I'll remember that if it ever comes to it." He stepped past the Leithian, who swung the door closed behind him.

Nagaro staggered to the bed in the darkness and dropped onto it with a groan, not bothering to undress. The last thought that drifted through his mind as he sank towards slumber was to marvel at the strange pattern of his life. Twice now he had begun a day by coming to the defense of Lankura and ended it by assisting the death of a member of the royal household. Vaguely he wondered if it might ever happen again. *If so, would he again be paid for his services with the gift of a shirt?*

# Chapter 7

# Farewell And Memories

Nagaro slept late into the following morning. He ate a late breakfast, for which he had little appetite, and spent a day of tedium and frustration. The guard at his door would not answer any questions, so he alternately sat or paced. He ate twice more because the food was brought and he knew he should eat. When darkness finally began to fall again, he lay down and eventually slept.

Early on the second morning, as he was bathing himself at the washbasin, a crisp knock sounded on the chamber door. Expecting the guard with his breakfast, he answered it, barefoot and shirtless, only to find himself subjected once again to Brandle's appraising gaze.

The Leithian stood with his hands apparently clasped behind his back. "I'm sorry to give you no better warning, Captain," he said. "But you must dress quickly. You are to ride today."

"Ride? Where? I don't understand."

"In the queen's funeral procession. And you'd best wear the silk shirt."

Nagaro crossed the room to retrieve the shirt the king had given him and hastily pulled it on. "But I'm a prisoner. I'm under arrest."

Brandle's teeth flashed. "Oh, I know. And there was a bloody great row in the Council about it from what I hear. But the princess begged, and the king insisted, and the Leithians had to give in since it was the queen's last request, made on her death bed."

Nagaro paused in the act of pulling on his boots. "I guess it was, at that. But she didn't understand the situation. She was confused... about a number of things."

"That doesn't matter. The princess promised her mother that you would have a place in the procession, and she's determined to keep her word." Brandle laughed. "An *honored* place, no less! So they've put you with *me*." He leered. "In the rear honor guard. Not being high-born, you couldn't ride in the procession itself."

Nagaro had finished with his boots and he now stood up. "That suits me well enough," he said, then frowned. "Though it occurs to me to wonder whether I am *guarding*, or *being guarded*."

This elicited another laugh. "Of course the intention is that you're being guarded—as far as anyone's concerned who thinks you need guarding. I know better, and so do most of the folk of Lankura. And for the sake of appearances—" Brandle paused dramatically "—so that it doesn't look to the townsfolk as if you're a prisoner…" He brought out his hands from behind his back. "You're to be allowed to wear *this*."

Nagaro's black leather sword belt dangled in the Leithian's grasp. The light of the hall lamp glinted off of the polished green stone in the pommel of the elegant Mahuk-made sword.

"*Not* inside the palace, of course," Brandle added as Nagaro started to reach for his weapon. "You'll have to wait until we're outside. And you'll have to surrender it again after the ceremony, before I bring you back under this roof." He shrugged apologetically at Nagaro's frown of annoyance. "I'm sorry, Captain, but that's the protocol. I didn't make the rules. Now if you'll follow me, I think they mean to give you something to eat before everyone gathers in the stable yard."

***

Outside, the morning was gray, heavy with mist and the smell of the sea. The stable yard was crowded with people and horses, and there were several carriages as well as the open horse-drawn bier that carried the body of the late queen, enshrined in a heavy casket of fragrant cedar wood. There was a subdued murmur of voices, further muted by the heavy dampness of the air. The drab colors of the mourners' garb were further dimmed by the diffuse gray light from a leaden sky.

Nagaro found himself at one edge of the crowd, surrounded by a loose knot of guardsmen. He'd been handed his sword belt and was buckling it about his waist when a voice spoke near at hand.

"Good morning, Captain Nagaro."

He looked up into the steely gaze of Lord Anduar and noticed that the surrounding guardsmen were studiously overlooking the Pact-Signer's presence.

"Good morning, My Lord," he replied rather coldly. He remembered all too well the Kelorin lord's intransigence concerning the assumed guilt of Pavo Maat.

Anduar's glance didn't falter. He smiled one of his quick, tight smiles—perhaps intended to convey good will—and said, "The sword, incidentally, was my idea."

"Was it?" Nagaro was unimpressed. "I'd say that it seems a rather superficial gesture."

The smile was a little tighter this time. "Symbolic, I would say, rather than superficial. But your attitude isn't surprising, all things considered. I am not your enemy, Captain. Indeed, I could be of use to you. The judges of the new tribunal will be the same as those who served on the previous one."

Nagaro eyed the Kelorin lord warily. "It doesn't matter who they are, as long as they do their work properly this time."

This elicited an arched eyebrow. "Yes, I recall that you didn't think they'd done so on the first occasion. I suggest you be careful to whom you express that opinion."

Nagaro shrugged. "The judges did not pursue the truth with due diligence the first time," he said mildly. "With the result that justice wasn't well served. Since a proper judge must be intent on discovering the truth, and I'm sure you wish to be a proper judge, My Lord, I expect you must be glad of the opportunity to correct a past error."

The steel-gray eyes bored into him for several seconds while Nagaro innocently returned the Pact-Signer's stare.

"It seems it would serve me ill to argue," the older man said at length with studied aplomb. "Though I think you are being more bold than ingenuous." He glanced suddenly in the direction of the stable in apparent response to a barked command that had come from that direction. "We will be mounting soon, Captain. Have they brought you a horse?"

"I don't know—" Nagaro was caught off guard by the change of subject.

Before he could say anything more, Anduar strode off and was quickly lost among the crowd. His voice was heard, however, raised commandingly. "You, there! A horse for Captain Nagaro. And see that you bring him something with some spirit."

"What was that about?" The question came from Brandle, who had materialized at Nagaro's elbow as if by magic.

Nagaro frowned. "Anduar being Anduar, it seems. He keeps trying to convince me that he's my friend—or at least that he's not my enemy, as he put it this time."

Brandle shook his head. "I'm not sure I'd sleep any better for hearing that man say he was my friend."

Despite his distrust of Anduar's motives, Nagaro had to admit that he did get a better horse thanks to the Pact-Signer's intervention. A tired-looking brown gelding had been intended for him, but just as he was about to mount it, a groom hurried up with a lively sorrel mare and a mumbled, "Compliments of his lordship."

From the mare's back, he at last caught a glimpse of Nevien just as she was getting into one of the carriages. She was all in gray, of course, except for the black veil that covered her hair and hid her face. Her head was down and she faltered a little on the carriage step. Elgurn was instantly at her elbow, helping her into the vehicle—supporting her as he had formerly supported his ailing wife. The sight brought Nagaro's thoughts back with a lurch to the dead queen and her grieving daughter, and he remained preoccupied with those thoughts for most of the next two hours while the funeral procession wended its way through the streets of Lankura.

Semorel was to be buried among the other honored dead within the palace grounds. The circuit through the city provided a formal ceremony that allowed the townspeople a chance to bid farewell to their beloved queen. What Nagaro remembered most about it afterward was the music. The crowds that lined the route were quieter than usual, allowing the instruments to be heard. The people's rustling and murmurs and occasional cries of grief were poignant punctuation to the measured pulse of the drums and the high, sweet song of the flutes. Someone had strewn flowers on the pavement, though these were crushed and trodden black by the time they came under the hooves of the horses of the rear guard. Nagaro rode in the middle of the front rank of that guard, with Brandle on his right and Delvin on his left and three more ranks behind him. The sorrel mare tossed her head and danced a little, glad to be out of her stall and in the company of other horses.

Nagaro, sitting erect in the saddle, eyes straight before him, guided the mare without thought or effort. His mind was full of memories of his encounters with the queen. The recent ones, when he'd been able to be himself, weren't many, so inevitably he found himself overwhelmed by recollections from his time as the idiot prince, Leyel Virden. Even from those dark days, he remembered Queen Semorel as being always kind and gracious. Her smiles had been meant as gentle encouragement, never mockery.

There was a lifting of the morning's overcast as the procession wound it way through the streets, and a noticeable freshening of the air as the somber cavalcade passed the midpoint of its circuit. By the time the procession swung west, on the final leg of its journey, the overhanging canopy of cloud had begun to thin and drift. And finally, just as the queen's bier passed beneath the arch of the city gate and into the wide courtyard in front of the doors of the palace, the sun broke through and shafts of light descended, bringing a sudden incongruous splendor to the mournful scene.

Nagaro found himself back in the stable yard, now brilliantly awash in spring sunlight. He shook himself free of the thrall of his dark memories and dismounted, delivering the mare's reins into the hands of a waiting groom.

"This way, Captain," Brandle murmured at his elbow. "From here, the processional order is the same, but we'll go on foot."

The queen's casket was lifted onto the shoulders of a dozen men and borne along a path paved with white stones between rows of rose bushes, just beginning to bud. The mourners came pacing after. Nagaro, among the rear guard, was one of the last to arrive at the grave site. It lay on the north edge of the garden, near the high wall that separated the garden from the slope leading down to the small cove on the far side of the peninsula on which the royal palace had been built.

The grave had been dug in a lawn of clipped grass under a spreading cedar tree. The light was clear as crystal. The breeze carried the scent of the sea. Nagaro, standing in the outer ring of those assembled, watched the casket being lowered into the earth. There were words spoken by some of those assembled, but he didn't heed them. His heart was too full. He saw Nevien drop bunches of flowers—white narcissus—into the grave. Elgurn scattered a handful of earth. Then everyone turned away, leaving the groundskeepers to finish the task.

As he turned, Nagaro's feet stumbled on a stone set in the ground. Glancing down, he saw that it was a grave marker, and as he moved his boots he came to a frozen halt. The letters carved on the flat stone read *Leyel Virden* with a date corresponding to the year of his escape from the palace and his bondage.

"Don't worry. You're not walking on his bones."

"I know—" Nagaro caught himself and glanced at Brandle, who had addressed him. "I mean, I heard they never found his body," he added hastily, resuming his forward progress.

"Huh! Didn't look very hard, I'd say."

"What do you mean? I heard they used dogs."

"I was here when they made the search." Brandle turned around and pointed. "See where those grape vines are trained against the north wall? No one could do it now, of course—because the wall is higher—but that's where he went over by all accounts. If it was him. A half a dozen witnesses said *someone* went over the wall, and two were *almost* sure it was the idiot prince. The dogs followed a scent to the stream, but they lost it in the water. As far as I know, they didn't even take the dogs across to the other side. It had rained, you see, and the stream was swollen. It looked dangerous. So they assumed the prince had fallen in and been carried by the water. They only looked downstream and along the shore where the stream spreads out and is easier to cross. The dogs never picked up the scent again, so they gave up the search. For my part, I think Leyel is alive somewhere."

"You do?" Nagaro licked dry lips, ducking his head to hide his face.

But Brandle wasn't looking at him. "*I* think he got tired of being laughed at and is having a good laugh himself, somewhere—or would be if he had the wit for it. Or, more likely, the poor fool got lost and couldn't find his way home."

Nagaro felt the familiar burning of blood in his face that came with a surge of mingled shame and outrage. He'd heard *that* theory before. "More than likely," he murmured, trying to cover his discomfort. If he'd gone over that wall the way Brandle had described, he had no memory of it. From the look of it, it would have been an impressive athletic feat, and he had his doubts. He hurried his pace, following the other mourners who had gotten ahead of them while Brandle had been speaking.

There were no drums now, but the flutes were playing again. The notes soared high and sweet, poignantly sad. With a sudden jolt, Nagaro realized that he recognized the melody as one the Lady Maramine had occasionally played on her harp and sometimes sung. A snatch of the words came to his mind:

*My love he was a Leithian, golden as the sun,*
*And good and kind as any man that ever maiden won...*

When he had been quite young, he'd asked her once whether the man she had loved had been a Leithian because of that song. She had answered no. Her love had been a dark-haired Kelorin, though the song had been written by a Kelorin woman who loved a Leithian. She liked the song, she'd said, because it was for anyone whose love was lost or unattainable.

He swallowed hard and walked on, following the musicians.

Brandle eventually conducted him to the palace's side door. There Nagaro stopped to unbuckle his sword belt. As he was handing it to Brandle, however, he realized he was being addressed, and when he looked up, he found himself face to face with Lord Madred Furthing, Brandle's father.

"You're very sober today, Captain. No waving to the crowd. No basking in their good wishes." The Leithian lord's tone was even, but he was looking down his fine patrician nose for all that. Brandle suddenly became very busy with the belt buckle.

Nagaro frowned. "It was a funeral, My Lord. A time to bid farewell to a great and noble lady."

The expression on Lord Madred's handsome features continued to be disapproving. "Yes, to be sure. Still, you managed to be included in the procession. And I have to say, Zirda, that your reputation is remarkably *resilient*. The common folk are saying that Captain Nagaro would not have brought his friend back if he didn't think he could prove him innocent.

They say this even though they don't know that Peldred has been accused by the nephew of the Mautep Emperor and that Kuran has been sent to Long Harbor to fetch him. I ask you, Zirda, why *did* you come back? What did you expect to find? And what do you think you can prove?"

Nagaro kept his voice level. "We were following a ship belonging to men who had taken my daughter, My Lord, until we saw that Lankura was under attack. Then we came to the aid of Edrovir. I didn't expect to find the Emperor's nephew among the attackers. And as for proving Pavo's innocence, I've always hoped that Peldred's conscience would lead him to tell the truth."

"And you claim that all of that is the truth?" Madred regarded him narrowly. "You would swear it?"

"I swear it on my honor and in Vothra's name, My Lord. I will swear it again before the Tribunal if you wish."

Lord Madred frowned and appeared to consider him keenly. Then he said, a little stiffly, "By all means, Captain, see that you speak truly before the Tribunal." With that, he turned on his heel and was gone.

Nagaro let out a long breath and glanced at Brandle.

The young Leithian cocked his head. "They were good answers," he said. "You've set him thinking. And my father does value the truth, whatever his shortcomings."

As they passed through the door into the hallway that led to the back stairs, they encountered another interruption. This time it was no less a person than the king, who appeared to have been waiting for them, since he immediately addressed Nagaro.

"A word, if I may, Captain."

Nagaro was looking for Nevien, but she clearly wasn't there, so he wrenched his attention back to Elgurn.

The king was impeccably groomed and dressed, his manner cool and brisk, his expression carefully controlled. The man had apparently completely regained his self-possession since the events of two nights previous. "I believe I know who has your daughter, Captain—which faction, that is," he said in a tone he might have used to discuss some detail of palace protocol. "The difficulty is that none of the men in question will admit to having her in his keeping. Since you came to our assistance, I believe they may be somewhat *embarrassed*. I've set Lord Madred to work on the problem."

"*Lord Madred?*" Nagaro couldn't hide his dismay.

"Yes, certainly." Elgurn's pale blue eyes were as unreadable as ever. "He has some influence with these men, and he's very well respected. Why? Didn't he mention it when he spoke to you?

"No. He didn't." Nagaro's mind was racing. The man who would be the chief judge at the tribunal had also been tasked with securing Narei's release!

"Ah well, no matter." Elgurn seemed unconcerned. "I have every expectation of a favorable outcome, but it may have to wait until the conclusion of the tribunal. You must be patient, Captain."

Nagaro could only murmur his thanks and stare after the king's retreating back. Beside him Brandle spoke with a show of confidence. "Don't worry, Captain. My father wouldn't have accepted the task if he didn't mean to see it through. You'll get your daughter back. But right now I'm afraid I have to get you back to your room."

***

The rest of that day was tediously uneventful. Nagaro tried to reassure himself regarding Narei's situation and to otherwise think about it as little as possible. The night brought a vivid dream he had never had before in which he paused, straddling the top of a wall, then dropped to the ground on the far side. The shouts of the men in the garden faded behind him. A brief downhill scramble through the bushes in the night, under the silver moon, brought him to the bank of a swift-flowing stream that cascaded down the slope, splashing noisily over rocks. Away to his left, the Mahuk ships lay anchored in the small cove and there were men moving along the shore. To his right, the hillside rose again. Beyond the watercourse lay the forest. It was clear what he had to do. Without hesitation he slid down the bank and stepped into the stream. The water was moving fast, but he balanced on the rocks and reached the farther side.

Standing on a water-slicked boulder, he laughed aloud. This was easy. And it was perfect too. The water would cover his scent. There was shouting now from the men on the beach below. Word of his escape must have reached them, but they were too far away to stop him. No, the men of the Mahuk Baar wouldn't catch him, and they weren't the ones who mattered anyway. Laughing again, he turned right and began to work his way upstream, his feet half in and half out of the cascading water, careful to use rocks that were at least wet with spray. It was slippery going but in his dream he was agile and confident.

He followed the stream in this way until he was out of sight of both the cove and the garden wall he had scaled. The shouts had faded once more. The woods came closer here, the trees arching over the stream. With another quiet laugh he abandoned the watercourse, slipping into the moon-shadow between the trunks. Silently, he began to run...

Nagaro woke with a gasp, and sat up in the darkness.

The dream stood so clearly in his memory, in all its detail, that he was certain it had to be a fragment of memory, triggered no doubt by Brandle's description of someone going over the palace's garden wall on the night of the first Mautep attack nine years before. There had been nothing about events inside the garden, only the sense that he'd come over the wall, a vague impression of scrabbling for viney hand- and footholds. It was enough to convince him that he had in fact been the person who'd climbed over the wall that night. And of course the dream fit well with those he'd had years ago of running through the forest.

He put his hands to his head and rubbed his temples. So, he had gone east, up the stream, and then must have run north for twenty miles until he'd collapsed in a fever in the woods near Taru's house. He sighed. It was all he was ever likely to get from his own memory. Standing in the garden over a year ago, looking at the wall from the inside, had only brought him fleeting images of men herding captives up the path that led to the hidden gate. And before that, there was the memory of the last time he'd been in the palace, under the sway of the accursed heskial. He winced at the memory of the blinding flash that had seared through his mind after drinking the wine the princess had given him—

*The princess!* He frowned. Nevien might be able to tell him more, but she surely had known nothing of the conspiracy that had enslaved him. *And of course he couldn't ask her.* Having realized that he loved her only made him more certain that she must never know the truth about who he had once been. The look he would surely see in her eyes was something he couldn't bear to think about.

*"Keshaal!"* He swore aloud. The only good thing about the dream was that it might give him something else to worry about besides Narei, the impending tribunal, and Nevien's grief.

He gazed around the darkened room. A faint light emanating from the high windows told him that dawn wasn't far away. Realizing that he wasn't likely to sleep any more, he rose and dressed in the gloom—this time in his own plain cotton shirt that still bore traces of blood stains—and began once again to pace the floor. He was still doing so an hour later when there came a knock at the door. The guard, a new man, thrust a tray into his hands, bearing a cold breakfast, and then gave him the news he'd been anxiously waiting to hear for days.

"Ye'd best eat and make yourself ready, Zirda. Ye're to stand before the Tribunal this very morning."

In fact it was nearly two hours before a knock came again and he was ushered out into the hallway and into the company of half a dozen waiting guards. He was surprised to see Taru and Pavo being brought out of their rooms and into the hallway as well. This was unexpected. Each witness had appeared alone before the previous Tribunal. This time the three of them were apparently being herded in together.

Taru gave him a jaunty smile that was noticeably nervous around the edges. "They take their bloody time, don't they, Nagaro?" the young Turo observed, only to be promptly admonished to be silent by one of the guards.

Pavo gave Nagaro a knowing look and an almost imperceptible nod of his head. Nagaro could detect the tension in the Hashtep's movements and in his eyes, though to the inexperienced observer Pavo would likely have appeared stoically calm.

They were marched in silence through the palace corridors to the small rear door of the Audience Chamber. When they arrived there, however, Nagaro was surprised to find another group of guards already waiting. In the midst of this group stood Roheed. The young Mautep was dressed in his full uniform, lacking only his sword and sword belt. He stood erect, unbound, his face impassive. Except for the fact that he was noticeably unshaven, he might have been waiting in attendance upon the Emperor of the Mahuk Baar.

Nagaro made him a small bow of acknowledgment, which Roheed stiffly returned. Their eyes met as the young Mautep officer straightened. "Now I will have chance to speak?" the young Mautep inquired.

"Yes. I think so."

Nagaro read relief, briefly, in the other man's face before it was wiped away and replaced by the familiar stoic mask. "That is good."

They both fell silent after that, since the guards were giving them frowning looks.

They were all kept waiting in the hallway for another half hour, trying not to exchange worried glances. Nagaro wondered what he should expect from this second Tribunal. At the first one, the judges had all clearly formed their opinions based on the testimony of Vell Sobring. They'd kept Nagaro waiting for days in frustrated ignorance, and hadn't been interested in hearing anything from him that contradicted the conclusion they had already drawn—that Pavo was obviously guilty. The Leithian lord, Odus Morbern, had been intent on embarrassing him, while the two Kelorin lords, Soren and Anduar, had been bent on protecting his reputation. Since there had also been an effort to protect the reputation of the deceased Commander Strad, whose ill-chosen actions had been largely responsible for the capture of the *Sword of Freedom*, Nagaro had always suspected there'd been some quid pro quo.

This time it looked as if he might actually witness the entire proceedings. The judges must be mainly interested in the testimony of Roheed and of Peldred, and Roheed was clearly being called for the first time. How much credence the judges would give to the testimony of the foreign prince would likely depend on what Peldred was willing to admit. If Peldred was already in Lankura, he couldn't have been there long. It was barely a week since Kuran had set sail for Long Harbor.

Nagaro's musings were interrupted when the door abruptly opened and a clerk leaned out. "You're to bring them in now," he told the guards. "The Mautep prince is to sit at the table on the right, closer to the judges. The other three are to be at the table on the left."

Chapter 8

# The Courage Of Peldred Gilforn

They filed into the Audience Chamber amid a flurry of murmurs from the folk seated in the gallery on the opposite wall. The long, high-vaulted room was lit somberly from above by the light from windows high in a clear-story. The light that filtered down to the level of the polished marble floor was augmented by ornate bronze lamps set in brackets at intervals along the walls. Between the lamps, the walls were hung with a series of large tapestries depicting the history of Edrovir. Nagaro glanced at Roheed as they advanced into the room and was gratified to see the young Mautep's dark eyes become momentarily less narrow as he gazed about him. The nephew of the Emperor of the Mahuk Baar was impressed.

Nagaro next turned his attention to the audience. The gallery seats opposite were nearly full. Most of those seated there were strangers to him, and he noticed a fair number of Leithians. He picked out the figures of the king and the lords Pendrik and Devral seated together in the front row. Nevien was nowhere to be seen.

The four judges were seated, as they had been on the earlier occasion, in a row of chairs behind a long table at the foot of the dais that bore the empty royal thrones. The High Judge, Lord Madred, placed to the left of center, was looking solemn and reserved. Odus, on his right, locked stiff and grim. Anduar, on the High Judge's other hand, leaned back with his arms folded, wearing an expression that on another man might have been mistaken for boredom. Beside him, the gray-haired Soren fidgeted in his chair in what appeared to be suppressed anticipation.

The two tables to which Nagaro and the other prisoners were conducted stood at right angles to the judges' table, facing the gallery where onlookers were seated. Nagaro noted that the other gallery, behind his back, was empty. Two more tables were placed across from where he was to sit. A pair of clerks with writing implements were seated at the one nearer the judges. The other was empty, without even chairs provided.

The only other thing of note in the room, besides the presence of several members of the Palace Guard, deployed strategically, was a group of a dozen men in the uniform of the Royal Fleet who stood stiffly in close ranks at the far end of the room. The doors of the Audience Chamber's main entrance were firmly closed behind them. Nagaro could see Lord Kuran at the front and center of the group, flanked by Vell and Captain Brodig, but he couldn't see Peldred Gilforn there or anywhere else in the room. This fact brought his brows together in a worried frown as he came to a halt behind the chair appointed for him.

He had been directed to the central one of three chairs placed at the left-hand table, with Pavo on his right and Taru on his left. Roheed stood stiffly behind the single chair at the other table, nearer the judges. With the prisoners thus in their places, the room became ominously quiet.

A bell was rung by one of the clerks and the judges rose, all together. Lord Madred cleared his throat and spoke sonorously into the waiting silence, declaring the Tribunal officially convened by order of the King of Edrovir, and so forth. The High Judge went on at some length, but Nagaro made no effort to follow all of the flourishes, being preoccupied with worrying about Peldred's absence.

The king proceeded then, without standing, to introduce the judges, which seemed to give them permission to once again be seated. After that, the prisoners were finally allowed to sit down. Nagaro's attention was brought back fully to the matter at hand when Lord Madred addressed himself to Roheed, instructing the young man to state his full name.

Roheed rose briefly to make a small, stiff bow to the High Judge before stating firmly, "I am name Roheed jir-Akaan."

"And by what oath will you swear to tell the truth to this Tribunal, Roheed jir-Akaan?"

Watching the young Mautep officer, Nagaro saw him frown briefly with the effort of sorting out the sentence before he made his answer. "I swear to tell truth by my honor and in name of great god Sheptuum."

Madred acknowledged this with an inclination of his head. "Tell us then, Roheed jir-Akaan, he said gravely, "why the family name you bear is the same as that of the Emperor of the Mahuk Baar."

This time there was no hesitation. "Emperor Baalkir is brother of my father, Lord High Judge."

This was apparently news to some of those present, for it drew murmurs from those in the gallery. Nagaro frowned afresh. The information established Roheed's noble status, and it also might suggest that the young man had the Emperor's ear—or that he had been following his orders at Osfaraad.

Madred was speaking again. "And how should we address you?"

"Ad-dress...?" Roheed was perplexed.

Anduar cleared his throat. "Should we call you *Lord?* Or *Captain?*"

Roheed nodded understanding. "I am *Heerukan.*" He frowned. "It is... more high than captain."

Anduar inclined his head.

Lord Madred made a note on a piece of paper in front of him. "Very good... *Heerukan,*" he said, pronouncing the word carefully. He spoke slowly as he continued. "Will you repeat for us please what you said to King Elgurn about the man Pavo Maat on the day of your surrender?"

Roheed nodded again, plainly prepared for this. "I have tell him Pavo Maat is not traitor to him or to land of Edrovir," he said, speaking clearly. "Pavo Maat did not tell Emperor plan for attack Sar Tipaal."

"And how do you know this?"

"Because I was there, Lord High Judge. At Osfaraad. I have see and hear everything."

Anduar shifted languidly in his chair. "Were you with the Emperor at *all* times, Heerukan?" he inquired pointedly. "During the *whole* time that Pavo Maat was in the Emperor's hands?"

Roheed's attention was transferred from Madred to the Kelorin Pact-Signer. "Yes, Lord," he said. "I was with Emperor from time when Captain Nagaro have made surrender to when Emperor ship have leave Osfaraad Island."

Nagaro let out a pent breath. So far, so good. Madred and Anduar were both being polite to Roheed and asking reasonable questions. And Roheed was doing quite well, both with understanding the questions and with framing his answers, despite having limited knowledge of the Common Speech. And the young Mautep appeared very self-possessed.

Nagaro had just begun to relax when Lord Odus cleared his throat and addressed the witness. "If you please, *Heer-ru-kan,*" he said rather sourly. "We have been told that your Emperor made certain threats and also certain *offers* to this Pavo Maat—this fisherman's son. What have you to say about *that?*"

Roheed had turned toward Odus, frowning in puzzlement. "I do not understand."

Anduar leaned forward in his seat. "Please tell us, Heerukan," he said smoothly, "what your Emperor said to Pavo Maat, and what Pavo Maat said to the Emperor."

Roheed frowned for a moment in concentration. "There is much," he said.

Anduar waved an encouraging hand. "Just tell us what is most important."

Roheed nodded, appeared to collect his thoughts for a moment, and began. "Emperor Baalkir first order Pavo Maat to tell us plan of lord who command all Droviri ship, but Pavo say he will not tell it. Emperor then say Pavo Maat will die if he do not tell, but Pavo say even if he must die, still he will not tell because he have swear oath of honor to land of Edrovir. So then Emperor say he will give Pavo gold and land and make him one of lord of Mahuk Baar if he will swear oath to follow Emperor. But Pavo say he have already find good man to follow—that is Captain Nagaro Kiraam Shaku-Tal—and he will not break oath he have swear."

Roheed ceased speaking and murmurs ran among the audience in the gallery. Nagaro was aware of Pavo sitting stiffly beside him. Not a muscle of the young Hashtep's face had moved, but there was a light in his eyes.

"Did not your Emperor consider this behavior to be treasonous?" demanded Odus acidly. "From a son of the Mahuk Baar?"

Roheed looked baffled. "What is he mean?" he asked, looking from Anduar to Madred.

Anduar cleared his throat. "Lord Odus wonders whether Pavo's loyalty to Edrovir is treason against your Emperor," he said blandly. "Since Pavo Maat was born in the Mahuk Baar."

Roheed immediately shook his head. "No, is not treason," he said emphatically. "Pavo Maat is Hashtep. He have not swear oath to Emperor. *He* is belong to Emperor, but his *honor* is not."

This pronouncement created a considerable stir among the various assorted observers.

Anduar raised an eyebrow. "An interesting distinction," he said smoothly. "But tell us, Heerukan, why Baalkir let Pavo go—if, as you say, Pavo Maat belongs to the Emperor?"

"Because honor of Pavo Maat belong to Edrovir, and honor is more strong," Roheed responded without hesitation. Then he added, "But before Emperor have let Pavo go, first he test Nagaro Kiraam to see, is he worthy to carry this honor."

This evoked signs of surprise from most of those present. All four of the judges reacted with movements of one kind or another. Even Pavo sat up a little straighter.

Anduar leaned over and spoke low into Lord Madred's ear, and it was the High Judge who fixed Roheed with a fierce blue stare and asked, "Please tell us, Heerukan, what was the nature of this *test?*"

Roheed simply nodded. "It is maybe eight year ago Nagaro Kiraam take ship away from Captain Urchak tok-Faar. Emperor have heard good thing about Nagaro Kiraam and bad thing about Urchak, but he do not know what is true. So he give Nagaro Kiraam to Captain Urchak for punish, to see what each man do. Nagaro Kiraam have show he is more good man than Captain Urchak."

Nagaro stared. *So it was true.* The Emperor had put him into the hands of a man with a whip and hot irons, whose ship he had stolen, to test them both. And *he* had tried to push Urchak hard enough to cause the man to lose control—*and it had worked.* The questions were still flying and Roheed was answering, though Nagaro scarcely noticed.

"Did your Emperor give you an order to stop this test before the other man killed Captain Nagaro?"

"No, Lord High Judge. He do not order me to do that."

"But you *did* stop it?"

"Yes, Lord."

"*Why* did you stop it when you did?"

That question penetrated sufficiently to bring Nagaro's attention back to the proceedings.

Roheed was looking earnestly at Anduar, who must have asked the question. "Because is very bad thing," he said, speaking slowly as if feeling his way, "for man who have very much courage and honor to be killed by man who have very little. Sheptuum surely will be angry if I let that happen. Maybe Sheptuum be angry with Emperor. Maybe he punish all of Mahuk Baar."

There was a stunned silence.

"You think your god would have punished your *whole country* if this man Urchak had killed Captain Nagaro?" This came from Soren and it was less a question than an expression of disbelief.

"I think, Lord, maybe yes."

"Roheed jir-Akaan." Anduar's tone was suddenly sharp, and his eyes narrow. "Captain Nagaro has told us you knew that Urchak had killed a woman—which is dishonorable."

"Yes, Lord." Roheed showed no hesitation. "I have see him do it."

"Did the Emperor—your uncle—already know this at Osfaraad?"

"No, Lord. I have not tell him." Still there was no hesitation.

Lord Madred leaned forward avidly. "*Why not?*"

"I was very new... sea-man... when it happen. Not officer." Roheed was struggling with the words it seemed, not the content. "Urchak was my captain. Sea-man do not tell such thing about captain. Officer can do it, but those officer that saw it do not want to tell it. But after Nagaro Kiraam have say it, *then* I can say I know is true. And if I do not say it—and Urchak kill Nagaro Kiraam—bad thing is sure to happen."

There was a buzz of conversation, but Lord Madred rapped on the table and raised his voice. "Silence, please!" The buzz subsided, and the Leithian lord squared the papers in front of him.

"So there was a code of honor that prevented you from speaking until the matter was otherwise revealed," he said briskly. "And I think that's enough about that little mystery." He cleared his throat. "We will now proceed, Heerukan, to the other matter we are met here to address—the matter of the accusation you made at the time of your surrender. If it was *not* Pavo Maat who revealed our plan to your Emperor, *who was it?*"

Nagaro sat tensely watching Roheed. He was glad to have learned so much about what had motivated the young Mautep at Osfarrad—and glad there had been no mention of the blood debt—but this wasn't really important beyond the fact that Roheed's confident and consistent answers bolstered the young man's credibility.

Roheed stood calmly again as he answered, perfectly self-assured. "Man who tell plan to Emperor is very young man," he said in a clear voice that carried to every corner of the room. "It is most young officer of ship. With yellow hair."

"And you were witness to this? You saw and heard?"

"Yes, Lord. I have see and hear."

"Tell us how it happened, Heerukan."

Roheed shifted a little, his eyes focused in concentration. "Urchak have ask Nagaro Kiraam many time to tell plan," he said carefully. "But Nagaro do not tell even when Urchak burn him with hot iron and beat him with whip until he fall down. There is very much blood. And Nagaro Kiraam get up and say Urchak kill woman, and Urchak burn him again and he make cry—and I have to stop Urchak from kill him—and they have carry him away with blood all over him. Then they take other officer with yellow hair that is more old, and they ask him two time to tell plan. And they put hot iron on him—here, and here." He indicated first his left shoulder and then his right. "He make cry, but he do not tell plan, and he fall down. So they put him to lie beside Nagaro Kiraam."

Roheed paused for air, and the room was so silent that his intake of breath was audible. "And *then* they take last man... most young man," Roheed continued. "And they say they are go to put hot iron *here*—" he touched his left shoulder, "—if he do not tell plan, and they are go to burn him again and again until he tell. First he say no, so they burn him, and he cry very much. And when they come again with hot iron, to burn him, then he say he will tell if they do not burn him again. And then he tell us Droviri ship are all go to meet at Paktaar, and are go to attack Sar Tipaal."

Nagaro bowed his head as a murmur of muted voices rose in the Audience Chamber. It was just as he had feared. The Mautep had made calculated use of fear and pain to break the most vulnerable man—the youngest officer, most inexperienced and untried. *They had left him to the last, forcing him to watch everything that came before.*

Madred was speaking again, and Nagaro raised his head to see what would happen next.

"Do you see this young man here, now, Heerukan?"

Roheed did not immediately answer. He surveyed the room with a gathering frown, similar to the one that clouded Nagaro's countenance as his eyes also swept the Audience Chamber. Peldred was still nowhere to be seen. *Was this a test?* There were several young Leithian men present among the scattered guards or the group of Fleet men at the other end of the room, but none of them looked much like Peldred.

Roheed turned back to the judges' table. "I do not think he is here, Lord High Judge," he said.

"Are you sure, Heerukan?" The question came from Lord Odus, with just a hint of insinuation. "All the officers who surrendered at Osfarrad are presently in this room."

Nagaro's frown deepened. *What were they playing at?* All he could imagine was that Peldred must be concealed somewhere. *Maybe among the group of Fleet warriors, in the back, behind the front rank...*

Beside him, Taru muttered under his breath. "The pissing little coward! Where's he hiding?" The guard standing behind his chair hissed a warning to be silent.

Roheed was searching the room again with his eyes. "I do not see most young man," he said, now with a trace of apprehension in his voice. "There is captain, and Pavo Maat." He indicated Nagaro and Pavo at the table to his left. "And *there* is more old officer with yellow hair, I think." He pointed at Vell, standing beside Kuran among the Fleet men. "I remember that yellow-hair man with—" Here he frowned and touched his own mustache. "But I do not see most young man. He is not so tall. No hair on face. Hair on head color like straw."

Lord Madred cleared his throat. "It is well," he said, "that you say you do not see him, Heerukan, since he cannot be seen. But it is time to bring him forth." The High Judge directed a sober glance to the opposite end of the room. "My Lord Kuran, bring him out for all to see!"

Nagaro saw Kuran turn and speak to the Fleet men, saw them bend their backs. He felt a sudden chill as of a premonition. The men straightened and began to move, following Kuran, Brodig, and Vell as they approached the judges.

"*No,*" he whispered, for he now saw that the men were carrying something, walking with a measured tread. He caught a glimpse of blue and white. A few paces farther, and he could plainly see the long bier, borne by two rows of Fleet warriors, draped in the flag of Edrovir—a cloth of deepest blue that shrouded the shape of a man lying in repose, the great white figure of a hawk with outstretched wings blazoned across the fallen warrior's chest, its pinions trailing on either side.

"*Vothra, no!*" Nagaro was on his feet. "I never wanted this!"

In the gallery, a woman began to sob softly. She wore a gown of deep burgundy, like old blood. A fine silk scarf covered her head, not quite concealing hair of silver-gold.

Taru murmured, "*Hamaei mata noa!*"

Someone behind Nagaro was pressing a hand on his shoulder, urging him to sit down, and he dully sank into his chair. "I never wanted him to die," he murmured. "I was trying to save him!"

The Fleet men carried their burden to the empty table across from where he sat, the one that lacked chairs. They set the bier down and stepped away, taking places at the table's foot. Kuran, Brodig, and Vell stood at the table's head. Together, Brodig and Vell reached out and lifted the blue cloth, turning it down to expose the pale face and straw-blond hair of Peldred Gilforn.

Lord Madred cleared his throat. "Roheed jir-Akaan, I charge you to look closely at this man and tell us whether he is the one you have spoken of."

Roheed rose and left his place. Accompanied by one of the guards, he approached the bier, where he stood for several long seconds contemplating the dead youth. At last he turned to face the judges' table. "Yes, Lord High Judge, this look like man who have tell Emperor plan for attack on Sar Tipaal."

Madred nodded somberly. "Thank you, Heerukan," he said. "You may return to your place." Then, even before the young Mautep had arrived at his appointed seat, he continued. "My Lord Kuran, will you please give us your report?"

Kuran bowed his head for the space of several heartbeats, then raised it, his expression grave. "My Lords," he said, "good people, I will tell you what I know of how this came to pass. My ships arrived at Long Harbor three days ago, near sunset, and I arranged at once to speak with Commander Geldoran concerning my orders to transport Peldred Gilforn to Lankkura for questioning. The Commander informed me that Peldred lay at that very hour close to death. It seems there had been an attack on Long Harbor three days earlier by four Mahuk ships—"

Roheed made a sudden movement, starting to say something, but was immediately silenced by one of the guards.

Kuran had been distracted by the motion, but he continued. "When Long Harbor was attacked by these Mahuk galleys, Geldoran's ships were caught in the harbor. The fighting was intense. The *Swift*, under Captain Brodig, was boarded. Her third mate, Peldred Gilforn, led a charge, an effort to win through to the rail and carry the fight onto the enemy's deck. It was a bold move—showing great courage. It was successful too. The Mahuk ship was taken, and the other three were ultimately driven off. But unfortunately, young Peldred took a wound during that charge that would plainly prove mortal.

"So it was that I was brought to see him where he lay in the officers' cabin on his death bed. Before I could say anything to him, he spoke to me, weakly. He said he had something he must say, and asked that a certain sealed letter be taken from his sea chest." At this point Kuran paused to withdraw a paper from his uniform tirka. "I have it here, and with your permission, Lord Madred, I will read it so that all may hear."

Madred nodded gravely. "By all means, My Lord, proceed."

Nagaro was watching the faces of the judges. *They aren't surprised by any of this,* he thought numbly. *They all know what is in that letter. Odus knows he has lost and Soren has won.* The judges, he realized, must have been told everything beforehand. This dramatic scene was a show for everyone else's benefit—and for Roheed.

Kuran cleared his throat and read:

*"To any who may wish to know these things: If you are reading this it means that, one way or another, I have paid for the sin of my cowardice. May the Gods be merciful. It was I who revealed the plan for our attack on Sar Tipaal to the Mahuk Emperor, and the place of the rendezvous. In the face of pain, and the fear of more pain, I was weak. For this I am sorry and ashamed.*

*"At first I hoped the Emperor would not be able to gather his ships in time, so that my weakness would not serve him. But it wasn't so. Then I thought that perhaps the Hashtep man had revealed the plan as well, so that my failing would have made no difference. I prayed for the Gods to save Pavo Maat if he was innocent, so that I would know, by whether he lived or died. When I heard the news that he had been carried away to safety by Captain Nagaro, who is surely the chosen one of Hrathgard, I knew what I had to do.*

*"I mean to seek an honorable death in battle. This is all I can do now to counter my shame and restore the honor of my house. The Gods grant that it may also serve to save my spirit from Hel. I will seal this letter and mark it to be opened after I am dead. To all those I love, forgive me and farewel. —Peldred Gilforn."*

Silence followed Kuran's reading of the letter. Nagaro emitted a muted groan that was clearly audible in the stillness. He bowed his head into his hands. In his mind he could still see Peldred standing on the deck of the *Sword of Freedom,* facing the foe, looking pale... *so terribly young... so undeserving of death.* That the young man had called him the chosen one of Hrathgard only made matters worse. *He had doomed Peldred by saving Pavo.*

Kuran spoke again, quietly, in the hush of the Audience Chamber. "I praised Peldred for his confession, and I told him that as far as I was concerned, all was forgiven. Within an hour of speaking to me, he was dead. The healer told me that he had lived for three days in pain, refusing opa, refusing all but the most minimal ministrations. No one can doubt his courage. As Lord of the Royal Fleet, I ask that he be buried in the Fleet Compound among the honored dead of the Royal Fleet of Edrovir."

A ripple of affirmation moved through the hall. Elgurn's voice was heard saying, "Let it be so."

*"Hakura!"* muttered Taru. "And to think I called him a coward!"

Madred cleared his throat. "The work of this Tribunal is hereby concluded. I speak for all the judges in this. The confession of Peldred Gilforn is accepted. Together with the testimony of Roheed jir-Akaan, it serves to prove the innocence of Pavo Maat. All previous judgements concerning this matter are set aside, and all warrants and charges are rescinded. This Tribunal is now dismissed."

Before anyone could move, Roheed raised his voice. "Please, Lord of Fleet, what color was flag on four ship that make attack on Long Harbor?"

Nagaro raised his head in surprise. All eyes turned to Roheed, for he had spoken urgently.

Lord Madred frowned. "If you please, Heerukan—" he began rather severely.

Roheed gestured impatiently. "There is no Mautep lord have order to attack Long Harbor. Someone disobey. I must know who!" He turned back to Kuran. "Lord, what color was flag of four ship?"

Elgurn spoke from the gallery. "You had best answer him, Kuran. The matter is of interest."

Kuran spoke low to Captain Brodig who stood beside him, and it was Brodig who answered. "Their colors were green and gold."

Roheed did not wait for anyone else to speak. "Green and gold is color of Lord Tuluptak, Lord King," he said, frowning. "Tuluptak have six ship in your water when we make attack on this place. His order is to not attack. It is to keep Nagaro Kiraam far away from here."

Elgurn leaned forward. "He was to keep Captain Nagaro away from our capitol while you made your attack on us?"

"Yes, Lord King."

"Can you tell us why?" This question came from Anduar, who was also sitting up and leaning forward.

Roheed turned to the Pact Signer. "Nagaro Kiraam have favor of Sheptuum. Emperor do not want to fight him."

Nagaro was staring at the young Mautep, oblivious to the new rustle of voices. *First Peldred and now Roheed!* First Hrathgard, then Sheptuum. And the Emperor had meant to keep him away from Lankura. It would have worked, too, if not for Narei's abduction.

Anduar's glance flicked from Roheed to the king and back again. "Thank you, Heerukan," he said quickly. "We will speak to you more of this later. And now, good people," he continued, addressing the general assemblage, "we ask that you be so good as to depart. Peldred's kinfolk may remain to attend upon his body and prepare it to be taken for burial. Also I ask that Captain Nagaro, Pavo Maat, and Taru Nareyo remain so that their swords may be returned to them."

Everyone was moving and talking at once. Folk were coming down out of the gallery and moving towards the main doors of the Audience Chamber, which now stood open.

Nagaro stood up. There was only one thought in his mind. He was looking for the woman who had been weeping, and caught a glimpse of deep burgundy near the table where Peldred's body lay. Without a word to anyone, he circled the table at which he'd been sitting and crossed the floor in a few quick strides to where the woman stood.

"I beg your pardon, My Lady," he said urgently. "Are you Peldred's mother?"

She turned to him, startled, and nodded. Her pale blue eyes were red-rimmed beneath the elegant sweep of her coiffured hair, straw-gold laced with silver. Yet her face was now composed and she bore herself very erect.

"I'm... *so sorry...*" he said brokenly. "I didn't want him to die. When we stood in final defense position at Osfaraad, he looked ready for the end. I believe he would have died bravely with the rest of us if I hadn't surrendered. I was trying to save him... to save them all—"

"Please don't trouble your mind, Captain." The high-born Leithian woman's voice sounded calm, almost triumphant. "My son lost his way for a time, but he found it in the end. He has reclaimed his honor, and I know I will see him in Seralind."

Nagaro could only swallow and duck his head, for he suddenly realized that he had nothing to offer this woman. Vothra had nothing to offer her that she had any need or wish to hear. "Of course, My Lady," he murmured. "Thank you." And he managed to bow and to step away from her, knowing better than to say anything to undermine the belief that gave her the strength to accept her loss with such dignity.

But the burden of his decision to surrender lay heavy on his heart. He would always carry it. He had intended that he himself would die and that Peldred would live, and it hadn't turned out that way. And it wasn't fair. Having Peldred's mother decline to blame him made it worse, not better. He was just going to have to accept that the young man's kin didn't consider his death unnecessary. Peldred, after all, had been raised to the same beliefs.

According to Vothrin teachings, of course, the young man's spirit would have another life, without the weight of a shame the whole world knew about. When Nagaro thought about that, it helped a little. Peldred's choice was not so hard to understand.

He had been moving while his thoughts spun, and his feet had retraced their steps across the Audience Chamber. Taru now came urgently around the table to meet him, with Pavo looming behind him.

"The guards took Roheed away," Taru said. "So it looks like *he's* still a prisoner. But it sounds like *we're* free t' go—as if it never happened!"

"Yes, I believe so." Nagaro still felt numb.

"And are we three also back in Fleet?" Pavo could not quite keep the disbelief out of his voice.

Nagaro shot the Hashtep a sharp glance. "As far as I'm concerned, we were never out of it. They really should apologize to you, Pavo—"

"Ha!" Taru barked a laugh. "Ye'll grow barnacles waitin' for that!" He turned to Pavo. "But at least ye've cheated the hangman! What are ye going t' do now?"

Pavo looked very serious. "First I go to find someone who help me write letter to Tenepti. Then I think I will go to bed and sleep until it is tomorrow."

"Captain, and Zirdas, I have your swords."

Nagaro turned around to meet Lord Anduar's infuriatingly bland smile. Three sword belts were draped over the man's arm.

"And there will officially be no objection to you wearing yours today, Captain," Anduar continued as he handed Nagaro his weapon, "for the brief time it will take you to exit the palace by the front door. If you go to the stable, you will also find a horse at your disposal."

Nagaro's teeth flashed ferally. "I'll accept those privileges only if the same are extended to my officers." He indicated Taru and Pavo.

Lord Anduar's smile became broadly magnanimous as he returned the other two swords to their respective owners. "Of course, Captain. Whatever you wish." He was already turning away.

"*Papa! Papa!*"

"*Narei?*" Nagaro spun around just in time to catch the raven-haired comet that came swooping towards him across the polished floor. He scooped up his daughter and held her with her knees against his chest and their faces level. "There you are, Ginger Pie!"

She threw her arms around his neck. "I knew they'd find you, Papa!"

"Find *me*? That shouldn't have been hard—" He stopped when he heard a discreet cough, and looked past Narei to find Elgurn standing in the spot just vacated by Lord Anduar.

The king held up a restraining hand. "There was... ah... a great deal of confusion after the battle," he suggested. "It lasted for days, but we've sorted it all out."

Nagaro set Narei down beside him, where she stood, hugging his leg as he rested a protective hand on her head. "Ah... yes. Thank you, My Lord," he managed.

"Will ye be long, Nagaro?" Taru asked impatiently. He and Pavo both looked eager to get out into the open air.

"You two go ahead. If the stablemen give you any trouble about the horses, I'll speak to them when I get there. And if not, I'll see you at the Fleet Compound."

Taru saluted, and the two friends strode off.

Elgurn spoke again, lowering his voice. "You should thank Madred Furthing—in private. Your daughter was delivered here to the palace yester-eve by a pair of unliveried men. It was a condition of her release that there be no names connected with this affair." The king paused, then added, "My daughter will explain the accommodations."

"Accommodations? Your daughter—?" Nagaro was confused.

Narei turned her face up to him. "Oh yes, Papa!" she chirped. "This is the king, and I met the princess too! She's very nice, even if she is very sad—and she's right over there with Omei. You have to meet Omei. She's very nice too!"

*Nevien...*

Nagaro was instantly looking for her, only half listening to the rest of Narei's prattle. He barely noticed that Elgurn was nodding, because suddenly, *there she was!* Standing only yards away. She was veiled and wearing mourning gray, and there was a Turowan woman at her side.

"I expect you will want to settle yourself immediately at the Fleet Compound, Captain," the king was saying, "and return to your duties. The Council will meet in a few days, and I'd like your advice concerning what's to be done with six Mahuk ships and a hundred and fifty Mautep sea warriors—not to mention the Emperor's nephew."

The last words fully reclaimed Nagaro's attention. For a moment he could only stare at the other man as he tried to digest them. There was a faintly satisfied glint in the king's shrewd blue eyes. When he found his voice, he said, "Very good, My Lord." *The tribunal was scarcely over and already the king had expectations of him.*

As he watched Elgurn walk away, he felt a tugging at his hand.

"Papa! The princess and Omei are coming!"

It was true. Nevien was indeed approaching with the other woman trailing a little behind.

Nevien reached up to put her veil aside and gave him a smile that was as weak as water. He could see that she was trying to show him that she shared his happiness at the reunion with his daughter. But it was clearly too soon for her, after enduring a parting that would be forever. *And her face was much too thin...*

"My Lady Princess," he managed to say, and bowed, remembering the need for formality in the nick of time.

Her smile tugged just fractionally wider, and there was genuine warmth in her eyes. "Captain Nagaro." She acknowledged his greeting. "I want you to meet Omei. Apparently she's been looking after Narei ever since the child was taken from Pakoa."

He tore his eyes away from Nevien's face to really look at the Turowan woman for the first time and found that she was studying him keenly. The woman was dressed simply, though she seemed not the least bit intimidated by all the departing noble folk or the grandeur of the Audience Chamber. She appeared to be between fifty and sixty, with dark hair pulled back into the traditional Turowan braid. There were streaks of gray at her temples, but her black eyes were bright and quick as a bird's. Her smile was like a well-kept secret. *And something about her seemed familiar.*

"So ye're Captain Nagaro," she said, before he could collect himself enough to say anything.

"Yes." He gave her a grave nod. "And I'm very pleased to meet you, Omei." *There was nothing at all familiar about the name.*

"Are ye?" she said. "Well, that's good t' know. I was afraid ye might not be, seeing as how I've taken money from them that carried off your little girl. They'd have taken her anyway, o' course, whether I was there or not. But she would ha' been all alone. The other women they asked wouldn't touch the task."

Nagaro frowned. He was trying unsuccessfully to think of where he might have seen her face. "I hope they paid you well," he said, "since that means less money in their hands and more in yours. For the rest, I trust Narei's judgement."

The woman's smile briefly became broad enough to show her teeth. "Ye're a wise man, Captain."

"I knew you'd like her, Papa." Narei was grinning.

Nevien cleared her throat. "I've arranged for Narei to stay here in the palace with Omei to take care of her, Captain, until you decide what's to be done. You couldn't have your daughter in the Fleet Compound, after all, and she and Omei seem to have quite taken to one another."

Nagaro looked at his daughter. "Is that all right, Narei?"

"Oh yes, Papa! And maybe I'll talk some more with Princess Nevien. I can see why you like her so much. She likes you too!"

Nagaro shot a reflexively panicked glance at Omei. But, though the woman's bright eyes were still watching him, he could read nothing in her face that he found alarming. "I'm sorry," he said, because he realized that he was staring. "I keep thinking that I've seen you somewhere before, but I've no idea when or where it could have been."

The woman smiled disarmingly. "Perhaps ye met my mother," she said easily. "They say I favor her. She was a medicine woman, and she traveled all about the country for years and years. Luka was her name."

"*Luka!*" The exclamation slipped out before he could stop it. This woman did indeed look like a younger version of the old medicine woman. *And Luka had recognized him despite his disguise. What might she have told her daughter?* He glanced at Nevien and saw with relief that she didn't seem to have taken any notice of his slip. And for her part, Omei showed no sign of trying to unmask him. Surely a great many people must have known Luka. "Yes," he said quickly, and as casually as he could. "That must explain it. I did know a medicine woman once by that name."

Nevien was giving him a warm, wan smile. "Well, I guess it's settled then," she said. "If you'd like to see it, Captain, I'll show you the room they picked out."

Nagaro allowed his eyes to linger on her face for the space of two seconds. He wasn't at all sure that returning to Lankura was a good idea, and the reason for his misgiving was standing right in front of him. He gave her a half bow and said, "Yes, please, My Lady."

"It's in a part of the servant's quarters," she said, "But it's near the kitchen and the garden. It's rather plain, but they both seem happy with it."

"Come on, Papa!" Narei pulled at his hand, bouncing eagerly and grinning from ear to ear.

Beside the princess, Omei was smiling a knowing smile.

***

When he arrived at the stable yard half an hour later, Nagaro saw no sign of Taru and Pavo. Presumably the stablemen had given them horses. After a moment's consideration, he decided not to request a mount for himself. The walk to the Fleet Compound was not so very long, and he hoped he might attract less attention on foot. Besides, he needed to think.

He set off with a purposeful stride, keeping his head down. Briefly he wished he had a cloak, but it was a sunny day and walking the streets with his hood up would probably have made him more conspicuous, rather than less. It was already mid-afternoon and once he had left the palace courtyard and the City Gate behind, he was moving among the normal flow of townspeople going about their business. Inevitably, someone recognized him, with a startled, "Captain Nagaro! It's good t' see ye back in Lankura!" He returned a minimal polite response, making it clear he didn't wish to engage in conversation. Other similar greetings occasionally penetrated his abstraction as he walked, but for the most part his thoughts ran on in circles.

Nevien had left them at the door of Narei's room and fled, as if the effort to keep up appearances in company were just too much for her. Nagaro had struggled to keep from going after her. It would have been completely inappropriate, but it had hurt to let her go. He wasn't sure whose mental state concerned him more—hers, or his own. *He wasn't sure which was more difficult for him, her presence, or her absence.*

It probably would be best for him if he didn't stay in Lankura. He should probably take the earliest opportunity to go to Kuran and resign his commission—but what reason could he possibly give? Everyone would expect him to stay. Taru and Pavo expected it. The king expected it. Kuran would, of course, expect it, as would Landros and Tredhold and all the other former pirates who had followed him a year ago when he'd joined the Royal Fleet. Once the news got out of how he had been vindicated by Peldred's confession and completely exonerated by the Tribunal, the good people of Edrovir would surely expect him to continue his service.

*Nevien would surely expect it too.*

And there he was... back around to Nevien again.

He looked up, startled, as he passed under the arch of the city's South Gate and came out beside the quay where the ships of the Fleet were moored. *He hadn't realized he'd come so far.* He searched with his eyes and found the *Sword of Freedom*, riding beside Kuran's flagship, the *Pride of Lankura*—where everyone would assume his ship belonged. Of the *Tiger* and the *North Wind* there was no sign. Moraga and Timegar would probably linger long enough in the waters around Lankura to get news from the fisherman of the Tribunal's verdict. But they would soon be gone, taking with them the members of the *Sword*'s more recent pirate crew. He didn't even have an easy means of departure.

He stood for a long moment on the cobblestones beside the quay—in front of the entrance to the Fleet Compound—feeling trapped, like a moth caught in the entangling threads of a spider's web. Then he drew a long breath and let it out again in an even longer sigh. It seemed that, at least for now, he really had no choice. It wasn't a final decision, after all. He could resign his commission at any time. He could stay for a while and tie up some loose ends, regarding the captured Mautep, for example. See Nevien through the worst of her grief... *He could prepare people for his decision, choose his moment...*

He squared his shoulders and crossed the paved area between the walls of the city and the Fleet Compound. As he passed through the compound's wide front gate, the two gate guards took a few seconds to recognize him without his uniform and then greeted him heartily.

"Captain Nagaro! Ye're back!"

"Welcome home, Zirda!"

Nagaro returned a salute, for an answer. *Home...* That was what they thought it was to him.

He had scarcely set his feet on the parade ground when Landros appeared as if from nowhere. The grizzled Fleet captain must have been waiting for him because he immediately called out, "Nagaro, lad! There ye are! Taru and Pavo blew in with their news more 'n an hour ago. So ye're tardy—not to mention being out o' uniform!"

Nagaro accepted a clap on the back and did his best to smile. "I suppose I'd better remedy that last," he said. "Is my old quarters—"

"—just as ye left it?" Landros finished the question. "Aye. Right down to the key ye left on the mantle. That's how much Kuran hoped to see ye back. He poked around in it, just a bit, before Estevad showed him that packet ye left that explained everything." Landros paused and lowered his voice, although the parade ground was nearly empty and there was no one within hearing. "Kuran stood your friend, lad, as much as he could, though ye did make the water a bit rough for him."

Nagaro ducked his head. "I'm sorry for all the trouble I caused. I'll have to make my apology—and thank him."

"Don't worry yourself, lad," Landros put in quickly. "The old salt-fox is used to navigating choppy seas. And all your old mates talked up your innocence the whole time ye three were gone. And now, o' course, Pavo's proved he was no traitor by fighting for us, and Peldred confessed on top of it—not to mention Roheed giving his testimony. So there's no room for argument."

Nagaro's astonishment showed in his face, and Landros chuckled. "I *did* say that Taru and Pavo brought the news. But the truth is, there's been rumors for days about which way the winds were blowin'. This verdict was no big surprise. And everyone's got something else on their minds right now."

Nagaro frowned. "What do you mean?"

"It's about this man that claims to be the lost heir o' the House of Loros—Tevren's son, and Darion's grandson. Everyone's so worked up about it that I figure they'll ha' forgotten about Peldred and Pavo and the whole second Tribunal in a week!"

Nagaro had all but forgotten about the heir of Darion, having been so focused for days on Pavo's fate, not to mention his own and Taru's. Now, however, everything he'd heard on the subject came back to him in a rush, and his frown deepened. Normally he would have been glad not to have his doings be a topic of conversation, but he thought the supposed heir of Darion was trouble Edrovir didn't need, and he said as much.

Landros nodded ruefully. "Ye'll get no argument from me."

Nagaro wasted no time after that in bidding Landros a heartfelt good day and making for number 14 Captain's Row. He got several more welcoming hails on the way, but was soon safely inside with the closed door between him and the world.

The key was indeed still on the mantle. He dropped it into his pocket, where it weighed like a piece of lead. The rooms smelled musty. He'd have to open the windows and air them out. *Maybe tomorrow...* The seaman's chest was still in his bedroom with his Fleet uniforms inside it, all neatly folded. He picked up a deep blue tirka and matching pair of pants and shook the creases out of them with a sigh, then set about changing his clothes. For better of for worse, he was back.

# Chapter 9

# The Pale-Eyed Man

It wasn't as hard as Nagaro had expected to settle back into the old Fleet rhythms. Landros' prediction that the Tribunal and its issues would be quickly forgotten proved accurate. At the same time, it seemed that the Fleet Compound was blessedly insulated from the rumors swirling around the man who claimed to be the heir of Darion, at least for the time being, with the result that politics were easy to ignore.

Nagaro had been reinstated as captain of the *Sword*, and Kuran wisely posted Taru and Pavo as his first and second mates. Most of his crew was composed of familiar faces with the rest being men who had been recruited the previous summer, and the task of molding this assemblage into a working team occupied most of his attention. There were drills and maneuvers, on land and sea, and of course there was always sword practice. Evenings meant games of King's Men with Taru and Pavo in Nagaro's quarters, and at week's end the three friends once again enjoyed their rides along the banks of the River Edro.

The king wasted no time in calling the promised meeting of the Council, and Nagaro and Kuran were summoned to appear before it together. This time, Nagaro was asked to present his recommendations immediately, without preamble or argument. The king and the council members heard him out and listened to Kuran's broad endorsement, all without comment, then dismissed them both. Nagaro tried not to think about it in the days that followed, as he waited for news of the official decision. If his suggestions were followed, his own participation would likely be required—another reason why he needed to stay in Lankura. It wouldn't be wise to trust the fates of Roheed and all those Mautep warriors to the whims of the council members and the vagaries of Edroviran politics.

Not thinking about Nevien was the most difficult task he had set for himself, but even this was facilitated by the fact that he saw nothing of her. It helped that no one else saw anything of her either, but he couldn't help wondering how she was bearing up under her grief. He visited Narei at the palace as often as he could get away from his duties. Each time he went, his thoughts were initially a curdled mixture of hope and dread at the possibility that he might meet the princess. But over and over, it failed to happen. So he pushed the thoughts aside each time and dutifully reminded himself that there was little he could have done to comfort her in any case.

He was just beginning to feel he could congratulate himself on how well he was managing, when he entered his quarters late one afternoon after a strenuous day of sea-maneuvers to find that a small envelope had been pushed under the door in his absence.

With his heart in his throat, he picked it up and discovered that it was a formal invitation to the Festival of Flowers, the annual celebration of spring, at the palace. He realized with a jolt that the event was actually less than a week away and he had managed to forget about it completely. At the bottom of the note, in a hand that he knew all too well, was written: *I look forward to seeing you there —Nevien Harlind*

The princess had troubled herself enough to not only see that he received an individual invitation, but to add a personal note as well. Neither one was necessary since Kuran always had a blanket invitation broad enough to accommodate all of the Fleet officers. His heart leaped at the thought that she wanted to see him, but then he mentally kicked himself. *Of course she wanted to see him, but that didn't mean he should go.*

Before finding the note, he had been planning to refresh himself and rest a little before it was time for dinner in the Fleet dining hall. He therefore stowed the invitation in his sea chest, fetched some water from the pump in his tiny back garden, and proceeded to wash his face and neck. He dried off with a towel and then stood staring at his frowning face in the mirror. It was still too early for dinner, but resting was out of the question. He was too tense. He needed to *move.* So he decided to go to the dining hall and get a cup of sothiril, and see if there was perhaps some cold meat.

There was in fact some cold meat left from lunch, as well as bread, cheese, and some early apricots, to go with his sothiril. Since there was no one else in the hall but the servers, Nagaro decided to have an early dinner, hoping that it would give him a chance to think without being disturbed. He made up a plate and took it to a seat at an empty table where he sat down and let his thoughts run as he ate.

He knew that he probably should not go to the Festival of Flowers. He should try to devise some excuse. The trouble was that he *wanted* to go. *To see for himself how Nevien was faring...*

He was so deep in thought that he failed to notice the sound of approaching footsteps until the presence of two men directly across the table from him became impossible to ignore. Then he looked up into the disconcertingly pale eyes of Lord Rastyl Korven. The second man, not surprisingly, was Rastian Korven. Both father and son were carrying steaming cups.

Rastyl smiled with what was probably intended to be warmth, though the paleness of his eyes made his expressions hard to interpret. "Welcome back, Captain," he said. "Do you mind if we join you?"

In fact, Nagaro would much rather have been alone than be forced to deal with the strange behavior he expected from the Kelorin lord. Unfortunately he had no polite way of saying so.

"By all means," he said, noting that at least the men had only sothiril to drink, not dinners to eat.

The two men sat down, Rastyl directly across from Nagaro, Rastian on his father's left. The younger man fumbled with his cup, and smiled ingratiatingly, though his eyes were wary.

Rastyl leaned forward, fixed Nagaro with his disturbing eyes, and addressed him in a low, intense voice. "Your return comes none too soon. We might have found ourselves in grave difficulties without you."

Nagaro finished chewing and swallowing, glad of the time it took since he had no idea what the man was talking about. "Difficulties?" he asked. "Without *me?*"

Young Rastian looked pained and raised his cup to take a swallow of sothiril.

Rastyl, however, leaned even closer. "Surely, Zirda, you see that if matters should deteriorate further, our cause may require a champion?"

Nagaro was not enlightened, and he was becoming increasingly uncomfortable. *There was something disquieting about sitting at a table, facing this man, something it reminded him of. Something he couldn't place...* "Your cause may require... a champion?" he repeated slowly, trying to feel his way to the meaning.

"*Our* cause," Rastyl corrected, and his eyes seemed to stab, the pale irises surrounding sharp black pupils. "I've been taking the measure of our best swordsmen," the man continued. "Some, like Rastian, have skill, but none compare to you. And of course none have your *other attributes.*"

This was fairly clear—up to the word *attributes*—but Nagaro was finding it hard to focus on Rastyl's words amid a rising anxiety that was somehow connected with the way the pale-eyed man was *sitting... leaning forward and looking at him.*

*Those eyes!* Nagaro yanked his gaze away to glance at Rastian, whose father had just belittled him, but he found that the younger man was studiously sipping his sothiril.

"I believe Rastian could do better if he didn't hold back," Nagaro said, remembering the last bouts he had fought with Rastian, more than a year ago. He tried to meet Lord Rastyl's eyes again, but found it hard to look directly into them. "Besides," he added, "a challenge should be a last resort—" Sitting with this man was bothering him so much that he couldn't think!

Rastyl's eyes just kept staring as his voice dropped another notch. "There is only one way to deal with men like Lothard Hurn."

Nagaro was trying not to flinch, while his mind spun. *Why were they talking about challenges? Why did it feel so wrong to have Rastyl across the table from him?* "I can't challenge Lothard," he protested. "He's a lord, and I'm not."

Rastyl was still holding his eyes, still leaning forward, and Nagaro felt an irrational urge to get up from the table to escape the situation. *To flee... To run away from this man...* His heart had begun to pound. Sweat prickled his sides. He realized that he was beginning to panic—

And just at that moment there came a sound of voices and boots on the flagstones as half a dozen Fleet men entered the dining hall. They milled about the counter, calling for food.

Rastyl shot a glance at the men, and Nagaro felt relief the moment the man's gaze was withdrawn from him. The Kelorin Lord frowned in annoyance. Then he straightened abruptly and the frown vanished. He turned back to Nagaro and spoke in a voice that was pitched at a normal level. "Of course, Captain," he said easily. "But there are *ways* that may be found to deal with that."

The pale eyes made one last stab at him and Nagaro instantly felt his uneasiness flood back in response, until Rastyl grasped his cup and stood up. "Our swords are ready whenever they're needed, and we will speak of this again another time," he said. "Come, Rastian." He turned away from the table, gesturing for his son to follow him.

Rastian rolled his eyes and shrugged at Nagaro. "Captain," he said, making a little bow before retrieving his own cup and departing in his father's wake.

Nagaro was too shaken to find words of parting. He kept his eyes down and therefore didn't see where the two men went. He tried to focus on his forgotten dinner, forcing himself to eat, although his appetite had completely deserted him.

As he finished his food, however, his agitation gradually ebbed and he began to feel a little foolish. What on earth had been wrong with him? The conversation had been strange, but no stranger than usual when speaking to Rastyl. It didn't seem to be the *words* that had disturbed him. Was it the *length* of the conversation, together with the paleness of Lord Rastyl's eyes, that had nearly elicited a panic like the one he'd felt years ago on Pakoa, trying to watch Tredhold use a bladder-thorn?

By the time he rose to leave, he had calmed down enough to wish he'd paid better attention to the conversation's content. Recalling things that Kuran had told him about Rastyl, he wondered if the Kelorin lord's words might have concerned the presumptive heir of Darion. It seemed possible, but he had no way of answering the question, so he did his best to mentally drop the matter.

Dinner was by now in full progress, but Nagaro didn't wait for Taru and Pavo. His friends would seek him in his quarters later if they wanted to play King's Men. Outside, the sun was just setting across the parade ground. It was a fine spring evening with stars just beginning to prick the arch of the sky. He realized, belatedly, that he'd made no decision regarding the spring festival. The encounter with Rastyl had completely driven the matter from his mind. He would, at the very least, need to inform Kuran that he had received an invitation.

Thinking of Kuran caused him to glance in the direction of the Fleet Lord's quarters, and he was just in time to see the door of it swung open and a man emerge into the light of the lamp that was already lit above the doorway. Nagaro's feet came to an immediate stop. Even from that distance, he recognized Lord Rastyl by his size and his manner of movement. He stayed where he was, having no wish to speak to the man twice in one day, but he needn't have worried. Rastyl immediately set off for the entrance of the Fleet Compound, walking at a rapid pace.

Nagaro frowned. He wondered why Rastyl Korven had sought a meeting with Kuran Kel, and he could not help thinking of the conversation in the dining hall. He hoped the two events were not connected. He stood in mental debate for half a minute before curiosity overcame him and he started towards the lamp-lit door.

Kuran answered his knock himself and let Nagaro into his study. where the Lord of the Fleet motioned him to a chair before sitting down at his own cluttered desk and turning his sharp black eyes on Nagaro.

"What brings you to my door at this hour, Captain?"

Nagaro began with the invitation. "It means you wouldn't need to include me on your list," he said, "since I have an individual invitation. And I also wanted to be sure there was no conflicting duty."

Kuran laughed out loud. "On the night of the Festival of Flowers? Hardly! And I expect you to be there. You've been properly reinstated, and I don't want anyone to forget it."

Nagaro was both relieved and grateful at having his hand tipped in this fashion, and felt instantly guilty for it. He swallowed, and decided to simply approach the other matter directly.

"I saw Rastyl Korven leaving this building just before I came, My Lord," he said. "And I couldn't help wondering what he had to say to you. I wouldn't presume to ask except that he and Rastian pinned me down in the dining hall about an hour ago to talk about something I didn't entirely understand."

Kuran sat for a moment, regarding Nagaro closely. Finally he said, in a casual tone that belied the watchfulness of his eyes, "Where would you stand if it came to war between the Leithian and Kelorin factions?"

Nagaro frowned at the question, but didn't hesitate. "I am sworn to the service of Edrovir," he said. "Such a war would serve Edrovir poorly, so my course would be to try to prevent it."

"Mmm." Kuran gave a small nod, though his expression remained carefully neutral. "And if that effort failed? If you couldn't prevent it?"

Nagaro frowned afresh. "In that case, My Lord, I would try to end it. But I hope you don't mean to ask me how. From where I stand right now, I can't see so far."

Kuran looked down and rearranged some of his papers. When he looked up again, his expression was grave. "The answers you've just given me are almost exactly the same as the ones I gave to Lord Rastyl when he asked me those questions. Does this surprise you?"

Nagaro blinked. "Not that you answered him so, My Lord. But it surprises me that he asked. Did he seem pleased by your answers?"

Kuran crooked a brow ever so slightly. "I'm not sure. He's a hard man to read."

Again Nagaro frowned. "When he spoke to me in the dining hall, he spoke of *our cause*, and of the need for a 'champion'. And he suggested there were ways that a man like me might fight a challenge against Lothard Hurn."

"Ah." Kuran nodded fractionally. "That last part is true. A man who isn't high-born may fight a challenge as if he were, if he's fighting—as a champion—on behalf of someone who *is*."

Nagaro digested this. "Do you think the cause he spoke of was that of the Kelorin Faction? Or of Darion's heir?"

"I couldn't say." Kuran's eyes narrowed and he fixed Nagaro with a penetrating gaze. "He did ask me one more thing, though. He asked what I knew about *you*—if I knew who you were."

Nagaro felt a chill, and his mouth went dry. "What did you say, My Lord?"

Kuran laughed shortly. "I told him that I don't greatly care *who* you are since I know *what* you are—which is an uncommonly good man. He then demanded to know how I could have given you a place in the Fleet under such circumstances. Since I don't like having other men tell me how to conduct my command, I politely directed him to the door."

Nagaro looked at the floor, overwhelmed by embarrassment and relief. "Thank you for the compliment, My Lord," he murmured.

Kuran coughed. "I don't suppose he's asked *you* who you are?"

Nagaro raised his eyes. "Actually, no, My Lord." He swallowed. "I suppose that now he may."

The lengthening silence that followed was awkward. Kuran seemed to be waiting for Nagaro to say more, and Nagaro fervently wished he could repay Kuran's trust by offering some further confidence. Unfortunately he wasn't willing to.

In the end it was Kuran who spoke. "Well," he said with surprising mildness, "I see that it's unlikely to avail him anything if he does—which gives me some satisfaction. And now I think I had best give my attention back to these infernal papers, Captain."

***

Nagaro found Taru and Pavo waiting at the door of his quarters. Since he couldn't make anything of Rastyl's enigmatic questioning, and his conversation with Kuran hadn't helped, he didn't trouble his friends with any of it. They played several games of King's Men before going to their beds.

He fell asleep easily enough, but later that night when a storm blew in from the sea that rattled the windows with thunder and lashed the roof with rain, his sleep became as restless as the night. There came a dream, in which a pale-eyed man was staring at him...

"Come," the man said. "Sit with me." And though he didn't want to sit with the man, he followed as if compelled, and sat in an elaborately carved chair at a long table in a cavernous room. The man sat down opposite him, and began to talk—*and to stare.*

He wasn't listening to what the man was saying and was trying not to listen to his own responses, which were all stiff and flat. He knew he could rely on the puppet part of him to give the man answers—*stupid answers.*

The pale-eyed man wore dark velvet with silver decoration. He himself wore a shirt of dark green silk—not as bad as the purple one. Around them, the Great Hall was full of finely dressed lords and ladies, and the walls were festooned with flowers, but he didn't care about any of that. All he wanted was a chance to get away—*alone*—to find a place to die. *It was the only way out of the nightmare.*

He tried to blink his eyes, as the pale-eyed man talked and stared, and his heart leaped when he found that he could do it. *The drug was wearing off!* Soon he could try to escape. But if he tried to move too soon, with his muscles incompletely under his own control, he might fall.

The man was still talking, leaning forward, still staring. *If only the fellow would tire of the puppet's stupid answers and go away!* He willed himself to count the seconds. He tried to voluntarily draw a breath out of sequence. *Yes! It worked!* He tried to move his foot under the table. *Again, yes!* Carefully he turned his head a tiny bit, so that by swiveling his eyes, he could scan the path to the doors on the other side of the room, doors that led to the terrace and the garden beyond. *The doors were open!* None of his three keepers was to be seen along the path he meant to take. His excitement rose.

The pale-eyed man had stopped speaking. The pale eyes still stared, but there would be no better chance and he didn't have much time. He couldn't speak, of course, to excuse himself. By the time he could speak his own words, he would be too wracked with pain to stand up or to walk. So he did his best with pantomime. Moving the muscles of his face into a pleasant smile, he nodded. He began to stand up, intending to bow—

*But there was resistance, though there shouldn't have been!* In rising panic, he struggled to overcome that unexplained resistance. *Struggled... and struggled...*

Until the desperate effort to move jerked him awake—

Nagaro sat bolt upright in his bed in the familiar darkness of the bedroom in his quarters on Captain's Row. He was shaking. The dream's images were still fresh in his mind, as if burned into his brain.

"*No!*" he groaned. "*Oh, no!*" The dream, he realized, had been riding on a long-buried memory, and something had just become horribly clear.

He stumbled out of bed and fumbled for his clothes in the dark, in too much of a hurry to go to the fireplace to light a candle. He found his shirt, pants, and boots, pulling them on with hands that shook, then groped his way to the front door. Taking his cloak from its hook, he wrapped it about him and stepped out into the night.

A cold, wet wind slapped him in the face. The rain had gone, and the pale moon, Talebra, was low in the west and nearly full, telling him that dawn was less than an hour away. Diamond-bright stars punctuated streaks of clear sky that were as black as the void of death. Moonlight and starlight glistened on the rain-slicked flagstone paths, the muddy ground between them, and the dark wooden roofs of the buildings that housed the Royal Fleet.

Nagaro ignored the cold, the wind, and all the other details of the scene as he struck off as fast as he could walk in the direction of the building where Taru and Pavo once again shared a two-room quarters. Reaching it, he rapped loudly on his friends' door—and again, more loudly, when no one came. He was about to beat upon it even harder, when it was wrenched open by Pavo, clad only in the long robe that served him in place of a nightshirt.

Pavo stared at him, blinking. "Nagaro! What is wrong?"

Nagaro pushed past him without a word, into the outer of the two rooms, the kitchen-dining room where a bed had been set up for Pavo. He heard the door close behind him, and the glimmer of moonlight was cut off. "It's Rastyl…" he said brokenly. "He… he recognizes me! I remember now. We met years ago. I saw it in a dream—"

"Wait Nagaro. I will get light." Pavo retreated into the darkness.

Groping with his hands, Nagaro found one of the chairs belonging to the room's small table, and he sank into it.

Light flared as Pavo ignited the wick of a small hand-held lamp using an ember from the fire grate. The young Hashtep came and set the lamp on the table, then sat down in one of the other chairs, studying Nagaro with serious dark eyes. "Now you tell me," he said. "You have dream that tell you Rastyl have recognized you?"

Nagaro shook his head. "No," he said, struggling to explain. "I had a dream about something that happened years ago—during *that time*. And I remember now how I met Rastyl—back then. He was *there*—at the Festival of Flowers. And I… I think he knows who I am!"

"Ye think Rastyl knows who ye *are?*" Taru was standing in the doorway of the bedroom in his nightshirt.

Pavo turned to the young Turo. "Nagaro have had *dream*," he said, the last word laden with significance.

"*Hamanei mata noa!*" Taru rolled his eyes, then was seized by a sudden shiver. "Let me get my cloak. It's bloody cold in here." He went to the hooks beside the door, and a moment later was sitting in the remaining chair with the garment wrapped around him. "All right, Nagaro," he said, turning a patient gaze on his friend. "What is it that's put ye on the edge this time?"

Nagaro raised a hand to massage his temples, trying to think how to explain what had just happened. It was complicated, and talking about it wasn't easy either. Eventually he began at the beginning—his encounter with Rastyl and Rastian in the dining hall, what had been said, and how seeing Rastyl sitting across the table from him had nearly put him into a panic. Then he related what Kuran had told him. When he got to the part where Rastyl had asked Kuran if he knew who he was, Taru gave Pavo a sharp glance.

Pavo returned Taru a puzzled look before turning back to Nagaro. "But if he have *asked* Kuran that, why do you think he already *know?*" he inquired patiently.

Nagaro looked at the table top. "Because of the dream I just had," he said carefully. "It was a dream about something that happened in the past," he added, glancing up at Pavo. "That's all the dream was. But after having the dream, I know why I didn't like sitting across from him. It's because I *remember* now that he was there years ago, at the Festival of

Flowers. He sat across the table from me, talking to me." Nagaro drew a long breath. This was a danger he had never thought of, because he hadn't remembered...

"What did he say?" Taru asked.

"I have no idea." Nagaro ran a distracted hand through his hair, which he hadn't bothered to tie. "I... I wasn't paying attention to him. I never used to pay attention if I didn't have to, because it was so awful listening to all the... the *stupid* things that came out of my mouth—" He stopped, unable for the moment to go on.

"You are sure it was Lord Rastyl at festival?" Pavo asked. "This was seven year ago, and you say you did not pay attention."

Nagaro drew a shuddering breath. "It was a Kelorin man of the same size, with very pale eyes—almost white—that seemed to stare. How many such men can there be?"

"But the man can't possibly be sure of anything, based on such a little thing," Taru put in, "as sitting and talking, one time, when it was so long ago!"

Nagaro shook his head. "He could have seen me any number of other times when I didn't notice," he said dully. "It wouldn't have been hard. And I remember some other things. Things that weren't in the dream..." He drew another breath, and let it out again. "The... the heskial.was wearing off. So I got up and left him, and that's where the dream ended. But I *remember* now that I got all the way out onto the terrace before Bron caught me... and... and knocked me down and held me. I was starting to shake. But from where I was lying, I could see that *the pale-eyed man had followed me!* He got close, too, before Kale stopped him and kept him away from me. And I heard Kale tell him that *there was nothing he could do.*"

Nagaro stopped to draw a breath before adding, "And when I was at the victory feast two summers ago—the first time I saw him again—when I introduced myself, Rastyl said, *'I've heard what name you go by.'* What would have made him think 'Nagaro' wasn't the name I'd always borne? He doesn't have a Turowan mother like Kuran does. I tell you, *that man knows who I am!*"

There followed a little silence. Then Pavo said, "Still I think maybe is not so."

But Taru's face had frozen. "Ye'd better hear this, Nagaro," he said slowly, giving Nagaro a worried look. "Last night—on our way t' your place—Pavo and I crossed paths with Rastian and Rastyl. I don't think they saw us, but we couldn't help overhearing some o' what Rastyl was saying."

Nagaro's stomach felt like lead. "*Go on.*"

Taru cleared his throat. "Rastyl said that Kuran had no idea what he had in his hand." Taru frowned with the effort of remembering the words.

"He said, 'If that man were to declare himself, he could bring Elgurn down and turn our whole world on its ear'." Taru shot Nagaro another look. "I had no idea what he was talking about when he said it," he went on quickly. "But now I'm thinking, '*that man*' could ha' meant *you!*"

Nagaro closed his eyes and sat in silence for several long seconds. "That would have been right after he finished talking to Kuran," he said hollowly. "I don't know what else he could have meant. *What am I going to do?*"

Taru exchanged glances with Pavo. "Let's have some breakfast," he said, with forced brightness. "Things are sure t' look better after ye've got some food in your stomach. The sun 'll be up soon, and no one's going back t' sleep. So I'll make a pot o' sothiril, and there's still half a bag o' those oat cakes we bought from the baker-woman."

Nagaro sat numbly while Pavo kindled a fire and Taru dressed and went out to the pump to put water in the kettle. Presently, when the sothiril was brewed, Nagaro found himself with a steaming cup of it to sip at while he gingerly nibbled an oat cake.

"Maybe you worry too much, Nagaro," Pavo said over his sothiril. "You think Lord Rastyl have know this thing for two year, but he have not done anything to hurt you. It does not seem he have told anyone."

Nagaro frowned. "He's told his son," he said grimly. "Rastian clearly knows. Besides," he added, "Rastyl may have kept his knowledge close so far because he hopes to make use of me—to serve his *cause*, or be his *champion*. What if I don't want to do either one?"

Taru was already on his second oat cake and now he gestured with it dismissively. "If he tried to tell anyone else, who would believe him? Everyone says the man's half daft, and anyone that looks at ye would think it's ridiculous."

Pavo nodded emphatically. "What Taru say is true, Nagaro."

Nagaro picked up his cup, still frowning. There was some truth to Taru's words. Any number of people had looked at him by now and *not* recognized him. "Maybe," he said doubtfully. "But if he's guessed I was being... drugged... he could explain it that way."

"But it still sounds daft!" Taru protested. "And no matter what the man thinks he knows, he can't be *sure* if ye don't tell him he's right. *So don't tell him!* Stay on your course, and give him the lie—and if he stares at ye, just look at him like ye think he's soft in the head! And ye can handle Rastian the same way. The father and son together are like one piece on the game board."

Nagaro swallowed a gulp of sothiril. *Could this actually work?* "I'm not a good liar, Taru. You know that."

"Well, that's true," Taru conceded. "Ye're not good with a flat-out lie. But ye've a way o' saying things that *aren't* lies, but *work* like lies, if ye know what I mean."

Nagaro grimaced. "That takes an awfully quick wit sometimes," he said ruefully. "And it's hard to do if someone asks you something straight out."

"Does Rastyl ever do that?"

"Well... no, he hasn't so far." In fact, Nagaro had to concede that Rastyl wasn't much given to straight speaking, and he realized that he might easily feign ignorance in most situations and use the man's odd behavior and dubious reputation to discredit him if he had to. And he'd only have to worry about it for as long as he remained in Lankura in any case.

He felt the tension ease in his shoulders. The night's terrors were fading in the face his friends' good sense. A year ago he had thought that everything was over when Fendar had identified him, yet nothing had come of it. And Rastyl surely knew much less about him than Fendar. He finished his oat cake and reached for a second. His appetite was improving in parallel with his mood.

Pavo frowned as he poured himself some more sothiril. "Still I do not understand why Rastyl say that if Kuran know who you are, it will make king fall."

Nagaro frowned in his turn. "He probably meant that's what *could* happen, if the whole country knew the truth," he replied. "I think it's an exaggeration. Though it wouldn't be good for Elgurn if everyone knew he'd committed such a crime—if he has enemies who want the crown, for example."

Taru leaned back in his chair, brushing crumbs from his beard. "Ye'd better see that Kuran doesn't find out, then," he observed. "He's the king's man because Elgurn made him Lord o' the Fleet and gave him a Wared. If Kuran finds out, ye'd best watch your neck!"

But Nagaro shook his head. "That's not a fair judgement of Kuran," he said earnestly, "although it's true that I can't tell him because it would put him in a difficult position. He does owe Elgurn a great deal, and he's in the king's confidence, but he's also been my benefactor. I believe he's a good man, but I don't know what he'd do if he knew the truth. He wouldn't wish to hurt me, but he might feel his duty fell counter to his wishes."

They weren't likely to come to any better understanding of the matter, so the three friends decided they might as well begin their day's activities. Taru and Nagaro set about rinsing the pot and washing the cups while Pavo got dressed.

Chapter 10

# The Festival Of Flowers

There were flowers everywhere in the Great Hall, their mingled scents perfuming the air. Graceful porcelain vases, set on mahogany stands at intervals along the walls, held blooms of pure white, deep rose, and various shades of blue and lavender. Garlands of flowers of the same hues framed the tall windows through which midmorning sunlight streamed. More garlands encircled the room, swooping in graceful arcs from hook to hook along the walls and girding the pillars that marched the length of the hall in two stately rows.

This was the Feast of the Spring Moon, also known as the Festival of Flowers. The people still mourned their beloved queen, and the colors of the flowers were a little more subdued than usual, but it had been agreed that Semorel would not have wanted anything to interfere with her favorite celebration.

Nagaro paused at the door to bow to Lady Merriel—the late queen's dearest companion—who was greeting the guests. Nevien might have signed his invitation, and added a personal note to it, but apparently she wasn't up to such a demanding social duty as this. Nagaro hoped to have a chance to talk with the princess a little, privately, and he tried not to frown as he forced himself to attend to the ritual pleasantries.

The diminutive Leithian woman in front of him was smiling brightly. "Captain Nagaro!" she gushed. "It's so good to have you back again in Lankura, and back in that uniform! We had missed you."

"It's a pleasure to see you again as well, Lady Merriel."

Another bright smile. "You're to sit at the match table, Captain. Lady Rianine will direct you to a seat."

"Ah... thank you, My Lady."

*The match table...* The name wasn't official, of course, and he wasn't sure how he felt about being placed there. It meant someone was still trying to 'match' him, and he wasn't sure who was doing it. *But, would Nevien be seated there?*

Merriel was already looking past him, her eyes lighting up like stars. "My Lord Kuran! It's *so* good to see you—"

Nagaro stepped away, moving towards the head of the Hall, past tables graced by matching floral arrangements. His eyes swept the room, looking for Nevien, grateful that at least he needn't worry about Rastyl tonight. The man was reportedly at home in Irvenen Wared. Near the head of the hall, the musicians were tuning their instruments. Soon there would be food and drink, music and dancing, but Nagaro hadn't come for any of that. Since Kuran had insisted he come, he intended to use the opportunity to find out how Nevien was bearing up.

The princess was not at the match table—only Rianine, standing at the head of it. He winced. The young Kelorin woman was wearing a gown of pale yellow satin and had her ebony hair done up in coiled braids and crowned with a little circlet of creamy white flowers in honor of the occasion. She was actually quite lovely, and she gave him a smile as he approached that would have seemed perfectly charming if he hadn't known her better.

"Good morning, My Lady Rianine." He gave her his best bow, not wanting to give her anything to criticize if he could help it.

"Ah, Captain Nagaro—always so charming." A little pause, then, "I see you're not wearing your medal."

"What medal?" he asked, before stopping to think.

"The one they didn't give you, of course," she said brightly. "For pulling their meat out of the fire—again."

Rianine had a way of putting people off balance, and worse, she seemed to enjoy it. There was laughter in her eyes. Nagaro took a breath. "Oh, that one," he tried experimentally. "I may not be wearing it, but at least I'm not wearing it with *pride*."

"Oh! Well done, Zirda!" Mirth was supplanted by approval. "Seriously, didn't they give you *anything?*"

"Other than restoring my full rank and privileges? No. Well, Kuran *did* issue me a commendation for preventing a serious miscarriage of justice. Fortunately, however, there's no medal for that."

"Fortunately?"

"I don't care for medals."

"Good for you." She gave him a wink, then said, "I'm here to tell people where to sit. That's your chair, on this side of the head of the table. Do make yourself comfortable."

He paused with his hands on the back of the chair and addressed her as casually as he could. "Will the princess be sitting at this table?"

She gave him a sidelong look. "Oh, no," she answered negligently. "Nevien will be on the dais with her father. There's a new girl who will be sitting across from you. *Do* sit down, Captain. There will be wine or sothiril, and cheese and biscuits served presently."

Nagaro sat down rather than risk being asked a third time. *On the dais... She wasn't there yet of course. She and Elgurn would probably make a grand entrance after most of the guests had arrived.*

He sat, brooding, while the room filled up with people. When the refreshments appeared, he absently poured himself a glass of ruby-hued sothiril and nibbled a ginger biscuit.

The princess's ladies began to arrive. Rather than sit, however, they all stood on the other side of the table, talking, and Rianine joined them. From the snatches of conversation that reached his ears, Nagaro could easily guess the topic.

"Does anyone know whether he's handsome?"

"My mother says he should be, considering who his parents were—if he *is* the son of Tevren and Lindra."

"What will he do, do you suppose, if he comes to Lankura?"

"Become king, of course—"

"Do you know if he's married, Rian? If he isn't, he'll be wanting a wife—a *highborn* wife! She should be a Leithian too, if he doesn't want to make the same mistake his father did."

"*I* wouldn't marry him even if he *is* the heir of Darion!

"Not even if he's king? Why not, Clarimel?"

"Brcause if he's from Irvenen, he's probably a goatherd or some such. I don't fancy being married to a goatherd!"

"Well, you've no need to fear then. If he's going to be king, he'll want to marry Nevien—"

Nagaro sat up at the mention of the princess's name, and set his glass of sothiril down with a frown. It hadn't occurred to him that the man who claimed to be Darion's heir would be another potential suitor.

Someone abruptly clapped him on the back, causing him to start violently in surprise.

"Ah, Captain!" Lord Soren sounded jovial. "I want to congratulate you on having your man completely exonerated—just as you said he should be!

Nagaro hurriedly pushed back his chair and stood up, turning to face the speaker. "Thank you, My Lord. Though I think you should have congratulated *him*."

"Ah yes. Quite, quite." Soren leaned close to him and whispered into his ear. "There'll be a gathering at the Golden Branch on Three Cedars Lane—at sunset on Eighth Day. If you care about the fate of Edrovir, you'll be there. That's Three Cedars Lane. The Golden Branch." He straightened, without waiting for any response, and resumed his jocular tone. "I congratulate you again, Captain. Well done!" And with that, the aged Kelorin moved off at a surprisingly spry pace through the gathering throng.

Nagaro stood staring after the man, frowning in annoyance. *The Kelorin Faction again... Still trying to win him over, it seemed.*

His thought was cut short by the sight of lords Anduar and Pendrik bearing down on him. Pendrik, slightly in the lead, was carrying a half-full glass of wine. Nagaro cast about a little desperately but saw no way to avoid an exchange with the two Pact Signers. Hastily, he bowed and said, "My Lords."

"Captain Nagaro!" Pendrik gestured with his wine glass. "There wasn't any chance to say it at the Council meeting, so I'll say it now. And I've brought my *esteemed* colleague so that I can have the pleasure of rubbing his nose in it." A second gesture indicated that the "esteemed colleague" was Lord Anduar.

Anduar emitted a long-suffering sigh. "As I have already told you, Pendrik, there is no need—"

"No *need?* How often do we get the chance to point out that someone else—" the wineglass sloshed in Nagaro's direction— "was right about something, and that *you* were wrong? I'm referring to the affair of young Peldred and that Mahuk-man." The last was spoken to Nagaro, or at least in his general direction.

Anduar cleared his throat. "What I had *started* to say was that there is no need to 'rub my nose in it' since I am pleased to admit my error." He turned to Nagaro. "I should have had more trust in your judgement, Captain. I'm delighted to have made that discovery."

"Ah... thank you, My Lord—"

"Pah! Pleased, do you say?" Pendrik gesticulated. "Delighted? You think you can wiggle out of it? You were wrong! Wrong, wrong, wrong!"

Anduar bowed. "Yes, Pendrik, I was wrong."

"Hah! That's more like it!" Pendrik raised his glass. "Much more like it! Ah ha ha!" He turned fleetingly to Nagaro. "Your health, Captain!" he declared, and drained his glass. "And now I need some more wine! Good day, gentlemen." And he was off, shouldering his way through the crowd.

Anduar shook his head. "This is what one must endure when one has the reputation of being right a good deal of the time. I advise you to bear that in mind, Captain."

Nagaro shrugged. "I've already noted the phenomenon, My Lord."

"Have you?" Anduar raised an eyebrow. "Yes, I expect you might. I would also toast your health, Captain, but I did not bring my glass. It seems you're an excellent judge of character."

Nagaro frowned. "I try to pay attention to people, My Lord. *You,* for example, from what I've seen, are highly intelligent and capable of seeing a great many things very clearly. But you seem also to have grown cynical, and I've noticed that cynical people can't always be relied upon to do what is right."

Anduar's gaze had become almost hungry for an instant, and there was something—a little flicker—as Nagaro ceased speaking. When the Kelorin lord spoke, however, his voice betrayed nothing. "You're very astute, Captain. But an inveterate cynic sees only brass even when gold is before his eyes, and you, Captain, are as close to gold as one is likely to find in this weary world."

Nagaro sighed. "I might find your words more flattering, My Lord, if you didn't make your purpose so obscure."

"It is what I do." Anduar smiled a small, tight smile.

Nagaro returned a mirror image. Then, just to see what response he would get, he said, "Lord Soren was here just before you, My Lord. He told me there will be a meeting this Eighth Day at the Golden Branch on Three Cedars Lane."

"Did he really?" One of Anduar's eyebrows arched slightly.

"Yes. He said I should attend if I cared about the fate of Edrovir."

Anduar's expression didn't change. "And do you? Care, I mean?"

"Of course—"

"Then I expect you'll wish to attend." The inflection was completely neutral, and the Pact-Signer continued with scarcely a pause. "I shall be otherwise engaged, but I look forward to hearing what you observe. I salute you again, Captain. Do take care."

With that, and a nod, the older man turned on his heel and departed.

Nagaro watched Anduar's retreating back and muttered, *"I don't understand that man."* The last time that Anduar had seen members of the Kelorin Faction trying to recruit Nagaro, he'd bidden them be off. Shaking his head, Nagaro sat down and picked up his glass of sothiril. *Would Anduar really have gone to this meeting if he could? Would he have been welcome?*

The clear, pure chime of a bell rolled through the Great Hall, cutting across all other sounds. A second bell followed a few seconds later, and after a similar interval, a third. There was a resulting modulation of the babble of voices as the standing clusters of brightly-clad folk moved towards tables and chairs and seated themselves.

There followed a brief flourish from the seated musicians, and King Elgurn and Princess Nevien entered the Great Hall and moved to take their places at a table on the raised dais at the hall's head. Elgurn was dressed for the occasion in deep green and rich dark brown—colors not quite of mourning, but subdued.

Nevien came on her father's arm. She had put aside her veil and her mourning gray in honor of the day, but not too far aside. Her gown was simple in line, executed in softly muted green, and unadorned by lace or embroidery. Her honey-colored hair was simply swept up on either side of her head and secured by a pair of ivory combs, to each of which was attached a single ivory-white lily. Nagaro followed her keenly with his eyes, trying to discern how physically strong she was and how well she was bearing up under her grief.

After the princess and her father mounted the dais, yet another bell was sounded. The king raised a hand to address the assemblage. "Good people!" he declaimed, "We bid you all welcome, and pray that you may continue as you were. We won't keep you from your enjoyment of the day with lengthy speeches."

The words drew murmurs of approval as the king and princess took their seats and the musicians promptly struck up a lighthearted tune. Nagaro's brow furrowed. Nevien had moved steadily to her place on the dais, but the smile she wore looked a little forced. Other than that, he hadn't learned very much.

"—I'll be glad to make you acquainted, Captain—"

With a jolt, he realized that Lady Merriel had apparently been speaking to him. "I beg your pardon, My Lady," he said hastily. "I'm afraid my mind was a hundred miles away." *Less than a hundred feet, actually...*

"That's quite all right, Captain." The flaxen-haired chaperon smiled indulgently. "I'd just said that I don't believe you know everyone at this table, and I was about to introduce you to the newest of the princess's ladies. She indicated the young woman seated directly across from him.

The table had filled up with guests while he'd been unaware. As usual, the side he was seated on held only young men, while the other side was graced exclusively by young ladies. Rianine had said he would be opposite "the new girl," and he now turned his attention to her for the first time, realizing that this was presumably the girl he was matched with. She looked terribly young to him—sixteen or seventeen—and her midnight-blue eyes were wide with something akin to awe as she stared back at him. He also took in her dark brown hair, worn loose and crowned with a circlet of scarlet flameflower, and her gown the color of ripe apricots.

"This is Delasin Virden," Merriel continued. "Virden is only a minor house, but one with a long and noble history."

Delasin looked at Merriel in some dismay, and the color rose in her cheeks. All Nagaro could think of was that this girl was possibly some relation to his own Lady Maramine. In fact, the Lady Delasin had the same unusual deep blue eye color, known as Kelorin blue. He found his voice and murmured, "I'm pleased to make your acquaintance."

Her eyelashes fluttered. "It's... it's such an honor to meet you, Captain," she said, sounding eager and breathless. Then she added, "And we're no relation to Leyel Virden—in spite of the name. You see, he was *adopted.*"

Nagaro felt a surge of outrage at this gratuitous denial. "Really?" he said before he could stop himself. "The tale I heard was that he was the Lady Maramine's son, begotten by her murdered lover. And in that case it becomes you ill to so disown him—" He stopped in shock at his own words. Both Merriel and Delasin were staring at him, aghast. Rianine was eyeing him with a raised eyebrow, though the other occupants of the table seemed oblivious to what had just occurred. "It's just a story," he said hastily, realizing belatedly that he'd put two stories together—the one the folk around Averwin had concocted, and the one Maramine had told him. "I shouldn't have repeated it," he went on in what he hoped was a conciliatory tone. "What I meant was that it's a bit unkind to be in such a hurry to deny any connection to an unfortunate young man, whose troubles weren't of his own making."

But the Lady Delasin's face was on fire. "*His* troubles!" she cried indignantly. "*He* never even understood that everyone was laughing! While my sisters and I— *Oh!*" Abruptly she burst into tears and then fled weeping from the table.

Rianine's eyebrow arched a little higher. "*That* went well," she observed dryly.

Nagaro was stunned. "I didn't mean to make her cry—" he began in utter dismay.

Merrial immediately broke in. "I'm sure you didn't, Captain. And I know it all happened years ago, but I'm afraid Varsyl Virden's children did suffer rather badly from ridicule as they were growing up. Delasin is the youngest and she's understandably a bit sensitive about it. But don't worry," she added reassuringly. "I'm sure she'll get over it."

Nagaro sat frowning. He knew that Leyel Virden had been anything but unaware of the laughter. In fact, he'd suffered more than Merriel or Delasin could possibly imagine. But he couldn't say so, and he couldn't help feeling guilty as well. Delasin's experiences represented an aspect of the whole affair that he'd never even thought about.

Merriel sighed. "Perhaps I shouldn't have mentioned the family, but I wanted you to know that she would be a suitable match for you. The Virden family are minor nobility, and Varsyl can't expect all three of his daughters to do as well as the eldest—she married Lord Anduar's son. *Not* that you aren't a good catch, Captain. You're very well respected now, even if your parentage is unknown—"

The woman chattered on as if a sheer density of words might fill the gaping hole left by Delasin's departure. Presently she moved on to a discussion of the other guests seated at the table and the changes in relationships that had occurred during his absence. Nagaro wasn't really interested in who was currently courting whom, but he tried to pay attention to spare himself future embarrassment.

He duly noted the fact that Tulevian and her beau were both gone—yes, married, Merrial explained in answer to his question. Brendet was gone as well, betrothed. The rest of the ladies were still there. Rianine was paired with a new Kelorin gentleman, named Hendrel, seated to Nagaro's right. The young man looked more than a little uncertain about the pairing, and Nagaro felt rather sorry for him. The two remaining Leithian ladies, Clarimel and Alliset, were seated to Rianine's left. Clarimel had an arrangement of yellow daffodils in her hair and wore a gown that matched the flowers. Alisset wore lavender silk and a crown of purple iris. The two blond gentlemen across from them—Rese and Vanhold—were familiar to Nagaro (although their pairings had been reversed). Kendira was at the far end of the table, gowned in periwinkle blue and crowned with daisies. She was seated across from a young Kelorin with a thin mustache named Geivian whom Nagaro faintly remembered as having been previously courting Rianine. Kendira was conversing with the man politely and not looking in Nagaro's direction—which suited him very well.

The conversation at the table took a predictable turn even before Merriel reached the end of her social summary, though this time it was carried on by the male guests.

"I say he's been routed." Rese voiced his opinion with casual confidence. "He and his followers have all fled into the forest. They've no stomach for real battle."

"Nonsense!" Hendrel countered with equal assurance. "The man's only gone into hiding while he regroups his forces."

"How can he hide in the woods with five hundred men?" demanded Geivian. "He must have some other plan—"

"I heard it was two hundred—"

"I heard four hundred at least!"

Vanhold leaned forward. "I say we should keep watch on the back roads, in case he tries to find another way south to Lankura."

At this point, Rianine apparently saw her opportunity. "But why shouldn't he come to Lankura?" she inquired airily. "It's no crime. Why are they all trying to stop him?"

"It's the *Leithians* who are trying to stop him," Hendrel muttered darkly.

Rese gestured angrily. "Of course we have to stop him! He means to be king! In defiance of the Council!"

"He should be king! He's Tevren's son, and Darion's heir!"

"He *might* be Darion's heir!"

"Gentlemen! Please!" Merriel spoke firmly. "We're gathered here in celebration of spring, as Queen Semorel would have wished. We shouldn't quarrel. Besides, I don't think any of us really knows who this man is or what he means to do."

Rese and Hendrel, feeling the rebuke, sat in frowning silence. Alliset, however, suddenly burst out with, "But Rianine *does* know who he is! Don't you Rian?"

"How could *she* know?" Vanhold demanded.

Alliset turned to stare at him, round-eyed and serious. "Have you forgotten? She's from Irvenen Wared! And she went home to visit at the turning of the year." The Leithian maid turned eagerly back to Rianine. "Tell them what you found out, Rian!"

All eyes turned to Rianine, who plainly relished the attention. "He comes from a village called East Fork," she said calmly. "He has worked as a blacksmith—*not* a goatherd." Here she shot a look at Clarimel, who returned her a haughty stare. "There has always been some mystery concerning his father, but the woman who claims to be his mother *did* come from Loros Wared."

"Does he have a name?" Hendrel asked.

"Of course. It's Kenthos."

"Kenthos?" Geivain looked thoughtful. "That means 'dextrous,' or 'skillful', doesn't it?"

"Ha!"exclaimed Rese. "That's a name for a tradesman, not a king's heir!"

"It could be just what he goes by," Rianine offered. "It wouldn't have been safe for him to use his real name."

Nagaro had listened silently up to this point, but he now cleared his throat and asked the question he thought mattered the most. "Do you know what his intentions are, Lady Rianine?"

She turned him a serious gaze. "There seems to be no agreement on that, Captain. Some say he means to be king, others say that he's only trying to get back to Loros Wared."

Rese slapped the table. "There *is* no Loros Wared!"

"That's hardly *his* fault!" Hendrel retorted. "If the Leithians hadn't murdered its lord and cut it in pieces—"

A piercing trill of flutes interrupted Hendrel's incipient tirade, and the voice of one of the musicians rang out in the suddenly quiet hall. "Good people! Lords and ladies! There will now be dancing to whet your appetites for the noon repast. Gentlemen, choose your partners for *Road to Seralind*."

There was an immediate sound of scraping chairs and a rising of voices. Most of the occupants of the match table seemed eager to escape the tense atmosphere of the interrupted discussion. Nagaro was one of the few who did not immediately stand up.

Rianine, on the other hand, must have left her chair immediately and gotten around the head of the table very quickly. "Will you give me the first dance, Captain?" she asked sweetly.

For a moment Nagaro could only stare at her. Conventionally it was the man who did the asking, but there was nothing conventional about Rianine. The reversal of roles didn't bother him so much as the lady herself.

"I didn't think you liked to dance," he ventured. "I can't remember seeing you do very much of it."

"How very observant. But don't worry, I won't slow you down. I'm quite a good dancer in fact. Are you going to say yes?"

He frowned, feeling trapped.because he couldn't think of a polite way to refuse. "I... well... all right." He rose and offered her his arm. Then, emboldened by her direct approach, he added, "But I really don't understand why you want to do this."

"*Don't* you?" She was suddenly coquettish, turning her face up to his with a flutter of eyelashes. "Let's just say I have my reasons." He had a moment of pure terror before she shed her flirtatiousness like a glove as she curled her fingers around his forearm. "You were *supposed* to dance with Delasin, you dolt! But you've frightened her off so completely that she'll have to be paired with someone else. If you want an excuse to be at our table, you'd best look like you're interested in *someone*."

"Oh. Right." He'd resisted the urge to protest being called a 'dolt,' reminding himself that Rianine delighted in making people feel foolish. He began walking towards the area set aside for dancing. "But what about Hendrel?"

"Him?" Rianine was contemptuous. "He's already had enough of me. Hopefully Merriel will send him off to look for Delasin and spare me any more effort to be rid of him."

Nagaro winced inwardly, but he was beginning to understand that bluntness could do him no harm with Rianine, so he added, "You don't really think anyone will believe we're interested in each other, do you?"

Rianine emitted a peal of laughter. "Oh, Captain Nagaro," she said. "I think I'm going to enjoy this!"

There were so many folk wishing to dance that two circles were being formed. Having caught a flash of periwinkle blue in the nearer circle, Nagaro promptly set his course for the farther one.

"Wrong circle." Rianine's fingers applied suggestive pressure to his forearm.

"I think not. And I'm steering."

"Pig!" She dug in her nails. "Kendira's in the other one."

"That's exactly why I'm avoiding it." He completed his course and maneuvered them into a starting position in the circle of his choice.

"Don't you want to rub it in just a little?" she hissed in his ear. "You're a much better dancer than Geivian, and prettier too. And she's wearing *your* pearls!"

"They're *her* pearls, and she can wear them whenever she pleases. And if she's found someone agreeable, I'm very glad of it."

Rianine eyed him narrowly. "You did that very well. I almost believe it was an honest answer."

"It was. I'm not a good liar."

"Really? Now there's a desirable trait in a man, though a very rare one in my experience."

With a series of invitational opening bars, the music began.

As it turned out, dancing with Rianine wasn't bad at all. To begin with, she really was quite a good dancer, and they moved together through the figures of Road to Seralind with ease. And there was the added advantage that she didn't try to engage in conversation while moving through the steps. The experience lacked the positive pleasure of dancing with Nevien, but it was much better than having an inept partner or one who insisted on being flirtatious. Rianine just smiled—a smile that was somewhere between smug and serene. He turned her under his arm with a flourish as the music finished and they spun to a stop facing each other.

Rianine gave him a thoughtful look. "Thank you, Captain," she said rather formally.

"Where did you learn to dance?" he asked, curious.

"At home in Irvenen. I did quite a lot of it when I was a girl. I used to enjoy it." She frowned abruptly and turned to snap at a young woman who'd been hovering hopefully. "You can't have him yet, my dear. I'm not through with him."

The young woman looked shocked and immediately backed away.

"That was rather rude."

Rianine shrugged. "I don't care," she said. "Why should I follow the rules? They were all made by *other* people—men, in fact. *For* other people—men, again! If you had liked the look of *her* better than *me*, you could have thanked me politely and asked her to dance. Or, if you liked *me* better than *her*, you could have ignored her and asked me for the next dance instead. While *I'm* supposed to meekly accept whatever you do. Well, you can stick that in the mud and spit on it!"

"It's not as easy as you make it sound," he protested. "And you could have just asked me."

"Really? *Good.* Will you give me the next dance?"

At that moment the flutist signaled the next dance by playing a suggestive snatch of the tune to the *Balandir*.

"I *suppose*." He moved reflexively to take up the starting position for the new dance.

"Good. I want you to tell me that story some time, by the way."

"What story?" He wondered whether the rules ever got a chance when Rianine was involved.

"The one about the murdered lover."

He made a face. "Please don't!" he begged. "It's only a story, and I *really* shouldn't have repeated it."

"It sounds deliciously shocking."

"*My Lady!*"

The musicians rescued him with the opening chords of the Balandir, and for a time he focused on the melody and the steps. When the dance came to a close, however, Rianine was ready before he had a chance to collect his thoughts.

"Next dance, Captain?"

"I... don't mind. But are you sure you wouldn't like to dance with someone else?"

"Positive." She gave him a sultry sidelong glance that sent an unpleasant chill up his spine. "Were you acquainted with Leyel Virden by any chance?"

"*What?*" The chilly fingers tightened their grip.

She cocked her head at him. "The way you leaped to his defense was quite remarkable."

"Oh. I, ah... We never met face to face. In fact," he added with sudden inspiration, "it would have been quite impossible."

"Just sympathy from one fatherless adopted child for another?"

"You could say so. I thought the way she said it was unnecessarily unkind."

"Well, I suppose it *was*, though I don't see why you care so much."

"Do you know anything more about this man Kenthos?" he asked, to change the subject.

She frowned. "Not really. He doesn't seem to be married yet, but otherwise there's not a lot that's really known about him. Some folk say he's too young to be the lost heir. Others disagree. That sort of thing."

A scrap of the tune to *The Ivy Vine*, plucked on a lute, signaled that the next dance was immanent, and Nagaro began to move into position as he asked, "Do *you* think he's the heir of Darion?"

Rianine shrugged. "I suppose it's possible, but I prefer not to make up my mind too quickly about people. For example," she added, giving him a meaningful look, "I thought at first that you were nothing but a rough-polished farm boy, putting on airs. But your sensibilities are much too refined for that."

He was spared the need to hear more of what she thought about him because the music started in earnest at this point and their conversation was interrupted for several minutes while they wove their way around the circle. The dance's conclusion brought the announcement that the afternoon's repast was about to be served, and the circles broke up as folk returned to their seats. Nagaro escorted Rianine back to the match table with considerable relief.

"Three dances in a row!" she said with a conspiratorial wink. "You must be quite smitten with me!"

"Meaning I should feel like I've been hit in the face?" He gave her a look of annoyance, to which she returned a sugary smile.

Being in love wasn't at all like being hit in the face, he reflected as he returned to his seat. It was more like being tangled up in something. He caught himself looking at the table on the dais.

*She was still there.* Hurriedly he pulled his eyes away.

The meal when it came proceeded in the dullest fashion. Everyone seemed determined to avoid the subject of the Heir of Darion, with the result that the conversation revolved around the food, which included glazed, roasted pheasant, new potatoes, and assorted spring greens—all of it excellent, of course.

Rianine was now seated across from Nagaro, having exchanged a meaningful glance with Lady Merriel before sitting down. Delasin, when she finally made her reappearance, sat across from Hendrel by default. The Kelorin maid avoided so much as looking at Nagaro, and seemed to be doing her best to be inconspicuous—not an easy feat for one dressed in orange silk with flame-colored flowers in her hair. Nagaro gave his full attention to the meal and said as little as possible.

When at last the dishes were being collected and the lead musician rose again to announce that the first dance would be *Analul,* Merriel drew Rianine away on some errand. Delasin smiled shyly when Hendrel offered her his arm, and Nagaro was quite happy to be left alone at the table while everyone else returned to the dance foor.

When he thought it was safe, he stole a glance at the dais and saw to his great disappointment that Nevien was no longer sitting there. Perhaps she had endured enough of the merrymaking and had gone upstairs to her chamber. He frowned at the thought, but how could he blame her?

There were still both wine and sothiril on the table so he poured himself a glass of the latter and sat, nursing the drink and staring moodily at the dancers. Analul was a sedate and graceful dance, well suited to full stomachs and there were more folk watching than dancing. From where he sat, Nagaro could only catch an occasional glimpse of periwinkle blue or apricot. Since both seemed to be happily in motion, he supposed that everyone was getting along quite well without him, which was just as well.

And suddenly *she* was there—settling onto the chair beside him with a rustle of dusky green silk and a hint of perfume.

"Here you are," she said breathlessly as she nudged the chair closer and leaned her head against his shoulder. "Oh, Nagaro, I can't *tell* you how glad I am to have you back!"

The physical contact sent a thrill along every nerve in Nagaro's body and it was all he could do not to gasp. Then, as the shock subsided, he had to exert all his will to resist the urge to put his arm around her shoulders. *"Nevien,"* he managed. And then, because her action really seemed unwise, he added, "I don't think you should do that."

"You're right, of course." She straightened. "Someone might draw the wrong conclusion."

Nagaro was more concerned that he might be tempted to do something that would cause people to draw the *right* conclusion.

Nevien turned her face up to his. "I've missed you so!"

He gazed into those wonderfully familiar green eyes. "I missed you too." *Vothra, how he had missed her!* He thought her face looked rather pinched. "How are you feeling?" he inquired, and added, "You look a little better." Then he kicked himself for the implication that she still looked unwell and had looked worse.

Nevien seemed un-offended. "I am feeling a little better, physically," she told him. "I'm getting more sleep, though I still haven't much appetite. I expect it will take time." She paused as a shadow passed across her face, then shook it off, and said, "I want to thank you for what you did for Mother."

He shook his head. "You shouldn't thank me. I wasn't sure it would work, and it's Vothra that makes it work, really, anyway."

Her eyes grew momentarily distant. "It was such an amazing thing," she murmured. "Feeling Vothra in my mind."

"Yes it is." He was suddenly immensely glad that she had joined the circle. *It was something they had shared. Something they would be able to talk about that had nothing to do with the past he dared not mention...*

"I'm sorry I didn't warn you better," she said, "about my mother's fantasies. I could have told you she imagined us to be courting—even being engaged. But I wasn't sure she'd speak of it, and—"

"It's all right," he said hastily. "I understand." He read nothing in her face but earnest concern. *Nothing to say that she wished those fantasies were real...* To change the subject he said, "You're not wearing mourning."

She shook her head. "How could I possibly wear gray today—for the Festival of Flowers? Mother would never have wanted that. I *am* still in mourning, though, officially. I've asked for six months before the courtships are allowed to begin again, and the Council has agreed."

"Well, that's something." In fact he was more glad to hear it than he dared admit. *There would be six more months before he'd have to endure watching other men doing what he could not.* He dragged his thoughts away from that yawning chasm, and said, "At least no one will expect you to dance today."

"No. And it's such a relief. I'm not ready to dance—not with *them*. It would be nice to dance with you, but you've been Devral's proxy, so we'd better not. I did see you dancing with Rianine, though."

"Yes. It was supposed to be Delasin, but I'm afraid I snapped at her."

"You did?" Nevien looked shocked. "Nagaro, that's not like you. Is that why she ran away? I thought perhaps she was ill."

"No, she's all right—except that I upset her. It was over something I really shouldn't have brought up. I tried to apologize, but it didn't seem to work. So I danced with Rianine—just for show. If I thought *she* was interested in me romantically I'd be looking for a fast horse and a short road out of town!"

Nevien actually laughed. "What? As bad as that?" She sobered. "You needn't worry, though. There's a... a woman back in Irvenen... that she speaks of sometimes. They can't be together, so she's not very happy I guess. I think she takes it out on the rest of the world."

"Oh. Is that it."

"She's really not a bad person."

They sat a little awkwardly in silence. Nagaro was trying to adjust to the idea of Rianine as a woman frustrated in love, and realizing with a shock that they had something in common.

Nevien must have had one eye on the dais because she suddenly said, "There's Father, huddled with some of the Council again. They're talking about Darion's heir, I'm sure. How can he do that so soon after losing Mother?"

"Maybe he's trying to take his mind off of the loss."

Nevien shifted in her seat. "That's what he *says*, of course, but she's not even a month gone—" The princess stopped, and hugged herself. "I can't stop thinking about her." Her voice caught and she looked away.

"*Nevien*—" He began to reach out, caught himself, and withdrew his hand just before his fingers touched her cheek. "I wish there were something I could do," he said helplessly.

She apparently hadn't seen the gesture, but she looked up, her eyes glistening with tears. "Actually, there... there *is* something you could do," she said in a choking voice. "If you're willing."

"Why? What is it?"

"You know that Mother had her charities? And I used to go with her?" Nevien spoke with hopeful urgency. "I... I'd let it all slip, and I have to pick it up again. I'm supposed to visit the Ivy House Orphanage on Eighth Day, and it would be wonderful if you'd come with me. It's... it's just so hard to face them alone, right now. I mean, Merriel will come, of course, but the children don't want to see *her*. They want to see the princess. If I bring them Captain Nagaro, they won't feel cheated if I'm not at my best." She was looking at him pleadingly. "You *will* come, won't you?" She made a move to wipe her eyes with the sleeve of her gown and seemed to think better of it.

A part of his mind knew it would be wiser to beg off—to say he was very sorry, but he had duties. But what he heard himself say was, "Of course I will, Nevien. I'd be glad to help."

"Oh, thank you!" The smile she gave him would have melted an ice flow. "You're a dear man, Nagaro!" She brushed at her eyes with the back of her hand. "But now I'm afraid I have to go back to the high table." She rose, giving his arm a grateful squeeze, and was gone in a rustle of silk, leaving him to wonder what trouble he'd just made for himself.

## Chapter 11

# Family Secrets

He sat alone with the scent of Nevien's perfume and a tightness in his throat. The perfume, he suddenly realized, was her mother's. She was doing her best to take her mother's place, to assume the dead queen's duties, become her mother, as it were. *She wasn't a queen yet, but she would be soon enough, and he could do nothing to rescue her from that fate.* He realized, then, that she wouldn't wish to be rescued. Nevien wasn't one to shrink from responsibilities. Such steadfastness was part of what he admired about her.

After a moment, he stirred. He really wanted to leave, now that he'd seen her, but he knew he ought to stay for a little while. *Dance a few more dances for appearances...* He pushed his chair back, stood up, turned—and nearly collided with a man who had apparently just stepped up to speak to him.

Nagaro had never seen the man before, yet he knew him—with a cold, gut-twisting certainty. The man was Kelorin, his age somewhere in the vicinity of fifty-five years, his black hair heavily peppered with gray, his eyes of deepest Kelorin blue. The expression in those eyes was deeply, tragically melancholy. The lines on the man's high brow and at the corners of his mouth were etched by some deep sorrow. All of this Nagaro took in instantly, but what struck him with such shocking force was the unmistakable family resemblance. Even before the man spoke, he knew without question that he was in the presence of the brother of his beloved Lady Guardian, Maramine.

"Your pardon, Captain," the man said solemnly. "Allow me to introduce myself. I am Varsyl Virden." He made a small bow and upon straightening put out his hand. "You met my youngest daughter, Delasin, earlier."

Nagaro returned the bow. "I... yes. I'm sorry, My Lord. I'm afraid that I upset her." He shook the proffered hand with what cordiality he could muster. *This man had hurt Maramine, and deeply.* Yet he saw none of the coldness or haughtiness he'd always imagined in the man. "I, ah, repeated something I'd heard, without weighing the impact of my words. It was very clumsy of me."

"Please say no more, Captain. Not here." There was a fleeting humorless smile. "But I would like to speak with you, if I may, in private. Will you accompany me out onto the terrace?"

Nagaro swallowed. "Of course, My Lord," he said, with rising dread. There was simply no excuse not to.

Varsyl led the way around the dance floor and between the tables on the hall's farther side, making for a pair of large double doors. The doors stood open to admit air, and the two men passed easily through them and out onto the terrace beyond. It was a small paved court, that was surrounded on three sides by wings of the palace. The fourth side faced the palace gardens and was separated from them by a fountain and a low wall pierced by a pair of gates. A dozen small tables were set out, scattered about the flagstone surface. It was afternoon and the day was fair and warm. Some of the guests had come out to take advantage of the fair weather, mostly couples who were crossing the terrace on their way to take a stroll in the gardens.

The terrace lay on the palace's north flank so that the building's shadow fell across a part of it. Varsyl determinedly made for one of the tables in that shadow, one placed some distance from the doors through which they had come. The Kelorin lord pulled out a chair for himself and gestured for Nagaro to take one opposite. Nagaro sat down, noting that no one else was near enough to risk their being overheard. He also noted for the first time, as Varsyl took his seat, that the man wasn't wearing a sword, though he surely had the right to carry one.

Varsyl regarded him appraisingly for a long moment during which Nagaro's apprehension continued to rise. Finally the other man said, "I have heard you are a fair-minded man, Captain. Indeed, I presume it was fair-mindedness that led you to speak to Delasin as you did."

"I meerly thought it needlessly unkind that she was in such a hurry to distance herself from Leyel Virden. That may have been what you call 'fair-mindedness', but it doesn't excuse my repeating rumors and unsubstantiated tales—"

Varsyl raised a hand to stop him. "That is fair all around, Captain, but I wonder where you heard the tale you spoke of."

Nagaro's apprehension began to congeal towards panic. "I... I don't recall exactly where I first heard it," he said hastily, and quite truthfully in the strictest sense. "It was a long time ago."

"Ah. Yes, it would have been." Varsyl appeared to relax. "Well, it's no matter," he said, sounding relieved. He sat for a moment, frowning at the table top, then raised his eyes and said, "There were never many who knew the true tale."

Nagaro swallowed. "My Lord?

Varsyl's gaze slid away, past Nagaro's shoulder, towards the fountain and the garden beyond. "It's been a carefully guarded family secret," he said quietly. "But it is time, I think, that the Virden family ceased to hide behind a lie."

"But, My Lord..." Nagaro had to swallow again, his mouth suddenly very dry. "Surely Leyel *was* adopted, just as Delasin said."

The deep blue eyes in the tragic face came back to focus upon him. "No, Captain. The true tale is closer to the one you just apologized for repeating."

Nagaro's mind reeled. *Maramine, his mother?* Blood pounded in his ears.

Varsyl apparently misinterpreted his thunderstruck look. "Yes," he said earnestly. "It's true. It was I who killed my sister's lover. Never, I think, has brother done sister a greater harm—and never regretted it more, of that I am sure. But I mean to tell you the whole tale, Captain, if you will listen. And you, who are known for your fair-mindedness, will be the first to judge it."

Somehow Nagaro managed to nod his assent. He so desperately needed to hear what Varsyl had to tell.

The Kelorin lord did not begin immediately, however. He dropped his eyes to the tabletop again as he seemed to collect his thoughts, then raised them to stare past Nagaro once more, focusing on some imagined vision. His expression was very grave when he finaly began to speak.

"I want you to know that I loved my sister dearly," he said. "She was five years my senior—intelligent, kind, beautiful... Our mother died giving birth to me, and Maramine took her place in rearing me from the time she was ten. I had most of my tutelage from her, as far as book-learning was concerned. Our father, on the other hand, had earned renown as a fighter in the border wars over the years, and he made sure that I was well tutored in the use of arms. As soon as possible, he sent me off to the southern border under the charge of his trusted captain-at-arms to 'prove' myself in combat against the Jinari, and be 'made a man.' I was still seventeen when I set forth, and barely nineteen when I returned from that campaign."

Varsyl sighed, pausing, as one who remembers most unwillingly. His eyes suddenly came back to Nagaro's face as he picked up his thread. "Looking back, I can see that I was terribly young and inexperienced," he said, "though I don't mean to excuse my actions, Captain, when I say that—only to explain them a little, to put them in perspective. I fancied myself quite the warrior, I'm afraid, having put my father's lessons to *practical use* in the south. I had shed the blood of foes, and I regret to say that I was proud of it. I'd been absent a year and a half, and I came home, all brashness and swagger, to find my father in a towering passion.

"I walked right into it. He was ranting with rage. My sister had been deflowered, he said, by a traveling minstrel who had played shamelessly upon her sweet nature and love of music. The man had gotten her with child and said he wished to marry her, but he was an itinerant bard. He would surely bring her low... abandon her... ruin her life."

Varsyl paused once more. Pain briefly contorted his features before he shook it off, and heaved a sigh. "Well," he said with a bitter grimace, "I took it all for perfect truth, I'm sorry to say—without troubling to get any information from any other source—and of course I was outraged. The situation plainly cried out for vengeance, and who better to mete it out than I, fresh from the southern battlefields with my sword at my hip?" Varsyl's mouth twisted. "The minstrel was easy to find—*unfortunately*—" Varsyl choked. "If only he hadn't been! If only there had been more *time!* Time for my temper cool... or if I'd spoken to Maramine—any number of things—and all might have gone very differently..."

Varsyl had been speaking with increasing anguish and now his voice trailed off. He put his hand to his brow and bowed his head as if overcome with emotion. When at length he continued, he spoke through his fingers, and his voice was tight.

"But no, Captain. I found him easily, as I said. I had grabbed a spare sword, since—being a minstrel—he didn't carry one. I told him I was prepared to die for my sister's honor and I hoped he was as well. He tried to speak to me—to say, I think, that no one needed to die. But I wouldn't listen. I threw the weapon at his feet and told him to defend himself, if he were a man. And I suppose his pride wouldn't let him do otherwise, or perhaps he thought that right would prevail."

Varsyl lowered the hand that was shielding his eyes. His gaze caught Nagaro's now and held it. "He'd had some training, as nearly every man does for the sake of practicality, And he fought hard—desperately, I would say. He had to, because I pressed him to the extremity of his skill and beyond it. And when I had him at my mercy, I... I ran him through the heart, thinking in my blindness that I was somehow putting the world right—" Varsyl's voice broke. "And *then*, only *then*, did I go to find my sister. *And do you know what she told me?*"

Wordlessly Nagaro shook his head. The other man's eyes were full of terrible pain.

"She told me that she and the minstrel—Beloras was his name—had been in love for more than a year. She said that Father was opposed to her marrying a man of such background, and that the getting of a child had been their plan. They'd hoped it would induce Father to relent. Instead, of course, it had brought this *catastrophe*." Varsyl drew a breath. "She told me that I had destroyed her love... her life... her every hope for happiness. She said she never wanted to speak to me again—that she wished never again to look upon my face—"

Varsyl broke off, closing his eyes. He brought his clenched fist to his mouth and bit the knuckle hard.

"I'm sorry..." Nagaro didn't know what else to say. This man had been one of the villains of his youth, but now that he'd met Varsyl and seen the depth of the man's remorse, that role seemed entirely undeserved.

Varsyl's eyes sprang open. "*You're* sorry!" he exclaimed. "You are much kinder to me than I deserve, Captain. Your tale called it murder, and that isn't far from the truth. Technically it was a challenge, freely accepted. We were equivalently armed, and only a half a dozen years apart in age, with him the elder. But Beloras was no great swordsman, whereas I—and I don't mean to boast—was well trained, well practiced, and gifted besides. It would have taken some trick of Lokundas for Beloras to have bested me. I wish with all my soul that he *had* bested me—even slain me—but Lokundas played me a far worse trick that day by allowing me to win that fight!"

Varsyl fell silent and sat staring straight ahead, unseeing.

Nagaro also sat silent, shaken. Finally he found his voice and asked, huskily, "What happened after that?"

Varsyl spoke leadenly. "Once I understood that Maramine was speaking from the heart about the love between herself and Beloras, I was beside myself with grief and remorse. I took to my chamber—even to my bed—for days. I'm not sure how many. I swore I would never again wear a sword, nor lay my hand on one—and I haven't, from that day to this. My father was very gentle with me. I think he was dismayed both by the extremity of my remorse and by the fatal outcome of the challenge. He may also have blamed himself for his intemperate words. In any case, he styled the whole thing as a terrible accident, and I believe he paid a substantial sum in recompense to Beloras' mother. The man had no father living, or things might have gone differently for me."

"And your sister?" Somehow Nagaro managed to get the words out. "She... she bore her child?"

Varsyl sighed. "By the time I reemerged into the light of day, she was gone. Father had sent her away to a small country estate called Averwin to bear the child. He wouldn't let me see her or even write to her. Eventually I learned that she had declared she would never marry, and that Father had allowed her to dwell alone at Averwin—to keep the child and rear it out of the public eye—on condition that she give him her word never to say that the child was her natural son. The tale she was to tell was that the child was adopted. That, you see, is how the lie began."

For a long moment, Nagaro felt as if the world had ceased to turn. Varsyl was staring past him again, abstractedly—which was just as well, because he couldn't at that moment have made any coherent conversation. *Maramyn had been with child when she'd come to Averwin. And if he hadn't been that child, what could have become of it?* But how could she have looked into his eyes and denied being his mother when he asked her directly? Surely she would have made an exception in his case to the promise she'd made to her father—*she who always spoke the truth... but who also always kept her word.*

He realized that Varsyl was speaking again and wrenched his thoughts away from the madly spinning paradox.

"—it was a lie my father cultivated all his life, with considerable success." Varsyl appeared to be speaking to a point somewhere past Nagaro's left shoulder. "I tacitly acquiesced to it, since I never openly contradicted it—though I never openly repeated it either. It was my father who made sure the lie was taught to my children. Their mother never even knew it wasn't true to the day she died." Varsyl's eyes sought Nagaro's at last. "It is only since my father's death last year that I have considered telling my three daughters the truth. *I* never gave my father any oath, after all, and I am now Lord of Virden Wared." Varsyl paused, his face suddenly full of concern. "Are you feeling unwell, Captain?"

Nagaro swallowed. "I... no, I'm fine." *How could she have lied to him?*

"Is it the story then? I've shocked you, haven't I?"

"What? How could you shock me? My own daughter was born out of wedlock." *If Maramine's own child had died, she might have adopted another... mightn't she?*

"But *you* never tried to conceal the fact!"

"That's true." Nagaro gestured distractedly. "But I... I couldn't very well have. Everyone on Pakoa knew what had happened." He paused, struck by the wretchedness in the other man's eyes. "Please don't ask me to judge you, My Lord," he said hurriedly. "You made mistakes, serious ones, but you know what they were. You can't undo them—" *If the man would just stop looking at him like that.* Nagaro felt he had to get away. He needed to think. "It's plain that you're sorry," he continued. "There's nothing more—"

"—except forgiveness!" Varsyl's face writhed. "If only I could have heard her say that she forgave me! I didn't dare to go to her. She'd said she didn't want to see me! I'd tried to write to her, but Father intercepted my letters! I thought there would be *time*, if I waited until Father died. But *she* died first! And now I'll never be able to hear those words!"

Nagaro licked dry lips. He pushed his chair back. "Talk to Vothra," he said desperately. "Vothra forgives everything—"

"But I'm unworthy!"

Nagaro shook his head. "No one is ever unworthy in Vothra's eyes. The Spirit told me that." He stood up. "Please just try! I... I'm sorry, Varsyl. I have to go—"

He turned and fled, not looking back—not wanting to see whether Maramine's brother might be following him. Entering the Great Hall, he paused just long enough to mark his course between the tables and around the groups of dancers. Then he walked, keeping his head down, moving as quickly as he could without drawing attention to himself. *He had to get away.*

He had the exit doors in view when his way was suddenly barred by a female figure in pale yellow satin. "Here you are, Captain," said Lady Rianine. "Someone said you'd stepped out with Varsyl Virden. It's time you gave me another dance."

"Please, My Lady, not now!" he begged. "I... I have to go—"

"So early?" She arched a brow at him.

"Yes. Rianine... *please!*"

For a moment she appeared to be contemplating some barb, but something in his face or voice must have changed her mind. "All right, Captain," she said, stepping aside. "If anyone should ask, shall I tell them that you're indisposed?"

"Tell them whatever you like."

He moved past her. It was a risky thing to have said, perhaps, but at that moment he didn't care.

Moments later, he had reclaimed his sword, and a few moments after that, his horse. The afternoon sun shown warm on the city streets. The cobblestones rang merrily under Thunder-Heels' iron-shod hooves, and there was a fine, gentle air from the sea. A few wisps of cloud, like spun sugar, decorated the brilliant blue arch overhead.

Nagaro was blind to the fairness of the day. He couldn't slow the whirling maelstrom of his thoughts, couldn't focus his mind. When the gate of the Fleet Compound rose before him, much too soon, he turned the stallion's head hard to the left, seeking the well-worn track that ran beside the river. He gave the horse his head then, and with a joyous snort, Thunder-Heels sprang away, devouring the ground in long eager strides.

***

Nagaro sat at the little-used writing desk in his quarters, frowning at a blank sheet of paper. It had been a long ride, a good ride. Some combination of the speed and rhythm, the wind in his face, and nearly two hours of reflection had brought coherence and a degree of clarity.

He had begun with his conviction that Varsyl had told him the truth as the man knew it. The story wasn't something a man would make up, and Varsyl had believed he was speaking to a disinterested stranger. The man's pain had simply been too raw to be feigned.

The assumption of Varsyl's sincerity had led to acceptance of the fact that his Lady Guardian hadn't told him the full tale of how and why she had come to Averwin. But accepting that he must be Maramine's son was another matter. It was the simplest interpretation of the facts known to Varsyl, but Maramine had specifically denied being his mother. Nagaro could understand her keeping certain details of her private life from him, but it was hard to think of her lying outright about something that concerned him so closely. Beloras also seemed an unlikely father for him from what he knew of the man—a minstrel, and a poor swordsman—though that was hardly conclusive.

Nagaro drew a long breath and rubbed his forehead, glancing at the un-stoppered ink bottle. It had taken him half an hour to conclude that Varsyl's information didn't resolve the issue of his parentage. The rest of the time had been spent wrestling with the memory of Varsyl's tormented face. The man's entire adult life had been lived under a burden of guilt for a single terrible mistake he had made at the age of nineteen. Maramine had come to terms with what had happened and moved on. Varsyl had been unable to do so—for nearly thirty years—all for the want of his sister's forgiveness. Nagaro had come to realize during his ride that he had it in his power to ease the man's suffering, if only he could find the courage to reveal his identity to this one person.

He knew with a moral certainty that he had to do this. Maramine would have surely wished him to, and the Vothrin Writings were clear: Pain *must* be answered with compassion, need with acts of kindness, remorse with forgiveness and mercy. To do any less was to stray from Vothra's Path. Nagaro frowned. He'd advised Varsyl to talk to Vothra. The Benevolent Spirit surely knew everything that Nagaro knew, and everything Maramine had known. Vothra could answer Varsyl's need—and Nagaro's questions as well, for that matter—but Vothra would do no such thing. Wisdom, not knowledge, was Vothra's stock in trade. No, Varsyl Virden's sole hope of finding peace before he died depended on Nagaro telling the man what he knew. He picked up the quill, fingering it distractedly.

Broaching the matter to Varsyl face-to-face, he knew was beyond his strength. But he could write the man a letter. He had come to that decision by the end of his ride, but he was having trouble putting pen to paper. Varsyl would doubtless wish to speak to him again, and he thought he could bear that, as long as the crucial fact of his identity were already known and didn't have to be repeated—but it would have to be a very carefully worded letter. Varsyl would only be likely to believe the message if he believed in the messenger, so Nagaro would have to make his identity clear without stating it outright.

Very deliberately, he dipped the quill into the bottle of ink. *It would take some time to compose this, but he had time.* Taru and Pavo had gone to Wotana and weren't expected back until the following afternoon. And he'd eaten well enough at the palace that he could easily skip supper. He withdrew the quill from the ink bottle, stared at the paper for several long seconds, and began to write. He started over half a dozen times before finally producing a letter that satisfied him.

It read:

*Zirda: I have undertaken to write these words only because I have reason to believe they may ease your mind, and I trust you will keep this letter in strictest confidence. Concerning your sister, I can tell you with certainty that she forgave you. I know this because she told me so on more than one occasion. Had she lived long enough for you to have sought her out, I believe she would have told you so herself.*

*I can tell you also that your sister found her own peace. Her life was full, and in no way wasted. She devoted her days to painting, to music, and to studying the teachings of Vothra. She also sewed clothes, cared for the sick, and performed many acts of kindness for the ordinary folk around her. All who knew her loved her.*

*I will always honor the memory of your sister for the sake of what she gave to me. She raised me, and cared for me. She taught me my lessons, and showed me by her example how to follow the Path. She moved through the world with grace and wisdom and serenity. And although her death was untimely, she bade me not to grieve long for her because her spirit was going to become one with Vothra.*

*Please know that you have my respect and my good will. I wish you well, and may Vothra bring you peace.*

He read the letter over carefully one final time to make sure it said everything he wanted it to say without containing anything that could do him harm if it were to fall into the wrong hands. Finally he signed it simply *A Friend*, folded it, and sealed it with candle wax to which he added no impression. Nor did he write any name or directive on the outside of the folded paper. The earlier drafts he put into the fire, making sure they were completely reduced to ash, which he stirred to powder with the poker.

By the time he'd finished, the evening had grown late, so he put the sealed letter into his seaman's chest for safekeeping, intending to find some unobtrusive way to deliver it. He then went to his bed, exhausted, but with a sense that he had chosen the right course.

# Chapter 12

# Rastian's Request

The carriage lurched as one of its wheels struck something in the roadway. Nagaro reflexively grasped the edge of the seat to steady himself. Nevien, seated across from him, did the same. In mourning dress again, her face was hidden by a black veil, but her startled intake of breath was audible. Lady Merriel, beside the princess, clutched at the seat and exclaimed, "*Mercy!*" She then drew the curtain aside from the coach window to put her head out and call up to the driver to have a care. The man's response was audible, but not intelligible.

Merriel drew the curtain back across the window. "Someone had turned up some paving stones," she informed them. "He said he couldn't swing wide enough to avoid hitting them." She paused, watching Nagaro. "Are you not quite comfortable, Captain?" she asked. "You seem rather quiet this afternoon."

"No. I mean, yes. I'm quite comfortable."

It was not entirely true, of course, but his present discomfort wasn't physical. It derived from the fact that he was riding in a carriage with Nevien, which inevitably reminded him of the last time he had done so, nearly eight years ago. He'd been married to her then, nominally at least. He'd been sitting beside her rather than across from her, and there had been no need for a chaperon—and not just because they were married. He'd been sitting exactly where instructed, rigidly upright under the control of heskial, facing the front of the carriage and making no physical contact with his wife—while she had been sitting as far away from him on the seat as possible without actually appearing to be cowering away. *Doubtless a consequence of his actions of the previous night—actions that hadn't been truly his own, but which he nevertheless remembered all too clearly...*

With a conscious wrench, he pulled himself back from the yawning pit that the memory had opened. He glanced at Nevien. She'd insisted that he should ride inside with her and Merriel, after thanking him again, warmly but rather formally, for agreeing to accompany them. She had swept aside his hints that he could ride beside the carriage on his horse. He sighed. She'd spoken no other words since, and he could make out nothing of her features through the veil. It was quite understandable that she was preoccupied, but he still wished that she would say something, and he didn't dare try to draw her out.

Merriel was also silent at the moment, apparently watching the princess solicitously.

With no distracting conversation, Nagaro's mind ran back over the events of the morning, which weren't actually any more comforting. *The letter might have been delivered by now.*

He had taken the opportunity to visit Narei briefly in her palace room before the visit to the orphanage, and then had sought out Brandle in the guards' quarters. Brandle had readily agreed to deliver the letter to Varsyl, who was staying in the palace. The big Leithian had scarcely raised an eyebrow at Nagaro's request to be sure there were no witnesses to the delivery, and that he keep the matter in confidence. He'd noted the absence of writing on the letter's exterior and asked, stone-faced, whether it was intended to be anonymous. Nagaro had explained that it was actually necessary that Varsyl be informed of the letter's origin. Brandle had then completely spoiled the effect of everything he'd done up to that point by giving Nagaro a broad wink and saying, "Well, I know this can't be what it looks like, because you're not that kind of man."

Nagaro caught himself frowning and hastily smoothed his features. He knew the letter was the right thing to do, but he squirmed at the thought of what it revealed and feared what what happen as a result. Taru's reaction to hearing about the whole thing that morning hadn't helped.

The young Turo had nearly choked, and said, "Ye wrote a *letter* to Lord Varsyl? Are ye daft? What if he tells someone?"

"I asked him not to—"

"*What if he does anyway?*"

"I don't believe that he will. Why would he turn about and hurt me when I'd just done him a service?"

"Ye think ye can *trust* him, when it sounds like he killed your father?"

"It's the right thing to do according to Vothrin teachings, Taru. And I don't actually think Beloras was my father—"

"Because he wasn't a swordsman?"

"Well, yes. I mean, he was a minstrel— and I can't sing or play. And Maramine *told* me she wasn't my mother!"

Hoping for reassurance, Nagaro had sought Pavo's opinion. Pavo's response had come with the young Hashtep's usual deliberate earnestness. "I think you are right, Nagaro. It is not good for man to think his sister hate him all his life. And how can mother bear to live all her life without hearing her son call her 'mother' even one time?"

Nagaro liked that argument—

He started, realizing that Merriel was speaking to him and he had caught only a few words. "I beg your pardon, My Lady," he said hurriedly. "What did you say about ships?

She gave him a politely indulgent smile. "It's not important, Captain. I just wondered if you know what they mean to do with all the captured Mahuk ships and men?"

"Oh, that." Nagaro was relieved to have a safe topic of conversation. "I suggested to the Council that they send all of the men, and all but two of the ships, back to the Emperor."

Lady Merriel's eyes widened. "Send them *back*, just like that? Why, Captain?"

"It's not 'just like that.' We would be sending the ships back *without* their slaves. And they paid a high price in men's lives in this attack, just as we did at Paktaar. Emperor Baalkir held his ships back at Paktaar when Kuran retreated, and then escorted our fleet to the edge of Mahuk waters. They could have sunk all the ships—killed everyone—but the Emperor had made his point. Now we've made ours."

"Oh. I think I see." Merriel looked impressed.

"It will also show that surrendering to us is a safe and honorable option."

"I see that, too. But why did you say we should return all but *two* of the ships, Captain?"

"Those two will replace the two that were destroyed when the shipyard was burned, which is reasonable. We'll still have to rebuild the shipyard, of course. We *should* build one or two more, besides, in other ports. I've told them that. And that we should send Roheed—the Emperor's nephew—back with a repetition of the message we sent before Paktaar: The Mautep must not violate our waters with intent to steal from us, or to attack our ships, our ports, or our fishermen. They must take no more slaves, and we will free any slaves that are brought into our waters."

Merriel pursed her lips. "It makes sense to me, Captain. Do you think the Council will do all that?"

"I don't know. Kuran told me they're calling it Lord Anduar's plan rather than mine, because Anduar is pushing for it."

Nevien moved suddenly. "I didn't know it was your plan, Nagaro. But they mean to do exactly as you just said." She reached up and twitched her veil aside. Her green eyes met his. "And I'm sorry I've not been better company."

"It's all right," he said quickly. "But how do you know what they're planing to do?"

"My father keeps me informed of everything he thinks is important."

"He shouldn't trouble you—" he began, and stopped because she was shaking her head.

"He has to," she said ruefully. "If I am to be queen, I may have to advise my husband—whoever he is. So I have to understand everything, though I've been so distracted lately that half of it goes right past my ear. Almost anything about Darion's heir goes past me—I'm *that* weary of it. But if it's about *you*, I pay attention. And this time he told me that they mean to keep two of the ships and send the others back with all the captured men. Kuran will lead the escort, and you and your ship are to be part of it. Apparently the decision was unanimous."

"*Unanimous?* I don't believe it!"

"Well, Father said it was."

Nagaro frowned. "It's such a complete turn-about for some of them—Odus and Pendrik in particular. Anduar must have been persuasive."

Lady Merriel had been looking out the window as they spoke. "I don't like to interrupt," she said, "but we're almost at the orphanage."

"Oh dear!" Nevien was instantly distressed. "We haven't told him what we want him to do!"

Merriel leaned forward and addressed Nagaro. "After the coach stops, the driver will come around and open the door, Captain. You should step down first, then hand me down, and then the princess. Do you know how that's done?"

"I believe so."

"Good." She gave him an encouraging smile. "Then all you have to do is talk to the children while Nevien and I oversee the unloading of the gifts we've brought. Tira Timbrel, the House Mother, will introduce you. There's a man who works there who will do the lifting."

Nagaro had noticed a number of boxes and baskets on the carriage top before they'd left the palace. "What did you bring?" he asked.

"Oh, just little things." Merriel waved a hand. "Some treats—fruits and nuts and sweet rolls. And some little things they can use, like combs, ribbons, leather belts and buckles, lacings for shoes..."

The carriage was slowing as Lady Merriel recited the inventory. She paused as the vehicle rounded a corner and came to a rocking halt. "Did you think to bring anything, Captain," she asked with sudden concern.

Nagaro shrugged. "Just some string."

"*String?*" Both women spoke in puzzled chorus.

Nagaro had no opportunity to respond, however, because just at that moment the door swung open, revealing the spry little figure of the driver, who bowed and ushered them out with a sweep of his arm.

Nagaro gave Merriel a hasty smile and stepped down from the carriage into a small walled yard, between two buildings, that contained some work tables, a cistern and water trough, and a little bit of struggling greenery. There was also a group of people standing in front of the orphanage's front door. The group consisted of two women, a man, and about fifteen children of both sexes, their ages ranging from toddler to stripling. They were all staring at him. If Nevien had hoped to surprise them with his presence she had clearly succeeded.

Behind him, Merriel hissed, "Captain, your hand, please!"

Hastily he extended a hand to help Merriel descend the two small steps from the carriage. Disappointed children's whispers were heard, saying, "*Who is that?*" and "*Where's the princess?*" followed by urgent shushing. He turned back to the carriage interior, giving Nevien a crooked smile as he helped her down to stand beside Merriel.

"There she is!" cried a childish voice. "I told you!"

Nagaro finally turned around and determinedly approached his small audience,

"And that's Captain Nagaro!"

"It *can't* be!"

"It *is!* I saw him in Market Street."

His gaze swept the astonished, awe-struck faces. "Hello," he said as he stuck his hand into his pocket. "Would anyone like me to show you some things you can do with sticks, a little string, and a pen knife?"

***

"Captain Nagaro, you're amazing! Is there anything you can't do?"

It was nearly two hours later, and they were in the carriage again, sitting in their respective seats and on their way back to the palace. Lady Merriel's round face was aglow as she regarded him across the confined space.

Nagaro laughed. "A great many things—sing, or play any kind of instrument, for example." He fell silent, suddenly serious.

The chaperon seemed not to notice. "You were perfect with the children! Wasn't he, My Lady?"

Nevien was resting her head against the high seat back. Her veil was still thrown back so that he could see that her eyes were closed. She looked tired, but she opened her eyes long enough to shoot Merriel a glance of acknowledgment. "Yes," she said. Her voice sounded tired too, but the smile that briefly brightened her face was genuine. "I thought he'd be good with children after watching him with his daughter, and I was right." Her eyes sought Nagaro's face. "They scarcely noticed the treats we brought."

Nagaro frowned. "They surely will, now that we've gone."

"Of course." Another fleeting smile. "I said I wanted you to distract them, and you did. Tira Timbrel wants you to come again the next time. She said the children all know you've had to make your way in the world without any parents or family, just as they'll have to do, and it's good for them to see how well you've managed. You will come again, won't you?"

"Yes," he said without hesitation. "I'd like that."

"He could come to the other orphanages, too," Merriel interjected.

Nagaro gave the older woman a startled look. "What, there are more orphanages?"

"Oh yes," Merriel informed him brightly. "This one takes all comers, but there's one devoted to the children of fishermen, and another for the children of men slain in the wars."

Nevien shifted in her seat. "I was going to ask if you could come with us on Fourth Day, next week, Captain," she said hopefully. "It's the Old Widows' Home, not an orphanage, but I remember that you mended an old woman's roof last year at Mid-Winter."

There was eagerness in her voice and a plea in her eyes, and Nagaro felt himself on slippery ground. "I'd be glad to do that," he said, honestly but cautiously. "But I'll have to speak to Kuran. The Fleet may have some other need of me."

"Oh. I understand." Nevien was plainly disappointed. "Of course you mustn't neglect your duties."

"I'll come if I can," he said hastily, because he couldn't bear seeing that look on her face. The words earned him a smile that made his heart sing.

"You're a dear man, Captain."

For a little while they rode in silence except for the rattle of the carriage as it jolted over the paving stones. Eventually Lady Merriel must have felt the silence becoming awkward, for she said, "I must say you held up very well, My Lady."

Nevien sighed. "Most of it wasn't too hard, until two of the older girls told me about how they'd lost their mothers. They said they had to carry on in spite of missing them, but that it got better after a while. They were trying to cheer *me* up—and they're only children! It quite put me to shame—" Her voice broke.

Merriel immediately reached for the princess's hand on the seat beside her. "There, there, dear. It's been hardly any time at all for you—and it *will* get better."

"Yes it will," Nagaro put in. "Though it will take time because you knew your mother for such a long time. I never missed mine because

I never knew her." He frowned. He'd *thought* he never knew her. He *had* missed Maramine, although he'd been distracted, first by the hel of heskial and then by being taken as a slave.

Nevien sighed. "You're both very kind," she said and gave them a wan smile. Her eyes were moist.

No one seemed to know what to say after that, and this time the silence stretched for several minutes, during which the princess closed her eyes again.

Finally Merriel said, "They liked your trick of making a net bag out of knotted string, Captain. Wherever did you learn to do that?"

"In Wotana. The pattern of knots is the same as for a fishing net. Any fisherman's wife on Wotana Bay knows how to make net bags to carry things, like apples or loaves of bread."

Nevien spoke without opening her eyes. "That Wotana is a fishing village isn't it? Somewhere north along the coast. Is that where you were learning to be a fisherman, Captain?"

Nagaro mentally kicked himself, then gave an inward shrug. It wasn't a secret after all, and what could she make of it anyway? "Yes," he said easily. "My friend Taru's family used to live there. Taru's father taught me to fish, but it was his mother who taught me to tie a net."

"You say they *used* to live there?" Merriel seemed to be desperately trying to draw out the conversation.

Nagaro swallowed and tried not to look at Nevien. "They're both dead. The Mautep raiders killed them when Taru and I were taken."

"Oh dear!" Merriel glanced at the princess and bit her lip. "I'm sorry to hear that."

"It's all right," he said hastily. "It was years ago. But I remember them well. They were good people, and I learned a great deal from them."

"Did they teach you how to make the little boats, too—from sticks and leaves and string—with nothing but your pen knife?

"No, that was the gardener. When I was growing up."

Nagaro risked a furtive glance at Nevien. She had her face turned towards the carriage window, but he saw to his dismay that her cheek was wet. He started to rise, thought better of it, and sat down, frowning. *What had he meant to do?*

Lady Merriel had caught his movement and followed his eyes. She shook her head urgently at him and made a little pantomime to show that they should just keep talking. "Well, wherever you learned it," she said with forced cheerfulness, "it was a stroke of genius to try floating them in the horse trough."

A few minutes more of desperate conversation brought them at last to the stable yard. Nevien dropped her veil over her face again as the carriage rolled to a halt. She allowed Nagaro to hand her down from the carriage as he had at the orphanage, but as soon as she had alighted she spoke a few murmured words to Lady Merriel and then bolted for the palace's side door.

Merriel gave him a weak, apologetic smile. "We had best let her go, Captain," she advised. "She wants to be alone." She saw the worry in his eyes. "You said yourself, Captain, that it will take time to get better. If you'll come up with me, though, I'll make a list for you of the charity visits we've planned, along with the dates and times."

On the way back down the stairs with the list, he encountered Brandle coming up.

In answer to his questioning look, the big Leithian patted his tirka. "It's quite safe, Captain," he said. "I've not had a chance to deliver it, ah, *discreetly*. But don't worry, I will." He was watching Nagaro's eyes, and he must have read something there because he added, "Unless you've changed your mind?"

Nagaro swallowed. "No," he said hastily. "I haven't changed my mind." Then he hurried on down the stairs before he was tempted to do exactly that.

***

All the way back to the Fleet Compound his thoughts were a maelstrom of memories and misgivings. It was late afternoon by the time he had returned Thunder-Heels to the stable and set out to return to his quarters. As he rounded the corner of one of the barracks buildings he came to a dead stop. There was a man waiting outside his door, pacing back and forth with obvious impatience. It took exactly one second for Nagaro to recognize Rastian, the son of Lord Rastyl Korven. He immediately broke into a sweat.

For a moment, he frantically considered simply turning around and finding something else to do. Before he could take any action, however, Rastian looked up and saw him.

"Ah! Captain, there you are!" The young Kelorin officer crossed the intervening space in half a dozen strides. His gray eyes weren't as pale as his fathers, but were still disconcerting, although his tone was jovial. He lowered his voice when he spoke again. "Do you know there's to be a gathering tonight at sunset at the Golden Branch?"

"I, ah, yes," Nagaro managed to answer. "Lord Soren told me at the Festival of Flowers." Other matters had put it completely out of his mind, but he now remembered, and it seemed a safe subject.

"Soren!" A frown creased Rastian's brow, to be banished an instant later. "Ah, well. You must come, of course."

"I *must?*"

Rastian gestured impatiently. "You *should* come," he ammended. "They'll be discussing what's to be done about the man who claims to be the heir of Darion."

"Oh." *So that was it.* "I... had assumed that this meeting was called by the Kelorin Faction."

Rastian shifted, frowning. "They're casting the net wider this time. Though it *will* be all Kelorin folk, I'm sure." He leaned closer, speaking earnestly. "You do mean to come, don't you, Captain?"

Nagaro stood his ground. "I hadn't decided," he said stiffly. "I'd like to know more about it. Who will be there? Is... ah... your father coming?"

"I don't know. I've had no word from him since he returned to Irvenen."

"Any other Fleet men?"

"Possibly."

"Lord Kuran, perhaps?"

Rastian glanced at a group of men who were passing by the other end of the barracks and seemed relieved that they were paying no attention. The pale gray eyes swung back to Nagaro. "No, he's too much of a king's man. They wouldn't have told Kuran."

"Ah." Nagaro's mind was moving towards a disquieting conclusion. "Then they wouldn't have invited Lord Anduar either, I expect?"

"*Anduar?*" Rastian laughed a hard little laugh. "If they trusted the Council to handle this, there wouldn't be any need for a gathering!"

"I see."

"Captain, please?" Rastian implored him. "We need to have some sensible people there. A gathering like this will attract all the hot-heads."

Nagaro considered. This was obviously important. Soren, Anduar, and Rastian all wanted him to be there—independently, it appeared. He made a decision.

"All right. I'll go—"

"Excellent!" The pale eyes glinted with satisfaction. "Do you know how to find the Golden Branch on Three Cedars Lane?"

"I've a general idea. Can you give me directions?"

"I'll do better than that. I'll show you. We can ride together."

"That really isn't necessary." Nagaro tried not to show his distaste. "I wouldn't want to trouble you."

"Nonsense!" Rastian smiled broadly in a way obviously intended to express comradery, but complicated by the oddness of his eyes. "It will be good to have someone to ride with. I suggest you have something to eat first. I'll meet you at the stable in an hour. Be ready!"

With that, Rastian strode away, leaving Nagaro swearing silently to himself. He couldn't even discuss the wisdom of what he had just agreed to do with Taru and Pavo since his friends had gone to Wotana again for the week's end and wouldn't return until the following day.

It wasn't that Nagaro disliked Rastian. He didn't know the young man well enough for that—chiefly because he avoided him whenever possible because of his association with his disconcerting father. The situation had grown worse now that he suspected the two men knew his history, but neither Rastyl nor Rastian had ever spoken the name of Leyel Virden in his presence nor made any reference to the idiot prince. The trouble was, he still didn't know their intentions. Rastyl had seemed to want something from him in the past, and was perfectly placed to threaten him with exposure if he so chose.

At least in this case Rastian's purpose seemed clear. And his desire to have sensible men present at the planned meeting was encouraging—which was a good thing since there was now no graceful way for Nagaro to avoid attending.

***

An hour and a half later, Nagaro and Rastian were riding together along the Great Circle Road—a wide, paved way that roughly circled most of Lankura, just outside the city wall. Rastian had chosen to turn into it as they had exited the Fleet Compound, rather than crossing the Circle Road and going through the city, explaining that there were fewer folk abroad outside the wall to observe them at that hour.

The route was only one of Rastian's precautions. He'd also insisted that Nagaro wear a hooded cloak—though the evening wasn't cold—and that he ride any horse but Thunder-Heels. The big gray tolerated no other rider and so was a dead giveaway. Nagaro was therefore astride a dark bay with a crooked blaze, having decided not to argue. The secrecy, in this case, was welcome. He and Rastian were an unusual pair to be seen together, and he had no wish to attract attention.

They had ridden mostly in silence, as if both were wary of the few folk who were passing along the portion of the Circle Road that ran between the river and the city's south wall. Presently, as they rounded the curve and moved away from the river, the land opened to the east into fields and pastureland, interrupted by low walls or by small stands of trees, and dotted with the scattered dwellings of farmers and herdsmen.

The sun was sinking westward beyond the city and the sea. The shadow of Lankura's encircling wall reached out across the land. Trees and fields glowed in the steeply slanting rays, and wildflowers—red, blue, orange, and yellow—bloomed along the roadside, shining like jewels. Nagaro could not help thinking that the land of Edrovir was very fair—verdant and fertile enough to provide plenty for all. He could think of no reason why Edrovir's people shouldn't live together in prosperity and peace.

Now that they were away from the river, there were very few folk about, making it easier to carry on a conversation without fear of being overheard. Nagaro decided to risk sounding out his companion to see what he could learn.

"I have the impression that you and your father don't consider yourselves members of the Kelorin Faction."

Rastian's eyes flicked in his direction and back to the roadway ahead. "We don't," he said. "There aren't as many who do anymore, but then of course, my father never did."

"Why?"

Rastian gave him another sidelong glance. "Why don't others, now? Or why didn't my father, then?"

Nagaro shrugged. "I meant the second, but those are both good questions."

For several seconds there was only the creak of saddle leather and the clip-clip of the horses' hooves on the paved roadway. Finally Rastian said, "My father was King Tevren's man, and Tevren didn't ally himself with any faction—any more than his father, Darion, did. The weakening of the influence of the Kelorin Faction has to do with Darion's heir, as much as anything."

"What do you mean?"

Rastian frowned. "The Kelorin have been waiting all these years for Tevren's son to appear. After Anduar persuaded the strongest lords to stop fighting and sign the Pact of Lankura, the rest of the Kelorin lords hadn't enough strength among them to do anything but wait. But it's been too long. Folk expected to see him come in seventeen or eighteen years—twenty at the most. After twenty seven years, most folk have grown weary."

"So, if he *has* come now, the remaining Kelorin Faction are hoping to regain some support?"

Rastian turned in the saddle and gave him an odd, searching look. "Yes," he said, and continued without taking his eyes from Nagaro's face. "Only they'd be following the wrong man, of course."

"You don't think this Kenthos is the heir of the House of Lorcs? How sure are you of that?" Nagaro was trying hard not to flinch under that gaze.

The pale gray eyes remained fixed on him for several heartbeats. Then abruptly Rastian turned back to the road ahead. "My father seems sure," he said. "And I have to trust him. I wasn't even born yet when King Tevren was killed."

Nagaro laughed. "Well if *I* was, it would have been only just," he said for the sake of conversation. "I can always figure out how old Tevren's son would be, since he was born in the same year I was—in the spring, too, it seems."

This time Rastian didn't turn. "Yes," he said quietly. "He was born in the spring." He paused again, then added as if his tongue were running on while his mind was elsewhere, "I was born that fall." He fell silent then, his brows knit in a frown.

Nagaro made a few half-hearted attempts after that to restart the conversation, but without success. Eventually he gave up. Rastian gave the impression of being deep in thought, except that he glanced at Nagaro from time to time as he rode. His expression at such times was impossible to read.

Lacking other distractions, Nagaro's mind soon slid back to Nevien and the dilemma she posed. He wanted to help her, but feared he might give away his feelings if they spent too much time together. His thoughts chased themselves in fruitless circles.

The shades of twilight were beginning to fall as they reached the crossroads where the Great Circle road met the New North Road. Rastian turned into the north road, leaving the city behind. As they rode on, the stands of woodland became larger and more numerous and they frequently passed through the deeper shadows cast by trees.

After about half a mile, they came to the three massive cedar trees that gave their name to Three Cedars Lane, a narrower path, branching to the right. The Golden Branch Inn stood at the crossroads, looming darkly in the failing light, its silhouette punctuated by the bright rectangles of lighted windows. Other men had clearly arrived before them. Two were just going in through the door as Nagaro and Rastian entered the inn yard, and at least two dozen horses were tethered at the hitching rails. Another small party appeared from the direction of the lane just as they were dismounting. Rastian tied his horse among the others and drew his hood closer about his face, motioning for Nagaro to do likewise.

Nagaro frowned as he tethered the bay beside Rastian's mount. "I don't like being so secret—" he began.

"Shh!" Rastian quickly motioned him to silence. "It will be best to just watch and listen for a while—see how the winds are blowing."

Nagaro shrugged as he adjusted his hood and followed. He was thinking that walking into an inn with one's hood pulled up was hardly inconspicuous.

As it turned out, he needn't have worried.

# Chapter 13

# The Gathering

R astian surveyed the room from the shadow of his hood, then motioned with a jerk of his head and led the way to a vacant table near the door. They sat down, facing the center of the room.

Nagaro looked about him. The common room of the Golden Branch was about twice as long as it was wide, with its front door near the end of one of the longer sides. It was larger than the common room of the Bay Tree Inn on Pakoa, though otherwise similar, with great hewn rafters supported by stone piers along the two longer walls. Halfway along the wall facing the windows, a fire blazed in a huge hearth, flanked by doorways leading to the kitchen. There was the usual array of long tables and miscellaneous stools. Some of those gathered there must have come early enough to order dinner, for several serving women were clearing away dishes.

The room was not very well lit. Although there were oil lamps in addition to the hearth fire, they were sparsely spread and it seemed to Nagaro that their wicks weren't turned up as high as they might be. The resulting gloom, together with the large number of hooded customers, combined to give a distinctly conspiratorial air. Nearly half of the men there apparently didn't wish to be recognized since they had their hoods up and were seated around the shadowy edges of the room. The ones who presumably didn't mind being identified were grouped nearer the hearth, where the light was better. Nagaro couldn't see the faces of any of the men sitting near him well enough to tell if he knew them, so he turned his attention to those near the fire.

He immediately saw Lord Soren Tuveilas, gaunt and gray-haired, sitting near the center of the room. The old lord was flanked by the younger lords Therin Oranil and Rathdar Sundorin. Therin, with his neat brown beard, was leaning his spare frame forward to carry on an animated discussion with Rathdar, a muscular, broad-shouldered, black-haired man who had propped an elbow on the table as if trying to appear to be at his ease, though there was tension in every line of his body. Soren was turning excitedly from one to the other of the two conversants.

These three men had once approached Nagaro at the midwinter festival, and Lord Anduar had referred to them as the heart, hand, and soul of the Kelorin Faction—though Nagaro wasn't sure which man represented which. Anduar had also suggested that no one within the faction had enough wit to represent its head.

There were other men sitting at the same table whom Nagaro didn't know, all listening avidly to the conversation. He supposed they belonged to the Kelorin Faction. There were also other groups at other tables, as well as men who seemed to have come alone. Among those who were showing their faces, Nagaro picked out Hendrel and Geivian. Another man, sitting across from the hearth with several companions, looked vaguely familiar though Nagaro couldn't place him. Soren and his companions occasionally gave the man frowning glances.

Nagaro turned to Rastian. "Who is the somber-looking elder man there with the neatly-trimmed gray beard?" he asked in a low whisper, gesturing with his head.

Rastian followed the gesture. Then he gave Nagaro a look. "That's Lord Endemar."

"Oh yes, now I remember. He has the keeping of Loros Hall, doesn't he?"

"Yes, he—" Rastian fell silent.

Men were still entering the room, singly or in groups, some by a back door at the other end of the room and others by the door through which Nagaro and Rastian had come. Two hooded men had just come in by the front door and were eyeing the table where Nagaro and Rastian were seated, apparently looking for an out-of-the-way place to sit. The one shook his head at the other and both moved on. Nagaro stared after them. He'd caught a glimpse of a scarred face under one of the hoods. Its owner moved slowly and carefully but couldn't quite conceal the fact that he walked with a stiff-legged limp.

Rastian leaned close. "Was that *Lord Devral?*" he breathed in an incredulous whisper.

"Yes, it was."

The pact signer and his companion had taken seats on the other side of the door in a pool of shadow. Nagaro saw Devral raise a hand to his mouth and heard a muffled cough.

"Did he recognize us?" Rastian asked.

"I don't think so."

"What is he doing here? He *can't* have been invited. He wouldn't be welcome—"

Their conversation was interrupted by the loud rapping of Lord Rathdar's knuckles on the table in front of him. He swept the assembled faces with a fierce gray gaze. "Quiet, everyone, please!" he cried. "The sun is gone. We should begin."

There were cries of, "Aye! Aye!" from various quarters.

Lord Soren stood up, the stiff erectness of his posture belying his advanced years. He appeared to murmur thanks to Rathdar. Then, as the clamor of voices sank to a hush, he addressed the gathering in ringing tones.

"My friends! Good people! This is a day we have long been waiting for—when the son of our dear King Tevren, the heir of the high House of Loros, has at last emerged from the shadows and into the light!"

This speech was met with murmurs of approval from many of those assembled, but there were also some frowns and questioning looks. Lord Endemar, in particular, frowned deeply and shifted in his seat. Nagaro noticed that Lord Devral had put his head close to the man he had come in with and was speaking to him.

Soren seemed not to notice. He paused no longer than necessary to draw breath and then continued. "All good Kelorin folk must now join together to support the man, Kenthos, who has come forward to claim his rightful place!"

Lord Devral's companion abruptly raised his voice, at the same time pushing his hood back from his head. "Your pardon, My Lord Soren. May I humbly ask what proof you have of this man's identity?" He was a smooth-shaven man, younger than Devral though still of mature years. He had spoken mildly, yet loud enough to be heard throughout the room.

Nagaro didn't recognize the man and neither apparently did Soren, for he frowned and said, "I don't know you, Zirda."

The man made an easy gesture with his hand. "I am called Menden, but it's of no consequence. You just said that Kenthos is the heir of the House of Loros, and I wonder how you know this. We've heard such rumors before."

Soren spread his hands. "There have been other rumors, yes, but this man is real. He has won battles. Men are rallying to him—"

"You have seen this?" The question came from someone on the other side of the room.

Therin spoke up eagerly. "It was one of Rathdar's men who found him and helped him to discover his history."

Rathdar promptly rose to his feet. "I've also spoken to men who witnessed the battles—trusted men. I tell you, we must put our swords together. Raise a force! Go to his aid!"

"Aye! Aye!" Nearly a dozen of the younger men present stood up or started to rise, fists punching the air.

Nagaro wasn't surprised to see that Hendrel was among the enthusiasts, but then another face caught his eye and he started from his seat. "*Simion?*"

He felt Rastian grab his cloak and pull him back down onto his stool. The room was very warm and he mopped his brow, half pushing his hood back in the process. In the moment before he could pull it forward again, his gaze met Lord Soren's and he read recognition—and satisfaction—in the old man's face. Soren inclined his head in acknowledgment. Nagaro returned him only the slightest nod, frowning.

In the meantime Rathdar had motioned his supporters back into their seats with murmured thanks. "You see, Zirda," he said to the man who had asked for witnesses. "Some are prepared to accept my word."

The man named Menden had been conferring with Devral, and he now said, "I don't understand what's proven by winning battles, My Lords, or by men following him. Can you explain this to me?"

"It isn't just the battles," Lord Therin volunteered. "The woman who has been passing as his mother was a maid-servant to Queen Lindra. So obviously Lindra must have given the child into her keeping before she and Tevren rode from Loros Hall on that fatal night."

"But winning battles is important too!" insisted Rathdar. "And so is rallying men. These are things you would expect from a man of Tevren's and Darion's lineage."

"*I* heard that they were more like skirmishes than battles, and that his followers come and go depending on his most recent fortune." This came from Geivian, who promptly ducked his head as if he expected to become the target of blows.

Lord Endemar's face had been showing increasing annoyance as the words flew back and forth, and he now stood up. All eyes turned to him immediately, for he was a tall, commanding figure. His voice when he spoke was measured, and as stern as his countenance. "Whether they were battles or skirmishes, or how many men follow him, is immaterial. Haven't I made it clear that the child of Tevren and Lindra is dead? He died within a few days of his birth. I have here the very letter in which Tevren gave me the sad news." He drew a folded piece of parchment from his tirka and held it aloft. "If you will allow me to read it aloud, the matter can be quickly resolved. It isn't long."

Menden leaned forward. "By all means, My Lord, read it."

Rathdar and Therin were frowning.

Soren looked sour. "You know my opinion regarding that letter, Endemar—" he began, but other cries cut across his words.

"Read it!"

"Yes, read it! We want to hear it!"

Endemar shot Soren a significant glance and proceeded to unfold the parchment with a flourish. "It is addressed to me by name," he informed his listeners gravely. "And it reads thus:

*"If I do not survive this night, it will be for you to tell the world that the babe who would have been heir of the House of Loros is dead. Look where the earth is turned in the garden, near the west wall, and you will understand."*

He lowered the paper. "It is signed simply, 'Tevren of Loros.' Surely you all now see the folly of giving support to this upstart, Kenthos."

Soren scowled at him. "I understand no such thing! I've always thought the letter either a fraud or a deception—"

"It was surely intended as a ruse!" Rathdar slapped the table in front of him, his sharply-chiseled face flushed with anger. "But it's *you* who stand to gain by claiming its truth, Endemar. You were given the rule of half of Loros Wared, and you stand to keep it as long as there is no heir!"

The blood came instantly into Endemar's face. "*How dare you, Rathdar!* —to accuse me of such a thing!" He turned on Soren. "And it is no fraud, Zirda!"

"Let me see the letter! I'll tell you whether it's genuine."

The last words were spoken by a new voice, and all eyes now turned to its owner. A moment before he had been only one of the many anonymous hooded figures at the shadowy edges of the room, but he had risen and stepped forward as others were speaking. His cloak and boots were spattered with mud, his graying hair was disheveled, and there was stubble on his chin. His strange, pale eyes were fixed on Lord Endemar.

Beside Nagaro, Rastian murmured, "*Father!*" He glanced at Nagaro and lowered his voice so as to be barely audible. "I swear I thought he was in Irvenen!"

Rastyl Korven continued his advance, moving into the area in front of the hearth. He extended his hand towards Lord Endemar. "I've often heard of this letter, My Lord," he continued. "But I have never had the opportunity to examine it—you've guarded it so jealously. Since you now bring it out, I can do you the service of confirming whether it is genuine. No man knew Tevren better than I."

Lord Endemar looked affronted. "I know his hand, Zirda!"

Rastyl flashed him a tight smile. "Of course. But it seems that some of those here aren't prepared to accept your word, Endemar. If the letter is genuine, as you say, you've nothing to fear by letting me look at it."

For perhaps three seconds the two men stood with eyes locked, and the onlookers held their breath. At last Endemar shrugged, though the smile he gave the other man was noticeably strained. "Very well, Rastyl," he said. "Though you may find that these three—" he indicated the lords Soren, Therin, and Rathdar, "— don't trust your word any more than they trust mine." He proffered the letter.

Rastyl took it, handling it almost reverently. "I swear to give you my honest judgement," he said. "On my honor and as I hope for a new life when my present life is done." He studied the parchment for several long seconds before making his pronouncement. "The words are exactly as Lord Endemar has reported them," he said, his voice taut with emotion. "And the hand is unmistakably that of Tevren Loros."

The room had been silent, but now there rose a babble of voices.

"The child must have died, then!"

"He *can't* have died! It must be a mistake—"

Soren was staring at Rastyl in open disbelief. "Surely you can't turn about *now*, Rastyl, and declare that Tevren's son has been dead all this time for the sake of those few words. Not you, who have claimed to be seeking him the whole length and breadth of Edrovir!"

Lord Endemar moved to retrieve the letter. "How can anyone do otherwise? You must all see that it's just as I've said. The heir of Loros has been dead these twenty-seven years. The man Kenthos is deluded."

But Rastyl backed away from Endemar. He brandished the letter in the air. "This doesn't say that Tevren's heir is dead!"

"What do you mean? Of course it does!" Endemar advanced. "Give it back to me!"

Rastyl retreated another step, now clutching the precious parchment possessively to his chest. "It does *not!*" he cried. "It says that's what you were supposed to tell the world! What did you find by the west wall of the garden? Did you even *look?*"

Endemar drew himself up. "Of course I looked! There was a place where the earth had been turned, just as the letter says—a fresh grave. I marked it with a stone."

"You marked it with a *stone?* You didn't look *in* the earth?"

"Disturb the grave? Of course not!"

"Why, you old fool!" Rastyl shook his head at Endemar. "If you never looked *in* the earth, it's clear why you never understood—"

"You insult me, Zirda!" Lord Endemar's face was livid. "Give me the letter! Tevren entrusted it to *me!*" He lunged forward and snatched the parchment from Rastyl's grasp.

Rathdar had risen, his eyes blazing. "Clearly Tevren should have found a wiser keeper for his message!" he cried. "Rastyl has got something right for once. It was a ruse, just as I said! The grave is surely empty. The child was given to Queen Lindra's serving girl—or delivered to her by the third man—and raised in ignorance of his true origins, until my man traced the trail and discovered the truth—"

"*Truth!*" Rastyl spat the word. "I tell you, Rathdar, I have seen the man Kenthos, and heard him speak, and if he's the heir of Darion, then I'm the king of Jinara!"

This drew nervous laughter from some of those present, and it was now Therin who leapt to his feet. "How can you say that, Rastyl! What makes you so certain?"

Rastyl spun to face the younger man. "Don't you think I would know the son of Tevren and Lindra if I saw him? If I heard him speak? I knew them both—better than any man here!"

"And yet you'd have us believe that Tevren told you nothing? That you weren't the third man? That you haven't had Tevren's heir in your keeping all this time?"

Therin had spoken with fine irony and Rastyl seemed to sag under the sting of it. He dropped his eyes. "Alas, it's true," he said quietly. "He told me nothing, left me no word. And I was not the third man." He drew a long breath and raised his eyes again, rallying. "I can only believe that he didn't send his son to me for the sake of the child's safety. He must have known Irvenen Wared would be the first place men would look."

"Oh, *that*'s convenient!" Rathdar flung up his hands. "You haven't got Tevren's heir because folk would have *expected* you to? Well, if you haven't got him, maybe we have! I think you're just put out because *we* found him first—in Irvenen, right under your nose! Or maybe it's because Tevren didn't trust you enough to give you the keeping of his son!"

Nagaro saw Rastyl stiffen, read the anger and hurt in the man's face, but Endemar spoke before he could respond. The tall, imposing lord raised both hands in a gesture that drew all eyes to him. "The heir of Darion is *dead!*" he cried in a commanding voice. "This talk of a ruse, and looking in the earth, is grasping at threads because you have no *rope!* And you call *me* a fool! I beg you all to put this folly aside now and pursue the path of reason!"

Rathdar snorted. "*My* reason tells me that we've found the heir of Darion! Let's not lose him now because we won't follow him!"

"Hear! Hear!" Some of the younger men voiced their agreement.

Nagaro glanced at Rastian, beside him, the blood clearly visible in his face as he watched his father's discomfiture. Nagaro frowned. He was learning some interesting things about the history of Darion's heir, but this wasn't why he had come. The discussion seemed to have strayed far from its appropriate purpose. He thought he felt eyes, and turned quickly to see Simion watching him surreptitiously. He realized that the young man hadn't joined the other voices this time when they shouted their support for Kenthos. Was Simion having doubts?

"Will none of you listen?" Lord Endemar's gaze was sweeping the audience and finding no support. "Then I have done with you!" he cried. "I won't stand here any longer to be insulted and shouted down—to have my judgement questioned. Take whatever path you will, but I'm going home to my bed!" With that, he turned and swept towards the door, gesturing to those who had presumably come with him. A handful of men rose and followed him, their heads held stiffly up.

Soren's voice rose briefly above the ensuing tumult. "My Lord Endemar, can we not—"

Nagaro turned in time to see Therin pull the old man back into his seat.

Rathdar was still standing. "Let him go!" he cried. "Let him go home to his Wared, to nurse his piece of parchment and guard an empty grave. We who know the truth will see the rightful heir placed upon the throne of Edrovir!"

Rastyl had been left standing, forgotten, but now he suddenly leapt onto one of the tables, drawing all attention away from Rathdar. "I tell you, Kenthos is not Tevren's heir!" he cried. "Place him on the throne, and you will regret your folly!"

Rastian uttered a groan. His father had never looked more like a madman, standing on the table, wild-eyed and disheveled in the firelight.

Lord Soren stood up. "My dear Rastyl," he began soothingly, "I urge you to calm yourself—"

"And get off of the table," put in Rathdar less kindly. "You're making a fool of yourself."

"Unless, of course, you can prove your claim by producing the true heir," added Therin, who hadn't left his seat.

Rastyl stood his ground on the tabletop. He very pointedly ignored Rathdar and turned instead to Therin. "Unfortunately I can't—"

"Because you haven't found him!" Rathdar took two steps to stand in front of Therin, forcing Rastyl's attention. "After twenty-seven years of searching!"

"I didn't say I hadn't found him!" Rastyl's voice cracked like a whip.

There were audible gasps. Soren, Therin, and Rathdar all gaped at him.

"Endemar is simply *wrong*," Rastyl declared dramatically. "The heir of Darion lives and breathes and treads the soil of Edrovir!"

"*Then where is he?*" Geivian asked the obvious question.

Rastyl spun about and dropped to the floor, taking two strides to stand over Geivian. "Where is he at this precise moment?" Rastyl asked, almost conversationally. "I couldn't say."

Rathdar threw up his hands. "*I couldn't say*," he mimicked. "*At this precise moment*. What about yesterday morning, then? Or a week ago last Second Day?"

Rastyl turned a cold glance on the other lord. "You mock me," he said stiffly. "But Tevren's son has never been in my keeping. He is his own man, as you'd expect of a lord of the House of Loros."

"Then tell us who he is," Therin offered smoothly. "Give us a name, if you're so sure that *we* have the wrong man."

Rastyl drew himself up, but his expression betrayed uncertainty. "It's for *him* to decide how and when he will reveal himself," he said. "I wouldn't presume to play his move for him."

Therin shook his head pityingly. "This is smoke and air, My Lord."

"Yes," agreed Soren. "You must give us substance if you wish to convince us, Rastyl."

"I'm afraid I can't—"

"Of course you can't!" Rathdar declared triumphantly. "You have never been good for more than words!"

Rastyl was searching the faces of his audience with his pale gaze. He apparently found no more support there than Endemar had, for he sagged and dropped wearily onto a stool, a hand to his brow. "The heir of Darion lives," he muttered distractedly. "He lives and breathes and treads the soil of Edrovir."

Rathdar laughed. "Well, I'd say that, right now, he treads that soil somewhere near the northern border of Hurn Hold. And Lothard surely won't let him pass unchallenged. That's why we have to raise a force to aid him!"

"Why must he cross Hurn Hold?" Wondered Geivian aloud. "Can't he go around it, through friendlier lands? Through Sedras and Tyronin Wareds, perhaps?"

"That would take too long," protested Therin.

"And it would be cowardly!" added Rathdar. "If he doesn't confront Lothard and win the field, he can't hope to win the throne, even if he comes to Lankura."

"That's not necessarily so," Soren opined. "He could pass through Sedras Wared, Fendred Hold, and Virden, gathering strength along the way—and *then* face Lothard at Lankura—"

"But that path would bring him close to Sobring Hold. Grimbold is strong. Grimbold would stop him—"

So the debate continued regarding the best course for the young Kenthos to take, while Nagaro sat, only half listening to the ebb and flow of words. Did no one else see what was wrong with this? Would no one say the obvious?

He looked around, noting that Rastyl was brooding on his stool, his head down as if scarcely aware of the discussion. Rastian was watching his father, worriedly chewing his lip. The man named Menden and the hooded Lord Devral were deep in whispered conversation with their hoods together. And Simion was still watching Nagaro.

"Now, if only Captain Nagaro were here, we could ask him what he thinks."

Nagaro started at the sound of his name. The voice had been Lord Soren's, and he saw that the old man was looking at him expectantly. Nagaro frowned sharply at this disingenuous ploy. Then without a word he pushed back his stool and stood up.

Someone said, "*There he is!*" And the room became suddenly so still that the snapping of sparks in the fireplace was plainly audible. The firelight flickered on startled faces, all turned towards him. Rastian tugged at Nagaro's cloak, trying to pull him back into his seat, but Nagaro shook himself free. *Hadn't Rastian brought him here to be a voice of reason?*

"Yes, I *am* here, My Lord Soren," he said, loudly enough to carry to the far end of the room. "And what I think, is that I've heard enough!"

There were small uncertain movements, furtive glances exchanged, a few hushed words. Soren cleared his throat, looking uncomfortable. "Perhaps you don't understand, Captain," he ventured. "I had hoped you might recommend some strategy..." The sentence dangled.

Nagaro's frown deepened even further. "I'd be glad to offer strategy if you proposed to fight against some enemy of Edrovir," he said curtly, "instead of your own countrymen."

Rathdar smote the table in front of him. "It's the cursed Leithians who insist on offering us battle!"

Nagaro sighed. "What would *your* response be if a party of armed men came marching through your Wared, My Lord? —talking about setting some unknown Leithian on the throne?"

There were some doubtful murmurs from several quarters now, and shifting of seats in the room's shadowy recesses. Nagaro could feel every eye. The reactions of the three leaders of the Kelorin faction ranged from Soren's dismay to Rathdar's frank disapproval. Lord Devral's eyes were two bright gleams under the shadow of his hood, while Simion watched with an avidity that was almost worshipful. Even Rastyl had emerged from his gloomy introspection and had stood up to fix Nagaro with a burning gaze.

And Nagaro wasn't finished. "I came here tonight because I care about the future of Edrovir, My Lord Soren," he said pointedly. "And I thought these others had come for the same reason. What I've heard instead, is men going on about the parentage of a man named Kenthos, as if it were all that mattered. —*As if it mattered at all!* While the two most important questions haven't yet been asked. First, *what is Kenthos' character?* Is he worthy of being followed? And second, *what are his intentions?*

Nagaro's eyes swept the room. "If you follow him, where will he lead you? Does he mean to meerely redress some old wrongs—to reinstate Loros Wared, perhaps? Or does he mean to seize the throne? Men like Lothard and Grimbold may indeed be spoiling for a fight, but other

Leithians surely are not. And yet, could you blame them if they didn't stand meekly by while Elgurn was cast down and a man they know nothing about was set in his place? Have you any reason at all to think that Kenthos would make a good king?"

Lord Soren apparently had no answer. The aging lord sat frozen, speechless.

Therin leaned forward nervously in his seat. "If he i the true heir of Darion, then he surely would," he ventured.

Nagaro gestured impatiently. "Sons are not always like their fathers—let alone like their grandfathers."

A definite murmur was now rising. Soren leaned over and spoke to Therin in a low voice. Both men looked distinctly uncomfortable, but Rathdar had been eyeing the gathered faces. Now he stood up defiantly. "What, then, *cowards?*" he cried. "Would you abandon the House of Loros in its hour of need?"

Nagaro threw up a hand and instantly every eye turned back to him. "Just think a moment, friends," he said reasonably. "Consider what you're proposing to do in the service of this claimed heir of the House of Loros. Will you try to force your will upon your fellow citizens by strength of arms? That path can only lead to the shedding of blood—Edroviran blood, spilled by Edroviran hands. That is not the way of Darion as I have understood the man. And I can't believe it's what Tevren would have wanted either!"

In the silence that followed, Devral's cough, muffled behind his fist, sounded disconcertingly loud. No one seemed willing to hazzard a response. Even Rathdar stood frowning, biting his lip. Nagaro hitched his cloak about his shoulders. "That's all I have to say, Zirdas," he said quietly, though his words reached every ear. "I hope you will consider my words. For myself, I want no part of anything that leads to strife between the people of Edrovir. Good night to you all."

He turned and made for the door. Behind him the room erupted in confusion. He heard some voices protesting what he'd said, others begging him to come back. Some of the men rose from their seats, but if they had meant to hinder him, they stepped back when they saw the look in his eyes. He felt a hand grip his arm, and his quick sideward glance caught a glimpse of a familiar scarred face, shadowed by a hood, before the hand was withdrawn. Three more strides, and he reached the door and flung it open. Amongst the voices behind him he heard two that were familiar as he crossed the threshold.

"No, Rastian, you stay and listen! I'll follow him—"

"I tell you, Father, he has no idea!"

Nagaro hurried across the inn yard to where his horse was tied, not wishing to speak to Rastyl. Deftly he disentangled the appropriate pair of reins from the hitching rail, then backed the horse clear of its fellows and swung into the saddle. Quick though he was, however, someone was right behind him. He caught a silhouette with disheveled hair against the light from the inn's windows as the man reached up and caught his horse by the bridle.

"Wait, My Lord!" The voice was Rastyl's.

Nagaro stared down in astonishment. The light was still behind the other man, and he couldn't make out the expression on his face. "Why do you call me that? he demanded. "I'm no man's lord."

"Your pardon, Zirda. It was a slip of the tongue." Rastyl still held the bridle. "Though you do have something of nobility about you."

Nagaro laughed uneasily. "Vestiges of my upbringing, I suppose." He pulled on the reins, trying to turn the horse.

"I think it's more than that." Rastyl had shifted his ground a little, though not his grip. He braced himself to hold the horse, frustrating Nagaro's efforts, and the light from the windows caught the gleam of his pale eyes.

Nagaro frowned anew. "What do you want of me, My Lord?" he demanded in desperation, though he dreaded what the answer might be.

"*I* want of *you?*" The eyes appeared to search his face. "Nothing!" There was a pause, then, "What do *you* want, Zirda?"

This was beyond Nagaro. He could make no sense of it, and this on top of everything else put him out of temper. "That you leave me alone!" he snapped. "And please let go of the bridle!"

For the space of several heartbeats, Rastyl didn't move. Then his fingers loosed their grip and he stepped back. "As you wish, Captain," he said, his voice oddly flat.

Nagaro didn't stop to analyze the response, being glad just to make his escape. He swung the horse around to face the new North Road and applied his heels. The beast sprang away, carrying him out of the inn yard in a spray of gravel. Since he didn't look back, he didn't see that Rastyl stood for a long time, staring after him, before turning to re-join the gathering in the common room.

Chapter 14

# Arrangements

Early the following morning, the Fleet Compound lay under a shroud of thick gray fog that had drifted in from the sea. The mist bedewed Nagaro's hair and dampened his clothing as he knocked at the door of Kuran's quarters. He had found a message waiting for him the previous evening, saying that the Lord of the Fleet wished to speak to him in the morning, as early as possible. He shivered as he waited for Kuran's clerk to answer the door. It was unusually cold for the season even given the earliness of the hour.

He stifled a yawn. It had taken him a long time to fall asleep, what with all of the previous day's events, and he'd awakened before dawn from dreams populated by the three leaders of the Kelorin Faction, by Rastyl and Rastian—*and by Nevien*. After lying awake for some time and finding that further slumber eluded him, he had risen, eaten a cold breakfast, and come to see if Kuran was astir. He was just beginning to think that he'd come too early when the door opened and the clerk appeared.

"Ah. Come in, Captain." Estevad stood aside and ushered him into the little hallway. "My Lord will return momentarily. He left word that you should wait in his study if you came while he was out."

"Thank you, Estevad." Nagaro gave the man a nod.

He stepped into the study, and stopped dead. The small room wasn't empty. His first thought was that the clerk had been mistaken in thinking that Kuran had not returned, until the man who was bending over the fire on the hearth at the end of the room straightened and turned to face him. It was Lord Anduar.

"Ah good, Captain, you're here. Pray come and warm yourself. I've just put on another log."

Nagaro frowned, but he crossed the room to stand beside the Pact Signer in the fire's glow, grateful in spite of himself for the invitation.

"Estevad didn't mention that you were here, My Lord."

Anduar's steel-gray glance didn't waver. "That's because the man follows instructions," he said mildly. "Kuran will doubtless return very shortly, but we needn't wait upon that event for you to begin making your report."

"My report?"

"Concerning events last night at the Golden Branch." There was the slightest twitch of the facial muscles. "You *did* go?"

Nagaro was annoyed. "As it happens, I did, My Lord. Though I easily might not have if Rastian Korven hadn't pressed me. You should not make assumptions. In fact," he added after a moment's hesitation, "in the future I would prefer that you not attempt to use me for your spy—at least not without having the decency to tell me plainly your intention. You would never have been invited to that gathering. I dare say there would have *been* no gathering if you'd made it known that you meant to be there."

There was a low whistle from the doorway. "*Well*," observed Kuran as he stepped into the room. "You don't mince words, Captain. And I'm curious to hear what you have to say in reply, My Lord."

Anduar had turned in response to the whistle. His eyes tracked Kuran coolly as the latter made his way to his desk, but he said nothing until the Lord of the Fleet had settled in his chair. Then he turned back to Nagaro. "Your objection is noted for future reference, Captain," he said smoothly. "Now, do you intend to tell us what you learned, or are you going to withhold the information as some form of retribution?"

Nagaro considered him steadily. "I will tell you," he said. "But if I refused, you could ask Lord Devral."

"Devral?"

Nagaro saw genuine surprise pass fleetingly behind the Pact Signer's eyes. Kuran's raised eyebrow indicated that he'd seen it too.

"He arrived shortly after I did. He was still there when I left, as well. He kept his head covered, but someone should tell him that his walk and his cough give him away."

"Ah." Anduar had recovered. "Did he say anything?"

"Not out loud, no. He was clearly trying to influence the meeting by speaking through another man who said his name was Menden."

"Menden?" Anduar glanced a question at Kuran.

Kuran shrugged. "The name isn't known to me."

"It likely isn't his true name." Anduar waved a hand. "So it doesn't matter. And Devral would have chosen a man for his mouthpiece whose face isn't widely known." He returned his penetrating gaze to Nagaro. "Will you tell us what else you observed, Captain?"

Kuran coughed. "Yes, but first won't you sit down, Captain? If you've finished warming yourself."

Nagaro ignored Anduar's peremptory request and acknowledged Kuran's courtesy with a slight bow. Moving to one of the plain wooden chairs that faced Kuran's desk, he repositioned it and sat down warily. Lord Anduar took one of the others, managing as usual to appear to be lounging at his ease even in a straight-backed chair.

Nagaro began to speak in response to an encouraging gesture from Kuran. "Soren, Therin, and Rathdar began the discussion and appeared to be in charge. They're all convinced that Kenthos is the heir of the House of Loros and are bent on raising a force of arms to go to his aid. Rathdar is particularly hot for it, and many of the men there seemed eager to follow him. Devral—speaking through Menden—was trying to undercut them."

He paused, frowning. "Then there was Lord Endemar, who brought a letter written by Tevren. He set off a great argument by saying that Tevren's son had died a few days after his birth. Rastyl Korven was also there. He's sure that Tevren's heir isn't dead, and just as sure that he isn't Kenthos. Rastyl also claimed he had *found* Tevern's heir, but no one believed him because he wouldn't give any details. What troubled me, though, was that all of them were talking as if the only thing that mattered was Kenthos' blood line—as if being Darion's heir was enough reason to follow the man, or even set him on the throne."

Anduar's expression had grown increasingly grim as he listened to Nagaro's summary and now he interjected a sharp question. "Did you speak?"

"Well, yes. I was trying to remain hidden at first, but Soren had noticed me and he wanted me to help them with a strategy for getting Kenthos to Lankura. I told him that I wanted no part of helping men of Edrovir to shed each other's blood. Then I left. I've been wondering since whether I should have stayed."

"What would you have gained by staying?" Kuran wondered aloud. "If they were all so set on their course?"

"I don't know." Nagaro sighed. "I stirred things up a bit with what I said, but they might well have shouted me down in the end."

"They would likely have asked you to leave." Anduar was leaning forward, no longer lounging. "You surely made yourself unwelcome. Did Devral or his man respond to you?"

"Not with speech. Devral caught my arm for a moment as I was going to the door—as if he wanted me to know he was there, but he kept his head covered."

"And you said he remained after you had gone. But you didn't stay and watch?"

Nagaro hesitated. He had no desire to bring up Rastyl's parting actions. "I had no wish to hang about, skulking in the bushes. I was too angry about what I'd heard."

Anduar's steel-gray eyes bored into him. "Were you, indeed?"

"Wouldn't you have been, My Lord?"

Anduar leaned back in his chair once more. "I rarely permit myself the luxury of anger," he said with a negligent gesture. "It serves little purpose. Is that all you have to tell us?"

Nagaro attempted to cover his dismay. *The man could be disturbingly cold-blooded.* "Yes, My Lord," he said. "Have you any more questions?"

"How many men were there?" Kuran inquired.

"Perhaps fifty."

"And how many of those seemed to support Rathdar and the rest of their Faction?"

"More than half. It varied, depending on who had spoken last and what argument had been made. I may have swayed a few."

"Well." Anduar stood up. "Let's hope that you did, since every man who was there will have gone home and told a dozen others." He stood for a moment, frowning at the window as if in thought. Then he brought his gaze back to the other two men. "I will leave you now, gentlemen," he said tersely. "I have some questions for Devral." With that, he turned and strode purposefully out of the room.

Kuran waited while they heard the outer door close, and the sound of boots on gravel that faded into the mist-wrapped morning. He then cleared his throat and said, "He has a great deal of respect for you."

"Really? He has a strange way of showing it."

Kuran smiled tightly. "He has a lot on his mind this morning. But I hear what he says about you when you aren't present. And of course you *did* rebuke him, just as I was coming in."

"He used me! And he maneuvered me into it by misrepresenting his intentions."

Kuran raised a placating hand. "I quite understand. But unless I'm very much mistaken, he won't do it again."

Nagaro sighed. "I certainly hope not. Did you know he was coming this morning? Is that why you asked me to come here?"

"No. He surprised me by turning up at such an early hour and was quite pleased to find that I was already expecting you, as it spared us the trouble of sending you a summons." Kuran paused. "I called you here to discuss our sailing orders."

"Oh?"

"Yes. We're to sail with six of our ships and four of the captured Mahuk craft, carrying all the Mautep sea warriors we currently have in our custody." Kuran leaned forward, watching Nagaro narrowly. "Our orders are to escort them safely to the border of Mahuk-controlled waters and to return, taking all precautions to avoid any armed confrontation. So the Council has followed your suggestions to the letter."

Nagaro returned the older man's glance. "Good," he said calmly. "When do you plan to sail."

"Tomorrow, if we can be ready." Kuran rubbed his chin. "I must say you don't seem very surprised."

Nagaro shrugged. "I had already heard about the Council's decision—from the princess."

"Nevien?" Kuran's eyebrows had shot up at first, but then he smiled. "Ah, yes. You were at the orphanage with her yesterday, weren't you? How did that go?"

"Well enough that she wants me to do it again, and to join her on visits to her other charities. Lady Merriel gave me a list, though I told them I wasn't sure how much I could be spared."

"I see." Kuran looked thoughtful. "Well, it's a noble duty. I'll spare you as much as I can. But the next occasion will have to wait until our return from this mission."

"Of course." Nagaro frowned. Something had occurred to him. "My Lord, could I possibly use this opportunity to return my daughter to Pakoa? The mission will take us past the island."

Kuran pursed his lips. "We could encounter trouble, even in our own waters."

"I know, My Lord, but the risk of meeting Mahuk ships is low, and I believe it would go against the Mautep sense of honor to harm a child. I'd take full responsibility for her presence, and I swear I wouldn't let it influence my decisions if it came to a fight."

Kuran nodded decisively. "Good enough. If I have your word on that last, I will allow it. And now, I'd like your opinion regarding how to handle Roheed."

Several minutes of discussion followed, until finally Kuran leaned back in his chair and said, "Very good, Captain. I think that should be all, and you may go about your duties." He picked up one of the stacks of papers on his desk with obvious distaste.

Nagaro rose and replaced his chair against the wall. He started to leave, then turned back. "May I ask you a question on a different matter, My Lord?"

"Of course you may ask."

"At the gathering last night, there was mention of a 'third man.' Do you know what that means? I hadn't heard of it before."

Kuran put down the papers. "You know that Tevren and Lindra were not alone when Reith Hurn and his men intercepted them on the road to Lankura?"

"Yes. According to Berinar Sundorin's account in his book titled *Rule of Loros*, there were two men with them—two trusted men of King Tevren's household."

Kuran nodded. "On that much everyone agrees. But several of the Loros family servants said there were *three* men with them when the king and queen left Loros Hall."

"Oh. I see."

"Yes. There has been a lot of speculation about who the third man could have been—*if* there was one—and what became of him. No one has ever come forward to identify himself as having been that man. Some have suggested it was Rastyl Korven."

Nagaro frowned. "He denied it last night."

Kuran shrugged. "He has always denied it. And there's evidence he was in Irvenen Wared at the time."

"What did the other two men say? Berinar writes that they tried to help Tevren and were 'subdued and restrained' to keep them from doing so. But they were not slain."

Kuran absently picked up a quill that was lying beside his inkwell. "They were older men, and both are now dead. They went to their graves swearing they knew nothing about a third man."

Nagaro frowned again. "They may have been sworn to secrecy."

Kuran twirled the quill in his fingers. "Well, obviously. The Kelorin Faction would like to believe that the third man carried the infant to safety, and of course the other two would have protected the child by denying any knowledge of it."

"That all seems to fit."

Kuran let the quill fall. "As far as it goes, yes. But it's twenty-seven years later, and where is the child? Very probably Endemar is right and the heir of Loros was already dead when Tevren and his queen rode out of the gate of Loros Hall."

***

Nagaro passed the door of the palace kitchen, from which came a rattle of pans and clink of china. He was on his way to visit Narei after surrendering his sword at the palace's front entrance. The young guard, Delvin, was by now accustomed to these visits and had passed him through with a nod, allowing him to move unescorted through the halls.

As he approached the open doorway of his daughter's room, he could hear Narei's voice, as well as the voices of two women. His heart thudded against his ribs when he recognized one of them as Nevien's. The other voice belonged to the Turowan woman, Omei. Treading softly, he closed the remaining distance and stopped in the doorway, surveying the scene within.

The modest room was graced by simple wooden furniture, with a slightly worn dark green rug on the floor. There were two narrow beds and a small table against one wall, a chest of drawers, and a padded bench at one side of the small fireplace. The table's two chairs had been placed in front of the room's single window and Narei and the princess were seated there, facing each other, intent on a game of string figures.

Omei was sitting on the bench, sewing. She looked up from her work as Nagaro appeared in the doorway, giving him a nod of greeting and one of her knowing smiles. Narei and Nevien, however, remained oblivious, and he watched as Nevien's slim fingers hooked the cris-crossing strings that Narei held. Her hands moved carefully, out, down, and up, as she took the string figure from the little girl, transforming it in the same motion. Narei stood up for a better view. Her quick brown hands darted out to grip the strings in just the right places as she moved her fingers out and around, opening downward to take the string and make a new pattern.

Nagaro cleared his throat softly and said, "Hello there, Ginger Pie."

Two faces turned towards him and two pairs of eyes lit up.

"Papa!" Narei bounced eagerly up and down. "Take it, Nevien! Take it!"

The princess shook her head, laughing, as she tried to find the right crossings on what had become a moving target. She made a valiant effort to take the string, but Narei's bouncing must have confounded her and the figure unraveled in her hands. "Oh dear," she said. "I must have gotten it wrong somehow."

Narei seemed only to care that her hands were free. She ran to Nagaro with outstretched arms.

He met her half way, caught her up, and hugged her to him. "You're going home, Narei," he told her. "You're going to sail on my ship with me when we take the Mautep and their ships back to the Mahuk Baar."

"I'm going with you on the *Sword of Freedom?* Hurray!"

"All the way to Pakoa." He set her down again.

"Oh good! I want to play by the sea-shore! They won't let me go to the sea-shore here, Papa."

"When will you leave?"

The question came from Nevien and something in her voice caught at Nagaro's heart. He saw that she had risen from her chair and was standing there with the loop of limp string in her hands. He swallowed. "Tomorrow, if we can be ready. I'm sorry, Nevien. Will you miss her?"

"I... Yes, I will. But it's all right. She must go home to her Auntie Ani and her cousins." The princess looked down at the string in her hands. With exaggerated care, she began to form it into a small tight coil. "I should go now," she said. "I'll leave you to talk about your plans." She set the little coil of string down on her chair seat and made for the door as if in a hurry to be gone, not meeting Nagaro's eyes as she passed him.

"You don't have to go—" he began.

She paused in the doorway. "It's all right, Nagaro," she said, still without really looking at him. And then she was gone.

*Keshaal!* He stared at the empty doorway, wishing that he had any excuse to go after her—to tell her, perhaps, that his daughter could stay another week or two.

Narei had been watching with a puzzled frown, and she ran to the door, stopped there, and put her head out. Then she cupped her hands to her mouth. "I'll miss you too, Nevien!" she called after the departing princess. She came back more slowly to her father's side. Looking up at him, she asked, "Why is she crying, Papa?"

He reached down and stroked the little girl's hair as he tried to explain, not wanting his daughter to feel guilty for going. "She's very sad all the time right now, Narei, because of losing her mother. Even little things make her cry. It will be that way for a while, but the day will come when she'll be able to remember the good things about her mother without being sad."

"Oh, I see." Narei nodded seriously. "I taught her how to play the string game, Papa—Picking-up-fish-nets. She said they call it Kitten's Cradle here, but she never learned it. Isn't that a funny name? Kitten's Cradle?"

"Yes, I suppose it is."

Narei's small brow puckered. "I want to write her a letter—when I'm home on Pakoa. Can I write her a letter, Papa?"

Nagaro smiled. "Of course you can. It's a wonderful idea, and I'm sure she would like that. But you'll have to practice your writing—and your reading, if you want to be able to read her answer."

"Ooh! Do you really think she'll write me an *answer?*"

He laughed. "I'd bet you a rin that she does. Now find something to do while I talk to Omei."

The Turowan woman had put down her sewing and risen from the bench. "Ye can take the basket, Narei, and go out t' the kitchen garden an' pick some lettuce—the way I showed ye, remember? But mind that ye stay where I can see ye from the window."

"Uh-huh!" Narei scampered to the table, pulled a basket from under it, and skipped out the door.

Omei went to the chairs by the window and sat down on one of them. Nagaro sat on the other, after picking up the coiled string from where Nevien had left it. Omei turned her calm gaze to him, and asked, "What was it ye wanted t' say, Zirda?"

He looked at the string in his hands. Omei hadn't said a word while the princess was in the room, but he was sure she hadn't missed any of the nuances. He met her eyes again. They were black, and bright as a bird's, in a broad brown face that had begun to be marked by time.

"I want to pay you something for looking after Narei."

She shook her head. "Ye don't need to, Zirda. I've had my keep while I've been here, and I've still got some o' what those Leithian's paid me."

"That may be true, but you'll have living expenses after you leave the palace, and I don't suppose you'll be going back to... to the Leithians you were working for. You'll have to find another position. Won't you accept some payment?"

Omei turned her head to look out of the window to where Narei's crouching figure was bobbing along among the neat rows of kitchen greens. The mist was beginning to clear, and beyond the planted rows, a great gnarled pear tree was plainly visible. Nagaro remembered that tree—unfortunately. Nevien had called it her mother's pear tree. *He remembered climbing in its branches, picking pears and throwing them down, one after another, after another.* He had picked far too many, because Nevien, after first suggesting that he pick some, had tried to politely hint that she didn't need so many instead of simply telling him to stop.

He was saved from the embarrassing memory by Omei's voice. "No, thank ye, Zirda."

She had her bright black eyes on his face again, and had put her head a little on one side in a gesture that suddenly reminded him very strongly of Luka, her mother. "There's only one way I'll take money from ye, Captain," she added. "Let me serve ye a little longer. Let me look after Narei on this voyage ye're about t' make."

"All the way to Pakoa?" He stared at her. "But surely your home is here in Lankura—or somewhere nearby. If you sail to Pakoa, you'll have to get passage back again."

Omei simply nodded. "That's why I'd be takin' your money, Zirda. To buy my passage home."

"Oh." He considered. "Well," he said after a moment, "for my part, I'd be glad to have you there to look after Narei. And I think she'd like it too. Of course, I'd have to clear it with Lord Kuran, but it's more than likely he'd allow it. It could be dangerous, though. There's a chance we could be attacked."

A secret smile twinkled in Omei's eyes. "Do ye still have the stone my mother gave ye?" she asked.

Nagaro froze as her words brought a cold twist to his stomach. *So she did know.* But he reminded himself that this was not unexpected, and she plainly meant him no harm. He put his hand into his pocket and pulled out the smooth, flat, gray pebble with the Turowan life sign cut into it. "Yes," he said. "Why? Do you want it?"

She shook her head. "Oh no, Zirda. I have one o' my own." Her hand disappeared into a pocket in her skirt and reemerged with a polished white stone in the palm of it. The sign cut into the white stone's surface was identical to the one on Nagaro's gray one.

"Oh," he said, thinking he understood. "You aren't afraid because you believe that will protect you?"

She smiled serenely. "Did ye have yours with ye at Osfaraad?"

"Well, *yes*..."

"And what happened t' ye there?"

"I was very nearly killed, but there were two men who saved me. Roheed struck the sword away, and the Emperor spared my life. I'm sorry," he added, "I really don't believe it was the stone."

Omei's expression remained unchanged. "Not the *stone*," she said patiently. "The *Spirits* that bless the stone. And who's t' say the Spirits don't go whispering in men's ears?"

Looking into her eyes, Nagaro gave up. There was no use arguing with the certainty he read there. "I'll speak to Lord Kuran and send you word in the morning," he told her. "We probably won't sail until after noon, but you'll need to be ready early just in case—both of you."

Omei chuckled as she slipped her life stone back into her pocket. "That won't be hard," she said. "We've little enough t' be packin'—either one of us."

Just then Narei's voice reached them through the window. "Omei! Papa! Look! I'm climbing in the pear tree!"

And Nagaro nearly choked on his tongue as he resisted the urge to tell his daughter to get down from there immediately.

# Chapter 15

# A Transformation

He went down the stairs under a bitter cloud. It would have been perfectly ridiculous to tell Narei to get down from the tree. She was agile and strong and had climbed dozens of trees at home on Pakoa. It was only because it was *that* tree... *the queen's pear tree.*

He reached the bottom of the stairs and had started down the central hallway, leading to the palace's front door, when a man's voice hailed him from one of the many side halls.

"Captain Nagaro!"

He checked his stride, turned to look, and suppressed an instant impulse to flee. The man striding purposefully towards him up that side passage was Varsyl Virden.

"Captain! Please wait— I must speak to you!"

Nagaro glanced quickly around. He could guess what Varsyl wanted to talk about, and he knew he must do it, but he didn't want to be seen. Fortunately there was only a guard standing at his post a little way along the central hall, and a servant passing some distance ahead of him. He stepped into the side hall to meet Varsyl. "All right," he said. "But not here, please. Is there somewhere more private?"

Varsyl nodded. His eyes were very bright. "Of course—my chamber. Come this way, Captain."

Nagaro followed the other man along the side hall to a closed door, which Varsyl opened and ushered him through before closing it firmly behind them.

The room they had entered was one of the palace's many guest chambers. Like all of them, it was richly appointed. The polished stone floor, dark-stained walnut furniture, and brocade upholstery stood in stark contrast to the room where Nagaro had so recently parted with the Turowan woman, Omei.

"Please sit down, Zirda." Varsyl gestured to one of two chairs that flanked a small table.

Nagaro sank onto the cushioned seat, his heart full of dread.

Varsyl sat down opposite him and searched his face with such intensity that Nagaro felt quite uncomfortable under the man's deep blue gaze. If Varsyl was seeking something, he apparently didn't find it, however, for he seemed to falter and passed a hand over his eyes. When he lowered the hand, the excitement in his face had been replaced by uncertainty. He spoke cautiously. "Captain, the letter I received yesterday... I understand that it came from you?"

Nagaro swallowed, trying to moisten a mouth that had gone dry as dust, and managed to say, "Yes."

"I must ask you... did you... write it? Or do you merely know the one who did?"

For a moment Nagaro felt a temptation to seize upon the escape the other man was inadvertently offering him. It would be so easy to simply deny authorship. But he knew it wouldn't work. Varsyl would want to know where Leyel was, would want to speak to him. One lie would lead to another. So he swallowed again and forced himself to articulate the words. "I wrote it."

Some of the light came back then, and with it the eagerness. "Is it true then? All of it? Do you swear it is the truth?"

"Yes, it's true." That, at least, was easy to say. "I swear it in Vothra's name. I wouldn't lie to you about such things."

Varsyl closed his eyes. "*Thank you,*" he breathed. "Thank you. I was almost sure it had to be. No one knew she painted. I never mentioned it to you, or that she was musical. Whoever wrote that *had* to have known her."

There was a pause while Varsyl stared abstractedly past Nagaro. But then he shook himself, found Nagaro's eyes, and continued. "I did try talking to Vothra, as you suggested," he said. "But only last night—*after* I read the letter. I tried calling the Spirit before I lay down to sleep, and I was answered in a dream. It was quite extraordinary." The older man shifted in his chair. "I confess I had hoped that I might speak to *her*. To Maramine's spirit, that is."

Nagaro swallowed. "What did Vothra say?"

Varsyl looked sheepish. "I was told—gently but firmly—that Vothra is much, *much* greater than any one spirit. And that the spirit that had belonged to my sister was much greater than only Maramine. And—" Varsyl drew a breath "—then Vothra told me that if I wished to know more about anything in the letter, I would have to ask the man who'd written it, because he had suffered much and it was for him to decide what else he was willing to tell."

The words hung in the air between them, and Nagaro closed his eyes to escape Varsyl's probing gaze. "What do you wish to know?" he managed huskily.

"Well, of course, I want to know what *happened*. How was it that you seemed so *different?*"

*Oh Vothra!* Nagaro's eyes snapped open again in alarm. He found himself looking into Varsyl's earnest, sympathetic face. *The man had a right to some sort of answer.* He struggled to respond. "I was... drugged. To... to... force me into marriage with the princess—"

"By *whom*—?"

This was too hard. Nagaro raised his hands as if warding off an attack. "No. *Please!* I'm sorry, but I don't want to talk about it!"

"All right. Of course." Varsyl was instantly solicitous. "I suppose you would want to forget all that."

"I'm sorry I didn't say anything when you first spoke to me. It was hard even to write the letter."

Varsyl nodded. "I understand," he said quickly. Then he tried a new tack. "Tell me more about my sister."

So Nagaro stared into those eyes that were so like Maramine's and talked, sharing his memories of the woman who had raised him, her gentle and graceful ways, the things she had taught him, the happy and peaceful life she'd made for them at Averwin.

Varsyl devoured the information. When Nagaro paused, he asked, "How did she die? I hope it wasn't a hard death."

Nagaro hesitated. He saw in his mind, vividly, the woman writhing on the bed. Heard the knife-edge horror of her screams. "Her end wasn't easy—" He faltered. "Don't ask me how it happened. It wasn't a natural sickness that took her, and... and there's danger in it becoming known—danger for me, and possibly for you. Her death was hard, but she didn't suffer long. And in her Death Dream, that she sent to me, she spoke only of her joy in anticipation of joining Vothra."

"She chose *you* for her Death Dream?" Varsyl's brow constricted, and hurt rang in his voice.

"I am sorry. She knew I was in need. And... and having had no word from you, she couldn't have known the depth of your trouble."

"Of course. Forgive me." Varsyl put a hand to his brow. "Of course she would send her Death Dream to her son."

*There it was.*

Nagaro drew a deep breath. "I don't believe I'm her son, My Lord."

The other man stared at him. "But, what else—?"

"She told me I was a foundling. When I heard the tale about being the child of her dead lover, and asked her, she denied it—to *me!*"

Varsyl considered him, frowning. "It does seem strange that she would hold *so* true to the promise she made to our father," he admitted, "—even in speaking to you. But she would have feared losing her place at Averwin if you said the wrong thing to the wrong person." He paused. "How old were you when you asked her about it?"

"Perhaps eight, or nine."

Varsyl relaxed. "Well, there, you see? A child of that age can't be trusted with a dangerous secret."

"But I was seventeen when she died! In seventeen years she never once called me 'son', and I never called her Mother!"

Varsyl regarded him seriously. "That is extraordinary, yes, but so was she. Father made her swear in Vothra's name to keep the secret. She would have felt bound by that, absolutely."

"So absolutely that she lied to me outright, My Lord? And though she was always very kind to me, she was somehow... distant. How do you explain that?"

Varsyl's deep blue eyes, so very like Maramine's, darkened with a sadness that was also familiar. "Perhaps it helped her to maintain the fiction, Nagaro. Should I call you that? Nagaro?"

Nagaro nodded. "Yes. Not *the other*. Never the other."

"All right." The dark eyes held his. "And you may call me Varsyl. But there is another reason, perhaps, Nagaro. How should I say this?" Varsyl frowned. "You are, I think, more like the men of the House of Virden, than you are like Beloras."

"Well, I'm certainly no minstrel. I can't sing a note. And Beloras was no swordsman. That's another reason why I don't think—"

"But that's exactly what I mean!" Varsyl leaned forward eagerly. "*I* have no gift for music either. Maramine had that gift from our mother, but it was never a Virden family trait. So you're not a minstrel, but a swordsman—like me, the man who slew her true love! You must have inherited your talent from your maternal grandfather, *through her*, but it would not have been a talent she'd have wanted you to have. Do you understand?"

And he did understand. Because it made sense, especially when he remembered how long she had resisted his pleas to be allowed to study swordsmanship. He'd begged her, over and over, for years. In the end, she had only relented because she'd said he should be able to defend himself! *And almost her last words to him, in the Death Dream, had been a warning against anger, against vengeance.* Another thought struck him. "She gave me a ring, when I was twelve," he said slowly. "I always thought it must have been left with me, on the doorstep, though she never actually *said* so. She just said it was from my parents. And she told me to keep it secret."

"What sort of ring?"

Nagaro started to reach into his shirt. "A man's ring—"

"Leave it then." Varsyl gestured for him to stay his hand. "It would have been from Beloras. I wouldn't know it, and I have no right to touch it. But don't you see how this fits? If you had been a foundling, why should you keep the ring secret? She wanted to give it to you, but couldn't tell you it's significance without being foresworn. So she told you to keep it secret, so the truth would not get out and her promise would remain unbroken."

"*Yes...*" Nagaro frowned. "I suppose so. But I wish I could be certain of this. Would Beloras have family who could identify the ring?"

"Perhaps. But alas, I can't even give you his family name. He came from far to the north, originally, from Irvenen Wared, I believe. My father would have known more, but he is dead. I'm sorry, Nagaro."

"Do I *look* like Maramine's son?"

Varsyl frowned. "I confess that I can't see anything of my sister in your face. And there's your *coloring...*"

"It's kuma stain. My skin is naturally fair."

"Ah. I thought it must be something like that."

"And Beloras? What did he look like?"

Varsyl sighed. "He was a very handsome man—that much I do remember—black-haired and gray-eyed. That much you share. But as for the exact shape of his features, I saw too little of him, and it was too long ago. Again, I'm sorry."

Nagaro stared at the tabletop. Was this the truth then? Had this been Maramine's fate—having to watch him grow up looking like Beloras and acting like her brother? "I don't know," he said finally, raising his eyes. "A lot of this seems to make sense, but even in the Death Dream she didn't say anything about being my mother."

Varsyl heaved a sigh. "Well," he said. "It doesn't matter whether the relationship is by blood or by adoption. I will always look upon you now as a nephew. And I hope you can think of me as an uncle. I'd like to offer you a place within the House of Virden, if you'll have it."

Nagaro swallowed. At that moment he was thinking of how nice it might be to have an uncle, and that he rather liked Varsyl. But it wasn't that simple. "I'm sorry, Varsyl," he said carefully. "I thank you for your offer, but I have sworn never to use *that name*. I don't wish to be known by it."

The older man sighed again. "I think I understand," he said. "And it's not as if you need us, after all. You have done very well on your own, despite all the cruel turns that Lokundas has put in your path. I'd be proud to claim your kinship openly, but if it can't be open, I must accept that. Perhaps I don't deserve it, after all, considering what I did."

"It isn't that," Nagaro told him hastily. "You're being very kind. It's just that I've buried the past. And also, I believe it would be dangerous to declare this openly."

An expression of resignation crossed the other man's face, though the deep blue eyes didn't waiver. "So be it," he said. "But it doesn't change what's in my heart. And if the world should change, my offer stands. If you ever need anything that I can give, you have only to ask, even though it may be in secret. The House of Virden owes you that much."

"Thank you," Nagaro murmured. "I'll remember it." He didn't know what else to say. His heart was full.

Varsyl nodded. "You are most welcome. And now I must go to finish what I'd begun to do—to say farewell to Delasin." He rose and extended his hand.

Nagaro stood up as well, and grasped the hand in his. As their fingers parted, he found his voice. "My Lord, I feel ashamed—"

"But *why?*" Varsyl frowned.

"Because I've always cast the family of my Lady Guardian as villains when I've told the story of my life. I've said they wanted none of me, but I never sought out anyone of your house to ask. And now I find it isn't so."

Varsyl smiled an understanding smile. "You can scarcely be blamed for that, Nagaro. And it *was* true, as far as my father was concerned—while he was lord of Virden Wared. But I am not my father. And see how promptly you responded when you found that out? And how kindly?"

"I could not have done less—not and count myself a good  follower of the Path."

Varsyl was moving in the direction of the door. "That's because you are a good man."

"And because your sister taught me well."

Varsyl flashed him another smile. "True enough. Indeed, she taught us both. But it seems you took the lessons more to heart than I. You have become what I once dreamed of being, a true defender of Edrovir."

"I don't think it is ever too late to choose right actions, Varsyl." Nagaro paused awkwardly in the doorway. "But I'm afraid I will have to continue to tell the same tale."

"I understand."

"And you will keep all that we've spoken of today in confidence?"

"Of course."

They emerged together into the corridor outside and started back towards the intersection with the central hallway. As they neared that crossing of ways, Varsyl turned once more to Nagaro, and said, "Whatever comes, Captain, I am forever in your debt. The gift you've given me today is beyond price."

"I'm very glad of it."

They stepped forward side by side into the central hallway—and nearly collided with two women.

"Oh!" Nagaro exclaimed reflexively. "Ladies, excuse me!" Further words then froze on his lips because he saw that the two ladies were Nevien and Lady Merriel.

He caught Varsyl's eye. The older man's glance flicked from him to the princess and back again. Silently he mouthed, *"Does she know?"* Nagaro made the barest shake of his head. He was aware that Nevien was staring at him, questioningly. Before he could think of anything to say, however, Merriel spared him the trouble by speaking.

The diminutive Leithian woman had been looking from one man to the other, and now she said, "Good afternoon, Captain Nagaro, and Lord Varsyl. I must say you're looking well, My Lord."

Nagaro could only manage a quick bow, directed generally to both women.

Varsyl was more self-possessed. "A very good afternoon, My Lady Merriel, and My Lady Princess." He smiled broadly as he bowed to each in turn. "It's always a pleasure to see you both. The captain and I were too engrossed in our conversation, I fear. We didn't mean to run you down."

"Oh tush!" Merriel waved a hand. "There was no harm done. But where are you off to in such a hurry, My Lord?"

"I must say goodbye to my daughter, and then take the road to Virden Wared. I regret that I can't stay longer to talk, but I've already been delayed and I've a dozen miles to cover before nightfall." He bowed again, beaming. "Farewell to you both, dear ladies." He turned to Nagaro. "And farewell to you, also, Captain. May the Benevolent Spirit be with you."

Nagaro inclined his head. "Farewell, My Lord. Vothra keep you on the way."

Varsyl moved graciously past Merriel and Nevien, and strode off down the central hallway in the direction from which the two women had come. There was a distinct spring in his step.

All three of those he left behind watched him go, the two women looking slightly stunned. It was Merriel who broke the silence. "Well," she said, *"that* was a pleasant surprise, I must say. Though I don't know what's come over him. Varsyl is usually so *grim.*"

"Morose, I would say." Nevien spoke for the first time. She turned to Nagaro. "Whatever did you do to him, Captain?"

The words were spoken lightly, and she managed what was obviously intended to be a teasing smile, though it looked a bit strained. He could feel the effort she was making to be jocular, and he winced, inwardly, both at her effort and at her question.

"Why, yes," Merriel chimed in. "You *must* tell us. I believe I heard him thanking you for something."

Nagaro made a panicked grasp at the only safe part of the truth. "I, ah, was able to give him some information that pleased him."

"Pleased him!" Merriel exclaimed. "Transformed him, I would say. Whatever did you tell him that has made such a difference?"

"It was of a private nature."

"Oh dear! I beg your pardon!" Merriel was instantly apologetic. "In that case you must keep it in confidence, of course." She suppressed her curiosity and continued brightly, "So, whither are *you* bound, Captain?"

"Back to the Fleet Compound," he said with immense relief. "We'll be sailing tomorrow to return the Mautep and their ships to the Mahuk Baar."

Merriel nodded her understanding. "Then we are all going in the same direction, for the moment anyway."

"Yes," Nevien put in. "Father has called a meeting concerning the man Kenthos." She gave a little sigh as she started forward along the hallway. "And I must go to it."

Merriel moved forward as well, beside the princess, and Nagaro fell into step at Nevien's other side.

"Narei will be going as well, Merriel," Nevien observed. "So if you want to give her the little apron you were sewing, you'll have to finish it tonight."

"What, she's leaving so soon?" Lady Merriel glanced at Nagaro for confirmation. He managed to nod, though he was watching Nevien.

"She must go back to her home of course," the princess explained. "It's not as if she came here on holiday." She gave a small brittle laugh that cut Nagaro like shards of glass.

He sought for something to say that might please her. "She says she wants to write you a letter, My Lady. I told her I thought you would answer it."

"Of course I will. That's sweet of her." Nevien turned away abruptly with a movement of her hand that suggested she had something in her eye.

Nagaro's heart sank. *He'd only made her cry again.* "I actually plan to bring her to Lankura to live someday, because I miss her so much," he said desperately. Their steps had carried them to the doorway of the Audience Chamber, where the two women stopped, and he stopped also. "I thought it would be in a few years' time," he continued. "But perhaps the time is now. After she spends a little time on Pakoa—" He stopped speaking because Nevien had turned to face him squarely. Moisture still glistened in her eyes, but her expression was resolute.

"No, Captain," she said firmly. "I know what you're trying to do, but it's quite unnecessary. Narei is a charming, light-hearted child, and I look forward to seeing more of her in a few years when she's old enough to leave her home. I've enjoyed spending time with her because she has distracted me from... other things... but I can find other distractions." She gave him a smile that was almost warm enough to thaw the chill that lay on his heart. "Now please don't worry about me anymore. I'm quite all right." She turned to the other woman. "Come Merriel," she said, as the two women entered the Audience Chamber. Then she added over her shoulder, "I wish you a safe voyage, Captain."

*Keshaal!* Nagaro stood for several long seconds outside the tall oak doors. *She was trying to be strong, and he wanted so much to help, but everything he said only seemed to make things worse.* And there was no way he could explain to her that nothing was right with him if she was suffering—because he couldn't tell her *why.*

Eventually he moved on, almost blindly, because standing there any longer might make people stare. It was all too much. *Nevien and Narei... and Varsyl's interpretation of Maramine and Beloras...* He scarcely knew what to think anymore, or what to do, except to go through the motions that were expected of him. *Perhaps it was just as well that he would be leaving Lankura tomorrow.*

When he passed through the palace entrance hall, Delvin had to call him by name and run after him. If not for the vigilance of the young guardsman, he would have gone out the front door of the palace and down the steps without reclaiming his sword.

Chapter 16

# Hostage Of Honor

Nagaro stood on the captain's platform on the stern castle of the *Sword of Freedom*, looking down with a mixture of pride and parental apprehension on a scene that was bathed in brilliant afternoon sunlight. Below him, on the main deck, Narei was squaring off with Taru in a mock battle with wooden practice swords. She wore a miniature version of fisherman's pants and tirkyl, her hair was tied back, and she held Nagaro's old practice sword clutched in her fist. Taru wasn't a big man, and the little girl was tall for a child not quite seven, but she still looked over-matched as the two of them circled like cats. The apparent unevenness of the contest was less evident, however, when the two combatants moved in and out with a clatter of the wooden weapons. The exchange was sharp, but no hits were scored.

The bout had drawn an audience. Various members of the crew who happened to be on deck had drifted over and now formed a semi-circle. Even Pavo had joined them, though he was still keeping one eye on the rigging. Roheed was there also. The young Mautep officer hung back behind the front rank, watching with a puzzled frown. Omei stood to one side with Narei's little apron neatly folded in her hands and her feet planted squarely against the ship's motion. A brisk sea breeze whipped her skirts as her dark eyes keenly followed the movements of the two combatants.

Taru darted forward again. Click-clack! Whack! Crack! The sticks rebounded off each other. An appreciative murmur arose from the onlookers as Taru danced back out, shaking his head.

"Don't be goin' too easy on her now, Taru," one of the men drawled. "Just 'cause she's half your size."

Taru risked a brief withering glance in the man's direction, then cried, "Hoi!" as Narei took advantage of his inattention to launch an attack of her own. He tried to dodge, but Narei pursued him without mercy.

Clack! Swish! Click-click-*clack!*

"A hit! A hit for Narei!"

The crowd bellowed with laughter as Taru spun away and came around, crouching low, on his guard. Narei stood on guard also, getting her breath back.

"Go on, Taru! Even it up!"

This time Taru wisely ignored the taunt. Instead he moved in again, making a couple of feints. Narei swung at him and missed. He made another lunge, coming in very low. Click-*clack!* And Narei's sword went spinning away across the deck. Half a dozen of the men leaped after it, laughing and shouting.

Taru straightened, then passed his sword into his left hand and extended his right to his small opponent. "Well-fought, Narei," he said a little breathlessly.

Narei took his hand and shook it with an exaggerated pumping motion. "Thank you, Uncle Taru!" She turned her face up to her father, grinning. "I hit him, Papa! Did you see?"

"Yes, Narei. It was a hit. But it wasn't very fair to attack when he wasn't looking."

Narei laughed. "All right, Papa. I won't do that next time."

Taru stepped away from the little girl and collected the second practice sword from the man who had retrieved it.

Omei promptly moved in. "If ye still want t' help the cook, Narei, ye'd best come now," she said, holding out the apron.

"Oh yes! I want to help!" Narei stood impatiently while Omei tied the apron around her waist. Then she ducked under the woman's arm and disappeared through the stern castle door. Omei went after her, shaking her head.

Taru laid the two swords at the base of the stern castle wall, then made for the ladder, mounted it in a few bounds, and came to stand beside Nagaro on the captain's platform.

"That daughter of yours is a little she-tiger," he remarked. "I swear she's nearly as fast as you, and all her attacks are so *low!*"

"It's only because she's short, Taru. It's an advantage she'll lose as she grows." He considered his friend. "And I know you were trying not to hurt her."

"Well, o' course! And that's not easy, without being roundly beaten. The other men can laugh, but I'd like t' see *them* try it. At least I can still disarm her."

"I would have thought those swords were gone forever. Where did you find them?"

Taru grinned crookedly. "Gama had them. She'd taken them out of Father's house. She kept them all this time and never said."

Both men stood silently for a long moment, remembering, as the *Sword of Freedom* cut her way southwards through the deep blue waters of the Great Channel. Below them on the main deck, the men went about their tasks. Pavo was directing his deck crew to make some adjustments to the lines. Roheed leaned against the port rail, amidships, looking across the water. From time to time the young Mautep glanced up at the two men on the captain's platform, but for the most part he seemed to be watching the coast of Edrovir slide past.

Nagaro frowned. There had been no opportunity to discuss the evemts of the week's end with his friends, since Taru and Pavo had returned too late the previous day and the morning had been filled with hurried preparations to sail. He cleared his throat. "How is Gama?"

Taru shrugged. "Well enough, I guess, for an old woman."

"And Hamani? Did you happen to see her?"

"Aye. She was there."

"What did she cook this time?"

Taru shot a glance at his friend, but Nagaro appeared to be watching the channel ahead and the other ships of their small fleet. It seemed an innocent question, so he answered. "Sausage rolls."

"The ones wrapped in pastry that melts in your mouth?"

"Aye, just like that."

"*Mmm...* I wish I'd been there. I love those. I'll have to go with you next time. But if she makes sausage rolls again, I might just offer her marriage on the spot." Nagaro turned to face his friend, who was gaping at him. "So how are you doing with courting Jitali?"

"I... that is, it's going well—now that I'm not under a warrant of arrest anymore."

"So her father wouldn't mind if I asked to court Hamani?"

Taru frowned. "Nagaro, ye wouldn't *really*, would ye?"

"Well someone's going to. What is it that Gama says? 'There's no blessing like good cooking.' Be sure to tell me the next time you plan to go, won't you?"

"Right. I will, o' course."

There was a pause. Nagaro allowed it to lengthen enough for a modest amount of reflection before he changed the subject. "I talked to Varsyl Virden again. That is, he wanted to talk to me. He was very decent, very grateful for the information. He even offered me a place in the House of Virden. He thinks I'm his nephew."

"Well so do I." Taru was suddenly all attention. "Don't ye agree?"

It was Nagaro's turn to become hesitant. "He said that I'm like the Virden men—a swordsman, not a musician—which could have made Maramine more distant, and explain why she told me to keep the ring secret, if it had belonged to Beloras."

"Of course! That makes perfect sense. So if Beloras was your father, what're ye going t' do about it?"

"I don't know. I've thought about going to Irvenen—where Varsyl said that Beloras came from. But it's a big Wared, and Varsyl couldn't tell me Beloras' family name. The next time I'm invited to Averwin, I'll try to look in Maramine's desk again to see if I can learn anything more."

"That's a good idea." Taru paused, then said, "Do ye mind if I tell Pavo what Varsyl said? *That'll* show him!"

"I don't mind, as long as you're careful that no one's listening."

"O' course I'll be careful! Don't be daft." Taru started to step away from the rail.

"You can also tell him that I don't think Rastyl will be troubling me anymore."

"What d' ye mean?"

"Remember that gathering at the Golden Branch that Lord Soren told me about?" Nagaro proceeded to briefly describe the event, with particular attention to his parting conversation with Rastyl.

Taru shook his head. "Huh! He *is* an odd one. But now ye've told him t' push off his boat, and it sounds like he means t' do it."

"He thinks he's found the real heir of Loros, and it isn't Kenthos."

"Just so long as he doesn't expect ye to fight for the man, eh?"

"I *might* fight for him, if he were the right kind of man. But I'll make up my own mind, and only after I know enough about him."

"Right ye are, Capt'n!" Taru gave him a mock salute. "I'm with ye there. And now I'm going below to see to the oar deck." Grinning, he turned and made for the ladder.

Nagaro stood alone on the captain's platform. The wind was out of the west and the island of Lapoa was slipping past to starboard. The six Edroviran ships and the four Mahuk craft they were escorting were moving down the center of the Great Channel, in formation. The *Sword of Freedom* was the middle of the three ships that made an arc in front of the tightly-clustered Mahuk galleys. The *Pride of Lankura* was cutting the swells thirty yards to port, while the *Sea Eagle* was running in an equivalent position to starboard. The three other Edroviran ships, *Tempest*, *Heart of Oak*, and *Harbinger*, formed a similar arc around the rear of the group of Mahuk craft.

Nagaro reached for the spyglass and scanned the channel ahead. There were sails here and there, all belonging to harmless fishing boats or merchant craft. He lowered the glass. So far all was going according to plan.

A movement on the main deck caught his eye and he looked down to meet the eyes of Roheed jir-Akaan, looking up. The Mautep raised a hand as if asking permission to speak. "Is permit that I come up, Nagaro Kiraam Shaku-Tal?"

Nagaro nodded acknowledgment. "You may go anywhere on the ship, Roheed."

Roheed frowned, but he made for the ladder, mounting it with lithe grace. Once on the stern castle deck, he approached the captain's platform more hesitantly. "I would make speak with you. Is permit?" he ventured.

"Yes. Of course." Nagaro stood aside to make a space on the small raised platform.

Roheed mounted to stand beside him. The young Mautep officer was a slim figure, erect in his scarlet and black uniform, shaven now, his mustache impeccable. His brows were constricted as if in thought, and after a moment, he said, "You say I can go anywhere—" He stopped, then started again. "Why I am here, on this ship? Can you tell me, Nagaro Kiraam? They have try to explain, but I do not understand."

Nagaro considered. "You are what we call a *hostage of honor.*"

"Yes. That is what they say. And I understand *host-age.* That is *turtaak.* But what is mean honor part of host-age?"

"It means we honor you by treating you as a guest—letting you go anywhere on the ship. We trust you not to try to escape, or to hurt anyone. And your men must trust that we will not hurt you." Nagaro paused. "I didn't think it was necessary to have a hostage, because I trust you as commander of your men. But those who have power insisted. So I suggested the hostage of honor arrangement and offered to have you on my ship."

"I understand now." Roheed nodded knowingly. "Thank you for do this. I like to see this ship." Roheed continued standing at the rail. At length he said, "I am very glad to see you look so well and strong, Nagaro Kiraam."

"Ah, thank you." Nagaro squinted out across the main deck to the glittering surface of the sea beyond. "I am grateful to you for stopping Urchak."

Roheed shrugged. "If I do not speak when I did, Emperor would have stop him."

Nagaro turned to face the other man. "He almost waited too long. I nearly died from the wounds made by the whip."

Roheed made a movement that was a kind of flinch. "I am sorry."

Nagaro swept the matter aside with a gesture. "I'm still grateful. I expected to die."

Roheed shifted his weight uncomfortably. "I have thought maybe it is your plan to die," he ventured awkwardly. "Maybe that is why you tell me Sindar is not dead."

"My *plan?* Why would I plan to die?"

"Maybe is to bring anger of Sheptuum down on Mahuk Baar."

Nagaro stared at the young Mautep for several stunned seconds. Then he shook his head emphatically. "No, Roheed," he said. "I don't think that way. I was trying to keep more men from dying—Droviri and Hashtep, both."

Roheed's narrow black eyes widened. "Then is it *true* you have find Sindar?"

"Of course it's true. I wouldn't lie to you. I didn't want you to think you still had to pay the blood debt."

Roheed's face registered complete astonishment "You think of such thing? In *that time?*"

Nagaro frowned, remembering the strange place where his mind had been. "I thought I was going to die. There were things I wanted to tell people before it was too late—like telling the Emperor that free men row better than slaves."

Roheed shook his head wonderingly. "You are very strange man, Nagaro Kiraam. Good strange."

Nagaro laughed a little. "I will accept that."

There was a short silence.

Then Roheed said, "Your daughter is very good fighter."

"She is only a child, but yes, she has talent."

"It is usual that Droviri woman are train to be warrior?"

"No it isn't. And I don't know that Narei will want to be a warrior. She likes to fight now, but when she is grown, who knows?"

"Why do you have her on ship with you? This is usual?"

"No. She was taken from her home on Pakoa. I'm taking her back again."

"She was taken?" Roheed was puzzled. "Who have take her?"

Nagaro frowned. *How to explain...* "It was some Droviri men who wanted to force me to come to Lankura that took her," he said after a moment's thought.

Roheed stared at him. "That is not honorable. Why they do it?"

"Because I broke the law when I took Pavo away. They wanted me to be punished. And Pavo too, of course."

"Is that why you have go to Lankura? For get back your daughter?"

Nagaro nodded.

"And Pavo Maat have go too?"

"He chooses to go where I go."

There was another silence while Roheed digested this. Finally he said, "So you have wife on Pakoa island?"

Nagaro swallowed, concerned about where this might lead. "No. I have no wife."

The other man's narrow dark eyes considered him. "How is it then you have daughter?"

Nagaro drew a long breath. It was the obvious question, and he was determined to explain. "Her mother played me a trick," he said at last, "when I had drunk too much wine. She pretended to want me, when really she wanted to get a child, to fool another man. When the other man wasn't fooled and didn't want the child, she came back to find me—"

"—So you have keep child, but not woman." Roheed finished the sentence for him.

"You could say that." Nagaro had expected some blame, at least some shock, but the young Mautep sounded as if this outcome made perfect sense to him.

"How many year have your daughter?"

"Ah... six. Almost seven now."

"I have son. Just seven year."

"Oh. So then, *you* have a wife?" Nagaro felt a fool for asking, but if Roheed could so easily accept that he hadn't married Narei's mother...

"Yes. My father have made good match for me." Roheed spoke with evident pride. "Maybe your daughter will be good match for my son?"

Nagaro had to struggle to keep his mouth from dropping open. Roheed's expression indicated he was quite sincere. "Ah—" he tried to find words "—if your son wanted to marry my daughter, when he is grown, he would have to court her. And if she wished to marry him, that wouldn't displease me, but it would be *her* choice." He floundered to a halt, hoping he hadn't insulted the other man.

Roheed's brows were knit in a frown. "Droviri do not make match for their child?"

"Some do. I don't."

Roheed's teeth suddenly flashed in a smile. "Ah," he said. "Daughter of Nagaro Kiraam Shaku-Tal must be *win*. Is very good!" He actually laughed. "And she is good with sword. So I will tell my son. What is name of your daughter?"

Nagaro was trying to cover his astonishment. "Narei," he managed.

"*Nah*-ray," Roheed rolled the name on his tongue. "Narei Kiraam Shaku-Tal. Is very good!"

Nagaro frowned. "Ah... Roheed," he began, carefully, "I do not like this... thing... that you call me—Kiraam Shaku-Tal."

Roheed frowned in his turn. "You say you do not have family, but for honor you must have family name. So I have give you one."

"I... see..." Nagaro chewed his lip. "But I have to tell you that in Edrovir we do not honor a man who takes things that don't belong to him. We call him *thief*. For us, thief is not a good word."

"You do not like I call you Kiraam?" Roheed's voice carried a note of dismay. "Kiraam is not bad word—"

"Not to your people," Nagaro put in quickly. "Pavo has explained that to me. *I* don't mind, really, if you say it in Hashti—and explain it if anyone asks. I know you didn't mean me any dishonor, but I thought you should know."

"*Yes...* is good that I know." Roheed stood for several long seconds, frowning. Then he added, "So your people think it is dishonor when Mautep take gold from Droviri ship or Droviri island?"

Nagaro nodded. "Yes, that is true."

Roheed returned the nod. "That also is good I know." He paused. "I will remember it. And you will remember what I have say about my son. He is name Kodaal jir-Akaan." Roheed smiled broadly. "Now I think I go to look at oar deck."

The young Mautep put out his hand, which Nagaro took. Then he made Nagaro a bow before turning to descend the ladder to the main deck.

Nagaro stared after the retreating figure. *"Vothra's Eyes and Ears,"* he murmured to himself. It seemed that Roheed had actually tried to arrange a marriage between Narei and his son! She was only six, and Roheed's son was only seven. And on top of that, she was Droviri while Roheed's family were high-born Mautep and Nagaro had made it clear that, Narei had been born out of wedlock! None of that seemed to matter to Roheed at all.

Nagaro shook his head, bemused. *Would he really have Kodaal jir-Akaan knocking on his door in ten or fifteen year's time, asking after Narei Kiraam Shaku-Tal?*

***

Three days later, the *Sword of Freedom* rested at anchor in Pakoa Harbor among the other ships of their oddly mixed fleet. Nagaro stood at the rail, waiting to descend the rope ladder to one of the longboats. He smiled faintly, remembering the clumsy movements of the Mautep ships as their sea warriors had tried to maneuver through the narrow passage into the harbor without any trained slaves at the oars. It was fortunate, he reflected, that the wind had been favorable all the way down the length of the Great Channel. They had made very good time without having to do much rowing.

Pavo was already sitting in the longboat, and Narei scampered easily down the rope ladder to join him. Omei stood for a moment, eyeing the ladder askance. Presently, however, she straightened, hitched up a bit of her skirt in the front, and tucked a strategic fistful of it into her waistband. Then she swung her sturdy legs one at a time over the rail and went down with relative ease.

Nagaro followed as soon as she reached the bottom. He took his seat in the longboat's bow, with his back to the shore and picked up one of the pairs of oars. Pavo, seated in the stern, deployed another pair. Narei and Omei were sitting between the two men, facing Nagaro, and he gave them as serious a glance as he could manage, addressing them with mock formality. "If you two ladies would just give us a warning when we get within a dozen feet of the wharf, I'd be very much obliged."

Narei giggled. "All right, Papa."

Omei gave him one of her knowing smiles. "I'll see she doesn't play ye any tricks, Zirda."

Narei first shot the woman a pouting glance, but then she grinned. And when the time came, she called out, "Now, Papa!" at just the right moment. Nagaro shipped his oars, grabbed a coil of rope, and stood up. He turned, balancing in the bow, and deftly sent the rope snaking out to be caught by one of the village men who served as a dock hand. A small cheer went up from the crowd that had gathered on the wharf. Nagaro raised a hand, saluting them, and drew another cheer. Then he set about helping to make the boat fast and assisting Narei and Omei to climb up the wooden ladder to the wharf. He got a third cheer when he climbed the ladder himself.

The loudest cheer came, however, when at last Pavo mounted the ladder and came to stand amongst the townspeople.

Tenepti was there at the front of crowd, right in the middle, her face wreathed in a smile and her eyes alight. She all but glowed with happiness as she threw her arms around her husband's neck. "Oh Pavo," she murmured, her face pressed against his chest. He reached up to stroke her hair, then her cheek. And then, as if husband and wife had the same impulse at exactly the same instant, she lifted her head and he bent his, and their lips met in a sweet, lingering kiss.

A collective sigh arose from the crowd, then another ragged cheer. And then there were people moving everywhere, with most of the folk bent on congratulating Pavo and Tenepti.

Nagaro stood and watched as the Hashtep couple thanked their well-wishers. It warmed his heart to witness their happiness, even though it seemed unlikely he would ever experience the same. Seeing Narei start to slip away, he made a grab for her. Bending, he said, "Stay close, Ginger Pie." When he straightened, he found Yuli, the innkeeper's wife, in front of him.

"Welcome home, Tor Nagaro," she said as she embraced him, then stepped back, smiling broadly. "Ye're looking well. And I see that ye've put everything t' rights—everything that can be, that is." She leaned closer as her smile faded. "We got word o' the queen's passing from the same ship that brought Pavo's letter for Tenepti, so we had the happy and sad news all at once. How is the princess taking it?"

"She is trying to be strong, but it's plain to see she's grieving."

Yuli nodded soberly. "All our hearts are with her."

"I'll tell her that when next I see her."

Yuli ducked her head, abashed. "As if she'd care what the likes of us think!"

He gave her a gentle smile. "She may not know you, Yuli, but she does care what folk are thinking.

"Oh well, all right." The Turowa glanced up at him almost shyly. "Ye take good care of her, Tor Nagaro. And take care o' yourself, too." Yuli made something almost like a curtsy as she withdrew.

Suddenly, Tulara was there with Habu, her husband, behind her. "Dear Nagaro," she said, stretching to give him a peck on the cheek. "It's good t' see ye back safe, and back in that uniform. But where is Taru?"

"On the ship." Nagaro read conflicted disappointment in her eyes. "One of the officers had to stay," he added hurriedly, "and, since he had no business of his own ashore, he volunteered."

"I see. But he's well, is he?"

"Oh yes, quite well."

"And happy t' be back in the Fleet? Back in Lankura?"

Nagaro shifted his feet. Tulara seemed to be probing. Habu was looking back and forth from her to Nagaro with a puzzled expression. "He seems to be," Nagaro ventured, then added, "Actually, he's courting a young woman in Wotana."

"Is he? Oh good." Tulara looked genuinely relieved. "Will ye tell him we're sorry we missed him?"

"Yes, of course. And it's good to see you both." Nagaro watched the young couple walk away hand in hand, glad he hadn't mentioned that the "young woman" was a stunningly beautiful girl of seventeen who let her sister do all the cooking.

Nagaro was just leaving the crowd with Narei in tow, when Dakuro, the Town Chief and blacksmith, strode up. "Captain Nagaro!" he cried jovially. "I must say it's good t' have ye back in our town." He glanced around. "Openly under the sun, I mean. And ye've brought both Pavo and your daughter safely back too, I see."

Nagaro nodded. "Yes. Luckily it all came out all right. But tell me, Dakuro, have there been any Mahuk ships sighted around here recently?"

"Besides the ones in our harbor right now, d' ye mean? I hope ye know what ye're doing, bringing them here."

Nagaro frowned seriously. "They have no slaves to row, and the warriors aboard them have no swords. We're escorting them back to Mahuk waters."

"Ah. Well and good." The burly Turo accepted this reassurance with an easy shrug. "As a matter o' fact, there were some Mahuk ships that snuck past us going south, three days ago. Four o' them, our watchers said."

"Did they see the color of their banners?"

"Ye always ask, so we always mark it. They were green and gold this time."

Nagaro nodded. "Those were Tuluptak's ships. They tried tc make an attack on Long Harbor while the Emperor's men were attacking Lankura, but they were soundly trounced. I expect they hung about until it was clear things had gone badly for Baalkir's fleet. They'll be carrying the news to the Emperor."

"Is that bad for ye?" Dakuro looked worried.

"Actually, no. I'd rather the Emperor had advance knowledge of the outcome of his little gambit."

"Ye would?" Dakuro's brow furrowed. Then he shrugged. "Well, I expect ye know what ye're doing, Captain. Will ye be staying long?"

"No more than a few hours. We may take on some water, but we're well-provisioned. And now, I must take my daughter home."

As he and Narei started towards the street, he noticed Omei standing stolidly, watching him with her quick dark eyes. He approached her and said, "I'd like to pay you now, Omei. I don't want to take a chance of forgetting." He dug into his purse and began counting out silver half-trokin coins. "I'd like to give you five hundred rins."

"The passage to Lankura's not likely t' be more'n three hundred at most, Zirda," Omei observed tartly. "I asked around."

"Really?" Nagaro paused, but only for a second. "But there was your service on my ship, and it may be days or weeks before a ship comes to carry you home. You'll have to live on something until then."

"Three hundred and fifty then."

"Four hundred," he said firmly, and he pressed the coins into her waiting palm.

The dark eyes considered him. "Please yourself, Zirda," she said, and the money disappeared into the pocket of her skirt.

"Narei! There ye are!"

"*Pilo!*"

Nagaro had let go of Narei's hand to count the money, so there was nothing to keep the little girl from darting away to meet her young cousin. The two children nearly collided, but Pilo thrust Narei away from him. "I've come t' take ye home," he said severely. "Mama couldn't come, so she sent me." Then he noticed the two adults, who had approached in the meantime. "Hallo Uncle Nagaro. Who's *that?*"

Nagaro smiled faintly. "This is Tira Omei, Pilo. She's been looking after Narei on the ship."

"Oh." Pilo stuck out his hand awkwardly to the woman. "Pleased t' meet ye, Tira Omei."

Omei solemnly took his hand and shook it. "I'm pleased t' meet ye too, Pilo. And I'll walk with the both o' ye."

Nagaro cleared his throat. "So will I."

Pilo immediately rounded on him. "Ye don't need t' come too! I'm thirteen! Don't ye *trust* me, Uncle Nagaro?"

"Of course I trust you, Pilo. And your mother obviously trusts you or she wouldn't have sent you. But I'm only going to be in port for a few hours, and I'd like to see her."

"Oh." Pilo was mollified. "Well come on then. If ye're in such a hurry, we'd best get started."

Narei tugged at his sleeve. "I want to tell you what happened, Pilo!"

"Ye can tell me while we're walking. Come on, little one."

The two children immediately started off along the dock. Nagaro glanced back and saw that the crowd was breaking up. Pavo and Tenepti were standing together, he with his arm encircling her shoulders. Pavo raised his free hand. "I am go to see my son now, Nagaro!"

"All right, Pavo. I'll meet you back here in two hours." Nagaro waved to his friend and then hurried to follow Pilo and Narei. Without a word, Omei fell in beside him.

Chapter 17

# What Omei Had To Tell

Nagaro frowned. "Are you sure you want to come, Omei?" he asked her. "We have to climb that ridge and cross the ravine on the other side."

Omei followed his pointing finger. "Oh, aye," she said easily. "I'm not so old I can't manage that. And I'd like t' meet Narei's Aunt Animara."

"All right then." Nagaro turned onto Front Street, following the two children who were already well ahead. He could see Narei gesticulating as she walked. It didn't seem to slow her down.

"I'd also like to meet Pakoa's medicine woman," Omei said, beside him.

"Tira Zomora? Why?" He turned to search her face.

She returned him a straightforward glance. "It's well t' pay one's respects," she said simply.

"That's true," he conceded. "In fact, it's a good idea, since you came with me and may be seen to be in my service."

"Have ye done something t' make Tira Zomora angry?"

Nagaro's eyes had returned to the children ahead of them, but he could hear the raised eyebrow in Omei's voice. "I have made a place for myself here," he said. "But it was Zomora's place long before I came. Her care for the safety of her people makes her suspicious of strangers and sharp in her judgements. I respect her, and I hope she respects me, but I'm not sure what account of me she might give you."

Omei laughed a short, dry laugh. "I suppose I'll have t' see."

They walked on for a while without speaking. To keep the silence from growing too long, Nagaro said, "You'll like Animara. I always enjoy visiting her house."

"Ye don't live there, then, when ye're here on Pakoa?"

"No, I have a house up on Hill Road." Nagaro twisted around and gestured. "I share it with Taru. Pavo lived there too, before he married Tenepti."

"I see." They walked on. "She's a good woman, this Animara?"

Nagaro answered without hesitation. "Ani is pure gold. She has the warmest heart you can imagine, and she's very wise too. For me it's been like having an older sister to talk to."

"Ah." Omei nodded. She gave him a sideways glance. "She knows all your secrets, does she?"

"No!" Nagaro's answer was reflexive and emphatic. "She does know *some* of them. But no one on Pakoa knows... what *you* know, for instance."

She gave him another sideways glance. "And that's how ye want it, Zirda?"

"Yes. Please." Nagaro swallowed. He realized that his agitation had made him slow his pace, and he pushed himself to quicken it. "My past is dead and buried, Omei. There are fewer than ten people in the world who know about *that*."

She studied his face as she swung along beside him. "All right then, Zirda," she said. "If that's how ye want it."

He released a breath. "Thank you."

He looked up just in time to notice their surroundings and to turn onto the Street of Kuma Mills. At the farther end of that street, Pilo and Narei were just turning into the trail that snaked its way up the side of the steep ridge they had to climb. The two adults walked on in silence for a time. They were halfway up the street before Nagaro thought of something else that it should be safe to talk about. "Omei, do you know who the men were that were holding Narei? King Elgurn wouldn't tell me. Keeping it secret was apparently a condition for her release."

Omei looked at him. "What would ye do if ye knew?"

He shrugged. "Just remember it. Vothra warns against vengeance. I can make guesses about who they were, of course, but I don't want to risk blaming the wrong people."

Omei nodded. "They told me I would be sorry if they heard I ever told anyone," she said. "But I know ye'll keep it close. Most o' the men who were holding us were Peldred's folk, but I heard other names too—names ye hear spoken of as Brothers o' the Blood."

"Which names?"

She pursed her lips. "Grimbold Sobring was one. And Lothard Hurn. And there was another man they spoke of a lot, a man named Torlung."

"Madred Furthing's Chief Minister?" Nagaro was picturing an oily Leithian he had seen with Madred in the courtyard of the lord's headquarters in Lankura.

Omei shrugged easily. "Aye. That 'd be the one."

Nagaro stopped dead as another realization struck him. "But the king chose Madred to negotiate for Narei's release! Elgurn said he would have some influence with the ones who'd taken her..." His voice trailed.

Omei shrugged again. "I guess ye could call that *influence*, couldn't ye? Lord Madred bein' Torlung's master?"

"Keshaal!" Nagaro recollected himself and started walking again.

They reached the end of the street and started up the narrow track that climbed the ridge. Almost immediately, the path grew markedly steeper. "Ye'll have t' pardon me, Zirda," Omei said, gesturing at the tiny figures of Pilo and Narei far ahead up the path. "But if ye don't want t' lose them, we'll have t' do less talkin' and more walkin'. I've not got breath for both."

Nagaro nodded. "You go first and set the pace," he said. "Most of the way, the path isn't wide enough for two."

They set out with a renewed focus on the climb, and Omei set a remarkably good pace considering her years and the shortness of her legs. Nagaro followed close behind, puzzling about what he'd learned. Was this the kind of game that Elgurn played? Or was it Madred, the respected and revered, who was playing games? —Or was it Tarlung? Brandle Furthing believed that his father cared about the truth. And when Nagaro thought back to that day in Lankura, when he'd vainly sought for Madred's aid in staying Pavo's execution, he remembered that Madred had been speaking crossly to Tarlung—*about something in which he saw no honor.*

Nagaro continued to mull over these thoughts, but could come to no conclusion. And the last part of the climb was so very steep that he had to focus on the effort, and on Omei. The Turowa went more slowly near the end, but didn't stop until she reached the top.

Narei and Pilo were waiting there, sitting on a rock, looking out over the little narrow valley that was their home. Omei stopped and bent over with her hands on her knees, to catch her breath. When she straightened, she surveyed the scene spread out below her, the kuma bushes on their terraced slopes, the cedar woods below, and the sturdy stone house on the farther side of the ravine. The beach was a pebbled arc with black rocks at each end and the sparkling cobalt sea beyond it. "Well," she said, "It looks like a fine place for a child t' grow up in."

"Oh, it is!" Narei affirmed as she stood up. "Come on, Pilo, let's race!"

Pilo laughed. "Not a race," he said. "The path's too narrow. But if ye want t' run, I'll come behind ye."

Narei sprang away with a peel of laughter, and the two children went leaping down the trail like wild deer.

Omei cocked her head at Nagaro. "Ye let them run like that?"

He sighed. "If I tried to stop them, I'd likely fail—and they'd call me an ogre. Besides, I did things just as dangerous when I was a child."

Omei shrugged. "Didn't we all." She pointed to their left along the nearer side of the ravine. "Is that the rest o' the family?"

Nagaro shaded his eyes. "Yes. I see Ani's husband, Sudano, and the other two children, Tavo and Bahiri. They're cutting dead wood out of the kuma bushes. Ani must be at the house preparing the mid-day meal, since it's nearly noon." He cupped his hands and shouted a greeting to the three hard-working Turowans. All three heads came up and Sudano raised a hand and waved back. Then the stocky Turo gestured to his two older children, and all three began to work their way down the slope.

Omei clucked her tongue. "So I'm invitin' myself to lunch?"

Nagaro laughed. "Yes, but don't worry. They had word the ships were in, and Ani will have made plenty to eat. She always does."

When they got to the house, they found Ani in the main room that served as both kitchen and dining room. It was bright with light from the two open windows. The gentle cross-breeze, flowing between them, wafted the aromas of savory herbs and baking bread.

Ani greeted Nagaro with feeling. "Here ye are at last, Nagaro," she said. "Safe and well, and back in a Fleet uniform. Narei's come in t' hug me already and run out again."

Nagaro nodded, unsurprised. "I saw her and Pilo playing on the beach, and the other three will be here any minute. Ah, Ani, this is Omei. She took care of Narei on the ship—both times."

The two women briefly sized each other up, then simultaneously opened their arms and embraced one another.

Ani spoke first as they stepped apart. "The Spirits bless ye," she said. "I was so worried that I couldn't sleep nights, thinkin' about how frightened Narei must ha' been."

"I'm glad t' bring her back to ye," Omei replied. "She's a happy child, and a good-hearted one—and I think I can see why."

There were voices outside, and Sudano entered with Bahiri and Tavo behind him. "Welcome back, Nagaro!" he cried, putting out his hand. "Ye're just in time for lunch—as usual." He took a step back after warmly clasping Nagaro's hand and gave him a broad wink.

Nagaro proceeded to introduce Omei to the other family members.

Sudano considered the new arrival with interest. "So ye looked after Narei, Tira Omei? For those Leithians? I'd like t' know how ye got mixed up with that lot."

Omei cocked her head at him. "I'll be glad t' give ye the tale, Zirda, but we'd best sit down for the telling."

"By all means, Zirdyn, sit!" Sudano pulled out the best chair for her at the head of the table.

Sudano then sat on one side of the table, and Nagaro on the other. Animara poured hot water into the tea pot and added dried yellow berries for sothiril tea, then sat beside her husband, when she wasn't taking the bread from the oven or stirring the soup. At a nod from her mother, seventeen-year-old Bahiri set about fetching cups and setting them on the table, while the three younger children sat on the hard earth floor playing with figures of men and horses made of braided straw

"I've been serving Leithians these past twenty-seven years," Omei began. "My family went with the land when it changed hands, so t' speak. We used to serve the lords o' Loros Wared, but the part o' the land where we dwelt went to Sobring Hold when Loros fell. There were some holdings in Lankura too—three big buildings on Broad Street—that went to Bron Sobring as well, and to his brother Grimbold when Bron was slain in the southern war. Grimbold's a crooked piece o' work, I don't mind telling ye—but that's another tale. I've worked most o' my days as a housekeeper in one or another o' the Broad Street buildings. Lately it's been the one they call Council Hall."

Nagaro straightened in surprise. "Is that *the* Council Hall? Where the Council of Lords used to meet?"

Sudano and Animara both turned to stare at him.

Omei nodded. "Aye, Zirda, that's what it was. But it's all been done over for offices, and meetin' rooms, an' such. The big room where the Council used t' meet is still there, but it stands empty most o' the time. Every now and then they have a banquet in it, but that's all the use it gets."

Nagaro shook his head. "I always wondered what happened to the Council Hall. I thought the Crown probably kept it."

"Ye'd think so, wouldn't ye? But it never belonged to the Crown. It belonged to the House o' Loros."

Sudano coughed. "That's all very interesting," he said. "But I want to know how ye found out that some o' these Leithian folk were fixin' t' make off with Narei."

"Did they plan it in the old Council Hall?" Animara asked.

Omei shook her head. "Not in the old Council Hall, but the building next to it. That one used t' be called the Gray Hall, but the Brothers o' the Blood have been meetin' there for two years, and they call it the 'Watch Tower'. It's only got three floors, so it's not much of a tower, but I suppose they're keepin' watch on what passes in Lankura."

"And these men who were plotting to take Narei—in this Watch Tower building—they were members of the Brothers o' the Blood, and some of Peldred's people?" Nagaro prompted.

"Aye. It was an easy place t' meet, I guess, since some o' Peldred's folk keep space in the third building—the one they call 'The Livery', because it used t' be a livery stable. The Livery belongs to the House o' Sobring, but they rent out parts of it t' other Leithian Houses—several o' the smaller ones."

"How'd ye come t' hear what they were planning?" Sudano asked.

Omei sighed. "The women that keep house in those three buildings are nearly all Turo, an' we all come and go by the same alleys, 'round the back and in between the three halls. So when the Leithians began asking the women that work in the Watch Tower if they wanted t' make a bit o' money doin' this little task o' theirs, we all found out about it." Omei paused to glance at Nagaro. "The other women all wanted no part o' kidnaping your child, Captain, so they found excuses to say no. But I knew those men'd take the child anyway, and I didn't like t' think o' the little girl bein' all alone in the hands o' that lot. So I let it be known I was willing. I pretended I just wanted the money, and they took me on." She spread her hands. "And that's the tale."

Bahiri had sat down on a stool at the foot of the table and had been shyly listening. Now she asked, "Why does the king let the Brothers o' the Blood meet in that building, if they're such bad men?" Then she dropped her eyes, abashed, as her elders all turned to look at her.

Omei shifted in her seat and frowned. "I don't know, child."

Nagaro had listened with interest to Omei's account. "I'm afraid I know the answer to that, Bahiri," he said. "Elgurn has only very limited power over the lords of the noble houses. They can come and go as they please, speak as they please, and make whatever assemblies they wish. Elgurn can't do anything unless they're involved in treason—something like plotting to kill him, or taking the throne by force, or giving aid to an enemy of Edrovir."

Animara had risen and she paused in the act of pouring the sothiril. "Elgurn has so little power as that?"

"Against the noble houses, yes."

"What about the King's Council?" Sudano asked.

Nagaro sighed. "Officially the members of the Council only advise the king, but I've learned that they have more power than that. They just don't exercise it openly."

Sudano shook his head in dismay. "It all sounds a right bloody mess to me."

"My mother would ha' called it a 'fine kettle o' stew,' Animara put in. "And speaking o' kettles, the soup is ready—and the bread, by the smell of it. Will ye fetch the bowls and spoons, Bahiri, while I take out the bread and cut it?"

"Yes, Mama!" Bahiri sprang to obey.

Nagaro rose. "Let me help with the soup, Ani. The kettle's heavy."

Tavo, Pilo, and Narei must have caught the words 'soup' and 'ready' because they came crowding around the table, finding stools for themselves. With Nagaro and Bahiri helping, Animara soon had a thick slice of bread, a steaming bowl of sausage-and-bean soup, and a cup of hot sothiril at every place.

For a time there was no conversation beyond praise for the food.

Finally Animara turned and asked Omei, "Will ye be going back t' work for those Leithians in the old Council Hall?"

Omei shugged. "If my place hasn't been taken by another."

"But why, Tira Omei?" Bahiri asked. "Why don't ye find someone nicer t' work for?"

Another shrug. "It's a useful thing for Minowei's People t' have one of us there."

"You mean to have a Turowan there?" Nagaro asked, frowning.

Omei shook her head. "I'm not *just* a Turowa. I'm one o' those whose ancestors pledged themselves t' Nevrath years ago—when Minowei's father died and Nevrath became their chief."

Nagaro gazed at the woman in amazement. "You mean Takuma's clan still exists? Do you know who else belongs to it?"

A fleeting smile crossed Omei's face. She inclined her head to him, her dark eyes bright. "The women keep the family lines," she said. "Some o' the women, that is, because it's our task. We're the *Ku Taihana*, the Keepers o' memory for our folk. We watch, and listen, and remember. The time was when Minowei's People all dwelt inside o' Loros Wared, but since the Kelorin folk of Loros Wared are scattered now, and other folk have re-drawn the borders, we live in several holds and wareds."

"It's wonderful that you've kept account of your people," Nagaro said, and he meant it. "If only someone had kept account of the Kelorin folk of Loros Wared, we might not be at the point of going to war over whether Kenthos is Tevren's son."

Omei's bright black eyes had not left his face. "We know that too, Zirda," she said. "They may be Kelorin, but they came t' be Minowei's People when Nevrath took Minowei to wife."

"Well, tell us then!" Sudano cried, and his fist hit the table, making the dishes jump. "*Is* Kenthos what he claims t' be?"

Narei and Pilo, who'd been engaged in mock swordplay with their spoons, looked up in astonishment. Tavo stared at his father, round-eyed.

Nagaro was just as interested as Sudano. "Yes," he said. "From what you say, he'd be the chief of Minowei's People as well as being the heir of the House of Loros."

Omei didn't answer but gave a little cough and a quick, meaningful glance at the three younger children. Animara cleared her throat and said, "Tavo, Pilo, and Narei, ye can go outside to play until it's time t' go back to work."

"Hurray! Come on, Pilo!" Narei jumped up eagerly, and Pilo almost upset his chair in his haste to follow his little cousin. Fifteen-year-old Tavo made a show of rolling his eyes at being included with the younger children but seemed glad enough to go for all that. Bahiri rose and began gathering up the dishes.

As soon as the door had closed behind the three younger children, Sudano leaned forward eagerly and addressed Omei. "Ye know something about Kenthos, don't ye, Tira Omei?"

The Turowa nodded gravely. "Aye," she said. "The man called Kenthos *is* one o' the scattered sons o' Loros Wared, but he's no more Darion's heir than ye or me. He was born in Irvenen Wared to one o' Queen Lindra's serving women who fled north after the king and queen were slain."

"What about his father?" Sudano pressed.

Omei sighed. "Well, that does get a little bit sticky," she admitted. "Kenthos must ha' been got in Loros Wared, 'cause he was born just half a year after his mother got to Irvenen. But she had no husband—that's why I wanted the children sent out. It's plain that Kenthos is no child o' Queen Lindra's. And he could only be King Tevren's son if Tevren was false t' Lindra and lay with her serving woman—"

"Which he never would ha' done!" Sudano finished emphatically.

Omei expressed her agreement with a decisive nod. "No man of Nevrath's line has ever been known t' be untrue," she said. "And those that knew him say that Tevren loved Lindra with all his heart."

"That sounds right," Nagaro put in. "He was pressed hard to marry a Leithian woman, but he insisted on marrying Lindra—on following his heart—even though it set the Leithians against him. I've heard folk say it was his ruin."

For a long moment there was silence in the room. From outside came the sounds of waves on the shore and the children's voices. The afternoon breeze wafting in the window bore the mingled scents of juniper and brine. It stirred Bahiri's hair where she stood frozen like a statue at the foot of the table with bowls and spoons in her hands. Finally she said, "Tira Omei, do the women of Minowei's folk... those Keepers... know where Tevren's son is?"

Omei turned her eyes, bright as a bird's, upon the young Turowa. "That's a secret, child," she said quietly.

"Well if they *do* know," Sudano observed gruffly, "It seems t' me they could save everyone a lot o' trouble by telling us!"

Nagaro stirred and spoke again. "Would it save trouble, I wonder?" he asked. "Or would it only make the trouble worse?"

"Worse for *him*, surely," observed Animara. "Wouldn't the Kelorin folk be wantin' to make him king, and the Leithians be wantin' him dead?"

Omei nodded wisely. "Aye," she said. "If someone was to tell the world where t' find the heir o' Darion, they'd be landing him right in the middle o' that kettle o' stew. And he might very well not like it."

Nagaro nodded. "From what I've seen of that kettle, it's not a thing *I'd* want to be caught in the middle of."

Omei's head bobbed. "Well, there ye have it," she said with an air of finality.

Sudano threw up his hands. "Never argue with women's wisdom," he said. "That's what I say."

Omei leaned towards Animara and said in a conspiratorial stage whisper, "I begin t' see why ye married him!"

***

A half an hour later, Nagaro and Omei were climbing the zigzag path up the side of the little valley on their way back to Pakoa Harbor. They reached the ridge crest and paused there to catch their breath. Omei's eyes followed a branching path that ran along the side of the narrow valley, crossing a small waterfall near the head of the ravine by means of wooden bridge, before winding its way up the farther side. "That looks like a pleasant path t' walk," she said.

"It is. You can go exploring that way if you like, but I have to go back to the harbor and the ship."

Omei stood a moment longer gazing at the little bridge. "No," she said. "I'll have plenty o' time for that later, no doubt. I'll just go back t' the harbor with ye this time."

"All right. Are you rested enough?"

"Aye."

They started down the path to the harbor, Omei leading with Nagaro following close behind. Feeling safe in the windswept solitude of that high country, Nagaro addressed the Turowa as they walked. "I've been wanting to ask you this," he said. "Is your mother, Luka, still alive?"

Omei shook her head. "She's been gone nearly two years now."

"I thought it likely. I'm sorry."

"No need t' be, Zirda. My father's spirit waited a long time for her in Hanuroa. And she went very peacefully in the end."

"Well, that at least is good."

They went on for a little way. The path was steep and Omei took it slowly.

Nagaro had been wondering about something else, and he finally asked, "Do Minowei's People have a chief now?"

Omei didn't falter in her stride. "O' course we do."

Nagaro frowned. "Then you must have someone to answer to for having left your place in the Council Hall—going away twice, for days at a time, to help my daughter and me?"

Still Omei kept walking. "Ye needn't worry about it, Zirda," she said without turning.

"But, we don't belong to your people."

Omei seemed to hesitate in getting past a rock that made a kind of small step in the trail. "How d' ye know that?" she asked.

Nagaro's feet stopped moving. "Well, I... I mean, I don't know who my parents were." He didn't want to mention Beloras. He didn't know Omei well enough, and he wasn't certain about it either.

Omei must have noticed that she no longer heard his booted tread, for she paused and turned around. She put her head on one side. "Don't ye know that ye grew up in a place right on the edge o' the old Loros Wared?"

Nagaro frowned. "No," he said, "I didn't know that. To begin with, my Lady Guardian didn't keep maps. And I've never known exactly where the boundaries of Loros Wared were. But Averwin surely belonged to the House of Virden."

"Aye, it did. The Yuna River was the border. 'Course the bit o' Virden with Averwin in it, and the bit o' Loros across the river, have both gone over t' the Crown."

Nagaro's brow furrowed. "And the northernmost part of Loros Wared went to Sobring Hold," he said carefully. "And the eastern part, with Loros Hall in it, went to Kildoran Wared under Lord Endemar. And the westernmost part became Kel Wared. So the old Loros Wared stretched all the way from the sea to the River Yuna and from the Edro to the old boundary of Sobring Hold."

"Aye. And when it fell, most o' the Kelorin men in it were slain or driven off, so don't be thinkin' it's got nothing t' do with ye, when ye grew up just outside the edge of it!"

Nagaro laughed at her seriousness. "Well, I won't object to your including me and my daughter in your clan if it means you don't mind having done us a service," he said easily. It hadn't actually occurred to him that his parents might have been refugees from the blood-letting in Loros Wared. He supposed it was possible.

They both began walking once more, and Nagaro's thoughts turned yet again. "The knowledge that your Keepers—your Ku Taihana—have, about the family lines of your clan... Have you written it down?"

Omei, in front of him, shook her head. "It's never been done that way, Zirda. None of us can write, anyway."

"But you *should* write it down. It's the beginning of a history, and it could be so easily lost. Surely you can find someone to write for you."

Omei laughed. "What? Someone t' write names down for a few old Turowan women?"

"Why not? I'd be glad to do it for you, if you like."

This time Omei stopped dead and turned around to stare up at him. For a long moment she searched his face. Then she turned back around and started down the path once more. "Ye mean it, don't ye?" she said in a bemused voice.

"Of course. Why wouldn't I?"

She shook her head silently to herself. After a while she said, "That'd be something, that would. I just might take ye up on it one day, Zirda."

By this time, they had reached the bottom of the track and were entering the outskirts of the town. Neither one of them spoke as they traversed the Street of Kuma Mills. On Front Street, many of the townspeople who were going about their business greeted Nagaro as they passed, and at length they came again to the wharf.

"Can ye recommend good lodgings, Zirda?" Omei inquired as they came to a halt.

"There's just the Bay Tree Inn, there." He pointed to it. "But you wouldn't find better lodgings anywhere on the mainland. Just tell Yuli, the innkeeper's wife, that you came with me, and she'll take you right to her heart."

Omei gave him a sidelong glance. "Thank ye, Captain. Ye're a good man. If ye ever need me for ought, ye've only to ask any Turo in Lankura and they'll tell ye where t' find me. And if ever ye do fetch Narei back to Lankura t' live with ye and ye need a housekeeper, I wouldn't mind taking the task."

Nagaro smiled. "I'll remember that. Thank you again, Tira Omei, and I wish you a safe voyange back to Lankura."

As the Turowa walked away in the direction of the inn, Pavo came up, breathless. "Have I make you wait, Nagaro?" he asked apologetically.

"Only for a moment. How's the baby—little Chotao?"

"Chotao is very good, Nagaro, thank you. He is already grow so much from last time I see. I have talk to Tenepti about coming to Lankura soon, so baby will not grow up without my see him do it."

Nagaro laughed as he made for the long boat. "I know what you mean. I hope she can come soon."

A quarter of an hour later, the last of the ships had cleared the entrance of the harbor and the fleet had turned south once more. The Mahuk captains had frantically shouted commands, oars had flailed, and the *Sea Eagle* had physically nudged one of the Mahuk galleys to keep her clear of the rocks. Atop the *Sword's* stern castle, Nagaro heaved a sigh of relief.

Roheed's voice hailed him from the main deck. The young Mautep did not ask permission this time, but simply came up the ladder to join Nagaro on the captain's platform.

"Good afternoon, Nagaro Kiraam," he said with a small bow.

"Good afternoon, Roheed."

"Is truly very good thing to be hostage of honor. I have go to oar deck and see with my eye that what you say is true. Free man do row better than slave."

Nagaro did his best not to smile. "Well, at least free men who are *trained* to row do."

Roheed's narrow black eyes were very serious as he nodded. "Yes, is true. Free man must be train to row. But there is big question I want to ask you."

"And what is it, Roheed?" Nagaro asked cautiously.

"How you have make oar deck so *clean?* I know this ship before. Always oar deck have smell very bad." Roheed made a face at the memory of it.

Nagaro laughed, but sobered quickly, remembering how it had been. "First we scrubbed it all *very* well. Then we let it air for three days. And then we painted everything with varnish—two or three times, I think. Does that answer your question?"

Roheed nodded seriously. "Yes. That is not so hard to do. Thank you, Nagaro Kiraam."

Nagaro frowned. "Do you think Emperor Baalkir might really try using free men instead of slaves?" he asked.

Roheed shrugged. "I do not know. But if he maybe think about it, he will want to know how can it be done. Is good I know how to tell him."

"Ah. I see."

Roheed moved to step down from the platform and made another small bow. "Thank you for talk to me, Nagaro Kiraam. Now I am go to place call *gah-lee*," he added brightly. "Cook say he will show me how to make Droviri food call *pan-kek*. Truly is good to be hostage of honor!"

# Chapter 18

# Facing Baalkir Jir-Akaan

Kuran leaned back in his chair. "You think Tuluptak's ships are three days ahead of us?"

"They were, My Lord. But it might be close to four by tomorrow morning, since we took some time at Pakoa and we also stopped early this evening to anchor for the night." Nagaro glanced at the open stern windows of the *Sword of Freedom's* great cabin. Outside, an opalescent dusk was falling on the quiet waters of a little bay. Lights shown warmly from the windows of Jinari fishermen's huts nestling amid fragrant juniper. This was the southernmost island in Jinari waters, and the ships of Lord Kuran's small fleet were resting in the same anchorage they had used on the last ill-fated mission to the Mahuk Baar. The local folk, usually inclined to be friendly, had disappeared at the first sight of Mahuk warships among the Droviri craft, but when nothing untoward had occurred after an hour or so, they had begun to reemerge and go about their business.

Kuran took a gulp of cold sothiril and set his mug on the table with a solid clunk. "Time enough, you think, for them to have sailed all the way down to Sar Tipaal and for the Emperor to have sailed all the way back up to his northern border?"

Nagaro considered. "Probably not, though the wind has been fair. But Baalkir may not have been at Sar Tipaal. He would likely have found an excuse to be at this end of the Baar, with a good part of his own fleet being overdue in returning from a raid on Lankura."

"So you think he'll be lurking close by?"

"I hope so."

Kuran nodded. "So do I. I don't like turning our captives loose at the border and just sailing away. And I'd also rather not sail very far into Mahuk waters looking for Baalkir. It might look like a provocation, and I'm not so confident that your presence would forestall an attack—no matter what our young Mautep prince may say."

Nagaro nodded his agreement, frowning. He knew that the members of the King's Council were counting on his possessing a kind of immunity in the Emperor's eyes, and Roheed did seem to believe it was so. It might be true, but he didn't want to take it for granted. He also wasn't sure that any immunity he might have would extend to anyone else who was sailing in his company.

"I think we should sail openly into the Baar, as far as the northern anchorage at Osfaraad," he said seriously. "If we don't encounter any Mahuk craft, we should just leave Roheed and the captured ships there, turn around, and sail out again—very deliberately and without any show of haste. If we *do* encounter Mahuk ships, we'll have to see what action they take, and choose our course accordingly."

Kuran fingered his cup. "That's a good plan," he said. "It's honest and bold, and I like it. Though I'm a little surprised that you've picked Osfaraad, considering your past experience there"

Nagaro shrugged. "It's logically the best place in the same way that this harbor is the best place for us to lie up tonight. Osfaraad is the closest Mahuk island with an open anchorage large enough for at least ten ships. It's a place where you can see, and be seen, for a good distance on several sides. And it's open, for an easy escape if that should prove necessary."

"Unlike the harbor mouth on the other side of the island where you were trapped the last time."

Nagaro grimaced. "There are also a fair number of former galley slaves living on Osfaraad who owe their freedom to the activities of my pirate fleet."

"Aha!" Kuran's smile spread knowingly. "Now *that* I didn't know." He stood up. "Thank you for your counsel, Nagaro. I will announce a meeting of all the captains on the *Pride* in an hour, to explain the plan. That should give everyone time to finish their dinners."

✳✳✳

Two days later, at about two hours before noon, Kuran's fleet was traversing the waters of the Mahuk Baar. The ships had been sailing close to the mainland coast, for ease of navigation, and they now had to steer a more westerly course and skirt the small island of Tetep to make for Nagaro's chosen anchorage on the northern shore of Osfaraad.

It took perhaps half an hour for the last of Kuran's ships to round Tetep's northern tip. Within a minute after that, one of the Emperor's ships emerged from behind the southeast shoulder of Osfaraad. The *Sword*'s lookout raised an immediate cry, his arm flung out, pointing.

"Ship! There! A point off the port bow!"

By the time Nagaro had the spyglass to his eye, the sails of three war galleys were already visible. As he watched from the captain's platform, one ship after another appeared from behind the island, until the total numbered eleven. The banners they bore were of several different colors, only three being the Emperor's own scarlet and black. Still, one of those three was the Emperor's flagship, surging along in the lead under the power of both sail and oars. Her course was clearly chosen to intercept the Edroviran ships.

A ragged cheer rose from the captured sea warriors on the craft behind him, but quickly subsided. The Mautep were perhaps uncertain what kind of welcome to expect from their lord.

"What're your orders, Capt'n?" inquired Bouno, at the tiller behind Nagaro.

"Steady ahead, steersman."

There was some milling about and excited talk on the main deck. Taru came striding through it, and raised his voice. "Ye want me below, Capt'n?"

Nagaro nodded, then shouted, "All oarsmen below! Hold her steady. We're not looking for a fight."

Taru gave Nagaro a salute as the oarsmen made for the doors, fore and aft, leading below decks. "I hope they feel the same," he said as he turned to follow his men. "They've got us outnumbered two t' one."

Pavo called up from his place on the main deck, "Do you want more sail, Captain?"

"No, Pavo. Let it be."

Nagaro reached for the speaking trumpet that was kept secured to the rail in front of him. He raised it and began shouting orders across the water to the five other Edroviran ships, with the result that the vessels drew together, tightening their ring around the four Mahuk craft in the middle of the formation.

Nagaro hung up the speaking trumpet and surveyed the progress of the Mautep fleet. The ships were distinctly closer. The flagship seemed to have slowed a little, and the others were beginning to fan out. He scanned Osfaraad, shading his eyes. Sunlight sparkled on the water and the safe anchorage beckoned straight ahead. The wind was brisk out of the west, very slightly in his favor if the Emperor tried to come between him and the island, but he hoped he needn't worry about that. As he had told his crew, he wasn't seeking a fight. Nor an escape—yet. He glanced at the tip of the *Sword's* main mast where a white flag of truce snapped in the breeze, just below Edrovir's banner—white hawk on a field of blue. Every Edroviran ship in Kuran's small fleet bore a similar white flag. *Surely Baalkir would honor them.*

But so far there had been no answering sign. He saw only the flags of various warlords, and the Emperor's fleet was still coming on, swinging out into a long arc with the flagship in the middle. The nearest of the craft was now less than a quarter mile away, ahead and to port.

Kuran hailed him from the *Pride of Lankura*, his voice carrying across the water, focused by a speaking trumpet. "Stand in the bow where you can be seen, Captain! With Roheed!"

"Aye Zirda!"

Nagaro made for the ladder to the main deck, even as he looked for the red-and-black-clad figure of the Emperor's nephew. He spotted the young Mautep, already mounting the ladder to the forecastle. It didn't take long to join Roheed there at the forward rail.

The young Mautep's gaze was scanning the advancing Mahuk fleet with eager attention. He turned when Nagaro came up beside him and said, "Now we must see what Emperor mean to do." Nagaro didn't find the audible tension in Roheed's voice reassuring, considering how often the young man had told him that he had earned Baalkir's respect.

He felt for the spyglass on its cord around his neck and raised it again to his eye, scrutenizing each Mahuk craft in turn. It was just as his glass found the flagship's main mast that he saw the sea warrior in the lookout's perch release a rectangle of white fabric, flying just below the pennant of imperial gold. Nagaro let out his breath, and a knot of tension eased between his shoulder blades. It was one thing to be sure that what he was doing was right and another to trust the Emperor of the Mahuk Baar to answer him in kind. Hurriedly he swung the glass from ship to ship, and saw white blossoming on one main-sprit after another. Nagaro lowered the glass.

"Look at the banners," he said, offering the spyglass to Roheed.

Roheed took the glass eagerly and focused it, tracking from ship to ship. When he handed the glass back there was obvious relief in his dark eyes. "Is good," he said. "Is very good."

"Lord Kuran wants you to stay here with me, where we can both be seen."

Roheed nodded his comprehension. "This also is good."

***

By noon, the island of Osfaraad's northern anchorage was full of ships—so full that Taru said, "If ye threw a stone, ye'd be as likely t' hit wood as water."

The description was evocative, if not literally accurate. The ships were necessarily fairly close together, although they were still arranged into groups. The Emperor's eleven fully-armed war galleys occupied the eastern half of the wide, shallow harbor, the disarmed Mahuk craft were grouped at the far western side, and the Edroviran ships were arrayed in between, rather like a fence, since the captured ships had not yet been officially returned to the Emperor's control.

Despite this last detail, the scene was outwardly quite peaceful. All the vessels rode quietly at anchor, with canvas furled and oars shipped. From a human standpoint, however, the tension was as tight as a drumhead.

Nagaro stood on the *Sword's* stern castle, watching what was happening on the far side of the main deck of the *Pride of Lankura*. Lord Kuran's flagship and that of the Emperor were drawn up side by side with as little water between them as was prudent. The two commanders stood, each at his own rail, facing one another across the gap. The Emperor had a pair of sea warriors at his side. Kuran had the *Pride's* captain, Ruald, and also Pavo Maat. Roheed was there as well, and an occasional gesture from him revealed that the young Mautep was involved to some extent in the conversation. All the other members of both ship's crews were manning their posts and therefore excluded from this meeting of leaders. Those who happened to be closest were doubtless straining their ears.

Nagaro let his breath out tensely and tried not to resent being one of those who were excluded. The command belonged to Kuran, of course, and it was entirely appropriate for the two commanders to speak to one another—well, *try* to speak. Neither spoke the other's language, which was why they needed Pavo and Roheed.

"Hsst! Capt'n!" Bouno hissed from behind him. "What're they doin' now?"

Nagaro sighed. "They're still talking. No, wait! They seem to have finished. Kuran just returned Roheed's sword, and now the Mautep are putting their longboat over the side to fetch him across. Kuran and Pavo are coming back this way."

The *Pride* and the *Sword* were anchored with their sides almost touching and their main deck rails overlapping for several feet, just forward of the *Sword's* stern castle. A long plank had been laid across the gap there, and a rope stretched across at a good height for a hand-hold. Pavo now came balancing nimbly across this makeshift bridge and was followed by Kuran.

The Lord of the Fleet squinted up at Nagaro where he stood on the stern castle. "You'd best come down, Captain. I'll be wanting to hear your recommendation—and needing the use of your great cabin."

"Aye, Zirda." Nagaro saluted and made for the ladder.

Shortly thereafter, Kuran and the *Sword's* three officers were seated around the table in the *Sword's* great cabin. Taru had made his appearance with such perfect timing that it would have been very awkward to exclude him. Kuran sat with a brooding frown. Taru fidgeted. Pavo, true to the way of his people, waited with stoic patience.

It was Nagaro who ventured to break the silence. "Has the matter not been entirely concluded, My Lord?"

Kuran pursed his lips. "Ah, *no,*" he said. "According to Pavo, Roheed delivered our message accurately, to the letter. The Emperor appears glad to have his nephew back, and glad also to have four ships returned with the surviving men. He seems to accept that he has lost the slaves and that we kept two of the ships. Regarding his own future conduct towards Edrovir, however, and the rest of our demands, he, ah, says he wants to talk to us some more, on the beach."

"On the beach?"

Kuran sighed and ran a hand through his hair. "He wishes to talk to me in a place where neither one of us has a ship full of men with swords at his back."

"Therefore, on the beach." Nagaro nodded. "That makes sense. How many are to come?"

"Each commander with four other men. He wanted my four to be the four officers of the *Sword of Freedom* who surrendered here a year ago."

"Ah." Nagaro nodded again, frowning. "And I assume you told him that Peldred is dead."

Taru had been sitting with a gathering frown and he spoke now, with some heat. "I say he's got a lot o' bloody nerve—wantin' the men he tortured t' come and sit on the beach with him!"

Kuran raised an eyebrow. "I wouldn't have put it so bluntly, but I rather agree. It doesn't please me to hazard Nagaro, in particular, a second time, in the power of a man who very nearly killed him once. I'm also not sure about that beach. There are fishermen's houses up among the trees and some fishing boats on the sand, but I don't see any people."

At this, Pavo spoke for the first time. "I think they all are hiding," he said quietly. "There are too many warship with different flag. They do not want to be in middle of fight."

Nagaro agreed. "Yes, that's quite likely. And as for hazarding me, I am willing."

"That's good of you, Captain, but I still don't like it. There weren't any small boats out in the open water when we approached, either." Kuran shook his head. "None at all. They managed to hide awfully quickly, and how do we know they're not hiding exactly where the Emperor wants them?"

Nagaro sighed. "They will have had plenty of advance warning, My Lord. We've been sailing openly, in broad daylight, and in clear weather for all to see. And Baalkir's fleet has probably been hanging about these waters for days. Fishermen will fish if they can do it safely, but they keep their eyes open. And they pass the word from boat to boat. If it looks like trouble is brewing, they get out of the way. Did the Emperor give you any guarantee of our safety?"

Kuran let out a long breath. "He swore on his honor and by his god that no harm will come to us. He said we would talk to him for an hour and then freely go our way. He even said we could bring our swords."

Nagaro leaned forward. "Then I think we should trust him. Isn't that what this is about, My Lord? Building trust?"

"Well, yes," Kuran admitted. "Though Pavo and Vell would have to also be willing."

Pavo calmly returned his commander's gaze. "I am willing, Zirda."

"Well, all right." The Lord of the Fleet rubbed his bearded chin. "That leaves asking Vell, though he'll be hard pressed now to say no. And we must choose a fourth man. I did explain that Peldred is dead, and Baalkir merely said I should bring someone else instead."

Taru spoke up. "Let me be the fourth man, Zirda."

Nagaro frowned. "*You*, Taru? It sounded like you didn't care for this venture."

"I don't like it one rin! But ye'll not be leaving me out of it this time!"

Kuran regarded Taru speculatively. "It's not a bad idea," he said. "You will all be serving as witnesses, after all, and this way all the free peoples of Edrovir will be represented. Good enough!" He slapped the table and stood up. "I'll send word to Vell on the *Harbinger*. See that you're all ready in half an hour."

Kuran gestured for the others to precede him from the cabin, then hung back to speak to Nagaro as Taru and Pavo went out the door. "So, you will have your right- and left-hand men this time, Captain," he said in a low voice. "I find some comfort in that."

"I hope they won't be needed in that capacity, My Lord."

"So do I. But the absence of the fishermen still worries me. You say that some would be friends to you. Could the Emperor have done them some mischief?

"I very much doubt that the Emperor knows their history," Nagaro replied earnestly. "They would have kept it strictly secret. They're probably just hiding."

"Ah. Well, I'll try to take comfort in that as well."

***

Nagaro stepped out of the longboat and into the shallow froth of a receding wave. The harbor was protected from the main force of the swells, and the waves broke gently here, making such an easy landing that the local fisher-folk needed no wharf or pier. In fact, it would have been difficult to build one on a beach where the high and low tide lines must be nearly twenty yards apart.

He stood for a moment on the hard, wet sand. It was very quiet, except for the swish of waves and the cries of the gulls wheeling overhead. A dozen small fishing boats were arrayed along the curve of the beach, drawn up safely above the high water line. Past the wet sand and a stretch of dry sand beyond it, patches of wiry grass anchored several ranks of dunes in place. A brisk breeze rippled the gray-green dune grass into silver highlights. Beyond the dunes, the land rose gently at first, then more steeply to form a modest hill with a ragged, rocky crest. Stands of mingled pines and cedars graced the lower slopes, some extending almost to where the dunes began. The fishermen's houses were tucked among the shadows under the forest's fringe.

Behind him, on the ships in the harbor, Edroviran and Mahuk warriors crowded the rails, watching. But in front of him, on the island of Osfaraad, there wasn't a man, woman, or child to be seen.

The other men had all stepped out of the boat as well. Taru and Pavo exchanged a single glance of silent understanding, gripped the longboat by the gunnels on either side, and dragged it a dozen feet farther up onto the sand. The tide appeared to be high and already turning, but the two fisherman's sons took no chances.

Kuran took a few steps boldly forward onto the sand. Pavo started to follow, then turned, waiting for the others. Vell paused beside Nagaro, who gave him a wry glance.

"Are you ready to impress the Emperor, Vell?" Nagaro asked.

Vell shot him a look. "I don't mind saying that I don't care for this," he said darkly. "But I'll be damned if I'll be the only one to hang back."

The Emperor's longboat was landing fifty yards away along the beach. As arranged, it contained four men in addition to the Emperor. Predictably, one of the men was Roheed. Taru had come to a stiff halt at Nagaro's right hand, staring at the Mautep in the boat. "I hope ye know what ye're doing, Nagaro," he muttered. "I'd ha' rather seen ye stay safe on the *Sword* no matter what the Emperor wants, or what he's sworn to. At least I'm here this time t' protect ye if that rotter tries anything."

"Nothing bad is go to happen this time." Pavo raised a hand to the flawless blue arch of heaven. "This time Sheptuum have smile."

Taru rolled his eyes, then muttered, "Have ye got that life stone with ye, Nagaro?"

"Yes." Nagaro frowned, but he knew there was no point in arguing with either of his friends. "Come on," he said, and moved to join Lord Kuran.

The Emperor had stepped out of his boat and was standing erect and resplendent in his striking tunic, half of scarlet and half of gold. He waited just long enough for the other men to disembark. Then he advanced to meet the Edroviran party with a measured stride. The four other Mautep followed him, one step behind. Like the Edrovirans, they all wore their swords.

Kuran motioned for the members of his entourage to move forward as well, and the two groups approached each other in such a way that they would meet on the dry sand roughly halfway between the two longboats. Nagaro walked at Kuran's right hand with Taru and Pavo behind him. Vell walked on Kuran's left. When they were still some paces short of the meeting place, Kuran leaned a little towards Nagaro and said under his breath, "They're all wearing different uniforms, do you see? He's also bringing witnesses."

Nagaro merely nodded. He had noticed this as well. Only Roheed wore the red and black uniform of jir-Akaan. One of the others wore Lord Angkat's gold and brown, the second wore Lord Tuluptak's green and gold, and the third wore orange and dark blue—colors that Nagaro didn't recognize.

Both parties came to a halt with about six feet of sand between them. For a long moment, no one spoke as they took each other's measure. As before, Nagaro found the Emperor of the Mahuk Baar impressive. Baalkir jir-Akaan appeared to be about fifty. While not a tall man, he was very broad in the shoulders, and he radiated a self-assurance that was extremely convincing. The narrow dark eyes in his broad, brown, well-favored face took in the world with a quick, sharp gaze that bespoke a penetrating intelligence. It was plain that the three unknown men with him were not his equals. Those in Angkat's and Tuluptak's colors were much younger men, in their thirties. They tried to move boldly and maintained stiffly impassive expressions, but subtle signs betrayed their nervousness. The man wearing orange and blue was much older, with gray in his hair and a weathered countenance. He made no attempt to conceal his deference to the Emperor. Only Roheed came close to matching his uncle's bearing.

It was Emperor Baalkir who at last broke the silence, speaking in his native Hashti, his voice richly resonant. "Here we will sit and talk." He gestured to the ground in front of him. Then, as if to illustrate, he proceeded to seat himself cross-legged on the sand, his sheathed sword coming to rest beside him. His four officers took their seats in a semicircle, two on either side. Roheed was at his uncle's right with Tuluptak's man beyond him.

Pavo translated the Emperor's words, though Nagaro had understood the simple sentence and had begun to sit even before Kuran made a move to do so. A flick of Baalkir's eyes took note of this, though he did not comment. Kuran sat down, and the rest of his officers followed his example, with Pavo and Taru flanking Nagaro so that Pavo was next to Kuran's right hand. Vell sat on Kuran's left.

The Emperor cleared his throat and proceeded to make his own introductions, which Pavo translated. "He have say you already know Heerukan Roheed. Man of Tuluptak wearing green tunic is Captain Hakor. Man of Angkat is Captain Ampao. Man in blue tunic is Lord Masataak. He is lord of this island."

Kuran listened intently, nodding to each man in turn, then made his own introductions. "You know Captain Nagaro, Lord Emperor, and his second mate, Pavo Maat. Beyond Nagaro, there, sits his first mate, Taru Nareyo, who was my first mate at Paktaar. Captain Vell Sobring, on my left, you may remember as Captain Nagaro's first mate when last you met here at Osfaraad."

Roheed had been murmuring a translation in the Emperor's ear as Kuran spoke. When the young Mautep finished, the Emperor leaned back and addressed Kuran in words that Nagaro understood. "So, Kiraam Shaku-Tal and Pavo Maat once again wear uniform of your royal fleet. That is good. Heerukan Roheed has told me how this came to be. And brave yellow-hair man is now captain." Baalkir nodded as if he approved of this also. "And other yellow-hair man, one who betrayed his commander's plan, you say is dead, which Heerukan Roheed has confirmed. Tell me, please, how he died."

Kuran responded as soon as he understood Pavo's translation. "He received a mortal wound in the fight with some of your men at Long Harbor. Before he died, he wrote his confession, and so reclaimed his honor."

Roheed frowned slightly at the reference to Long Harbor and glanced at Tuluptak's captain, Hakor. His translation, however, was word for word without elaboration and Hakor sat through it stonily with nothing more than the slightest flicker in his eyes.

The Emperor frowned and leaned close to Roheed. There followed a rapid exchange between uncle and nephew which was not translated. Nagaro caught only enough to suggest it concerned the details of the attack on Long Harbor. He heard the words "banners of green and gold" after which Baalkir gave Captain Hakor a significant look that seemed to promise more attention at a future date, before he turned back to Kuran.

"Your pardon, Lord of Fleet," the Emperor rumbled. "There is small matter I must deal with later. But now we talk." He settled himself more comfortably in the sand. "So we begin to trust each other. You give back my Heerukan. I sit within reach of your demon swordsman." A small gesture of his hand indicated Nagaro.

Having clearly understood the Emperor's words, Nagaro frowned. "I doubt you would have let me live if you thought I was demon, Lord Emperor," he said levelly.

"This man speaks Hashti?" The Mautep in the blue and orange was apparently so astonished that he spoke aloud.

Nagaro turned to the man. "I speak a little, Lord Masataak. Not so much as Pavo Maat speaks Droviri."

Pavo had been frantically translating in a low murmur for Kuran's benefit, and Kuran now loudly cleared his throat. "We are all men here, Lord Emperor. I bring no demons to this meeting."

Roheed rendered Kuran's utterance into Hashti, then leaned closer to his lord to add more words that were too low and rapid for Nagaro to follow. Baalkir listened narrowly. Then he inclined his upper body to Kuran, spread his hands, and made a rather long reply of which Nagaro caught only a few words.

Pavo shifted position. "Emperor say he does not mean Nagaro Kiraam is demon. But he has seen Nagaro fight. If Nagaro have man with sword on his left and on his right—way that I and Taru now are sitting—surely he can kill Emperor and all man with him if Lord of Fleet order him to do it."

Kuran frowned. "Assure him that I have no intention of giving such an order—provided he and his men do nothing to warrant it. Remind him that it was he who proposed the number of men in our party and suggested that we bring our swords. You might also point out that we have come ashore to talk with him at his request and that the ground on which we sit is part of his territory, not ours."

Pavo needed some time to translate this rather lengthy speech. The frown of concentration on Roheed's face plainly showed that it would have taxed the young Mautep's linguistic skills. The Emperor lifted an eyebrow ever so slightly. "Lord of Fleet," he said very distinctly in Hashti, his eyes fixed on Kuran, "this land belongs to Lord Masataak, not to me. And you can see there is nothing here to fear." With a sweeping gesture he indicated the sand dunes and the trees beyond them. "There is no one on this island but fisherman, and they are not brave."

Nagaro waited through Pavo's translation out of deference to Kuran before placing his hands on his friend's shoulders and saying in Hashti, "These man both began as fisherman, Lord Emperor. You should not judge your own people by saying they are not brave."

This remark drew startled intakes of breath from several members of the Emperor's party, who all turned to see Baalkir's reaction even as Pavo hurriedly rendered the exchange into the Common Speech. Taru muttered, *"Hamanei!"* under his breath, and Kuran stiffened fractionally where he sat.

The Emperor's eyes narrowed as he considered Nagaro for the space of several heartbeats. Then, abruptly, he emitted a low, rumbling chuckle. He swung his gaze to Kuran, and said, "Your man speaks his mind very plainly, Lord of Fleet. Do you find this inconvenient?"

As soon as he understood, Kuran replied, "Yes, Captain Nagaro does speak plainly at times. For the most part, it is something I have come to value."

"Ah. So." Baalkir nodded in response to Pavo's translation, then he abruptly leaned forward to strike the sand with his hand. "Enough of small word! Time passes." He straightened, barely allowing Pavo time to translate these words before launching into a much longer speech of which Nagaro could make nothing.

Pavo listened intently with a gathering frown and finally cautiously raised a hand to ask for a pause. He turned to Kuran. "Lord Emperor does not make apology for having put three man to torture," he said cautiously. "He says he needed to protect Mahuk Baar, and he needed to know what Lord of Droviri Fleet was doing in his water with so many ship. He says he have regret that it have happened, but he also have regret that Droviri King have made it necessary."

"I see." Kuran's eyes were hard. "Ask him if he would use torture in dealing with men he held in honor."

Pavo nodded and promptly put the question. For answer the Emperor made Kuran a small bow where he sat, and said, "It is true I would not. And now that I have seen that these two man have honor—" he gestured to Nagaro and to Vell, "—I make apology to them for pain they have suffered." This concession brought murmurs from the two Mautep captains and Lord Masataak. When the words had been translated, Taru murmured *"Hakura!"* Vell muttered *"I'll be bodjered!"*

All of these reactions were ignored by Emperor Baalkir, who resumed speaking, his eyes fixed on Kuran. He spoke slowly this time, and Pavo was therefore able to translate line by line.

"Now I have some question, Lord of Fleet. You say that you will swear not to bring Droviri warship anymore into water of Mahuk Baar if I will swear that Mautep will no longer bring warship into water of Edrovir. This is correct?"

Kuran nodded as Pavo's translation ceased. This was part of the message Roheed had been instructed to deliver, since there had been no certainty of a face-to-face meeting with Baalkir. "Yes, Lord Emperor, that is correct," he said. "There must be no more robbing of our merchant ships, or our gold ships, or our ports. There must be no more taking our people to be galley slaves. If you will swear on your honor to do this, our King Elgurn gives you his word of honor that there will be peace between Edrovir and the Mahuk Baar."

The Emperor waited for the end of Roheed's translation. "So," he said. "Then there will be no more stealing of slave and other thing from warship of Mahuk Baar?"

When he understood, Kuran made a small, cautious gesture. "That is correct, Lord Emperor, if they stay in your waters. But there is more. There must also be another meeting with you before the summer's end to arrange for the return to us of all of the Edroviran citizens that are held within your borders against their will. These men committed no crime against you nor against any law of the Mahuk Baar, and it is the position of the King of Edrovir that they were wrongfully taken and are being wrongfully held."

This speech required some time to translate, with Roheed pausing several times to ask Pavo for assistance. In the end the Emperor regarded Kuran narrowly and asked, "Does King of Edrovir value fisherman so much?"

Kuran's response when he understood was, "Fishermen or farmers or merchant seamen, they were born free men of Edrovir."

"And does Kiraam Shaku-Tal also swear by his honor that if all of this is done, he will not any more come into our water and attack our ship to make slave free?" Here the Emperor's gaze swung to Nagaro.

Nagaro drew a long breath. "I would rather see all slaves free, everywhere," he said in the Common Speech because he was more sure of the words. "But I have given my oath to Edrovir, and I will abide by the decisions of Edrovir's king. If your warships come into our waters with slaves aboard them, that is a different matter since we allow no slaves in Edrovir. But if your warships do not come to steal gold or take slaves, this difficulty should not arise."

The Emperor appeared to consider after hearing the translation. "You must understand," he said, and his gaze flicked sharply back and forth between Nagaro and Kuran. "That what you ask is not easy. The place of all these Droviri man must be filled by other man."

Nagaro answered him, again in the Common Speech. "It is true, Lord Emperor, that if you wish to keep sailing the same number of galleys, you must replace all of these men, one way or another—"

"How you replace them is not our concern," Kuran put in hastily. "We are prepared, at the meeting we propose, to work out the timing of the release, and it need not be done all at once."

Roheed translated with help from Pavo.

"Ah. I see." The Emperor appeared to be thinking. His narrow black eyes played over the faces of the group of Droviri seated before him, while the sea birds cried and the wind ruffled the dune grass. Presently he said, "There is question I want Kiraam Shaku-Tal to answer."

Kuran frowned slightly and shot a glance at Nagaro before saying, "Very well."

The black eyes shifted to Nagaro. "Heerukan Roheed has told me you were in fight at Lankura."

Nagaro nodded. "Yes, Lord Emperor."

"Why did your people kill so many of my man? Heerukan Roheed tells me almost half of them have not come back to me. Was it because we killed so many Droviri at Paaktar?"

"No, Lord." Nagaro had understood the Hashti and answered in the same, aware that Pavo was translating for his comrades. "It was because they would not surrender—until I killed their commander. When Roheed became commander, he agreed to surrender. If he hadn't done that, probably we would have had to kill them all."

The Emperor made a small forward inclination of his head in acknowledgment. "So," he said. "Why do you think first commander refused to make surrender?"

Nagaro met the black gaze levelly. "He did not trust that he and his man would be treated with honor. He did not trust the King of Edrovir."

"Heerukan Roheed trusted King of Edrovir?" The Emperor raised an eyebrow.

"He trusted me, Lord Emperor. I told him he could trust our king."

The black eyes narrowed. "You were certain of this?"

Nagaro drew a breath. "Certain enough. And I did not want more man to die—Mautep or Droviri."

"Ha!" The Emperor sat back. His expression seemed fleetingly to register satisfaction, and he turned his head to left and right, taking in the reactions of his own officers. Roheed's face was impassive. Masataak looked impressed. The two captains were frowning as if the direction of the conversation were unexpected.

Baalkir turned back to Nagaro. "I have other question, Kiraam Shaku-Tal," he said, leaning forward and pinning Nagaro with his gaze. "King of Edrovir asked once before that there be no more taking of gold and slave, but before he had heard my answer, he sent many ship to attack my city. Why should I this time trust King of Edrovir? How do you answer this, man who speaks so plainly?"

Nagaro could feel the eyes of his comrades on him when they understood the translation. He drew a long breath. "I will answer that, Lord Emperor, if you will tell me why you sent some of your ship to attack Lankura after you had already sunk many Droviri ship and killed many man at Paktaar—and escorted the remaining ship out of your water." It was a question to which he thought he knew the answer.

There was some muttering among the Mautep officers during Pavo's translation, but Nagaro kept his eyes on the Emperor. Baalkir considered him intently, apparently ignoring his men, before scanning the sky. There was not so much as a wisp of cloud to be seen anywhere, though at that moment there came a little gust of wind that rustled the blades of dune grass and sent tiny cascades of sand skittering down the leeward slopes of the dunes. The tension in the air was palpable.

The Emperor's eyes came back to Nagaro's face. "Answer is not simple." he said, and the words felt carefully measured. "There is only one emperor in Mahuk Baar, but there are many warlord—who all speak to emperor. They make suggestion, and emperor must decide what to do—what is good suggestion, and what is not, and what will happen if he do this, or that. Does this answer your question, Kiraam Shaku-Tal?"

"I think so." Nagaro spoke in Droviri, slowly to make Roheed's task easier. "It is similar in Edrovir. There is only one king, but there are many lords, and some of them also make suggestions. This plan you have heard twice was my suggestion. The first time, the king liked it, but some of the lords made a different plan and spoke very strongly in its favor—"

"Other plan was to attack Sar Tipaal?" Baalkir interrupted sharply when the translation caught up to Nagaro's words. "Plan you refused to tell me?"

Nagaro nodded. "Yes, Lord Emperor."

"So why do you come now again with first plan?"

"The consequences of the second plan were not so good," Nagaro said carefully. "So the king and the lords have all agreed now to try the first plan."

The Emperor's eyes narrowed. "They will not change their mind again?"

Nagaro sighed. "This time they will wait to see what you do, Lord Emperor." He risked a glance at Kuran. The Lord of the Fleet gave him an approving nod.

The Emperor sat still, frowning, for several long seconds when he understood. Everything was very quiet. His own officers seemed to be holding any response in abeyance, their faces rigid. Roheed's expression was carefully neutral. Among the Edroviran party no one breathed. Even the wind seemed to hold its breath.

At last, Baalkir cleared his throat and addressed Kuran. "Peace between honorable man is good thing, Lord of Fleet," he said sonorously. "So we will try this plan that you propose. This I swear by my honor and in name of Sheptuum: So long as Droviri King does not break his word, no warship of Mahuk Baar will sail into Droviri water by order from my mouth. If you find any there, Lord of Fleet, you will know they do not act in my service. Do with them what you will, and with every man on board, free or slave. And tell your king that I will meet with him at last full moon of summer, at island of Chitaopa that is in water of no country, to return first hundred of your people. Then we will speak of how many more there are and when they will be returned. Tell him also to send this man who speaks very plainly—this Kiraam Shaku-Tal. Is this good plan, Lord of Fleet of Edrovir?"

Nagaro was watching the faces of the Emperor's men as the speech unrolled itself and Pavo translated line by line. He read shock in the eyes of Hakor and Ampao, though their faces remained as immobile as masks. He saw Lord Masataak's jaw go slack in astonishment. He felt Roheed meet his eyes and saw the heerukan smile the smallest of smiles and incline his head ever so slightly in congratulation.

And then Kuran was making his reply, declaring that, yes it was a good plan, and swearing on his honor and in Vothra's name that he would faithfully transmit the Emperor's words to the King of Edrovir.

A moment later, they were all standing up and the Emperor stepped forward and put out his hand to Kuran. The Lord of the Fleet took the Emperor's hand and shook it.

The Emperor then turned and extended his hand to Nagaro.

Without hesitation, Nagaro took the single step necessary to close the distance and put his hand into the hand of the other man. This brought them for the first time eye to eye. Baalkir had a grip like iron, but he didn't abuse it. As he released Nagaro's hand, he spoke. "Nagaro Kiraam Shaku-Tal, test I made for you was more cruel than you deserved. It pleases me that Sheptuum chose to spare you."

For a long second Nagaro measured the sincerity of this man who had placed him in the hands of his bitter enemy. "Tell me, Lord Emperor," he said then, quietly. "What did you do with Urchak?"

The Mautep's black eyes never faltered. "He will sit on my oar deck and row for three year. Does this punishment please you, Nagaro Kiraam?"

Nagaro frowned and looked at the ground. Beside him he heard Pavo suck in his breath. He knew that his Hashtep friend was following every word, though he wasn't translating. At his other side, he could feel Taru vibrating with tension as his eyes flicked back and forth between the two speakers. Kuran and Vell were at a little distance, watching warily. Nagaro raised his eyes again to the Emperor's face. "It is justice that he do this labor for a time, but I do not like to see any man used as slave."

The Emperor made a dismissive gesture. "He is not slave. He does not belong to me—"

Nagaro stiffened, scarcely noticing that Pavo and Taru both flinched at his movement. His eyes flashed. "I bear your mark on my body, Lord Baalkir, but never have I belonged to you!"

A flick of Baalkir's glance took in the position of Nagaro's sword hand, which had not moved. He inclined his head. "If there is anything you want that I can give you, Kiraam, I will give it," he said.

This was so unexpected that Nagaro could only fall back on his natural response. "There is nothing I want that you can give me, Lord Emperor."

"Nothing?" The Emperor raised an eyebrow. Roheed stepped close to murmur something in his uncle's ear. Baalkir nodded fractionally and said, "Heerukan Roheed tells me you have no wife, Nagaro Kiraam. I can choose one for you from woman of my House."

For an instant Nagaro felt only shock. If it weren't for Roheed's earlier attempt to make a match between Narei and his son, he might have thought he had misunderstood the Emperor's words. He heard Pavo, beside him, gasp. He looked at Roheed, hoping for some guidance, but the young Mautep only returned him a look that said, *well?*

Nagaro swallowed. "You do me great honor, Lord Emperor. And woman of Mahuk Baar are very beautiful. But I—" He hesitated, then took refuge in the truth. "My heart has already made choice for me." He waited, watching the Emperor's face, worried the man might be insulted.

Baalkir was frowning, his straight dark brows coming together darkly. His black eyes fixed Nagaro with a penetrating stare. Then, abruptly, his face relaxed. "So," he said, in what seemed an amiable tone, "Father of this woman must be very pleased."

To this Nagaro could make no answer, so he bowed—one of his best bows—stepping back as he straightened.

The Emperor merely gave him a nod of acknowledgment and turned back to Kuran. More bows were exchanged, and then the two parties separated, each moving back towards the appropriate boat.

Nagaro let out his breath as the knot in his stomach eased. He passed a hand across his brow. Kuran clapped him on the back. "By the Eyes! Well done, Captain! It seems your plain speaking has won us an agreement. It's quite a concession the man is making, too, promising to return men he's been holding for years. It was clever asking him why he attacked Lankura after letting me leave Paktaar with half my ships. It seems the Emperor has politics of his own to deal with!"

Nagaro smiled wanly. "I thought he might."

They had reached the longboat, and Taru and Pavo promptly seized hold of it and slid it back across the sand into the gentle surf. They were just holding it for the other members of the party to embark when a shout went up from the direction of the Mautep boat.

Nagaro looked up and saw that one of the Mahuk captains was pointing towards the dunes. All eyes turned, following the pointing hand to see that a man was standing just behind one of the first row of dunes, dressed in the garb of a Hashtep fisherman and holding a knife in his hand. As they all watched, a second fisherman stood up from behind a neighboring dune, then a third, a fourth, and a fifth. Within seconds there were a score of men standing in plain sight between the fishermen's houses and the place where the meeting had taken place. Sand gently cascaded from their clothing and they all carried something that could be used for a weapon— a long fisherman's knife, a heavy garden hoe, a blade lashed to the end of a pole.

"*Bloody Hel!* What trickery—?" Kuran began, and then stopped as a torrent of angry words burst from one of the Emperor's officers.

It was Lord Masataak, who claimed jurisdiction over the island. His words were not intelligible to the Droviri, but his tone unmistakably echoed Kuran's. He was clearly demanding that the fishermen explain themselves.

For answer, the man who had first stood up, who appeared to be the leader, turned to face the Droviri longboat. He raised his fisherman's knife aloft and cried, "Long life to Kiraam Shaku-Tal! May Sheptuum protect you!"

Nagaro, standing beside the longboat with the sea foam swirling about his boots, raised his hand and shouted back, "Thank you, friend, for your word! Go in peace!"

He heard Pavo translating for the benefit of his companions. He watched as the other Hashtep fishermen joined in their leader's salute, then turned towards the trees and departed, slipping quietly into the shadows of doorways that were suddenly open to receive them.

"Come on, lads," muttered Kuran. "Best be on our way while the Emperor's men are still wondering what to make of that."

Seeing the wisdom of this, Nagaro stepped into the longboat and took his seat beside Taru. He risked a glance over his shoulder at the Mautep longboat as he picked up an oar. The other boat still lay on the wet sand, the Emperor's officers gathered around it, gesticulating. The Emperor himself, however, stood still and erect as a statue, watching the departing Droviri craft. Across the distance, Nagaro felt their eyes lock. He raised one hand to the man in a gesture of salute and had the satisfaction of seeing Baalkir jir-Akaan raise his hand in answer. Then he thrust the blade of his oar into the sand and pushed hard, joining the effort to push the boat clear.

Kuran was the last one aboard since he claimed the place in the bow. He waded out, pushing the boat until it was well into the surf before boarding nimbly. Soon they were all paddling, turning the boat about, and rowing for the ships. They had taken several good pulls before Taru suddenly burst out laughing. "Fishermen aren't brave!" he chortled. "I guess they showed him!"

In the bow, behind Nagaro, Kuran grunted. "We're lucky those Mautep didn't decide that it was somehow our doing."

Vell twisted about, trying to look at Nagaro over his shoulder as he rowed. "You and the Emperor had a bit of a chat, Nagaro," he puffed between strokes. "What was that about anyway?"

"Aye. I'd like t' know that too." Taru shot Nagaro a look.

Nagaro shrugged. "Several things," he said evasively. "None of them very important."

But he hadn't reckoned on Pavo. The young Hashtep was sitting next to Vell with his back to Nagaro, and he didn't bother to turn around. "Emperor offered to give Nagaro woman for wife," he said triumphantly. "Woman from his own House!"

Vell missed a stroke. "A *wife*, Nagaro? All he offered me was an apology! What did you say, man?"

"I said no, of course."

"To the *Emperor?* That was risky!"

"I hope you were diplomatic about it," Kuran put in. "Powerful men sometimes don't take no for an answer."

"I know *that* well enough," Nagaro muttered darkly, then hurriedly added. "I said it as politely as I could. He seemed to accept it."

"But what did ye *tell* him?" Taru wanted to know. He'd slowed the rhythm of his rowing and Nagaro had to slow down to match, to keep the boat straight, with the result that the blade of his oar knocked against Pavo's. Nagaro shook his head. "It doesn't matter."

"He say his heart have already chosen—" Pavo began.

"No!" Taru's oar blade came to a halt poised above the water as he gave Nagaro a look of astonished incredulity. "Ye *lied*, Nagaro? The plain-speaking man just *lied to the Emperor?*"

Pavo shook his head. "I do not think—"

"We're losing way!" Nagaro cut in desperately. "Call the strokes, Taru! Set the rhythm."

"Yes," Kuran added archly. "I don't want the Emperor to think that we don't know how to row."

"Aye, Zirda!" Taru swung his oar forward. The other oarsmen, watching, moved their oars in parallel. "One, two, three... *stroke!*"

***

Half an hour later, Nagaro was back on the captain's platform of the *Sword* and all six Edroviran ships had left the anchorage at Osfaraad's northern shore and were rapidly putting the island to stern. None of the Mahuk craft had tried to hinder their departure in any way.

Nagaro heaved a sigh. The sun was high, the wind was fair out of the west, and there wasn't a cloud in the sky. They should be safely out of Mahuk waters before sunset. He allowed himself a brief smile of satisfaction. The negotiations had gone better than he had hoped. He should be very pleased.

His smile faltered and died. If only Pavo hadn't told the men in the longboat what he'd said when the Emperor offered him a wife. He could only hope that none of them would be curious enough to pursue the matter.

# Chapter 19

# The Envoy

Kuran intended to return to Lankura as quickly as possible, passing through Jinari waters by skirting the islands, making only such stops as were strictly necessary. They made good time until they were passing the strait that separated the Jinari isles of Atadalba and Janidi, on a flawless morning, when a shout went up from the lookout in the crow's seat of the lead ship, the *Pride of Lankura*.

Standing atop the stern castle of the *Sword*, which was running just off the *Pride*'s stern on the landward side, Nagaro turned to the east, to follow the man's outstretched arm. A boat was approaching from out of the strait. It looked like one of the larger single-masted fishing craft the Jinari used, with a permanent wooden cabin aft, making a kind of low stern castle. From the mast was flying not only the yellow, red, and green flag of Jinara, but also a second bright red flag and a long white pennant of the kind generally used to signal peaceful intent.

As the boat moved into a better position relative to the sun, Nagaro put the spyglass to his eye. Besides several crewmen, there were two dark-skinned Jinari men, standing on the stern castle, who weren't dressed like fishermen. One wore a black tunic, the other a long robe-like garment of crimson. Nagaro frowned and lowered the glass, still watching the boat's approach. As the vessel changed course to make directly for the *Pride of Lankura*, the man in the black tunic began to gesticulate.

Abruptly Nagaro started and hurriedly raised the glass again. "Vothra's Eyes!" he exclaimed. "That looks like Utabala!"

"Where?" Taru had mounted the ladder and stepped up beside him.

Nagaro handed the glass to his first mate and pointed. "On that boat. It looks as if he's part of some official delegation."

"Aye, it does. It's a trim little craft too, and she's headed straight for the *Pride*."

There were shouts back and forth between the men in the boat and those on the deck of Kuran's flagship, and presently Kuran took up his speaking trumpet to inform his captains that the fleet would be anchoring nearby along Janidi's shore so he could meet and talk with the men aboard the smaller craft.

Nagaro was frowning as he gave orders to follow the *Pride*. Just a few months before, he had told Utabala that the High Council should send out a boat to meet Lord Kuran if they wanted to discuss the subject of secret trade. *And now, here was a boat.* "I may know what this is about," he told Taru, as the young Turo headed for the oar deck. "Tell Pavo to ready one of the longboats."

It wasn't far to the intended anchorage, and the fleet was soon safely harbored there. Nagaro didn't wait to ask permission, but rowed across to the *Pride* as soon as the *Sword* was secure. As quick as he was, the two official occupants of the Jinari boat had reached the deck of the flagship before him. Nagaro went up the same ladder that had been left dangling in anticipation of their eventual departure. As he came over the Pride's rail and approached the place where Kuran stood with the Jinari delegation, Utabala turned and raised a hand in greeting.

"Ah, Captain Nagaro. May de One Whose Name We Do Not Es-speak keep you ever in his favor. It is good to see you again." The merchant's agent spoke with measured reserve, though the warmth in his eyes was clearly genuine.

Nagaro's response matched the other man's tone and glance. "Well met, Utabala. May fortune smile on all your dealings."

Kuran cocked an eyebrow as he looked from one man to the other. The man in red who stood beside Utabala was also looking from one of them to the other, a frown marring his aristocratic countenance.

"We heard dat your ship was among de Droviri Fleet dat sailed past, going south to de Mahuk Baar," Utabala continued as Nagaro came to a halt beside Kuran. "I hoped dis meant dat you were once again in de good graces of de King of Edrovir. And I see dat it is so—praise to de Un-Named One."

Nagaro touched the front of his dark blue uniform tirka. "Yes, he said. "I've been reinstated, as you see."

Kuran cleared his throat. "Well," he said pointedly. "We *were* just in the process of making our introductions."

The man in red leaned towards Utabala and rattled off a string of rapid syllables in his native tongue that ended in a rising inflection and was accompanied by gestures in the direction of first Kuran and then Nagaro.

Utabala immediately responded with a staccato barrage of Jinari accompanied by similar gestures. When Utabala finished, the other man made a small, satisfied grunt, nodded, and stood waiting expectantly. Utabala turned to Kuran. "I ask your pardon, Lord Kuran. As I have said,

I am Utabala, a humble merchant's agent, and it has pleased de High Council of Jinara—may de Unnamed One hold dem in His Hand—to place me in de service of dis gentle-man." He indicated his companion with a sweeping gesture. "He is Hota Radavan Janavidi—may he be blessed in all dat he does. He is de official Envoy of de High Council. We were sent to seek de Lord of de Droviri Fleet, to es-speak to him about a matter of *concern* to de government of Jinara."

Kuran made a low bow to Radavan. "I am honored to welcome you aboard my ship, Zirda. I will do my best to serve you. Captain Nagaro—" and here he gave Nagaro a penetrating glance "—will be joining us. He is one of my most trusted officers, and I assure you that anything you wish to say to me can safely be said in his presence."

Utabala turned to the Envoy to relay the response in another string of rapid Jinari. The Envoy seemed to have rather a lot to say in return, and his black eyes flicked several times to Kuran and to Nagaro.

While the two Jinari were speaking, Kuran leaned close to Nagaro. "I'll excuse your inviting yourself," he said dryly, "since you seem to know the interpreter. What can you tell me about him?"

"We were slaves together." Nagaro spoke under his breath. "He's a trustworthy man in his own right, but right now he's acting in an official capacity and is likely to be under specific orders from his government."

"Ah." Kuran returned his attention to the two Jinari. When there was a pause in their discourse, he said, "Tor Utabala, if you and the Envoy will join us in my great cabin, I can offer you refreshment and give you an hour of my time."

Utabala glanced quickly at Nagaro before pulling his eyes away. Nagaro read tension in the man's movement and wondered what it meant. The merchant's agent recovered his aplomb, however, and made Kuran a small bow before translating for his companion. The Envoy made a brief rejoinder. Utabala turned back to Kuran, his face carefully neutral. "Hota Radavan says dat dis is very good, Lord Kuran. If you will please show us de way, we will follow."

Kuran bowed and led the other men across the deck and through the door into the stern castle. They were all soon seated at the table in the *Pride's* great cabin, Kuran and Nagaro on one side, Utabala and Radavan on the other. The *Pride's* cook, obviously skilled at handling unexpected contingencies, had produced a pitcher of cold sothiril which Kuran served up in stemmed glass goblets.

Nagaro studied the two Jinari over his glass. The men were similar in age and had superficially similar features, to an unpracticed eye. Like all those of their race, they were very dark-skinned, with sleek black hair, hawk-like noses, and black eyes. Nagaro could easily see differences, however, which went beyond the obvious half-inch wide strip of beard on the Envoy's chin. Radavan's face was more fleshy, his brows more beetling, and his hair had a light sprinkling of gray throughout, while Utabala's was gray only at the temples. There was also something a little calculating in Radavan's eyes, though he appeared more watchful than nervous. Utabala still seemed tense, though he covered it with polite small talk about the sothiril.

Kuran had also been studying his guests as he drank. Now he set down his glass. "And now, Zirdas," he said, sweeping both men with his sharp, black eyes, "What is this matter that your government finds of such concern?"

Utabala did not apparently need further instruction from the Envoy. "If it please you, Lord Kuran," he said, "Before we es-speak of dat, Hota Radavan wishes to inquire what brought you into de waters of Jinara some days ago wit six ships of de Droviri Fleet and four ships of de Emperor of de Mahuk Baar?

"Ah. Of course." Kuran nodded. "Please tell him that we were escorting captured Mahuk ships and some two hundred Mautep sea warriors, taken during a raid they made on our capitol. Our purpose was to return them to the Emperor and gain speech with him if possible. We hoped to improve our relations with the men of the Mahuk Baar, and we have secured an agreement that should end the Mautep practice of taking slaves from among our people and robbing our lands and our merchant ships. We are now bound for Edrovir once more to make our report to the king."

Utabala's sharp-featured face registered surprise as he turned to the Envoy, and his surprise was soon mirrored in the other man's face as the latter listened to the translation. Radavan frowned when Utabala had finished and seemed to consider. When he spoke again it was rather more slowly and his face wore a carefully fixed smile. Utabala's smile was similarly cautious, if a little less stiff, as he translated the other man's words.

"The Envoy says dat de government of Jinara also wishes to have better relations wit de leaders of de Mahuk Baar. De sea warriors of de Baar have also robbed our ships and taken our men captive. It would be pleasing to de High Council—blessings be upon dem—if you will tell dese tings to de Emperor when next you es-speak to him. Dis will make even better de good relationship dat we have now between de land of Jinara and de land of Edrovir."

Kuran made a small bow where he sat. He swept both men's faces with a smile that was only slightly stiff around the edges. "If the opportunity arises," he said carefully. "I will certainly convey your sentiments and concerns to Emperor Baalkir. And now I would appreciate it if we could discuss the matter that has brought you here, for the sun is moving higher and we are eager to be on our way."

Utabala spoke a few quick words to Radavan, who nodded. The merchant's agent then cleared his throat. His eyes flicked once, uncertainly, to Nagaro's face before snapping back to Kuran's. "It is dis," he said rather more slowly than usual, as if feeling his way. "It has come to de attention of de High Council—blessings be upon dem—dat dere has been for some time a secret trade dat goes on between some men of Jinara and some men from Edrovir."

Although he had expected this, Nagaro felt his apprehension rise.

Kuran coughed lightly. "While I don't care for secrets," he observed, "I would generally regard trade between our two lands as being desirable. May I ask why you bring this matter to me rather than to the King of Edrovir?"

Utabala moistened his lips, still without looking at Nagaro. "Partly it is because you are *here* in our waters, and we assume dat you represent your king. But also it is because dis trade is coming and going by *sea*."

"Ah." Kuran's brows descended slightly. He drummed his fingers on the table. "I have not been aware of the trade that you desribe. Trade is not, usually, my concern. Is there some particular reason why your High Council is worried about this secret trade?"

Radavan's frown had been deepening, and at this point the Envoy leaned towards Utabala and made a short, sharp utterance that ended in a rising inflection.

"I ask for your pardon, Lord Kuran," Utabala said quickly. "I must ek-es-plain to Hota Radavan what we have been saying."

"By all means, Zirda."

There followed a brief, intense exchange between the two Jinari. At length the Envoy lapsed back into an alert silence and Utabala fixed his eyes once more upon the Lord of the Fleet. "Lord Kuran," he said, speaking very precisely. "I must tell you dat de members of de High Council of Jinara—may dey ever prosper by de hand of de Unnamed One—look wit great disapproval upon any secret dealings, no matter if dey be between two Jinari or between a Jinari and a man of anoder land. Partly dis is because it is trade dat does not pay de tax."

"Ah yes, I see." Kuran tapped his glass with a fingernail.

"But dat is not all." Utabala licked his lips. "In *dis* case de matter is more serious because some of de tings being traded are tings dat are forbidden by de law of Jinara for a man to buy or sell. And we have very recently learned dat de Droviri men have purchased a quantity of a particular forbidden ting—an abominable sub-es-stance known as *hasakila*, dat I believe your people call *heskial*."

Nagaro had been quietly listening, but he flinched involuntarily at the mention of the drug that had once enslaved him. A chill like a wave of cold water washed over him, and he made a hasty grab for his glass, hoping to cover himself by taking a sip of sothiril. *This was new.* He had never spoken to Utabala specifically about heskial.

Utabala's eyes hadn't left Kuran's face, but the muscles of his jaw tightened visibly. Radavan glanced at Nagaro with a questioning frown and he rattled a rapid question.

A slight turning of Kuran's head revealed that he also had noted Nagaro's movement. He didn't wait for Utabala's translation. "Captain," he said quietly, "Have you some knowledge of this substance?"

Nagaro swallowed his mouthful of sothiril. "I've heard of it," he said vaguely, which was true as far as it went. Utabala was looking at him now and looking distinctly relieved. What had the man been fearing? Nagaro's mind raced. *The High Council of Jinara looked with great disapproval upon any secret dealings...*

Utabala leaned over to hastily murmur a translation for Radavan's benefit.

Kuran rubbed his beard. "I confess this is disturbing," he said. "What does this substance do, by the way?"

Nagaro hesitated, caught between not wishing to answer and not wishing to lie by saying that he didn't know. Fortunately Utabala came to his rescue.

"It causes one man to become an es-slave to anoder man's will," Utabala supplied. "I tink dat *abomination* is a good word for it."

Kuran looked troubled. "I assure you that I don't at all like the idea of such a drug making its way into Edrovir. Can you tell me anything more about the secret trade? How is it being carried out?"

"It *was* coming and going from de port of Patamtala, Lord Kuran. Until de High Council—blessings be ever upon dem—sent men dere to es-stop it. Unfortunately, we tink it is es-still continuing, but dat dey have moved de place. De Droviri always come and go in de night, in es-small boats, coming from de nort. Dis we know. And dey are all men wit yellow hair."

"*Bodjer!*" Kuran grimaced. Turning to Nagaro, he muttered, "I was afraid of that." He composed his features with a visible effort and turned back to his two guests, who had exchanged some words in their own tongue and were now watching him narrowly. "You may be assured, Zirdas, that King Elgurn will be informed, and inquiries will be made into this matter," he said rather stiffly. "It is not a thing that Edrovir wishes to see continue. I am sure you understand, however, that it can be difficult to put a stop to secret activities. Your government has already tried once and been thwarted."

Utabala nodded ruefully, and made his translation. Radavan responded briefly, and Utabala spoke again to the Lord of the Fleet. "May we say dat de High Council can depend on de cooperation of Edrovir in dis matter?"

"I cannot speak offically for the king without first consulting him, but I believe I can safely say so, yes."

There was another rapid exchange between the two Jinari, and Utabala inclined his head. "Dis is good, den. We do most humbly tank you, Lord Kuran, and we will not keep you any longer from your mission. "May your way ever be es-straight under de sun." He rose then, and the Envoy rose as well.

Kuran and Nagaro also stood up.

The two Jinari bowed, and Radavan addressed some words to Kuran. Utabala put his palm to his forehead. "The Envoy wishes de blessings of De Unnamed One upon you both, Lord Kuran, and Captain Nagaro."

Kuran and Nagaro each bowed in their turn, and Kuran voiced some appropriate platitude before escorting their guests back to the open deck. Once there, they all proceeded to the part of the rail where the small Jinari craft was made fast. While the Envoy was descending the rope ladder to the deck of his own boat, Nagaro managed to catch Utabala's eye and draw him aside. "I'm sorry, Utabala, I never thought about the tax," he said, speaking in a low voice. "Did you pay tax on all of our transactions?"

"Oh yes," Utabala assured him. "De tax was always paid, dough sometimes I had to write a different name in de book. Do not worry about dat, Captain." The Jinari leaned closer and continued urgently. "When I learned about de heskial, I had to do some-ting. So I made sure de tax collectors found out about it. But dey must not find out that I have known about de trade for years wit-out reporting it. I was protecting my master— he transported secret cargo years ago wit-out knowing what it was—"

"I understand, Utabala. And don't worry." Nagaro put out his hand. "May fortune favor you, my friend."

Utabala shook the hand warmly, then quickly followed the Envoy down the rope ladder.

Nagaro leaned on the rail beside Kuran, watching the departing boat. The morning sunlight glittered cheerfully on the widening stretch of water between the *Pride* and the small Jinari craft, but he felt a chill on his heart. There were a few crewmen on the deck, going about their tasks, but none was within earshot. He cleared his throat and said, "There is more to tell, My Lord."

Kuran turned towards him. "What do you mean?"

"Utabala clearly didn't want me to speak of it in front of the Envoy, but I know that he's been tracing this secret trade for several years. He told me about it some time ago."

"You've had other dealings with him then? Besides being slaves together?"

"Yes, My Lord. Before joining the Fleet, I did business with him at times to sell things taken from Mahuk warships—things for which there was little market on Pakoa or in Harmoth."

"I see." Kuran looked grave. "What else did your friend Utabala find out?"

"That the trade involved things a lore master might want: Herbs, or scrolls about herbs—some of them poisonous—equipment for distilling the virtue from plants..." Nagaro hesitated, then added, "bladder-thorns." He swallowed and continued. "Utabala learned that the Leithian men brought lists of what they wanted, with merchant's marks on them. He managed to get copies of the marks, and this spring he showed them to me."

Lord Kuran was so silent that Nagaro risked turning to look at him. The older man was regarding him with a piercing stare, his jaw muscles tight.

"You have these marks?"

Nagaro shrugged. "They're in Lankura. When I got them, I thought I might try to make inquiries concerning them, but at the time, well, it was too difficult. And since then, the press of other events had put the matter out of my mind."

Kuran coughed. "All quite understandable. Have you told anyone else about this?"

"Only my two friends, Taru and Pavo."

"Those two? I hope you've sworn them to secrecy."

"I have, and I will again, My Lord. But I haven't been sure who else I could safely tell. Considering the source of the information, I wasn't sure that I would be believed. And up until today, the only thing unlawful about it, that I knew of, was the fact that some of the trafficking was done in time of war—which I've done, myself, in trading with Utabala."

Kuran's expression softened. "As it happens, it's safe to tell *me*," he said. "And as far as trading in time of war is concerned, I think I can grant you dispensation—provided you weren't dealing in weapons."

Nagaro shook his head. "It was jade, silk cloth, Jinari carpets... some jewelry..."

Kuran waved this aside, then added in a voice a notch lower than the one he'd already been using, "I assume you have some sense of the implications of this?"

Nagaro glanced at the older man, reading deep trouble in Kuran's eyes. He swallowed. "The nature of the things being traded originally made me think of Dreigen," he said. "They were things a lore master would value, as I said, and Dreigen is the most *conspicuous* lore master in Edrovir—"

"*Notorious*, I would say," put in Kuran. "*And* he's half Jinari."

"Well...yes. There's that." Nagaro paused uncomfortably. He also wondered what King Elgurn might know about it, but he wasn't going to say that to Kuran. "Also, the fact that the Edroviran men involved are Leithians makes it possible that politics are involved," he added, because the point was too obvious not to mention.

"*Possible?*" Kuran snorted. "I'd put it a bit more strongly."

Nagaro shrugged. "Now that I've been reinstated," he said. "And have been reminded of the matter, it occurs to me that there is someone I know in Lankura to whom I could show the merchant's marks. Someone I trust to be both discreet and thorough." He was thinking of Simion.

Kuran frowned and started to say something, then stopped. "I was about to say that *I* know merchants and their marks," he said. "But it will be less conspicuous, and less politically fraught, if I am not visibly involved in the initial inquiries. So I will charge you with the task, Captain. See to it at your earliest convenience once we return to Lankura, and report to me what you discover."

Nagaro stepped a little back from the rail and bowed. "Very good, My Lord. I'll do that."

"Right. And now it's time we put this island to stern of us."

"Aye, Zirda!" Nagaro saluted and went down the rope ladder.

## Chapter 20

# In The Service Of Edrovir

T hree days later, on a fine, blustery morning, Lord Kuran's ships sailed into the mouth of the River Edro and came to anchor at their usual moorings near the gate of the Fleet Compound. A small gathering of folk watched their arrival from the quay.

This was not unusual. The fisherman of Lankura kept their eyes open when plying their trade and often passed news to men on shore, making it relatively easy for Lankura's common folk to get accurate information about movements of the Royal Fleet. Nor was it difficult for members of the noble class to keep themselves informed if they were lodging in the city where they could get news from the palace. A man on the third floor balcony with a spyglass could, after all, see a long way up or down the Great Channel.

What was unusual, on this occasion, was the number of noble folk among the waiting crowd—nearly two dozen—that and the fact that they were all armed men on horseback, equipped with saddle rolls and saddlebags.

Nagaro took note of the assemblage from the *Sword's* stern castle as the ship was being made fast, and frowned. The frown deepened when he identified the man at front and center of the mounted group as Lord Anduar. When the Kelorin lord maneuvered his horse to the foot of the gangplank of the *Pride of Lankura*, Nagaro headed for the ladder to the main deck. Anduar's business was apparently with Kuran, and Nagaro's best chance of learning anything was to be present when the two men met.

Lord Kuran was just descending the gangplank when Nagaro strode along the quay to the place where Anduar had dismounted to speak closely with the Lord of the Fleet. When the Pact Signer noticed Nagaro's approach, he transferred his attention long enough to point to a spot beside him on the flagstones. "Stand here, Captain," he commanded. He then extended the hand in greeting to Kuran as Nagaro stepped into the indicated spot.

Kuran clasped the proffered hand. "I'm able to report a successful mission, My Lord Anduar. The Emperor has promised to comply with everything we asked, and we owe our success in no small measure to Captain Nagaro here, who is a fair hand at diplomacy in addition to standing high in the Emperor's esteem."

"That's all well and good."Anduar's manner suggested that what he had just heard was a mere formality. "But I must speak with you on a more important matter."

Kuran looked taken aback. "More important than peace with the Mahuk Baar?"

"I dare say so. Certainly more urgent. You must not allow your men to disperse, My Lord, until you've found fifty of them who can ride a horse and whose loyalty to their oaths to Edrovir is beyond question."

Kuran stiffened. "All of my men are loyal, My Lord! But they're sea warriors, not horse-soldiers. What's this about?"

Anduar met the other man's offended glance with a steely stare. "The king requires a force of arms to ride immediately in defense of the peace of Edrovir," he said. "I am to lead it. It must be a force that won't be seen to favor either the Kelorin or the Leithian side and must be made up of men who won't hesitate to draw a sword against a countryman—be he Kelorin or Leithian—if ordered to do so."

Standing at Anduar's side, Nagaro felt his heart go cold. "Do you anticipate bloodshed, My Lord?" he inquired.

Anduar swung to face him. "I hope to *avoid* bloodshed, Captain. Or I should say, *further* bloodshed."

"I think you'd best tell me what has happened while we were gone, My Lord," Kuran put in dryly."

"Yes," Nagaro agreed. "Choosing men who won't take sides will be easier if we know what we're facing."

Anduar considered him sternly. "If you had stayed at that meeting at the Golden Branch until its conclusion, Captain, you might have some inkling. But you stormed out, after speaking your piece. Yes, I had the whole tale from Devral," he added, seeing Nagaro's expression. "Who *did* stay." His eyes flicked back and forth between his two listeners. "Rathdar was there to raise a force to aid his man, Kenthos, against the forces being raised by Lothard Hurn and his lot. He was on his way to succeeding too, it seems, when a certain well-known captain of the Royal Fleet stood up and invoked the name of Darion to argue against it."

Nagaro stiffened. "I said that Darion would not have wanted blood shed between citizens of Edrovir, My Lord, which I'm sure is true. And I told them to *think* before they acted!"

Anduar fixed Nagaro with his steel-gray stare. "Well, a great many of them apparently *did* think, Captain. A large part of Rathdar's support melted away after you left. He'd hoped to lead a force of two hundred men, and he rode out with little more than fifty—most of them from his own Wared. Unfortunately, Lothard and the Brothers of the Blood were able to gather four times that number. When the two forces met, the Kelorin were broken and scattered, and the Leithian force is bent on hunting them down and most probably slaughtering them all. *This* is what I hope to prevent.

Nagaro was stunned. "My Lord," he managed, "I swear I will ride with you and bring every man of my crew who can sit a horse, but surely I can't have had so much influence—"

Anduar's glance impaled him. "When the 'Hero of Osfaraad' invokes the name of Darion, you don't think men will sit up and listen?"

Nagaro shook his head. "I don't call myself that! I've *told* them I'm not a hero."

Kuran took a half step forward to interpose himself between the two men. "A man can't choose what others call him," he said quickly. "Nor how he's perceived. And it's unfair, Anduar, to suggest that Nagaro made matters worse. If he hadn't spoken, and two larger forces had met, there would likely have been more lives lost and much less that could be done about it."

Anduar's glance sharpened, but then he seemed to catch himself. "I don't fault him for trying to talk sense into those hot-heads," he said in a milder tone. "But his report to us failed to convey the extent of his success. By the time I found out how effective he'd been, valuable time had been lost." He turned to consider Nagaro keenly. "The fault was not willful on your part, Captain, but it's time you became aware of the power of your words."

Nagaro bit his lip. "Yes, My Lord. I see that."

Kuran spoke again. "How soon do you need this muster you've spoken of, My Lord? And where should we gather?"

"As soon as possible. In the Fleet Compound. I hope to ride out this afternoon. These men—" he gestured at the group of horsemen who were waiting patiently just out of hearing "—are hand-picked citizens of my Wared. They're my contribution, which I want you to take charge of for the present. Each of the other Council members is charged with providing a similar number. I am bound immediately for the palace to see what I can glean from the Palace Guard. I only wish I had better knowledge of it's members."

"You should talk to Brandle Furthing, My Lord."

Anduar's eyes came back to Nagaro, who had spoken. "Brandle Furthing?" he said doubtfully. "Lord Madred's son?"

Nagaro inclined his head. "Brandle is no partisan, My Lord, whatever his father's sympathies. And he can probably name others of a similar mind."

Anduar arched an eyebrow, but nodded. "All right. I'll keep that in mind, Captain.

"What should we tell the men, My Lord?" Kuran asked. "They will want to know what they're riding into."

Anduar frowned. "Unfortunately, you must tell them as little as possible. I don't want the news spreading to the men who aren't chosen—the ones who *will* take sides. Just tell them it's a mission for the king, in the service of Edrovir. And now I must go. I hope to see both of you again within an hour."

Anduar turned briskly and remounted his horse. He spoke briefly to his horsemen before spurring his mount into a rapid trot and making for the nearby city gate. His men saluted him and turned their own mounts towards the Fleet Compound.

Kuran turned to Nagaro. "Well, lad," he said. "That was scant praise for a task well done. But perhaps we'll hear more about it later. Go see who you can draw from the *Sword* and the *Sea Eagle*."

"Aye, Zirda!" Nagaro spun on his heel and strode off along the quay. He couldn't help reliving in his memory the final scene in the dark inn yard—how glad he'd been to escape from Rastyl. The effectiveness of the words he had spoken in the common room of the Golden Branch had been the last thing on his mind.

***

The sun was already noticeably past its zenith by the time Anduar returned from the palace accompanied by ten men in the livery of the palace guard, all mounted and equipped for travel. Brandle Furthing was riding stone-faced at their head. They included five Leithians, four Kelorin and a Turowan.

Standing with Kuran at the head of the mustered Fleet men, Nagaro made note of the numbers. "How many have we to offer?" he asked Kuran out of the side of his mouth.

"Forty-three, including you, me, and the other three captains."

Nagaro nodded fractionally. Those other three captains were Landros, Vell, and Ruald—so the officers were nearly evenly divided between Kelorin and Leithian. He disliked keeping the tally, but he knew that appearances could be important. He had drawn mostly Kelorin from his own crew, though he'd included as many non-Kelorin as he could find.

Pavo and Taru stood behind him, as well as Tredhold, old Rubo the cook, and a Turowan named Haruda.

"I'd have called more Turowans if I could," he murmured, "but most of them don't ride."

Kuran grimaced his understanding. "The Turo are great swimmers, seamen, and fishermen—a fair hand as farmers and hunters—but they aren't horsemen."

Anduar had been reviewing the chosen Fleet warriors, and he now came to a halt in front of Kuran and Nagaro. "You've both done well under the circumstances, My Lord... Captain."

Kuran made a small bow. "What of the other Council members?"

"They'll meet us on the road."

"Ah. Will you address these men, My Lord?"

"Yes, if you don't mind."

Anduar turned and strode to a spot in front of the center of the first line of assembled Fleet warriors. Once there, he raised a hand for their attention. The whisper of voices among the ranks instantly ceased.

"Men of the Royal Fleet!" Anduar's voice rang in the silence. "You have been chosen to aid in the important task of maintaining the peace of Edrovir in the king's name. I charge you to remember your oaths, and to follow the orders you are given, whatever they may be. This is a land mission, not a sea mission. You will each have a horse. We'll be riding out in a half hour's time, and I expect we'll be gone for several days. You must be prepared to eat and sleep in the field, so I suggest you use the half-hour to gather whatever gear you can that will serve that purpose and that can be carried on your back, behind your saddle, or in your saddlebags."

As Anduar ceased speaking, Kuran stepped out of the front rank to stand beside him and addressed the men in his turn. "Are there any questions, before you are dismissed?"

"Can't ye tell us what this is about, Zirda?"

The speaker, a man in the ranks behind Nagaro, was not identified, but his question drew an appreciative murmur from the other men.

Kuran hesitated and Anduar answered, frowning. "It's about maintaining the peace, as I've said. That's all you need to know for now."

"But My Lord—" This came from a new speaker, a Kelorin in the front row who was one of Nagaro's crew. "We've heard rumors of trouble in the north—between the man who says he's Darion's heir and some o' the Leithian Faction. They're saying men have been killed. We'd like t' know, was it Kelorin killed by Leithians, or Leithians killed by Kelorin? And what are we likely t' be ordered to do?" The man wasn't challenging the Pact Signer so much as seeking clarification.

Anduar didn't immediately answer, and it seemed to Nagaro that he was uncertain how to deal with this frank request for information.

Nagaro personally thought the Pact Signer should simply say what he knew, since the men knew so much already. It wasn't wise to seem to be keeping secrets. So when Anduar's gaze swept the ranks and met his eyes for an instant, Nagaro mouthed, *Tell them!* The next instant, the contact was broken and at the same time Kuran leaned close to Anduar to mutter something in the Kelorin lord's ear. At last Anduar spoke.

"There have been roughly a dozen men slain, according to my information, and they've fallen on both sides. I can't foresee exactly what orders you may be given, but I will say this: It's not your task to avenge the dead—nor punish their slayers. Your task will be to prevent more bloodshed, if that's possible. Are you answered, Zirda?"

The man who had asked the question eyed Anduar appreciatively and saluted. "Aye, My Lord. Thank you."

"I've another question, Zirda."

This time the voice came from behind Nagaro and he recognized the gravely voice of old Rubo.

"Yes?" Anduar's steely glance found the speaker.

Rubo was apparently undaunted by the look. "What d' ye mean t' do for food, Zirda—beggin' yer pardon? Ye've said nothing about provisions."

Anduar cleared his throat. "We'll take what we can carry on horseback, and obtain more along the way. We may have to forage."

"Would that be like—shootin' the king's deer, Zirda?"

"For example, yes." Anduar's response was acerbic. "The king—or any other lord—can spare a deer to men in the service of Edrovir."

Rubo let out a hearty guffaw. "*Hakura Kili!* I think I'm goin' to enjoy this!"

Anduar gave the old Turo a stern look, but let the matter go.

Kuran raised his voice. "Time is flying! If you haven't eaten, get something from the mess hall, and more that will travel. I want to see you back here in half an hour with no more than you can carry. You are dismissed!"

There followed a kind of restrained chaos. As Nagaro turned to make for his own quarters, Taru gave him a wicked grin as he hurried past. Behind him, Nagaro heard Anduar giving orders to his own men, and those of the Palace Guard, to assist with mustering the horses.

Brandle suddenly loomed over him, on his horse. The big Leithian leaned down to ask, "You mean to tell me that old Turo can ride a horse?"

Nagaro squinted up at the guardsman. "He's never done it before, but he swore he'd still be there at the end of the ride as long as I got him up on top of the beast and pointed it in the right direction."

"You *trust* that? I'd say you've saddled yourself trouble."

Nagaro shrugged. "If I have, so be it. My guess is we'll be glad to have him regardless of any trouble he may be. Rubo can cook *anything* so you don't mind eating it."

***

When the troop of horsemen finally rode out, they headed north, to no one's surprise. They didn't pass through the city of Lankura, but followed the road that ran around outside the city wall and past the crossing where the Golden Branch Inn stood with its landmark cedar trees. At that crossing they were joined by Lord Pendrik at the head of twenty-seven mounted Leithians. Nagaro added their number to his mental tally with some relief as it made the balance more even.

After passing the Golden Branch, the road wound on through country that was mostly wooded, passing out of land held by the Crown and into Kel Wared. At length, as the sun sank westward and the shadows lengthened, the leaders of the party chose a place to make camp for the night. The spot was off of the road a little way, among the trees, where the cooking fires wouldn't be seen from the roadway and where there was a stream and a little grassy meadow for the horses.

Nagaro swung easily off of Thunder-Heels and moved to help Rubo dismount from the small, sturdy gelding that had been found for him. Rubo grimaced as he stretched his legs. "Ye can give me a boat over a horse any day o' the week," he growled. "Even in a bloody gale!"

Nagaro smiled wanly as he set about unsaddling their two mounts. He had ridden close to the man the entire distance, keeping an eye on the uncertain horseman. "I said you'd be sore. But you'll get used to it." He paused and leaned close. "To tell the truth, I was miserably sick the first time I was in a boat, and that was on a calm morning in sheltered water."

Rubo stared at him. "Now, by the Spirits, Capt'n! I'll never believe that!"

Nagaro laughed. "You can ask Taru if you don't believe me." He unbuckled Thunder-Heels' bridle and slipped it off. "But first go find whoever is in charge of the cooking and make yourself useful."

Before Rubo could answer, Nagaro was hailed, and he turned to find himself confronted by Brandle. The man thrust a bow at him and a quiver of arrows. "Your friend Taru says that if there's any hunting to be done, you're the man for it, Captain. Assuming there's any truth to that, I suggest you take your own advice and make yourself useful. I fancy some meat tonight." The big Leithian was grinning wolfishly.

Nagaro laughed as he took the bow and quiver. "And how will you make *yourself* useful, Brandle?"

Brandle made a face. "After handing out the bows, I'm assigned to picketing the horses." By way of demonstration, he took Rubo's horse by the bridle. When he approached Thunder-Heels, however, the big gray tossed his head and sidestepped. "Here now!" Brandle said to the beast, disapprovingly, "Where's your bridle? We can't have you wandering off."

Thunder-Heels backed away, ears flattening.

"Whoa, Thunder." Nagaro stepped between, putting a hand on the stallion's neck. The big horse lowered his head and Nagaro spoke softly into one velvety ear. He turned then to the astonished Brandle. "Thunder needs no bridle or hobble. He'll follow you to wherever the other horses are pastured, and he'll stay with them."

Brandle gave him a sideways look. "Since you're the one saying it, I'll take it for truth," he said wryly. "And it'll be on your head, not mine, if you can't find him in the morning."

The Leithian set off then through the trees, leading Rubo's gelding. Thunder-Heels gave a wiffling whinny and followed.

Rubo cackled and slapped his thigh. "Well if that don't beat fish tales! Ye knows your horses, Capt'n, an' that's a fact!"

Nagaro looked up from stringing the bow and impaled the man with a carefully stern look. "Off to the cook fires with you, Rubo! Step lively!"

"Aye, Zirda!"

After half an hour of stalking among the tree trunks and undergrowth in the fading light, Nagaro returned to the camp and located Rubo at one of the cooking fires. He deposited two rabbits and several assorted fowl beside the old Turo. "That's the best I could do, Rubo, without losing any arrows," he said apologetically. "If there are any deer out there, they must have heard me coming. Perhaps some of the other hunters have had better luck."

Rubo glanced up from sorting various little piles of green leafy things by the light of the fire. "Not much," he observed. "And some o' them *did* lose arrows. Ye can put the bow over there with the others, Capt'n. He examined Nagaro's take. "Hmm... If we stew the rabbits an' roast the birds..." He pushed the fowl towards Haruda, who was sitting cross-legged beside him. "Just start pluckin' these, will ye, lad?"

"Hoy, Nagaro! Over here!"

Nagaro turned to see Taru sitting with Pavo, Landros, Tredhold, and the other sea warriors who had been drawn from the two former pirate ships. He put the bow and quiver in their place and joined his friends. "What have you been doing?" he asked.

"Gathering firewood." Taru jerked his head to indicate an impressive pile of dead branches near the cooking fire. "That's what they set most of us t' doing."

"Well, it's an important task. Where is Kuran, by the way?"

"Over there." Taru pointed to a fire at the edge of the encampment. "The lords are all over there 'taking council'—in private. I tried t' get close enough to listen, on account o' being a first mate, but that wasn't good enough for 'em. Maybe ye can find out something since you're a captain."

"That didn't do *me* any good, lad." Landros must have been listening. He squinted up at Nagaro from his seat on the ground. "But Kuran's been taking Nagaro into his confidence lately. There's no harm in trying."

At this, Pavo spoke up. "Lord Kuran came to look for Nagaro, while he was hunting with bow."

Taru brightened. "Ye just go tell 'em that, Nagaro. Tell them Pavo told ye about it."

Nagaro frowned. "All right," he said. "I'll see if I can learn anything."

He started off in the direction of the council fire, although he didn't like the appearance of being Kuran's favorite. The Lord of the Fleet had been asking his advice quite a lot lately, but he attributed this to his knowledge of Roheed and of the Mautep Emperor. He knew next to nothing about the supposed heir of Darion.

There were several guards positioned around the council fire, and one of them immediately told Nagaro to halt, identify himself, and state his business.

Nagaro answered loudly enough, he hoped, to be heard by the men at the fire. "I'm Captain Nagaro, and I was told that Lord Kuran was seeking me."

To his surprise, the man simply said, "Pass," and stepped aside.

It turned out there were six men seated around the council fire. Anduar, Pendrik, and Kuran were three of them, but the others were dressed in rough clothing of colors that blended with the forest undergrowth. Their ages varied. Two were Kelorin, but the oldest man was Turowan.

Kuran must have heard Nagaro's voice, for he raised a hand and called, "Come and sit with us, Nagaro. These men have just finished."

Nagaro advanced into the circle of firelight as the three roughly dressed men rose to depart. The first two ducked their heads respectfully to him as they passed, and one murmured, "Vothra keep ye, Zirda."

The last man, the Turowan, paused to look Nagaro up and down. "So ye're Captain Nagaro," he said, sticking out his hand. "I'm Jato, and it's a pleasure t' meet a man what speaks for the Turo."

Nagaro took the hand. "Well met, friend Jato," he said as he shook it. "And I speak for all the common folk of Edrovir whenever I can."

A broad smile cracked the man's seamed brown face. "Ye just keep doin' that, Zirda," he said, and made a kind of stiff little half bow before following his two companions into the shadows under the trees.

Nagaro shook his head and approached the fire, where he sat down cross-legged in the space the three others had vacated. Kuran was on his right. Anduar and Pendrik were across the fire. He was aware that all three men were watching him.

Pendrik emitted a low chuckle. "So you speak for the common folk of Edrovir, do you, Captain?"

Nagaro earnestly returned the Leithian's gaze. "I try to, My Lord. And I'd appreciate it if someone would tell me who those men were."

Anduar cleared his throat. "They're three of my scouts, Captain, and they're very good at gathering information. In this case, they've told us that both Devral and Odus have been delayed in raising the required men in Sedras Wared and Morbern Hold. We've also learned that, as recently as yesterday afternoon, the forces under the command of the Brothers of the Blood were in the vicinity of Glenarl in Harland Hold, roughly fifty miles northeast of here."

"What about Kenthos and his followers?"

"They hadn't been located, as of yesterday—"

"And they won't be!" Pendrik cut in. "They're *hiding*. That's the problem!"

Kuran coughed. "We've had some discussion regarding the best course of action, Nagaro," he said carefully.

"Yes, we have." Anduar stepped in smoothly "It's been pointed out that taking Kenthos under our protection will be difficult if he's making himself hard to find. On the other hand, if we confront the Brothers of the Blood instead, Kenthos and his men may slip away and go unapprehended. Have you any suggestions, Captain?"

Nagaro considered the three lords. Anduar was lounging against a fallen log, his expression blandly questioning. Kuran was watching Anduar warily. Pendrik was scowling. Nagaro frowned. He doubted that Anduar really wanted his opinion. More likely this was some sort of test, but he wasn't sure of what or whom. It seemed wisest to answer as best he could.

"The ideal thing would be to bring both parties together in one place," he ventured. "So that we could do our best to resolve the matter where everyone could hear what was said."

Pendrik gestured angrily. "This matter is for the king to resolve!"

Nagaro shrugged. "In that case, My Lord, the leaders on both sides should be escorted to Lankura to stand before Elgurn. But it would still be best to bring both sides together first, to explain to them what is being proposed. And the difficulty is the same in either case—finding both parties before they find each other." He turned to Anduar. "Do you think your scouts will be able to locate Kenthos and his men, My Lord?"

Anduar continued in his lounging posture. "It's hard to say. The land around Glenarl—and between here and there—is broken woodland, forest and pasture intermingled. The area is large, and the number of scouts limited."

Kuran stirred. "We can add to the number of the scouts from among our own force once we get closer."

Anduar considered. "A good thought," he observed calmly. "Though the men we have are soldiers, guards, and sea warriors, not foresters or woodsmen."

"I believe some of my men could do it." Nagaro spoke his thought aloud. "—those who served with me before joining the Fleet, I mean," he added hastily.

"Pirates again," growled Pendrik.

Anduar ignored the Leithian. "That's good to know, Captain, but the matter remains uncertain, nevertheless."

Nagaro nodded. "Of course, My Lord. Which means that our best course is to track the Leithian force while the scouts make every effort to find the fleeing Kelorin. That way, if the Brothers of the Blood find Kenthos's men before your scouts do, at least we'll be close by."

"Excellent, Captain!" Anduar gathered himself and stood up in a single movement, the litheness of which belied his years. "What do you think of that, Pendrik?"

"Huh!" Pendrik clambered less gracefully to his feet. "If I didn't know better, Anduar, I'd say you had coached the man!"

"Nonsense, my friend." Anduar began to move around the fire, back towards the rest of the encampment. "It's only that superior minds think alike."

"Superior minds! You class yourself with the pirate? Where are you going, Anduar?" Pendrik started after the Kelorin Lord.

"To assess the disposition of the camp, my dear Pendrik. If you wish to accompany me, we can continue this discussion—"

"Discussion be damned! This has been your mission all along, and you know it! Are you quite sure there's no wine?"

Nagaro stared after the two Pact Signers as they moved away from the firelight and into the shadows under the trees, their voices fading. "Well, so much for my opinion," he observed. "It's obvious Anduar had already decided before he asked me."

Kuran chuckled. "They had a wager between them. Anduar said he'd stake a bottle of wine—which of course he doesn't have—that you'd agree with him. Pendrik said that if you did, he'd concede command of the mission to Anduar—which of course he'd already done. But Anduar does value your opinion. You've a reputation for sound judgement."

"Not with Lord Pendrik, it appears."

Kuran considered. "Perhaps even with Pendrik. He was jesting when he called you a pirate."

Nagaro had his doubts, but decided to let the matter pass. "It seems they were both jesting—about a rather serious matter," he said disapprovingly. "Although I suppose jesting is better than coming to blows, since they're on the same side."

"You're right about that. And you won't see such levity, I'm sure, when we get closer to Glenarl."

Nagaro leaned closer and dropped his voice. "My Lord, do you know any more details about the situation or its history?"

Kuran laughed shortly. "That was very direct," he said. "But then you tend to be. I do know a bit more, and I'm willing to tell you—knowing you'll pass it on as you deem appropriate." He paused as if to order his thoughts, then continued.

"The main confrontation occurred three days ago, in the afternoon, and word of it reached Lankura yesterday morning. What happened, apparently, was that Kenthos and his followers tried to come south openly along the border of Hurn Hold. They were stopped by a modest Leithian force—led by Lothard, himself, we believe—on the road as they approached Glenarl, and were then set upon from either side by more Leithians who'd been hiding in the forest. One of Anduar's scouts actually witnessed the attack."

"The Kelorin weren't the aggressors, then?"

"Not in this case. Although they apparently were quite ready to draw their weapons at the first sign of trouble. There was some bloody work done, rather briefly, and then either Kenthos or Rathdar gave the order to withdraw, and they took to their heels back up the road and off into the woods on the eastern side of it, which is the territory of Harland or of Sedras."

"So the Kelorin leaders are Kenthos and Rathdar?"

"Apparently, yes."

"Where are Soren and Therin?"

"We're not sure. They may have gone to their Wareds to gather more support."

Nagaro shook his head. "That's Tuveilas Wared to the east, and Oranil, which is west and south. And they may not know where to find Kenthos when they return. So they'll be blundering about searching for him just as we are. And Lords Odus and Devral will be, too, by the sound of it."

Kuran nodded grimly. "It's a bad business and no mistake."

For a long moment they both sat staring into the fire. Nagaro was first to break the silence. "I confess I really don't understand this."

"What do you mean?"

Nagaro's brow was furrowed in perplexity. "I don't understand why there are so many Kelorin who are so eager to follow someone they think is Darion's heir. I don't agree with the Leithians' ideas, or with what they're doing, but at least I understand that the Brothers of the Blood have their traditional notions about the inheritance of leadership and power. And they think their traditional ways are being threatened. But the equivalent Kelorin tradition comes from the Third Corner of Kelorin Law, which says that men should choose their leaders. Even if they've really found King Tevren's son, why are they be so determined to support him? Being Tevren's heir doesn't make him heir to the throne. Or at least it shouldn't."

Kuran sighed. He got up to toss some more wood onto the fire, and a shower of sparks erupted, spiraling up to die in the darkness. "It helps if you know something about Darion," he said, as he reseated himself. "What he was like and what he meant to the people of Edrovir, to the Kelorin people in particular."

Nagaro shifted closer to the fire. "He died before I was born."

"Yes, so I would have imagined. I was a very young man then, but I do remember him." Kuran was staring into the fire, which now blazed brightly, but his eyes were not focused on the flames. "Darion was a remarkable man. To begin with, he was physically impressive—half Turowan as I am, but a full head taller and solidly built. Dark, of course, though he wore his hair in the Kelorin fashion. And he was an extraordinary swordsman as everyone knows. But those aren't the things that made him a great king. No, it was his intellect, his temperament, his fairness. He had read the Writings, and he followed them. He was a thinker. He knew when to speak, and when to listen. And he never did anything to serve himself, but always for the good of the people of Edrovir..." Kuran's voice trailed.

Nagaro spoke into the pause. "Are you saying that folk are looking for another Darion?"

Kuran turned to him, frowning. "In a way, I suppose they are."

"So they chose his son, Tevren, to be king, and now they're looking for his grandson?"

Kuran shook his head. "It's not that simple. Tevren was a good man, but not his father's equal. There was too much of his mother in him. Darion was steady as a rock, with a mind as cool and clear as water. His wife, Selfira, had a spirit like a flame, and was as changeable as the wind. That's what they say, at least. She died young. Tevren was bold and courageous, but he was also like his mother in that he tended to be quick to act and to judge. To his credit, he was also very quick to admit error, and generous in making amends, but he lacked his father's thoughtful, deliberate ways."

"Didn't folk see this?"

"Yes, they saw it. The choosing of Darion to be king was very nearly unanimous. Tevren's choosing was much less so, but many folk were placing their hopes in Lindra."

"Tevren's queen?" Nagaro was puzzled.

Kuran sighed. "Lindra was Tevren's perfect complement. She had the thoughtfulness he lacked and a wisdom beyond her years. And Tevren listened to her. He was a wise enough man to know his own shortcomings. Ruling together, they could have governed Edrovir well. And also there was great hope for the issue of their union. If the child of Tevren and Lindra were to bring together his father's boldness and his mother's measured reasoning, then the world might indeed see another Darion. Or so men reasoned. And so, when the word leaked out during that long-ago spring that Lindra had borne Tevren a son at Loros Hall, a spark of excitement ran through the hearts of the men of the Kelorin Faction, while the men of the Leithian Faction felt only fear. They had accepted Darion because he was just and even-handed, but they didn't want a Kelorin dynasty. The result, of course, was the fatal confrontation on the road to Lankura, where the royal couple with their two retainers were met by Reith Hurn and a company of his followers—"

"Ending with Tevren and Lindra slain, and no sign of the child."

"Exactly."

Nagaro thought he understood. "So men like Rathdar believe that the son of Tevren and Lindra is out there somewhere, and that he will manifest his parents' better qualities?"

Kuran picked up a stick to poke at the fire. "I'm not sure exactly what Rathdar Sundorin believes," he said with a sigh. "But his father, Berinar, had a hope that amounted very nearly to certainty."

Nagaro nodded. "Yes. I have read Berinar's book, *Rule of Loros*. He was very clear about his views—if not about his reasoning."

"If you've read his book, then you know he was a great supporter of Darion. He nearly worshiped the man. And Rathdar grew up steeped in that worship, up until the age of twenty-five when his father died under mysterious circumstances—was murdered, many believe—"

"To balance the numbers of Kelorin and Leithian Pact Signers."

"Or because of his views on the House of Loros. Or both. It doesn't really matter. The point is that, for Rathdar, finding the heir of Loros and demonstrating his worth, and maybe setting him on the throne of Edrovir, would vindicate his father, or give meaning to his father's death. And there are other men, less prominent and powerful than Rathdar, whose fathers told them tales of Darion—or who, like Soren, remember the man and hope that the mingling of the blood of Tevern and Lindra will produce a great king—a king to end all woes and bring back a golden age. And of course, to the Brothers of the Blood, the whole idea is anathema."

Nagaro shook his head. "That's far too much to expect of one man," he said. "And it's ironic too. The Brothers of the Blood believe that everything is or ought to be inherited, and yet here we have Kelorin wanting to stake everything on heredity—and the Leithians don't like it!"

Kuran nodded grimly. "But there *is* an important difference in the way Kelorin and Leithians think about heredity. The Kelorin looked at Tevren and at Lindra and tried to think what a child might inherit from each of those two specific people, while for high born Leithians it's all about noble blood, and mostly the blood that's carried in the male line, at that. They want a woman to be of good family, of course, but as for her traits, it's enough if she's beautiful, fertile, and stays in her place." He sighed. "And of course the Leithian answer to inconvenient blood lines has always been to cut them down with a sword—as Reith Hurn did on the road to Lankura."

Nagaro winced. "*So*," he said thoughtfully, "if Lothard Hurn is now seeking to slay Kenthos, he may see it as following the path set by his father—finishing his father's task, as it were?"

Kuran nodded. "Very likely, although Reith did profess remorse for the slayings of Tevren and Lindra. He may have been sincere—at least with respect to Lindra, since killing a woman, even 'accidentally', gains one little favor. Personally, though, I think Reith Hurn's 'remorse' was a convenient way of avoiding the consequences of his actions. He would not have gotten a place among the Pact Signers if he hadn't formally expressed regret for those slayings."

"I see." Nagaro sat frowning.

Kuran face twisted into a wry smile. "There's one more little piece of irony. You know that some of the Leithian Faction wanted Tevren to wed a Leithian woman?"

"Yes, I had heard that."

"Well, they had a particular woman in mind—the Lady Jessafel of the House of Glenmark. She was a beauty, and of very good family, and so on. But Tevren detested her. He said she was 'petty, vain, and stupid. And not fit to be queen'."

"That's rather blunt."

"Yes. And it may not have been wise, though it was accurate, by all accounts. In any case, he soon rediscovered Lindra—whom he'd met as a child when he traveled to Irvenen Wared to visit relatives. And once he'd set his heart on her, there was no turning him." Kuran paused and cocked an eye at Nagaro. "So what do you think became of the Lady Jessafel?"

"I've no idea."

"Reith married her. She's Lothard's mother. He studied at her knee, and to my mind it shows."

"You two are talking about my cousin Jessafel?" Pendrik's rumbling voice interrupted them as he and Lord Anduar suddenly emerged into the firelight.

"Your least-favorite cousin, I believe," Anduar put in pointedly.

Pendrik made a face. "That's true," he said. "She's a stubborn, spiteful woman. Do you know that she still insists it would have sullied our House to mingle her blood with Tevren's? I say she's just bitter because she wanted to be queen." He turned to Nagaro. "Why are you still here, Captain? Hadn't you better go speak for some common folk?"

Nagaro stood up. "There's no immediate need for that here in this camp," he said easily. "So I'll have to be content with speaking *to* some of them. Thank you, My Lord Kuran, for the information. And now, please excuse me, My Lords." He swept the three other men with a bow and quickly made his exit.

As he walked away under the trees, he heard Pendrik's loud, if somewhat belated, guffaw and cry of, "How droll!"

Chapter 21

# Night Watch

Nagaro found Taru, Pavo, and his other friends where he had left them. He quickly sketched what he'd learned about the situation they were riding into.

Taru shook his head. "It sounds like a bodjering big game o' cat an' mouse," he said. "Except there's more than one cat, and some o' the cats are hunting each other."

The others agreed with this assessment.

A short time later, dinner was handed around. Rubo's cook-fire served the Fleet men, and they found themselves well-served, with the game birds well roasted and the rabbit stew surprisingly flavorful. Many of the men had brought bread in their saddlebags, so they made a good meal of it.

Nagaro was sitting with his back against a fallen log, facing the cook-fire and turning over in his mind what Kuran had told him, when Brandle strolled over from the area where the members of the Palace Guard were gathered. The Leithian dropped onto the ground in front of Nagaro with a bowl of Rubo's rabbit stew in his hand. He gestured with the bowl. "You called this one well, Captain," he observed. "The stew's first rate. You have my permission to keep your Turowan cook." He downed a mouthful with a sigh, then added, "And I understand I have you to thank for being invited along on this little stroll in the country."

Nagaro gave him a wry look. "I'm afraid so. Anduar wanted men who wouldn't take sides, and I suggested your name. I hope you don't mind."

"No, on the contrary. I *won't* take sides since this isn't my fight, and guarding the palace is really quite dull. I welcome the chance to give my sword arm some exercise."

"I hope it won't come to that."

"Ha!" The big Leithian grinned wickedly. "You and Simion!"

Nagaro winced and asked in a low voice, "Where is Simion, by the way?" He knew how protective Brandle was of his lover.

"In Lankura."

"You're, ah, sure of that?"

Brandle stopped with his spoon halfway to his mouth and gave Nagaro a hard look. "Is there something you need to tell me, Captain?"

Nagaro shifted uncomfortably. "It's just that I saw him at the Golden Branch tavern a week and a half ago, at a gathering that was called to try to whip up support for Kenthos."

Brandle looked relieved. "I know all about that. He went out spitting fire and came back with his tail between his legs—saying it wasn't what Darion would have wanted." The spoon completed its journey to his mouth. Then he added, around the mouthful of stew, "Anyway, Simion is no warrior."

Nagaro frowned. "He'll fight for something important, Brandle. Something he believes in. He fought for our freedom that day on the Mahuk galley."

Brandle stood up. "He fought for *you*, Captain," he said. "Don't think I don't know it!"

"What do you mean by that?" Nagaro felt an unwelcome twist in his stomach.

Brandle stood looking down at him, his face hard to read in the dim light. "Simion falls in love," he said quietly, "with people—and with causes—and he'll do almost anything for them. He didn't want to let you down that day on the slave galley, because you'd asked him to help. If you don't want him to get hurt, don't ask him again!" The Leithian turned away.

"I don't intend to—" Nagaro began, but Brandle was walking away towards the fire, clearly not listening. The big Leithian paused to joke with Rubo as he returned his empty bowl.

Nagaro sat frowning. He had been the one who'd said that Darion wouldn't have wanted to see Edrovirans shedding each other's blood. *He'd said it to the whole room, but...*

"Seems Brandle took your question amiss. He's not jealous, is he?"

Nagaro started at Taru's question. The young Turo had moved closer without his being aware. He looked at the ground. "He knows better than that."

Taru snorted. "I don't know, Nagaro... Ye're not married yet. Ye're not even courting—*or are ye?*"

Nagaro shot his friend a dark look. "No, I'm not courting anyone."

"So what ye told the Emperor really was a lie?"

Nagaro caught what sounded like worry in Taru's voice, but he wasn't ready to tell his secret. *Not to Taru anyway.*

To his immense relief, they were interrupted by Kuran's raised voice.

"Men! I need your attention!" The Lord of the Fleet was standing beside the cooking fire, drawing the eyes of all the Fleet men gathered around it. "There'll be three watches tonight. The men under Lord Anduar—including the Palace Guard—will contribute three men to each watch, as will Lord Pendrik's men. From my contingent—our own Fleet men—there'll be six for each watch because there are more of us. The men under each Lord will guard their own segment of our perimeter, and two of ours will guard the horses. I'll take volunteers for tonight, and whoever doesn't stand tonight will stand tomorrow. Is that clear?"

Rubo stuck up his hand. "Why so many watchmen, M' Lord? Ye're not expecting an attack, are ye ? Here in your own Wared?"

Kuran turned to the old Turo. "The border of Sobring Hold is a quarter mile in that direction." He pointed north, in the direction the road was taking them. "And Lord Grimbold Sobring is allied with Lothard Hurn. I don't think an attack is likely, but if any fleeing Kelorin were coming this way, they might be traveling by night and could stumble on us in the dark. And if there were Leithians searching for them, *they* could blunder into us too. It's not likely to happen, but I don't want us coming to blows with anyone before they know who we are. Are you answered?"

"Aye, Zirda."

Kuran swept his eyes over the gathered faces. "Anything else?" There was no response. "Very well then, do I have any volunteers for tonight's watches?"

Nagaro knew he wasn't ready for sleep so he stood up. "I'll stand a watch."

"And I."

"And I."

It didn't take long to fill up the three shifts. Nagaro, Taru, and Favo all drew the first watch, and Nagaro asked for duty with the horses because no one else seemed to want it. He expected that Taru might join him so he could ask more questions, but Pavo quickly said, "I will do watch with Captain Nagaro," and Taru merely gave Nagaro a look and a shrug.

"Good enough." Kuran gave the Hashtep a nod. "That decides everything. Those on first watch, to your posts! The rest of you, bed down and get some sleep."

Nagaro and Pavo immediately headed for the meadow where the hobbled horses were pastured, skirting the edge of the camp. When they reached the grassy area, they hailed the two men who had been on guard during dinner, and the two gratefully picked up their bowls and spoons and departed in the direction of firelight and voices.

The two friends sat down at the meadow's edge with their backs to the glow of the nearest cooking fire. The meadow was faintly illuminated, more by starlight than by the firelight that found its way between the tree trunks. The horses were dim shapes, the lighter colored ones the most visible. Nagaro found the large gray silhouette of Thunder-Heels, moving along the downhill side of the meadow near the bank of the stream that was a sinuous darker ribbon cutting across the silver expanse of grass.

Here, away from the camp, the night was quiet. The low snorts of the horses reached their ears, along with the distinctive sound of the animals grazing—grass stalks being gripped between strong incisors and torn off with quick, short jerks.

After a time, Pavo spoke. "It is very dark tonight, Nagaro."

"Yes. It'll be lighter when Talebra rises and gets clear of those trees."

There was a little pause, then: "Naru have almost catch up with Talebra."

Nagaro shifted a little. "Yes." He wondered where the conversation was going. The smaller, darker moon, Naru, moved slightly faster than the larger, brighter Talebra. For many months, the smaller moon had been drawing closer to the larger one, seeming to move on the same track. Naru passing Talebra was the most dramatic part of a repeating cycle that took years to complete.

"Do you think maybe Naru will hit Talebra?" Pavo sounded worried.

Looking at his friend, Nagaro could see the whites of the young Hashtep's eyes. He shook his head. "No, Pavo, you needn't worry. Usually Naru passes just above or below Talebra, but in the rare cases when they don't completely miss each other, the dark moon always passes across the face of the bright one."

"You have read this in book?"

"Yes. The lore masters who study the heavens have records going back a long time, and the two moons have never hit each other."

"Oh." Pavo sounded relieved. "I am glad to know that."

For a time there was no sound but the movements of the horses. Then Pavo said, "Can I ask you something else, Nagaro?"

"Of course."

A pause, then, "Did you tell truth to Emperor when you say you do not want wife because your heart have already choose?"

Nagaro felt a chill. "Did Taru tell you to ask me that?"

There was a longer pause before Pavo answered. "It is true that Taru and I have talk about it, but I ask because I want to know. At first Taru was sure you have told lie. But then he remember you have told him how much you like Hamani, and now he think maybe woman you choose is Hamani."

"*Keshaal!*" Nagaro closed his eyes. This was the last thing he wanted. And it left him little choice but to tell Pavo the truth. "I told Taru what I admire about Hamani because I want him to see that she's a desirable woman. She's loved him for years, and she'd make a good wife for him if he'd just look beyond the fact that her face is plain."

"But if you have not choose Hamani, does it mean you tell lie to Emperor?"

Nagaro drew a long breath in the darkness. He was glad that Pavo couldn't see his face. "I didn't lie to the Emperor. It just isn't Hamani."

"Oh." There were several heartbeats of silence before Pavo said. "Then it must be princess."

Nagaro turned on him. "Why do you say that?" He could tell that Pavo was looking right at him. The whites of the young Hashtep's eyes gleamed faintly in the starlight.

"Because you talk to her so much." Pavo spoke with unruffled confidence. "And it will make good end of story if you marry princess."

"But I *can't* marry her, Pavo!"

"Why not? Already she is your wife once. Her father have choose you once for her. Why he cannot choose you again?"

"Oh, Pavo..." Nagaro brought his hands to his face and continued speaking through his fingers. "He must only have considered me before because he thought the Lady Maramine was my mother—"

"But you think maybe she *is* your mother."

Nagaro dropped his hands. "I can't prove it, even if it's true! And besides, I'd have to admit that I was... *him!* And I can't!" He felt his chest tighten.

Pavo was watching him, his expression unreadable in the darkness. "You are not go to court her?"

"*No!* If I tried, I'd be dead in a week! But that doesn't even matter. Don't you see? I could never court her without telling her *everything*. And I can't do that! *I'd die if she ever found out!*" Nagaro stopped. He was shaking. "You mustn't tell anyone about this, Pavo! Please!"

"I cannot tell even Taru?"

Nagaro drew a breath, striving for balance. "*Well,* I suppose you should tell Taru whatever you think is best. I don't want him to think he can't court Hamani. *But no one else!* Swear it, Pavo!" He saw the other young man nod.

"I swear it in name of Sheptuum."

"Good." Nagaro drew up his legs and wrapped his arms around them to stop them from shaking.

Pavo didn't speak for several long seconds. Then he said, "But this is not how story should end—"

"*Bishka!*" Nagaro released his knees to gesture impatiently. "There's nothing that says every story has to have a happy ending, Pavo! The ones that do just get repeated a lot, that's all—because it makes everyone feel good." He gathered his feet under him and stood up. "We've been talking too much, Pavo—not being good watchmen. You stay here. I'm going to walk over to the other side of the meadow.

He set off without waiting for a reply, picking his way shakily through the grass, past the looming shapes of horses. His heart was beating too hard and too fast. It was always this way when he thought too much about... *those things*. He drew several long breaths and let them out, forcing his legs to keep moving. By the time he'd reached the stream, he was feeling steadier, though his mind was still dodging unwelcome memories.

The watercourse was neither wide nor deep. He crossed it easily on some large stones that glimmered palely in the starlight. Thunder-Heels came splashing across after him and walked beside him for a little way, nuzzling his ear with a velvety muzzle and blowing warm, grass-scented breath on his neck.

Nagaro reached up to pat the gray's head distractedly. "How is your new herd, brother of the wind?" he murmured. "Are they all at peace? Is everything quiet this night?"

Thunder-Heels nickered softly and nuzzled his ear again. Then the big gray moved on ahead of him, lifting his feet briefly in a beautiful, floating trot that carried him like a cloud, then splashing back across the stream to join the other horses. Nagaro walked on, fervently wishing everything were quiet in his own mind. In two and a half hours the watch would change and he would have to try to get some asleep. Edrovir might need fresh men on the morrow.

*That's it! Think of Edrovir and her troubles, of Kenthos and Rathdar and the Brothers of the Blood.*

He kept walking. As often as his thoughts strayed to places they shouldn't go, he dragged them back to more desirable territory. He crossed the stream again and kept walking until he came to a place on the opposite side of the herd from where he knew Pavo was sitting. There he paced back and forth and listened for any suspicious sounds. But the night was still, except for the usual night noises—insects chirping, the stirring of air among the leaves of the trees. Gradually his pacing slowed.

He thought about the leaders of the two factions whose quarrel had brought Lord Anduar's little army here. About Rathdar and Lothard—and Kenthos... He didn't know nearly enough about Kenthos. Except, of course, that he wasn't the missing heir of Darion if you believed Omei. And for some reason, he did believe her. Perhaps it was because, among all those who had expressed an opinion, she seemed to have the least stake in the answer. Her opinion placed her in agreement with Rastyl Korven, of course...

Nagaro almost laughed aloud at that, for the two of them could scarcely be less similar. And yet, they also both claimed that the heir of the House of Loros was alive and that they knew where he was. Nagaro shook his head. He could hardly imagine that Omei and Rastyl had both found the same person. And if the true heir of Darion was alive, *then where was he?* What did he think about what was happening—about this trouble in the land? If he were a true son of Tevren and Lindra, he must surely care. But perhaps he knew he was not what men like Rastyl assumed he would be. Perhaps he saw the wisdom of keeping his head down, of not becoming the seed of even more trouble.

Nagaro's thoughts at last spun themselves out. He found a rock and sat down. He listened to the night and watched the horses, now sleeping on their feet as horses do. Talebra rose, gibbous, above the trees on the eastern edge of the meadow, suffusing the scene with silver light. A short time later, Naru's dim disc—also gibbous—rose in hot pursuit.

Eventually, Tredhold Ferth came to relieve him. Nagaro recognized the healer as he approached by his small stature, his manner of movement, and his short sandy hair that shown palely in the moonlight.

"Has there been any sign of anyone passing?" Tred inquired as he came to a halt beside Nagaro's rock.

"No, the night's been very quiet. Who are you paired with?"

"Landros. Pity we can't pass the time by spinning yarns, but it's better to watch like this—one on each side o' the herd."

Nagaro stood up and gestured at the sky. "It really does look as if Naru will cross Talebra's face this time. Pavo was worried they'd collide."

Tred considered the two partial discs. "Well, the Leithian lore masters say it's time. Remember the tale I told once? That Kroneg—the god of war—rides Naru, and Lissafel—the goddess of love—rides Talebra? What you see there, is Kroneg pursuing Lissafel. Usually she evades him, but once in a while he catches her and they embrace."

Nagaro smiled. "Is that what they call the conjunction?"

Tredhold nodded. "When Naru crosses in front, and Talebra's disk shows all around its edge, that's the embrace. The story says that, when it happens, one or the other will have their way—that there'll be either war or peace among men."

For a long moment, the two men stood looking up at the moons. Then Tredhold shrugged. "It's ironic it should be happening now," he said. He spoke lightly, but his voice sounded a little strained.

"It will still take a few months for those moons to come together, I think," Nagaro offered. "We should finish this mission within a few days, and with luck we can resolve the conflict."

"I hope so." Tred sighed. "But I doubt that solving this little matter will put everything to rights."

Nagaro also sighed. "I suppose not," he conceded. "So there's still time for the moons' embrace to mark some dire event. I hope men don't take that portent seriously."

Tredhold shrugged. "There's some that do, but not so many in these days as there used to be. But I shouldn't keep ye in talk any longer. Go get some sleep."

"I'll try. Good night, Tred."

"Good night, Nagaro."

Nagaro found Landros sitting where he had left Pavo earlier and exchanged greetings with the grizzled Kelorin. When he reached the area where the Fleet men were bedded down, he found Pavo and Taru already stretched out and rolled in their blankets. He retrieved his own blanket from his saddle and lay down not far from his friends, wrapping the blanket around him and pillowing his head on his folded cloak. He'd already done his thinking for the night, so he closed his eyes and emptied his mind of everything but the peaceful image of horses dozing in the meadow under the moon.

# Chapter 22

# Encounters

T he southern part of Sobring Hold was indistinguishable from Kel Wared in terms of terrain and vegetation. The troop of horsemen under Lord Anduar's command passed the crossroads that marked the boundary between the two territories shortly after breaking camp. After passing through rough, wooded country for more than an hour and passing the side road that led to Sobring Hall, they came to the stone that marked the border of Hurn Hold. A few miles farther on, they turned into a road that angled off to the east and would eventually connect with the road that led north to Glenarl. Some way beyond that turning, they came to a village.

There were fewer than a score of small slate-roofed stone houses clustered around a modest inn and a mill for grinding flour. Anduar and Pendrik, who were in the lead, drew rein in the village square in front of the latter two buildings. The ranks of horsemen came up behind them, half filling the little square. At this hour of the morning, the majority of the town's inhabitants were working in the fields. Those few who were visible were all Leithians, as one would expect. A few stopped to stare at the newcomers, but most avoided the horses and continued about their business with their heads down.

Pendrik spoke to Anduar, in a voice loud enough for all to hear, proposing that they stop long enough to ask the innkeeper about buying some wine. Anduar made some reply in lower tones. Then, as Pendrik dismounted and prepared to enter the inn, Anduar raised his voice to announce his intention of purchasing other more substantial supplies.

This finally drew a response from one of the villagers who had stopped to watch, a man of middle years clad in rough pants, dusty boots, and a faded red tunic. He now approached Lord Anduar, who still sat astride his horse, and addressed him deferentially.

"Welcome to the town o' Huring, My Lord. I'm Tor Gunder, the Town Chief's deputy. Did I hear ye say ye wished t' buy victuals?"

"That's right, Zirda."

"Enough for all o' these?" The man's gesture took in the troop of waiting horsemen. Behind him, a number of other men and women had begun to gather, obviously curious to see what was afoot, though they remained silent.

Anduar shrugged languidly. "We wouldn't expect you to sell us more than you can spare. But for whatever you *can* spare, we'd be grateful, and we'll pay a fair price. You'll also have the satisfaction of knowing that you've served your king and country."

Gunder stiffened slightly, and there were some  murmurs from the little crowd behind him. "Ye're about the king's business then, are ye, My Lord?"

Anduar inclined his head in a small affirmative gesture. "Yes. We are here by direct order of King Elgurn. I am Lord Anduar Tyronin of the King's Council. The gentleman who just went into the inn is Lord Pendrik Glenmark, another Council member. And the gentleman there on the bay horse is Kuran Kel, Lord of the Royal Fleet."

These revelations drew more murmurs and urgent whispers from the onlookers. The Town Chief's deputy looked rather uncomfortable. "I'd best take the matter t' the Town Chief, My Lord," he said hurriedly. "If ye'll be so good as t' tell me what business of the king it is that brings ye to our poor village, I'll go straight away and tell Chief Halbert. I'm sure he'll do whatever he can t' serve ye."

Anduar considered the man. "You may tell your Town Chief, Zirda," he observed coolly, "that we have come to find Kenthos of Irvenen and escort him to Lankura to stand before the king."

This drew excited looks and hissed comments from the villagers. An alarmed expression crossed Gunder's face, and he immediately raised his hands to silence the crowd. "Ye lot had best go about your affairs," he told the onlookers with evident annoyance. "This doesn't concern ye."

The crowd promptly began to disperse, amid audible muttering. Gunder waited until there was a little more space around him, then squinted up at Anduar. "My Lord," he ventured cautiously, "do ye mean that ye'll be putting the man under arrest?"

Anduar raised his hand in an equivocal gesture. "*Arrest* is such a strong word," he drawled. "Let's just say that the king wishes to ask the man some questions."

"I see. Ah, very good, My Lord." The Chief's deputy was suddenly obsequious. "I'll just go and tell Chief Halbert what ye've said. This is his house, right behind me."

So saying, Gunder bobbed a bow and turned around. Stepping up to the door of the indicated house, he rapped sharply twice. The door was immediately opened by someone who couldn't be clearly seen, and Gunder quickly darted inside. The door closed promptly behind him.

Anduar turned in his saddle to address the company. "Take your ease, men," he said curtly. "I expect you'll have a few minutes to stretch your legs."

There was murmured conversation, punctuated by groans, as stiff men dismounted from their horses. Nagaro had paid close attention not only to Anduar's exchange with the Chief's deputy but also to the behavior of the other villagers, trying to gage their mood. Now he swung easily out of the saddle, dropped to the ground, and stood by Thunder-Heels' sleek flank. From there, he continued to observe the townspeople as they went about their business. He watched a pair of Leithian women who smiled and were outwardly friendly as they passed near the horesemen but exchanged furtive glances and whispered words as soon as they thought they were unobserved.

Frowning, Nagaro took Thunder-Heels' bridle and worked his way to where Kuran was standing at the edge of the troop, near the house into which Gunder had disappeared. "The villagers seem very nervous," he observed in a low voice.

Kuran nodded. "The folk in Lankura have been tense, too, but not like this. I wonder why the man, Gunder, asked our business—as if it would make any difference as to whether they'll sell us any food. And he jumped at the name of Kenthos."

"Well, they would surely have heard of Kenthos. Do you think they know that Lothard is hunting for him?"

"I think it's likely."

"I wonder what they might know about Lothard's movements."

Kuran made a wry face. "Not much, I'd imagine, unless Lothard and his men are very close by—which I doubt. The Lord of Hurn isn't one for sharing his plans with the common folk, though he makes no secret of his views."

Nagaro digested the implications of this in silence.

In the meantime, Pendrik had triumphantly emerged from the inn with a bottle of wine. He worked his way around the press of men and horses to where Anduar still sat in the saddle. The Kelorin lord hadn't followed his own advice about dismounting, but he now did so to more easily speak privately with Pendrik. The two lords stood with their heads together, conferring in low tones, a few paces from where Nagaro and Kuran were standing. Nagaro couldn't make out the words, but the content of the men's conversation could be easily guessed from Anduar's occasional slight jerk of the head in the direction of the closed door of the Town Chief's house.

Kuran shifted from foot to foot, frowning. "Our friend Gunder is taking rather a long time," he muttered, "considering he said he'd be quick."

The Lord of the Fleet had scarcely finished speaking when muffled voices and a series of loud thumps were heard, emanating from behind the closed door of the house. This was followed by a splintering of wood as the door burst open and a dark haired man hurtled out, his arms awkwardly behind him. He stumbled a few steps and fell sprawling in the dirt just a dozen feet from Kuran. Once the man was down, it was plain to see that his wrists were bound behind him. He struggled to roll onto his side, twisting so that he could look up at the Lord of the Fleet. "My Lord!" he gasped. "You must tell them who I am!"

"*Rastian!*" Nagaro and Kuran both started towards the fallen man with simultaneous cries of recognition. They each grabbed an arm, helping him to his feet. Behind the young man, three worried-looking Leithians had come to a halt just outside the Town Chief's front door. One was Gunder. Another—who was older, grayer, stouter, and also wearing a red tunic—was presumably the Town Chief. The third was young and muscular, with the look of someone who prefers to follow orders rather than figure things out for himself.

Kuran's attention was still on Rastian. "Why weren't you in Lankura?" he demanded. "There was a muster, and you were missed."

"My Lord, I'm sorry! I was called away on my father's business. I wrote you a letter. Estevad said he would put it on your desk."

Kuran's frown eased. "I left without taking time for paperwork," he muttered. "But what are you doing *here?*"

"I was looking for you! My father had word that you'd ridden out under Lord Anduar with a company of sea warriors. I have news of—" He caught himself, then hastily added, "Please, My Lord! Tell these men that I am not Kenthos and have nothing to do with him! They won't believe a word I say!"

Lord Anduar had been listening to the entire exchange from a few feet away with a faintly amused expression. Now he intervened. Turning to face the three Leithians squarely, he addressed the older man in red. "You, I presume are the Town Chief? Tor Halbert?"

The man licked his lips. "Aye, Zirda, I am."

Anduar sighed. "I am Lord Anduar. Lord Pendrik stands with me here, and Lord Kuran there, as you may have guessed. And this man—" he indicated Rastian "—is Rastian Korven, an officer of the Royal Fleet and also the son of the ruling lord of Irvenen Wared."

The Town Chief had turned pale. "We were, ah, just discussing the matter of releasing him to you, My Lord," he stammered.

Rastian moved impatiently, jerking his bound wrists. "They were arguing about whether they should even tell you I was here!" he cried hotly. "I decided not to wait for them to make up their minds."

"I see." Anduar emitted another sigh. He turned back to Halbert and Gunder. "I won't ask which of you was taking which position," he said coolly. "That way I won't have to decide which of you to arrest—provided, of course, that you promptly remove that rope."

Town Chief Halbert blinked. He swallowed visibly. "Ah, certainly, My Lord!" he managed. "See to it, Harth, and be quick!"

The burly young Leithian had been gaping, but he recovered quickly once someone told him what to do. Pulling a knife from his belt, he stepped around behind Rastian and used it to saw through the rope that bound the young Kelorin's arms.

Rastian shook himself free and stood scowling and rubbing his wrists. "And my horse?" he inquired resentfully.

Chief Halbert flinched. "Harth, fetch the gentleman's horse."

"Aye, Zirda!" Harth saluted and hurried off to do his master's bidding.

Anduar appeared to be thinking. "I must say," he said, addressing the Town Chief, "that I'm curious to know what prompted you to seize him in the first place."

"Ah, well, these are rather uncertain times, My Lord." Halbert was sweating.

Gunder, however, stuck out his chin. "He was caught skulking around one of our henhouses last night, Zirda. And Lord Lothard has put out orders t' detain any man suspected o' following Kenthos of Irvenen. This man admitted to hailing from Irvenen Wared, My Lord, and I might point out that he's not wearing a Fleet uniform."

Anduar turned a questioning glance on Rastian. "Well, Zirda? What's your side of it?"

Rastian had not stopped scowling. "Being from Irvenen doesn't automatically make me a follower of Kenthos! And I was only trying to skirt the village in the dark, leading my horse, when I slipped down an embankment and fetched up against the wretched henhouse. The birds started squawking, and the next thing I knew there were men and dogs all over me!"

Lord Pendrik spoke for the first time. "Why were you skirting the village?" he rumbled, instead of riding through it like an honest man?"

"Because I was in haste! I'd already lost *hours* from being stopped over and over by folk demanding to know who I was and where I was going—and that was on the open road under the sun!"

Anduar raised a hand before anyone could respond to this. "I believe I've heard enough," he said. "These are, as Chief Halbert pointed out, *uncertain times.* One might say, *distrustful* times. Let us be grateful that no harm has been done, though I might point out that Lord Lothard has no authority to arrest or detain citizens of Edrovir without having reasonable cause to believe they've committed a crime."

"Are ye saying there's no crime in what Kenthos and his lot have been doing, My Lord?" Gunder inquired, and it was plain from the look Halbert gave him that the Town Chief would have rather he'd kept his mouth shut.

Anduar's steely stare impaled the deputy. "It's not a crime to travel the roads of Edrovir, Zirda. Nor to go in company. Nor to bear arms," he said levelly. "But preventing honest citizens from doing those things *is*." He returned his attention to the Town Chief. "And now, Tor Halbert, perhaps we might discuss the matter of purchasing some provisions."

***

An hour later, Anduar's company had put the village of Huring out of sight behind them. The Town Chief had been generous, and a number of the horses were newly encumbered with baskets of bread or dried meat, and sacks of flour or potatoes. The men were generally in good spirits, with the notable exception of Rastian. Nagaro was keeping Thunder-Heels at a distance from Rastian's mount, hoping to avoid having to speak to him. Once, when he glanced at the young man, he found Rastian's pale eyes focused on him, but for the most part the young Kelorin rode with his head down and an air of intense preoccupation.

The day was very fair, the troop had been making good time, and there were even a few complaints from the ranks when Anduar called a halt. The place the Pact Signer chose was just past a sharp bend in the road, where a stand of trees hid them from the view of travelers on the road behind them. In addition, Anduar led the company off the road and down a little slope to a place flanked by dense thickets. "Rest a little, and eat something if you can," he instructed the men. "My Lords and I must speak to Rastian."

Rastian's head came up at that, and he quickly dismounted and moved to join the three lords as they stepped to one side and stood a little way from the rest of the company. Anduar hung back, however, his eyes sweeping the ranks until they found Nagaro. "You too, Captain," he said shortly.  Then, almost as an afterthought, he added, "And you, Lieutenant," as his gaze fell on Brandle.

The big Leithian threw Nagaro a sharp, questioning look as soon as Anduar's back was turned. Beyond him, Vell and Ruald stood together, frowning. Plainly they had seen what had just happened and didn't understand why some were being included and others not.

Nagaro merely returned Brandle a shrug, being preoccupied with the conflict between wishing to hear Rastian's news and the discomfort he felt in the man's presence. He followed Anduar but stopped and stood just outside the circle made by Rastian and the three lords. Brandle stopped beside him.

Anduar wasted no time once his intended audience had assembled. "Well, Zirda," he said, turning a steely glance on Rastian, "Why were you seeking us, and what can you tell us about the whereabouts of Kenthos, or Lothard, or the men who are riding with either of them?"

Rastian returned the look. "I was seeking you for the purpose of telling you that, My Lord," he said sourly. "My father and I encountered Lord Rathdar, traveling with Kenthos and a half dozen men, yesterday afternoon. Actually, one of their scouts found us. They were lying concealed in a dense stand of woods a quarter or a mile east of where the Old North Road crosses South Hurn Way—the road we're now traveling."

Anduar's eyes narrowed even as his lips curled into a small smile. "So we're going the right way."

Pendrik snorted. "A stroke of luck, I call that!"

Rastian didn't smile. "It was the middle of yesterday afternoon, My Lords," he said. "And they were only waiting for sunset before moving on, so we won't find them where I left them."

"Huh! You see, Anduar?" Pendrik gestured triumphantly.

Anduar eyes had not left Rastian, and he wasted no breath on a response to the Leithian lord's outburst. "Did they say which way they meant to go?" he inquired.

"*Yes*—"Rastian hesitated. "Rathdar, ah, said they were making for Loros Hall."

"What do they mean to do at Loros Hall?" Pendrik demanded. "Lay claim to it in Kenthos' name?"

Rastian bit his lip. "I'm not sure. It might be so. There was, ah, also something said about 'digging up the earth by the garden wall.' I think Rathdar would like to show the world that Tevren's child isn't buried there."

Kuran shook his head and spoke for the first time. "Endemar has the Hall in his charge, as well as the gardens and all of the lands around them. He believes the child's grave is in the garden, and he'll never allow them to dig it up."

Pendrik frowned. "They may not even bother to ask Endemar's permission."

"What do you mean?" Kuran sounded shocked. "Will they break down the gate? Or climb over the wall?"

Lord Anduar held up a hand. "We are wasting time," he said. "We haven't come to talk about digging up gardens. We've come to prevent bloodshed. We should ride to this crossroads as quickly as possible and then turn south towards Loros. My scouts may be able to learn more in the meantime. Rastian, can you tell us anything about the position of Lothard and his men?"

Rastian shrugged. "Only that Rathdar thought they were searching the lands north and east of where he and his men were hiding."

Nagaro stirred. He had been listening, and thinking, and now he voiced the thought that was uppermost in his mind. "What did you see of Kenthos? What manner of man does he seem to be?"

All eyes turned to him, but the only gaze he felt was Rastian's. The young Kelorin's pale eyes regarded him with an expression that was hard to interpret.

"Well?" Anduar prompted. "Answer him, Zirda.

Rastian cleared his throat. "Kenthos is a big man, as you'd expect of a blacksmith—tall and strong, but weary to exhaustion. Wounded, I think, and trying not to show it."

Nagaro frowned. He would rather have been out from under that gaze, but this was important. "What character did he show? Did he say anything?"

"Nothing that I heard, Captain. It was Rathdar who did the talking. Kenthos was keeping his feet and walking among the men to keep their spirits up. But if you want to know the truth, he looked to me like a man nearly spent."

"So," Pendrik interjected. "It sounds as if Rathdar is the real leader of these men."

Rastian turned to the Leithian lord, releasing Nagaro's eyes. "I can't say it has always been so, My Lord. But right now I'd guess that Rathdar is making the decisions."

Anduar had been listening intently and now he spoke. "What about the men who are with them? Half a dozen, you said?"

"I saw six, My Lord, but there may have been others on watch, or out scouting. Those I saw seemed to be Rathdar's men. At least, they answered to him as if accustomed to doing so."

Anduar frowned. "We know there were a great many more. Did you learn what happened to them?"

"Mostly scattered in small bands—told to do so for their own safety. As least that's what Rathdar said."

"And where is your father?"

Rastian flinched and seemed to balk, but Anduar's steel-gray eyes held him on the point of their gaze.

"He has, ah, gone north, My Lord."

Pendrik pounced. "Gone *north?* When we need him *here?* To what purpose?"

Rastian drew himself up, instantly defiant. "He went in haste to Irvenen to seek a witness, My Lord Pendrik. One who knows Kenthos' true history."

"Who does he think he'll find?" Pendrik didn't trouble to keep the contempt out of his voice.

The blood rose in Rastian's face. "He knows where to find the man's mother," he said stiffly. "She refused to speak with him before, but he believes she will speak to him now that her son is in danger of losing his life."

"Very likely she will." Anduar's words were slipped coolly in before Pendrik could respond. "It's a good thought, Rastian, and the effort may well serve us if it's successful. And now, gentlemen, we should be away before more time is lost."

They rode on, with greater haste, through country that was gently rolling and intermittently forested, passing through other villages without stopping. The inhabitants of these hamlets gaped at them or ducked out of sight as the troop of horsemen rode past.

Nagaro still avoided Rastian, riding instead beside Kuran. He was thinking hard about everything he had learned in the past two days. When Anduar finally called a halt to water the horses where the road crossed a stream on a little bridge, Nagaro dismounted and stood beside Kuran waiting for their chance at the water. Turning to the older man, he asked, "How accurate is Berinar Sundorin's account of the death of Tevren and Lindra? Do you know?"

Kuran's brow furrowed. "It's based on the accounts of the two men who rode with them," he said, speaking carefully. "And it might, therefore, be biased. Certainly it differed from the tale that Reith Hurn told. The other Leithians supported Reith's version, as you'd expect. Except for Edgold Furthing. He broke with the others and confirmed the details of the Kelorin account."

"Wouldn't that give credence to the Kelorin version?"

Kuran nodded. "That's always been the position of the Kelorin Faction. Unfortunately, Reith and Edgold had previously quarreled, and Reith claimed that Edgold sided against him out of spite."

"Ah. An impasse then."

"Yes."

"What exactly were the differences in the two accounts?"

Kuran squinted in thought. "Whether Tevren's two men were prevented from aiding him, or merely stood by—that was one—and whether the three Leithians who challenged Tevren before Reith fought him were acting on their own or following Reith's orders. And then, of course, there's the matter of how accidental the queen's death was."

"She's supposed to have put herself between Tevren and Reith Hurn, trying to save her husband. Do the Leithians contest that?"

Kuran shook his head as he moved forward to let his horse drink. "No. Tevren went down after fighting three other men, and then Reith. He was wounded in several places and bleeding. She threw herself on top of him, begging Reith not to strike. The Leithians claim that Reith was already moving and couldn't stop his lunge. The Kelorin claim that he didn't begin his lunge until after she had thrown herself on her husband and spoken her words."

Nagaro let Thunder-Heels lower his head to the water. "That makes a great deal of difference."

"Yes. Of course the end is the same, either way. A single sword stroke pierced two hearts at once, and they died together. They had just come from Loros Hall, where they'd gone for Lindra's lying-up, so their bodies were carried back there and laid in a single grave."

Kuran had spoken somberly. Now he backed his horse away from the stream to make room for the next, shaking his head. Thunder-Heels raised his dripping muzzle and Nagaro drew on the stallion's reins and followed the older man.

Kuran swung back into the saddle, but sat there abstracted, his eyes shadowed. "That was a dark day for Edrovir," he murmured, under his breath.

Nagaro remounted as well, but left the Lord of the Fleet to his thoughts for a moment before finally asking, "What about the child?"

Kuran shook himself. "The child was not with them. Lindra had carried a bundle in her arms, and from the way she cradled it, they all thought it was the child. But she let it fall when Tevren went down, and it turned out to be only a bundle of clothes."

"Was she carrying it to fool them?"

Kuran sighed. "Perhaps. Who knows?"

"And the two Kelorin men who were with them knew nothing about the fate of the child?"

This time Kuran shrugged. "They both swore so to the end of their days."

At this point, the order to ride interrupted Nagaro's final question. He had to press Thunder-Heels close to Kuran's horse as they climbed the stream bank so that the other man could hear him above the snorts of horses and jingle of gear. "And they also knew nothing of the third man?"

Kuran leaned closer in his saddle as they topped the bank. "Aye. They swore that too."

***

Another hour's hard riding brought them to the crossroads of which Rastian had spoken, and they stopped there to rest and reconnoiter. Anduar immediately dispatched Rastian and two other men to scout the place, just off the road within Harlind Hold, where Rathdar and Kenthos had last been seen.

It was a perfect late spring day, bright and fair and rather warm, and laden with the scent of growing things. The sun was near its zenith. Insects sang in the grass at the road's edge, and birds chirped in the trees and the bushes that formed dense screens along both sides of the paving. The men paced, or stood on the Harlind side in the shade of several large oaks that arched over the Old North Road at the southeast corner of its intersection with South Hurn Way. Some pulled food from their packs and ate where they stood.

Nagaro slipped the bit from Thunder-Heels' mouth and let the stallion graze along roadside. He stood near the big gray, a little apart from the rest of the men, gazing north, the direction they did not intend to go. The Old North Road was a broad track, well traveled and well maintained. A hundred yards of it could be seen from where he stood before it curved and disappeared from view among forested hillsides. After a time, Pavo and Taru came to stand beside him.

Pavo was the first to speak. "Do you think Lothard and all his man are coming down that road, Nagaro?" he ventured.

Nagaro shook his head. "No. I expect they're already well to the south of here, where we have to go if we mean to find them."

"Why d' ye stand here then?" Taru asked.

Nagaro heaved a sigh and turned, putting his back to the scene he had been contemplating. "Irvenen Wared lies that way," he said simply.

"Ah. Ye're thinking o' Beloras, that was your father—"

"*May* have been my father," Nagaro corrected. "And yes, I *was* thinking of him. I was thinking that he must have had a spirit that loved to roam, to have traveled all the way from Irvenen to Virden Wared plying his minstrel's trade. It's quite possible he came down this road."

Pavo nodded understanding. "Maybe someday you will ride up that road, Nagaro. To look for more of your family."

Nagaro shrugged. "Maybe, Pavo. But not today."

They were interrupted by the return of the three-man scouting party. Rastian pulled his mount to a halt in front of Anduar, and Nagaro stepped closer to hear the report.

"It is as we expected, My Lord," Rastian began. "The campsite is abandoned. They've all gone south."

"You're certain of the direction?"

"Yes, the tracks are plain. They didn't even try to conceal which way they'd gone."

"Could you see any sign that they were being tracked?"

Rastian made a wry face. "It would take more skill than I have to tell that, My Lord. There were single tracks going in and out in several directions, but we know they had scouts."

"All right then." Anduar swung into his saddle and raised his voice. "To horse, men! We ride south! And keep your eyes open. There could be scattered bands of Kenthos' followers about."

As Nagaro swung up onto Thunder-Heels, he gave the empty north road one last lingering look. He imagined Beloras there. *Riding south in search of his heart's desire, and finding it in Virden Wared—only to lose his life after first planting a single seed...* He frowned and pressed the stallion forward to find his place beside Kuran.

***

The sun was nearly half-way down the sky when Lord Anduar's party encountered the first group of fleeing Kelorin. At first the men had been keenly eyeing the stands of woods on either side of the road, but as the miles had dragged by, their vigilance had waned. So it was that the column of riders came to a startled halt when five dark-haired men abruptly stepped out from under the trees on the Hurn Hold side and hailed them.

"Help us, Lords! Please protect us! We fear for our lives!"

Nagaro had been riding with Kuran on the side of the road where the men emerged. His attention had been drawn by their movement even before any of the men cried out, but now he started in recognition. "Hendrel!" he exclaimed. "Thank goodness you found us!"

Hendrel looked up at him with harried eyes. The young man's hair was unkempt and his clothing torn and streaked with mud, though he looked otherwise unscathed. "Captain Nagaro!" he cried, glancing from Nagaro to Kuran and back again. "I thought you were away on a mission in the south—you and Lord Kuran both."

"We returned yesterday."

"Yes," Kuran put in dryly, "And we were immediately drafted for this rescue mission."

This brought a chorus of voices from the fugitives. "Rescue? Vothra keep you, Zirdas!"

"Have you come to save poor Kenthos?" Hendrel gazed up at them with relief and gratitude.

Anduar had ridden back along the line of horsemen after calling for a halt, and now he reined in his mount and sat looking down at the ragged little band of Kelorin with his cool gray stare. "We have come to forestall further bloodshed," he observed tartly. "Do you know anything of the whereabouts of Kenthos or Lord Rathdar?"

Hendred miserably shook his head. "No, My Lord. We parted from them yesterday morning. They told us to go—for our safety. We thought better of it, and tried to make our way back to them, but we were cut off by the men from Furthing Hold."

"Furthing Hold?" Anduar leaned forward in the saddle, his voice taking on a steely edge. "Lord Madred leads troops here?"

"I— I don't know about Lord Madred, himself, My Lord." Hendrel was flustered. "We never saw him. But the men were in Furthing livery."

"When did you see them? And where?"

"Late yesterday afternoon. At sunset. We blundered into them at a curve of the road. They chased us, and we hid in that thicket, there, last night, because it was the first good cover we found. We didn't like being on Hurn land, but we've been afraid to move all day for fear of being seen—until you and your men came along."

"I see." Anduar straightened, picking up his reigns. "Do you have horses?"

"Aye, My Lord. They're hidden in the trees. Give us a minute and we'll join you!"

Anduar's teeth flashed briefly. "You'll ride with us, but you are *not* joining our force! You're under escort, and you are not to enter into any conflict that may arise unless I, Lord Pendrik, or Lord Kuran gives you a direct order. *Is that clear?*"

Hendrel swallowed visibly. "Yes, My Lord."

It took little more than a minute to bring the horses out. Two more men came with them. Nagaro was surprised to see that one of these was Geivian. The young man mounted a sorrel gelding, his face grim, and took a place among his fellows about half-way along the column in the midst of Anduar's troops. As they rode forward again, Nagaro maneuvered Thunder-Heels to a position at the sorrel's side.

"Well met, Geivian," he said, raising his voice above the trample of hooves and jingle of gear. "I didn't expect to find you here. At the gathering, you sounded skeptical of supporting Kenthos."

Geivian, whose clothing was in no better condition than Hendrel's, shot him an almost guilty look. "I came to see for myself what manner of man he was."

"Well that at least is a good reason." Nagaro gave the other man an encouraging nod. "Now that you've seen him, what do you think?"

Geivian shook his head bitterly. "The truth? He's just a blacksmith. A big man, and handsome, but a blacksmith."

"He has courage!" Apparently Hendrel, riding on the farther side of Geivian, had overheard. "You have to admit that."

"Oh well, aye, he's brave enough," Geivian conceded. "Though he's scarcely a swordsman. If he weren't so big a man, no one would fear his blade. And he's no lord—no leader of men—and he knows it! Do you know what he said when he told the other men to go? He said, 'I tried to do something that's too big for me, and I'm going to die for it. But there's no sense in the rest of you lads dying too'."

Nagaro reigned the long-strided Thunder-Heels in a little. "Those are good words," he said. "They show both humility and a care for others."

Geivian shook his head bitterly. "He's humble all right. He doesn't believe he's Darion's heir—not any more, at least. You can see it in his eyes, whatever Rathdar says."

"Rathdar still believes it then?"

"Aye," Hendrel interjected. "He still holds to it, or maybe he's just carrying on now that old Abeidos is gone."

Nagaro frowned. "Who is Abeidos? I haven't heard that name before."

Geivian answered. "He was Rathdar's man—Berinar's man, before that—and as keen to find the heir as his old master. Abeidos was the one who traced Kenthos' history and put the idea in his head that he was Tevren's son."

"What happened to him?"

"He's dead," Hendrel supplied, "Killed when we met Lothard on the road."

Geivian nodded. "He was an old man, and he died thinking that he'd found Tevren's son and had set him on the path to his destiny, so there's no need to grieve for him over-much."

Geivian fell silent then, and Hendrel didn't contradict him. Nagaro decided not to pursue the matter further, so they rode on, each occupied with his own thoughts.

The countryside glowed in the late afternoon sunlight. Pastures and fields unfolded, tucked among the bits of woodland. Cattle grazed, and farmers' plantings sprouted in rows, new-green and tender. The air shimmered with a golden haze, and the shadows of trees began to stretch cool blue fingers across the dusty road. All the world seemed at peace, the hurrying troop of armed horsemen the only incongruity. Watchful though he was, Nagaro saw no sign of any other fugitives, nor of their pursuers. The farming folk he saw seemed a little more furtive than would be expected if nothing were amiss, but it might have been only wariness at seeing a troop of armed men riding by.

And then, at last, came another hail, this time from a pair of scouts in the green and brown of foresters who stepped out of a willow thicket where the road crossed a stream on a narrow stone bridge. Anduar immediately called a halt and directed his troops to water their horses while he, Pendrik, and Kuran held a huddled consultation with the two men at the far end of the bridge.

Nagaro recognized one of the scouts as the old Turo, Jato, who had been one of those bringing news to the encampment the previous evening. Since he hadn't been invited this time to join the council, Nagaro rode Thunder-Heels upstream a little way to get around the press of men and horses. He dismounted to let the gray stallion drink long and thirstily while he knelt to refill his flask where the cool water slid over bright stones. By the time he returned to the bridge, the scouts had departed and the lords were watering their horses on the farther bank of the stream. When Nagaro caught Kuran's eye, the Lord of the Fleet beckoned to him, and he rode across the bridge to join the three men.

"What news?" he asked from astride Thunder-Heels when he reached the other side.

"Rathdar and Lothard are still both before us, and still traveling south," Kuran informed him. "And Lord Madred is indeed here with a force of men. The old Turo thinks he'll join with Lothard's forces before nightfall."

"What of Odus and Devral?"

Anduar answered before Kuran could speak again. "Devral is some two hours behind us, on this road, with forty men. Odus is rumored to be farther east, on another road, and we're not certain of his numbers. And before you ask, there's word of a force led by Lord Soren to the east or south of us. If Soren has good scouts, and hears of Rathdar's intentions, he'll likely make directly for Loros Hall. Therin may do the same if he gets wind of what's afoot, but we've had no word of his whereabouts."

"Thank you, My Lord."

"Enough of this standing about!" Pendrik interrupted impatiently as he swung onto his horse. "Let's ride!" He reined his horse around onto the southward road and put his heels to his mount, leaving the bridge behind him.

Kuran muttered an oath as he put his foot in his stirrup and swung astride. Nagaro made out a fleeting frown on Anduar's face as the Kelorin lord pulled his horse's head around and sprang into the saddle. "I'll catch him," the Pact Signer muttered with annoyance. "You two gather the men and get them moving. We can camp in Harlind Hold, but I'd rather not be right across the road from Lothard's territory, and we're still a distance from the border of Fendred Hold."

The troop was quickly mustered. Within a quarter mile, they had overtaken Anduar and the impatient Pendrik, but they didn't slow, riding on hard down the road, racing the westering of the sun. The shadows were stretching long and purple and the sun was on the point of dipping below the treetops when they passed the stone on the right-hand side of the road that marked the border between Hurn and Fendred Holds. Even then, Anduar did not slacken the pace.

The troop was rounding a bend in the road as it skirted a steep hill when they surprised a second band of fleeing Kelorin, this time nearly a dozen of them. These men were afoot on the road, and they immediately leaped into a ditch on the Harlind side with frightened shouts, then scrambled up the farther bank, turned, and drew their swords.

Anduar halted his troop as they drew abreast of the men where they stood at bay, then called for Hendrel to come and talk to his former comrades. It didn't take long for Hendrel to convince the weary band of foot-soldiers to put their weapons away and accept the protection of the Anduar's mounted warriors. It scarcely took any longer to determine that the men had no news that Anduar didn't already know. Their lack of mounts was dealt with by putting each of them up behind one of the riders.

Nagaro took one behind him on Thunder-Heels. The harried and bedraggled young man in his twenties clambered gingerly up onto the stallion's rump and clung to Nagaro's waist when the horse began to move. Once Thunder-Heels hit his stride, Nagaro attempted to converse with him.

"What's your name, friend?"

"Lored." The man spoke between clamped teeth.

"Where do you hail from?"

"South o' here!" This time the answer was a gasp.

"Which Wared?"

"Kildoran! *Ai!*" The man's grip tightened even further as Thunder-Heels leaned into a turn.

"And the others with you? Are they also from Kildoran?"

"Most o' them, Zirda. *Oh, Vothra!*"

Thunder-Heels had swerved suddenly to the left, jostling amongst the other horses. Nagaro, who had his boots in the stirrups, easily adjusted to the movement, but Lored had begun to slip in his seat and only saved himself by his hold on Nagaro's waist. After this near mishap, Nagaro decided to forgo further conversation and concentrated on trying to keep Thunder-Heels' movements more steady.

He and his passenger rode in silence the rest of the way to Lord Anduar's chosen camp site at the edge of a ragged strip of woodland. Since the light was failing fast, Nagaro let a grateful Lored down, relieved Thunder-Heels of his saddle, and found a bow as quickly as he could. His efforts at hunting in the failing light met with less success than the previous evening. In spite of this—thanks to Rubo's skill—they had a fine rabbit stew, this time with potatoes roasted in their jackets among the coals.

Night came on quickly, and quiet stole over the camp. There had been no further news, and everyone was too weary for talk. The watches were quickly set and those who could were advised to seek slumber. Since Nagaro, Taru, and Pavo had all stood a watch the previous night, they had every expectation of enjoying a full night's sleep. Their talk to one another had been limited, confined to the events of the day, and it occurred to Nagaro as he lay down and tried to compose his mind that Taru hadn't plied him with questions concerning the state of his heart. There was also no sign that Pavo had told Taru anything about the previous night's conversation. Perhaps they would both forget about it.

Nagaro had settled himself on his side, facing east, and there were no trees to block the eastern horizon from his view. The stars were out, brilliant diamonds in a deep blue velvet sky. Talebra was already there as well, shining like beaten silver. Her trailing edge was still ragged, but he knew she was waxing. Smaller and dimmer, Naru rode just above the horizon, not quite nipping at Talebra's heels. The conjunction was coming.

*Kroneg or Lissafel, war or love... Which would prove the stronger?* Nagaro frowned in the moonlight and muttered to himself, "We'll just have to make bloody sure there isn't a war." Then he rolled over, turning his back to the rising moons, and very deliberately closed his eyes.

# Chapter 23

# The Hunt

"Wake up, Captain!"

"Mmh?" Nagaro's mind clung for an instant to the shreds of a dream in which he'd been riding up the Old North Road on his way to Irvenen Wared. But the image faded and he found himself staring up at Kuran. The Lord of the Fleet was bending over him, shaking him by the shoulder. The sky framing Kuran's face had the pale glow of very early morning.

Nagaro blearily raised himself on his elbow. "What is it, My Lord? Has something happened?"

Kuran gave him a tight smile. "Get up and join the council, Captain. We've just learned that Lothard's force is camped less than two miles away, on the Fendred side of the road!"

Nagaro hastily flung off his blanket, got up, and donned his cloak. The council, when he joined it, turned out to include Brandle again, in addition to the three lords and himself. Jato was there as well, squatting beside a fire newly kindled among the ashes of the old one, the smudge of its smoke tainting the fresh morning air. The grizzled old scout was stolidly holding his peace, waiting, listening. Pendrik was pacing and ranting.

"So close! In a field right beside the road! They've been there all *night*, and you waited for morning to come and tell us? *Why*, man?"

Jato didn't twitch a muscle. "It was after dark when I found 'em, M' Lord," he said laconically. "And I didn't know *ye'd* got so close. And they'll not be goin' anywhere for two hours at least. They've met that other lot—under Lord Madred—like we thought they would, an' there's two hundred men in that camp. Ye can't shift two hundred men in anything like a hurry."

Pendrik stared for a moment in mute astonishment, then flung up his hands. "If one of *theirs* and one of *ours* had gotten up to take a piss at the road-side, they'd have gotten each other's shoes wet!"

Jato blinked at the Leithian lord and shrugged as if he considered Pendrik's jest unworthy of any other response.

"Do sit down, Pendrik." Anduar indicated a conveniently located tree stump. He himself was enthroned upon a rock, languidly stretching his boots to the fire. "Two miles isn't as close as all that. Jato did well, getting up before dawn and working his way around them to find us."

Nagaro was now wide awake and impatient with inconsequential talk. "Where are Rathdar and Kenthos?" he asked. "Does anyone know?"

Jato turned at the sound of Nagaro's voice. His expression immediately became noticeably more respectful. "They'll be away farther t' the south, Zirda," he said. "Pedran was still trackin' 'em when I turned back t' find the Leithian camp."

"And where is this Pedran now, then?" Pendrik demanded. He had grudgingly sat down on the stump, but wasn't inclined to abandon his belligerence. "I don't see him here to give his report."

Jato blinked again. "Still on th' trail, I reckon."

"If he hasn't lost it overnight!"

Jato gave the Leithian lord an indignant look. "He'll not ha' lost the trail *they're* leavin' M' Lord! "But he can't be everywhere at once. He'll stay on 'em 'til he's sure they're makin' for Loros Hall."

At this, Kuran spoke up. "The Leithians will be following that trail as well, I suppose?"

Jato spat. "If they ain't fools."

Kuran frowned. "Won't they also still be trying to catch any other Kelorin who were out with Kenthos?"

Anduar coughed. "I'm afraid they have enough men to do both, especially since Madred has joined them. We, on the other hand, can't afford to divide our strength."

"It's a pity we can't draw any men from Harlind," Pendrik growled. "We could use more blond heads. But of course we can't have Elgurn's people involved in this directly."

There was a somewhat gloomy pause, which Nagaro spoke into. "How far ahead do you think Rathdar and Kenthos are right now, Jato?"

The old Turo squinted thoughtfully. "They'll be well into Kildoran, I'd say. They're stayin' off the road, which slows 'em down, but they're pressin' hard. They traveled all day yesterday, an' they didn't stop when the sun set. They was still goin' when I left Pedran, like I said."

Pendrik scowled. "They have to sleep sometime."

Anduar sighed. "They may plan to sleep when they get to Loros Hall. By the sound of it, they could be only a few hours from it right now—"

"And we have some time before the Leithian forces begin to move." Nagaro was thinking aloud.

"We could try to get around them before they do." Brandle spoke for the first time, putting a cautious verbal toe into the conversational water.

Pendrik nodded. "I like that plan."

Anduar, however, shook his head. "We might not manage it without alerting them to our presence. And even if we got around them unobserved, all their attention is focused in front of them. They'd be likely to notice us moving ahead of them before we could overtake Rathdar—which would almost certainly provoke a confrontation."

Pendrik scowled. "Well then, Anduar," he countered. "Suppose you tell us *your* plan."

Anduar considered the other lord. "We should stay behind Lothard and Madred," he said levelly. "And follow them as closely as we dare."

Pendrik angrily smote the top of his stump. "That isn't better than my plan, it's worse! They could catch Kenthos and strike him down before we could do anything about it!"

For the second time, Anduar sighed. "Every plan has drawbacks, Pendrik. We'll counter that particular one by making good use of our scouts."

"What if Lothard's men discover us?"

"It will be much easier to claim that we came there by chance if we're *behind* them than if we're between them and their quarry."

Pendrik threw his hands in the air. "But we haven't enough scouts!"

Anduar's eyes shifted instantly to Nagaro. "As I recall, Captain," he said blandly, "you said some of your men might serve in that capacity?"

"Yes, My Lord." Nagaro had been thinking as he listened. His expression was serious and his gaze sharply focused. "I can get you at least four from my crew, I'm sure. But you'll need to use the men from Kildoran Wared, as well—"

"The men from Kildoran?" Anduar arched a brow. "What are you suggesting, Captain?

"That we assemble a party of scouts and send them around the Leithian force before it begins to move. Jato can lead them south—along Kenthos' trail—and position them at intervals in places of concealment, making a chain all the way to Loros Hall if need be. Then, as each man is passed by the Leithian line, he has only to wait until he's in the clear and then come straight back to find us."

Anduar actually smiled. "That, Captain, is the best thinking I've heard this morning." The smile vanished as quickly as it had come, however, to be replaced by the familiar steely stare. "Unfortunately, the men from Kildoran Wared are partisans."

"I know, My Lord. You'll have to decide whether they can be used this way, but I see little risk if they swear to follow your orders. They'll be too few and scattered to be a fighting force, and they'll be highly motivated to perform the task well and to avoid capture. Since they're from the area ahead of us, they will also know the terrain, and this is a task for footmen so it doesn't matter that they don't have horses."

Anduar stroked his chin. "They'll be at considerable risk if caught."

"Any men who serve as scouts will be at some risk—unless they're Leithians—My Lord. I'll lead them myself if you wish."

At this, Anduar leveled a forefinger at Nagaro. "That you will *not*, Captain! I want you with me!"

"My Lord?" Nagaro frowned.

"I won't have you making your own solution to this affair!"

Nagaro's frown deepened. "I assure you I have no intention—"

"Of course you don't." Anduar stood up, his cool gaze still fixed upon Nagaro. "But opportunities have a way of presenting themselves." The intensity of his gaze softened, however, in the face of Nagaro's offended innocence. "I'm not saying your solution wouldn't be a good one, Captain. But the king's order rests on *my* shoulders. In this time, and in this place, I represent the Crown, and whatever choices are made must be seen to flow from that authority. Is that clear?"

Nagaro had drawn himself up. His eyes still met Anduar's, though he could feel every other eye upon him as well. "Yes, My Lord," he said evenly. "I understand, and I will do my best to follow your command."

"Good." Anduar's eyes released Nagaro as he swung his gaze away to fasten it upon the old Turowan scout. "What do you think, Tor Jato? Can you do this?"

A wide grin split the old man's seamed face. "Aye, Zirda, I can. An' I'll be more 'n happy to."

"Good, again!" The gray eyes turned next to Brandle. "I charge you, Lieutenant, with the command of this chain of scouts. Do you understand the Captain's plan?"

"Aye, Zirda!" Brandle saluted stiffly. "If I might make a suggestion, My Lord, shall I see if I can recruit a few Leithians to place at the nearer end of the chain—in Harlind and Fendred Holds?"

"Yes. A good thought, Lieutenant. Take Jato with you and see to it. I want your party to set out as soon as possible. If you happen to find Rathdar and Kenthos, tell them whatever you know about Lothard's movements—but don't be caught doing it by Lothard's men. Do you understand?"

Brandle nodded very gravely. "Aye, My Lord. What shall I tell them about what our force is doing?"

Anduar's eyes narrowed. "Only that we're coming behind the Leithian force. Do *not* promise them rescue."

Brandle's shoulders stiffened. "Aren't we to use our swords then?" he asked. "To prevent bloodshed?"

The narrow gray eyes grew hard. "Only if you can be sure of success, Lieutenant. If you're dealing with only a few men, for example. Don't try to intervene against Lothard or Madred and their army."

The muscles of Brandle's jaw tightened. "Aye, Zirda!." He saluted stiffly.

Anduar's gaze turned to the other lords. "Pendrik, Kuran, we must rouse the rest of the men. Bid them eat something and be ready to ride within the hour."

With that, the council broke up.

Nagaro immediately set off to find Taru and Pavo, but Brandle came up beside him with Jato in tow. "So, Captain," he ventured. "You got the praise, but not the posting. Are you angry?"

Nagaro shot the Leithian a glance. "No," he said seriously. "Though I wish I could be there. And I didn't like his last words to me. I understand full well that he has to have the final authority. He needn't think I'd try to usurp it."

At this, Jato laughed shortly. "The old goat don't want the young goat bein' too bold, eh, Zirda? Ain't that always the way of it?"

Nagaro shook his head. "Lord Anduar is never that simple."

"If I didn't know better," Brandle put in, "I'd say he was saving you for Lothard."

Nagaro stopped walking. "What do you mean?"

"In case it comes to a confrontation—a challenge. You're the only man in Edrovir with a chance of taking Lothard in a fair fight."

Nagaro frowned sharply. "You're surely exaggerating." He resumed his walk.

"I don't think so." Brandle lengthened his stride to catch up. "I know Anduar couldn't do it. Or Pendrik, or Kuran."

Nagaro stopped again, considering Brandle. "Even if that's true, Lothard would never challenge me. I'm a commoner."

Brandle shrugged. "Maybe, but it's still a good reason for Anduar to keep you close to him, and to his plans."

Jato had been listening closely, his dark eyes flicking back and forth between the other two men. "Ye don't think it's because the Captain has a good idea or two?" he ventured.

"Well, yes, there's that too," Brandle conceded. "Either way, though, it's better than his reason for including *me*."

Nagaro frowned at the Leithian. "What are you saying?"

Brandle smiled crookedly. "That I'm here to balance *you*, because my hair is blond and yours is black. He can pretend I represent the Palace Guard, so he calls on me instead of Vell or Ruald, but what he really wants is another Leithian to balance all the Kelorin faces around the circle.

That's why I got this command too—*balance.* Another Leithian doing the king's business."

Nagaro considered. "I'm sure he thinks you'll do a good job of it, Brandle."

"And I will, too!" Brandle's teeth flashed. "Especially if I have your help speaking to the men from Kildoran Wared. I'd like you to explain to them what they're going to have to swear to, and why. And you can help me pick the other men for the task too."

Half an hour later Brandle was ready to leave the camp with his hand-picked band of scouts. It included most of the unmounted men they had overtaken on the previous evening, four former pirates, and a handful of Leithians culled from among the members of the Palace Guard. The men who had been followers of Kenthos had listened gravely to Nagaro's explanation that they were to act as scouts only, not combatants, and had duly sworn an oath to that effect. All seemed prepared to do the task proposed. Nagaro still had a nervous knot in his stomach as he watched them prepare to steal away. He pulled Jato aside.

"Try to put my men in the most doubtful positions," he advised. "And the others in the safer places."

Jato winked. "Don't ye fret, Zirda," he said conspiratorially. "I knows what I'm about."

Nagaro did his best to smile. "Good luck to you, Jato. And to you, Brandle," he added more loudly when he realized the Leithian was watching them. "I wish I were going with you."

That earned him a broad grin and a salute.

After Brandle and the scouts were gone, Nagaro finally sought out Taru and Pavo, who naturally wanted to know all the news. Landros and Tredhold were with them and anxious to hear as well. Since he hadn't been told to keep the matter close, and could see no harm in it, he told them the entire plan in detail.

"So." Taru cocked his head. "We're to tag along behind this great Leithian army all day?"

"More or less. But if the Leithians catch Kenthos, or anyone else, I'm sure Anduar will make some more decisive move."

"How are we t' know if they catch anyone if all our scouts are way out in front o' the army and have t' come all the way 'round?"

"Aye," Landros agreed. "And they'll still have to find us, while we're trying not to get too close to the Leithians."

Nagaro turned thoughtful. "That's a good point. Anduar could use one or two scouts on this side of the Leithian line as well, who know where we are."

Taru's eyes brightened. "Now there's a task more t' my liking than trudging along in the Leithians' dust!"

Nagaro smiled. "You may find you can have the task if you offer, Taru. There's Anduar, right over there."

Taru's glee turned to immediate apprehension. "I don't know," he said. "That man is as sharp as a nail and as cold as an icicle!"

Pavo grinned. "I am not afraid of him, Taru. And I also want to do this. Come with me, and I will ask him!"

Taru stiffened. "I didn't say I was afraid. I'm just thinking he'll likely say no, and none too nicely. Who needs t' be treated like a lump o' dirt?"

Pavo's grin widened. "Maybe he will say yes. Only way to find out is to ask. Are you going to come with me?"

Taru's jaw set in a hard line and he managed a shrug. "I suppose there's no harm in trying. Lead on, Pavo."

Nagaro smiled faintly as he watched them go. Tred was smiling broadly. Landros chuckled, then quickly turned sober. "Looks like it's time to saddle up, lads," he said grimly.

Nagaro gave the old sea-dog a nod of agreement, then turned quickly and went to saddle Thunder-Heels.

***

It turned out that Lord Anduar was perfectly willing to accept Taru and Pavo as scouts for the task they proposed. It also turned out that as close as their force dared get to the Leithians was anywhere between half and three quarters of a mile, depending on the terrain. And Nagaro soon found that Anduar had meant it quite literally when he'd said that he wanted Nagaro close to him. The Pact Signer set him to ride at his left hand, with Pendrik on his right and Kuran beyond that. The four of them formed the troop's front rank. Nagaro supposed that he and Kuran, both in Fleet uniforms, might appear to be an honor guard for the two lords in between, but he felt a little out of place as the only one of the four who couldn't count himself among the nobility. His position also meant there was no one he could possibly talk to except Anduar.

The arrangement did have one advantage. He was necessarily privy to everything Anduar heard or said. The first time that Anduar called a halt, it was in response to a report from Pavo, who appeared at the side of the road ahead of them, rising from behind a farmyard wall. Just as Nagaro drew abreast of him, Pavo stepped out into the road to address Anduar.

"My Lord, you must wait here for report from Taru. Leithian are almost ready to move, but if you go around bend right now, they will see you."

Anduar nodded his comprehension and raised a hand for a halt. "Well done, Zirda," he said. "Please return to the front."

Pavo saluted, ducked back behind the wall, and was gone.

The halt lasted nearly half an hour. Pendrik had soon had enough and bore his impatience with ill grace. "Where's Devral?" he grumbled. "We were told he was right behind us yesterday afternoon, and we're being slow enough that a turtle could catch us. And where has Odus gotten to? We're tracking a force of over two hundred with scarcely sixty men!"

Anduar cast the other Pact Signer a cool glance. "We may hear something soon, Pendrik. My other scouts have yet to report."

Nagaro frowned, astride his horse. How many scouts did Anduar have? He had heard men say that Lord Anduar had eyes everywhere, and he was beginning to believe it. "What about the Lord of Fendred Hold?" he asked. "These are his lands to the west of us."

Pendrik snorted derisively, but Anduar turned to Nagaro with a mild glance. "I'll send a messenger to inquire when we're closer to his hall, but I don't expect much from Fendale. Fendred Hold is small, and nearly defenseless against the power of Hurn Hold on their northern border."

At length Taru appeared, just as Pavo had, with the news that the Leithian force had begun its march. "They're spreading out, My Lord," he reported breathlessly. "Lothard's men are at this end o' the lines, and Lord Madred's on the other side. If ye go ahead now—but not too fast—ye should be safe."

"Good man." Anduar acknowledged the report with a salute, then raised his hand to signal the advance, simultaneously setting his heels to his horse's flanks and crying, "All forward!"

They hadn't gone half a mile, however, before they had to halt again. As they were waiting, they were overtaken from behind by another of Anduar's scouts, the one who'd been sent to locate Lord Devral's men. As it turned out, Devral was close on the scout's heels with forty armed warriors.

This addition to their force raised everyone's spirits, and the new arrivals were cheered and clapped on the back as they joined the ranks. Pendrik was especially pleased by the development. When Devral joined the other lords, at the front of the newly enlarged force, the Leithian Pact Signer welcomed him quite jovially. "Well met, my friend! You nearly double our numbers."

Devral's scarred face cracked into a wolfish leer. "Here's something new under the sun," he growled. "Pendrik is glad to see me. Or is it only my men at arms? I was told to bring a dozen, and I've brought three times that number!"

Pendrik let out a guffaw, then shot back, "It's only a pity they're not Leithians!"

Devral's grin grew slightly toothier. "Kelorin folk are all we grow in Sedras Wared."

Anduar, who'd been silently listening, smiled faintly. "All jesting aside," he said, "it would be better for the look of things if we had more blond heads. I hope Odus finds us before matters come to a head and that he brings as many as Devral. The force we're following numbers two hundred."

"Two hundred!" Devral was surprised. "Has Lothard really brought so many just to hunt down a handful of men?"

"Not Lothard alone, he and Madred together," Anduar replied. "Fortunately we don't need to outnumber them—or so I hope. Madred at least is a reasonable man. We only need a force large enough that it can't be safely ignored."

Nagaro frowned as he listened. Apparently Brandle was right about balance.

At that moment, Taru appeared and beckoned them forward. Anduar gave the order to move, and they rode forward again, though cautiously.

A little farther on they met the first of Brandle's scouts. He came trotting around a bend in the road and stood catching his breath while the troop of horsemen closed the distance. He was a Leithian with a brown cloak worn over the white tirka of the Palace Guard.

"My Lord," the man said, and saluted, when Anduar drew rein in front of him.

"Your report, Zirda?"

"They've spread out on both sides of the road, My Lord. Mostly t' the east of it. Just a few t' the west. They're following the same trail we were following, and beating the bushes as they go. But the plan worked like oiled leather, My Lord. I was hid up a tree and they rode right under me!"

Anduar smiled tightly. "What need to look up, eh, when you think your quarry is mounted? You can't hide a horse in a tree."

"No, My Lord. Ah, should I mount up, Zirda?"

"Not yet. Walk with us until we pass the place where you were hiding."

So they proceeded, moving first between pastures, then between two copses of trees where the Leithian indicated that he had been concealed just off the road in the branches of a huge oak.

The Leithian scout had barely found his mount when Pavo appeared from among the trees on their left with the advice that they ride only as far as the crest of the next hill and wait, before topping it, until Taru came to tell them it was safe. This they did, and the second of Brandle's scouts found them while they were waiting for Taru's word. His report was very much like the first except that he told of finding a little group of fleeing Kelorin.

"We warned 'em what was coming, My Lord," he said earnestly. "They struck off right away, t' the west. Brandle reckons they'll get clear."

Twice more the pattern of stopping and proceeding repeated itself. Another man from the chain of scouts found them with the report that the trail continued and that he'd also seen a small party of Kelorin slip the net by bolting to the west into Fendred Hold while the Leithian force moved ponderously on.

When they reached a crossroads at about mid-morning, Anduar sent one of Brandle's men spurring down the side road, westward to Fendred Hall. They waited for the man's return, and it wasn't long before he came back, alone, which surprised no one. He did however bring news.

"Lord Fendale says to look out for Grimbold Sobring, My Lord. His people have seen a mass of fifty or sixty men heading south on the Sobring side of their border."

Anduar's eyes were hard as he nodded his acknowledgment. "All right, Zirda. Well done. Do you think you can find the chain again on foot?"

The man, a Leithian, nodded. "I reckon so, My Lord."

"Then leave your horse, and carry this news of Lord Grimbold to Lieutenant Brandle."

Devral turned to Anduar as he watched the man dismount. "We've already passed the southern border of Harlind, and ridden almost completely past Fendred Hold," he growled. "We'll have Kildoran Wared on both sides of the road pretty soon, and Endemar would surely aid us. Should we send word to him?"

"Endemar?" Anduar's face remained impassive, though his gray eyes narrowed. "The effect of his presence would be uncertain. He'll defend his Wared—and Loros Hall, for that matter—against any armed intrusion. And he won't wish to see blood spilled on his soil—"

Kuran cleared his throat. "Remember that some of his folk have been out with Kenthos."

Anduar face grew grim. "Which was surely against their lord's wishes. And there are others in Kildoran Wared who will also be tempted to take Kenthos' side if their lord calls them to arms to turn aside an invasion of Leithians. It's some distance from Endemar's seat to Loros Hall. With luck, he won't have gotten word of what's afoot, and if we don't want bloodshed, I don't think we should tell him."

Nagaro shifted in the saddle and spoke what was in his mind. "What about Varsyl Virden, My Lord? We must be very close to Virden Wared."

Pendrik snorted loudly.

Devral laughed outright. "Varsyl doesn't even carry a sword," the scarred old Kelorin pointed out.

"And he keeps only a very small defensive force." Anduar made a dismissive gesture. "There's little use in asking him for aid. But here's your man Taru, Captain—come to tell us we should ride on."

So the slow pursuit continued, with the men from the chain of scouts who came to them now being Kelorin. The sun arced upward. The air grew very warm. Whenever they stopped to wait they were surrounded by birdsong, the humming of insects in the grass, and the scents of fresh earth and wildflowers. During one of these pauses, at mid day, Lord Anduar issued an order for the men to eat, and whatever dry meat and bread they still had was passed around.

When next they moved on, they passed the stone on the right-hand side of the road that marked the border of Kildoran Wared. Shortly thereafter the road entered a dense stand of oak trees so tall and broad that their branches arched over the road, nearly meeting in the middle overhead. The troop passed gratefully into the resulting tunnel of shade.

The rear guard had scarcely gotten under the overarching boughs, however, when two men appeared around a bend in the road a little way ahead, coming at a half run. One was Pavo. The other, a Kelorin, was staggering visibly and leaning on Pavo for support. Nagaro thought he looked like one of the men from Kildoran Wared, and he pressed Thunder-Heels forward, fearing the man was wounded. Anduar pushed forward also, staying abreast of him.

When Pavo saw how quickly they would meet, he stopped in the middle of the roadway, letting the other man rest, bent over, hands on his thighs. As it turned out, the man was merely winded. Anduar pulled to a halt in front of him with Nagaro beside him and the other lords a few paces behind.

"What news, Zirda?"

Pavo answered. "This scout have found Kenthos, My Lord! He say maybe ten mile from Loros Hall."

"How long ago was this?"

Pavo nudged his companion. "You must tell it. You know better."

The Kelorin straightened, his breathing still ragged. "You must save him, My Lord!" he gasped. "Ride now! Ride fast!"

Anduar's face remained stony. "Answer my question, Zirda! *How long ago did you see them?*"

The man drew himself up, staring at Anduar as if in disbelief. For a moment his fists clenched, but then he seemed to master himself and he un-knotted them. "It was an hour, My Lord. Maybe more. I came as fast as I could!"

Anduar nodded fractionally. "That I believe," he said cooly. "And where were they? Can you name the place, or describe it?"

"They were lying hid, in a cowbarn, My Lord," the man gasped. "Outside the town o' Devenrul. They'd ridden all day yesterday. Most o' the night. They only stopped 'cause they couldn't go farther without sleep! I pray ye make haste!"

"Will we find them in the same place? Or are they moving now?"

"They'll be moving, My Lord, o' course—now they know Lothard's bloody lot is two miles away! Lieutenant Brandle told them so."

"All right." Anduar turned to one of the men behind him. "Get this man onto a horse." He turned around again. "Pavo Maat?"

Pavo jerked to attention. "Yes, Lord!"

"We will follow you, Zirda. Lead us as close to Lothard's rear guard as you can."

"Aye, Zirda!" Pavo spun about and set off back the way he had come at a jog-trot.

Anduar hung back to let him get a little way ahead, then followed him at a distance. As the road wound through the woods, Pavo's figure moved on before them through flickering shade and patches of sunlight, sometimes passing out of sight briefly at a bend in the road.

After perhaps a quarter of an hour, the company rounded such a bend to find Pavo standing in the middle of the road, in conversation with another Kelorin scout who was gesticulating wildly. Anduar immediately signaled a halt.

"Who is that man?" Pendrik demanded.

Nagaro answered, having recognized the man who'd ridden behind him the day before. "Another of the men from Kildoran Wared. His name is Lored."

At that moment, Pavo turned and came jogging hurriedly back to join them, the Kelorin man close on his heels.

"Lord Anduar!" Pavo's normally impassive face betrayed excitement. "Some of Lothard's man have seen Kenthos and Rathdar and all of their man! They are making chase!"

"Please, Lord!" Lored cried. "Ye must ride quickly! Ye must save him!"

Anduar regarded the Kelorin levelly. "*Who* exactly has seen them?" he inquired. "And *who* is chasing? Is Lothard among them, or is it still possible that he doesn't know? And what of Lord Madred?"

Lored drew a ragged breath. "I didn't see Madred or Lothard, Zirda. It was some o' Lothard's men—his livery—out in front, the bush-beaters. They shouted, '*There they are!*' and '*Get them!*' —and they started t' run. And the men behind them heard, an' they started running too! Please, Zirda! Please hurry! They'll kill him!"

Lord Devral started to say something, but Anduar raised a hand for silence. "How long ago was this?"

Lored shuddered and glanced desperately at the narrow bit of blue sky that showed between the overarching tree limbs as if trying to guess the angle of the light. The sun wasn't visible through the gap, being elsewhere in the sky. "I don't know, My Lord! Maybe a quarter hour—maybe half. I waited just 'til the line went under my tree and dropped an' came as fast as I could! They might ha' caught them by now! Please, Zirda! I've kept my oath. Give me a horse and let me go after them!"

"That I will not, Zirda!" Anduar spoke sternly. "I hold you still to your oath, and you'll find it much easier to keep it if you're here with us. One of the men will take you up behind him— *Not you, Captain!*" The last was spoken to Nagaro who had begun to urge Thunder-Heels in the man's direction.

"He may be needed to guide us, My Lord," Nagaro pointed out.

"Ah. Yes." Anduar nodded, his eyes narrowing. "But I don't want *you* encumbered." He ran his gaze over the first rank of men immediately behind the line of lords. "You." He pointed at Tredhold. "You're small, and your horse looks strong. Take this man up and follow us closely."

Tredhold saluted. "Aye, Zirda!" He swivelled his horse and extended a hand to Lored.

Anduar turned back to Pavo. "And you, Zirda, find your horse and mount up! We've come to the end of this cat-and-mouse game."

***

The hooves of their horses thundered on the beaten earth as they galloped on under the trees, until, at length, they burst from the shadow of the wood into bright afternoon sunlight. A verdant valley opened before them with green pastures and plowed fields. Not far away to their left—to the east—the roofs of a town showed through a copse of trees.

Pendrik twisted in his saddle to shout a question at Lored. "What town is that?"

"Devenrul!" The Kelorin gasped his answer. "They were hiding in the cowbarn over there!"

Part of the building in question could be seen among a nearby cluster of trees, but Anduar made no move to approach it, and the reason was readily apparent. Ahead of them, a stream wound through the valley, marked by bordering sedges and reeds. The road crossed the stream on a solid stone bridge beyond which the land rose, gently at first, then more steeply, culminating in a range of hills that were intermittently wooded. Figures were moving uphill on the rising ground beyond the stream, men on horseback, a long ragged line of them, going quickly. It was just possible to make out that they wore light-colored tirkas with red sashes.

"Lothard's men!" Lored was pointing. "There! Hurry!"

The road dipped downhill toward the watercourse. The bridge was narrower than the roadway, and they clattered across it, the lords leading, four abreast. Nagaro dropped back briefly into the second rank, between Tred and Lored on the one hand, and Pavo on the other. The Hashtep gestured at him. "I do not like it," he shouted. "I do not see Taru!"

The lords spread out again on the farther side of the bridge, reining in a little to let Nagaro rejoin them, then dragging their horses to a halt in a spray of dust as another of the Kildoran scouts suddenly emerged from a hiding place under the bridge. The man pointed unnecessarily at the riders on the other side of the valley and gasped, "They're climbing the hills! Hurry, My Lords! Ye must stop them!"

Pendrik swung his horse around to face the man. "Have they caught Rathdar or Kenthos?"

"They can't ha' done, M' Lord." The scout wrung his hands. "Or they wouldn't still be riding on like that!

"Where is Taru?" Nagaro asked. "Have you seen him?"

"The young Turo? He told me to wait here, Zirda. He went after the Leithians."

Anduar fixed the man with his steely gaze. "Where is Lieutenant Brandle?"

"Still out there in front o' them somewhere, M' Lord. He said he meant to press on to Loros Hall."

"Had he gotten the word that Lord Grimbold is coming from the east?"

"Aye, M' Lord."

Anduar nodded grimly. "All right. Find someone who'll take you up on his horse." He surveyed the assembled ranks behind him as the scout dove in amongst them. "Are all the men clear of the bridge?" There came answering cries of, "Aye, Zirda!" Anduar gave a short nod. "Then forward!" He spun his horse about and set his heels to the beast's flanks.

Anduar rode with redoubled speed past a crossroads leading to the town of Devenrul. The other lords pressed their mounts to keep up and Nagaro kept Thunder-Heels among them. The troop came close behind as the road began to rise and wind into the hills. At the first turning that yielded a view of the valley behind them, Nagaro swept it with his eyes and caught movement. He let out a shout and pointed.

"Whose men are those?"

A large body of horsemen could be seen massed on the southern side of the town. The troop was large enough to amount to a small army, and even before Nagaro's words had died, a distant shout carried over the fields and the army began to move. Its leader chose a course straight up the hillside to the east of the winding road that Lord Anduar had chosen.

Anduar checked his mount just long enough take in the scene. "Green and white—Madred's colors!" he cried. "*Forward!*"

The road took them first westward, then turned again and climbed, going among trees once more. Even if they had not needed all their attention for the turnings of the road, it would have been impossible to get a clear view of the higher slopes where they'd earlier seen Lothard's men ascending in a scattered line. Nagaro found himself clenching his teeth, imagining those Leithians having already reached the crest of the hills and started down the other side.

The road turned eastward again and they thundered along it. Then suddenly, Taru leaped into the roadway in front of them. He must have been coming straight downhill, rather than by the road, for he came out of the bushes at the top of a bank on the uphill side, landed in a crouch, then straightened and saw the troop of horsemen bearing down on him. He ran directly at them, waving his arms madly and shouting, "*Hold! Hold!*" Before Taru reached them, a second man, a Kelorin in the uniform of the Royal Fleet, came sliding down the bank, scrambled to his feet, and charged after Taru. Nagaro recognized the second man as Olendar, one of his own former pirates.

Anduar and the other lords raised their voices and the troop of horsemen came plunging to a panicked stop, nearly colliding with one another. Taru was in amongst them in an instant. "Where's my horse?" he cried frantically. "There's been a fight!"

"*A fight?*" Anduar, Pendrik, and Devral all converged upon Taru, hemming him in with their mounts.

"*Who?*" Anduar demanded.

"Some o' Lothard's men against Rathdar and Kenthos and their lot!"

"How many?"

"Less 'n a dozen on each side—*Let me get t' my horse!*"

Anduar, however, was coolly focused. "Stand! Where did this happen?"

"Just the other side o' this ridge." Olendar spoke for the first time. "It wasn't much more 'n a skirmish. The ground was too steep for a proper fight."

"Aye, but we saw Rathdar go down!" Taru seemed to have forgotten about his horse. His gaze was now locked on Lord Anduar.

"*Rathdar down!*" exclaimed Devral. "Not dead, I hope?"

Taru shook his head. "No. They got him up on his horse again and made off down the hill, but he was hangin' on t' the beast's neck! It didn't look good."

Anduar's steely gaze swung to Olendar. "You saw the same?"

Olendar mopped his brow with the back of a dirty hand and nodded. "Aye. Rathdar took a sword cut. I couldn't tell how bad—"

"And Lothard wasn't there?"

"No, Zirda."

Anduar raised his gaze to take in the front rank of men. His expression was set. "Get these men onto horses!" he snapped. "Now!"

Several men leaped to obey.

Nagaro addressed Olendar, who was closer. "What did Kenthos do in this skirmish? Did he fight?"

Olendar nodded. "Aye, Capt'n. Least he tried to. He cut the man that wounded Rathdar. I think he was angry—"

"More like desperate," Taru put in. "He's no great swordsman and he looked t' be hurting too, but the Leithians were hanging back from him."

"Why should they hang back?" Pendrik demanded.

Taru turned to the Leithian lord. "On account o' Lothard saying he wanted t' kill Kenthos himself, I expect."

"Kill Kenthos himself? *By the Blood of Kroneg!*" Lord Pendrik swore vigorously.

Anduar turned the full intensity of his gaze upon Taru. "You said Lothard wasn't there!"

Olendar hastily answered. "We heard one o' the men say it!"

"Aye—My Lord." Taru belatedly remembered his courtesy. "One o' them said Lothard was just over the ridge, and he'd be there any minute, and that Lothard wanted t' kill Kenthos himself—like he was reminding them not t' get in their lord's way. And *then* they realized the man they'd hurt was Lord Rathdar an' they all pulled back. If they hadn't done that, Kenthos and his lot never would ha' got away."

At this point, Taru's and Olendar's horses were finally brought. The two men were in the saddle in an instant and the whole cavalcade spurred forward again.

As they rounded the next bend and started up yet another stretch of road, Devral shouted to Anduar over the beat of hooves, "It would be shorter off the road! Go straight up the ridge like Madred was doing!"

"Shorter, but not faster!"Anduar shot back. "And this way we won't injure our horses!"

"But Loros Hall is *east*, after ye top the ridge, M' Lord!" Lored all but screamed from behind them. "An' that;s where Madred's men are going over the top!"

To this Lord Anduar made no reply except to urge his horse to greater speed.

Chapter 24

# The Road To Loros Hall

They met no one else before they topped the ridge, where the road brought them onto a promontory, nearly bald of trees. There they drew rein to let the horses breathe and to survey the scene spread out before them. The land fell away in tumbling tree-covered slopes to green pastures and fields that stretched away into the blue distance. Among them, running roughly east to west, lay the undulating silver ribbon of the River Edro. The afternoon sun was beginning its descent and its rays struck at an angle, limning every copse, every hedge or wall, every outcropping of stone, with violet shadow. Colors were kindled to brilliance by that light. Overhead a few snow-white wisps of cloud decorated a sky that was otherwise an achingly perfect azure.

Nagaro caught his breath. *In days to come*, he wondered, *will anyone remember that it was on such a day as this that these events unfolded?*

"Where is Loros Hall?" he asked.

"There, Captain!" Lored, still seated behind Tredhold, pointed ahead and to the left, east by northeast. "Down on the flat land, near the great river."

Nagaro shaded his eyes. "I see a building with towers, some trees, and a little space with a wall around it."

"*That* would be the infamous garden where the child is said to be buried," Devral put in dryly.

"If only they can reach it in time!" Lored's words were a breathless prayer.

"Where have Lothard's men got to? That's what I want to know!" Pendrik was bluntly practical.

Lord Anduar had been scanning the hillsides below their perch with narrowed eyes. "I can see men on horseback," he said, "there, and there, and there." He pointed. "Wearing red, white, and black, the colors of Hurn Hold. They appear to be moving towards Loros Hall."

"Just as we were told Kenthos would!" Devral punched his thigh. "Do these Leithians have the same information that we do? Or do they guess?"

"Perhaps it's only that they are very close upon the scent," Anduar observed calmly.

Lored's gasp of alarm in response to this suggestion was plainly audible, though Anduar ignored it.

Nagaro had been making his own observations. Now he pointed in a different direction, westward along the line of the hills. "There's a road, there, and a company of horsemen coming along it! Do you see?"

All eyes turned to look. The road in question skirted the base of the range of hills on which they stood. The horsemen were yet a few miles away but approaching at a rapid pace.

Devral shaded his eyes. "What are their colors?" he asked tensely. "Can anyone with younger eyes make them out? If they're Grimbold's men they'll be wearing purple baldrics over white. If they're Therin's they'll be wearing russet and blue."

"They may not be in uniform," Anduar pointed out. "Particularly if they're Therin's men."

Nagaro squinted. "I see white tirkas—or shirts," he said. "But white shirts are common."

"They're surely Grimbold's," Pendrik declared. "We should ride!"

The Leithian lord began to urge his horse forward, but Anduar raised a hand to stay him. "Not so hasty, Pendrik," he said. "There may be more to be seen from this height. Once we're down among those trees, we won't see anything until we're on top of it—or it's on top of us."

Anduar had scarcely finished speaking when Kuran flung out a hand, pointing to the southwest. "I see another body of men! Not so close and nearer the river. They seem to be approaching, but they're much too far away to see any colors."

Anduar leaned forward, straining his eyes. "I see them. That would be the River Road, that passes Loros Hall on the river side. That could well be Therin's force. Do any of you see anything to the east besides Madred's men? Soren might come that way, to Rathdar's aid. And Odus should be bringing us reinforcements from that direction."

They all turned eastward, and several men immediately pointed to mounted figures, in the green and white of Lord Madred's livery, moving among the trees, further east than Lothard's but also going towards Loros Hall. Then there were long seconds of tense silence as all eyes scanned the land for any other signs of movement.

Suddenly Lored pointed and cried, "Over there! Far to the east—moving along the river!"

"Yes!" Pendrik cried. "Also on the River Road. A large force, I'd say!"

"Hmm... *yes*..." Anduar was leaning in the saddle again, peering keenly. "But too far away to make out details. We may hope that's Odus. Does anyone see anything else?"

It seemed that no one did, and time was slipping. The riders among the trees below them had all this time been moving steadily downslope, though their progress was slowed by the steep, wooded terrain.

Anduar spoke: "We dare wait no longer. Lored, can you tell us the shortest way to Loros Hall?"

"There's a narrow road that branches from this one, M' Lord. The second or third leftward turning. I'll know it when I set eyes on it."

"Good." Anduar turned and spoke to Tredhold, who bore Lored behind him. "Come forward, Zirda, and ride on my right hand." Then he raised his hand, and his voice. "Forward, men! Now we must ride!"

And ride they did.

Nagaro would long remember it. The road led downhill, sometimes steeply, and they plunged along it at a breakneck pace, the horses sometimes jostling dangerously at the turnings. So they descended rapidly, sometimes hearing shouts or catching glimpses of moving men when there were openings in the trees ahead. Always Lothard's men were before them. Nagaro, moving with the press, astride Thunder-Heels, tried to picture in his mind the Leithians' sweep towards Loros Hall as he rode, and the simultaneous convergence of the other three forces they had seen from the crest of the hills.

Gradually the slope of the land became less precipitous and the road less winding. Far from slackening the pace, however, Anduar and the other lords only urged their horses to greater effort. They passed a place where a road joined theirs on the right and Lored shouted breathlessly that it was the road Grimbold's men were on. Shortly thereafter, a second, narrower, way crossed theirs, but Lored shook his head, crying, "Not that one!" At the next turning, Lored pointed eagerly, nodding, and Anduar slowed, gesturing for the company to turn left.

They had nearly passed out of the foothills by this time, and the side road—a modest dirt lane—led past a stand of woods that covered a sloping shoulder of land. Coming around that shoulder, at the edge of the wood, the land opened before them into a stretch of meadow fifty yards across, with the road cutting southeast through the middle of it. The grass was vibrantly green and thick with spring flowers, snow-white queen's lace, scarlet columbine, and deep blue larkspur. The lengthening shadows of the trees on the riders' left stretched across the roadway where it entered the meadow.

Just beyond the edge of that shadow, a gray-cloaked figure crouched by the side of the road. The man stood up when he saw the company of horsemen, raising his hands as if in supplication. His movement revealed the form of a second man lying in the grass at the roadside.

The horsemen were moving so fast that the company was nearly on top of the two men before anyone could draw rein. "Whoa! Whoa! Halt! Halt!" Several voices cried out in chorus.

Nagaro's voice rose over the rest. "It's Haruda! One of our Fleet men!"

The standing man, a Turowan, was in fact one of Nagaro's former followers, though he'd discarded the dark blue tirka of the Fleet uniform. His cloak was torn, and there was a smear of bright red blood like a silent scream across the front of his white shirt. His attention was instantly drawn by Nagaro's shout. "Captain!" he gasped. "Help me! Hurry!"

Nagaro's stomach tightened. "Are you hurt?"

Haruda shook his head. "Not me. It's Pedran!" He pointed at the man sprawled on the ground.

"*Pedran?*" Anduar spoke sharply, and in the next instant he had swung from his horse and was striding towards the fallen man.

"Let me see him!" Tredhold spurred forward.

Haruda seemed to see the healer for the first time. "Tred!" he cried. "Praise the Spirits!"

Tredhold was off of his horse in a second and hurriedly unstrapping his healer's satchel from the side of his saddle. Lored slid to the ground so as not to hinder him. The Lords Kuran, Pendrik, and Devral dismounted as well and all gathered around the fallen man.

Nagaro swung down from Thunder-Heels and followed, though he hung back to let Tred do his work. Still, he caught a glimpse of the wounded Pedran, Lord Anduar's tracker, as the healer knelt beside him in the knot of other men. He saw a black-haired Kelorin some years past forty, his face pale as chalk, his shirt stained with blood. His hands clutched feebly at a wad of blood-soaked cloth pressed against his stomach.

"I tried t' stop the bleeding. Tore a piece o' my cloak..." Haruda was babbling.

Nagaro swept his eyes over the meadow, so peacefully bathed in afternoon light that was as rich as liquid gold. The tumbled remains of walls running parallel to the roadway suggested the grassy expanses on either side had once been pastures, though they now appeared abandoned. He frowned. The grass grew tall and uncropped, with flowers everywhere in profusion—except where they were trampled, in a broad swath leading from the uphill edge of the meadow to the road just beyond where Pedran lay. That trampled grass must surely tell a tale.

Abruptly Tredhold stood up, drawing Nagaro's attention back to the group around the wounded man. The healer met Lord Anduar's frowning gaze and shook his head. The pain in his eyes and the set of his jaw spoke plainly even before the words were formed on his lips. "I'm sorry, My Lord," he said. "This wound is beyond a healer's skill. If ye've anything to say to him, say it quickly. He's not got much time."

Anduar gave Tred just the slightest nod before dropping to one knee beside his tracker. He took one of the man's bloody hands in his. "Pedran," he said in a voice both gentle and urgent. "Pedran, can you hear me?"

The man's eyes flickered open. His wavering gaze found his master's face. "Yes... M' Lord..." The words came with difficulty, formed around pain.

"Report, Zirda."

The eyes closed again as a spasm crossed Pedran's face. "Brandle's got... to Loros Hall. Kenthos... be there... soon."

"My Lord!" Haruda bent down urgently. "He's told me everything he knows! Ye needn't—"

Anduar cut the Turowan off with a gesture. "Well done, Pedran. You've always given me good service. You can be proud of that."

Pedran's eyes opened again, though now their gaze appeared unfocussed. "Thank ye, Lord. My wife... my sons?"

"They shall want for nothing. You have my word."

"Thank ye..." The eyes were staring up at the perfect blue sky.

Lord Anduar leaned closer, his eyes fierce. He put his other hand on Pedran's shoulder, shook him, and spoke commandingly. "Pedran! *Who did this?*"

Pedran seemed to rally as if pulled back into the world by the sharp tone of Anduar's voice. His eyes came back to focus on the lord's face. "Leithian... officer. Lothard... ordered it."

"Lothard ordered one of his officers to kill you?"

"Yes. I told him... serve you. He said it... wouldn't save me."

"I saw it all, My Lord," Haruda put in. "From the woods."

Once more Anduar motioned Haruda to silence. He shook Pedran again, and then harder, because the man was obviously drifting. "Pedran! Did you tell Lothard what you were doing here?"

"*mmh*... I said I was... tracking Kenthos. Wasn't... with him." Pedran drew a ragged gasping breath. "He... called me... liar!" Another ragged gasp.

"It's all right, Pedran. You've told me all I need to know. You can rest now."

Pedran's eyes closed. His voice scarcely audible, he murmured, "Thank ye, M' Lor'—"

The words ceased as the wounded man shuddered and grew still. Tredhold knelt down and felt for a pulse. "It's over," he said. "He's gone."

"Vothra guide his spirit in its passing." Nagaro spoke his thought. The voices of the other Kelorin present murmured an echo of his words.

For the space of half a dozen heartbeats, Lord Anduar remained kneeling, holding the tracker's hand. Then he laid the hand on the man's chest, and when he stood up his face was rigid. His hard gray gaze swept the circle of watchers, lingering on Pendrik, the Leithian Pact Signer. "You are witness to this! This tale of arrogant disregard for life and law," he said sharply. "Pedran was no fighter, and he was unarmed." Then, before any of them could respond, his glance snapped to Haruda. "*Now* it's your turn, Zirda. Tell us what you know!"

Haruda was visibly intimidated by the intensity of the Kelorin lord's gaze. "I–I was hiding in the woods, over there," he stammered, indicating the stand of trees they had ridden past. "He was comin' back t' give me news, when I saw the Leithians take him. They came down the hill—out o' the trees up there—and rode him down as he was crossin' the meadow on the road."

"You didn't go to his aid?" Lord Anduar's question was crisp.

Haruda gave him a look of agony. "It would ha' been one sword against a dozen, My Lord! And I didn't think they'd *kill* him! He was a *tracker!* An' besides, it was over in less 'n a minute. I caught some words—Pedran sayin' your name—three times. An' I heard Lothard say, '*Finish him!*' An' then the other Leithian just pulled out his sword an' ran poor Pedran through the belly, and they left him where he fell!"

"They left by way of the road?"

"Aye, Lord." Haruda wrung his hands. "He didn't want me t' leave him, Lord. If I'd only come and fetched ye! Or if I'd known what t' do for him—"

Tredhold put a hand on Haruda's shoulder. "Nothing could have saved him," he said gently. "He may only have lived long enough to speak to us because ye stayed here talking to him."

Devral coughed. "It may be too late for your man, Anduar, but there are others in need of saving."

Anduar nodded grimly. He turned to Haruda. "Find someone to take him up and bear him on their saddle bow. There's no time now to bury him with proper honor, and I won't leave him here."

Nagaro stepped forward. "I'll do it, My Lord. He's a small man, and my horse is strong, so I won't be much hindered."

For a moment it seemed that Anduar would forbid it, but then he nodded, his jaw set, his gray eyes cold as a winter sky threatening snow. "Very well. To horse!" He turned on his heel and strode away. Behind his back, the three other lords exchanged significant glances.

Nagaro looked from one to another of them. "Anduar seems really angry—" he ventured. It was something he hadn't seen before.

"Oh yes," Kuran replied grimly. "Anduar is the kind my mother always called 'slow to anger and slow to mend'. And Pedran was one of *his*."

Devral gave a dark nod of agreement, then turned and called after Haruda. "How far to Loros Hall?"

Haruda turned back long enough to answer. "No more 'n two miles as a bird flies, M' Lord."

Nagaro knelt, tugging at Pedran's cloak, trying to free enough of it to wrap around the man's body. Tredhold knelt also. "Here," he said. "Let me help ye with that."

***

Most of those last two miles to Loros Hall were afterwards a blur. Nagaro's attention was divided between keeping Thunder-Heels in his place beside Lord Anduar's mount and making sure that Pedran's body didn't slip from its position across the saddle bow in front of him. When he could spare any attention for the surrounding country, he noted tangled patches of woodland and rows of trees, interspersed with pastures and fields that, as often as not, were overgrown with weeds. Here and there were farmhouses, some tenanted, others abandoned, their desolate shadows stretching longer over the green land as the sun moved westward.

"Why so many empty houses?" He shouted the question to Lored.

The Kelorin clung to Tredhold's belt and twisted his neck to answer. "The Leithians killed all the men o' Loros or drove them off!"

"Didn't any come back?"

"Not many. Lord Endemar holds the lands open for the rest—hopin' they'll come one day."

At that moment, there were shouts as the men in the front rank caught glimpses of riders some distance ahead—some on the road, some off of it—all moving in the same direction they were going. Then, a little later, the company's rear guard cried out in alarm that they had glimpsed horsemen at a distance behind them on what had to be a stretch of the very road they were riding on. These could only be Lord Grimbold's men.

Anduar immediately pressed for more speed, then called suddenly for a halt as they passed into the shadow of a copse of trees and discovered a man's body lying in the roadway.

Nagaro, in the front rank, had to pull Thunder-Heels up sharply to keep from riding over the fallen man. A wave of anger rose in him, echoing the outraged cries of the others. The dark-haired Kelorin lay face down with an arrow in his back. From the way he'd fallen, it appeared he had been coming from the direction of Loros Hall when he'd been shot down.

Kuran dismounted and knelt by the body, turning up the dead man's face up for all to see. Lored immediately cried out in anguish, recognizing one of his companions, a man of Kildoran Wared. Nagaro felt a pang of guilt. It had been his idea to press these men into service as scouts.

Pendrik shook his head. "This is a bad business," he said. "What kind of man shoots men down like animals?"

Anduar grimaced. "One who believes that common folk warrant no respect," he said tightly.

"The poor fellow was probably bringing us news," muttered Devral. "What was it, I wonder?"

Kuran rose, and drew out the arrow, then remounted his horse with the grizzly prize. "The markings may name the bowman," he observed grimly.

Lord Anduar offered no further comment. His eyes were hard, his jaw rigid.

The Kildoran men all clamored to be allowed to bury the man, and Anduar grudgingly assented to this since he didn't wish to carry another corpse. He chose two men for the task, keeping Lored with him. "Pick a spot out of sight of the road," he told the men. "Don't let Grimbold's men catch you, and I charge you to come after us when you can do it safely."

The company rode on quickly after that. They could already hear occasional shouts from the horsemen on the road behind them.

Before long, they got their first clear glimpse of Loros Hall, a long roof and two small turrets that appeared for a time above the trees.

And a short time later, Jato abruptly rose out of a ditch on the right hand side of the road and hailed them.

Anduar instantly drew rein. Leaning down, he extended his hand to the woodsman. "Get up behind me!" he grated. "Speak as we ride."

So Jato delivered his news from the precarious perch behind Lord Anduar's saddle, and Nagaro was privileged to hear the whole exchange since he rode on the Pact Signer's left hand. Anduar's utterances were sharp and clipped. Jato's were lengthier, if slightly breathless, as he clung to Lord Anduar's belt.

"Report, Zirda!"

"There's a kind o' path, M' Lord. Leads off t' the right. Among some trees. Ye must take it!"

"Why leave the road?"

"The path goes t' the gate—of the Hall's back garden. That's where ye'll find Kenthos! Didn't the last messenger tell ye? We sent one o' the Kildoran men."

"The man's dead, Jato."

"Dead? *Hamanei!* What about Pedran, that we sent before him? Did he find ye, Lord?"

"*We* found *him*—dying of a sword wound. His corpse rides with the Captain, there."

"*Hamanei mata noa!*" Jato cast a horrified glance at the bundle that lay across Nagaro's saddle bow. "Not Pedran too! The Spirits protect us! But, turn, *turn*, My Lord! Here's the path!"

Lord Anduar gave a shout to those following even as he spurred a little ahead and turned off the road onto the path Jato had indicated. Nagaro and the other lords swung in behind him, and it soon turned out that what Jato called a 'path' was a really a kind of wooded lane where the riders could still go three abreast. The rest of the company crowded together and thundered after the front riders.

"Kenthos is at the garden gate?" Anduar continued his interrogation. Nagaro still rode on his left flank. Pendrik was on his right, while Kuran and Devral had dropped behind with Tredhold, but were close on their heels and doubtless straining their ears to catch every word.

"Aye Lord. Least he was when I came t' seek ye."

"How many with him?"

"Seven, M' Lord.That's not countin' himself an' Lord Rathdar, that's wounded."

"Where's Lieutenant Brandle?"

"Hidin' in some trees where he can watch the gate. This path 'll take ye there."

"Good. What of Lothard and Madred? Their men?"

"They've joined together and are makin' for the *front* gate, M' Lord."

"Ha! What of Lord Odus?"

"He's near, M' Lord. Him an' Lord Soren, together. Comin' down the River Road from the east."

"And Lord Therin?"

"Comin' up the River Road from the west, from what we hear, Lord. But not so near."

"Ah. Well done, Jato. And Grimbold was close behind us before we turned. It's all coming together."

The path had been cutting through the stand of trees like a cool green tunnel, and it now descended into a broad gully that opened on their left hand. It forded a stream at the bottom, and then continued along the far side of the watercourse. Anduar had to slow the pace because of the uncertain footing where parts of the stream's bank had slipped and slid onto the path. The trees dropped away on both sides of the deepening gully, and almost immediately the track plunged into a thicket of willows that grew densely along the margins of the stream.

The ground was firm there, but the willows encroached on the path so closely that the horses could only go two abreast. What with the willows and the increasing height of the streambanks, it was impossible to get any view of the surrounding terrain, which of course also meant that the company of riders was invisible to observers on the wooded land above them.

Nagaro had been forced to drop back behind Anduar and Pendrik, and if there was any more talk, he couldn't hear it. His thoughts were thus free to run. He could hear in his mind the way Anduar had said, *"It's all coming together."* The words had an ominous ring, the more so because of the satisfaction with which they'd been uttered. Nagaro had suggested days ago that both opposing parties should be represented at the finish, but the large numbers of armed men now converging on Loros Hall seemed to him to threaten trouble. *And Anduar was angry.*

"How much farther?" Pendrik's impatiently shouted query interrupted Nagaro's meditation.

"Not far, Lord!" Jato answered over his shoulder.

Looking ahead, Nagaro could make out a stand of trees on the stream's left, or east, bank—the side on which lay Loros Hall. When they came abreast of the trees, they found that the willows grew less thickly there, and the bank was less steep where the trees topped it. A narrow branch of the trail angled up this gentler bank to disappear among the clustering trunks.

Jato called for a halt, indicating they must follow this side trail, and within a minute the entire company was crowding into the stream, the horses splashing and eagerly putting down their heads to drink. The sun was well down the western sky, and both banks of the stream lay in deep shadow. Only at the very top of the eastern bank did the sun's rays brighten the pale green grass that grew among the half-exposed tree roots.

Jato slid down from Lord Anduar's horse. "Ye'd best lead the horses from here, M' Lord," he said. "Ye can't ride up in those trees 'cause the branches hang too low. Up there's where I left Lieutenant Brandle."

Anduar nodded grimly. He waited only until the horses had drunk, then told Jato to lead on.

The old Turo started up the slanting trail, the lords following one by one, leading their horses. Nagaro considered the steepness and narrowness of the path and the precariousness of the burden that lay across his saddle bow, and then went up the incline seated in the saddle, dismounting only at the top where there was just a little level ground before entering the trees.

At first there was dense undergrowth under the trees, but farther in, where light couldn't penetrate, the space under what turned out to be a grove of cedars resembled a dimly lit, many-pillared hall—but one certainly not meant for riders. Too many branches hung too low, just as Jato had said, and the trail they were following clearly had never been intended as a bridle path. Nagaro followed the horse of the man in front of him—Kuran, as it happened—through the gloom for a way, until he became aware of light ahead between the trunks.

A moment later, the trees ended abruptly as the trail passed out into a clearing about thirty feet across, encircled by trees but open above to the deep blue sky. Simultaneously Thunder-Heels' hooves rang on stone, and Nagaro looked down and saw the explanation for this treeless space. A low-domed outcropping of gray stone, nearly smooth on top, broke the surface of the soil and prevented any trees from growing. Around the edges of the stone, on several sides, grew mounds of berry brambles, the thorny canes sprinkled with white blossoms like scattered snowflakes.

The four lords had halted in the middle of the clearing. Pendrik, staring about him, exclaimed, "You could hide a small army in here!"

"Very small," Devral affirmed dryly. "Fortunately that's what we've brought."

Jato, standing at one side, nodded. "The Kildoran men call it the Stone Circle," he said. "The story goes that King Tevren an' Queen Lindra passed this way afore dawn on *that day*. Ye'd best wait here, M' Lords. I'll fetch Lieutenant Brandle." With that, he turned and disappeared between the trees that framed the continuation of the trail on the other side of the peculiar clearing.

Nagaro and Tredhold made use of the pause to carefully lift Pedran's body from the back of the gray stallion and lay it down on the smooth stone, composing the limbs. Tredhold then went to join Taru, Pavo, and Landros, who were standing together and talking in low voices. Nagaro would have joined them as well, but Anduar called to him to stand with the waiting lords instead, and a moment later, Jato reappeared accompanied by Brandle.

The Leithian's relieved expression changed to an angry frown when Anduar briefly described the death of Pedran and the finding of the slain Kildoran scout.

"This is ill," he said. "We sent several groups of Kenthos' followers out of harm's way. I thought we'd done well. And now this!" He shook his head.

Anduar's jaw clenched. His glance had daggers in it.

"Don't berate yourself, Brandle," Kuran said. "It's hardly your fault that Lothard and his lot have stooped to killing unarmed men."

"Where are Kenthos and Rathdar?" Pendrik asked impatiently.

"At the Hall. Or rather at the gate to the back garden, which is about thirty yards beyond the edge of these trees."

"What are they doing there?" demanded Devral.

"Trying to get in. It seems the gardener won't open the gate."

Anduar's gaze had been flicking from face to face. "How close are Lothard and Madred," he asked sharply.

Brandle turned to the steel-eyed Pact Signer. "If they aren't already at the Hall's front door, they soon will be, My Lord."

Anduar seemed to be holding himself on a tight rein. "When they find no one there," he said, "they'll circle the place. We have to be where we can see. Is it possible to get a troop of mounted men around between Kenthos' men and the River Road without them being seen?"

"Yes," Brandle answered. "There's an old apple orchard—one of our scouts is in it, watching for Lord Therin. You can reach it by following the path on down along the stream and then cutting across. Jato can show you."

"My Lord Devral!" Anduar turned to the other Kelorin Pact Signer. "Take your men and horses around that way and make sure Kenthos and his men don't get away. Stay out of sight as long as you can."

Devral flashed him a humorless smile. "Very good, My Lord." He turned and called to his men, drawing them after him.

Anduar raised his voice. "Those who aren't with Devral, hear me! We'll leave the horses here, under guard of one man from each contingent. The rest, form up and prepare to follow me! We'll have to spread out but stay as close together as we can. And whatever you do, keep out of sight."

# Chapter 25

# What Happened There

Anduar halted the company under the farther eaves of the trees, where the undergrowth still hid them from view. There they spread out to either side of the path, keeping well concealed. Nagaro stood with Anduar and Brandle near where the trail emerged from the cedar trees. Behind him stood the ranks of Anduar's contingent, the members of the Palace Guard, and Kenthos' followers. He was aware of Kuran to his left, with the other Fleet warriors arranged in ranks behind him. To the right of the trail, stood Pendrik with his Leithian warriors.

In front of them was an expanse of grass, cropped short as if by grazing sheep. The shadow of the cedar grove stretched across the nearer half of it, with the farther half in sunlight. About thirty yards away was the infamous garden wall, with Loros Hall looming beyond it. The apple orchard, in which Devral's men would soon be hiding, lay to the right, two hundred feet from the walled garden—southward, in the direction of the river.

The ancestral home of the House of Loros was a graceful, two-story edifice built of local stone and surrounded by small stands of oak, ash, and pine. The late afternoon sunlight picked out every detail of the high-arched windows and towers with crystalline clarity. Tall, violet-shadowed buttresses stood in sharp contrast to the silver sheen of the sunlit stonework. Where the west-facing windowpanes reflected the sun's light, they glanced like gold.

The hall's main entry faced east and was thus at the opposite end of the building. Anduar's company stood nearest to the northwest corner. They had a clear view not only of the garden wall and rear facade, but also the north flank of the building, farthest from the river, although scattered trees partially obscured it. The garden wall was plain and smooth and taller than a man. It formed three sides of a rectangle, with the rear of the Hall making the fourth side, and enclosed an area about a hundred feet square.

"They're right over there." Brandle indicated a group of men and horses clustered near the north-west corner of the garden wall where a high gate of solid wood stood between stone gateposts. "It doesn't look as if they've seen us."

This appeared to be true. Nagaro could see a man lying on the ground at the base of the wall beside the gate with several men kneeling by him. The recumbent man, he supposed, was the wounded Lord Rathdar. Another man, tall and broad-shouldered, stood motionless a few paces farther from the wall, facing the river with his head down. That would be Kenthos. The remaining half-dozen men stood between the lone man and the wall. Their stances and movements suggested uncertainty.

"This Hall has no defenses!" Vell exclaimed in obvious surprise. "Unless you count that little ring of raised earth."

The earthwork in question was little more than an undulation in the grass that appeared to encircle both the hall and the garden. It's closest approach was only a few yards from where they stood.

Remembering something that he'd read, Nagaro said, "That must be the foundation for Tevren's wall. Darion never wanted one, but Tevren lived in more hostile times. The work had gotten no further than raising a ring of earth at the time of his death." He stopped because a number of those nearby were staring at him.

Anduar smiled fleetingly. "Your information is accurate, Captain." The Kelorin Pact Signer turned his gaze eastward to sight along the hall's north flank. "Beyond those trees, I can see what looks like a body of horsemen massed at the front of the Hall," he said. "They probably don't know Kenthos is back here."

Nagaro scanned past the scattered trees and saw the gathering of men in question, at the hall's farther end. He could also make out glimpses of the road that led up to the building's front gate. As he watched, another troop of horseman appeared on that road, emerging from a larger stand of trees and moving to join the force that was already assembled.

"Whose are those?" asked Captain Ruald, who must have also seen them.

"Grimbold's." Anduar's response was clipped.

Geivian, Lored, and the other former followers of Kenthos were crowding forward, trying to see over the shoulders of those in front of them. Now Geivian spoke. "My Lord Anduar," he said urgently. "Won't you warn Kenthos and Lord Rathdar of the danger?"

"No." Anduar's response was cool. "Let the game play out."

"Look!" Kuran pointed. "Some of those Leithians are coming this way!"

About a dozen riders in the livery of Hurn Hold had detached themselves from the gathered mass and were threading between the trees, approaching at an easy trot along the inner side of the low earthwork.

Up to this point events had been unfolding slowly, but this was beginning to change. One of Kenthos' men had gone to the corner of the garden wall to look around it and he now cried, *"Stand ready! They're coming!"*

Immediately there were urgent movements among the fugitives, though the one who must be Kenthos remained where he stood. One of those who had been bending over Rathdar sprang up and began beating on the gate with his fists, shouting, *"Open in Vothra's name! They mean to kill us!"* His frantic cries carried easily across the grassy field.

The gate remained closed, but the man's cries must have been heard by the approaching horsemen because they shouted and spurred their mounts to a canter. The fugitives, in turn, must have heard *those* shouts, for they raised more cries and became visibly more agitated. One of them ran to Kenthos, clutched at his shoulder, and seemed to remonstrate with him. The words couldn't be heard, though the gestures were eloquent. The tall man raised his head, gestured vaguely at the fugitives' horses and said something indistinct, but still didn't move from where he stood. The other man gave up, retreating to Rathdar's side—just as the Leithian riders swept around the corner of the garden wall.

The Leithians rounded the corner, moving in a wide arc, reining in their horses when they saw their prey. One who appeared to be their leader shouted orders to the rest. "Spread out! Don't let them escape!" And, to another man beside him, "Ride back! Tell My Lord Lothard that we have them!"

The second man spun his horse and galloped away, even as the others maneuvered their mounts to form a semicircle around the little group of Kelorin and their mounts. Swords flashed as the Leithians drew their blades. The Kelorin, most of whom were now gathered protectively around the wounded Rathdar, drew their swords as well, holding them defensively, crouching at bay.

Kenthos turned slowly to face the Leithians. He reached hesitantly for the hilt of his sword and his hand fell upon it, but he didn't draw it.

Behind Nagaro, Lored moaned, *"Oh, My Lord!* Go to his aid! Save him, I beg of ye!"

Anduar gestured the man to silence.

The encircling Leithian riders held their places, awaiting orders. The Kelorin by the gate made a frozen tableau. Hidden under the cedar trees, Anduar's company all held their breaths.

It seemed an age, though it could not have been long, before the Leithian who had been dispatched came galloping back with Lothard riding at his side. Lothard was tall, blond, and muscular, but his handsome features were twisted in anger and he leaned forward avidly in his seat as he rode. Reaching the grassy space where his men held the fugitives cornered against the garden wall, he swung down from his big bay horse and strode towards Kenthos. His sword caught the horizontal rays of the sun as he drew it, flashing red.

"*You!*" he cried furiously. "I have you now! Stand and fight!" He stopped a dozen paces from Kenthos and came on his guard.

Kenthos swayed a little. Then he took two painful, limping steps toward Lothard. His hand faltered again on his sword hilt. The other Kelorin called to him to come back and join them, even as they drew more closely around Rathdar.

The encircling Leithians, taking their cue from their leader, dismounted and stood at their horses' heads, swords held ready.

Nagaro, watching, remembered that Lothard's men had orders to leave Kenthos for their lord to deal with. He risked a glance at Anduar. The Pact Signer's eyes were fixed on the would-be combatants, His face was set. There were angry murmurs from some of the men behind him, but Anduar raised a restraining hand.

Lothard flourished his sword impressively. "*Well?* What are you waiting for?" he demanded. "Spawn of Loros! Come and fight!"

Kenthos made no answer. He took one more unsteady step. The two men were separated by fifteen feet of greensward. Physically, they looked well-matched, being of equal height and similar build. But the way they moved told a different tale. Lothard crouched, coiled and taut, a hunting cat ready to kill. Kenthos looked like a man in a walking dream, lost, not ready for any kind of a fight.

Lothard's anger was steadily increasing at finding his intended opponent so uncooperative. "Come on, *coward!* Show some fight!" he snarled, brandishing his sword. "I'll show you what I do with men who go trampling my fields! Killing my deer! Attacking my men! I'll teach you to invade Hurn Hold with your pathetic army!"

For the first time, Kenthos spoke. "I have no army," he said dully. "I told them to go home—"

Behind Nagaro, Lored groaned. "My Lord, help him! He means to die!"

Taru's voice came, in a stage whisper. "*What're we waiting for?*"

Anduar made no verbal response, only raising his hands to indicate that no one should move.

It was at that moment that the rest of the Leithian army reached the corner of the garden wall. They pulled up at the northern edge of the semicircle formed by Lothard's men, their leaders calling for them to wait.

Nagaro picked out Lord Madred at the head of the new arrivals, on his white horse, as well as a big red-faced man whose resemblance to Bron Sobring marked him as that man's brother, Lord Grimbold.

Grimbold started to ride forward, through the ring of horsemen, but Madred called him back and the two sat on their horses, arguing, while Lothard toyed with his prey.

"Devral must not like this," Pendrik growled to Anduar, pointing to the south. "His men are coming out of the orchard. They're advancing—Wait! Therin's men are with them!"

"*Vothra's Eyes!*" Anduar swore under his breath. "And Soren's will be here soon, as well," he added, keeping his voice low. "With luck, it will take them some time to figure out what's happening." He stepped out of the trees just enough to sign to Devral to halt his advance and to hold back those who were with him.Then he spoke to his own company. "All forward! Slowly. Stay behind me, and be silent!"

So the company began to advance, out from the eaves of the cedar grove, edging towards the assembled men around the garden gate but halting again just inside the edge of the shadow cast by the cedar trees. With the dazzle of the setting sun behind them, they would have drawn few eyes even if anyone had been looking for them. As it was, none of those assembled near the gate—neither Kelorin nor Leithian—appeared to notice the movement. The men were either turned towards the garden wall, or each other, not facing the cedar grove. And their attention was focused on the drama unfolding nearer at hand.

Lothard hadn't even looked around when his two fellow lords had arrived, either not noticing or not caring. He was still inching forward, throwing taunts at Kenthos and growing angrier by the minute. "*Dog's get!*" he raged. "*Coward filth!* Where's your great House of Loros now?"

Nagaro frowned. Lothard was obviously trying to goad Kenthos into attacking him—which couldn't end well for the commoner. *And why was Anduar still holding back?*

Lothard's mention of the House of Loros must have wakened some spark in Kenthos, for he seemed for the first time to notice that his hand was on his sword hilt. Awkwardly he drew the blade, but he didn't crouch. Instead he stood, with the sword in front of him, both hands on the hilt as if to steady it. "Don't speak ill o' the House of Loros!" he said, his voice tight with emotion.

"*Ha! Yes!*" Lothard chortled in triumph. "I'll finish you, at last, you whelp!" He danced forward, narrowing the gap between them.

"*Oh, no!*" Lored groaned. "*Help him!*"

"Anduar? My Lord?" Kuran's tentative query went unanswered.

Pendrik said, "*Steady men—*"

Kenthos swayed, his sword-point weaving. Several of the other fugitives inched forward, blades up, faces desperate, resolute.

Nagaro's mind raced. *If Lothard closed with Kenthos, Kenthos would likely die. If the other men tried to avenge him, there would be more deaths. All those Leithians would be drawn in, as well as the Kelorin forces waiting.* He flicked a glance towards the orchard and plainly saw men in different liveries with naked swords, moving, stealthily. Time hung in a shifting balance. His eyes spun back to Lothard's menacing advance and Kenthos' ineffectual defense. He flicked a glance at Anduar. The Pact Signer's gaze was coldly fixed on the two men, his jaw rigid, and Nagaro felt a rising horror. *Let the game play out*, Anduar had said, and he was angry—at Lothard. Kenthos couldn't possibly defeat Edrovir's greatest swordsman, even if he weren't at the end of his strength. But if Lothard killed Kenthos—

Nagaro spoke into the thundering stillness of the moment. "We have come here to prevent bloodshed—" He was seeking confirmation. *Or contradiction—*

He received neither.

Kenthos' voice came again, across the greensward, drawing all eyes to him. "No!" he said. And then again, louder and more firmly, "*No!* I won't—" And with that, the country blacksmith opened his hands and let his sword fall to the grass. He spread his arms wide.

Lothard swore vilely in anger and stepped forward, his sword-arm cocked, the point of his blade leveled at Kenthos' unguarded chest.

Cries sprang from several quarters. Belatedly men began to move.

But Nagaro was running even before Kenthos' sword struck the ground. Sprinting across the grass, his own sword in his hand, it took just seconds for him to cross the intervening space, dodge between two of Lothard's circling Leithians, and interpose himself between the two combatants. Even as he skidded to a halt, he was turning, swinging his blade. Steel rang on steel as he struck Lothard's sword up and to the side. "*No!*" he cried in a voice that rang above the confusion. "*You shall not kill this man!*"

It had not been a disarming blow, just a turning of the blade, and Lothard recovered quickly. The point of his blade swung swiftly around to hover in front of Nagaro's face. "*Get out of my way, pirate!*" he snarled. "*Let me finish my father's work!*" Then, sidestepping Nagaro with the speed of a striking snake, the Leithian lord once more drove his blade at Kenthos, this time hard and low.

There were shouts flying all around him, a confused cacophony of sound, but Nagaro could spare none of his attention as he moved to counter Lothard's lunge. The universe consisted of himself, Kenthos, and Lothard.

Kenthos continued to stand frozen in the face of Lothard's second thrust, his arms still outstretched, his jaw slack, eyes unfocused. He looked like a man beyond reasoned thought, in a trance or on the verge of fainting. Lothard's sword would have pierced him easily if Nagaro hadn't moved as swiftly as the Leithian. His blade whipped out to catch Lothard's, deflecting it in the nick of time. "There will be no spilling of blood!" he gasped. It was just as Kuran had once told him. The man was amazingly fast, considering his size.

Lothard spun upon him. "I'll spill *yours* if you hinder me again, *mongrel!*" he screamed. "*Get out of my way!*" His face was contorted with rage. When Nagaro failed to move, the big man moved sideways around him in the other direction and leveled his sword at Kenthos a third time.

Nagaro dove between the Leithian and his prey, twisting, shielding Kenthos with his body, his sword held defensively before him. "There will be no killing! I have orders!"

"*What do I care for your bloody orders!*" This time Lothard went for Nagaro, a darting, hooking thrust, lightning-quick.

Nagaro simultaneously dodged and struck the blade down so that it bit the turf, a purely defensive stroke. *Amazingly fast, yes, but he'd be more dangerous if he weren't so angry. If he were thinking more...*

And suddenly a third sword was inserted into Nagaro's universe. Brought down decisively between the other two drawn blades as if signaling the end of a bout.

"We must have an end of this, gentlemen." Anduar's voice was like polished ice. "Be so good as to sheathe your weapons. *Now.*"

The external cacophony ceased. The universe expanded.

Nagaro drew a long breath as he straightened from his defensive crouch. A flick of his glance verified that the man on the other end of the third sword was in fact Lord Anduar, and he was suddenly aware that there were a great many more men around him, standing much closer than they had been. The sun was so low in the west as to be nearly blinding if one looked in that direction. Still, he could make out Kuran on that side, with some of the Fleet men. On the south side of the circle he saw the Lords Devral, Therin, and Soren, looking visibly shaken. On the other side, Lord Madred stood, cold and frowning, restraining a red-faced, scowling Grimbold Sobring with a hand gripping his shoulder.

Warily Nagaro stepped away from Lothard, moving two steps closer to Kenthos. He gave Anduar the barest of nods as he slid his blade back into its sheath.

Still Kenthos had not moved. He was very pale, his eyes unfocused. His arms had fallen slack at his sides, and now he staggered a little as if his legs would no longer carry him. Two of Rathdar's men suddenly appeared on either side of him, catching him, bearing him up.

Lothard had been startled out of the heat of his rage by Anduar's iciness. He seemed also to have become aware of the large number of onlookers. Still he was not a man to be easily turned from his purpose. He frowned and gestured angrily at Kenthos with his naked blade. "Am I to have no justice? he demanded. "This man invaded my Hold, made war on my people—"

"—And trampled your fields, and killed your deer. Yes, we heard what you said, My Lord Lothard." Anduar smiled a brief, tight smile that did not extend to his eyes. "But your challenge has been declined," he continued mildly. "And I have orders to bring all involved parties to stand before My Lord the King."

"I'd much rather settle it here!" Lothard scowled. "This man must be punished!"

"If punishment is required, the king will decide it. And there are likely to be complaints on both sides."

"*Both sides?*" Lothard was highly indignant. "What do you mean, *both sides?*"

Madred moved forward. "My dear Lothard," he said soothingly. "There are *always* two sides. But we can trust Elgurn to be evenhanded, can't we?"

Lothard frowned. "Well, if the king will punish him..." He shrugged and moved grudgingly to sheathe his own sword. Then his eye fell on Nagaro and his frown deepened as he leveled a finger. "*That* one must be punished too! A mere commoner—a *pirate!* He dared to interfere with me!"

Anduar gestured dismissively. "Captain Nagaro was acting on my order—under authority from Elgurn." His voice was smooth as satin, though anyone who knew him could have sensed the steel underneath. His cool gray gaze flicked momentarily to Nagaro. "Thank you, Captain. That will be all. You may return to your company."

So now he'd been acting on Anduar's order? Nagaro's resentment stirred. He didn't like being so summarily dismissed, but he checked himself, knowing it would be imprudent to show his annoyance. This had become a matter for the lords. Since he was not a lord, and had served his purpose, he was no longer to be included. He managed a bow and a salute before withdrawing.

The surrounding ring of men parted before him.

Lored suddenly appeared in front of him, grasped at his hand and pumped it, beaming with gratitude. Other hands reached out simply to touch him as more men pressed in. Kuran met his eyes with a glance of approval. Devral gave him a broad wink. Brandle saluted him.

Landros, behind them, was grinning. "Well done, lad!" he muttered as Nagaro moved past him.

He caught a glimpse of Rastian, staring at him hard with his pale eyes, and suddenly Varsyl Virden was standing in front of him with a dozen men in livery, his hand extended. Nagaro gaped at the Kelorin Lord even as he took the hand. "Varsyl?" he murmured. "They said you wouldn't come. Because you don't fight."

Varsyl smiled. Releasing Nagaro's hand, he touched the gilded hilt of a sword swinging at his hip. "I've reconsidered some things of late," he said quietly. "I think I can trust myself to fight in a good cause, but fortunately there seems to be no need to fight today—thanks to you."

Nagaro frowned. "I prevented one man from being killed," he said quickly. "And now I have to find Tredhold the healer. There are two men back there who need his services."

At this point, shouts were heard, coming from the south, beyond the garden. The shouts grew nearer and then were joined by the sound of hooves and the jingle of harness. Nagaro looked over the heads of the crowd to where the rays of the setting sun just caught the top of an approaching carriage with two men on the driver's seat.

The crowd parted as the carriage stopped barely twenty feet from where Nagaro stood. The driver mopped his brow while the horses snorted and blew. The second man, a graying Kelorin in travel-stained clothes, leaped down, and Nagaro caught a glimpse of pale eyes in a familiar face as the man moved to open the carriage door. A man stepped out of the carriage and immediately turned to hand down a well-dressed Kelorin woman in a dark blue gown and a gray traveling cloak.

Behind him, he heard Anduar's voice rise above the murmur of the astonished crowd. "Ah, here is Rastyl Korven, bringing Kenthos' mother, if I'm not mistaken. Now we'll hear the truth concerning the identity of the man's father."

The Pact Signer had scarcely finished speaking when there came more shouts from yet a different quarter.

"Look, it's Lord Odus! Come at last!"

## Chapter 26

# In The Garden

E ventually some semblance of peace descended upon Loros Hall. The
sun had set, the stars were out, and it was a fine, clear night. In the
garden, the rapidly cooling air was filled with the mutter of men's voices
and the clatter of spoons against tin cups and wooden bowls. Here and
there, the light of cooking fires flared under stately trees or between neatly
arranged flower beds. Across the garden, the top edge of the high garden
wall stood out sharply against an uneven orange glow that indicated
the presence of many similar fires on the other side of it. While nearly a
hundred men were encamped within the garden, there were many times
that number encamped outside.

Nagaro sat with his Fleet friends on the grass, eating a helping of
Rubo's very fine stew and dumplings from a wooden bowl.

"It's not fair!" Taru declared, stabbing at his dinner with his spoon.
"All those folk gettin' here when they did, and puttin' everything else out
o' men's heads. Everyone's forgotten what ye did, Nagaro."

Nagaro shrugged uneasily. "Maybe that's for the best." The memory
of the look in Anduar's eyes when he'd dismissed him kept coming back.
The more he thought about it, the more glad he was of the interruptions
that had turned everyone's attention away from him.

In fact, there had been one final arrival after Lord Odus. It had turned
out that the gardener of Loros Hall hadn't opened the gate to Kenthos
earlier because he had slipped away nearly an hour before on the only
horse still kept in the Hall's stable. Never having had a party of armed men
at the garden gate asking for sanctuary before, the poor man had ridden
off to the nearby Kildoran Hall to ask the man who paid his wages what
he should do about it. He'd returned in the company of Lord Endemar
himself, and a dozen men at arms, just as the sun had finally dipped
behind the cedar grove.

This last arrival had interrupted an impromptu interrogation of
Kenthos' mother. A great deal of discussion had ensued, and the gate had

finally been opened, along with a portion of the lower floor of the Hall. Amid the general chaos, the decision had been made to quarter the men commanded by Anduar, Pendrik, and Kuran in the garden, together with the men who were identified as Kenthos' followers. Following that, the various lords had all gone into the Hall together, and they were still there now.

Nagaro sighed. He felt sorry for the gardener. The poor man, who was obviously dismayed by the sheer number of men with swords that were invading his usually peaceful domain, had retreated behind the closed door of his tiny cottage in one corner of the garden.

"But ye pulled Lord Anduar's meat out o' the fire!" Taru persisted. "I never heard that man swear before, but today I heard it twice—once when Devral an' Therin started coming out o' the apple orchard, and once when ye started to run. He'd almost waited too long, and he knew it!"

Nagaro winced. "Did anyone else try to intervene?"

Landros grinned wolfishly. "Kuran started after ye, and Anduar went after *him*, and the rest of us pretty much followed. But Anduar wouldn't let Kuran step in—laid hands on him to keep him outside the Leithians' circle. I saw Devral, Therin, and Soren moving too, out o' the corner o' my eye, but Anduar waved them back."

"Did any of Rathdar's men try to protect Kenthos?"

Pavo raised his voice. "Two of them made move almost same time you did, Nagaro. But three Leithian warrior moved to stop them with their sword, and Rathdar's two man move back. I think they were afraid."

Landros snorted. "They should be afraid! If not of those Leithian warriors, then of Lothard Hurn. Anyone with a speck o' sense is afraid of Lothard."

Pavo's frown had been gathering as he listened. "I do not understand, Nagaro," he said. "Lord Anduar said you have act on his order when you stop Lothard—but I did not hear him give you order."

Nagaro had finished his stew. He studied the empty bowl. "He, ah, didn't—not this afternoon. In Lankura, he told us our task was to prevent bloodshed, which seemed like an order at the time, but this morning he said everything must be seen to come from him because the king had put everything in his charge."

Landros had put his plate aside and was watching Nagaro narrowly as if trying to read his expression in the glow of the firelight. "So ye took the action, and Anduar takes the credit? Is that it? Has he thanked ye, lad?"

Nagaro toyed with his spoon. "No."

"Why d'ye think he didn't order us in sooner, Nagaro?" Taru asked. "What was he waiting for?"

Nagaro was glad that the empty stew bowl gave him something to do with his hands. "He said he wanted to let it play out."

"Play out!" Landros was indignant. "Maybe he thought there'd be some other end to it, but I say Lothard would ha' killed that man if ye hadn't stopped him, sure as tides and taxes!"

A silhouetted figure loomed suddenly between them and the nearest cooking fire. It was Tredhold, come to join them. The wiry little Leithian held a bowl and spoon in one hand and carried his healer's bag in the other. He dropped the bag on the grass and sat down beside it.

Nagaro was glad to change the subject. "How are your patients, Tred?" he inquired.

"Both doing as well as can be expected." Tredhold blew on his stew. "I've just come from the Hall where I was checking again on Lord Rathdar. He took a nasty sword thrust to his thigh earlier today, and he'd had no doctoring for hours when I first looked at him. I was just making sure I'd got the bleeding stopped."

Landros stretched his legs nonchalantly. "Will he be well enough to travel tomorrow?"

"Aye, as long as Anduar doesn't set too fast a pace. When I left him, he was conscious, sitting up, and talking—which is a deal more than he was doing when I first set eyes on him."

"Ye mean to say he missed Nagaro's little demonstration?"

Tredhold nodded at Landros as he swallowed a mouthful of stew. "Most of it. But don't worry. I gave him the details, and at least *he* seems grateful."

Nagaro shifted his seat on the grassy turf. "What about Xenthos, Tred? He seemed pretty dazed—and in pain."

The healer grimaced. "There's a wound in his side that looked pretty ugly when I first saw it. But I got it cleaned up and properly dressed, and he should be all right—physically, at least." Tredhold paused to give his attention to his dumpling.

"What do you mean, *physically?*"

Tred's spoon came to a halt halfway to his mouth. "The wound should heal, but I can't answer for the state of his mind. He thought he was going to die and had worked himself into a kind o' trance from anxiety, I think, waiting for the stroke to fall. When I first started working on him, I wasn't sure he even understood what I was saying. He came out o' that, some, as I talked to him, but I got fewer than a dozen words out of him all together. Then they let his mother talk to him, and she was in tears—putting her arms around him and begging him to forgive her for not having told him the truth about his father, and so on—but he, well, he hardly seemed to respond."

Nagaro frowned. "Where is he now?"

"They're holding him over there under that great oak tree." Tredhold pointed with his spoon. "Well, not *holding* him, exactly. He's not a prisoner. But they don't want him going anywhere, and they're not letting his followers get near him."

Landros leaned forward. "Can ye tell us what the lords are talking about in the Hall, Tred? Did ye catch any bits o' news from the big fish?"

Tredhold grinned. "A few," he admitted, "since they'd put Rathdar's couch close enough for him to be part of it. I think Lothard's starting to find things a bit hotter than he'd like. I walked into an argument about whether there was a challenge or not, and whether it was refused. And then Lord Anduar started going on about Pedran."

"*Ah-ha!*" Landros grinned maliciously. "What did Lothard have to say about *that?*"

"He's making it out to have been a *misunderstanding*—though he's mostly keeping his mouth shut and letting Madred do the talking. But there's more news." Tredhold glanced significantly around the circle of faces. "There's going to be one new grave dug and one old grave opened in this garden tomorrow morning."

Taru frowned. "The new one will be for Pedran, but what's the *old* one?

Nagaro drew a breath. "The place by the wall where the earth was turned," he said softly.

Landros slapped his thigh. "The place where Tevren is supposed to have buried his son! Endemar always swore the babe was buried here, but there's others say the grave is empty."

"Aye," Tredhold affirmed. "Ye've guessed it."

Nagaro shook his head. "I'm surprised Endemar would allow it."

"Well he didn't look very happy," Tredhold admitted. "But he seems to see the need of showing who's right—him, or men like Rastyl and Rathdar. Having Edroviran blood spilt because some men think the heir of Loros is still alive seems to have convinced him."

"Well," observed Taru, with a yawn. "With all that digging going on, I guess we won't be getting an early start for Lankura tomorrow."

"And a good thing too." Landros was grinning. "I'm a sailor, not a horse-soldier. I've been in the saddle far too much o' late for my liking."

"An' I could use a good night's sleep, for once."

"Aye, and a hot breakfast!"

Nagaro sighed. The conversation had digressed to trivial matters. He stood up. "If you're all finished," he said. "I'll take back the bowls and spoons."

***

Nagaro handed the dishes to the dishwashing crew at the cook-fire and was turning to go when Rubo called after him, "Do ye fancy a cup o' hot sothiril, Capt'n?"

"Sothiril? Of course, Rubo." He took a closer look. "Why, that's a proper teapot you've got to brew it in. Where on earth did that come from?" The pot was a large one, finely but simply wrought of red-brown earthenware.

Rubo grinned conspiratorially. "I wheedled it out o' the gardener, Capt'n, but it ain't his. All he had was a little one, living all alone as he does. This one came from *that* house over there." Rubo pointed across the garden in the direction of the river to a place where there was a mass of trees and shrubbery. A bit of wall showed amid the foliage, and the firelight glanced off the panes of a window. Rubo lowered his voice to a whisper. "That there's the house what Lord Nevrath built for Princess Minowei. And *this*," he raised the teapot from which he'd just poured a cup, "must ha' been Minowei's teapot! The cups too."

Nagaro closed his hand almost reverently around the cup. He was holding a little bit of history and the thought sent a shiver up his spine. The cup clearly matched the teapot, unadorned, but finely crafted. "Minowei's cups and sothiril pot," he murmured. "I hope you're being careful with them, Rubo."

"O'course I am!" Rubo was affronted. "They're on loan for tonight, an' I'll see 'em back where they belong tomorrow morning, safe an' sound!"

Nagaro took a sip of sothiril. His eyes strayed to the spreading oak tree where Tredhold had said that Kenthos was to be found. Tred's words about Kenthos' state of mind came back to him.

"Can you pour a second cup, Rubo? There's someone I'd like to share it with."

"It'll be a pleasure, Capt'n."

A moment later Nagaro was threading his way across the garden towards the oak tree with a cup of sothiril in each hand. The two men nearest the tree were presumably supposed to be keeping an eye on Kenthos, though they were sitting a dozen feet away where the light was better. They wore the uniform of the Palace Guard and were sitting cross-legged. Their two heads, one blond and the other raven, were bent over a game of King's Men played with marked pebbles on a board that looked like a handkerchief with squares drawn on it. When Nagaro drew close, the Leithian raised his head and Nagaro saw that it was Brandle Furthing.

"I thought I would try talking to Kenthos. I've brought him some sothiril." Nagaro held up one of the cups.

Brandle shrugged and waved a hand vaguely. "Go ahead, Captain," he said. "Maybe for you he'll stop acting like a stunned rabbit."

Kenthos was sitting propped up against the trunk of the oak in a position that was made a little more comfortable by a pair of very dilapidated leather saddle bags. He was awake, but staring at nothing. He looked up in a startled, worried way when Nagaro loomed over him.

"Would you like a cup of sothiril?"

Kenthos gave him a glance of pure amazement, as if surprised at being asked. He nodded. "Yes, I... Thank you." He extended his hand to take the cup. The movement was hesitant but the grip seemed steady.

Looking down as he released the cup, Nagaro noticed a spoon and bowl on the ground beside Kenthos. Both were polished clean. "Did you like the stew?" he inquired in an effort to keep up the conversation.

Kenthos had both hands around the cup now. He regarded Nagaro over the rim of it. "Yes..." He spoke the word as if relinquishing it, but the single syllable seemed to pull others hesitantly after it. "I–I haven't been hungry. But tonight it... tasted good."

The answer raised questions, but Nagaro merely shrugged. "That would be the magic of Rubo's cooking," he said with a smile he hoped was encouraging. "Nobody makes stew and dumplings like Rubo." He gestured at a patch of turf beside the empty bowl. "May I sit?"

This query elicited a wary look, but Kenthos nodded an uncertain affirmative.

Nagaro sat down and drew his knees up in front of him. He made a show of taking a sip of sothiril, then rested the cup on one knee and gazed out across the garden.

The silence lengthened.

"It's a beautiful garden," he ventured at length. "You can't tell so easily in the dark, but I saw enough of it before the light faded. It would be peaceful, too, if it weren't for all the men in it. It will be quite lovely, I think, in a few hours when the moons rise above the trees." He paused and lifted his cup for another sip.

Still there was no response from Kenthos.

"I'm glad to have had the chance to see Loros Hall," he continued. "I've read a little bit about it. The big building was built by Darion, of course. It was dedicated to the people of Loros Wared and was intended to be the seat of the lords of the Wared. I knew it was built on the site of Nevrath's homestead, but I didn't realize the original house was still here. I've just been told it's that building over there. You can barely make it out through the trees." He motioned with his cup.

Kenthos moved beside him. "Why are ye talking to me?" he asked. "And who *are* ye? I thought I saw ye... out there. Were ye the one who—" The words came to a halt in embarrassed silence.

Nagaro turned to meet the other man's eyes. "I'm called Nagaro," he said easily, and took advantage of the moment to study Kenthos' face more closely. The man was handsome, gray-eyed, and black-haired. The young blacksmith was also very much in need of a shave, though the incipient beard was coming in so evenly that it did little to spoil his looks.

The gray eyes now went wide. "*Ye're* Captain Nagaro?"

Nagaro shrugged again. "Yes."

Kenthos' hands began to shake, and he nearly spilled his sothiril. "*Oh Vothra!*" he murmured. "The healer said it was Captain Nagaro that turned the sword aside, but I didn't believe him! I–I mean—what are ye doing here? I thought ye wanted nothing t' do with me. And, and... ye're so *famous!*"

Nagaro had to laugh. "So are you, if it comes to that."

"Not like *you!*"

Nagaro heaved a sigh. "I'm just a man, Kenthos. I do what I can with what I'm given, and other men make more of it than they should."

At this Kenthos cast him a look that clearly said he knew how *that* went. Then the blacksmith took a long drink of sothiril and came up for air frowning. "I–I suppose I should thank you. For saving my life."

Nagaro's brow furrowed. "I suppose that depends on how glad you are to have been saved," he said. "If dying was what you intended, then I may have done you a disservice."

When there was no immediate response to this, he remembered Anduar's words, and added, "You asked what I was doing here. I'm part of the force of men under Lord Anduar's command. We were sent here with orders to prevent more bloodshed. And as for wanting nothing to do with you, what I said was that I wanted nothing to do with a cause that involved men of Edrovir killing one another."

"Oh." Kenthos looked at the ground. "We didn't set out planning to do that—killing, I mean. At least I didn't. But when it seemed that some o' the Leithians wanted t' kill *us*, we, well, we decided t' fight back." The young blacksmith paused, still not meeting Nagaro's gaze. Several seconds ticked by. Finally he said in a low voice, "I thought I was going to die—out there. I didn't *want* to. And I *don't* want to. But if I have to die anyway, I thought a sword thrust would be quick, and then it'd be over. Is hanging quick, d' ye think?"

Nagaro stared at the other man. If Kenthos believed he had only been spared one death to face another, it went a fair way to explaining why he was so subdued. "Is that what you think?" he asked. "That they're going to hang you?"

This time Kenthos earnestly raised his eyes to meet Nagaro's. "Yes."

"Why do you think they would do that?"

The other man sagged, hanging his head over his sothiril. "For pretending to be Darion's heir," he said miserably. "And for riding about the country with an army. And for killing those men."

"Are you truly guilty of all those things?"

This brought Kenthos' head back up again, frowning. "Well, maybe not *all* o' them, but they'll say I am, so it's the same thing."

Nagaro sighed. "Maybe you should tell me what you actually *did*. And what you were trying to do."

For a moment Kenthos just stared at Nagaro. Then he took another gulp of sothiril and sat staring into the dark liquid in the cup.

"I, well, the first thing I did wrong was listening to old Abeidos. I can see now that it was a mistake, but when he first came 'round—talking about me being Darion's heir, and gathering all the scattered men so the House of Loros could rise again, and everything, it all sounded so wonderful. I thought it was true—or I hoped it was—because I wanted to make all those other things happen. And I know men kept joining us because they thought I was the heir, like Abeidos said. And o' course, now everybody knows that Abeidos was wrong. I'm not the heir, and I didn't bring back the House o' Loros, either. And Abeidos is dead. There's nothing left o' the dream. An' they're surely going to hang me! I wish I'd never listened to him! I wish he'd found somebody else!"

The blacksmith's broad shoulders shook. "And there's my poor Saminda—that I just married. She didn't want me t' go! She was afraid I'd come t' harm, an' she was right! *Oh Vothra*, I wish I could see her again! To tell her I'm sorry!"

For the space of several heartbeats Nagaro considered the bowed head. It was amazing how such a big man could seem so small and defeated. "Kenthos," he said at last, "*Thinking* you're someone, when you aren't, isn't the same thing as *pretending* to be him."

Kenthos made a choking sound. He gestured distractedly. "That's just words."

Nagaro shook his head. "No," he said patiently. "This isn't just words. This is about what's *true*. They're not going to hang you for being honestly mistaken about who your father was, and it shouldn't make any difference to that judgement whether you're a commoner or high-born. As far as I know, it's not a capital offense."

The other man's head came up. "A *what?*"

Nagaro sighed. "A crime punishable by death. There aren't very many. Have you committed murder? Or treason?"

Kenthos looked bewildered. "There were those men that died..."

"Did you kill them yourself, or order them to be killed?

Kenthos frowned. "Most o' the time, Abeidos gave the orders—or Lord Rathdar. But when all of the Leithians came charging at us with their swords drawn, I told the men t' stand and defend themselves." He paused. "And I think I killed two o' them. There was one I stuck my sword through, and the one I cut in the throat. I–I'm pretty sure they both must ha' died."

"But they were attacking you with swords when you went against them—and they knew how to use those weapons," Nagaro persisted. "Did you ever kill unarmed men?"

"Of course not!" Kenthos' frown deepened. "If they'd been unarmed, it would ha' been *wrong!*"

"And did you ever attack them first?"

"Well... maybe once—because we were trying t' go south by the road, to get here t' Loros Hall, an' they blocked our way. But that was after there'd already been a few fights. We weren't trying to make trouble, but they seemed t' think we were."

Nagaro nodded in satisfaction. "So mostly it was either a fair fight or it was defending yourselves while trying to freely travel the roads. That really doesn't sound like murder to me."

Kenthos' mouth was hanging open. After a moment he gulped some more sothiril to cover his confusion. Then he swallowed visibly. "What about treason, then?" he asked warily.

Nagaro considered. "That would be either betraying Edrovir to her enemies or plotting to overthrow the rightfully appointed ruler. Were you planning to try to cast Elgurn down and set yourself up as king?"

"*No!*" Kenthos shook his head emphatically. "I never wanted that! There was some talk about it, I know, but I set the men straight every time I heard them say it."

Nagaro spread his hands. "No murder. No treason. If you've told me the truth, you haven't done anything that would give them cause to hang you."

Once more Kenthos gaped at him. "But... what about Lord Lothard? He was going t' *kill* me!"

Nagaro's teeth flashed in his feral smile. "Lothard is not the King of Edrovir." Then he sobered. "You *are* going to have to stand before King Elgurn—and probably the Council—and tell your story."

Kenthos looked panic-stricken. "I can't tell all o' this t' the King and his Council!" "They'd never believe me!"

"Are there people who will confirm it? Who will back your story?"

"Well, I–I think so. Lord Rathdar, and any o' the men that were with us..."

Nagaro drew a breath. "Then you can do this," he said firmly. "You have to. Just tell them the truth. Be respectful, but don't let them intimidate you. Remember that you have a right to be heard."

"Just tell them the truth?" Kenthos looked as if he were having some difficulty coming to grips with the idea.

"That's what I've always tried to do. It's worked fairly well for me—most of the time, anyway."

"Tell the truth—about the dream we had? About making Loros a Wared again? And choosing a new lord? Ye don't think they might still let us *do* it, do ye?"

Nagaro frowned. "I don't know," he said seriously. "Lord Endemar is only holding Loros Hall and the lands around it under stewardship. If enough men of Loros Wared could have been found, after Tevren's death, to choose a new lord, Endemar would have stepped aside, I'm sure. It's been twenty-seven years now, but the law hasn't changed. If there are enough men and women who are descendants of the folk of Loros Wared and who want to come back, and they choose a lord, the same principle should still apply. It's a fine dream, and it seems to me worth trying."

This time Kenthos sat staring across the garden, his gaze focused inward. "*By the Eyes,*" he murmured. "If this is *true*... If we could still do it after all—" He turned back to face Nagaro. "It's surely too wonderful to be true," he said. "But even if it isn't *all* true, if I am to live, it's enough to have seen this place and be able to go home t' my wife. It's more than enough." He paused, then added, "Thank you, Captain Nagaro, for saving me!"

Nagaro swallowed past a tightness in his throat. "You are more than welcome. And I was just following orders, remember?" He looked away, letting the silence flow in between them. Nothing appeared to have changed around them. The glows of the cooking fires still punctuated the night. Men were still going about their appointed tasks. Brandle and his fellow guard still had their heads bent over their makeshift game of King's Men.

At last he drew a breath and said, "And you've found out who your father really was. How does that feel?"

Beside him, Kenthos sighed. "Oh yes," he said, with quiet joy in his voice. "Even before ye told me all these wonderful things, I was thinking that at least I'd been given that before the end—so I wouldn't have t' die not knowing." He sighed again and it was a sigh of contentment. "My father was the son o' the blacksmith of Loros Hall. He lived in the village, not half a mile from here, and he would ha' wed my mother an' been the blacksmith o' *this* place in time, like his father before him if he hadn't died fighting the Leithians after they killed Tevren."

Nagaro nodded. He already knew the story that Kenthos' mother had told to Anduar outside the gate where everyone could hear. "So she had made up a different tale?" he ventured.

"That's right," Kenthos' eyes shown in the darkness. "To protect me, because the Leithians were hunting down and killing any son of Loros Wared they could find. She told a tale about a passing stranger that took her against her will." Kenthos paused. He drew a long breath and went on in tones not quite so glowing. "And she fled to Irvenen and met the man she finally married. She didn't want t' ask him to raise me—the child of another man she'd loved before him. So she fostered me to a blacksmith and his wife, so I'd be brought up in my father's trade."

Nagaro sat frowning. "And she didn't tell you the truth until today? That seems hard. The danger was surely long past, and you would have kept the secret. And if she'd told you the truth, you probably wouldn't have listened to Abeidos."

Kenthos shifted in the dark. "She said she was sorry," he said defensively. "She said it got harder t' tell the truth the longer the lie had lain there. She cried on my neck and said she knew it wasn't right. It's not as if she didn't care about me, after all. She came to see me twice a year 'til I was twelve, and once a year after that 'til I was seventeen."

Nagaro stared across the garden. The fires were beginning to burn down and the night seemed darker. The camp was growing quiet. "Well," he said, "at least you know the truth now. I'm glad for you."

Again the silence stretched. This time it was Kenthos who finally broke it. "The tales I've heard say that ye don't know who either your father *or* your mother was. Is that true?"

"Yes." Nagaro could feel the other man's eyes on him, but he didn't turn.

"Ye've no idea at *all?*"

Nagaro shrugged. "I have some hints," he said cautiously. He felt that Kenthos had earned a little confidence, though he knew he should be careful what he said. "There's a chance the woman I called my Lady Guardian was really my mother. She had a lover, who was slain. But she always said that she wasn't my mother. Her lover was a minstrel from Irvenen Wared. The man was no swordsman, and I have no music in me. I just don't know." He sighed. "It's likely I was born out of wedlock, though, the same as you.

"Maybe ye're another son o' Loros Wared," Kenthos suggested. "Maybe your real mother fostered ye t' hide ye, just as mine did."

This time Nagaro did turn to meet the other man's eyes. "I'd like to believe that," he said. "But if she did, she never came to see me—not once in seventeen years—" He caught himself, frowning at the slip, and added, "I prefer to think that both my parents are dead. It's easier."

"Well that could be true, too, if they were from Loros Wared." Kenthos didn't seem to want to give up his idea. "The Leithians killed a lot o' men. And women can die. And there seem t' be children of Loros Wared scattered all across the land."

Nagaro frowned, suddenly remembering. "Do you know," he said, "I met a Turowan woman not long ago who said she came from Loros

Wared. She told me there are some women among her people who keep in their memories the histories of all the scattered people of Loros. She knew your name, and that your mother was a serving woman at Loros Hall. She said you were born in Irvenen Wared, but gotten in Loros. Your mother must have guarded her secret well, though, because this woman didn't know who your father was. She just said it could not have been Tevren because he would never have been untrue to Lindra."

"That's amazing!" Kenthos was obviously impressed. "What did she say about you?"

Nagaro shrugged. "She seemed to think it possible that my parents came from Loros, but she didn't say she *knew* it. She seemed very sure about you."

"Oh." Kenthos sounded disappointed.

"It doesn't really matter, since I'm not likely to ever find out for certain." Nagaro stood up. "If you're finished, I'll take your dishes back to the cooks."

"Oh. Yes." Kenthos handed up his cup, bowl, and spoon, eyeing the bowl a bit wistfully.

Nagaro took the bowl, putting both cups and the spoon into it. "If you're still hungry, I could ask Rubo if there's any more stew and have someone bring you some if there is."

Kenthos nodded eagerly. "Would ye please? And thank ye for everything."

Nagaro grinned. "I'd offer to get you more sothiril too, but I'm afraid Rubo has to wash the cups and return them. They came out of Nevrath's house."

He left Kenthos staring after him in open-mouthed astonishment.

As he moved towards the fire, a woman suddenly emerged from the shadows and stepped up to him.

"I'll take those cups, Zirda," she said. "There's no need for you to wash them, since I can do that myself, and I'd hate to see them chipped." There was a smile in her voice as she said it.

He could see that she was Kelorin by the paleness of her face and the darkness of her hair, and by her voice she wasn't young. But that was all he could be sure of in the dark. He held out the cups. "Was it you that lent them to the gardener?" he asked. "The cups and the teapot that goes with them?"

He heard her draw a startled breath, and she moved around him a little, as if to let the light from the nearby fire illuminate his face. The movement allowed him to see her better, too, as her face and form were lit in profile. He saw narrow Kelorin features, the lines on her brow, and that her hair was caught loosely at the back of her head. But what struck him was the way she was looking at him, as if she would devour his face with her eyes. *"Is this him?"* she breathed.

Nagaro frowned. "Were you seeking someone, Zirdyn?"

She appeared flustered for an instant, but then quickly smiled. "I was seeking Lindra's tea set," she said, taking the two cups from his hands. "But I confess I also hoped to catch a glimpse of the man everyone is talking about."

"Kenthos? He's back there. Under the oak tree." Nagaro gestured in the direction from which he had come.

She barely glanced in the direction he had indicated, and her eyes came immediately back to his face. "Oh," she said. "And you would be—?"

He tried not to frown again. "I'm called Nagaro."

"The one who frees slaves," she murmured. "Of course." She nodded a satisfied sort of nod. "My name is Theseline. I help to keep Minowei's house in order, and I'm glad to have met you, Captain Nagaro."

"Well met, Tira Theseline," he said, and gave her a small bow, then watched as she turned and walked away—not toward the oak tree, but in the direction of the house that Nevrath had built. Perhaps, he thought, she meant to return the cups to their place and then come back to collect her glimpse of Kenthos. He shook his head and went to tell Rubo why he couldn't return the cups.

After satisfying himself that Kenthos would get his second helping of stew, he turned his back on the cooking fire and came up short when he saw that Lord Anduar was standing just outside the ring of firelight, watching him intently.

"I've been looking for you, Captain." Anduar's tone was curt, his words clipped. "Walk with me. I wish to speak with you."

"Yes, My Lord." Nagaro fell in beside Anduar with a sense of deep misgiving.

The Pact Signer chose to take an un-peopled path through the dark garden, giving him a sharp glance. "So. Once again you've found your opportunity."

"I don't understand, My Lord."

Another sharp look stabbed him. "Don't pretend you don't know what I am talking about," he said coldly. "There may have been a great many distractions this afternoon, but men won't forget what they saw: Captain Nagaro saving the life of the heir of Darion at the very gate of Loros Hall. That's how the tale will be told, and I won't be surprised if it spreads to every corner of Edrovir within a week."

Nagaro frowned. "Kenthos is not the heir of Darion."

Anduar gestured his annoyance. "Would-be heir, then. It doesn't matter. The point is, I brought you here, together with an assemblage of carefully chosen men—some of them very important men—for the purpose of bringing this matter to a conclusion, openly and visibly, under the auspices of the King of Edrovir. And what will be remembered? Another of *your* exploits, Captain. Assuring that your legend continues to grow."

Nagaro stopped dead in the darkness under the trees. "My Lord Anduar," he said, his voice tight with anger. "For a man as intelligent as you plainly are, it sometimes astonishes me how little you understand."

Anduar stopped also, turning to face Nagaro. In the shadows under his brows, his eyes reflected the ruddy glow of one of the distant fires. "You think I'm mistaken about what the people of Edrovir will make of what you did today?"

Nagaro sighed. They were quite alone where they stood. It was too dark to make out the other man's expression. "I don't know about that," he said quietly. "But you're very much mistaken if you think it's what I intended. I have said that I acted on orders, and I will continue to say it."

There was a little pause.

"Very well, then." Anduar's tone suggested he was not completely mollified. "I suppose I must accept that. But tell me, Captain, did you hear me tell everyone to stay behind me, when we stepped out of the cedar grove?" The Pact Signer's voice was level in its pitch, but edged none-the-less.

"Yes, My Lord." Nagaro met the glint of Anduar's eyes with a steady gaze.

"And I didn't order you to turn Lothard's sword aside. Yet that's what you did. Exactly what order were you following?"

Still Nagaro held the other man's eyes. "The one you gave us three days ago in Lankura when you told us our task was to prevent further bloodshed," he answered evenly. "I thought it encompassed the entire mission, and I understood it to come from the king."

"I see. Did you stop to consider the possible consequences of acting as you did?"

Nagaro frowned in the darkness. "If one stops too long to consider, My Lord, the chance for action is lost."

"Is that what you imagine *I* did?" Anduar's words were spoken coolly enough, but it seemed to Nagaro that an unwary man might be cut on them.

"It would be more charitable than imagining that you meant to sacrifice Kenthos' life, My Lord," he said calmly. "Although that possibility has also occurred to me."

This time there was no pause, and the other man's fire-lit eyes seemed to drill into him. "What perhaps did not occur to you, Captain," Anduar began, in the tone of one instructing an erring pupil, "is that, had Lothard slain a man who plainly couldn't defend himself—showing his true character in front of several lords and a few hundred witnesses—he would have compromised his honor. The King and Council could then have censured him for dishonorable conduct, undermining his standing among the Leithians and weakening support for the Brothers of the Blood."

Nagaro frowned. "But Kenthos' death would have been unjust, My Lord, and one shouldn't justify what is unjust by what is convenient. I have spoken with him. And from what I can see, he meant no harm to Edrovir by anything that he did. He and his men may have defended themselves rather aggressively at times, but they apparently were not the initial aggressors."

"He's only one man, Captain, and he was prepared to die." The two fire-lit sparks were unblinking. And the answer was cool to the point of cold-bloodedness.

Nagaro felt a wash of ice in his stomach, followed by a hot surge of outrage. "So was I, in the hands of the Emperor of the Mahuk Baar, My Lord! Yet I was spared, and I was very glad to be! Kenthos has a mother to grieve for him. And did you know that he has a new wife waiting for him in Irvenen Wared?"

Now the two sparks faltered and shifted as if the other man had blinked or looked away and back again. "No." The coolness was gone. "I'd heard nothing about a wife. Still, I think we may have cause to regret that you acted on your high principles today, Captain—just as you placed last year's mission in jeopardy by acting on your principles at Osfaraad."

Nagaro felt a shadow on his heart. He looked at the ground, but then raised his eyes. "My Lord," he said, "We can never know what would have happened had we done differently, but we still must choose how to act. A year ago at Osfaraad, I thought I could save all of my men without affecting the course of the mission. But the mission was affected—because I put too much trust in the honor of a man whose honor hadn't been proven to me—and young Peldred paid the price for my mistake. I will always carry his death on my conscience. I can't undo my action, but I can strive to build a better house on that bloodied foundation. If I have done harm this day, I'll do whatever I can to mitigate it."

He paused, then added, "But if Lothard *had* killed Kenthos, and *that* news had spread the length and breadth of Edrovir—that a Leithian had hunted down and slain a son of Loros Wared at the very gate of Loros Hall, as you put it—and the agents of the king had failed to prevent it, then surely passions would have been inflamed on the Kelorin side. You might have brought Lothard down and yet we still might have found ourselves closer to war."

He heard an indrawn breath as he stopped speaking, and the twin glimmers of firelight went out as Anduar bowed his head.

"*Vothra's Eyes, you're right,*" Anduar murmured. After a moment, he added, "And it shames me that I had to hear those words from you before the thought could enter my brain. I've been too preoccupied with Pedran's slaying—and with knowing that, when all this over, I must bear the news to his wife and sons. *Now let me think.*"

Nagaro caught the movement of the other man's form and the crunch of his boots as Anduar took three paces away, turned, and came three paces back. "Here is a conundrum," he muttered. "Lothard has been prevented from making a serious mistake, but he's also been thwarted in his desire. Madred will try to instruct him in the path of wisdom, but how apt will the pupil prove? And even if Lothard claims he meant only to frighten Kenthos, or wound him, his actions have seemed to belie that. On the other hand, the Kelorin Faction have had their supposed heir of Loros exposed as a fraud, but the man has been saved from falling to Lothard's sword. The balance is delicate. What must be found is a way to punish both sides for the spilling of blood, but not too heavily, and as equally as possible—"

Anduar stopped, and his gray eyes caught the firelight again as he returned his gaze to Nagaro. "It seems that once more, Captain, you have shown that you are a thinking man as well as a man of action. It's a useful combination. But I also see that Kuran was right to warn me that you can't be kept on a short chain. What would you have done if I had explicitly ordered you not to interfere?"

Nagaro heaved a sigh. "I'm very glad you didn't, My Lord. I wouldn't like to defy you, but I'm not made of such stuff that I can watch a man who isn't defending himself be slaughtered and not try to prevent it. For the future, If you don't want me to follow my conscience, I suggest you not include me in the mission."

"*Ha!*" It was a short, barking laugh. "And still far too honest! Yet I continue to like you in spite of it, Captain." Anduar scarcely paused before adding, "There will be Pedran's burial tomorrow at first light, and another event to follow. I want you there for both, but not too prominently, do you understand?"

"Ah, yes, My Lord, I think I do."

"Good. Do you have watch tonight?"

"Second watch, yes."

"Very good. Go get some sleep. I have matters to discuss with several others."

And with that, Anduar turned on his heel and was gone, leaving Nagaro to make his own way along the dark paths of the garden to the place where the men of the Royal Fleet had settled for the night. He found the workings of Anduar's mind too divergent from his own to fully fathom. It was a relief to be back in Anduar's good graces, even if he wasn't comfortable with how it had come about. It seemed that the Pact Signer had indeed been focusing his formidable mental powers on punishing Lothard. Now that he'd seen the error in this, he was taking a broader view, which was at least an improvement.

Rubo had finished banking the fire for the night. Its light had sunk to a ruddy glow. Taru, Pavo, and the others had already found themselves places to sleep. Nagaro fetched his cloak and blanket from his saddlebag and found a place beside his friends. To Taru's murmured question he replied vaguely that he had talked to Rubo and Kenthos at some length and then gone walking. He would have to decide what, if anything, he should say about Lord Anduar in the morning.

He awoke several hours later, a little before his watch, to find the garden bathed in moonlight. Every blade of grass, every leaf and flower, was limned in silver. Perhaps it was the light that had wakened him, for he could see from where he lay that the two moons had only just risen clear of the trees that overarched the house that Nevrath had built for Princess Minowei. He lay gazing up at the moons. Naru's palely glimmering shape, almost a full circle, trailed Talebra's brilliant orb by only a few lengths. So Kroneg would soon catch Lissafel, according to the Leithian legends. Nagaro frowned. Talebra was clearly larger than Naru, so when Naru passed in front, the bright moon would show around the edges. So Lissafel would hold Kroneg in her embrace, until Naru moved on and Kroneg broke free. But during the span of that embrace, what message would the world of men take from that image of interlocking light and dark?

Darkness and light... War and peace...

Nagaro shook off the spell. He could see Haruda coming to tell him it was time to change the watch. With a yawn he stood up and drew his cloak around his shoulders.

# Chapter 27

# The Place By The Wall

The dawn was dimmed by a low-hanging canopy of cloud, and a faint mist drifted among the flower beds and stone-paved pathways of the garden of Loros Hall. The trees were gray ghosts with arms uplifted. There had been a heavy dew. The grass was soaked with it and water dripped from the leaves of rose, lilac, and jasmine. The slightly more luminous gray of the clouds to the east suggested that the sun had risen, though it remained shrouded by the overcast. Among the bushes beside the central path, the long, slender farusia blossoms hadn't yet sensed the sun and remained tightly furled.

A group of about two dozen men gathered near the garden's northern wall where the grass was marred by a long, narrow hole with a fresh pile of earth beside it. The two diggers, men in Lord Endemar's livery, must have begun their work by predawn light. They'd finished only moments before and now stood on the dew-drenched turf with their heads bowed over their shovels beside the corpse that had been laid out next to its final resting place. All the lords who had converged on Loros Hall the previous afternoon were present for the burial—Kelorin or Leithian, partisan or not. Lord Anduar was presiding, and his influence was such that none of them had dared to be absent.

The other three Pact Signers, Pendrik, Devral, and Odus, flanked Lord Anduar while the representatives of the Kelorin Faction, Therin, Soren, and Rathdar, were grouped behind them. The wounded Lord Rathdar was leaning on Therin's shoulder. Lothard, Grimbold, and Madred, representing the Leithian Faction, stood together, as far from the open grave as they felt they dared. The demeanor of the three Leithians betrayed varying degrees of disdain for the proceedings. The remaining four lords, Kuran, Rastyl, Varsyl, and Endemar, were scattered about the fringes of the gathering.

Jato and the other trackers crowded forward, close to the grave's edge, to honor their fallen comrade. There were also a number of other men whom Anduar had hand-picked from those under his command. Nagaro was one of these, the others being Brandle, and the three Fleet captains, Vell, Landros, and Ruald. And lastly, Nagaro had brought Haruda because the latter had wanted to come. Lord Anduar had raised an eyebrow at this, but had made no objection.

Anduar knelt beside Pedran's body. His hands moved deliberately, parting the edges of the fabric of the cloak that wrapped the dead man and carefully removing three objects from the body: the belt with its buckle in the shape of an oak leaf, a small hunting knife in a plain leather sheath. and a carved stone pendant bearing the Sign of Vothra that had lain on Pedran's cold breast, strung on a simple leather cord. The Pact Signer gently drew the cloak back over the still form, then took the objects in his hands and rose.

"These things I will take," he said in a voice that was low, but loud enough for all to hear. "I'll carry them to Pedran's wife and his two sons, so they will have something to keep in remembrance of their husband and father. For myself, I will hold in my memory the image of his face in the last moments of his life and the words he spoke to me. His death was wrong, and I will not rest until that wrongness has been in some measure redressed."

Nagaro, standing unobtrusively in the second rank, glanced at the three members of the Leithian faction, gaging their reaction. He saw a flicker of annoyance briefly displace Lothard's supercilious sneer. The man's expression suggested that he considered Anduar's concern over a mere tracker to be nothing but political posturing. Grimbold, already scowling, scowled a little harder. Only Madred managed to show no reaction. His chiseled aristocratic features were fixed in an expression of solemn attentiveness, though to Nagaro's eye the look appeared rather forced. His son Brandle stood half a dozen paces away, but Madred took no more notice than if he'd been a stranger. Brandle similarly ignored his father.

Anduar was speaking again, and Nagaro returned his attention to the words.

"I will remember Pedran well, for he served me seventeen years with skill and diligence. There were times when I sent him into danger, not always realizing how great, yet he always went where he was bidden without complaint." The Pact Signer paused and sighed audibly. "We know that his spirit is gone from this life," he continued, "passing into the void, into the realm of the Benevolent Spirit. I pray that Vothra may guide that departed spirit into a new life so that it may walk again in peace and joy under the sun. The flesh that lately bore Pedran's spirit we now lay in the earth, as is fitting. For the *onam* of every man must return to *onam* of the earth. For those who knew Pedran during his life, and who grieve, we pray for comfort." He bowed his head. "May Vothra give us peace."

There was an answering murmur from the other Kelorin men who were present. "*May Vothra give us peace.*"

Anduar raised his head and stepped back, nodding to Pedran's fellow trackers who moved forward together to lift the body and lower it carefully into the grave. The men with the shovels stepped forward then, but Jato urgently begged them to wait while he hurriedly picked up an armful of freshly cut greenery. Haruda stepped forward with a similar bundle. The two Turowans stood together and tossed green boughs, one by one, into the grave so that they covered Pedran's body where it lay at the bottom. In answer to a questioning look from Lord Anduar, Jato offered a shrug and muttered, "It's t' catch the earth, M' Lord, so it doesn't lie so heavy on him."

Anduar nodded gravely. "Thank you, Jato and Haruda." He signaled for the two men with the shovels to resume their task. "And thank you again, My Lord Endemar, for allowing us to lay Pedran's body in this place. His mother was born in Loros Wared and it will mean something to his family to know that his body is buried here."

Hearing this, Grimbold snorted. Lothard rolled his eyes. Anduar, however, turned away from the grave, giving no sign that he had noticed either reaction. The trackers remained behind to witness the filling of the grave as Anduar led the lords away with a silent beckoning of his hand. Brandle, Nagaro, and the other Fleet men followed.

Anduar stopped on the broad flagstones of the nearest path and the other men gathered around him, frowning, puzzled or expectant. "We must wait here for Endemar's men with their shovels," Anduar explained. "They have another task to perform this morning, of heavier import even than this burial."

"Of heavy import indeed," Endemar interjected.

"We shall see, My Lord," put in Rathdar significantly.

Anduar made no response to either comment. He bent close to Kuran's ear and Nagaro overheard him mutter, "Keep both eyes on the warring parties, My Lord, while I consult with the Council." Then he signaled the other Pact Signers with a look and all four men withdrew a little from the larger group to huddle in low-voiced conversation.

The remaining men stood awkwardly, waiting. Some avoided each other's eyes. Others exchanged glances. After the distraction of the burial ceremony, the tension in the air was now palpable and Nagaro couldn't help noticing that Lothard was giving Rathdar sneering looks. As he watched, the big Leithian said something out of the side of his mouth that drew a snigger from Grimbold and caused a pained expression to cross Madred's face. Rathdar, supported on either side by Soren and Therin, shot Lothard an answering glance that was pointed enough to impale a man, and muttered something to his two companions that elicited wary smiles followed by an exchange of words in hushed voices.

Before long, the two groups began to quietly edge away from each other so they could converse in low tones without being overheard. No sooner had they done so, than Nagaro saw Grimbold casting frowning glances at his nephew, Vell, who stood among the remaining group, looking acutely uncomfortable at being the object of his uncle's attention.

Before anything else could happen, Anduar raised his voice to call Endemar, Rastyl, and Vell to join the Pact Signers' discussion. The two Kelorin lords had been standing silently, Endemar with his head bowed, Rastyl staring moodily across the misty garden. Now they responded to the summons without a glance at one another. Vell went after them, looking worried and chewing his mustache.

Nagaro was now left standing with the remnants of the neutral party, consisting of himself, Kuran, Varsyl, Brandle, Ruald, and Landros. Varsyl's eyes followed the three retreating backs. "So," he said dryly to Kuran, "Apparently you and I are too unimportant to be included in Anduar's councils, although we are governing lords. Should we be insulted?"

Kuran smiled wryly. "Personally, I don't find it worthwhile to be insulted by the slights of highborn folk," he said, "particularly since I usually find the company of commoners more congenial."

Varsyl laughed at this. "I often find it so as well."

Brandle nodded with a faint smile. "I have one boot on each side of that fence, and I agree," he said. Then he added, "But being a lord does have a few advantages. What's this mysterious other task? Do either of you know?"

Nagaro thought he did, but he hadn't been officially informed, so he kept silent.

Kuran exchanged a glance with Varsyl. The latter shrugged, and the Lord of the Fleet lowered his voice to reply. "I don't see why I shouldn't tell those of you who haven't heard," he said, "since you will all know soon enough. They mean to dig up the place where Endemar believes the infant son of Tevren Loros was buried."

"What, is it here?" Ruald asked in surprise, he being perhaps the only one besides Brandle who had no inkling.

Landros convincingly contrived to appear as surprised as Ruald. "Do ye know where the place is supposed to be, My Lord?"

"Inside this garden, by the west wall." Kuran gestured with a jerk of his head. "Tevren and Lindra are buried there as well, just a few paces away."

Nagaro decided to voice the question uppermost in his mind. "Does Anduar want all these folk as witnesses?"

Kuran shrugged. "Some he wants as witnesses, I'm sure, others are here to balance the numbers on both sides. I also suspect that he doesn't dare let the two 'warring parties' out of his sight."

Landros chuckled. "Aye. Bringing all the lords *inside* and leaving their warriors *outside* was a stroke o' genius. None o' the troops will ha' dared pick up their saddlebags in the night and leave their lords behind. And the lords are in no position to give them any orders."

Kuran smiled mirthlessly. "It was the only way."

Nagaro frowned. "Will all those men ride west with us to Lankura?"

Kuran shook his head. "Each lord will be allowed to take only seven men. And you'd scarcely believe how hard it was to decide on that number. Anduar and the other Pact Signers wanted fewer—to avoid trouble—but there were lords of both factions who wanted to bring more—for 'protection,' as they put it."

"The limitation only applies to those who were partisans in this affair," Varsyl put in. "I came with half a dozen men, but I could send back to Virden Hall for forty if I chose. I have no intention of doing so," he added. "My presence in Lankura isn't required, and I'll be returning to my Wared instead—although I confess I am curious to know how this affair will be resolved."

Kuran shot him a look. "I only hope it *is* resolved," he said grimly.

The conversation was interrupted at this point by the return of Anduar and the others, just as the two diggers rejoined the group. Anduar gave a nod to Endemar, and the dour old lord immediately set off down the path in the direction of the garden's west wall with the diggers and the rest of the men coming behind him. The men of the Kelorin Faction, and Rastyl, followed the old lord eagerly, and the three members of the Leithian Faction crowded close on their heels. The four Pact Signers followed the factions like sheep dogs. Nagaro, Kuran and the other non-partisans, brought up the rear.

The mist was already thinning as they passed through the camp, although the overcast still lingered and the light was subdued and gray. The camp was waking up and the cooks were preparing breakfast. The scent of smoke mingled with that of spring vegetation in the damp air. Some of those stirring the pots stared curiously at the passing company. But when Anduar's glance swept over them, they quickly averted their eyes and became busy with their tasks.

As Endemar approached the west wall, he left the paved path and continued across a stretch of dew-sprinkled turf to a place where a plain white stone was sunk in the ground beside a little grassy mound. There he turned and stood waiting while the other men assembled expectantly in a semicircle before him. The two men with shovels took up positions at either side of the mound.

"You stand in a place of remembrance," Endemar informed them solemnly. "Over there lies the grave of Tevren and Lindra of Loros." He gestured to his right, where, a dozen paces away, a larger stone marked a larger mound. "And this stone at my feet marks the place where I have always believed the bones of their infant son lie buried." He raised a hand to silence Lord Rathdar who had appeared about to speak. "I know you disagree, My Lord, and I know you're not alone in that. But hear me out, for it is I who have stewardship of this place." He paused to sweep his eyes over his audience. "One of the last acts of King Tevren's life was to send me a letter," he continued. "In it he told me what I must do in the event that he should be killed. And I'm sure he foresaw his end was immanent because that letter came into my hands on the very day that he and his wife were slain on the road to Lankura."

At this there was a mutter from several of the Kelorin present and a number of resentful glances were cast at Lothard. The big Leithian flung up his head haughtily and said, "Why do you look at me? It was a challenge that my father fought according to law. Everyone knows that."

"Law perhaps, but hardly honor!" retorted Soren.

"Peace, My Lords!" Anduar's voice cut across the rising murmur before Lothard could inflame passions further with some angry retort. "These are old matters, long since laid to rest by general agreement, if not to everyone's satisfaction. We are here in hope of shedding light on a different question." He turned to Endemar. "It would be best, My Lord, if you confine your words to the matter at hand."

"I have no wish to stir up old grievances," Endemar replied coolly. "But it's scarcely possible to explain what we're about to do without making certain references."

Anduar raised his hands placatingly. "Please continue, My Lord, but try to be circumspect."

Endemar inclined his head to Anduar and cleared his throat. "The point I was trying to make," he said, "is that word reached me of Tevren's death at about noon of that day, and I came to this place with all haste because of the letter I had received that morning. In the letter, Tevren spoke of the death of his infant son and bade me come to this garden to see where the earth had been turned near the back wall."

Rathdar moved impatiently. "It didn't say the child was dead!" he said sharply. "Only that you were to say that to the world. And it told you to look in the earth so you would understand!"

The blood rose in Lord Endemar's face. "It says 'look where the earth is turned!' Not 'look *in* the earth!'"

"*My Lords!*" Anduar interrupted for the second time, his cool gray glance impaling first one man and then the other. "I have seen the letter.

The wording is ambiguous. If it were clear, we wouldn't be standing here with shovels."

Nagaro was standing at one end of the semicircle of watchers where he had a very clear view of Lothard and Grimbold. He couldn't help noticing that the two Brothers of the Blood were exchanging smug glances, clearly pleased to see the Kelorin men arguing amongst themselves.

Rathdar, however, leaned forward avidly. "The letter's wording is *purposefully* ambiguous, My Lord! Tevren was using a ruse to protect his son from a pack of bloody-handed butchers since he knew the letter could have fallen into the wrong hands! The meaning couldn't have been made clearer without risk to the child!"

This was too much for Lord Madred. He advanced a step towards Rathdar, very nearly treading on the grassy mound, and his hand went to the hilt of his sword. "Are you suggesting, My Lord," he said, his words edged with ice, "that a Leithian would stoop to slaying a helpless babe? If you were not wounded—"

"Madred! Rathdar! Please!" Anduar raised his hands imploringly. His glance flicked to Pendrik and to Devral. Those two lords both moved subtly but significantly so as to interpose themselves between the two bristling men. Anduar continued standing with his hands upraised. "I'm sure we are all honorable men here," he said, his tone bland but the words carefully measured. "And I know that no one wishes to see blood spilled in this place—a place of remembrance, as Endemar has pointed out. Therefore, I suggest we all return our attention to Lord Endemar, who is attempting to explain, *according to his own understanding*, why he first came to this spot and what he found. My Lord Endemar, please continue."

There was a collective release of pent-up breath. Madred bowed stiffly to Anduar and retreated a pace, his hand returning to his side. Rathdar gave Madred a faintly apologetic nod and drew back as well. His own right arm, which had tensed visibly, relaxed once more.

Endemar nodded respectfully to Anduar. "Thank you, My Lord," he said gravely. "I was endeavoring to explain that I came as swiftly as I could to Loros Hall after learning of Tevren's death. I arrived a full hour before those who came bearing the bodies of Tevren and his queen. I came immediately here, to the back west wall of the garden, as the letter directed me. And I found one spot—and one spot only—where the earth had been disturbed. It was this spot." The graying lord indicated the position of the small mound at his feet. "The turf had been cut away, and not replaced. Moreover, the earth was mounded up as you see it, and showed marks of boots where it had been trodden on to tamp it down. Also there was a scattering of loose grains of earth in the grass on the side closest to the wall. So it was clear that the earth had been piled up as the hole was dug and then shoveled back to fill it up again. Those were the signs as I read them."

Here he paused to sweep his audience with a challenging stare. "I *understood* that I had found the grave of Tevren's infant son," he continued with a pointed glance at Rathdar. "When the men came bearing the bodies of Tevren and Lindra of Loros, I grieved greatly to see that father, mother, and son were all dead. I directed that the parents should be buried near the child, but far enough away that the digging of the one grave wouldn't disturb the other. In the days that followed, I directed the gardener to place turfs of grass over both mounds and to be sure the turf was given water. I had the carved stone placed at the other grave. And I found this fair, white stone and placed it here with my own hands—though I left it un-lettered because I didn't know what name the Lady Lindra had given her child. So I have performed my duty as I understood it, tending this grave and the other one. That is my tale."

Lord Endemar stopped speaking and stood with his gray head bowed and his eyes solemnly cast down.

Nagaro caught a movement and turned to find Rastyl's eyes on him, the pale-eyed stare as enigmatic as always, until the man looked away. He wondered why Rastyl had so far been silent, when he'd been so adamant before in his insistence that the heir of Darion still lived.

Rathdar cleared his throat a little cautiously. "My Lord Endemar should be commended for the care he has taken," he said with an apparent effort at respect. "But the day waxes, and we should be about this task if we mean to learn the truth of the matter."

Anduar nodded gravely. "Yes. We have some hours' ride before us to reach Lankura. Thank you, Endemar, for your words and for your service. If there is nothing more to add, we should begin."

Endemar appeared to pull himself reluctantly from his reverie. He gestured to his two men-at-arms who still stood ready with their shovels. "Dig now, Zirdas," he said. "But go gently."

"Yes," Anduar affirmed. "If this is a grave, it was evidently dug in haste. There may have been no time to fashion any casket or box, and the bones of a newborn child would be thin and delicate."

The two men exchanged glances, evidently feeling the gravity of the moment. Then they bent and shifted the white stone out of the way and began to cut the sod into turfs with their shovel blades and to pile the turfs to one side. They laid bare the top of the mound and then began to dig in earnest. They were both Kelorin, being men of Kildoran Wared. One was fairly young, the other older, with hair as grizzled as that of his lord. They must also have been chosen for this duty because of some relevant experience for they worked quickly and carefully, removing the dirt in layers, a few inches at a time and piling it in a growing heap between the hole and the garden wall. The approach was systematic and it was hard for Nagaro to imagine that any object larger than a small pebble could be missed.

The observers gathered around the deepening hole, watching in silence for the most part, with only occasional murmured comments. Nagaro briefly surveyed the audience, noting that Soren, Therin and Rathdar were all intent on the diggers. So was Rastyl, now that the digging had actually begun. Among the members of the King's Council, Devral and Pendrik were also fully focused on the deepening hole, while Anduar and Odus were watching the watchers. Lothard and Grimbold at first tried to appear bored, but had more and more trouble maintaining the pretense as the work progressed. For his part, Madred stood haughtily with his arms crossed, his eyes nevertheless following every movement of the shovels.

Vell, who was standing near Nagaro, broke his silence. "What do you think they'll find?" he asked in a low voice.

Kuran shrugged. "I don't know," he murmured. "Something must be in there—even if it's only another stone—since the earth was mounded up."

"Unless there was some dirt brought in from another part o' the garden," Landros suggested. "To make it *look* as if something had been buried."

Vell frowned. "Endemar said the earth had only been disturbed in this one spot."

"No, only in this one spot *along the back wall*—"

"*Ahem!*" Lord Endemar, who had been standing at the margin of the circle of viewers, cleared his throat preemptively and shot a reproachful glance at Vell and Landros. The two guiltily fell silent.

Brandle inched closer to Nagaro and put his mouth to his ear. "Why is he so solemn?" he whispered. "If Kelorin folk think that spirits go on to another life, what do graves and bones matter?"

Nagaro answered in the lowest whisper he could manage. "They don't matter to the dead, but graves are places where the living come to remember those who died, and Endemar *knew* Tevren and Lindra."

The hole was growing deeper by slow, careful inches. Each small shovelful of earth that was cast up was strewn loosely across the rising pile. Many of those in the audience were growing increasingly tense, leaning forward each time a shovel bit into the dirt. As time passed and the diggers still found nothing, Therin abruptly knelt down beside the pile of earth and began to run his hands through it, sifting it with his fingers.

"What are you doing?" Rathdar inquired sharply.

"There should be *something* burried here," Therin muttered without looking up. "Some sign, or message for us..."

It was at that moment that the older of the two diggers thrust in his blade and everyone plainly heard a soft, dull thud that was clearly not the sound of iron striking stone.

The man froze. "*Vothra!*" he breathed, exchanging a look with the younger digger. Then he withdrew his shovel, cast it aside onto the ground, and squatted down beside the hole, probing with his fingers in the place where his shovel blade had struck something.

Eager voices rose on several sides.

"What is it?" "What have you found?" "Is it a box?"

"Well, it's wood," the man replied, rising and taking up his shovel again. "Menoril, ye work at finding that end, and I'll find this one," he added, speaking to the younger digger. "But have a care. It feels rotten."

The two diggers worked urgently now, alternately bending over the hole with their shovels or kneeling beside it to dig with their hands. The watchers crowded closer, craning their necks.

"Is it a casket?" Endemar asked while the two men were still bent to their work.

The older man glanced up. "It looks more like some kind o' chest, My Lord. With brass hinges and a brass latch. But it's all gone black an' rotten.

"If there wasn't time to fashion a proper casket," Anduar put in, "they might have made use of anything they had to hand."

"Or more likely Tevren put his message into this chest," snapped Rathdar. "You've got it half uncovered now, Zirdas. Stand aside and let us see!"

"Aye." Devral agreed. "Let us all have a look."

The two diggers immediately straightened and obediently stepped back, revealing a blackened oblong object at the bottom the hole, with square corners and an arched top. It protruded four or five inches clear of the earth and was about fourteen inches long by ten inches wide. The remains of hinges and latch were only distinguishable because they still showed traces of the blue-green patina of weathered brass.

"Now see!" Therin exclaimed. "The body of a newborn child could never have fit in that!"

"Curled up, it might have," Anduar observed calmly. "I'm afraid we are going to have to open it, Endemar."

The older lord had moved closer and stood staring down, frowning, at the little chest. "Yes," he said somberly. "We'll have to look inside. It isn't what I expected. I may have been mistaken..." His voice trailed off.

Anduar turned to the diggers. "Can you free the rest of it and lift it out?"

The older man ducked his head respectfully. "I'm sorry, My Lord, I don't think it'll stand t' be lifted. The wood's that rotten."

"Well then, can you open it where it stands?" Devral demanded.

The man eyed the scar-faced lord uncertainly. "We could *try*, My Lord. But I don't think the latch an' hinges are still in working order, if ye know what I mean."

"Then *break* it open!" Rathdar's impatience flared. "If the wood is so rotten, it should be easy enough. Here, I'll do it myself!"

The Kelorin lord took a limping step forward and came up short as pain contorted his face. At the same time, Soren stepped forward, first to restrain and then to support him. "Hold, Rathdar!" he admonished. "Endemar should open it. It was left in his charge."

Endemar looked stricken. "I—I hesitate to touch it," he quavered. "It's lain undisturbed for twenty-seven years—"

"I will do it." Anduar's voice cut crisply across the other man's. "I stand on neither side of this argument, and I have the command here besides. Let any disturbing of whatever may be inside be on my head."

So saying, the Pact Signer stepped into the hole, straddling the decaying box. He briefly tried prying up the lid with his fingers, then drew a strong, sharp hunting knife from his belt. He proceeded calmly to pry the corroded fragments of the latch free of the rotting wood, then did the same with the hinges. Finally, he fished a fist-sized rock from the pile of earth beside the hole and gently hammered the point of the knife into the approximate place where the crack between the lid and the bottom of the chest must have been, striking first on one side, then the other. At last, the top of the box came free, shifting visibly under the force of the blows. A gasp was heard from the onlookers.

Anduar slipped the knife back into its sheath, then gingerly reached out to grasp the decaying black lid of the chest. Carefully he lifted it and moved it aside.

There was a collective movement forward, followed by a collective indrawn breath—and all eyes turned to Endemar.

The gray-haired lord gave a little strangled cry. "*Empty!*" he moaned. "By Vothra's Eyes and Ears, I've been a fool! It was a ruse after all!"

He sagged and staggered, and might have fallen if Varsyl had not moved to support him. "Don't berate yourself, My Lord," Varsyl said soothingly. "The letter was easy to misunderstand."

"There may be no bones in this chest, yet it is not quite empty," Anduar observed quietly, as he reached into the box and drew forth a few thin, flat flakes of brownish material. "Though for us it might as well be. This was paper—parchment, actually, I think." He held the fragments up to the hazy daylight and examined them closely. "I can see traces of writing," he said. "But the ink has faded and the paper darkened so that I can scarcely distinguish one from the other. Besides that, it's all broken and falling to pieces. I see no possibility of reading any of it."

"Let me see those!" Rathdar reached out, eager to lay his hands on the moldering bits of parchment.

"Let me look at the rest of it!" Therin jumped into the hole and dropped to his knees beside the box, bending over it.

Soren approached the edge of the hole and bent his aging frame stiffly to look as well.

"By all means, see for yourselves." Anduar stood aside, handing the fragments he was holding to Rathdar with an air of resignation.

It did not take long for Soren, Therin, and Rathdar to confirm the Pact Signer's assessment. The box had contained at least one sheet of parchment paper bearing writing, but whatever message had been written there was utterly lost, destroyed by the ravages of time.

Rathdar disgustedly dropped his bits of brown paper back into the rotted chest. "What a pity," he declared. "That paper surely would have told us where the child was sent for safekeeping!"

Anduar sighed. "That's very likely," he said. "The tale of the child being dead was indeed a deception—directed at the world, I'm sure, and not at Endemar."

"Pah!" Grimbold spat. "What does it say about this King Tevren that he'd stoop to such a trick!"

Anduar rounded on him. "What does it say about all of us that he felt he needed to?" he said sharply. "And while I'm sure he wanted the child to be safe, I imagine he was also trying to avert the war he could see was brewing—and he might have succeeded if he'd lived. The bloodletting didn't begin until after Tevren was killed. The Kelorin folk rose up in anger over his slaying, and some of the Leithians could honestly say they needed to defend themselves, while others undeniably engaged in butchery. They may not kill newborn babes, as Madred says, but some of the Kelorin youths they slew were beardless boys. And after what we've seen happening in the last few days—over a man who turns out *not* to be the heir of Darion—how likely is it that Tevren's real son would have survived to manhood if his whereabouts had been known?"

Anduar ceased speaking and for a long moment all were silent. Grimbold's silence was sullen, but Rathdar looked abashed, and Madred wore a troubled frown.

It was Odus who spoke into the silence. "It was an ill time," he said soberly. "And ill deeds were done. All good men must now wish not to see such deeds repeated."

Anduar sighed. "The conflict was complicated," he said. "As conflicts usually are." There had been steel in his voice before, but now it was softened.

"Then let's put it all behind us," Pendrik said placatingly. "Are we finished here?" He gestured at the open hole. "I, for one, want breakfast."

Anduar squared his shoulders. "Yes, I believe we are finished. We've seen what there is to see, and I won't keep anyone any longer from his meat. We must make ready as soon as possible to take the road to Lankura."

The group began to break up, with roughly half its number moving off in the direction of the cooking fires. Notably, all of the Leithians departed, with Pendrik leading a group that included Ruald, Lardros, and Brandle. The members of the Leithian Faction, Lothard, Grimbold, and Madred, took their own path, walking close together and talking among themselves. Odus and Devral exchanged glances, then followed on the heels of the three Leithian lords like watchdogs.

The three members of the Kelorin Faction, Soren, Therin, and Rathdar, stood talking quietly beside the open hole. Varsyl and Rastyl also lingered, looking pensive. Kuran gave Nagaro a significant glance. "Stay a moment," the older man murmured.

Anduar turned to Endemar. "What would you have them do with the box, My Lord?"

Endemar shook his head. "Bury it again," he said bitterly. "Cover up this testament to my folly! And I humbly apologize to those who knew Tevren and Lindra and who would have given protection to their child if they had known where he was. Most especially, I apologize to you, Rastyl," he added, turning to the pale-eyed lord. "You knew Tevren best. He surely left some message for you on that lost paper, and all these years you've been cheated of it. I am most truly sorry."

Rastyl cast him a somber glance. "I accept your apology, old friend," he said. "You acted out of love and loyalty, believing that you understood the letter. I'm sorry we've had such a falling-out over it."

Endemar sighed. "Thank you for your good grace, Rastyl," he murmured. "I will go now to do remembrance at Tevren's grave. That, at least, I know is real. Will you join me?"

"Aye, very gladly."

The two men moved off, shoulder to shoulder, in the direction of the other grave.

Anduar addressed Endemar's two men with their shovels. "Put the top back on the box, Zirdas," he said. "And fill in the hole. Put everything back as it was."

"Even the stone, My Lord?" the older man asked.

Anduar shrugged. "Yes. The heir of Loros probably has a real grave somewhere else, but we're never likely to know where. So let this one stand."

Varsyl frowned at this, and said, "You can't be certain he's dead, Anduar. All we have learned is that he didn't die as a babe. He may be alive, and he could be anywhere!"

"Unfortunately yes," Anduar observed dryly. He turned away from the hole as the diggers set to work, and added, "It would have been far better if we had found bones here. And now I'm going to pay my own respect to Tevren's memory. You all may join me if you wish."

Nagaro was glad when everyone elected to follow the Pact Signer. He had been hoping to visit the place where Tevren and Lindra lay.

Soren spoke up as he hurried after Anduar. "How can you wish him dead, My Lord?" he asked querulously. "If he were alive, he might combine the best natures of Tevren and Lindra—"

"Or their *worst!*" Anduar cut the old man off as he came to a halt beside Endemar and Rastyl in front of a simple stone grave marker. "We would do better to put the whole thing to rest."

Rathdar, who had come to a halt, leaning on Therin, growled, "He'd teach Lothard and Grimbold a lesson! Maybe put *them* to rest!"

"He'd be someone worth following," added Therin. "He'd bring the Kelorin folk together!"

Kuran had come up beside them. "Shouldn't we be looking for someone that *all* Edroviran folk could follow?" he asked archly. "Not just the Kelorin ones?"

"But he *would* be that!" cried Soren. "Like Darion was—"

Anduar cut in coldly: "Darion's like will not come again. We must find our own path to peace, rather than looking for Darion's grandson to find it for us. It's been twenty-seven years, without a sign of him."

"Rastyl said he had found him," Soren pointed out. "He was quite loud about it at the gathering not two weeks ago."

"That's right," agreed Therin. "What's the matter, Rastyl?" he added, addressing the pale-eyed lord directly. "Have you decided that you're as mistaken as I was?"

Rastyl had been standing with his head bowed, but now he impaled Therin with a look. "I am not mistaken," he said coldly.

"Then where is he?" Rathdar demanded. "And why hasn't he shown himself?"

Rastyl's glance swung from one face to another, touching briefly on Nagaro's and flicking away again to focus on a nearby flower bed. "The heir of Darion belongs only to himself," he said quietly. "Therefore let him be." And with that, the graying Kelorin turned away, hunched his shoulders, and stalked off across the grass.

Endemar had been listening with a gathering frown, and now he cast a reproachful glance at Rathdar. "Shame on you, Zirda!" he said. "You should have more consideration for what that man has suffered—all those years of fruitless searching for want of the words on that paper. What peace can he ever have but to imagine that he's found Tevren's heir? You may think it a fantasy, but don't berate him. He deserves more kindness." And without waiting for a response, Endemar turned away from the grave and followed Rastyl's retreating figure with a stiff stride.

Anduar cleared his throat. "This spot is a place of remembrance, gentlemen," he said coolly. "I don't know why each of *you* is here, but *I* would appreciate a few moments of peace." He turned his face away then, and stood with his head up and his eyes closed.

The three representatives of the Kelorin Faction all had the good grace to look abashed. Exchanging guilty glances, they turned back to the grave and bowed their heads in silence. Varsyl also bowed his head. Kuran gave Nagaro a wink before composing his features and dropping his gaze.

Nagaro turned his attention to the grave, tracing the words on the roughly polished surface of the stone:

"*Tevren of Loros, born 20$^{th}$ of Vedorel, 505*," was written at the top, and below it:

"*Lindra of Loros & Irvenen, born 16$^{th}$ of Oteyin, 506*"

Below that was inscribed:

"*Died together on the 3$^{rd}$ of Evrel, 533.*"

It was the same year in which Nagaro had been born, though he had long known that and took no great notice of the fact. He performed a quick subtraction and was surprised to discover that Tevren had been just twenty-eight years old on the day of his death—only a year older than Nagaro was himself—and that Lindra had been only twenty-six. He hadn't realized just how young they had been when they died, and he felt a wave of sorrow at the thought of lives cut so short because of the fears of men who needn't have feared and the anger of men whose anger had been unjustified.

As he stood in somber silence with the other men, remembering how Kuran had described the young king and queen, a sense of deep quiet stole over him. It was a peaceful place. The mist had nearly all evaporated, and angled rays of thin morning sunlight cast the men's shadows across the grassy mound and simple gravestone. The air was very still. The birds had scarcely wakened, and the sounds of men stirring in the camp behind them seemed muted and far away.

At length the three representatives of the Kelorin Faction stirred and left the grave site, murmuring to one another as they went. Anduar and Varsyl went after them and Kuran moved to follow. Nagaro stood for a last lingering moment, with head bowed, before turning to follow Kuran.

Soren, Therin, and Rathdar glanced over their shoulders as they walked away, as if wary of Anduar's ears, but by the time they were halfway to the nearest cook-fire, their voices had risen as their enthusiasm waxed and it became apparent that they were again discussing their hopes of finding the heir of Darion.

Anduar, coming behind them, appeared to ignore their words, but then he cut their conversation short by raising his voice to address them. "We must make haste to have our breakfasts, My Lords," he said. "I mean to leave within the hour. The gate will soon be opened so that you can speak to your men and choose those who will accompany you to Lankura."

The other lords all promptly made small bows and expressed their acquiescence before moving off in various directions. Varsyl lingered long enough to bid Lord Anduar farewell, since he would be returning to his own Wared. He apologized for having arrived so late and with so few men. "If ever I can be of service to Edrovir," he added. "You need only ask."

"Thank you, My Lord," Anduar responded gravely. "I am glad to know that Edrovir can count on you in the future. Even a few men—or one good man such as yourself—can sometimes make a difference. But I am curious as to why you are now willing to take up arms after foreswearing them for so long."

Varsyl smiled faintly. "I have done sufficient penance for my past error," he said simply. "And I've become aware of the country's need."

When Varsyl had gone, Anduar turned to Kuran. "Be quick with your preparations, My Lord," he said. "I want all of our company to be mounted when the gate opens. The lords may be honor-bound to stand before the king, but I want no trouble. The Fleet men will ride as rear guard when we march, to prevent stragglers. And inform Lieutenant Brandle that the Palace Guard will be traveling immediately in front of you, escorting Kenthos. I don't want the Brothers of the Blood to be able to say that a commoner was given precedence over the high-born."

Kuran's smile was sardonic. "Meaning that I don't count as such?"

Anduar's face didn't even twitch. "Meaning that I know you won't complain, My Lord," he said. "You have your orders."

"Aye, Zirda." Kuran stepped away to see to his charge.

Before Nagaro could follow him, Anduar stepped between them, blocking his path. "You've been very quiet, Captain," he said, his steely eyes probing.

Nagaro returned the stare. "I thought that was what you wished, My Lord," he said mildly.

"Yet you don't always do as I wish. Have you no opinion about any of this?"

"I didn't say that, My Lord. But the other men have all lived longer than I. They remember things that I've only read about."

"Ah. A good point. How many years have you, Captain? Thirty?"

"Twenty-seven."

"So few as that? Still, Captain, I would hear your thoughts about this morning's discovery—and about this conflict." The steel-gray eyes never wavered.

Nagaro frowned. "Then, I agree with you, My Lord, that men should seek their own way to peace rather than hoping that Tevren's son will lead them to it."

"So *now* you agree with me." Anduar arched a brow. "Do you also agree that it would have been better if we'd found bones in that hole?"

This time Nagaro shook his head. "Only in the sense that the men would then have had to stop looking for Tevren's son, My Lord," he said earnestly. "I can't bring myself to wish that Tevren's ruse failed to buy a life for his child. But Rastyl is also right. Tevren's son doesn't belong to us. If he doesn't wish to show himself or aid us, we have no right to demand it of him."

Anduar studied him narrowly. "What if he doesn't know his parentage? Should he be told?"

Nagaro frowned in concentrated thought. "I would have to know the man to answer that, My Lord," he said after a moment. "A man has a right to know his parentage. Certainly I would like to know mine. But Tevren's son might well be happier not knowing, so that he doesn't feel the weight of other men's expectations. And of course, no one would then attempt to slay him."

Anduar's mouth twitched with the hint of a smile. "If ever I meet him in the flesh, I'll be sure to introduce him to you." The Pact Signer sighed and all trace of humor died. "But in the meantime, I still think it best to proceed on the assumption that he is dead, and to persuade as many men of it as possible for the sake of peace. And now I've held you long enough. Make your preparations—and your orders for the time being are to keep well clear of Lothard Hurn, lest his temper flare or your conscience be tweaked."

Left alone, Nagaro stared across the brightening garden. Beyond the figures of men moving along the paths among the flowerbeds he could make out the shadowy outline of the house that Nevrath had built, nestled among the trees. The mist was completely gone now, and the dew was fast evaporating. He was glad that he hadn't told Anduar about the woman, Omei, who was as certain as Lord Rastyl that Tevren's son was still alive and who had hinted that Darion's grandson didn't know his parentage. Anduar had recently been prepared, at least for a time, to sacrifice a man's life for what he had considered to be the good of Edrovir.

## Chapter 28

# The Road To Lankura

It was a long cavalcade that set out for Lankura from Loros Hall at about the third hour of the morning, its various constituent groups painstakingly arranged to avoid giving offense to any of the parties involved. The men who would not accompany them to the capital—some Leithian, some Kelorin, and all wearing the livery of their diverse lords—had been directed to return to their Holds and Wareds by various roads, all under strict orders to go directly and refrain from further hostilities.

The carriage bearing Kenthos' mother was positioned near the front of the column, and Rastyl still rode atop it. Kenthos, on the other hand, was riding near the rear, escorted by Brandle Furthing's troop of Palace Guard. Nagaro got a good look at Kenthos as the contingents were lining up and found the young blacksmith looking much improved. He had managed to get a shave, and although he winced visibly when mounting his horse, he held his head up and looked about him with obvious interest in his surroundings.

Tredhold, who was sitting his horse awaiting the order to move forward, turned to Nagaro astride Thunder-Heels and asked, "What did ye say to Kenthos that brought him around, Nagaro? He said ye'd talked to him."

Nagaro shrugged. "He'd assumed that he would be executed and I told him it was unlikely."

The sandy-haired Leithian's eyebrows shot up. "Well *that* explains a great deal. I could have given him the same reassurance if he'd told me what he was afraid of, but I couldn't get him to say more than a dozen words. Even this morning, I got little better."

Nagaro sighed. "Try not to take it personally, Tred. He was being pursued for days by Leithians bent on killing him. I suspect he has yet to learn that not all Leithians are his enemies, but he'll learn it soon enough."

The seven men from Sundorin Wared who had stood with Rathdar at the garden gate were allowed to ride with their lord, but Lord Kuran and his Fleet warriors had charge of those of Kenthos' followers that had been rounded up along the road. Kuran had told them sternly that they were potential witnesses and should be careful what they said during the ride to Lankura, since anyone who heard them speak might bear witness before the king. As a result, the men were being very quiet. Some, like Hendrel and Geivian, had their own horses and were riding, surrounded by mounted Fleet warriors. The others, who had no horses, were riding behind the saddles of some of the Fleet men. Tredhold had taken Lored behind him as he'd done the day before. The senior Fleet officers rode in front, five abreast, with Kuran in the middle of the line, Ruald and Vell on his right, and Nagaro and Landros on his left. They were positioned just behind the rearmost of the Palace Guard who encircled Kenthos. Immediately behind them came Tredhold and the others who bore Kenthos' horse-less followers.

The cavalcade started out at an easy pace out of consideration for those, like Rathdar and Kenthos, who were wounded. Even at such a pace, it would only be a few hours' ride to Lankura. They could pause to rest several times and still reach the capital city before mid afternoon. At first the Fleet men rode in silence, but before long, Landros asked, "Why was Lord Anduar in such a rush this morning? He seems in no hurry now."

Kuran motioned for Landros to lower his voice. "Anduar sent a pair of riders ahead to warn Elgurn of our coming," he explained. "But he couldn't send them until the party was all chosen and had started to march, so they could tell Elgurn what time we left Loros Hall, our speed and numbers, and who is coming."

"Ha!" Landros shook his head. "I should have known."

Ruald twisted in his saddle to address Kuran. "I'm surprised that all these lords are riding together so peaceably and going so willingly to appear before the king, after all that talk of war."

Kuran snorted. "They're only going peaceably because each party believes it has the upper hand. That the other side will fare the worse with Elgurn. After the testimony from Kenthos' mother—which she will repeat to Elgurn—it's plain that Kenthos doesn't even have a claim to noble blood, let alone to being Darion's heir. So the Brothers of the Blood think that the Kelorin Faction has lost and that Elgurn will uphold their grievances against a mere commoner. And the members of the Kelorin Faction are quite willing to concede their mistake with Kenthos because they think the king will punish the Brothers for using excessive force against them."

Ruald maneuvered his horse a little closer to Kuran's and asked, "Which way do you think it will go, My Lord?"

Kuran shrugged. "I doubt that either side will get its way entirely. Elgurn was a true follower of Darion and doesn't hold the traditional Leithian view that common folk have no rights. At the same time, he knows there are many Leithians who aren't among the Brothers of the Blood but who will still be offended if he punishes Leithian lords too heavily for following traditional ways."

Nagaro had been frowning as he listened. "Do you think Elgurn will punish Kenthos at all?" he asked.

Kuran shrugged again. "Not by executing him. You were right in what you said to Tredhold."

"Won't he *have* to punish Lothard, though, My Lord?" Landros asked. "After what those townsfolk did to Rastian—and what Rastian told us—we know that Lothard has been giving unlawful orders. And there've been bloody things done too—like the killing of Pedran."

Kuran's jaw tightened. "Lothard is now calling Pedran's killing a mistake. He's saying that his own man misinterpreted his order."

Landros bristled. "Surely ye don't believe that!"

"No. But unfortunately we can't prove anything."

Vell spoke for the first time: "What does he say about the man that was shot in the back, My Lord? Did you show them the arrow?"

Kuran looked sour. "I did. We were told the man was mistaken for a deer in the poor light."

"A *deer?*" Landros jerked so hard in the saddle that his horse sidestepped. "That's absurd, My Lord!"

"Yes, how can they claim they were hunting deer at such a time?" Vell asked. "And in the middle of the road?"

Kuran scowled. "There was some complaint about the Kelorin men killing deer in Hurn Hold, so they're saying that Lothard's men thought they were shooting a deer in payment. They say the man was shot while under the trees where they couldn't see him clearly and then ran out into the roadway where he fell dead and was seen to be a man."

Landros swore. "You said he was pierced through the heart, My Lord! He couldn't ha' run two steps!"

Kuran's jaw tightened. "We may doubt their tale, but we can't say with certainty that it happened otherwise," he said grimly.

Landros shook his head. "That Lothard is a slippery eel!"

"It does seem so." Vell sounded puzzled. "But I never thought he was so quick with his wit."

Kuran shot the young Leithean a look. "His *wit* here lies in choosing among the tales that Madred was putting forward."

Vell frowned. "If Madred is making excuses for Lothard," he said, "its a kind of crookedness that I've never heard of before from *him*."

"Aye," Ruald agreed. "Madred's reputation is better than that, My Lord!"

Kuran laughed bitterly. "I don't think Madred was *purposefully* making excuses for Lothard. He was offering possibilities—desperately, I think—hoping one might be true, and Lothard seized on whatever suited him. Madred hasn't challenged Lothard's veracity since then, but he must have doubts. It seems to me he's been growing less enamored of Lothard by the hour."

Something else had been troubling Nagaro, and now he said, "When Lothard was attacking Kenthos at the gate, My Lord, he said he wanted to 'finish his father's work.' What does he say he meant by that?"

Kuran shook his head. "I know it sounds damning to you and me since Lothard's father killed Tevren, and assuming that Lothard believed Kenthos was Tevren's son. But the Leithians cast it in a different light, and Lothard has changed his story on top of it. First he said he was trying to punish the man for making a false claim and taking action against lords when he was a commoner. Then, when that defense met with disapproval, he changed his tale to say he was deceived by the claim and thought the man his equal. In that context, he's been trying to claim he was angered by Kenthos' cowardice in refusing to fight him and that he meant to punish him for that. Reith Hurn was well known to have detested cowards, whom he considered dishonorable, and Lothard certainly did accuse Kenthos of cowardice at the gate."

Nagaro scowled. "It is hardly cowardice to stand and willinsgly bare one's breast to a sword!"

"I agree." Kuran hunched in the saddle. "But honor can require a man to fight to show his courage. So it could be argued that Kenthos didn't show honor—"

"But surely one can't expect honor from a man who was raised as a commoner!" objected Vell.

Nagaro stiffened. "*Why not?*" he asked sharply.

Kuran raised a placating hand. "Kelorin and Leithian folk have different expectations, both for how honor is shown, and for who is expected to show it. Our best hope, actually, is that this lack of common understanding between the two peoples may serve the cause of peace in this case. Everyone, you see, can claim misunderstanding."

"But Lothard was going to kill an unarmed man, My Lord!" Landros protested. "How can even a misunderstanding excuse that?"

Kuran sighed. "Lothard claims that he wouldn't have actually killed him. And since Nagaro interrupted him in the deed, he can't be proven a liar, although we may think him one."

They rode on in silence after that, each man occupied with his own thoughts. Nagaro's were revolving uncomfortably around his actions at the gate.

The cavalcade had followed the road from Loros Hall south to meet the River Road, there turning west to follow that wide, paved way along the course of the River Edro. It led them sometimes nearer and sometimes farther from the watercourse. Where they were now, there was room for narrow fields and copses of trees between the river and the road. All hint of clouds had by now completely burned away and the morning was clear and warm.

They were still passing through what had once been Loros Wared, and the land was as sparsely peopled as what they'd seen the day before. They passed tumbled walls, overgrown fields and pastures, and farm houses with fallen roofs or dark windows staring emptily. Other farms and pastures were plainly tended and a few folk were abroad in the spring sunshine, but Nagaro noticed more women in the fields than was usual, and very few men. Even fewer men were older than himself, unless they were so much older that they were gray and bent. He guessed this was evidence of history: Twenty-seven years after the slaying of King Tevren, it was still possible to see consequences of the slaughter and scattering of the men of Loros Wared.

The folk they passed also appeared unusually wary. Though many paused in their labors to watch the cavalcade pass, those who were close to the road retreated a distance before doing so. More than once Nagaro saw young women call to their children, or saw folk duck into the shelter of open doorways or stands of trees. He wondered whether they had heard rumors of the trouble to the north, or of the coming of Lothard and his Leithians. Even if they hadn't, it was likely they had seen Therin's armed warriors riding eastward the previous evening.

The folk were a little bolder in the single village that the company passed through that morning. They stopped their tasks and stared curiously, though they kept well out of the way of the horsemen and made no attempt to speak to any of the riders. Again there were very few older men and more women than men overall. It seemed the village had been built to house perhaps twice as many folk as now inhabited it. There were buildings with windows boarded up and others that stood open to the elements. Nagaro frowned at this further evidence that the wounds of Loros Wared remained unhealed.

A little before noon, they crossed what had been the western border of Loros Wared, marked by a stone with lettering. Soon after that, Anduar called a halt to rest and to water the horses at a place where the road crossed a good-sized stream on an arching stone bridge. The surrounding area was more wooded than open, and there were no dwellings immediately at hand. Their party was large, and riders sought the water both upstream and downstream of the bridge, and on both sides of the stream. The Fleet men and their charges dismounted on the nearer side, where they still found themselves last in line to approach the stream bank.

Kuran plucked at Nagaro's sleeve. "Would you like to see the spot where the king and queen were waylaid?" he asked in a low voice. "It's nearby, and there's water there as well."

Nagaro lowered his voice also. "All right," he said. "There are plenty here to keep charge of Kenthos' followers and it will take some time for all of the horses to drink."

The two men crossed the road to the upstream side, leading their horses. Once there, Kuran led the way to a stand of trees where a path plunged down a little slope between the trunks. It was cool under the overarching branches, though no trace of morning mist remained. Within a dozen yards, light showed between the trees ahead and the path emerged into a sheltered glade. The shadows of the trees darkened the eastern end of the long, narrow swath of grass, while sunlight fell on the western end that sloped downwards to meet the bank of the same stream they had left. The watercourse here ran broad and shallow. A profusion of flowers grew among the grass in the little glade, and near the center of the meadow there was a low, rounded gray stone half buried in the earth.

Kuran stopped. "This is the place," he said.

Nagaro drew up beside him. "The stone marks the spot?"

"Yes. It's said to stand upon the very spot that was stained with their blood. Kelorin folk set it here for remembrance' sake. It bears no inscription, save the date, because it was felt that words might inflame the passions of those who read them."

Nagaro stepped forward, leading Thunder-Heels, to stand beside the stone. "I'd always heard they were waylaid on the road," he mused. "How did it happen that they came to this place?"

"The two men who were with them, and who survived, said they had caught sight of men on the road ahead and turned aside to ford the stream here and avoid them. The move was apparently anticipated."

Nagaro raised his eyes to gaze about him. "It's a fair place for such a dark deed," he said. "And it was spring then, too, so it must have looked very much as it does now—unless it was a stormy day."

Kuran shook his head. "They say it was fair. But come, let's water the horses."

The two men led their mounts down the slope to the stream's shallow brink, where they let the horses have their heads before kneeling, themselves, to cup water in their hands and slake their own thirst while the animals drank.

Nagaro straightened and stood up. "If there's nothing more to see here, we should rejoin the company."

They retrieved the horses' reins and began to retrace their steps. As they crossed the glade, Kuran spoke, his tone carefully casual. "I know Anduar spoke to you, Captain. Did he happen to tell you why he withheld so long from stopping Lothard?"

Nagaro halted beside the stone marker. There was moss growing on it, but he could read the numbers cut there: *533*. He hesitated, frowning, thinking that Anduar might not like to have his reasoning revealed. But he was inclined to trust Kuran with the truth, and Anduar had not sworn him to silence. "I believe he hoped that Lothard would kill Kenthos," he said at last. "Because the Council could have censured him for it. He was angry with me at first for stepping in rather than waiting for his order, but after I pointed out that we might have had war as a result, he thought of some new course of action that pleased him."

"Ah." Kuran nodded. "I suspected something of the kind—regarding his reason for allowing Lothard to continue."

Nagaro sighed. "I meant to do right—"

"You *did* do right!" Kuran gripped Nagaro's shoulder. "You mustn't doubt it."

Nagaro frowned. "For myself, I don't. I can't just watch a man be cut down, who isn't even defending himself. And having spoken to Kenthos, I find him a decent fellow—ill-advised and misled, but innocent in his intent. His dream of restoring Loros Wared appeals to me, besides. But you said, yourself, that nothing can now be proven against Lothard, regarding his intent, because I interrupted his action."

"It *needed* to be interrupted, Captain!" Kuran had let his voice rise and he lowered it again, although there was no one to overhear. "You *know* Therin and Soren were in the apple orchard with their men. Devral had a devil of a time keeping them from rushing to Kenthos' aid when Lothard was only threatening him! If Lothard had *killed* Kenthos— or even *wounded* him—nothing could have kept those men in check. And if *they* had moved, the Brothers' forces would have charged in too, and we would have had a bloody battle on our hands! With so many lords arrayed on both sides, and more companies of men on the way, the war we've feared so long could have started right there, if not for you."

Nagaro shook his head. "You tried to stop him too. I'm told you were right behind me, but that Anduar prevented you—"

"He stopped me because you'd already gone! I hesitated too long, waiting for his order, while *you* stepped in without the order and prevented a bloodbath. Even Anduar knew you were the best man for that, both because you're a match for Lothard and because you've taken no side in this. The irony is that you have to go about saying that you acted on an order that Anduar never gave."

Nagaro frowned. "I've meant the order to prevent bloodshed that Anduar gave us before we left Lankura—an order that came from Elgurn. *That's* why I don't feel that I'm lying. I believe I acted in accordance with our mission. But I'm still glad you think I did more good than harm by it." He paused, glancing at the position of the sun and added, "We should go."

Thunder-Heels and Kuran's mount had both put their heads down to graze while their riders talked. Nagaro now pulled the gray stallion's head up and started towards the path by which they had entered the glade. Kuran tugged on the bay's bridle and followed. Nagaro spoke again in a low voice as he walked. "It was at least partly anger over Pedran's slaying that made Anduar hold back. It worries me to see that in one who is usually so cold."

Kuran sighed. "Anduar seems cold because he's at pains to keep a cool head. He isn't one to erupt, but he smolders. And he has detested Lothard for a very long time. He found much to object to in Reith Hurn, as well, yet he endured that man as a Pact Signer and a member of the Royal Council for years before Reith was slain in the border war. Almost from that day, he's had to contend with Reith's first-born son, and I once heard him say the son was worse than the father."

They had reached the entrance to the path through the trees and Nagaro paused because the leafy tunnel was too narrow to go abreast. "Do you mean to say that Anduar has been looking for a way to be rid of Lothard for some time?" he asked.

Kuran shook his head. "I'm sure he'd dearly love to be rid of the man, but maintaining peace has always mattered more to him. He takes very good care of his people, like Pedran, but he wouldn't ordinarily put one of them before the good of Edrovir. If he did that briefly at the garden gate, it was an aberration. He stumbled, but it seems he has recovered his balance." Kuran moved ahead, ducking under the trees. "We should hurry," he said. "They could be looking for us already."

In fact, they found that the men were just beginning to form up once more in preparation to set out. As Kuran and Nagaro approached the reassembled Fleet contingent, they found just one man waiting on his horse, a little to one side, watching for them.

It was Rastian. "So you visited the Slaying Place?" he asked when they drew near enough to hear. He seemed to address himself to Kuran, though his pale eyes flicked repeatedly to Nagaro.

"Yes. Nagaro wished to see it," Kuran responded easily. "And we watered our horses there."

Rastian's eyes suddenly came to rest fixedly on Nagaro's face. "You hadn't been there before, Captain?"

"No, I hadn't." Nagaro turned away and mounted Thunder-Heels. He hoped that Rastian would return to a place among the men, but when he looked up again the young Kelorin was still studying him.

"What did you think of it?" Rastian asked.

Nagaro's gaze slid away. "I thought it too pretty a place for such a bloody deed, and farther from the road than I expected," he said lightly, then spurred Thunder-Heels past Rastian's horse to follow Kuran's, just as the order came to march.

The River Road grew wider as the cavalcade wound westward along it, within sight of the banks of the Edro. The sun reached its zenith and began to arc downward. The party halted just long enough to distribute some cold food for the midday meal, which the men ate as they rode.

The Fleet men talked amongst themselves as the miles passed, and Landros wondered aloud whether the entire company would be taken into the audience chamber for King Elgurn's judgement. Vell voiced the opinion that only the lords would be present.

Kuran shook his head. "The lords will certainly go in," he said. "But there'll have to be others as well, to bear witness to the actions being judged, though not the whole company, of course. Most of those here don't have any useful testimony that someone else couldn't give just as well."

After this, the Fleet warriors fell to speculating about who would be included or excluded from the royal audience. Nagaro listened with only half an ear as he mentally reviewed his confrontation with Lothard at the garden gate, his conversation with Kenthos, what Anduar had said to him, and the most recent conversation with Kuran. He was trying to foresee the course of events. As the talk around him subsided, Nagaro studied Kenthos, who rode a little way in front of him, surrounded by members of the Palace Guard. Every time he caught a glimpse of him, the young man's head was turned to one side or the other as he eagerly took in the passing scenery with the interest of a man who anticipates a long life before him. Nagaro knew he had convinced Kenthos that he wouldn't be executed, and he desperately hoped he'd been right in doing so.

The land they now rode through had changed. To begin with, it was fully populated. There were more men than women in the fields, and most of the folk simply stopped what they were doing and stared curiously at the passing spectacle as if it were a parade. There was also more traffic on the road, and the travelers they met were more likely to stand to one side of the roadway while being passed, rather than leave it altogether. The cavalcade had to squeeze itself past horse- or ox-drawn carts, strings of pack horses, men with packs on their backs—and, in one case, an entire flock of sheep.

When the road came nearer to the riverbank, it could be seen that the river was wide and liberally dotted with boats and barges laden with goods. The downstream-bound boats were either drifting with the current or were rowed in a desultory fashion. Most of the upstream-bound boats were propelled against the current by the serious application of oars, but in some cases were pulled by teams of horses moving along a tow-path on the river's farther bank. All of this, Kenthos clearly viewed with interest, and his interest doubled when the riders reached the bridge at Stone Island. There he stood in his stirrups to see how the horse-drawn barges were gotten under the bridge's great arch—by dropping a rope with a float from a pier upstream and letting the current carry it under the bridge to the anchored barge, downstream, while the horses were led around the bridge to be re-harnessed to the upstream end of the rope.

The company of riders did not cross the bridge, since that way led south, but continued west along what was now called the High Road. Here there were throngs of people. Since most of them were Lankura folk, they were not shy. They stood to the side to let the carriage and the riders pass, but watched them with inquisitive stares, murmured comments, and pointing fingers. Some must have heard physical descriptions of Kenthos because more than a few fingers were pointed at him and this finally seemed to discomfit the young blacksmith, who sat self-consciously upright in the saddle with his eyes straight ahead.

When presently the walls of the city of Lankura came into view, however, with the great East Gate in the midst of them, the young man's self-consciousness was forgotten as it gave way first to surprise and then to wonder. As the cavalcade approached the walls that seemed to tower ever higher, Nagaro saw the young man from Irvenen Wared lean over to ask some question of one of the guardsmen who escorted him, pointing at the East Gate. The man answered him with laughter and a condescending smile.

Lord Anduar did not lead the company into the city by the East Gate, which would have taken them through the very heart of Lankura and drawn the maximum amount of attention. Presumably he hoped to avoid making a stir, for he gave the order to turn left, southward, into the Circle Road when the vanguard arrived at the crossroads in front of the East Gate's massive flanking towers.

As the vanguard and the carriage bearing Kenthos' mother, swung around the turn, Kuran turned to Nagaro, raising his voice above the thudding of hooves. "He means to bring us in through the South Gate. Some of the men will be left at the Fleet Compound—to make a smaller party."

Nagaro nodded comprehension. The East Gate was open, its two great wooden doors swung wide. Beyond the arch, he could see a broad sunlit street filled with people and flanked by buildings of two or three stories on either side. He could only imagine what Kenthos, accustomed to the sparsely-peopled northern Wared of Irvenen, might make of the sight. The gate loomed over him as he reined Thunder-Heels into the turn. The facades of the towers and the wall were sunk in deep blue shadow as the sun angled westward, and he saw the tilt of Kenthos' head as the young man looked up. Following his gaze, Nagaro's eyes were dazzled by the sun that etched the edges of the crenelations topping the towers and the flanking walls. Against that brilliance, he could just make out the heads and shoulders of city guardsmen high above, and caught the silver flash of their steel-tipped spears.

The way around by the Circle Road did not take long, for the paving was wide and comparatively uncrowded. Kenthos kept glancing at the city wall, and at the wall of the Fleet Compound when they reached the stretch of road that ran between them, and he now looked worried. When the company paused in the paved space between the city's South Gate and the gate of the Fleet Compound, the young blacksmith sat his horse in the midst of the men of the Palace Guard, looking very subdued.

Anduar's orders to those men who were sent into the Fleet Compound were made so quickly that it was clear the decisions had been made in advance. Pendrik, Devral, and Odus kept only seven men each, and Kuran dismissed all but fifteen of the Fleet warriors. The remaining Fleet men included all of the officers, Nagaro among them, as well as every man who had served as a scout or who had borne one of Kenthos' followers behind him on his horse. Tredhold was therefore included, as were Taru and Pavo. Those left behind at the Compound were sent to the Fleet dining hall to wait and refresh themselves after first being strictly instructed not to discuss the events of the past several days with any one who hadn't been there. The carriage was, of course, intended to continue to the palace, and enough horses were provided so that everyone who remained with the party might ride.

When Kenthos saw that some of the Fleet men were being dismissed he became agitated, looking desperately about until his eye lit on Nagaro. He then appeared to relax, seeing that his protector would remain with the party.

At length, the reduced company of horsemen rode on, passing through the South Gate and into the city. Now they were in between rows of shops and residences, and folk quickly began to line the street to watch them pass. Nagaro continued to keep one eye on Kenthos as they rode, but he was aware of the gathering crowd of onlookers as well. At first it was composed of folk who happened to be passing in the street—Kelorin, Leithian, or Turo. Before they had gone very far, however, Nagaro began to notice that they seemed to be attracting Kelorin onlookers disproportionately, and the Leithians who were present began to look about uncomfortably. Among the gathering Kelorin, there were men and women, young and old, and they were not silent. They raised their hands and shouted to one another, and many of them moved along the street, following the riders. Second-floor windows were flung wide, and folk leaned out, eager to see. They pointed at Kenthos as he rode past, and at Nagaro as well, and raised their voices.

"Kenthos! Kenthos! Son of Loros Wared!"

"Look! There's Captain Nagaro!

"Nagaro! Nagaro! Defender of Loros!"

Nagaro frowned, and he noticed that Kenthos was also disturbed by the attention. The young blacksmith had stopped looking about him at the city sights. He had been ill at ease from the beginning, but now he held his eyes straight before him and he seemed to cringe at the cries of these Kelorin folk who seemed to know him, or know something about him.

Kuran reined his horse closer to Nagaro's, his brow darkening. "I don't like this, Captain," he said, over the noise of the crowd.

"Nor do I. Can they have already gotten word of what happened at Loros Hall?" Nagaro remembered with chagrin Lord Anduar's recent assertion that the news of what he had done would spread throughout the country by the end of the week.

"Clearly." Kuran sounded annoyed. "And anyone who saw what happened yesterday at the garden gate could have gotten here before us by riding ahead while we were watching graves being dug and filled. We must put a stop to this talk. It can only stir up trouble among the lords who are with us."

These words from Kuran echoed Nagaro's thought so exactly that he immediately turned Thunder-Heels sharply aside, leaving his place in the Fleet ranks and making for a particularly vocal group of Kelorin on the side of the street closest to him.

"See if you can quiet them," Kuran called after him. "But don't tell them anything!"

Nagaro rode almost into the little knot of Kelorin, drawing rein only when Thunder-Heels was all but breathing in their faces. Those who were closest fell silent in dismay and some backed up, crowding into the ranks behind them.

"Good people!" Nagaro raised his voice enough to be heard by those nearby, but not so much that his words would reach the ears of the lords in the cavalcade. "I pray you to hold your peace, if you don't wish to do harm!"

Those who were immediately in front of him backed away some more, muttering, but one man close to Nagaro's age—dressed in travel-stained pants and boots with a fresh gray tirka and white shirt—stepped closer instead and addressed him boldly.

"We only speak the truth!" he proclaimed. "That's Kenthos, there, on the chestnut horse, whose father and mother both came from Loros Wared, and who led other men of Loros from the north, trying to reach the home o' their fathers. And *ye're* the defender of Loros who saved Kenthos' life by turning aside the sword of the Leithian lord that would ha' killed him. I dare ye to deny it!"

Nagaro considered the speaker, noting a dark red weal that looked like a half-healed sword cut at one side of the man's chin. "You or I might say it is so," he said severely, "but King Elgurn's judgement is yet to be given. *He* will hear the witnesses, and decide the fate of those who ride in this company. Do you wish to bear witness before him?"

The man faltered. "Nay," he said quickly. "I have no witness I wish to give."

"Then bid these others hold their peace, in Vothra's name!"

The man still held his gaze. "Very well, Captain," he said, and bowed awkwardly as if unaccustomed to it. "I'll do as ye say."

A woman of middle years, who was standing nearby, raised her voice, however. "Is it true, Captain Nagaro? Did ye turn the Leithian's sword?"

Nagaro turned his eyes to her. "I acted under orders from the king to prevent bloodshed, Zirdyn, and to preserve the peace. It was for that purpose that we rode north three days ago under Lord Anduar, and it's for that purpose that we now go to stand before the king. If you would do good rather than harm, I suggest that you pray for a good judgement." He raised his voice again to be heard more generally.

"Good people, I beg you to hold your peace, and pray for peace. Pray that all may yet be well in Edrovir!"

With that he spun Thunder-Heels about and rode up the street at a canter, quickly closing with the rear of the column, which had not stopped to wait for him. He took his place once more beside Kuran. Since he did not look back, he didn't see how the man he had spoken to melted back into the crowd and slipped stealthily into a narrow side alley that passed between two houses.

"What have you done, Captain?" Kuran inquired a moment later. "The shouting has stopped."

It was true. There were still more Kelorin than Leithians among those who watched them, and some of the watchers still appeared to be following them, but there was now no more than a low babble of voices coming from the crowd.

Briefly Nagaro sketched what had been said.

"Ha! You spoke to one man and one woman, where a few dozen folk could hear you. Is it possible this is the result?"

"It's the man's doing, I think. The woman was plainly just a citizen of the city, but the man looked as if he had incompletely changed his clothes after being on the road under rather rough conditions. And he had a cut on his face that suggested he'd been in a fight within the last week."

"Ah!" Kuran arched an eyebrow. "So you had the good fortune to address a messenger or news-bearer. A man who was out with Kenthos, perhaps?"

Nagaro sighed. "He was that, certainly, but it wasn't mere good luck. He put himself forward and addressed me. I only had to answer."

The quieting of the crowd might have allayed Kuran's concerns, but it did nothing to put Kenthos at his ease. The young blacksmith sat stiffly, staring fixedly at his horse's ears, all the rest of the way to the Palace Gate, through it, and into the broad plaza in front of the palace. Only when he obeyed an order to dismount did he look up, and then up again, his astonished gaze traveling from the high portico and massive palace doors at the top of the great flight of steps, all the way to the top of the three-story marble facade. That facade rose regally above them, snow white stone as cool as ice, with the sun behind it, ornamented with embellishments in hues of jade and ebony.

In dismay, the poor blacksmith spun around to gape at the size of the open square in which they stood, and which completely dwarfed the company of horsemen. From astride Thunder-Heels, Nagaro watched Kenthos' growing agitation with a gathering frown. A small army of grooms emerged from the stable yard to take charge of the horses, but Kenthos clung to his mount's bridle, only relinquishing his grip when Brandle approached and spoke pointedly to him. Even then, his eyes followed the animal, as it was led away, with the expression of a man marooned on a deserted island who is watching the ship that had been carrying him sink inexorably into the sea.

Nagaro could stand it no longer. He swung easily from the saddle, handed his reins to one of the grooms, and shouldered his way through the disorganized press of men to Kenthos' side. "Don't worry," he said when he caught the man's distracted eye, "They'll bring the horse out again when it's time to leave."

Kenthos grabbed desperately at his arm and held on as if he feared a flood might carry him away. "Captain Nagaro!" he cried. "This is too much!" Then he lowered his voice because some of the Palace Guard had turned to stare at him. "How can they imagine that I can do this? I can't go in *there!*" He jerked his head in the direction of the palace. "It's even bigger than Loros Hall!"

Nagaro gave him a sympathetic look. "It's probably the biggest building in Edrovir," he said, smiling crookedly. "So once you've been inside it, you'll have nothing more to fear for the rest of your life as far as buildings are concerned. But what does size matter? You're a bigger man than I am, after all."

Kenthos stared at him for a moment, and then his eye traveled up and down Nagaro's frame as if he were taking note of it for the first time. "That's so," he said after a moment. "Ye're not a very big man, are ye?"

Nagaro laughed outright. "No," he said, "I'm not. Though I have generally found myself big enough for the task at hand."

"And ye've been in there?" Kenthos glanced again anxiously at the portico and the great doors. Rastyl together with Anduar and Pendrik and their men at arms were already starting to escort Kenthos' mother up the steps.

"Yes—many times—in and out, and none the worse for it. It's a very big building, but still only a building. And the Audience Chamber is a very big room, but still only a room. And King Elgurn is a man no bigger than I—"

"—and what does size matter, hey?" Kenthos laughed nervously, but he looked better.

At this point Brandle appeared beside them. "We'll be going in soon," he informed Kenthos. "Do you think you're strong enough to get up those steps?"

Kenthos nodded, though he paled a little at the prospect. Brandle shrewdly considered him, noting the looks that passed between Kenthos and Nagaro. Then he said, "The captain will steady you. And once we're inside, I'll have the healer take a look at your wound."

So they went up the steps, going slowly, with Kenthos' arm across Nagaro's back and his fingers tight on Nagaro's shoulder. Nagaro took advantage of the moment to probe the other man's perceptions. "Are you satisfied that the healer has done well by you?" he asked.

"The healer?" Kenthos frowned. "Aye, he knows his work, seemingly, and his hands are gentle enough for all that he's a Leithian. But he tries to talk to me, and I don't know what to say. He wears a Fleet uniform, but how do I know who he reports to?"

Nagaro laughed. "Tredhold Ferth reports to Kuran Kel—and to me, somewhat. He's my ship's doctor, and a good friend besides."

"A friend? *Your* friend?" Kenthos was so astonished that his feet momentarily stopped moving on the steps. He was promptly prodded from behind and started up again.

"Yes. We were galley slaves together, and I would trust him with my life. In fact, I already have. You should listen to what a man says and watch what he does before you decide if he's friend or foe—or something in between. You can't fairly judge a man by the color of his hair—"

"—or the number of his years, or the style of his tirka, or the town he hails from," Kenthos finished ruefully. "The Writings say that, don't they? I forgot."

They had reached the top of the steps, and stood together under the portico. Kenthos released his grip on Nagaro's shoulder and straightened to stand on his own. Nagaro met his eyes seriously. "Yes, the Writings do say that. And now that you've been reminded of it, try to hold onto that thought when you go into the Audience Chamber. From what I have seen, the members of the Council truly desire peace, and everyone says King Elgurn was a devoted follower of Darion in his time. The world may be a little more complicated now, but they're all still trying to do right. Don't imagine that the king must be against you because you're Kelorin."

"I won't." Kenthos spoke earnestly. "And thank you for your advice."

At this point, Brandle moved between them and beckoned for Kenthos to follow him into the entry hall.

# Chapter 29

# To Stand Before The King

In the entry hall, those who were neither lords nor members of the Palace Guard surrendered their swords into the keeping of young Delvin, who was the guard on duty. Kenthos had not been wearing his blade since he'd dropped it on the grass outside the garden gate of Loros Hall. One of the guardsmen had been entrusted with it, and the man now handed it over, indicating to Delvin who the owner was.

"I'll keep it safe for ye, Zirda," Delvin dutifully informed Kenthos. "Ye'll have it back when ye go out again."

Kenthos shook his head. "I'm just a blacksmith," he muttered. "I should ha' kept to working steel, not trying to wield it. But where is this Audience Chamber?" he added, looking about nervously. "If I must do this, I want it over an' done with."

As it turned out, they were made to wait. The preparations weren't quite complete, they were told, for the inquiry that was to be conducted. Kenthos' mother was whisked away to a suitable chamber somewhere, in the company of several serving women and a guard to stand at the door. Only Anduar and Pendrik were summoned to the Audience Chamber. The remaining members of the company, including the lords Odus and Devral, were at first left standing in the Compass Room.

Roughly forty feet square, this chamber functioned as a kind of anteroom to both the Audience Chamber on one hand and the Great Hall on the other, as well as communicating with the rest of the palace by way of the door that was straight ahead as one entered it and which led to the central hallway. The Compass Room had been designed to impress visitors, and those who hadn't seen it before were still gaping at the huge compass rose set into the marble floor and the richly paneled walls with their decorative hangings when the palace Chamberlain arrived to usher them on into the pillared Great Hall.

There, the less experienced members of the company marveled afresh at this new room's vast dimensions. They would have been even more impressed, of course, if they could have seen it at festival time. While the Compass Room had been illuminated by both decorative lamps and a series of windows high up near the ceiling, the Great Hall was presently lit only by the light from the tall, arched windows set in the north wall. Devoid of festive finery, the room was dim and cavernous, a place of gray stone, dark, polished wood, and the smell of fine old leather. It echoed hollowly to the tread of their booted feet.

The various groups making up the company each chose tables and chairs for their use. Kuran gathered his Fleet warriors at two tables near the door by which they had entered. The former followers of Kenthos sat at several nearby tables with Brandle and some of his guardsmen seated among them. Kenthos was kept at a table apart from his men, surrounded by more members of the Palace Guard. Nagaro was therefore unable to speak further to the young blacksmith and hoped that Kenthos could look after himself for a while. He heaved a sigh and gave his attention to his fellow Fleet men.

Since no one had dictated the seating arrangements, those who sailed under Nagaro gravitated together at the end of one of the Fleet tables. Nagaro, Taru, and Pavo sat with Landros and Tredhold, although Tred was almost immediately called away to examine first Lord Rathdar, and then Kenthos.

As Tredhold departed, Pavo asked, "What have you and Kenthos talk about so much, Nagaro?"

"Nothing very important. He's very nervous about standing before Elgurn, and I was trying to put him more at ease."

"Ha!" Taru's laugh was short and derisive. "I've had to stand in the Audience Chamber, before the King's Tribunal. It wasn't so terrible!"

"You didn't have to speak," Nagaro pointed out. "Kenthos will certainly be expected to, and I'm sure that's the main reason why he's so nervous."

"Still, I was up for treason! I could ha' been hung!"

Olendar and Haruda, sitting nearby, looked impressed, but Landros swept Taru's words aside with a wave of his hand. "Pavo was up before the tribunal twice! *And* he had to speak. Didn't ye, Pavo?"

Pavo regarded them all impassively. "First time I had to speak very much," was all he said.

At this point, they were interrupted by Kuran's arrival. He settled into the seat that Tredhold had recently vacated. "I've just finished giving some advice to our fleet men at the other table," he observed as he glanced around the faces of the seated men. "And now I'll give you the same. Some of you are going to be called into the Audience Chamber—others not. And of those who are called, some will be questioned and others won't. I don't want you guessing at why you're called or not called, or why they do or don't question you. But if you *are* questioned, I want you to answer truthfully and with as few words as possible. Don't volunteer any information beyond what's asked. If there's something more that needs to be said, *I'll* say it. Or I'll ask you about it myself. Is that clear?"

There were nods and murmured affirmatives.

"As much as it's likely t' matter," Haruda remarked with a fatalistic shrug. "They'll not be wantin' to talk to *me*."

Kuran turned to the Turo. "If they want to know about Pedran's killing, they certainly will want to talk to you, Haruda."

Haruda shook his head. "High-born folk never take the word of a Turo."

Kuran's eyes acquired a steely glint. "You're a sworn warrior of the Royal Fleet, Haruda, and I'll see they don't forget it! They should want to talk to you about Pedran's death, and to Taru and Olendar about the skirmish in the hills where Rathdar was wounded, because there were no other witnesses to those events who weren't partisans. As for the rest of us..." He shrugged. "It's anyone's guess."

Landros raised a grizzled eyebrow. "Will ye at least tell the rest o' this lot what ye told us on the road, My Lord? About what Lothard has been saying?"

Kuran considered. "Yes," he said. "I think I should. If you've already heard it, you'll find it easier not to choke when the Leithians say it."

Nagaro sat, deep in thought, only half listening as Kuran sketched once again the arguments he had heard from Lothard and Madred. His mind was running ahead to other things. It struck him that if he were questioned, it might prove difficult to tell just the right amount of truth. Also, the more he reflected on all that he had heard and seen in the last three days, the more it seemed to him that Kenthos' desire to see Loros Wared restored ought not to be denied.

Presently, serving women entered from the kitchen bearing candles that were set on the tables, where they shed small pools of light, as well as trays of food and drink. Fine-grained bread, pale cheese, cold meat, and dried fruit were all set before them, as well as steaming teapots full of hot sothiril. While he ate, Nagaro tried to get a glimpse of Kenthos at the table with the guards, but he couldn't see enough to judge the man's state of mind. When Tredhold came back to join them, reclaiming the seat that Kuran had now vacated, he reported with evident satisfaction that both of his patients were doing well. He had also made a full report of his observations to Lords Odus and Devral at the other end of the room.

"Does Kenthos seem steady in his mind?" Nagaro asked when Tred stopped speaking and picked up his cup of sothiril.

The healer held up a hand to express equivocation. "He's nervous, but he controls it—for now at least. And he did talk to me this time—gave me more than the shortest answer to my questions. He even thanked me for my care!"

Nagaro smiled faintly. "I told him that he shouldn't judge men by appearances—and that you're a friend of mine, Tred."

"Oh?" Tred gave him a wry look. "So I must be *your* friend before he'll treat me decently? Still, I'm glad you took the trouble for my sake."

"Not for your sake, Tred, I'm afraid. It was for his. He'll fare much better before the king if he doesn't look askance at every man with fair hair. And, actually, what I said reminded him of things from the Vothrin Writings."

***

After nearly an hour and a half, Lords Anduar and Pendrik finally entered the Great Hall. They immediately sought out the other two members of the Council and all four put their heads together. After some discussion, they called for all of the other lords who were present to join them. In due course, Kuran returned from that discussion to the Fleet tables. He informed Captain Ruald, old Rubo, and a handful of others that they were to remain in the Hall, "To help keep an eye on the others who will be staying." The rest of the Fleet men he told to quickly finish their bread and sothiril, as they would soon be returning to the Compass Room.

As it turned out, Nagaro and all the other designated sea warriors had to wait while everyone else who had been told to expect a summons was called first, so they had considerably more time to sit and fret. When they finally did arrive in the Compass Room again, they found themselves joining a chaotic assemblage there. Despite having left men in the Great Hall, there were nearly sixty men crowded together on the side of the room near the Audience Chamber doors. Some, notably the lords, were eager to pass through those doors. Many others were reluctant and were trying to hang back but being prevented from doing so by the men who were guarding them. There was enough whispering and muttering to create an impressive din and to give a distinct impression of confusion despite all the efforts to keep order.

At last, the huge carved doors of the Audience Chamber swung open, and the press began to move. Nagaro had not yet taken a step, when he became aware of Kenthos beside him. The young man bent down to bring his lips close to Nagaro's ear. "Ai, Captain," he muttered nervously, "ye must tell me how I'm to do this. What am I to say?"

"They'll ask you questions," Nagaro returned, also speaking low. "Just tell the truth and use few words. That's what Lord Kuran told us to do."

"Use few words?"

"Yes. No more than you need to answer the question. But I'll add some advice of my own: Speak boldly for your cause, but humbly for yourself. It's the best way."

"Boldly for my cause?"

"Yes. And humbly for yourself."

"Boldly for my cause, and humbly for myself..." Kenthos repeated the words as if trying to commit a formula to memory.

"Come along now, Zirda!" Brandle grasped the young blacksmith's shoulder. "They're waiting for us."

"Will ye be there?" Kenthos called over his shoulder as he was hustled away.

Nagaro threw a wry look after him. "Best not to count on it!"

A moment later, Brandle's guardsmen had passed through the doorway with their charge. Nagaro hung back among the Fleet men who encircled the knot of Kenthos' former followers. Kuran, at the head of his men, was looking through the doorway, intent on something Nagaro couldn't see. He seemed to be waiting for some signal from inside the Audience Chamber. Presently he must have gotten it, for he beckoned them forward.

And then, abruptly, Anduar was standing in the doorway. The Kelorin lord stepped to one side as the Fleet men moved past him, but when Nagaro stepped forward, the Pact Signer planted himself firmly in his path. "Captain," he observed coolly, indicating with a motion of his hand that Nagaro should step out of the line. "I would speak with you."

Nagaro frowned even as he complied. The other Fleet men continued to file past. Taru checked, throwing him a worried look, until Anduar's cold stare made it clear that his presence was not desired. Hurriedly then, the young Turo returned to his place and disappeared through the doorway into the chamber beyond. In another moment, the last of the other Fleet men had crossed the threshold.

"My Lord?" Nagaro allowed a certain urgency to enter his voice.

Anduar wasted no time on preliminaries. "I wish you to wait here, Captain. Remain close, but do not attempt to enter unless you're called."

"But My Lord, *why?*"

"Let's say there are times when excessive honesty isn't desirable. Besides, everyone knows what you did, Captain, and why you've said you did it. The Pact Signer's tone was bland and didn't change when, in answer to Nagaro's deepening frown, he added, "Oh don't look so accusing, Captain. I've already made a full confession to My Lord King, and been chastised. And forgiven."

Nagaro stared in astonishment. He had been worried about the questions he might be asked and how to maintain his honesty, but this solution seemed too extreme. "I meant no accusation, My Lord," he protested. "But why bring me so close if my testimony isn't needed? I could have been left in the Great Hall with the others."

"True. You are, however, a deft hand at turning aside a blade, and someone must be left to guard the door."

"Someone without a sword, My Lord?" Nagaro raised an eyebrow.

"That will be attended to." Anduar smiled, but not with his eyes, then turned and strode through the open doorway into the Audience Chamber, leaving Nagaro standing mute and frustrated.

Two guards who had been standing to either side of the huge doors began to swing them closed, moving in such a way that they would be on the inside when they were finished. They had very nearly brought the edges of two doors together when there came some quick words from inside and one panel was swung back a little, just long enough to allow another man in the uniform of the Palace Guard to exit the chamber. As it turned out, the man was Brandle Furthing.

The big Leithian grinned wolfishly and jokingly saluted Nagaro. "At your service, Captain."

Nagaro frowned darkly at the closed doors. "Have they tossed you out too, Brandle? At least *you* have a sword."

"I do. *And* I have orders to hand it to you if they call for help from in there."

"*What?*" Nagaro turned on Brandle in astonishment. "If I were you, I'd find that insulting!"

"Not at all." Brandle actually laughed. "If they call for *your* sword, it will be because Lothard has drawn *his*—in which case, better you than me!"

"Anduar could at least have picked someone less senior than you!"

Brandle shrugged. "I'm used to being insulted, and I know well enough why I was chosen for this post."

"Balance, again?"

"*That*, and the fact that I'm an embarrassment to my father. He probably asked that I be excluded."

"Oh." Nagaro's shoulders sagged. "I *had* noticed that your father treats you like a total stranger, when he isn't ignoring you altogether. What does he do when you go to Furthing Hold? Are you even permitted there?"

"Oh yes. I'm as free to come and go there as any member of the family. I haven't been disowned. It's just that I'll inherit as if I were the second son. My younger brother will have what would have been mine—including the lordship when our father dies."

"You don't sound as if you mind."

Another shrug. "I don't—very much. I don't think I'd like being lord of the Hold."

"I see."

They both fell silent after that. Brandle stood stiffly, guard-fashion, in front of the double doors, which were so thick and solid that they allowed no hint of sound to pass. Nagaro began to move about, pacing tensely. His eyes swept the room, taking in the patterned hangings, the panels of dark wood, the lamps burning in their sconces along the walls. His thoughts whirled in circles, touching on Kenthos, or on Taru and Pavo—or Landros, or Tred—all possibly facing questions. And the answers to those questions were terribly important. Everything stood poised beneath the overarching threat of war.

The time passed, crawlingly. Brandle must have been following Nagaro's movements, for he suddenly spoke. "You'll never make a good guardsman, Captain, if you can't stand still."

Nagaro came to a halt and turned to face the man. "I have no desire to be a guardsman," he said with some annoyance.

"A man of action, eh?"

Nagaro frowned darkly. He was never happy being styled so. To him, the term suggested someone who didn't *think*. "I have friends in there," he muttered, "—several old friends, and a new one—facing things I can only guess at. And there are other men in there trying to bend the shape of those things to their wills." *And if the wrong things are asked, or answered, or acted upon, the whole country may slide into war.*

"You don't still fear for Kenthos' life, do you? After what Kuran said?"

Nagaro shook his head. "No. But I don't know what will become of his plan for Loros Wared if he's too nervous or frightened to speak on his own behalf."

"Or if he says the wrong thing?" Brandle ventured.

"Not the *wrong* thing, no. If he says no more than what he said to me, it should go well for him, I think. He's simple enough and honest enough, if he just isn't too nervous to put the words together."

"Simple and honest!" Brandle laughed. "If he's simple and honest, it's no wonder he's come to grief!"

Nagaro frowned afresh. He tried briefly to think how he might explain what he meant to the cynical guardsman, but he wasn't in a patient mood. He soon gave up and asked instead, "What's the guardsman's secret then? How do you stand so still?"

Brandle shrugged. "I just don't think about any of it."

"Ha!" Nagaro felt something akin to relief. "*That's* a trick I hope never to master!"

He turned away, this time circling the room, trying to find some distraction in a closer examination of its furnishings. He was studying the inlaid surface of a small table beside the open doorway leading into the long central hallway, trying to identify the different materials used in the design, when he heard his name spoken low and urgently, and near at hand, by a voice that made his heart jolt against his ribs.

"Nagaro! I've been looking for you!"

"*Nevien!*" He spun, eagerly, seeking her and found that she was standing just inside the central hall, beside one of the large doors that could be used to separate it from the Compass Room but which were currently wide open as was normal during daylight hours. Where she stood, she was out of Brandle's sight as she peered around the polished doorframe. Her slim brows were drawn together, the sharpness of the little line between them marking the acuteness of her distress.

"I looked in at the back door of the Audience Chamber," she said, agitatedly. "But the main doors were closed, and you weren't inside! Then I peeked into the Great Hall from the kitchen, but you weren't there either. Come here, quickly!" She beckoned. "I have to talk to you." And she withdrew further back around the door post.

Without a word or thought, he followed her, stricken by the pain in her voice. Once in the hallway, he felt her hand on his arm. There was a side hall running to the left just outside the chamber door, and she drew him urgently into it just far enough to be out of the line of sight of a guard stationed in an alcove some distance along the central hall. As soon as they were safely out of sight, she stopped and turned to face him, searching his face.

"Oh, Nagaro!" she cried. "My father is going to let the courtships begin again! He's not going to wait!" In her distress, she started to reach for him.

Nagaro's own arms moved to enfold her, and his heart leaped ecstatically at the prospect. But in the next instant he checked himself, shocked at how easily his feelings might betray him.

"Nevien," he murmured. "My Lady—not here! If anyone should see us—" He gently pushed her away.

"Oh! You're right, of course." She drew back, sounding resolute now. "I'll have to do without leaning on you so literally—at least until I can arrange an outing to River House. It's just that my father's decision has fallen on me like a weight from above." Distractedly she brushed back a strand of hair. "He's going to make the announcement within a week!"

"A week!" Nagaro's mind reeled. "I thought you'd have months!"

"It's because of this affair of the false heir of Darion. He says the people need something else to think about—that *certain men* need to be distracted from their quarrels. He considered reopening the border war with Jinara, but we'd lose too many good men that way."

Nagaro stared at her as his mind filled up with the enormity of this misfortune. "But," he began desperately, "if the meeting in the Audience Chamber goes *well*, then surely—"

She shook her head. "Even if it goes as well as can possibly be expected, he says we need the courtship. If the meeting went *badly*, I might actually be spared, because there would be war, but I can't wish for that!"

"No, of course not." He knew she was right, but he wasn't prepared for how little he wanted to see her married again. How could her father use her so? "Nevien, I... I'm sorry about this," he murmured. "I wish there were something I could do."

"But there is!" She smiled wanly at him. "You can help me be strong. I only need someone I can talk to. You'll do that, won't you?"

"Of course. I'd do anything for you." The words were absolutely true, and there wasn't the slightest reflection behind his uttering them. He reached for her, in spite of himself, only to realize what he was doing and hastily withdraw his hands.

She seemed not to notice. She was speaking eagerly. "I'll plan an outing as soon as I can, so we can talk properly. I have *so* missed talking to you, Nagaro—my dear, dear friend—the way we do at River House. And it will be all right. I'll find the strength. I always have, and I'm sure I can again if you help me."

She reached for his hand and squeezed it. And then she was gone, gliding away down the side hall, deeper into the palace's warren of rooms and hallways. He took two steps after her before he could stop himself, but she disappeared around a corner leaving him standing there, aching.

"*Keshaal!*" He slumped against the wall and pressed a hand to his brow. He was sweating. "*By the Eyes and Ears!*"

*Didn't she feel it the way he did? If only she would— No! Don't!* He bitterly chastised himself. *He mustn't wish for her to love him! It was as bad as wishing for war!* She had enough troubles without adding to them. And he mustn't ever let her know his feelings either.

Hard on the heels of these thoughts, came the realization that he had to return to the Compass Room. He straightened, and turned—and stopped dead.

Brandle was standing not twelve feet away in the Compass Room doorway, his face the expressionless mask so carefully cultivated by all guards everywhere. The Leithian's position was such as to let him keep one eye on the door of the Audience Chamber while at the same time witnessing all that had passed between Nagaro and the princess.

Nagaro's first thought was to wonder how long the man had been standing there—how much he had actually seen and heard. But in the next instant, he realized that Brandle would naturally have followed him to be sure he could call him back to the Audience Chamber if needed. And Brandle was the commander of the Princess's Guard, besides. As soon as he realized she was there, he would have moved to protect her.

All of this flashed through Nagaro's mind in the frozen instant before he took another step. His first impulse, then, was to speak to the man in his own defense, to offer some explanation for what Brandle must have witnessed—but he quickly thought better of it. Since he'd done nothing actually wrong, protesting his innocence could only make matters worse. Besides which, Brandle was standing in a place where Nevien must surely have seen him. The fact that she had said nothing about it could only mean that she trusted Brandle's discretion.

Nagaro took a deep breath. It seemed he must also trust Brandle. He squared his shoulders and strode past the guardsman without meeting his eyes, back through the doorway into the Compass Room. Brandle stepped back half a pace to allow more room for his passage, but spoke no word as he fell in behind Nagaro and followed him back to the place where they'd been posted outside the door of the Audience Chamber. Once at his station, Brandle promptly returned to his guardsman's stance.

Nagaro returned to his pacing, but made no further effort to interest himself in the room's contents. Instead he made a track a dozen feet long in front of the carved double doors, taking his paces and turning at each end of the track with the tautness of a caged tiger.

He first tried to keep his thoughts away from Nevien, to focus on what must be passing behind the double doors, imagining the hearing in the Audience Chamber. When this only agitated him more, he tried *not* to think about it, as Brandle had suggested, only to find his thoughts immediately returning to Nevien's predicament. When he tried not to think about Nevien, his mind snapped back to Taru, Pavo, and Kenthos and the threat of a war that he must not wish for. Brandle, who was watching him while studiously trying not to appear to do so, read the look of thunder on Nagaro's face and wisely refrained from comment.

Perhaps as much as an hour passed this way. The shifting quality of the light from the high window marked the afternoon's progress. Then, at last, the latches of the door rattled, and one of the two big doors swung open. Nagaro and Brandle both stood hastily aside as there emerged a company of about twenty men that included most of the Fleet Warriors. Landros brought up the rear of the group, and the door closed with a solid thud behind him.

Most of the group milled about, muttering to one another excitedly in low voices. Landros, however, addressed Nagaro. "They've decided that they have no more need o' me, or any of this lot, so we're to return to the Great Hall to wait," he said. "Ye and Lieutenant Brandle are to remain here until they're quite finished."

"Is all the testimony done?" Nagaro's eyes swept the faces. He saw Taru, and Pavo, as well as Haruda and Olendar—but didn't see Tredhold, Kuran, or Vell.

"Aye." It was Taru who answered. "I said my piece, and Pavo and Olendar and Haruda did too."

"Was there any trouble about any of it?"

"Grimbold called me a liar. But Lord Madred gave him a look that shut him up." Taru demonstrated a fierce stare, slightly cross-eyed, that made some of the other men smirk. "And o' course Olendar backed my tale," he added, "and it went better after that."

"Aye," agreed Haruda. "They let me say my piece too. *All* of it."

Landros cleared his throat pointedly. "Our orders were not to stay and talk."

Nagaro turned back to him. "But what have they decided? What's left to do?"

Landros shrugged. "They've decided what to agree on, but they have to work out the *details*." He turned to the rest of the men. "Go on, Zirdas! To the Great Hall!"

Grumbling a little, the men formed a line and began to move in the intended direction. Nagaro hung back surreptitiously at the rear, where Landros waited like a sheepdog herding sheep. He lowered his voice and asked, "What have they *really* decided, Landros?"

The old sea warrior gave him a sour look. "It's froth and foam, mostly. They're saying that it was all a *misunderstanding*. That there were *mistakes made on both sides*—in *similar numbers*. That's important—similar numbers. They couldn't say *equal* numbers, and neither side would admit to making more mistakes than the other. They've agreed that the killings were *unfortunate*, but there's been no apologies. When they sent us out, they were haggling over the price of a man's life, so as to pay recompense. If ye ask me, they don't want us commoners to hear any more o' their bickering."

"So there'll be no war?"

"I shouldn't think so." Landros had begun to move forward.

Nagaro followed. "What about Kenthos? Did he speak of his plan?"

Landros turned back for a hurried answer. "They asked him a cargo o' questions, and he answered 'em straight. There was something about leading his men back to what used to be Loros Wared."

"How did he sound?"

"Nervous at first. He got steadier." Landros had to raise his voice to fling the last reply over his shoulder as he disappeared through the doorway into the Great Hall.

Nagaro returned to the space in front of the Audience Chamber doors. Brandle was still standing there. His expression suggested that he had heard everything and was trying not to show how much he cared about it. He gave Nagaro a wry look and dug into his pocket to pull out a small cloth-wrapped bundle. "Shall we have a game of King's Men, Captain?" he asked. And with that, he dropped to the ground in front of the doors to sit cross-legged. He proceeded to undo the bundled cloth and spread it out, revealing the squares ruled upon it and the ink-marked gray and white pebbles it contained.

Nagaro recognized these odd objects as the same improvised game set he had seen the Leithian using the night before. He stood over the other man, shaking his head. "Is this approved behavior for a guard?" he asked with mock severity.

Brandle shrugged. "No, but it's better than watching you wear out the floor. The Chamberlain might even thank me."

Nagaro glanced down at the polished marble beneath his boots, and laughed. Then he sighed and sat down cross-legged across the cloth game board from the other man. "All right," he said. "I'll try. But I doubt I'll play very well. I can't concentrate."

Over the course of the next hour, they played two games. Brandle won both, and Nagaro suspected the games had only lasted as long as they did because the Leithian had purposefully blundered several times. He had to confess, though, that focusing even imperfectly on the game provided some distraction. They had just begun a third game when the door handles rattled again and they both hastily jumped up. The true cleverness of the makeshift game board and tiny playing pieces was revealed by the swiftness with which Brandle scooped up the cloth with the pebbles inside it and stuffed it back into his pocket.

# Chapter 30

# The Fate Of Loros

They were scarcely on their feet when doors burst open. The first men to come through the doorway were Grimbold and Lothard with Madred close behind. Lothard's gaze lit upon Nagaro and the man's blue eyes narrowed in recognition and intense dislike.

"Out of my way, pirate!"

Nagaro had already stepped aside before the words were out of the Leithian's mouth. Rather than retort, he inclined his head to the man in a small stiff gesture of formal respect. He refused to match offense with offense. Lothard's lips twisted into a sneer and the blue gaze swept on.

Madred's glance came next, equally blue and subtly disdainful. Still, the older lord saw fit to try to smooth the waters that Lothard had roiled. "I beg your pardon, Captain," he said, with the barest forward inclination of his head. "I fear My Lord Lothard is somewhat out of temper. I'm sure he doesn't truly wish to give offense."

Nagaro smiled faintly and answered, "That is well, My Lord, since I have no wish to take it."

This response earned him just the slightest flicker of what might have been approval and a small half-bow, which Nagaro returned. Then the Lord of Furthing Hold was gone, lengthening his stride to catch up with the two Brothers of the Blood.

Soren, Therin, and Rathdar emerged next, moving slowly due to Rathdar's limping gait. Tredhold was hovering at the wounded man's elbow, watching the way he moved with professional interest. The three representatives of the Kelorin Faction walked with their heads close together, deep in conversation. Their expressions were serious, but not angry—or so it seemed to Nagaro, who studied them closely as they passed. None of them paid him the slightest heed, so intense was their concentration, though Tredhold spared him a nod.

Soren paused long enough to look about and see where Lothard, Grimbold, and Madred had gone to stand and await their followers. He then pointedly directed his two companions in a direction that took them as far from that location as the confines of the Compass Room would allow.

After the three Kelorin lords and the healer, there came a large crowd of other men who could be identified by their liveries as warriors in the service of one or another of the lords who had preceded them. These spread out in quest of their masters, as more men emerged from the Audience Chamber, spilling into the Compass Room, milling about amid a rising babble of voices.

Nagaro looked worriedly for Kenthos but couldn't find the young blacksmith in the growing crowd. Abruptly Rastyl brushed past him with Rastian in tow. The older man gave Nagaro an enigmatic glance with his pale eyes before crossing the room in the direction of the door leading to the palace's entry hall. Rastian did not follow his father, however, but stopped and stood a short distance from Nagaro, his eyes wandering over the assemblage. Nagaro noted the young Kelorin's proximity with annoyance at first, but since Rastian's attention seemed to be focused elsewhere, he soon resumed his own efforts to locate Kenthos.

As he continued to survey the crowd, he saw Devral and Pendrik standing apart from the press, keeping watchful eyes on the lords who had so lately been combatants. He saw Vell standing to one side, talking intently with Odus Morbern, and wondered fleetingly what common interest those two men might have. After a moment, Commander Worling of the Palace Guard startled him by appearing from somewhere and drawing Brandle away with a curt gesture.

Then Nagaro caught sight of Kuran. The stocky sea warrior had just stepped through the open doorway of the Audience Chamber and was moving in his direction. And then he saw Kenthos, coming close behind the Lord of the Fleet and deep in conversation with Lord Endemar. The young blacksmith looked a little dazed as he nodded a response to whatever the old lord was saying, but he didn't appear frightened, much to Nagaro's relief. As Kenthos and Endemar moved forward, Nagaro got a glimpse past them into the Audience Chamber, where only Lord Anduar and King Elgurn now remained, just a dozen paces beyond the doorway and approaching with their heads together. At that moment, however, Nagaro was more interested in Kenthos.

Kuran had paused nearby and was also eyeing the young blacksmith and the old lord of Kildoran Wared, clearly trying to stay close to them without intruding on their conversation. Hoping to get some information, Nagaro stepped boldly up to the Lord of the Fleet.

"So, My Lord, has the matter of the recompense been settled to everyone's satisfaction?"

Kuran gave Nagaro a pained look. "Hardly," he said. "And yet, it *is* settled. Elgurn has been adamant that each man slain must be paid for—in equal coin. It's also been decided that the payment shall be termed *recompense*, and that there will officially be no *punishment*, as such. So the Leithians are angry because, although they're happy to receive payment for their own slain men, they think this should be done to punish the Kelorin Faction while *they* should pay nothing, because the Kelorin Faction, in their view, started all the trouble. And the Kelorin Faction are unhappy because, although they approve of recompense being paid by both sides, they believe the main problem was caused by the excessively belligerent behavior of the Leithians, who should therefore be punished in *addition* to paying recompense. So neither side is fully satisfied and a balance has been achieved only because both sides are dissatisfied in equal measure."

"This, no doubt, is what men call a political solution?"

"Of course."

Nagaro shook his head. Perhaps it was better that he had not been in the Audience Chamber, to have been forced to endure hours of testimony and argument only to come to this cautious and convoluted construction. "And there'll be no war?" he asked.

"For a while at least."

"And the price of a man's life? What's it to be?"

"Fifty silver trokins." Kuran's tone eloquently expressed his view of the arbitrary figure. "Five thousand rins. The Leithian's say it's too much for the life of a commoner, and the Kelorin say it is too little for anyone's life. So again both sides are dissatisfied. Lords Odus and Devral are charged with overseeing the exchange of payments, with Pendrik as a mediator. They must record the official lists of the slain men's names, and make sure that the correct amounts are paid at the appointed time. Lothard and Rathdar are each charged with gathering the necessary funds from their sides and delivering them to Odus and to Devral. They may gather the money in any way they choose as long as the amount is correct, and they're also to distribute what they each receive to the dead men's families."

Kuran paused to draw a long breath. "Of course, since the number of men slain on the two sides is very nearly the same, the sums of money exchanged will be very nearly equal. So there will be a great deal of fuss and counting of coins with the end result being of very little substance."

Nagaro's brow furrowed. "It isn't a pointless exercise," he said. "The dead men's families *will* be compensated. The money might just as well have come from their own lords, perhaps, but each side is, in concept, paying for the men they killed rather than providing for their own dead. And if the Brothers of the Blood give even a little thought to the needs of the families who receive the money, they may come to a better understanding of the value of the life of a common man."

Kuran chuckled. "You reason like Anduar. He said very much the same thing—though in his case I always wonder if he's got some other motive behind his words."

"Nagaro! Captain!" Kenthos suddenly intruded himself into the conversation, his face a picture of guileless delight. "This is so wonderful that I must tell you! I'm to go free! I'll have to work to pay for part of the recompense—but that will serve to ease my conscience. And I had to swear never again to make claim to the name of Loros—but I was glad to do that, because the claim was false anyway. And the *best* part is that I will be allowed to live in Loros Wared!"

Nagaro and Kuran both stared at the young Kelorin. "You mean, to live in the lands that formerly *belonged* to Loros Wared?" Kuran inquired carefully.

"Yes, yes!" Kenthos nodded excitedly. "I, and any of the other scattered folk of Loros, are free to do it. And Lord Endemar just told me that if twenty good men of our folk can be found to return and live there, the land can be a free Wared again and we can choose a new lord! And it will surely be easy to find twenty men! Oh, Zirdas, I didn't dream I'd live to see it come to pass! Not after these horrible weeks and all the ill that's happened—and I owe everything to Captain Nagaro!" Kenthos reached for Nagaro's hand, captured it, and began to pump it up and down.

"But I don't see how it is *my* doing," Nagaro protested. "I wasn't even in the room! I think you must have spoken very well to have achieved so much." He managed to extricate his hand.

"Oh, but ye told me what to say—well, *how* to say it, at least—an' besides that, ye stopped me from letting myself be killed when I thought everything was lost! Oh I know ye had orders, but it was *your* hand that saved me. And ye explained t' me last night how everything *wasn't* lost. And it's all true! Every word! And the king is a good man even though he's a Leithian, just as ye said. And Lord Pendrik and Lord Odus, too. How can I ever repay ye?"

Nagaro gaped at the man in pure astonishment.

Kuran looked from Kenthos to Nagaro questioningly. "Did you really do all that, Captain?" he inquired.

Nagaro shook his head. "I am glad if I've served you well," he said, addressing Kenthos. "Though what I did was really not so much as you seem to think. And I have thanks enough in seeing that the outcome has been good, and that you're pleased."

"Oh I'm more than pleased! And I'm in your debt, whether ye think so or not. But this is what we've come to expect from Captain Nagaro. Ye're always humble in the face of praise. I must study how to be the same."

At that moment, they were interrupted by a shout that made everyone look up to see that Kenthos' former followers were being led away under an escort of Palace Guard. And at the same time, Kenthos' mother appeared in the doorway from the central hall, accompanied by two of the queen's former ladies and another pair of guards. As soon as the woman had a clear view of the crowd in the Compass Room, she began agitatedly scanning it with her eyes.

"Mother! Here I am!" Kenthos waved frantically and began half threading, half shouldering, his way through the press of bodies.

Nagaro craned his neck to watch with satisfaction as the massive young blacksmith folded the slender woman into a hearty embrace. The image tugged at his heart, for he remembered Tred's description of their earlier meeting.

Beside him, Kuran coughed and murmured, "Very touching."

"Yes." Nagaro nodded. "I'm glad to see it."

"Pleased with yourself, are you, Captain?"

Nagaro started as he recognized the voice that had just spoken near his other ear. He hadn't heard Lord Anduar's approach. He spun to regard the man. "I said I was glad, My Lord, that's all."

"Ah." The sharp gray gaze impaled him even while the muscles of the man's face were set in an expression as mild as milk. "I wonder sometimes, Captain, why I delude myself with the notion that I have any vestige of control."

"My Lord? I don't understand."

Anduar sighed. "Always so innocent." The hint of a sardonic smile played about the Pact Signer's lips. "I had thought to exclude your influence from the proceedings by excluding your person. Obviously a foolish notion."

Nagaro frowned. "I don't believe—"

Anduar raised a hand to interrupt the protest. "The young blacksmith from Irvenen has just, with seeming simplicity, managed to turn a King's Court of Inquiry to his advantage. And now I learn that he owes his success to *you*."

Nagaro gestured impatiently. "He exaggerates, My Lord."

Kuran found it necessary to suppress a chuckle. Anduar ignored the Lord of the Fleet. His eyes remained locked on Nagaro, measuring him. "Does he? What of this plan to reestablish Loros Wared?"

Nagaro shrugged. "That's *his* plan. His dream. He told me about it last night."

The Pact Signer arched an eyebrow. "It hasn't, perhaps, been your dream also?"

"Before last night, I hadn't thought about it—though it seems a just cause."

Anduar continued to consider him. "There is no authority by which the King or Council can forbid the descendants of the folk of Loros Wared from returning to their ancestral lands, Captain," he said levelly. "Did you know that?"

Nagaro continued to meet the Pact Signer's eyes. "No, My Lord, though it seems both reasonable and just."

"And the rule about twenty good men being needed to constitute the government of a Wared or a Hold has stood since the founding of Edrovir."

"It's in the Charter, then?"

"In Darion's Charter, as some call it, yes. You didn't know this either, Captain?"

"I've never seen the document, My Lord, to know its details. I can see that this means that Kenthos' dream is lawful and should be readily achieved, but I don't understand why you're questioning me about it."

Anduar coughed. "I suppose it's because I have difficulty believing that you're as ingenuous as you appear."

Nagaro gave the other man a pained look. "Then perhaps, My Lord, you are rather too inclined to see your own mind mirrored in the minds of others."

At this, Kuran laughed outright and slapped his thigh. "I think I must mark a point for the Captain there, My Lord! And haven't I assured you on numerous occasions that he can be trusted?"

The steel point of Anduar's gaze was transferred to the Lord of the Fleet. "Your opinion has been previously noted, My Lord Kuran." The cool gaze swung back to Nagaro. "Let me be blunt, Captain," Anduar continued, "so that you will understand the cause of my concern. I'm not opposed to the restoration of Loros Wared—*in principle*. But the *timing* is inopportune. If the rise of a new Loros Wared comes too close upon the heels of recent events, in the present climate of mistrust, it will appear to the members of the Leithian Faction that Kenthos has been rewarded for his actions."

"But if it's all according to the law—"

"Not *everyone* is as impressed as you are with the law, Captain. And as I see it, there is nothing to prevent Kenthos from bringing twenty descendants of Loros Wared to Kildoran Wared within two weeks' time!"

"Oh come now, Anduar," Kuran interjected. "It won't be as quick as that. Remember that Kenthos is going to be escorted to the Fleet Compound this afternoon and housed there until his wound is fully healed. You can trust me to see that Tredhold is *thorough* on that point. And then the man must go first to his home in Irvenen Wared to carry his news to his wife. Once there, he must pack all of his possessions, set all of his local affairs in order, and finally move and resettle his household.

Any others who intend to move must all do the same. All of this will take time."

"And even once that's done," Nagaro added, "the choosing of a new Lord isn't something that should be hurried."

"Also true," Kuran agreed. "Ah, but look at Kenthos," he added, for he had been watching the young blacksmith with one eye. "He's finished speaking with his mother, and with her husband, and now Rastyl is about to escort the couple out by the front door. It's time that Kenthos was on his way as well. If you'll excuse me, My Lord, I'll retrieve my sea warriors from the Great Hall to provide his escort to the Fleet Compound."

With that, the Lord of the Fleet made a swift but elegant bow to Lord Anduar and hurried off across the Compass Room.

Anduar watched the other man go for perhaps two seconds before he returned his chilly gaze to Nagaro. "You will be part of this escort?"

"I assume so, My Lord."

The Pact Signer regarded him narrowly. "Very well," he said a length. "I also have business to attend to. But if you have occasion to speak further with Kenthos, Captain, I trust you will remember what I've said." So saying, Anduar turned on his heel and was gone before Nagaro had time to do more than pay him the courtesy of a hurried bow.

Nagaro watched the Kelorin Lord's retreating figure, frowning uneasily. He suspected that Anduar's concerns had merit, despite Kuran's optimistic interpretation. At the same time, he didn't like Anduar's presumption regarding what he might do.

Still frowning, he looked about him. Most of the crowd had already left the Compass Room, including Devral and Odus, the members of the Kelorin Faction, and Madred and the Brothers of the Blood. Rastian must have followed his father. Kenthos stood near the doorway of the central hall with his followers grouped around him, all engaged in animated conversation. They were still flanked by half a dozen members of the Palace Guard, and Nagaro saw Brandle there. The big Leithian was watching him and now made a beckoning gesture with his head.

Nagaro considered the suggestion only fractionally before crossing the inlaid marble floor to join the Lieutenant. "So," he said when he halted beside Brandle, "are you still guarding this lot?"

Brandle grinned wolfishly. "Until we can hand them over to Lord Kuran and the rest of your fine Fleet men," he answered, speaking low. "They're free to go their ways, but we're watching to see which way they go."

"What of the six lords—the trouble-makers? I didn't see where they went. Are they also free to go?"

"Absolutely." Brandle winked broadly. "But they won't go far this night since they're all to be lodged here in the palace as a 'courtesy'. Six separate rooms, in two different wings, and each room will have a 'guard of honor' at the door. There'll be no coming and going in the night that we don't know about."

Nagaro sighed. He supposed it must be the nature of political solutions that they required so much effort to make certain that they would *stuck*. He became aware that Kenthos was watching him.

The young blacksmith stepped closer when Nagaro caught his eye. He was frowning slightly. "May I ask a favor of ye, Captain?" he inquired in a nervous whisper. "While there aren't any lords about?"

"Yes, I suppose so." Nagaro felt some trepidation.

"Can ye tell me the name o' that Turowan woman ye spoke of last night? The one that knew my history and that said she knows where all the lost and scattered folk of Loros Wared are t' be found?"

Despite the whisper, several of Kenthos' followers clearly pricked up their ears. Nagaro saw that Geivian and Hendrel were among the ones who were watching him closely. Lored, behind them, looked expectant. Nagaro hesitated. He thought that the delicately balanced compromise the King and his Council had crafted fell short of full justice. The political solution was both tenuous and incomplete, and the latter fact offended his sensibilities. Like a broken mast, hastily spliced with weak timbers and lashed with thin rope, this solution might fail if asked to bear too much strain. *Still*, a crudely patched mast might also carry a vessel safely to calmer waters where a proper repair could be made. *And then there were Anduar's concerns.*

Nagaro drew a long breath. "I will tell you that," he said, "on condition that you use the information wisely. You must promise to go slowly with your plan for restoration, and to take care. Wait until all the scattered folk have been contacted, and those who wish to return have settled safely, before you consider calling on them to choose a new lord. Don't attempt a choosing until at least a full year has passed."

There was an angry murmur among Kenthos' followers at this, but the blacksmith raised his hand to silence them. "Wait," he said. "Captain Nagaro has given me good counsel before. He must have a good reason to say this."

Nagaro looked around at their questioning faces. "The law favors you," he said earnestly. "The rules for instituting a Wared and choosing a lord are set forth in the Charter of Darion, which the King and the Council still respect. But all of that will still be true in a year's time. You'll eventually get what you want if you're patient, and the need for patience lies simply in the fact that today's peace is precarious. Tempers are still hot. If you rush to accomplish the goal that worried the lords of the Leithian Faction in the first place, you'll have them up in arms again, and the Kelorin Faction will come rushing to your defense, and so on. A year from now we can hope that tempers will be cooler. Besides, isn't it a matter worth approaching with care?"

Kenthos nodded. "I'd say that it is." He glanced around for approval and read it in the other men's faces. "We should give everyone that wants to a chance to come. And we should have gathered as many as possible to choose a new lord before we hold the choosing. It'll likely take a year to do it right, anyway, so I'll give ye the promise ye ask for, Captain." He stuck out his hand.

Brandle had been listening. "Is this another order you're following, Captain?" he asked. "Lord Anduar had a lot to say to you just now." He cocked an eyebrow, though his tone was casual.

The question evoked frowns and some muttering among Kenthos' followers. The young blacksmith stood with his hand still extended. "What does he mean, Captain?"

Nagaro sighed. "Lord Anduar has given me no order concerning this, Kenthos. Only what you might call a broad hint. I think Anduar understands that I will do what I believe is best in any case, and in this case I believe I've given you good advice." He reached for Kenthos' hand and shook it. "Since you've given me your promise, I will keep mine. The woman's name is Omei. She's been employed at the old Council Hall on Broad Street. Everyone in Lankura knows where that is if you ask. I most recently left her on Pakoa, but she meant to return. If she isn't here by now, she should be soon."

"Omei. Council Hall. Broad Street." Kenthos repeated the names, apparently trying to commit them to memory.

"Does this Omei know where to find the heir of Darion, by any chance?" It was Geivian who asked the question.

Nagaro sighed. It was a reasonable question, but one he must answer with care. "She might or might not," he said cautiously. "And don't expect her to tell you if she does. In fact, you shouldn't ask. It was the possible appearance of Darion's heir that brought the Leithians down on you in the first place and caused all the trouble. Both he and you are safer if he remains unknown."

"Unknown!" Lored exclaimed. "But Captain! He's the rightful lord of Loros. He'd raise up the honor of the Wared, and lead all our people wisely. He'd stand up against our enemies, if only we knew who he was!"

But Nagaro raised his hand. "No," he said. "You're asking too much of him that he should live up to such expectations? And besides, the rightful lord of a Kelorin Wared is whoever the people of the Wared choose, not the son of the previous lord."

At this point the conversation was interrupted by the arrival of Kuran and the Fleet warriors who had been waiting in the Great Hall. There followed a most informal changing of the guard.

Brandle gave Kuran a rakish salute and declared, "They're all yours, My Lord."

Kuran countered with, "Off you go then," and a casual gesture of acknowledgment. Then he cast his eyes about and asked with some annoyance, "Where has Rastian got himself off to now? I left him in this room."

Brandle shrugged. "I can't speak to his purpose, My Lord, but I saw him go out after his father."

Kuran shook his head. "That man needs to sort out just who it is that he's serving," he muttered. Then he sighed, and addressed the company. "Well, we can't wait for him. Let's be on our way."

Delvin returned their swords in the entry hall. He first delivered Landros' blade with a quickly murmured, "Here's yours, Uncle Landros." Nagaro's elegant weapon, on the other hand, was brought forth reverently, cradled in both hands, and handed over with a breathless, "And this is your sword, o' course, Zirda. It's always an honor to hold it for ye."

Nagaro took the sword and sword belt with an exasperated laugh. "It's only a sword, Delvin." He buckled the black belt about his waist with a quickness born of long practice.

Kenthos watched him, awkwardly holding his own weapon, just returned. "Anyone can see you're meant t' be a swordsman, Captain," he said as Nagaro straightened to stand at his ease with the weapon at his hip. "I just hope I never have to use this thing again." He gestured with the belt and scabbard in his hands.

"I'd prefer not to have to use mine either," Nagaro informed him. "But you never know when Edrovir's need may call."

"You'd best put yours on, Zirda," Kuran told the young blacksmith. "There's a symbolism to your walking out of here wearing it. It says more plainly than any words that you are a free man."

With a rueful shrug, Kenthos buckled the belt around his waist. The other Kelorin men who had followed him did the same. And so it was that when Kenthos and the remnant of his followers ventured out through the tall front doors of the palace of Lankura into a late spring afternoon, they walked like the free men they were, with their swords at their sides.

Nagaro paused within the portico outside the palace's front door to look around and draw a breath. The sun was already close to setting. The air was cool, the sky a pale, luminous violet. The long blue shadow of the palace stretched across the expanse of the paved courtyard that separated the palace and its stables from the city wall and the sun-gilded towers of the tall city gate.

At the foot of the flight of steps that descended from the portico, there waited several dozen horses and what seemed a small army of grooms.

Just as Kenthos' party and their escort reached the foot of the steps, a voice was raised to meet them. "Here he is at last! Kenthos, our champion!"

The man who had spoken stepped eagerly out of the waiting crowd of stablemen to clap Kenthos on the back and clasp his hand. Nagaro immediately recognized the speaker, a young Kelorin man, by his fresh shirt and tirka contrasted with his travel-worn pants and boots, as well as by the sharp red sword cut on his chin.

"Venerev!" Kenthos greeted the new arrival with undisguised astonishment. "What on earth are ye doing here?"

The man gave him a broad wink. "I was in Lankura long afore ye were, Zirda, and I know one or two o' the stablemen." He grinned. "I got through the city gate over there along with a cart carrying a load o' hay."

"Have ye been waiting here all afternoon?"

"Aye. And it was a weary, fretful time. But I finally saw the lady, your mother, come out half an hour ago, and ride off in that lord's carriage. I knew by the look on her face that ye must ha' won. But what's it to be, Kenthos?" He leaned close. "What word should I spread among the lads tonight?"

"A-*hem!*" Kuran had been standing behind Kenthos with a gathering frown.

Kenthos glanced worriedly at him over his shoulder and back at Venerev. "I, ah, don't think..." he began uncertainly. "That is, ye shouldn't be telling anyone that we've *won.*"

"Not won?" Venerev looked alarmed.

At this point, Nagaro, pitying Kenthos' confusion, spoke up. "No one has won, Zirda," he said quietly. "And no one has lost either. What happened here today wasn't a fight to be won or lost. It was a sorting out of things in such a way as to reduce excessive heat and avoid further conflict."

Kenthos rallied. "That's right," he said. "We were brought here t' stand before the king, and we've done it, and as ye can see, we've come out as free men with our swords on. But I've got to find a way to raise fifty trokins t' pay for one o' the Leithians that was killed. They've, ah, got to pay for our dead lads as well," he added hurriedly, seeing Venerev's expression.

"Fifty trokins!" Venerev whistled. "That's a fair sum o' silver! Still," he added, "I can put the word about for our folk t' dig into their purses. We'll take up a collection—"

Kuran cleared his throat again. "How Kenthos goes about raising the money is entirely up to him—as long as there's no thievery involved, that is. Right now, though, I'd like to see this lot mounted so we can make our way back to the Fleet Compound in time for dinner."

"The Fleet Compound, Kenthos? They mean t' give ye dinner?"

Kenthos nodded gravely. "Yes. In fact, I'll be lying up there 'til my wound is healed. Then I'll ride back to Irvenen Wared—with a Fleet escort, although I don't expect there'll be as many as this." He gestured at the Fleet warriors who stood waiting. "But I'll tell ye what ye must tell any of our men that ye meet. Tell them I'll be going back to Kildoran Wared—to the part that used t' be Loros Wared—with my wife, and that I mean to dwell there. And any others that'd like to do the same can come and find me—in a month or two."

"A month or two!" Venerev breathed, his eyes alight. "Is that the plan? What d' ye say, Captain Nagaro, Defender of Loros?"

Nagaro frowned severely. "What I say, is that I don't accept this name you've been trying to put on me. I'm a defender of Edrovir, like all the other men who wear the Fleet uniform."

"Ah, just as ye say, Captain." Venerev raised a placating hand. "Just as ye say."

"And as for what Kenthos said," Nagaro continued, still frowning. "I might add that you'd be wise to tell those others to come one at time, and not to make a great noise about what they are doing or why they are doing it."

"Heard and heeded, Captain. Heard and heeded."

Nagaro relaxed. "Good," he said. "I believe I see your horse over there, Kenthos. And mine."

By the time that all the members of the party were in their saddles, Venerev had slipped quietly away. Kuran maneuvered into a lead position, snapped out the order to ride, and they all set heels to their horses.

Kenthos nudged his mount close to Nagaro's stirrup as they set their backs to the palace and the setting sun. "I've been wondering, Captain," he said earnestly. "When I ride north to Irvenen, do ye think ye'll be one o' the escort?"

Nagaro gave the other man a startled glance. "I hadn't thought about it. My Lord Kuran will have orders for me, I expect."

"But ye could ask for the duty, couldn't ye? I mean, I was thinking... Ye did say that your father might ha' come from there. Ye've done me such a service. Maybe I could help ye look for his folk?"

Nagaro stared at the young blacksmith's eager face, then he hastily looked away. *His father... Beloras, Maramyn's love...* In an instant, his mind was several days' ride and many miles away. He was sitting astride Thunder-Heels, gazing northward up that beckoning road that wound between the trees—the road that led to Irvenen Wared and possible clues to his own history. With Kenthos to aid him, he just might learn something, even if it was only to rule out a possibility.

The prospect was tempting. But in the next instant, Nevien's troubled face rose before his eyes as he remembered the urgency of her request. And he remembered his promise. Twisting in the saddle he looked back at the pale, looming face of the palace that Darion had built, silhouetted against the rosy glow of the sunset. Already lights showed in some of the upper-floor windows. They glowed like watching eyes, peering into his soul.

He wasn't sure how to help Nevien, or whether, in fact, he even could, but he knew in that moment that he didn't really have a choice. He could no more walk away from her now to pursue some personal quest than he could have failed to draw his sword to prevent Kenthos' death at the hands of Lothard Hurn. He turned back to Kenthos. The young man was watching him, expectant, hopeful.

"No," he said quietly. "Although I thank you, Kenthos. But I'm afraid I am needed here."

***

Later that night, something awakened him. Perhaps it was the pale moonlight flowing like clear water through the window of his quarters in the Captains' Row. Restless, he rose and padded across the floor, barefoot, clad only in his nightshirt. He opened the back door and stepped out into his tiny walled garden. It was a far cry from the large and elaborate garden he had so recently visited at Loros Hall. Aside from a little patch of grass and the moss around the base of the water pump, there were only a few violets growing along the north wall and the lilies that he had planted, grown from the bulbs given to him months ago by Chula, the gardener of River House.

*Of Averwin...* Those lilies represented the only legacy that he had of Maramine, his Lady Guardian. They were blooming now, their long slim flowers gleaming like pale wax in the moonlight.

The garden looked to the east, and the two moons had both risen in the eastern sky, high enough to float clear of the garden wall and the roofs of the next row of officers' quarters. Gibbous, waning, both showed as ragged-edged partial disks, Naru still trailing Talebra but closing... closing...

Nagaro gazed long at the two moons, considering their ambiguous portent. War or love. Kroneg or Lissafel. The Warrior or the Lady. The moons neither knew nor cared. This time, war had been averted, and he had played a part in that. And that was good—yet still the war might come. The image of Nevien's face rose yet again in his mind. For himself, he had little hope of love, and neither had she. Still, he supposed he could hope that Edrovir might fare better than the princess or a captain of the Royal Fleet.

Nagaro sighed as he turned to re-enter his quarters and return to his waiting bed. One thing at least was clear: All those who sought to maintain peace must remain vigilant—and he must be among them. He would do what he could to help Nevien, but not at the cost of peace. No matter what the personal price, to her or to him, in this one matter he knew where he had to stand.

# Glossary

**Abeidos** (ah-BAY-dose): An older Kelorin man in the service of Lord Rathdar Sundorin. A leading member of the Kelorin Faction.

**Alam Shufa** (AH-lahm SHOO-fah): An uninhabited point on the coast at the very northern edge of the Mahuk Baar.

**Alisset** (A-lihs-seht): Alisset Sobring. A high-born young Leithian woman. One of the princess's ladies. Daughter of Bron Sobring and sister of Vell.

**Ambras** (AHM-brahs): Master Ambras, a Kelorin healer, personal physician to Queen Semorel.

**Ampao** (ahm-PAH-o): A Mautep captain serving under Lord Angkat.

**Anduar Tyronin** (AHN-doo-ar teer-O-nihn): Lord Anduar. A Kelorin lord. One of the Signers of the Pact of Lankura and a member of the King's Council. Also ruling lord of Tyronin Wared.

**Angkat** (AHNG-kaht): A powerful Mautep warlord whose men have twice attacked Lankura.

**Animara** (ah-nih-MAR-ah): A Turowan woman, called Ani for short. Sister of Jila and Narei's aunt. Wife of Sudano and mother of Bahiri, Tavo, and Pilo.

**Atadalba** (ah-tah-DAHL-bah): One of the larger outer Jinari islands, south of the island of Janidi.

**Averwin** (AV-er-wihn): A small country estate in Verdin Wared. Nagaro's boyhood home, now belonging to the Crown and known as River House.

**Baalkir jir-Akaan** (BAHL-keer jeer-ah-KAHN): Emperor Baalkir. A powerful Mautep warlord who has become Emperor of the Mahuk Baar. Uncle of Roheed.

**Bahiri** (bah-HEER-ee): A young Turowan girl. Daughter and oldest child of Animara. She is cousin to Nagaro's daughter Narei and therefore is Nagaro's niece.

**basirah** (bah-SEER-ah): Hashti for "enough".

**Beloras** (BEHL-or-ahs): A Kelorin man, Maramine's murdered love.

**Berinar Sundorin** (BEHR-ih-nar SUHN-dor-ihn): A Kelorin lord. One of the Signers of the Pact of Lankura. Former ruling lord of Sundorin Wared. Father of Rathdar. Author of *Rule of Loros*, he died under mysterious circumstances.

**bishka** (BIHSH-kah): A relatively mild but expressive expletive in Hashti.

**bodjer** (BAH-jer): An expletive derived from a Leithian expression that was originally much cruder. It means roughly to "do an injury to" as commonly used in the Common Speech.

**Boka Omei** (BO-kah O-may): Northernmost major island of the Lomoan archipelago. It has two large harbors on the leeward side: the Bay of Omei and Boka Bay.

**Bouno** (bo-OO-no): A freed Turowan slave, formerly a merchant seaman. A follower of Captain Nagaro who also joined the Royal Fleet of Edrovir.

**Brandle Furthing** (BRAND-l FUR-dhing): A young Leithian, lieutenant (commander) of the Princess's Guard. A "crossed man," the older son of Lord Madred Furthing. ("dh" denotes the voiced "th" sound in "this")

**Brendet** (brehn-DEHT): A high-born young Leithian woman. Formerly one of the princess's ladies.

**Brodig Fane** (BRO-dihg fayn): A Leithian man. A captain in the Royal Fleet of Edrovir.

**Bron Sobring** (brahn SO-bring): A Leithian lord and former ruling lord of Sobring Hold. One of Leyel Virden's "keepers." Father of Vell and Alisset, he was killed in the border war.

**Chitaopa** (chih-TAOW-pah): A small uninhabited island off the coast of Jinara, not claimed by any nation.

**Chotao** (choe-TAH-o): Infant son of Pavo Maat and his wife Tenepti. (Turowan)

**Chula** (CHOO-lah): A elderly Turowan man, gardener at Averwin. He taught Leyel how to plant things and make things out of sticks and string.

**Clarimel** (CLAR-ih-mehl): A high-born young Leithian woman. One of the princess's ladies.

**crossed**: English translation of a word in the Common Speech used as a term for homosexual.

**Dakuro** (dah-KOOR-o): A Turowan man, Chief of the Pakoa Town Council. Also a blacksmith.

**Darion** (DEHR-ee-ahn): King Darion, called "Darion the Great." Ruling lord of the House of Loros and of Loros Wared. Chosen to be the first king of Edrovir. Son of Nevrath and Minowei. Father of Tevren.

**Delasin Verdin** (DEHL-ah-sihn VER-dihn): A high-born young Kelorin woman newly added to the princess's ladies. Youngest daughter of Varsyl.

**Delvin** (DEHL-vihn): A Kelorin youth. A member of the Palace Guard, well known to Landros, whom Nagaro met during the second Mautep attack on Lankura.

**Devenrul** (DEHV-ehn-rool): A small town in Kildoran Wared.

**Devral Sedras** (DEHV-rahl SEHD-rahs): Lord Devral. An aging Kelorin. One of the Signers of the Pact of Lankura and a member of the King's Council. Also ruling lord of Sedras Wared.

**dokan** (do-KAHN): A gold coin of Edrovir. There are ten trokins to the dokan, and one hundred rins to the trokin.

**Dreigen** (DREHY-gehn): A man of mixed Kelorin and Jinari heritage, the king's Lore Master. He is an expert on poisons.

**Droviri** (dro-VEER-ee): Name used by the inhabitants of Jinara and the Mahuk Baar for the Edroviran language (the Common Speech), or the people of Edrovir. Also an adjective meaning "pertaining to Edrovir."

**Duleyin** (doo-Lay-ihn): Seventh month of the Edroviran calendar, equivalent to July.

**Dunrel** (DOON-rehl): Sixth month of the Edroviran calendar, equivalent to June.

**Edro** (EHD-ro): River Edro. Largest river in Edrovir, flowing roughly northeast to southwest and emptying into the sea at Lankura where its mouth forms a major port.

**Edrovir** (EHD-ro-veer): A country inhabited by the Kelorin, Leithians, and Turowans, stretching from the Gorietha mountains in the east to the western sea, and from the Kor Vaskol mountains in the north to its borders with Jinara and Hran in the south.

**Elgurn Harlind** (EHL-gurn HAR-lihnd): King Elgurn. A Leithian lord chosen by the Pact Signers to be the third king of Edrovir. Also the ruling lord of Harlind Hold.

**Elyan** (EHL-ee-ahn): Prince Elyan. A high-born Kelorin man, third husband of Princess Nevien, he was fatally wounded while defending Lankura during the second Mautep attack.

**Endemar** (EHN-deh-mar): Lord Endemar. An older Kelorin, ruling lord of Kildoran Wared, to whose territory was added the tract encompassing Loros Hall, the ancestral seat of the House of Loros, which was left untenanted since the slaying of King Tevren.

**Estevad** (EHS-teh-vahd): A Kelorin man. Clerk to Kuran Kel, the Lord of the Royal Fleet of Edrovir.

**Evrel** (EHV-rehl: Fourth month of the Edroviran calendar, equivalent to April.

**Faranos** (FAH-rah-nos): Either of two island chains off the northern and central coast of Edrovir.  The Inner Faranos is the shorter, more northerly chain. The Outer Faranos partially overlap the Inner Faranos, lying farther off shore and extending farther south.

**Farano's Mouth**: Strait separating the southern end of the Faranos from the Lomoas.

**farusia** (fah-ROO-see-ah): A plant bearing large white trumpet-shaped flower, or the flower itself.

**Fendar** (FIHN-dar): A Kelorin swordmaster who was Leyel Virden's instructor, now serving as Swordmaster to the Royal Fleet.

**Finorel** (FIHN-or-ehl): Twelfth month of the Edroviran calendar, it is equivalent to December.

**Furthing Hold** (FER-dhing hold). The territory governed by the Leithian lord Madred Furthing. ("dh" denotes the "th" sound in the word "this")

**Gama** (GAH-ma): An old Turowan woman, Taru's grandmother. (The word *gama* means "grandmother" in the Turowan tongue.)

**Geivian** (GAY-vee-ahn): A young high-born Kelorin man who has a seat at the "match table" because he is courting one of the princess's ladies.

**Geldoran Finrad** (GUEHL-dor-ahn FIHN-rahd): A Kelorin commander in the Royal Fleet, second in command to Kuran Kel.

**Genorel** (GUEHN-or-ehl): First month of the Edroviran calendar, it is equivalent to January.

**Glenarl** (glehn-ARL): A major town in Harlind Hold.

**Great Channel**: Channel separating the various island chains from the mainland of Edrovir.  It is generally broader than any of the north-south channels separating the various islands and island chains from one another, hence the name.

**Grimbold Sobring** (GRIHM-bold SO-brihng): A Leithian lord. Brother, and successor of Bron Sobring as ruling lord of Sobring Hold. Uncle of Vell and Alisset. A member of the Leithian Faction and one of the Brothers of the Blood.

**Gunder** (GUHN-der): A Leithian man, deputy chief of the town of Huring in Hurn Hold.

**Hakor** (HAH-kor): A Mautep captain serving under Lord Tuluptak.

**Hakura Kili** (hah-KOOR-ah KEE-lee): Guiding Spirit of the Turo, who also tend to swear by the name. The exclamation "Hakura!" expresses awe or excitement.

**Halbert** (HAL-burt): A Leithian man, Town Chief of the town of Huring in Hurn Hold.

**hamanei mata noa** (hah-MAH-nay MAH-tah NO-ah): A Turowan exclamation, literally meaning 'Spirits protect us.' Also shortened to just "Hamanei!" It expresses alarm.

**Hamani** (hah-MAH-nee): A young Turowan woman who lives across the road from Taru's grandmother in Wotana. Her name means "spirit". Older sister of Jitali.

**Hanuroa** (HAH-noo-RO-ah): Turowan name for the afterlife. Equivalent to heaven.

**Harmoth** (HAR-mahth): Southern-most major port city in Edrovir.

**Haro** (HAHR-oh): One of the inner (landward) islands at the southern end of the Lomoas.

**Haruda** (hah-ROO-dah): A former Turowan merchant seaman from Pakoa Island, a follower of Nagaro. One of those who also joined the Royal Fleet.

**Hashtep** (HAHSH-tehp): The common folk of the Mahuk Baar. Also the general word for their race, which includes the Mautep or warlord class.

**Hashti** (HAHSH-tee): Language of the people of the Mahuk Baar (both Hashtep and Mautep).

**heerukan** (HEER-oo-kahn): A Mautep sea warrior rank roughly equivalent to "commander" in the Royal Fleet.

**Hel** (hehl): In Leithian belief, a place of punishment for the spirits of those who have transgressed in life.

**Hendrel** (HEHN-drehl): A young highborn Kelorin man who has a seat at the "match table" because he is courting one of the princess's ladies.

**heskial** (hehs-kee-AHL): A Jinari drug that enslaves the will while sparing conscious awareness. Derived from the heskia vine, it is presumed to possess "spirit magic."

**Hranji** (HRAHN-jee): An inhabitant of Hran. Also used as the plural, or to denote the people of Hran.

**Hrathgard** (HRAHTH-gard): Patriarchal god of the Leithians, King of the Heavens and Lord of the Wind. He is the patron of kings and rulers.

**Huring** (HOOR-ring): A small town in Hurn Hold.

**Hurn Hold** (hern hold): The territory governed by Lord Lothard Hurn.

**Idrin** (IHD-rihn): Seven-day-long thirteenth month of the Edroviran calendar, surrounding the winter solstice and marking the 'turning of the year'. Commonly considered unlucky.

**Inside Passage**: Irregular north-south path running between the islands of the Lomoa chain.

**Irvenen Wared** (ir-VEHN-ehn WAH-rehd): The territory governed by Lord Rastyl Korven, lying in the extreme north of Edrovir.

**Jaamra** (JAHM-rah): Strait of Jaamra. A passage between two islands on the Mahuk Baar. Site of a sea battle between two rival Mautep warlords, Baalkir and Angkat, during which Nagaro led his fellow slaves to seize the *Fist of Death* and make their escape.

**Janidi** (jah-NEE-dee): One of the more northerly of the outer Jinari islands, lying north of Atadalba and south of Judaba.

**Jato** (JAH-toe): An older Turowan man working as a tracker for Lord Anduar.

**Jila** (JEE-lah): A beautiful and notorious Turowan woman. Animara's sister. Mother of Narei.

**Jinara** (jih-NAH-rah): A coastal country lying between Edrovir and the Mahuk Baar, involved in a long-running border dispute with Edrovir.

**Jinari** (jih-NAH-ree): Edrovirin name for the inhabitants of Jinara. Also their language and an adjective meaning "pertaining to Jinara".

**Jitali** (jee-TAH-lee): A young Turowan woman living in Wotana. Younger, prettier sister of Hamani, and Taru's latest romantic interest.

**Judaba** (joo-DAH-bah): Northernmost major island of the Jinari isles. The port of Patamtala is near its northen tip.

**kajadeem** (kah-jah-DEEM): Hashti word meaning "honor."

**Kale Fendred** (kayl FEHN-drehd): A highborn Leithian, boyhood friend of King Elgurn. One of Leyel Virden's "keepers" who is now insane.

**Kapala** (kah-PAHL-ah): One of the outer, seaward, islands near the southern end of the Lomoas.

**Kel Tierna** (kel tee-EHR-nah): Port city on the southern coast of Edrovir, south of Lankura and north of Harmoth.

**Kelorin** (KEL-or-in): A fair-skinned, dark-haired people originally from the isles of Kelor in the far western sea. Also their language, or an adjective meaning "pertaining to Kelor or the Kelorin people".

**Kendira** (kehn-DEER-ah): A young Kelorin woman. One of the princess's ladies. Nagaro had been paired with her at the match table.

**Kenthos** (KEHN-thos): Kenthos of Irvenen. A young Kelorin blacksmith believed by some members of the Kelorin Faction to be the long lost heir of Darion.

**keshaal** (keh-SHAHL): An expletive in Hashti, fairly strong.

**kia kaar hanuk-tak** (KEE-ah kahr HAHN-ook-tahk): Hashti phrase meaning "put down your sword."

**Kiraam Shaku-Tal** (KEER-ahm SHAH-koo-TAHL): Name given to Nagaro by Roheed. In Hashti, it means "one who takes slaves." Rendered in the Common Speech as "Thief of Slaves."

**Kildoran Wared** (kihl-DOR-ahn WAH-rehd): The territory governed by Lord Endemar. It includes some lands that were formerly part of Loros Wared before the latter was broken up following the killing of King Tevren.

**Kroneg** (KRON-ehg): Leithian god of war. Arbiter of the outcome of armed conflict and ruler of the dark moon, Naru.

**kuma** (KOO-mah): Kuma stain or ointment. The ointment stains the skin brown and is made from the nuts of the kuma plant. Used by fair-skinned seamen to prevent sunburn.

**Kunoa** (Koo-NO-ah): A young Turowan fisherman's son from Pakoa. A freed former slave and member of Nagaro's crew who joined the Royal Fleet but left it when Nagaro went into exile.

**Kuran Kel** (KOOR-ahn kehl): Lord of the Royal Fleet of Edrovir. A man of mixed Kelorin and Turowan blood, from a merchant family but elevated by King Elgurn to the status of Lord of the House of Kel. Also ruling lord of Kel Wared, a territory the king created for him from part of the former Loros Wared.

**Landros Torenin** (LAN-dros tor-EHN- ihn): An older Kelorin sea warrior, former officer of the Royal Fleet of Edrovir, then a slave and one of Nagaro's followers who rejoined the Fleet. Captain of the *Sea Eagle*.

**Lankura** (LAHN-koor-ah): Capital city of Edrovir, located at the mouth of the River Edro.

**Lapoa** (lah-PO-ah): A small island near the northern end of the Lomoa chain on the landward side. "Lapoa Passage" refers to the strait between Lapoa and an adjacent island and is contextual since it could be either north or south of Lapoa.

**Leithians** (LAY-thee-ens): Fair-skinned, light-haired people originally from a land called Leith. "Leithian" denotes either a single individual or is used as an adjective meaning "pertaining to Leithians."

**Leyel Virden** (LEHY-ehl VER-dehn) Name given to Nagaro by the Lady Maramine Virden, under which he was ridiculed as the "idiot prince" during his marriage to Princess Nevien.

**Lindra** (LIHN-drah): Queen Lindra. A Kelorin woman, wife of King Tevren. Killed, supposedly accidentally, along with her husband by Reith Hurn.

**Lissafel** (LIHS-ah-fehl): "The Lady," maiden goddess of the Leithians. Ruler of the hearts of men and women, and of the pale moon, Talebra.

**Lokundas** (lo-KOON-dahs): The "Turner of Worlds," Kelorin personification of fate. One of the old gods of the Cloud Mountain People from before the founding of Kelor.

**Lomoas** (lo-MO-ahs): Archipelago off the southern coast of Edrovir. The Lomoa islands lie south of the Inner and Outer Faranos, across the gap called Farano's Mouth.

**Long Harbor**: Most southernly gold port, located at the northern end of Little Farano Island, at the harbor formed by the channel that incompletely separates Big Farano from Little Farano.

**Lored** (LOR-ehd): A Kelorin man from Kildoran Wared, one of the followers of Kenthos.

**Loros Wared** (LOR-os WAH-rehd): A former Wared, lying on the northern bank of the River Edro, near its mouth. Founded by Nevrath Loros, father of Darion and grandfather of Tevren, it was cut into pieces after Tevren's death.

**Lothard Hurn** (LO-thard hurn): A Leithian lord, son of one of the Signers of the Pact of Lankura (Reith Hurn) and currently ruling lord of Hurn Hold and lord of the House of Hurn. A member of the Leithian Faction and one of the Brothers of the Blood.

**Luka** (LOO-ka): An old Turowan medicine woman known to Nagaro from his childhood at Averwin. Mother of Omei.

**Madred Furthing** (MAH-drehd FUR-dhing): Lord Madred. A highly respected Leithian Lord, the ruling lord of Furthing Hold. Father of Brandle and a leader of the Leithian Faction. ("dh" denotes the "th" sound in the word "this")

**Madrel** (MAH-drehl): Third month of the Edroviran calendar, equivalent to March.

**Mahuk Baar** (MAH-huke BAR): A coastal country, and islands, lying beyond Jinara to the south of Edrovir. Inhabited by the Hashtep people with their Mautep warlords and ruled by an emperor. "Mahuk" is often used for the nationality, as in "Mahuk warships" or "Mahuk waters". It is also used (ignorantly) for the people of the Mahuk Baar.

**Maramine Virden** (mar-ah-MEEN VER-dehn): A Kelorin lady, former mistress of the estate of Averwin, estranged from her family. Nagaro's lady guardian, she was smothered by Elgurn to end her suffering during what would have been fatal heskial withdrawal.

**Matapili** (MAH-tah-PEE-lee): A Jinari man with a small boat who often carries messages for Utabala.

**Mautep** (MAH-oo-tehp): Ruling warrior class of the Hashtep people of the Mahuk Baar.

**Masataak** (MAH-sah-tahk): Lord Masataak. A Mautep warlord under Emperor Baalkir. The territorial lord of Osfaraad.

**Medrin** (MEHD-rihn): Fifth month of the Edroviran calendar, equivalent to May.

**Menden** (MEHN-dehn): Name given by a Kelorin man acting as Lord Devral's mouthpiece.

**Merriel** (MEHR-ee-ehl): Lady Merriel. A high-born Leithian woman, one of Queen Semorel's ladies and chaperon to Princess Nevien and her ladies.

**Minowei** (mih-NO-way): Princess Minowei. Daughter of a Turowan chief, Takuma, who married Nevrath, founding the House of Loros. Mother of Darion.

**Moluaro** (mo-loo-AR-o): Largest island in the southern half of the Lomoas, lying on the landward side of the Inside Passage.

**Moraga** (mor-AH-gah): A Turowan former merchant seaman and freed slave. One of Nagaro's followers who did not join the Royal Fleet. Captain of the *Tiger*.

**Nagaro** (nah-GAR-o): Captain Nagaro, also known as Nagaro the Pirate, and Kiraam Shaku-Tal (Hashti for "Thief of Slaves").

**Narei** (NAR-ay): Daughter of Nagaro and Jila.

**Naru** (NAR-oo): The dark moon, smaller of the world's two moons. It travels slightly faster than the bright moon, Talebra, overtaking her at times in what the Leithians consider a portentious conjunction.

**Nevien Harlind** (NEHV-ee-ehn HAR-lihnd): Princess Nevien, daughter of King Elgurn and Queen Semorel.

**Nevrath** (NEV-rahth): A Kelorin man who left the House of Tyronin and founded the House of Loros after a falling-out with his brother Hindrath. Nevrath married the Turowan Princess Minowei. Darion was their first-born son.

**Nondorin** (NOAN-dor-ihn): Eleventh month of the Edroviran calendar, equivalent to November.

**Oapa** (o-AH-pah): A small island on the landward side of the northern Lomoas, immediately south of Lapoa Island.

**Odus Morbern** (O-duhs MOR-burn): Lord Odus. A Leithian lord. One of the Signers of the Pact of Lankura and a member of the King's Council. Ruling lord of Morbern Hold.

**Olendar** (O-lehn-dar): A Kelorin man, a freed galley slave, one of Nagaro's followers who also joined the Royal Fleet.

**Omei** (O-may): Tira Omei. A Turowan woman, one of Minowei's people who lived in the former Loros Wared. She is a *Ku Taihana*, one of the "keepers of memory" of her people.

**onam** (O-nahm): The physical substance, or matter, of which the world is composed. In Vothrin belief, it refers to the flesh as opposed to the spirit, know as *anim*.

**opa** (O-pah): A potent drug used to relieve pain, noted for giving vivid "opa dreams."

**Osfaraad** (ose-far-AHD): An island belonging to the Mahuk Baar, near the northern border of Mahuk waters, where Nagaro's ships had put freed Hashtep slaves ashore. Site of Nagaro's surrender to Emperor Baalkir that led to the torture of three Edroviran Fleet officers, one of whom betrayed the Fleet's mission to the Emperor.

**Oteyin** (oh-TAY-ihn): Eighth month of the Edroviran calendar, equivalent to August.

**Pakoa** (pah-KO-ah): An island off the southern coast of Edrovir where Nagaro made his home during his pirate period. Southern-most inhabited isle of the Lomoas. Pakoa Town, on Pakoa Harbor, is its only significant town.

**Paktaar** (pahk-TAR): An island belonging to the Mahuk Baar, close to Emperor Baalkir's capital port city of Sar Tipaal. Site of the disastrous battle in which the Edroviran Fleet's mission to attack Sar Tipaal ended in defeat.

**Patamtala** (PAH-tahm-TAH-lah): A trading port on the northernmost Jinari island of Judaba.

**Pavo Maat** (PAH-vo MAHT): A Hashtep fisherman's son and former slave. Follower and close friend of Nagaro who also joined the Royal Fleet. Not tortured by the Emperor at Osfaraad, he was falsely convicted of treason and rescued by Nagaro and Taru, resulting in their exile.

**Pedran** (PEHD-rahn): A Kelorin man, a tracker working for Lord Anduar.

**Peldred Gilforn** (PEHL-drehd Gihl-forn): A young high-born Leithian Fleet officer, assigned to Nagaro's crew as third mate. One of those tortured by Emperor Baalkir at Osfaraad.

**Pendrik Glenmark** (PEHN-drihk glehn-MARK): Lord Pendrik. A Leithian lord, one of the Signers of the Pack of Lankura and a member of the King's Council. Also ruling lord of Glenmark Hold.

**Pilo** (PEE-lo). A young Turowan boy. Younger son of Animara, brother of Bahiri and Tavo. Cousin of Narei and one of Nagaro's nephews.

**Radavan Janavidi** (RAH-dah-vahn JAH-nah-VEE-dee): A Jinari man, official Envoy of the Jinari High Council, he bears the title "Hota" (HOE-tah).

**Rastian Korven** (rahs-tee-AHN KOR-vehn): A young Kelorin officer in the Royal Fleet of Edrovir. Son of Lord Rastyl Korven.

**Rastyl Korven** (rahs-TEEL KOR-vehn): A Kelorin lord with unusually pale gray eyes. Ruling lord of Irvenen Wared. Father of Rastian.

**Rathdar Sundorin** (RAHTH-dar SUN-dor-ihn): A Kelorin lord, son of the deceased Pact Signer Berinar Sundorin. Current ruling lord of the Sundorin Wared. One of the leaders of the Kelorin faction.

**Reith Hurn** (rayth hurn): A Leithian lord, previous ruling lord of Hurn Hold. Father of Lothard. A Signer of the Pact of Lankura and former member of the King's Council, he was killed in the border war with Jinara.

**Rese** (rees): A young high-born Leithian man, suitor of Alisset and one of those seated at the "match table."

**Rianine** (REE-ah-neen): A young Kelorin woman, called Rian for short. One of Princess Nevien's ladies and her frequent confidant.

**rin** (rihn): A small copper coin, the base unit of Edroviran currency. There are one hundred rins in one trokin and one thousand rins in one dokan.

**Roheed jir-Akaan** (ro-HEED jeer-ah-KAHN): A young Mautep officer, Emperor Baalkir's nephew. He speaks some Droviri, having been raised by the Kelorin slave woman, Emril. The apparent death of Emril's infant son, Sindar, formed the basis of a "blood debt" requiring Roheed to save the life of someone who was orphaned.

**Ruald Grinard** (roo-AHLD grihn-ARD): A Leithian officer in the Royal Fleet of Edrovir. Captain of Lord Kuran's flagship, the *Pride of Lankura*.

**Rubo Atatya** (ROO-bo ah-TAH-yah): An older Turowan man, retired as a sea warrior/cook with the Royal Fleet of Edrovir. One of Nagaro's followers who e-joined the Fleet as a first mate under Landros.

**Saminda** (sah-MIHN-dah): A young Kelorin woman, wife of Kenthos.

**Sar Tipaal** (sar tih-PAHL): A major sea port of the Mahuk Baar and the country's capital under Emperor Baalkir. Site of his famed shipyard.

**sea passage** (or seaward passage): "Taking the sea passage" means sailing north or south on the seaward side of any of the island chains. Not a channel, as such, but a course easily followed by seamen who lack the skill to navigate out of sight of land.

**Sedrin** (SEHD-rihn): Ninth month of the Edroviran calendar, equivalent to September.

**Semorel** (SEHM-or-ehl): Queen Semorel. A Kelorin woman, wife of King Elgurn and therefore queen of Edrovir.

**Seralind** (sehr-ah-LIHND): Name for the place of reward after death in Leithian religious belief. Equivalent to paradise or heaven.

**shaku** (SHAH-koo): Hashti word meaning "slave."

**Sheptuum** (shehp-TOOM): God of the Hashtep people, including the Mautep class.

**Simion** (SIHM-ee-ahn): A young Kelorin crossed man, Brandle Furthing's lover. Former Fleet warrior and galley slave who escaped in the slave mutiny led by Nagaro.

**Sindar** (SIHN-dahr): A young Kelorin man held captive since infancy in the Mahuk Baar who escaped and is under Nagaro's guidance.

**Soku** (SO-koo): A small island adjacent to Boka Bay on the island of Boka Omei, lying on the seaward side of the north end of the Inside Passage.

**Solbrid** (SOL-brihd): The Leithian mother goddess. Ruler of earth and giver of life.

**Soren Tuveilas** (SOR-ehn too-VAY-lahs): Lord Soren. An elderly high-born Kelorin, the ruling lord of Tuveilas Wared and one of the leaders of the Kelorin faction.

**sothiril** (SO-thur-ihl): Kelorin tea-like drink made by steeping the dried berries of the plant of the same name.

**Strad Olbern** (strahd OL-burn): A high-born Leithian who was a commander in the Royal Fleet of Edrovir during the incident at Osfaraad. He was subsequently lost at Paktaar.

**Sudano** (soo-DAH-no): A Turowan kuma farmer. Husband of Animara and father of Bahiri, Tavo, and Pilo. Narei's uncle.

**Talebra** (tah-LEHY-brah): The bright moon, larger of the world's two moons.

**Tambali** (tahm-BAH-lee): A major port city near the northern border of Jinara, Utabala's home.

**Taru Nareyo** (TAR-roo nar-AY-o): A Turowan fisherman's son. Nagaro's first friend from Wotana Bay who was enslaved with him by the Mautep sea raiders, freed in the slave mutiny. Nagaro's first mate, he joined the Fleet but went into exile with Nagaro.

**Tavo** (TAH-vo): A young Turowan boy. Older son of Animara and brother to Bahiri and Pilo. Cousin to Nagaro's daughter Narei and therefore one of Nagaro's nephews.

**Tenepti** (tehn-EHP-tee): A young Hashtep woman of Pakoa. Wife of Pavo Maat.

**Tevren Loros** (TEHV-rehn LOR-os): King Tevren. The young second king of Edrovir, killed by Reith Hurn in an event that sparked a civil war. Son of Darion the Great, he was mostly Kelorin but carried some Turowan blood through his grandmother, Minowei.

**Therin Oranil** (Thehr-ihn OR-ahn-ihl): A Kelorin lord, ruling lord of Oranil Wared and a leader of the Kelorin faction.

**Theseline** (THEHS-ehl-een): An older Kelorin serving woman at Loros Hall.

**Timegar** (TIH-may-gar): A Kelorin man from Pakoa. A former Fleet warrior, retired, who joined Nagaro's followers and became captain of the pirate ship *North Wind*.

**Tira** (TEER-rah): Respectful from of address for a woman, roughly equivalent to "Mrs.", but with no implied marital status. Always used before a given name.

**tirka** (TUR-kah): A men's short-sleeved upper outer garment, opening down the front, and cut long enough to cover the hips. Generally worn over a long-sleeved shirt and usually belted.

**Todrin** (TOE-drihn): Tenth month of the Edroviran calendar, equivalent to October.

**Tor** (tor): Respectful form of address for a man, roughly equivalent to "Mr." Always used before a given name.

**Torlung** (TOR-luhng): Minister Torlung. A Leithian of the House of Furthing, Chief Minister to Lord Madred.

**Tredhold Ferth** (TRED-hold furth): A Leithian healer, called Tred for short. A former Fleet warrior and ship's doctor who was held as galley slave, freed in the slave mutiny led by Nagaro. One of Nagaro's followers who rejoined the Fleet. Ship's doctor on the *Sword of Freedom*.

**trokin** (TRO-kihn): A silver coin worth one hundred rins. There are ten trokins to the dokan.

**Tulara** (too-LAR-ah): A young Turowan woman, employed at the Bay Tree Inn in Pakoa Town. A previous (unsuccessful) romantic interest for Taru.

**Tulevian** (too-LEHV-ee-ahn): A young Kelorin woman. Formerly one of the princess's ladies.

**Tuluptak** (TOO-loop-tahk): A powerful Mautep warlord.

**Tunapa** (too-NAH-pah): A Lomoan island on the eastern side of the north end of the Inside Passage.

**Turo** (TOOR-o): The Turo. Turowan name for their people, also use to refer to a Turowan man.  Turowa (toor-O-wah) is the female equivalent.

**Turowans** (toor-O-ahns): A brown-skinned, dark-haired people native to the coastal region and islands of Edrovir. Called by themselves "the Turo". The word "Turowan" can refer to a single male individual and is also used as an adjective to describe anything relating to the Turo.

**Urchak tok-Faar** (UR-chahk toke-FAHR): Captain of the Mautep war galley *Fist of Death*, taken in the slave mutany led by Nagaro and re-christened the *Sword of Freedom*.

**Utabala** (OO-tah-BAH-lah): A Jinari merchant's agent and interpreter, a freed galley slave who returned to the service of his employer and sometimes also serves the Jinari High Council.

**Vanhold** (VAN-hold): A young high-born Leithian man, presently a suitor of Clarimel and therefore one of those with a seat at the "match table."

**Varsyl Virden** (vahr-SEEL VIR-dehn): A Kelorin lord, brother of Maramine, who slew her love, Beloras in a sword challenge. He is now ruling lord of Virden Wared. Father of Delasin.

**Vedorel** (VEHD-or-ehl): Second month of the Edroviran calendar, equivalent to February.

**Vell Sobring** (vehl SO-bring): A young Leithian officer in the Royal Fleet of Edrovir. Son of Bron Sobring. Nephew of Grimbold Sobring who is currently the lord of Sobring Hold since Bron's death in the border war. One of three officers tortured at Osfaraad.

**Venerev** (VEHN-er-ehv): A Kelorin man, a follower of Kenthos.

**Vothra** (VO-thrah): The Benevolent Spirit of the Kelorin, an entity composed of the combined spirits of many individuals all of whom have lived multiple lives. Vothra's wisdom, collectively referred to as "the Path" is recorded in the Vothrin Writings. Vothra has an unusually strong connection to Nagaro's spirit.

**Wared** (WAH-rehd): Kelorin word for the territory governed by a lord. Equivalent to the Leithian word "Hold".

**Wotana** (wo-TAH-nah): A small town on the bay of the same name, located on the Edroviran coast about twenty miles north of Lankura. Taru's home town.

**Yuli** (YOO-lee): a Turowan woman, wife of the keeper of the Bay Tree Inn on Pakoa.

**Zirda** (ZUR-dah): A respectful masculine form of address, roughly equivalent to "Sir" in modern casual usage.

**Zirdyn** (zur-DEEN): A respectful feminine form of address, roughly equivalent to "Madame" in modern casual usage.

**Zomora** (zo-MOR-ah): Tira Zomora. Pakoa's Turowan medicine woman, and an unofficial power on that island and throughout the southern Lomoas.

# Acknowledgements

I am ever grateful to my fans, who give me hope that I am on the right track, and to my first reader, Kristie McCue. And of course I must thank those who gave me input on the manuscript including especially my test readers for the final version, Suzanne Coulter and the Read Warriors of ScHoFan. As usual, the members of ScHoFan, a critique group under the auspices of the Greater Los Angeles Writers Society (GLAWS), gave me feedback on versions of the early chapters. In alphabetical order, they are Carol Ann Alves, John Gwinner, Ken Hughes, Scott Kilburn, Katy Mann, Carmen Mendivil, Robin Reed, Taguhi Tavitian, and Garrett Weinstein.

I continue to be grateful for the support of my husband and the other members of my family, who by now have gotten used to this. I'm also grateful for the continuing support of my dear friends, Suzanne Coulter for her support and encouragement, and Anne Bannon for support, encouragement, and the gift of her knowledge and expertise.

# About the author

Carol Louise Wilde is the author of the fantasy adventure series the *Nagaro Chronicle*. She long led a double life: biology research scientist by day, and by night, chief archivist for the nation of Edrovir and its neighboring states. The *Nagaro Chronicle* covers but one brief period in the long and eventful history of this world and its inhabitants. Ms. Wilde lives in Southern California with her husband of forty years. They have two sons to carry on the tradition.